D0999781

NS' EMPIRE
REGION

JIN-CROLAH

Ghosting
Settlement

The Sanctuary

JIN-SUKAR

JIN-WONTA

JIN-HIDAL

JIN-LAHAM

Desert

THE
FINAL
STRIFE

THE FINAL STRIFE

A NOVEL

SAARA EL-ARIFI

NEW YORK

The Final Strife is a work of fiction. Names, places, and
incidents either are products of the author's imagination or
are used fictitiously. Any resemblance to actual events, locales,
or persons, living or dead, is entirely coincidental.

Published in the United States by Del Rey,
an imprint of Random House, a division of
Penguin Random House LLC, New York.

DEL REY and the CIRCLE colophon
are registered trademarks of Penguin Random House LLC.

LIBRARY OF CONGRESS CATALOGING-IN-PUBLICATION DATA
Names: El-Arifi, Saara, author.
Title: The final strife / Saara El-Arifi.
Description: New York: Del Rey, [2022] | Series: The final strife;
book 1
Identifiers: LCCN 2021055840 (print) | LCCN 2021055841
(ebook) | ISBN 9780593356944 (hardcover; acid-free paper) |
ISBN 9780593356951 (ebook) | ISBN 9780593501009
(international edition)
Subjects: LCGFT: Fantasy fiction. | Novels.
Classification: LCC PR6105.L429 F56 2022 (print) | LCC
PR6105.L429 (ebook) | DDC 823/.92—dc23/eng/20220128
LC record available at https://lccn.loc.gov/2021055840
LC ebook record available at https://lccn.loc.gov/2021055841

Map illustrations: © Kingsley Nebechi

Printed in the United States of America on acid-free paper

randomhousebooks.com

9 8 7 6 5 4 3 2 1

First Edition

Book design by Alexis Capitini

To those who dream in color

A Duster is built for labor. Their submissive nature, which I believe to be an element of their blue blood, means they are best suited for the plantation fields. Ghostings, stripped as they are of communication, make the best servants, their translucent blood a clear indicator of adaptability, although a Duster may be substituted if needs must, given the rarity of Ghostings. Embers continue to be the superior race, proving without a doubt that those with red blood are born to lead.

—Extract from *On Race and Color* by Hamad Al-Olar, Warden of Knowledge, year 378 of the Wardens' Empire

Stolen, sharpened, the hidden key,
We'll destroy the empire and set you free,
Churned up from the shadows to tear it apart,
A dancer's grace, a killer's instinct, an Ember's blood,
    a Duster's heart.

—The plantation chant of the Stolen

THE
FINAL
STRIFE

PROLOGUE

The tidewind came every night.

It billowed in from the Marion Sea between the clock strikes of twelve and two, moving from one wave to another, from the sea to the sand dunes of the Farsai Desert. Salt air and blue sand collided within its swirling midst, weaponizing each grain into something deadly.

It blew through the Wardens' Empire and the thirteen cities within, destroying everything in its path not strong enough to withstand it.

To the south, it swirled through the capital city, Nar-Ruta, running along the invisible seams that separated the citadel into four quarters. It weaved up toward the Keep, the smallest and most affluent quarter, where the four wardens, the leaders of the empire, slept soundly behind the iron walls of their fortress. Nothing entered the Keep without the wardens' knowledge.

In the Ember Quarter wreckage rolled through the cobbled streets, soiling the pristine courtyards of the nobility. The tidewind pounded on their lavish doors, but the metal shutters were steadfast.

The tidewind moved on to more fruitful ground, across the Ruta River, which separated rich from poor, red blood from blue and clear. It battered the wooden doors of the Duster Quarter and thrust its tendrils through poorly repaired windows. Brooms stood ready for the morning's cleaning. The residents, worn down from the plantation fields, were used to backbreaking work.

The wind moved east toward the final district of Nar-Ruta, the Dredge: the impoverished ruins and rubble home to Ghostings and Dusters. It moved toward the maiden houses where the fake cries of the nightworkers' pleasure drowned out the tidewind's wails. It swept through the shadows of the joba seed drug dens where the small red seed was consumed under the cover of the Dredge's crumbling structures. There it lingered, ready to shred the skin of any who had the misfortune of finding themselves outside as the tidewind blew. Then gone would be their dark skin and blood. The tidewind took it all, leaving nothing but bones and the tattered remains of who they once were.

And the wind had been getting stronger in recent weeks. Hungrier.

The residents of the Dredge not to be found in the maiden houses or joba seed dens could be found in the Maroon, the largest tavern north of the Ember Quarter. Set into the tunnels beneath the city, the tavern was protected from the tidewind's havoc.

Inside the Maroon, a drumbeat shook the blue particles of sand that had slipped through cracks and under shutters, until the sand danced like the plantation workers within.

They were all Dusters. The workers swayed, their brown faces smoothed by the fleeting freedom of the dance. Heels pounded the floor, turning outward left and right with a flick of their wrists. Backs arched, not in pain now but in defiance, their faces snapping to the rafters of the tavern. They stamped their scythes on the ground, adding to the cacophony of the drums. The blades were sharp enough to cut bark but blunt enough to make their Ember overseers feel safe. And if their limbs were covered with welts from the whip and their backs stooped from carrying heavy loads, the Maroon's shadows hid all that.

And if it didn't, the firerum would.

Griot Zibenwe took to the small wooden stage and signaled for the band to stop. He held a small djambe drum and wore a shawl patterned in bright reds and greens, well made if a little threadbare. His graying locs, which fell down to his waist, shimmied back and forth as he beat a new rhythm on his drum.

Griots were storytellers, Dusters who had taken it upon themselves to preserve their heritage in poetry, prose, and rhythm. Many of them worked in the plantations during the day, but at night they came alive with their stories.

There was a collective inhale as the energy from the dance shifted into anticipation of a new tale.

The drumbeat reached a crescendo and then abruptly stopped.

The audience stood on their heels, waiting with readiness for the griot's words. The silence pulled taut, the tension building, and just when the crowd thought they couldn't take it anymore the griot pounded the djambe three times.

Thump. Thump. Thump.

Then he spoke:

"Listen well. Sit close. This story will be told once, and only once. So listen well. Sit close."

Thump.

"Too close!"

Those sitting closest flinched, then laughed as a wicked grin spread across the griot's face.

He continued, "Let me take you to a time not too long ago, but not yesterday. A moment when the space between the peoples of the empire fractured a little more. Eighteen years ago. Not long ago at all."

Thump-ba-da-thump.

"There is one thing in life that weaves us all together. No matter your blood color, no matter your quarter—we are all birthed into this world as babes, naked under Anyme's sky."

"Absolve me of my sins, Anyme." The prayer was an instinctual reflex from the crowd.

"But when the babe cries the weave holding us together unravels. The colored threads of the empire pull apart, pull away. But there are those who resist the patterns laid down for them. And so, to the story I promised you today."

Thump-ba-da-thump.

"You may have heard of the Night of the Stolen, though the wardens tried to strangle the whispers on the wind. But for one night I will pry the wardens' grip from our necks and let the story free. It is a story about thieves in the night; about a rebellion brewing; about our wardens' home breached."

Thump.

"Duty."

The audience grumbled.

Thump.

"Truth."

The audience booed.

Thump.

"Strength."

Fists were raised in the air.

Thump.

"Knowledge."

The audience screamed their dissent to the beat of the drum.

Thump-ba-da-thump.

The griot stopped and leveled his gaze at a newcomer. "My stories may fill your mind, but they don't fill my coffer. Latecomers, pay up, stories aren't free. One slab apiece."

The griot paused until he heard the sound of a coin hitting his trinket box.

"Now, back we go. To the Wardens' Keep, where the court resides and the patrons sleep. Here we find three unwelcome shadows: a mother with her child, and the leader of their crimes, sneaking through the gates."

The griot's voice dropped to a whisper. "Do you know who

they were? The couple who crept in? Fleet of foot and quieter than a breath?"

"The Sandstorm!" a young Duster cried. Instead of a toy, she clutched her scythe.

"Eyoh! You have it right. Indeed, you have it right. The *Sandstorm*," Griot Zibenwe whispered the word and winked. "Just in case the officers hear your cheers.

"The Sandstorm had a plan that night. They crept into Ember houses and the Keep and cut down anyone in their path. And so, the three shadows moved through the Keep, death in their wake. Blue was their blood, but that night the Keep ran red."

Thump-ba-da-thump.

"Up and up the stairs they went. Toward the chambers where the nobility slept. Toward the chambers, where the babies were kept."

The griot lifted his hands from the drum and sliced them through the air. "The leader slashed his scythe through the nursemaid's neck. Blue blood stained the wall."

"He killed a Duster?" the young girl in the front cried.

The griot nodded sadly. "Yes, my friends, he killed one of his own. But I tell you this: love may give you strength, but retribution gives you purpose."

Thump.

"There in the center of the bedchamber, another baby lay. A babe whose blood ran red, unlike the blue-blooded child the mother held. Two years the Sandstorm had planned for this moment. The mother placed her Duster babe next to the other. Red and blue threads in the Sandstorm's plan. The Duster a decoy for the other, a life sacrificed to allow them to escape.

"The leader lifted the other baby. The child whose blood ran red. This new child, swapped, was the key to bringing down the empire. Neither looked back at the Duster child they left behind as they ran from the warden's home."

Thump.

"If you looked outside that night you might have seen other couples in flight. For the Sandstorm knew their craft. The craft of people wronged. Twelve children they stole and disappeared into the beyond."

The griot's voice softened, grew weaker, like he spoke his musings to himself.

"And that is where their story is silenced. A tale with no ending. What happened to the children they stole? Their doom impending."

He raised his head, his eyes shimmering.

"Dead is what the wardens say, destroyed like every rebellion. But sometimes I wonder, what was the Sandstorm's plan? And that of the stolen?"

The griot stood, the moroseness that had burdened him vanquished with a mischievous grin. "Remember, my friends: love gives you strength, but retribution gives you purpose."

Thump-ba-da-thump.

The audience cheered and stamped their scythes as the tale came to an end. The griot stood and reached for his trinket box, now brimming with slabs. He looped the strap of the djambe over his other hand and made his way through the crowd who congratulated him on his tale.

As he ascended the steps to the street above he listened for two things. First, to check whether the tidewind's wrath had quietened for the night, and secondly to hear the distinctive thud of an officer's boots. It was easy to know if an officer was nearby, as few people in the Dredge owned shoes.

When he heard neither, the griot pushed open the door to the Maroon and slipped out into the blackness of the night.

PART ONE

TRADE

Each of the thirteen cities of the Wardens' Empire specializes in different exports, creating a sustainable cycle of resources within a single market. Every city must meet its trade quota each mooncycle, often resulting in a higher death toll among those who labor in the fields. Sacrifices must be made in order to ensure economic stability within the empire; blood will always flow when an empire thrives.

—Extract from *Economic Independence* by Sibul Abundo

CHAPTER ONE

THE DAY OF DESCENT

I have been searching for any trace of the Sandstorm to complete my tale. Though the wardens claim to have killed them some years ago, I have no confirmation of where or when. It may be my aging eyesight, but I can't see the end of the story. The rumors are thin, wisps of smoke that I can't grasp. I will continue to search. I will continue to hope.

—Note found in Griot Zibenwe's villa

Bang-dera-bang-dera-bang.

The drumbeat still thrummed through Sylah's veins as she weaved her way back home.

The raw pink of dawn promised a blistering heat, and Sylah tilted her head and basked in the sun's rays. The trinkets in her braids chimed.

She ran her tongue over the joba seed tucked in the gap between her front teeth. The warmth induced by the seed was dissipating, leaving her cold. Hugging her arms to her chest, she noticed for the first time she held an empty bottle of firerum. She threw it at the wall of a derelict villa, which was filmed with blue sand. It had been a strong wind last night. At times its pounding had even eclipsed the drums.

But not the drumbeat in her memory.

Bang-dera-bang-dera-bang.

The sound came again and with it an unmistakable tremor of fear that woke people from their beds. Now Sylah listened and realized she knew the cadence of the rhythm, and it wasn't from the song in her mind. It was the pounding of the Starting Drum, indicating the beginning of a trial.

It was the sound of death.

Bang-dera-bang-dera-bang.

Dredge-dwellers began to seep out of their decrepit homes and stream toward Dredge Square. Sylah found herself being carried along in the current.

The square was full of Dusters and Ghostings, blurry-eyed from a night of drugs, sex, or alcohol. Or in Sylah's case, all three. A dozen officers of the warden army stood to attention in front of the rack, the wooden device used for executions. Like ripe bruises, the army's purple uniform was enough to instill fear in anyone north of the Ruta River—anyone without red blood.

Sylah spotted Hassa in the crowd and pushed her way toward her.

"How's it hurting?" Sylah greeted the Ghosting girl.

Like the beetle she had been named after, Hassa was small with dark eyes. The color was unusual for a Ghosting, as light-colored eyes were often a feature of their translucent blood. But it didn't matter if you were a Ghosting or a Duster, everyone who lived in the Dredge had the same hollowed-out look. It was a mandatory uniform, an expression of squalor and poverty enforced by malnutrition and childhood labor.

You look like shit. Have you even slept? Hassa signed.

Sylah ignored Hassa's observation and pointed toward the officers. "Have you seen this guy's talent?"

Hassa followed Sylah's gaze to the officer with the Starting Drum strapped to his chest. He was beating the rhythm with absolute dedication, his muscles clenching and releasing with military precision.

He was born to play the drums, Hassa agreed.

Sylah snorted. "Bet he wanted to join the playhouse, but his mother made him enlist in the army. Poor little Ember."

Hassa smiled, revealing the spongy flesh of her severed tongue. Her tongue, like her severed hands, had been taken from her at two mooncycles, like they were for every Ghosting in the empire. Their limbs and tongues were cut off and sent to the wardens to tally against the number of Ghosting births as a penance for a rebellion four hundred years old. As a result, Ghostings had developed a complex language that used all elements of their body. It was a subtle language, one invented in defiance of the rulers that still condemned them.

The drum stopped, though the vibrations of dread rippled out for moments afterward. The captain, identified by his striped green kente epaulettes, stepped forward.

"In the name of the four wardens, blessed by Anyme, our God in the Sky, we bring forth the accused."

A prisoner in shackles was brought forward between the officers' ranks. Sylah inhaled sharply between her teeth. "A griot."

They raided his villa a few strikes ago, no warning, Hassa signed. *He told his final story last night.*

Sylah vaguely remembered a griot entering the Maroon, but she had been preoccupied with chewing a record number of joba seeds.

"What did they get him for?"

Writing letters.

"Bastards."

Bastards, Hassa agreed, using her left wrist against her shoulder in a slashing motion.

Sylah scowled up at the podium where the officers stood. How she hated them and everything they represented: fear, oppression, pain. She rubbed her neck as the captain continued.

"The accused deliberately and maliciously plotted and engineered acts of rebellion against the Wardens' Empire through the written word. A crime punishable by death. May Anyme be our guide. May Anyme absolve you of your sins."

The griot's head hung low, his gray locs trailing the dirt in front of him.

"We pronounce you guilty of treason."

Sylah muttered, "They're *always* guilty."

Hassa nodded sadly. The trials always ended the same way.

A hush fell over the crowd as a ripper was spotted.

Rippers were Dusters, forced to turn on their own kind. It was their job to turn the lever that separated the two jaws of the rack. Their uniform was deep blue. Less washing that way.

Sylah shivered and ran her tongue over her teeth, probing for any residual joba seed juice, but the husk was dry. She spat the remains onto the ground.

"Ach." Hassa bared her teeth at the globule on the ground.

It's turning your teeth Ember.

"Ember?"

Hassa signed the word again. Sylah had been learning to understand the Ghosting language since she'd met Hassa six years ago, but she still stumbled now and then. "Ah, red." The two words were differentiated by an additional turn of the elbow. "Well, I don't care."

You should. The drug is very bad for you, it could kill you. The sign for "kill" was a wrist across the throat. For some reason the gesture made Sylah smile.

It's not funny.

Sylah met Hassa's stare and reached into the satchel at her waist. She pulled out her final seed and, with precision, squished it into the gap between her front teeth. The bitter juice took effect immediately, and she closed her eyes for a blissful moment.

The euphoria vibrated through her veins faster than the tide-wind. The feeling was so loud, so all-encompassing, that she was carried away from the scene before her.

But she'd seen enough rippings to know what happened next.

The prisoner would be chained to the rack's wooden bed with four manacles separating their limbs wide. Then the ripper would turn the lever and with each turn spread the wooden bed—and with it, the prisoner's limbs—even wider. First you would hear the prisoner's joints popping, then the cartilage tearing. Eventually, the skin would rupture, blue blood dripping. Sometimes a larger chain was wrapped around their midriff, so that their limbs were left intact, but their vital organs cleaved apart with each *click, click, click* of the lever.

Embers were never subjected to the horror of a ripping; their trials involved courtrooms and juries, although occasionally Embers would cross the Ruta River to watch those who had been condemned for doing something particularly nasty. The rack was tilted toward the audience for this very purpose. Nothing better than a family outing to watch a rapist get ripped to shreds.

If Sylah were in charge, the rippings would be the first thing to go, the racks broken, the splinters scattered like confetti.

Sylah opened her eyes, her blissful contentment at odds with the horror: fourteen turns of the rack and the griot was still alive.

Sylah whistled softly. "This griot's got some real stomach." A laugh burst out of her. "Well, no, I guess he hasn't." She gestured to the entrails on the ground.

People around her murmured sounds of dissent.

"Oh, fuck off, it's not like you haven't seen it before. They do it once a mooncycle."

Sylah. Hassa tugged on Sylah's arm. *Be quiet, you're going to draw the officers' attention.*

But the joba seed saturated Sylah with confidence.

"Why should I be quiet? What's the point when it could be *any of us next?*"

Hassa turned to Sylah and pushed her backward through the crowd. Though Sylah stood two handspans taller than Hassa, the joba seed robbed her of her stability, and Sylah drifted backward like a feather.

Sylah, get up. Hassa was standing over her.

"When did you get up there?" The warmth of the joba seed enveloped her, and as exhaustion settled within her bones she lay backward, her plaits fanning out.

They were braided with trinkets, fragments of a family she no longer had and that carried with them the frayed threads of memories and so were cherished above all else. Some she wove lovingly in her hair each mooncycle. Others, a leaf, a melon rind, had simply appeared uninvited and masqueraded as valued tokens.

Two sheer pebbles of glass, dangling from her fringe. The mottled remains of a woven scarf that had been absently stroked to tatters. Strands of a bow string and a quill knotted side by side at the end of two braids. The shell of a sand snail behind her ear.

When she tilted her head, her hair clacked like aching bones knocking together.

The skeleton of all the pieces of her.

No lice, though. Sylah was proud of that.

The braids were shorter, the hair coarser, angrier, where they frizzed around the scar that ran ear to ear across the back of her neck. A puckered smile from the officers who had cut her.

That had cut them all down in the end.

She rubbed the keloid skin absently. Six years, and still the scar refused to fade.

Hassa kicked Sylah in the shin.

"Ow, go away. Can't you see I'm sleeping?"

Sylah, you can't sleep here.

"Why not?"

Because you're in the middle of the street.

Sylah turned her head left and right, and saw, through the molasses of her daze, that she was indeed in the middle of the street. The crowds from the ripping had already begun to disperse, some stepping over Sylah without a qualm.

Sylah, get up. Hassa offered her wrist, and Sylah took it reluctantly.

As much as she wanted to sleep, the officers were still on patrol, and despite her earlier outburst, Sylah didn't want to be their next victim. Though sleeping on the streets wasn't an offense, she was sure the officers wouldn't simply step over her. And their boots were *heavy.*

Come on, let's get you home.

Hassa began to lead the way through the Dredge toward the Duster Quarter, Sylah resting her elbow on Hassa's shoulder.

Are you going to go to the Descent later? Hassa asked.

Sylah growled low in her throat. For a moment she had forgotten it was the Day of Descent. But now she looked around and spotted the signs of the holiday sprouting like weeds in the streets. Limp kente cloth flags and dirty rope streamers were strung from roof to roof. The breeze carried the smell of candied plantains, boiled in sugar that had been hoarded just for the occasion.

But no matter how hard the bakers tried, the aroma couldn't

mask the Dredge's pungent smell of unwashed bodies and filth. Even if you were lucky and the wind blew the other way, you'd get the acrid smell of raw latex from the rubber plantation fields outside the city's walls. Depended if you preferred spoiled cheese or shit, really. Sylah barely noticed either scent anymore.

"The Descent? Ha! No. I'm not going to watch four people walk down some stairs and call it a festival."

It's not just four people walking down some stairs, it's the changing of the government. The disciples taking their holy seats as wardens. Hassa's eyebrows pulled her shaven scalp toward her ears as she frowned.

"Blah blah blah."

It only happens every ten years. I don't remember the last Descent Day.

"'Course you don't, you were only seven."

You were only ten, Hassa shot back, mischief alight in her dark eyes.

"Exactly, so I don't need to go again. I remember it all." In fact, she'd tried to forget it many times.

Sylah ran her tongue over her teeth. "Hassa, I've run out of joba seeds."

I'm glad.

"I need to buy more."

Sylah, I'm not trading with you anymore. You're taking too much.

"It's not for me, it's for my friends."

You don't have any friends.

Hassa's eyes were hollow. Sylah reached for them, and Hassa batted her away with her wrist.

Promise me, promise me you won't take any more this week.

"I promise."

Hassa was visibly torn. *Do you have any slabs?*

Slabs were the currency of the empire. They were made of whitestone and stamped with the faces of previous wardens, just in case the citizens forgot who was in charge.

Sylah did not have any slabs. She'd lost another apprenticeship the night before, and she'd been drinking and chewing away her troubles all night.

"Trade?" Sylah offered.

Trading was the Ghosting way, more so than their roles as servants, because they chose to trade. Servitude to Embers was thrust upon them. Most Ghostings traded and smuggled goods. Drugs, firerum, materials, kitchen utensils—if you needed it, a Ghosting could get it, and Hassa was one of the best.

Fine. What have you got to trade? Hassa turned to access her stash from her bag, the opening large enough for both of her forearms to rummage in. Sylah stumbled as soon as Hassa let her go. The joba seed juice would thrum through her blood for some time yet.

"I have this." Sylah pulled out the runelamp from her satchel. Blown from the azure sand of the Farsai Desert, the lamp was a circular glass shell. It was no better than a fufu bowl without the bloodwerk that marked it: dark blood crafted into runes. Once activated, the runelamp created a deep red glow that was used instead of fire torches.

Bloodwerk was what really set Embers apart from the rest of the citizens. Red blood, when written into specific strokes and dashes, had the power to manipulate and move objects. It was the true power that placed Embers above the rest of them.

Sylah, that's broken.

"Shit, I must have smudged the runes in my bag." She hadn't; she'd found it that way. The chain of crimson runes were damaged, rendering the lamp useless. Sylah copied them down anyway; maybe one day she'd figure out how to bloodwerk. She could then sell runelamps by the dozen, making her a lot of slabs.

And more slabs meant more joba seeds.

"Will you still trade it?"

No, I can't sell this, Sylah. If you want to get the bloodwerk fixed, I will trade for it. Not until then. I hear a new master of blood has moved into the Duster Quarter. Doing penance, I'm sure.

"Oh, come on, Hassa, you know every master of blood charges Dusters double."

He charges Ghostings triple.

Sylah swore.

Find me something I can trade.

A couple of Ghostings emerged from their ramshackle villa and waved at Hassa. If the beige of their servant uniforms didn't set them apart, then the gray-brown pallor of their skin did. Ghostings had always seemed like beautiful dolls to Sylah. Dolls whose hands and tongues the empire had severed and then discarded at the bottom of their toy chest.

Hassa signed back to them, then turned to Sylah. *I have to go. If I don't see you at the Descent, I'll see you at the Maroon later?*

Sylah scowled, frustrated that her friend wouldn't trade with her for joba seeds. She'd have to find another dealer.

CHAPTER TWO

It is my fervent belief that severing the hands and tongues of Ghostings benefits their well-being. Those whose wounds fester are weeded out young, their frail countenance discarded before they become a nuisance to their masters. Those who survive understand the power of pain and the importance of subservience.

—Journal entry by Aveed, Disciple of Duty

The Day of Descent and Ascent were two of the few holidays Dusters and Ghostings were given. The Dredge would be emptying soon; everyone making their way up to the Keep to watch the four wardens abdicate to their disciples, their seconds-in-command. Sylah didn't care for it. One Ember was the same as the next, no matter who ruled. The ceremony would bring the wardens' decade-long reign to an end and start the reign of the new wardens. The other holiday was the Day of Ascent, in six mooncycles, once the new disciples were determined through a set of trials. At least on that holiday Sylah could make some money betting on who'd win.

She hawked, her phlegm carrying the husk of the seed she had been chewing. Her last one. The ecstasy from the joba seed now slid into a feeling of deep emptiness that was like stepping backward from a fire: you could see and smell the flames, but their warmth was a mere memory cooling on your skin.

Sylah needed to find something to trade, and quick. Not having any seeds in reserve put her nerves on edge. Hassa was wrong. She wasn't having too much.

There was only one place in Nar-Ruta for Sylah to find something to barter: the empty villas that lined the outer streets of the Dredge. The villas had once been full of Ghosting families, but they now stood empty as a disease known as the sleeping sickness decimated the Ghostings' numbers. The illness seemed only to affect those with translucent blood, stopping their hearts in their sleep. Dusters, not to forgo an opportunity—you had to take them where you could in the Wardens' Empire—had begun to occupy the Ghosting villas they left behind.

And so the district that had once been known as the Ghosting Quarter became the Dredge: an amalgamation of the two blood colors and yet somehow less than both. It was rare to find a business there that didn't trade in sex, alcohol, or drugs.

The houses in the Dredge were made of limestone, cheaper and less robust than whitestone, which was the only substance used in the Wardens' Keep and the Ember Quarter south of the Ruta River. The tidewind had sanded most of the unoccupied villas down to the bare bones of their foundations. Their skeletal remains lined the street as if it were a Ghosting graveyard.

But Sylah knew it for what it really was, a treasure trove.

Sylah entered the first villa on her right, stepping lightly over a crumbling doorframe into a common room thick with blue sand from the Farsai Desert and the night's tidewind. Pushing around the rubble, wood, and debris, all she could find was a rusty old spoon. She pocketed it just in case.

The next villa was painted with the black cross of the sleeping sickness. Sylah reached out and touched it, her finger coming away black.

"Still wet." Whoever had lived there had died of the disease that morning, and now no one could enter. The disease was said to be so contagious that their bodies had to be burned within moments of them dying, even though it was a holiday. Sylah looked at the horizon where smoke curled up to the sky beyond the city's walls—a pyre.

Sylah sighed and swirled her tongue around her mouth. The seed's bitter juice had waned completely, leaving her with an aching gap between her teeth. The effect was fading faster and faster these days.

She took extra care searching the next villa, which, with more than three rooms, was bigger than most. It was once the home of a rich Ghosting, though a rich Ghosting was still poor compared to a Duster and utterly deprived by Ember standards.

"Ah!" In the third room, a picture frame nestled in the corner. Blue sand had burrowed into its furrows, but when she turned it over the painting was still intact.

A young family looked back at her. They were Ghostings, their gray-brown complexions captured in paint. But something was . . . different.

"One, two, three sets of hands . . . even the baby." That meant the painting had been made before the Siege of the Silent. The picture was nearly four hundred years old, before the Ghostings started paying penance for an uprising against the wardens. They had lain siege to the Keep for two mooncycles, rebelling against the wardens' rule. It took time, but in the end the wardens recruited a squadron of ten thousand soldiers, forming the first warden army, led by the Warden of Strength.

Though the rebellion had happened centuries ago, the Ghostings still suffered for the deeds of their ancestors.

Sylah's fingertips ran up and over the strokes of paint until they found the corner of the canvas, and then she slipped her finger under the painting's lip and pulled down, ripping it from the frame. Sylah surveyed her prize. The frame looked like oak, a tree that was hard to cultivate in the harsh weather of the empire. If it was, it would be worth a lot.

Sylah smiled. Today was a good day.

As she got up to leave, Sylah stooped to pick up an aged piece of parchment next to her that had slipped out from behind the frame.

The parchment was old, but sturdy, the wording archaic and decorative. Her heart soared at the thought of more treasure but sunk just as quickly when she saw the words "Marion Sea." It was just a map of the empire.

Sylah splayed her hand across the illustration of the Wardens' Empire. There it was, in the palm of her hand: the whole world. The capital city of Nar-Ruta lay to the south, its four quarters divided by the blue line of the Ruta River. A spiderweb of trade routes spread northward from the capital to the other twelve cities. Sylah traced her finger northward past the coal mines of Jin-Kutan and the salt flats of Ood-Lopah. Up, up her dirty fingernail went, to the northwest of the continent to the village of Ood-Zaynib, where she grew up.

"The Sanctuary," she whispered. The Sanctuary was where she was raised.

Though the map didn't show it, she could see the Sanctuary's whitestone building ringed with sand dunes and fields of rubber trees.

The Marion Sea surrounded the empire. The sea was a death trap, and the map captured its dangers with jagged blue and black waves churning around the island. But Sylah had to laugh when she saw the gray drawing of the Tannin; the mythical sea creature was the subject of many children's nightmares but few grown-ups believed in it.

And then her fingers ran along the jagged edge of one side. Half of the map had been torn away.

But there in the top right corner, was that the swirl of another letter? The smudge of another land?

No, it couldn't be, there was no more land beyond the empire. The island was all that was left. Everything else had been consumed by the Ending Fire.

Sylah snorted. So not only was the map torn, it was inaccurate too. She rolled it up and added it to her satchel. Maybe she could paint over the corner and trade it.

By the time Sylah had finished scavenging, the usual joba seed dens were empty, the customers dispersed to the Keep to watch the Descent.

"Clockmaster, what's the time?"

The clockmaster slumped on his stoop at the streetcorner, a bottle of firerum dripping amber liquid from his limp hand. There was only one clock in Nar-Ruta, and few had even seen it. It stood in the cloisters of the Keep, and as the bell rang at each strike, the first clockmaster would call out the time to the next clockmaster in the chain. Sluggishly, with no urgency, the cry would travel through the Ember Quarter, across the Ruta River, and over to the Duster Quarter, eventually making its way to the Dredge.

So don't ever expect a Dredge-dweller to be on time.

There was one other place she could try: Maiden Turin's. She didn't like dealing with the maiden, but she had an aching hunger between her teeth that couldn't wait until she next saw Hassa. She bit down on the familiar scars of her cheek, pulling in her already gaunt face. Blood flooded her mouth.

MAIDEN TURIN'S VILLA was the largest in the Dredge. Years ago she had settled her business within walking distance of every tavern and seed dealer in the Dredge.

As soon as Sylah's knuckles rasped against the wooden door, a Ghosting answered with a smile as manufactured as a rubber sole. Their forearm was looped through the wide handle, the door designed to swing back and forward on oiled hinges for a Ghosting's ease of use. Sylah recognized them as one of the people who had helped raise Hassa, though she couldn't remember their name. They were a musawa, neither man nor woman, like the God Anyme. Sylah recollected this Ghosting preferred the pronoun "they," though some musawa went by "she" or "he."

They stepped back from the door, letting Sylah enter the maiden house.

From the moment a Ghosting's hands and tongue were severed, they were assigned a noble household where they would cook, clean, or do whatever else the Embers wanted. But some Ghostings were rejected by their Ember masters, for being lazy or for spying or some other ridiculous accusation, and simply thrown out on the streets to die.

So maiden houses like Turin's sprang up, welcoming discarded Ghostings with open arms. Embers turned a blind eye—in fact, they were some of Turin's most devoted clientele. Sylah had often seen their shrouded carriages waiting outside the maiden houses, and she and Hassa frequently made a game of throwing rotting fish through the windows.

"Sylah? Be that you?" Turin wrapped a silk overall across her bare body, her movements as calculated as a desert fox's. Her braids, woven tightly and precisely, fell to her waist, and her features were as bold as they were round. She jutted her chin at the Ghosting who had answered the door. "Go put on some coffee beans."

"I'm just w-wondering," Sylah stammered. Her body began to quiver, a symptom that often followed a night of particularly heavy joba use. There was only one remedy. More joba seeds.

"You're either in or out, Sylah, no loitering on my doorstep." Turin had already disappeared into the bowels of her home.

Sylah scratched the scar at the back of her neck and followed.

The living room hadn't been cleared of the night's revelry, and the heavy musk of sex still clung to the shadows.

"I assume you're here about a job? Heard you lost your apprenticeship at the glasskeep?" Turin tossed her braids backward, her silk overall slipping from her shoulder.

"No," Sylah answered quickly. "I'm sorry, I mean, no thank you." Working at the glasskeep had been a disaster, which Sylah only endured in order to learn as many bloodwerk runes as possible from the runelamps she had to wash. And even though she was in need of work, she'd rather toil in the fields than work for Turin.

The maiden leaned back in her chair and surveyed Sylah. Her gaze was like a claw dragging along her skin, and Sylah winced.

"We're closed for the Descent, but I can make an exception for you. You've made me enough money in the Ring. What will it be? Tall, small, old, bald?"

The Ghosting came in with the coffee. She used her foot to remove the leather harness from the table and plonked down the tray.

"I'm not here for a . . ."

"Nightworker?" Turin offered. "Didn't think this was your type of establishment; you should try Maiden Sefar down riverside." She pulled out a radish leaf cigar, lit it, and took a drag. "Less . . . particular, some might say."

Sylah's shaking fingers spun in knots on her lap. "Might you have any joba seeds to sell?"

"My, my." Turin's eyebrows lifted through the smoke.

"I could trade you this frame." Her offering looked pitiful next to the silver coffee set.

"That frame's worth about half a slab." Turin took a drag, her eyes shriveling to half-moons. "It's cheap rubber wood." She exhaled a cloud. "Besides, trading's not really my thing. I leave that to the rabble." She gave a pointed look to the Ghosting who was pouring the coffee.

Sylah looked at the map in her bag. Maybe Turin would be interested in that? But then Sylah looked around at the lavish oil paintings that covered the walls. Probably not.

"When are you next fighting in the Ring?"

Sylah hadn't realized how long the silence had stretched until Turin sliced it with the knife of her words. Sylah closed her satchel and replied, "Next week."

"Marigold," Turin barked.

Marigold, that was their name . . . Sylah recalled.

With no voice and no hands, it was impossible for Ghostings to name themselves something *convenient* for Dusters and Embers to say. So Dusters and Embers chose names for them, often after animals or flowers, things that the Ghosting servant reminded them of.

Marigold appeared. Their chin was dusted with the shadow of a beard beneath their counterfeit smile.

"Marigold, go and get my stash of joba seeds. The one for customers."

Turin turned back to Sylah.

"Marigold's one of my best, you know. They like the whip." Turin winked, and Sylah dipped her eyes toward her coffee cup. She doubted very much that Marigold liked the whip.

"I'm glad I've still got Marigold. I've been losing nightworkers to the sleeping sickness for the last two years."

"Oh, yeah?" Sylah hated small talk.

"Indeed. It's strange how the sleeping sickness only kills off the weakest of the empire."

Sylah had nothing to say to that. While it was true that no Duster or Ember seemed to get the sleeping sickness, Turin's attitude was all too common—that Ghostings were lesser than everyone.

They sat in silence until Marigold returned to the room holding a small packet. Too small a packet, in Sylah's opinion.

Turin held the packet out to her, and Sylah snatched the joba seeds and put them into her satchel.

"How much is it?"

"Thirty slabs."

Sylah swallowed her shock with a gulp.

"I don't—"

Turin smiled. "You have until the tidewind to pay me back."

Midnight? Surely Turin knew that would be impossible. The feeling of safety the seeds had given her was fading already like the smoke from Turin's cigar.

"I c . . . can't do that." Sylah handed them back.

Turin closed Sylah's hand over the packet of seeds.

"Why don't you fight in the Ring tonight? Surely you could make some money that way?"

Sylah understood now. Turin always placed her bets on Sylah. But she wasn't due to fight for another week. She'd have to go see Loot . . .

She nodded weakly.

"Thirty slabs, Sylah, before midnight. Don't want to get caught in the tidewind now, do you?"

Sylah shook her head and slipped a joba seed out of the packet. She didn't want to think about what would happen if she didn't pay the maiden back. The tidewind was the perfect cover-up for any murders committed in the Dredge. But that was a worry for another time that the anticipation of her next joba seed smothered.

"May Anyme protect you." The maiden of the house waved her away with a blessing, the cigar smoke, like an extended talon, following her out.

Now creaking floorboards and the patter of bare feet were the only sounds in the maiden house. Ghostings crossed Sylah's path in diaphanous fabrics. Bandages, like flags of conquered armies, littered their skin—tokens of the type of clientele Turin catered to.

Coffee and bile and anger raged in Sylah's throat. That's the thing with having transparent blood.

No one could see you bleed.

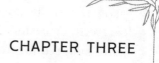

CHAPTER THREE

Warden of Truth—To preach and incite justice.
Warden of Duty—To nourish and maintain the land.
Warden of Knowledge—To teach and discover all.
Warden of Strength—To protect and enforce the law.
Warden of Crime—To resist and sow chaos.

—The Wardens' Vows

Sylah lingered outside the maiden house, a joba seed between her finger and thumb. Her hand lurched toward her mouth, but she held off biting down, savoring the rawness of reality for the briefest of moments.

The maiden house faced away from the Ruta River, toward the plantation fields outside of the city walls, where, on a clear morning, you'd be able to see the lines of rubber trees and the specks of Dusters toiling in the sun. Some of the field workers were as young as ten, the age at which a Duster's schooling was complete and they were deemed old enough to go to work.

Ghostings didn't go to school at all. Instead, they were forced into service as soon as they could walk. Sylah had seen Ghosting children wandering around in beige uniforms too big for their bodies, their maimed arms hauling coal or sweeping courtyards with brooms adjusted with horizontal handles for their forearms to grasp.

Most cleaning tools had been adapted for Ghostings' use. It wasn't out of kindness; simply put, the Embers wanted the job done well. Occasionally a Ghosting would come across a tool that wasn't adapted for them. It was why every Ghosting kept a pair of soft leather straps on their person, as tying the tool to their forearm was sometimes the only way to complete the task.

It wasn't an uncommon sight to see a Ghosting child's forearms strapped into a dustpan and broom, the implements bigger than their heads.

At least Dusters had ten years of childhood before they were assessed and categorized under one of the four guilds of the empire: strength, knowledge, truth, or duty.

If the empire needed more foot soldiers, you were assigned strength, even if you were crippled by malnutrition. If they needed teachers, you were assigned knowledge, despite having only a handful of years of schooling. If they needed Rippers, you were assigned to truth to tear down the flesh of your people while an officer watched. If they needed more field workers, you were assigned to duty, where your skin was routinely torn open by an overseer's whip. It was where most Dusters ended up, laboring for cotton, rubber, or sugarcane.

Once your role was appointed, the guild mark was then branded onto your skin. A reminder of your worth.

Sylah scratched the grooves on the underside of her wrist. A memory roiled through her: of charred flesh, hot metal, and salty blood.

Papa had offered her the iron. She remembered how her hand had shook with the weight of it, the brand glowing red. She didn't cry as she pressed the brand against her wrist, though she wanted to.

Papa hated tears.

"We need you to be able to blend in with Dusters when the time comes," he said over the sound of her sizzling skin.

She was six years old.

Sylah bit down on the joba seed. The release of the drug washed away the smell of burning flesh from her memory.

She closed her eyes to the world around her, reveling in the euphoria. The atrocities of the empire were not the reality she wanted to see. Once, long ago, she'd been promised more. But no longer. Better to blunt the sharp edges of the realm with drugs.

This was all that mattered now.

THE FESTIVE SPIRIT of the Day of Descent permeated Sylah's high as she weaved her way through the Dredge. She waved to a few children flapping kente flags, though one of them ran away in tears screaming that Sylah's "mouth was full of blood."

Once the peak of the drug had lessened, Sylah made her way to Loot's in the center of the Dredge. She needed to pay back her debt to Turin, and this was the only way to do it.

"How's it hurting, Fayl?" Sylah greeted Fayl, the watcher at the door.

"Easing up now you're here, Sylah." Fayl handed her a flask of firerum. His muscular arms were scored with intricate blue blood-ink. Dusters weren't allowed to write, but bloodink tattoos had become a small type of rebellion. The swirls, if you squinted really hard, almost looked like words. "You?"

"Flaming rough. I've seen piles of shit that I liked better than this day," she grunted. The rum burned her throat, bringing her out of the joba seed numbness. "You not going like the rest?" She took another swig.

"Eyoh no, seen four Descents in my time. Saw Kalad make the Descent two decades ago. Made sure I had a prime viewing spot for him . . ." He raised his eyebrows. "If you get what I'm saying."

"I always get what you're saying, Fayl."

"Aho, don't judge me. At the end of the day Dusters, Ghostings, Embers, they all look the same as any nightworker in a maiden's house once you get them nekkid. Two arms, two legs, no hands for the Ghostings, I guess, but they all have the same—"

"Fayl." Sylah grimaced.

Fayl's face went slack in innocence. "What? I was just going to say they all have the same bananas under their clothes. Some are bigger than others, some are plantain, if you—"

"Get what you're saying? Yes, Fayl." Sylah rubbed her brows.

"Well, my thoughts is this, I don't give one fuck what blood pumps in their veins. Who cares if the Embers can bloodwerk? Why do they get to rule? I say us Nowerks should have a shot at the top."

Sylah winced at the name Nowerk. It was an insult used by Embers toward Ghostings and Dusters, but Loot's guild members, the Gummers, had begun to reclaim it, manipulating it into a term of camaraderie.

Sylah sucked her teeth. "That's dangerous talk, Fayl. Can't be saying things against the wardens."

He shrugged, his hair frizzing around him in soft waves.

"There's only one warden I've pledged to follow. And it ain't those shits sitting in their fortress and the four guilds they lead. He might not be elected through the trials, or have a seat in the court, but he's the one we chose. The one us Gummers follow: 'To resist and sow chaos.'" He chanted out the Warden of Crime's mantra.

Sylah heard other Gummers echoing Fayl's vow down the tunnels behind him. The words had the lilt of a prayer.

But Loot wasn't just Fayl's watcher. He was Fayl's husband.

Sylah spat out a joba seed.

Fayl looked at it and frowned. "Sylah—"

"Strong tidewind last night." She cut him off. Sylah liked Fayl, as he was a good watcher. His bulk scared away the rabble. But behind his size he was a kind-hearted man who was always willing to share his firerum with those he liked. Still, Sylah didn't need another lecture. After all, she had Hassa for that.

"They've been getting stronger for a while. You heard it killed another person? They were coming out of a joba den last night." Fayl looked at the sky. "Never known it to kill this many, in all my years, Sylah, I tell you. Three in the Dredge this week alone. Nasty way to die, tearing skin from flesh, think I'd prefer the rack."

Sylah thought of the griot and wasn't sure she agreed with Fayl.

"How's Lio?" Fayl asked.

Sylah soured at the mention of her mother. "Fine." She'd have to tell Lio that she'd lost another apprenticeship. "Is Loot in? Putting my name down."

"Yeah, he's in, head on down." Fayl moved out of the way to let Sylah past to the stairway beyond. "Oh, and Sylah, watch out, he's in a terrible mood."

"Perfect."

"My bet's on you, Sylah."

Sylah wondered if it was true, if Loot even let him bet.

"Thanks."

The damp stairway led Sylah to the maze of tunnels under the Dredge affectionately known as the Intestines, probably because of all the shit that went down them. There were many pathways under the city, but no one truly knew where they all led. Countless Dusters had gone missing over the years, led astray by the myth that one of the tunnels led to the warden treasury under the river. If they ever got there, though, they never got out again.

Sylah was careful to follow the pattern she had memorized. Left, left, right, middle. Loot said if you weren't smart enough to memorize the sequence, then you weren't worth Loot's time. He valued wit above all else.

The tunnels led to Loot's headquarters, which he called the Belly. There the soft orange glow of the runelamps was like the rays of a permanent sunset, and the room was claggy with a soft haze of incense. Books, dozens, hundreds, ran from floor to ceiling, with not one speck of dust mottling their crisp pages.

And in the middle of it all, the self-proclaimed Warden of Crime sat on a three-legged stool. Word on the tidewind was that he had stolen it from the Warden of Strength's privy room. Sylah once checked. The initials Y. E. were stamped into the underside. It was a statement, proof his network could get anywhere, even into the Keep.

Of course, it was just as likely it was a story he'd crafted, that the wooden stool was nothing but a piece of junk and he'd carved the initials himself. He loved theatrics.

"Loot." Sylah nodded.

He closed the book he was reading with a snap.

"Here she is, my glorious fighter. What a surprise." Loot had the slightest lisp that somehow made him even more august. He was smiling widely. Not a good sign.

Loot was dressed like one of the wardens themselves in a rich mustard suit, and his brown eyes sparkled as she walked into the light. A spider brooch was pinned to his left breast, the glittering black diamond eyes twinkling in the runelamp light. At forty-five he was young to have founded a dynasty. But it would be a mistake to assume that made him inexperienced.

"By the blood, you look like a pile of eru dung."

"Steaming on a cold winter's morning," Sylah added, brushing a braid from her eyes, the glass beads clicking together.

"Ha!" Loot snorted. "Always the poet." Loot pushed his gold spectacles up his nose with a manicured finger. That was the thing with Loot: everything about him was elegant. From the well-groomed beard to the tips of his eru leather shoes. His obsidian skin was a flawless black mirror.

The crime guild token dangled by Loot's waist. It was a cross engraved in a coin of metal—the only letter Dusters were allowed to use, and even then, it was mostly used to sign death certificates. The emblem was a mockery of the guild tokens given to Embers when they chose their guild at twenty years old.

Choice? Sylah didn't know what that felt like.

A Ghosting servant, their brown uniform tied at the waist with a yellow band, brought out an opulent teapot. Like the wardens themselves, Loot had Ghosting servants, and he branded them as his own with a yellow sash. Sylah wondered which Ember official he bribed to get them assigned to him and not a noble Ember.

The servant's wrist was threaded through the large handle of the steaming, gilded teapot while they supported the base with their other limb. It was rumored that the teapot was the vessel Loot had used to poison the former crime lords of Nar-Ruta. It clinked as it touched the marble table in front of Loot.

"Tea?" It wasn't really a question. You didn't say no when Loot asked you if you wanted tea.

Sylah nodded, and he waved at a nearby chair and she sank into it. She twirled the braid with the scarf woven in until it pulled painfully at the root.

Whistling, Loot tipped a small sachet of powder into the tea. It was poison, though Sylah didn't know what type. He filled two flowery teacups to the brim and spooned three lumps of sugar into his. Sylah reached for hers, and Loot's brown eyes watched her above the rim of the teacup as she sipped.

Once she'd swallowed the poisoned tea, Loot continued. "So I'm guessing you're not here just for my famous tea."

"No." She tipped her head, her plaits falling around her face like curtains. "I want in on the Ring."

"You're not due up until next week."

"Bring me forward."

"I'd have to bump Ows. You know he doesn't like that."

"I . . . I need the money." Her fingers itched to fondle the remaining joba seeds in her satchel.

"Aho, did you burn down the glasskeep too?"

Sylah scowled, "I never burned down anything."

"That's not the story Abod the baker is telling."

"Just a bit of bread, that's all."

"So you didn't burn down the bakery, or steal the silk from the tailors, or misplace all the vegetables from Kala's mart? They just couldn't keep on such a bright young woman through no fault of her own."

"Exactly." Sylah drank more of the nectar tea. It was always sickly sweet. It had to be to mask the bitterness of Loot's sordid games.

"You know the rules, though."

Sylah nodded, keeping her black eyes on her teacup.

"Can't have you winning again, so this time, win one, lose two. I've got One-ear Lazo up tonight. It'll be a good match. He might even beat you."

They both guffawed.

"Be at the Ring at seventh strike. We'll settle after." Loot downed his tea and picked up his book, waving at the servant to clear the table. Sylah clutched her teacup in her hand, refusing to part with it when the servant reached for it with their limbs.

"Before," Sylah said. She didn't want to be in debt to Maiden Turin longer than she had to.

"Pardon?" He didn't look up from his book.

"We'll settle before, or I won't lose. I'll win them all and leave with the prize money."

Loot was faster than she expected. If she hadn't had the joba seeds and firerum, she might have been quicker. But as it was, he grasped a fistful of hair, sending her beloved trinkets clattering around her on the stone floor.

She twisted to meet him face-to-face, careful not to pull on her hair. He was holding a dagger up to her face, and two Gummers had stepped out of the shadows. The dagger wouldn't do much damage. She'd fought off worse without a weapon.

"Now, I have no doubt you can get out of this. I've seen you tackle three men to the ground with little more than your fists." His smile was wide, the whites of his teeth like stars in the night sky of his skin. "But the thing is, in about two strikes you'll start to feel a smidge queasy. Then you'll get a headache, right here, that'll make your brain feel like it's being carved in two." He ran the blunt side of his blade down her forehead, his smile roguish. "Then blood will start running out of your nose and ears. You'll start vomiting, incessantly." The word ran together with his lisp, but Sylah didn't laugh. "Until your vomit runs blue from the blood of your guts disintegrating within you. Then, finally, after two more strikes of the purest form of agony, you'll die."

He stared deep into her eyes, shifting back and forth between them. Looking for something; she wasn't sure what.

She forced a smile, and he grimaced. "Your teeth are going red. I thought you were better than that." He shoved her away, knocking her dainty teacup over.

She pulled in a ragged breath, "I don't know why people say, 'better than that,'—who's 'that' and why should I listen to them?"

Loot scrutinized her, then burst into laughter. "You really have got fire in your blood."

She nodded; if only he knew.

"Bring it to the Ring. Then we'll talk money." Sylah didn't remember seeing his Gummers melt back into the shadows.

He pulled out the antidote seemingly from thin air. The small glass vile held droplets of a liquid that could just as well be water. She downed it straightaway. Better to be safe than dead.

"See you later, Loot."

He had already turned back to his book.

CHAPTER FOUR

*Submit to my leadership or perish. In numbers we thrive.
To resist and sow chaos.*

*Yours,
Loot, your new Warden of Crime*

—Letter sent to every crime lord in the empire, year 403

The Ring wouldn't open until the moon rose, so Sylah had some time to waste. She couldn't wait it out at home. Her mother would be the only one in their neighborhood guaranteed not to have gone to watch the Descent. She'd have to report her unemployment to the duty office, but Sylah was more fearful of reporting it to her mother.

Sylah consumed another joba seed and let her limbs drift her along with the last few Dusters and Ghostings still heading toward the Keep.

The army's presence increased the farther away she got from Loot's headquarters. They speckled the landscape purple, like a disease that could kill you at any moment. There were generally fewer patrols in the Dredge than in the Duster Quarter. Some assumed it was because of the smell, but Sylah had her own speculations. In the six years she'd lived in the city, not once had she seen a Gummer on the rack. Loot must have made a deal with the wardens, she was sure of it.

An officer caught Sylah's eye as she made her way into the Duster Quarter, and Sylah stuck her tongue out at her.

"You!" She had a runegun, a weapon powered by bloodwerk runes on the shaft, and unwound her hand from it to point at Sylah.

"Fuck," Sylah swore under her breath.

The other people on the street hunkered down into their shoulders and quickened their pace.

"I said, you! You stinking Nowerk. Get over here." Her gloved finger jabbed at the air like a miniature knife.

"Officer?" Sylah felt herself tilting to the side, and she leaned forward on the officer's shoulder.

"Don't touch me, you filthy Duster." She brushed off Sylah's touch like *she* was the disease. "Empty your bag."

Sylah jammed her hands into her satchel, expecting the bag to be empty, but then she felt the parchment. The *map*. Her heart stopped. If they found her with written words, they might assume she wrote them. Why had she kept that blood-forsaken map?

She fished around in the dusty crumbs at the bottom of the bag, buying herself some time.

Sylah looked around, but there were too many of them. And they had runeguns. So Sylah withdrew the only other thing in her satchel. The one thing that might stop them looking further.

"Knew it, could see your red stains from a league away." The officer grinned, revealing too big teeth for her mouth, and then unbuttoned her breast pocket, where she put the packet among the other seeds she had confiscated.

Sylah's anger burned, kindled by the drug. *How fucking dare they?*

The next words slipped out of Sylah's mouth before she could contain them.

"What do you do with them? The drugs you take from us? Do you trade them? So eventually they make their way back to my hand, but you're all the richer?"

The cold butt of the runegun struck Sylah's midriff, sending her reeling.

"Next time you talk back to an Ember, you'll be on the rack. Now scatter, you Nowerk scum. The wardens have begun their Descent, and you owe them your *respect.*"

Sylah was bent double, her breath coming out in uneven puffs. She didn't feel the pain; she rarely did when chewing joba seeds.

Sylah righted herself and let herself be herded toward the river.

The Ruta River was a swirling mass of cobalt quicksand that bisected the city, with the Keep and Ember district on one side and the Duster Quarter and the Dredge on the other. And suspended five hundred handspans above the Ruta was the black iron bridge called the Tongue.

The trotro, the bloodwerk-powered trolley used to freight goods, clattered through the dust and debris left from the tidewind on one side of the Tongue. Its crates, normally full of goods going to the Ember market, were empty as every merchant made their way to the Keep.

Sylah fingered the three joba seeds left in her satchel. She'd coaxed them from the packet before handing over the rest to the officer. Her eyes darted to the next squadron of officers up ahead. They lined the Ember side of the Tongue as she neared. Their stance was different here, still alert, still ready to trigger their runeguns, but somehow more at ease on their own ground.

"Keep up the pace, Nowerks, stick to the main street," an officer barked.

Sylah complied for the moment, following the throng of Dusters and Ghostings until she found an opportunity to slip away.

"Get out of the way! Move!" The driver's shout was unnecessary. Everyone could hear the carriage thundering down the middle of the bridge, pulled by a jade-colored eru.

Fifty handspans long and at least ten handspans wide, the large lizards were the main mode of transport in the empire. The more experienced riders could saddle the big animals and ride them, but Sylah was not one of those. She hated traveling by eru, as she'd never mastered the skill to manipulate the large beast with reins or words. Most Embers, like this out-of-towner, preferred the comfort of drawn carriages strapped to the lizard's hindquarters.

The jade eru's tail hooked under the carriage as it scurried through the street, black claws tapping on the metal floor of the Tongue.

Sylah watched it amble off the bridge, the carriage bouncing on the cobblestones. Silver filigree wrapped around the roof of the carriage in ostentatious swirls. Sylah spotted a kente flag of green and yellow weave, flapping maniacally from a pole on the driver's platform. She recognized the pattern of the imir of Jin-Sukar. Imirs were the Ember leaders that governed the twelve districts north of the capital. Despite some of the areas being many weeks' ride away, the imir's puppet strings were long, the warden's rule absolute.

As the carriage drew level with the platoon of officers, she took the opportunity to slip away into a side street.

Pristine white villas sprawled along the road, the domed roofs sending shadows across immaculate courtyards. Sylah breathed in and scowled at the clean air. When she looked back, she couldn't even see the plantation fields.

How nice it is to be so blinded by your own riches that you can't see whose back your home is built upon, she thought.

Every villa had a joba tree growing in a small fenced patch of sand. The large trees were thought to be a conduit to the God Anyme, tall and high in the sky as they were. The taller the tree, the higher the family's status—the age of the tree being an indicator of generational wealth. Of course, the wardens were the first to settle in the Keep, so their tree was the largest and grandest. In the Duster Quarter you'd be happy with a six-handspans bush. Sylah's mother had managed to coax theirs to seven handspans.

Sylah clasped her trembling hands behind her and looked up past the white bark and wide, spindly arms to the canopy, looking for the red fruit the trees produced during the sixth mooncycle, knowing that there wouldn't be any, but hoping anyway.

The fences that surrounded each of the joba trees varied in size and opulence. Some were even locked to prevent thieves from stealing the decoration that dangled from the branches. Some Dredge-dwellers placed sad little sticks in front of their doors in poor replicas, like wealth would come to them if they manifested it through imitation.

As she weaved through the cobbled lanes, her palms began to

sweat. If she had to watch the Descent, she'd do it from familiar ground, not within the walls of the enemy, but it had been a long time since she'd been to the water tower.

It was haunted for her by the ghouls of her past.

Her feet knew the way even though it had been years since she'd last been there. Scouting the street one last time, she ducked behind one of the larger villas and found her way to the bottom of the steps.

The tower was the only ugly thing in the Ember Quarter. It had been abandoned after the Warden of Duty implemented a new irrigation system. Sylah spat out a joba seed. Dusters and Ghostings still had to haul their water from wells. She was surprised they hadn't torn it down: Embers hated unsightly things. It was why Dusters and Ghostings lived across the river.

She looked up from the bottom of the steps, worn smooth from exposure to the tidewind. A chant from her childhood limped out of her mouth.

"Stolen, sharpened, the hidden key,
We'll destroy the empire and set you free,
Churned up from the shadows to tear it apart,
A dancer's grace, a killer's instinct, an Ember's blood,
    a Duster's heart."

For a moment she saw Jond's smiling face.

"COME ON, NO one will know we took a break."

"But Papa, he told us to go right back. We should saddle Huda and go meet him."

"She's right, Jond. We've got the books he asked us to get." Fareen was frowning, the expression so rare on her usually carefree face.

"Eeyah, Fareen, stop copying everything Sylah does. Here, grab my hand, I'll help you up. The view will be worth it, I promise."

Jond held out his hand, and Sylah clasped it. Firm and warm, it was calloused like hers. He winked at her as he held hers for a second longer than was really required.

Fareen followed not far behind.

She sniffed and wiped her nose with the back of her hand. They were both dead. Just Lio and her left, and even then Sylah often wondered if her mother really wanted her. She probably wished another child had survived.

She popped a joba seed in her mouth and bit down. Two left.

The drug floated her up the dusty steps to her memory of the view above. When she reached the top, she steadied herself on the stone wall. The joba seed turned the cheers of the crowd into a liquid frenzy in her veins.

Thousands of Dusters and Ghostings had gathered in the courtyard. It was one of the few times Dusters were allowed to enter the Keep, usually barred from everyone but Ghosting servants and Embers. Today, the army kept them in check in a segregated section away from the Ember nobility who sat on seats at the front.

The four wardens stood at the top of the five hundred steps that led to the great veranda. Truth, duty, strength, and knowledge: the four pillars of the empire. They were stoic figures dressed in fine silk suits. Most wore heeled boots. Not the Warden of Strength, though. At sixty-eight she was always prepared for combat. Her boots were well worn, stained blue with the blood of many a rebellion.

As was customary for Embers, each warden had one obscenely bejeweled bracelet on their forearm. Bloodwerk required easy access to their blood. So although elaborately decorated, the cuffs, known as inkwells, were also functional with a space for a stylus to be inserted to pierce the wearer's vein and draw blood to the tip. The bracelets were bespoke to the wearer's writing arm. Sylah had once tried to make an inkwell with a sharp knife and a brass cuff she'd stolen from the market. It did not go to plan.

The four disciples had already begun their ascent from the courtyard below. Disciples trained under their warden's guild for ten years before taking over as warden themselves. They were second-in-command but also a ready replacement for any warden who met an untimely demise. It was rare, but it happened. Not often enough, in Sylah's opinion.

The Disciple of Strength was leading the way up the five hundred steps. Sylah could just make out the sneer that painted the Warden of Strength's face as her disciple, her daughter, ran toward her. Yona had first won the title of disciple forty years ago and had reigned as warden twice since then. Uka, her daughter, had won her Aktibar trials at fifteen—the youngest disciple to enter the court. The Elsari family was a force of nature stronger than the tidewind. Sylah wondered if Uka's daughter would be entering the Aktibar this year.

"The Aktibar." The words sent sparks flying in Sylah's mind. "The Aktibar." She repeated. "The Aktibar, the Aktibar, the Aktibar." The words merged together into a low drone.

"The Aktibar is the reason you exist," Papa Azim had once said to her. And she knew the words to be as true then as they were now.

It was why she chose this semi-existence. She had lost the one purpose in her life.

Sylah's gaze fixed on the four wardens until her eyes stung, their expensive silks blurring together.

What tests would they set for the competitors this Aktibar? It was always the same skills, but the trials varied each decade. The trials for the guild of strength started with aerofield, where competitors had to showcase their skill in ranged combat. The tactics trial would be next, where competitors had to showcase their military maneuvers. Stealth was the third skill tested, and the trial always involved a covert mission. The mind trial challenged the competitor's mental stamina, and the bloodwerk trial their ability to use runes.

The final trial was the combat trial. First to blood.

Six mooncycles. Six trials.

"And only one Disciple of Strength!" Sylah added her cheers to those below. It dripped with sarcasm and self-loathing.

It was meant to be Sylah. It could still *be* Sylah.

The Day of Descent marked the opening of the Aktibar. Any Ember over the age of fifteen could enter. Sylah ran her hands through her braids and thought of them, her family. Guilt clouded her mind, and she let her braids go, dragging her eyes back to the courtyard.

Uka Elsari, disciple turned warden, was halfway up the steps, showing no indication of slowing down. The woman was built like an eru, all muscle and bone. She even zigzagged up the steps with the same grace as the large lizards. She didn't have the scaled skin or the long tail, though. Sylah checked.

Uka's suit was gray, like the roots of her afro. The slits of her trousers were crisscrossed with string to keep them out of her way as she ran.

Sylah spat over the edge of the water tower and cried out when her joba seed went with it.

"Monkey's hairy bollocks." She leaned over the edge as if peering at it would somehow will it back between her teeth. It had at least half a strike of juice left in it.

"Not quite sure what monkey's hairy bollocks have to do with anything," a voice commented behind her. A voice she knew like the thunder of her heartbeat. She turned around.

Her eyes couldn't be telling the truth. She'd been the only survivor to make it out of the massacre alive. It must be the drug. She looked at her hands. They were shaking, the joba-seed high receding. And she could smell him, fresh basil and jasmine. Could she touch him? She reached out a quivering finger and poked him hard.

"Ouch," he grumbled. How could she hear him when he was dead? He poked back harder. It hurt in all the places she'd hidden away.

It hurt like a smile breaking chapped lips.

"Jond?"

CHAPTER FIVE

*If the Wardens' Empire were an orchard, the Embers would be the
fruit at the top. Red and ripe, most revered, the four wardens
crowning at height.*

*The Dusters, we'd be the fallen apples, bruised blue, the color of
our blood. Weavers, field workers, laborers, and griots too.*

*The Ghostings, like their translucent blood, they cannot be
seen, they are down below, the roots of the tree. Deep under the
earth, but essential to the empire, here to serve in their beige attire.*

And so is the way of the orchard of all.

But don't forget. Keep in mind.

The apples at the top have the farthest to fall.

—*The Orchard of All* as spoken by Griot Sheth
on the third Moonday of the year

Sylah's fist flew through the air before she knew what she was
doing—partly to test her theory that Jond wasn't an apparition,
but mostly to cause him pain. A fraction of what she'd felt when
she'd lost him.

He let her punch connect with his face with a thud. She struck
him just above his sharp jawline now dusted with the shadow of a
beard. He was smiling, despite the blossoming of a bruise marring
his face. Her hand went slack and fell to her side.

They looked at each other for a heartbeat. Like Sylah, Jond had
always been muscular, but in their years apart his body had broad-
ened. If it wasn't for the lopsided grin, he'd look dangerous. As it
was, his good looks were near fatal instead.

His dark eyes bored into hers, and she let him assess her, enjoying the feel of his gaze lingering on hers. Then they were skidding into each other's arms, the sand beneath them lifting in a gust of wind and engulfing them in a blue tornado. Jond held fistfuls of Sylah's tunic as they held each other.

He held her at arm's length, and she let him take her in. "How's it hurting?"

Sylah dipped her head and pressed her ear against his chest.

"What are you doing?"

"It works. It really works." Her hair brushed his beard as she stood, the tight curls entwining with one of her braids.

"What?"

"Your heart, it's actually beating. You're alive. Jond, you're really alive."

"I hope so."

"I don't understand." The impact of the ground meeting her ass knocked her teeth together. The truth was too heavy to stay standing.

Jond crouched in the dust next to her. He was smiling. Jond was smiling, and it wasn't a dream.

"Yes, I'm alive."

"Hello, alive-Jond." She gave him a watery smile and wiped her nose on the edge of her tunic.

Jond squeezed her hand.

"You didn't die?"

"No, Sylah. I didn't."

"Does Mama know?"

"No, but I'll go see Lio later."

"Who else survived?" Joy blossomed and spread its tentacles through her body, rushing between the hairs on her skin.

His neck twitched, his eyes downcast. It was all she needed to know. "Just me."

The joy was snuffed out by grief, as fresh as the day her family had died six years ago.

Jond reached for Sylah with sadness in his eyes and pulled her up from the ground. She looked down at their intertwined hands. Neither one of them had lost the thick calluses from their years of training.

Sylah pulled in a ragged breath, and her chest caved in, pulling in her tall stature. She didn't want Jond to see what she had become, how she had failed everyone who meant anything to her. Her hair fell forward, the braids jangling with the memories of the people she had lost.

"Jond," Sylah rasped. "How did you survive?"

A knot appeared between his brow but was smoothed out by the beginnings of a smile. "*We* survived, Sylah, we survived."

"I saw the runebullets strike you. I thought I saw your last breath."

Jond sat back on his haunches and lifted up his shirt. The bullet holes had healed into three perfect silver spheres. Sylah reached out to touch them, her fingers running over the grooves of muscle toward the scars. He shivered at her touch, and she pulled away. He gave her a shy smile before continuing, "I was close to death. So close I could hear Anyme calling my name. But it was someone else who came to my aid." He held the hand Sylah had placed on his chest. "Papa Azim's body had fallen on me, hiding me from the officers. His blue blood protected me."

There was applause in the courtyard followed by the chant, "To protect and enforce law." The crowd screamed the Warden of Strength's vow as Uka Elsari reached the top of the five hundred steps—the first one to do so.

Sylah loosened her lips to spit.

Jond continued. "Do you remember Amud? The farmer that Papa traded with? He came to the Sanctuary that evening." The crinkles around his eyes softened. "He had a box of two dozen eggs he wanted to trade for fresh latex. Instead he found me, strapped me to the back of Anka, and took me back to his farm."

The image of Jond on the back of Anka the goat should have been funny, but Sylah didn't laugh.

He continued, "After two mooncycles I woke from my coma. After three more I could stand. It took me a year to cough without drawing blood."

Sylah stiffened. "He knew?"

"Of course, but he protected me, hid me from prying eyes. Told anyone who came by that I was his nephew. He was alone on the farm."

"Why didn't you come find me?"

"I thought you were dead, Sylah. Amud, he told me the army had killed you all and taken your bodies away."

"Mama—" Sylah stumbled over the shape of her memory. She swallowed, started again. "I thought only Mama and I escaped . . . Did you go back? To the Sanctuary?"

"No." His voice cracked.

Sylah's eyes flickered to the scene in the courtyard beyond, anything to tear her eyes away from the grief, raw and bleeding, reflected on Jond's face.

Jond continued, "One day I woke and Amud's house was empty. I went outside and found him. His mind had been going for some time, he was losing his balance more often, forgetting who I was, where he was." Jond swallowed. "He had fallen and hit his head. I wasn't sure if he had passed before or during the tide-wind."

"It's been getting worse."

Jond nodded. "I set a pyre for him and continued to run the farm alone."

They looked at each other, the unspoken words just within grasp, if only one of them would reach for them.

More cries rang out, and they both turned their eyes to the scene below.

All four disciples had now reached the top of the steps, and the crowd had erupted into cries of joy. The wardens shook hands with their disciples, ending their ten-year reign. Sylah's hands clenched by her waist.

The former wardens began their descent into the bowels of the crowd. Even the Dusters and Ghostings were cheering, caught in the infectious patriotism of the event and the reverence they felt for their leaders.

Sylah didn't hear cheers. She heard the cries of newborn Ghostings having their hands and tongues severed, she heard the creaking of the rack as Dusters were torn limb from limb, she heard the snap of the whip from the plantation overseers.

"Are you okay?" Jond's hand touched her wrist.

Will I ever be?

Sylah nodded.

Yona Elsari, the now former Warden of Strength, led the way down the steps. Sylah couldn't drag her eyes away from her lithe run. Sixty-eight never looked so good.

"The Sandstorm are still fighting, Sylah," he said the words quietly, but they screamed in her ears.

"What?" Her head snapped toward him, braids clacking with the symbols of their childhood. "The Sandstorm are gone. Dead and gone." Her hand reached into her satchel pocket and rolled the two joba seeds left there.

"They came to the farm. They found me."

"Who found you?" Sylah didn't understand. They were dead. All dead.

"The Sandstorm."

She shook her head, harder and harder, shaking the confusion from her mind. The Sandstorm were dead. *The Sandstorm were dead.* She hadn't realized the words had come out of her mouth until Jond replied.

"Our faction died, yes, but the ideology lives on, Sylah." Jond took a deep breath. "As babes we were taken from our families and set on a path to tear down the foundations of the empire. The Sandstorm crafted us into leaders with *one* purpose: to destroy the empire from within. We are the Stolen, born to Ember parents but made by Dusters. And we cannot be unmade. Just because you turned your back on who you are doesn't mean the fight has stopped." That's the thing with unspoken words: sometimes they reach for you.

Shame stung Sylah's eyes, but he saw it. The guilt she had nursed over the last six years was hard to miss; it shone as bright as the red stains on her teeth.

"There was nothing to turn my back on," she shot back. "Where are they, this so-called Sandstorm?" The scorn screwed up her features.

"They're here in the city. We're going to infiltrate the court, win the Aktibar, just like Papa Azim planned. There might not be twelve Stolen anymore, but there's us, and that's enough to change the world."

Sylah smiled bitterly. "I thought about it, once or twice." Her thoughts turned to the griot who had been ripped earlier that day, "But then I opened my eyes to reality. Nothing gets past the wardens. They crush every rebellion. No, they *rip* them apart without a thought. Change the world? No, Jond. This will end in death like it did for the Sandstorm, like it does for every Duster and Ghosting held in the jaws of the rack. Papa's plan will never work, just as it didn't before." Sylah's eyes drifted to the courtyard of murderers below.

Jond cleared his throat. "It wasn't just his plan, Sylah. There were many players. He was just a small part."

Sylah looked at him. It was the same Jond, yet this fire was new. But there was no way he could pull this off without Papa Azim, without their family.

"Once you're warden, what then? There's still the Ember courts that we'd have to influence." Then she said the words she had come to terms with a long time ago. "The Sandstorm is nothing without Papa to lead. The Sandstorm is dead."

Jond flinched. "We're fulfilling what I was born and trained to do. What *we* were trained to do, Sylah." He splayed his hands toward the Descent below. All four former wardens were now at the foot of the five hundred steps. They were no longer wardens, just regular folk. Regular red-blooded Embers. The crowd parted to let them through as they walked up to the largest joba tree in all of Nar-Ruta.

It had been eighteen years since Sylah had been stolen from her crib by the Sandstorm. From the moment she was taken at two years old she was fated to battle for the title of Disciple of Strength. Trained, crafted, and honed into the perfect competitor for the Aktibar. It had been the Sandstorm's plan all along, to raise twelve Embers to do what Dusters couldn't, weren't permitted to: lead. To stand where those in the courtyard below now stood. But that was before the Sandstorm died. Before they were cut down, the rebellion slaughtered.

Twelve children, three chances to win each Aktibar.

Now just two left.

An Abosom priest, dressed all in white, chanted out a prayer. Sylah couldn't hear the words, but she recited them from memory anyway.

Jond whispered them beneath his breath. Like Sylah, he had been taught the prayer, hoping that one day it would be them up there—ending their reign with a better world.

"And to the earth the blood shall flow, and to the sky I returneth. Anyme, we thank thee for what you give us, we praise thee for where you lead us. Anyme, we serve thee for how you punish us. The blood, the power, the life." The citizens chanted alongside the Abosom, the collective worship making its way through the crowd. It haunted Sylah into a memory.

THE VIEW WAS *worth it. They could see more of the Wardens' Keep than they had ever seen before.*

"One day that'll be our home," Sylah said in the silence.

Jond's grin was toothy. "It'll be your home, you mean."

"Any one of us could win," Sylah protested.

"But you're the best." Jond rested his hand on her leg.

She had nothing to say to that. It was the truth, and Papa told them not to lie.

"Will you come and live with me?"

"Of course, you can have the whole right side, and Fareen can have the left side," said Jond.

"And where are you going to live?"

"In the joba tree, of course! I'll make a tree house bigger and better than your chambers."

"Remember when I said I was going to live in the joba tree?" It had been six years, but Jond still had the uncanny ability to know what she was thinking.

Sylah tried to laugh, but instead her lips drooped in a poor replica of a smile. She didn't want to talk about the Sandstorm anymore. There was no changing this world. It had taken the Sandstorm's deaths for her to realize it. She was better off chasing oblivion. She was good at it too.

Her hands shook as she balled them into fists. Damn, she needed another joba seed.

Her eyes darted to Jond's. He scrutinized her until she looked back to the scene below.

Submissions for the Aktibar had opened as they always did

after the ceremony. A line of Embers began to snake its way around the courtyard as they queued to enter their name into one of the four trials: strength, duty, knowledge, and truth. Submissions would end on the morrow.

Jond put a hand on her shoulder as he followed her gaze down the line. "Enter the Aktibar with me."

She had been waiting for those words. Hoping for them, maybe?

"Sylah, we trained for years for this, it's in our blood. It's what Papa Azim wanted us to do." She could hear the smile in the tone of his voice.

Sylah hawked and spat over the edge, pressing her shaking hands into the stone wall. "I gave up that dream, Jond. When I realized I was just the tool and had no idea how to wield it." She couldn't take it anymore. She was taking a joba seed.

Jond watched her as she crunched the seed and tucked it between the gap in her front teeth. That was better. That was much better. It was easier not to think, easier just to feel. A slow moan escaped her as the ecstasy was released into her bloodstream.

Only one left.

Sylah's head lolled forward, her lips going slack as she vibrated with the blissful energy the joba seeds gave her. This was what she was born for.

She laughed.

"What's funny?" Jond asked, but she had already forgotten. He was still watching her.

"Are you crying?" Sylah had never seen Jond cry, but there he was crying. Tears dripping down his cheeks like pearls. She wondered if she could string them together and gift them to him. Her fingers reached for them, and he let her touch the wetness on his rough cheeks. "You are, you're crying." With each drip she collected, the euphoria lessened.

"I'm sorry, Sylah."

"What for?" She cocked her head at him.

Jond cleared his throat, but his voice still came out husky. "For not coming sooner."

Sylah took a step back, but she was unsteady on her feet. The drug-induced dizziness would last for a little while longer. Jond reached for her, but she backed up to the crumbling wall of the water tower. Sylah fought the fogginess in her mind for a moment of clarity.

"How long have you known I was alive?" The question crept in between the folds of silence.

"I had to prepare—"

"How long, Jond?"

He looked at her, his response quiet. "Two years."

"Two years?" She clenched and released her fist by her side.

"I wasn't here, Sylah, I was training, you don't understand, let me explain."

"Two fucking years you knew I was alive."

"I only came to Nar-Ruta yesterday, to sign up for the Aktibar. They wouldn't let me—"

The blow gave him a matching bruise on the other side of his jaw. They grappled in the sand that had, moments before, danced in their embrace. Sylah clutched Jond's shirt in her fist and felt it tear.

"Peace, Sylah, peace."

She hissed through her teeth at him, and he peered forward to get a closer look.

"What has happened to you, Sylah?" He had seen the red stains.

"Nothing, not a damn thing." She forced a smile, and it was as raw as the two sides of an open wound. "It's been six years of bliss."

She launched herself off the water tower, stumbled across to the barn roof and over to the street beyond. She felt the ghost of her memories laughing at her.

The two of them used to do that jump together.

SYLAH CONSUMED HER last joba seed and moved on to firerum, which flowed thick and fast in the Maroon. But it didn't quite fill the gap between her teeth. The patriotic spirit had followed the revelers back from the Keep, and the energy in the tavern buzzed around Sylah as she hunched over her drink by the bar.

We cannot be unmade.

Jond's words infiltrated her thoughts, and she scowled. How dare he raise his sorry ass back up from the dead? Even if it was a very fine ass. And now he wanted to act like nothing had changed, that they were right back to the plan that had been set for them.

But Sylah had long veered off course, and she was content with the life she led. Besides, she had other things to concentrate on, like making her money back for Maiden Turin.

Three strikes had passed since sundown, and she was going to be late for the Ring. But she couldn't leave yet; she had just stolen half a bottle of firerum and no one had noticed.

"It is curious how they forget the wardens' tyranny." The voice was as deep and as cavernous as the coal mines of Jin-Hidal. "In the light of the new day it'll strike them harder than the overseer's whip. You and I cannot begrudge them their happiness. Brief as it is."

Sylah looked at the speaker. Beads hung around his neck and down from his ears, and patterned silks swept back his braids, which were dusted gray. He was as decorated as a joba tree in the Ember Quarter.

"Hello, Griot." Sylah leaned forward and clinked her stolen treasure against his glass. She didn't notice the mess her unsteady hand made. "Aren't you paid to be happy?"

"Today, I mourn." He growled into his glass, his thick lips a straight line of pain.

"Oh yes, the griot who died in the square."

He nodded. "When a griot dies, so do his stories."

"Not really," Sylah countered. "Not if he told them right. People remember."

"Do they?" Sylah noticed his teeth were perfectly straight, like dice lined up. "Or is that my job? To remember for them?" His eyebrows quivered upward, pulling his wrinkles into the start of a smile.

"How do you become a griot, anyway?" She eyed the trinket box by his hip. Maybe being a griot paid more than the Ring.

"Those who know tell. Those who tell are griots."

"But where do you get your stories from? You just make them all up?"

"A curious Duster you are."

"No, I'm not—" She nearly corrected him. But the Maroon wasn't the place to announce her identity. Not ever. Not unless she wanted the warden army knocking on her door, and a one-way trip to the rack for being one of the Sandstorm.

When it was clear she wasn't finishing her sentence, he continued, "Griots tell no lies, child. A griot looks at the truth and pulls it tight." He twisted his arthritic hands in front of his face. "So tight it oozes with adventure, weeps with romance, and bleeds with horror."

Sylah picked between her teeth with her finger, hoping to find the shell of a joba seed she'd missed. "Nice words. You should be a griot."

He snorted, his smile spreading.

"You know,"—Sylah flicked back her hair and nearly fell off her stool—"I thought I was going to rule them all and make things better. Because I have a Duster's heart, a dancer's grace, and one more thing . . ."

"Indeed?"

"Yeah."

"Seventh strike!" The clockmaster called out into the Dredge.

"Seventh strike . . ."

"Seventh strike . . ."

The murmur moved through the crowd with a practiced chant, ensuring everyone knew the time.

"What time is it?" Sylah asked suddenly, struck by the panic that she needed to be somewhere.

"Seventh strike, girl." The griot's voice churned like gravel.

She weaved through the Maroon muttering to herself, "Nice chat, got to go."

The Ring was in the northernmost tip of the Dredge, where Loot's Gummers reigned. She was at least half a strike away. She hated being late, it meant skimming across the rooftops and you never knew when you'd end up knee-deep in someone's shit.

Plumbing in the Dredge was not as sophisticated as in the Ember Quarter, or even the Duster Quarter. Bloodwerk runes, when they worked, pumped the sewage upward to septic tanks on the roofs. It had been a project that a Warden of Duty had spearheaded a few decades ago in the hopes of "clearing up" the Dredge. Sylah wasn't sure that moving shit closer to the sky counted as clearing up.

She climbed up the nearest ladder and began hopping across the tightly packed villas. Occasionally she came across a roof that was too decrepit, and she'd have to make her way down and through the bustling street parties that had started after the Descent, before making her way back up.

When the Ring came into view, Sylah jumped down from the rooftops and shook her pantaloons. At one time her trousers, woven by the old grandmothers in the Duster Quarter, had been patterned in blues and reds. Over time layers of dirt and sand embedded their way into the woven fabric, and now they were covered in sewage. At least she'd only fallen in one septic tank. Thankfully, the smell of firerum around the Ring was so strong it singed her nostrils and drowned out the smell.

A small bonfire burned by the side of the crowd, all waiting for the combat to begin. The audience was bigger than normal, and rowdier from the brief freedom of the holiday, but Sylah didn't have any nerves. This was what she had been trained to do since she was two years old.

What would Jond say if he saw her now? She imagined his jaw going slack as he watched her sell her skills for entertainment. His mouth would twist with righteousness. She could feel the phantom of his disapproval lace up her spine.

"Fuck you, Jond. You left *me*," Sylah whispered to herself. The anger caused by Jond's betrayal eclipsed the shame she felt. Anger she could use.

She slithered through the crowd, nodding to the odd audience member here and there. There were lots of regulars, and some irregulars—all drawn to the Ring for the thrill of playing the odds. She felt them assessing her, their greedy eyes calculating their chances. Sylah spotted amber eyes she knew. The golden hue was unmistakably Turin's.

"You're late." Turin's dress was as voluptuous as what was in it. It was richly woven, with waterfalls of fabric echoing the Ember court fashion.

"Nice boobies." The words were out of Sylah's mouth before she could stop them. They were, after all, piled right there in front of her. Thankfully, Turin laughed, a breathy sort of laugh that set Sylah both on edge and off it.

"Sounds like you finished the rest of my stash."

"No."

Turin winked. "Hope it doesn't hinder you in the Ring. I'm betting big tonight."

"Good, I'm planning to win." Sylah swaggered past Turin's circumference of lace, toward Loot. He spotted her and smiled. He'd brought his stool and was sitting by the side of the Ring watching the bets exchange hands. Fayl stood within range of Loot, the two of them aware of the space around each other, while surveying the crowd. Loot twirled the crime guild token through his long fingers.

"I know, I'm late," Sylah said as she circled the charcoal border that gave the Ring its name. It was drawn into the compacted ground every night, fifty handspans wide, just enough room to fight in. One-eared Lazo was standing to the side of Loot, his mass of muscle enough to stop anyone in the street. As his name suggested, he only had the one ear. He lost the other in a fishing accident, of all things, where he grew up on the coast. Sylah told him more than once to doctor the story to something more sinister. A "fishing wire getting caught in your hair" didn't have the same ring to it as "fighting off a rabid desert monkey with a knife."

"Indeed, you are late. And drunk and probably on drugs." Loot was still smiling, but the anger carried under his breath.

"I can still win." Sylah matched his whisper.

"Well, don't, lose this round."

"The first one? Who'll bet on me after that?"

"Well, it doesn't matter, because we have an agreement, Sylah. Fifty slabs a night whether you win or lose."

She hated this charade. "Fine." It was enough to pay off her debt to Turin, and buy another day or two's worth of joba seeds.

"Don't question me again." His smile was brittle as he cast his eyes to the crowd and stood up.

She felt the echo of Jond's disappointment crawl back up her spine. *No one* threatens one of the Stolen. Not the Embers, not the wardens, and especially not Loot.

"Fuck you," Sylah said to herself. "I'm going to *win*." It might not be the Aktibar, but at least with the full prize money from the Ring she could purchase enough joba seeds to forget that she was meant to be anything more. Sylah steadied herself as best she could, the firerum doing its best to replicate the need between her teeth, and followed Lazo into the Ring.

"Dusters, have I got a treat for you. On this sacred day, the first day of celebrations for our honorable wardens, I give you a fight like no other." He let the crowd roar. They cheered just like they did in the courtyard.

"Lazo, the reigning champion of the Ring, takes on our serpent in the dust, Sylah." Lazo punched his right fist in the air while the crowd cheered. Like Lazo, most fighters were trained in the martial art of Dambe, a form of boxing where the opponents used their strong arm as if it was a spear. The odd fighter in the Ring had been trained in Laambe, which was more defensive and favored an open-palm technique to force the opponent back. The rarest discipline in the empire was Nuba.

A regimented code of physical formations that were implemented through strict mental codes, Nuba practice was difficult to master. The user had to reach a state of complete control and focus, known as battle wrath, in which anger fueled the Nuba artist to create precise movements that become deadly when paired with a weapon.

Sylah had been a master of all three forms of combat by the time she was ten.

Loot continued, "As always, the rules are simple. Get your opponent out of the Ring without any weapons." He dropped his voice, luring the crowd in like a griot. He had a knack for pulling you into the world he'd created from the blood and pain of others. "Three rounds, one winner. Are you ready? Then let's carve the dust!"

That was their cue, and Sylah wasted no time. Yes, she was a little drunk, and no, her last joba seed hadn't fully worn off, but this was what she was made for. This was what she was born to be: a fighter.

Lazo smacked her on the side of the face, and she went flying. She saw the charcoal ring beneath her as she scrambled and fell over the line.

"Ahhhh." She thumped the ground with her fist. Did she just lose?

"Round one to Lazo!" Loot called out.

"That was a quick round." Fayl jogged over to her and offered her a hand up.

"Thank you for pointing out the obvious."

"Loot says win the next round."

"Yeah. I will." Sylah did a quick inventory of her body, making sure there was no broken skin. She had never lost by mistake before; it was always a calculated move. It had to be to make sure she never bled in front of the crowd. How many joba seeds did she have that day?

"And make it last longer," Fayl added.

"Tell that to Loot tonight."

Fayl laughed and clapped Sylah on the shoulder before sauntering back to his beloved. Sylah dusted herself off and re-entered the Ring opposite Lazo.

"All right, Sylah?" he asked with concern. Lazo was a nice enough fellow. He just had a lot of muscle dragging the blood away from his brain.

"Yeah, all right, Lazo. You ready to go again?"

"You bet." He grinned and showed off his three remaining teeth.

Sylah took a deep breath and reset her focus into battle wrath: the Nuba meditative state of pure rage. All she needed to do was think of Jond.

Two years he knew I was alive?

"Round two, commence," Loot barked.

This time Sylah was ready for the punch that flew her way. She pounced to the left and dropped into a crouch. Lazo's right arm kept coming, left, right, left, right. The meaty fist missing her by a handspan. Lazo's momentum propelled him close to the edge of the Ring. She could have ended it there, but she knew Loot wanted a show.

Sylah leaped onto Lazo's back, her nails drawing blue blood as she clawed him to the ground. He threw a kick at her, but she flipped backward through the air. Her aerobatics skills always made the crowd cheer. But agility simply required practice. Her real skill was in the forceful movements and manipulation of her body weight that she had learned by mastering all three martial arts.

And manipulate she did. He went left because she wanted him there. He threw a back kick, because she wanted to duck it. Sylah had always been the fastest of the Stolen. Not always the strongest, but always the smartest in combat.

Once, her skills would have been used to bring the empire to its knees, baring the neck of those who had brought injustice to each and every Duster. She would have severed the head from the body, and out of the chaos a new world would have been born. A world where Jond—

Sylah faltered, and a kick to her guts sent her sprawling to the edge of the ring. Jond was alive. The anger, fueled by his betrayal, dissipated in a moment of pure joy. Jond was *alive*.

She saw Lazo just in time, her legs kicking outward to propel his bulk up and out of the Ring.

"Round two goes to Sylah."

Sylah caught the eye of Turin in the crowd smoking a cigar and blowing red smoke into the face of the man next to her. A sly smile spread across Turin's face when she saw Sylah looking.

"Didn't take you for a fan of Turin's maiden house." Fayl handed her some water. She rinsed the sweat from her face and blue blood from her hands.

"Trust me, I'm not."

"She never smiles at me."

"Just settling a debt." She wiped her wet face with her tunic.

"That was a good show. Loot's really happy. People are betting big on you now."

"Yeah? What's the prize money for the winning fighter today?"

"Two hundred slabs."

Sylah whistled.

"Doesn't matter, though. Loot will settle the fifty slabs with you after. Lose this round, but don't make it quick." Sylah was no longer listening. Two hundred slabs was a lot of joba seeds.

Loot and Sylah had entered into their partnership six years ago. When it was clear she was going to win every round, Loot knew he had to ban her or lose out on profits. The preplanned outcomes were Sylah's idea. Anything to keep her in the Ring. To fight and feel normal. At least her years of training could make her some money.

Savior turned entertainer.

"Round three, commence."

Sylah wasted no time. She went on the offense and landed two kicks to Lazo's gut. Although it was as hard as whitestone, he moved ten handspans closer to the edge. He growled and launched for her waist. Sylah dropped to the ground and rolled, springing up in time to kick him in the back.

He was one kick away from the edge, but she had to make it look like a mistake. She pranced to the side and let him gain ground, giving her enough time to flip backward. But instead of landing the flip, she twisted her body to the side, landing heavily on her hip in front of the edge of the ring.

But Sylah had timed it perfectly. Lazo launched a kick at Sylah's midriff and she caught the heel in her hands. From Loot's view it simply looked like Lazo had tripped, but those on the other side of the ring could see the trick Sylah pulled.

Lazo, robbed of his balance, flew forward and out of the ring.

The crowd was deafening.

"Fairly won, Sylah." Lazo pulled himself up and shook her hand.

Sylah was grinning, soaking in the fever of the crowd. "Thanks, Lazo."

"The winner is . . . Sylah." Loot sounded like he was choking on his own words. Sylah caught his eye, and his stare promised violence. She didn't care; the crowd had piled in around her, people touching her hair, handing her firerum and compliments. Shame no joba seeds.

By the time she made it to Loot, he was well and truly steaming.

"Well played, Sylah."

"Thank you."

"You broke our contract." Two Gummers moved in behind her. One of them, the woman, had a scar running from the bridge of her nose to the tip of her collarbone. She smiled at Sylah, making her shiver. They were in public; he couldn't do anything.

Could he?

"He slipped, I tried to—"

"I'm not an idiot, Sylah." He pulled off his gold spectacles with a sigh. The black spider brooch watched her with its glittering diamond eyes.

The evening's entertainment over, the crowd dispersed, and a Gummer handed the winnings to Loot. He rummaged through the bag and pulled out fifty slabs.

"Here's your lot."

"That's fifty."

"As we agreed."

"But I won."

"Did you? I thought it was a mistake?" Loot took out a pipe and lit it.

Sylah took the slabs, the smooth stones cool on her skin. She turned to leave.

"Oh, and Sylah, don't come back to the Ring." His words hit her harder than Lazo's punch. Fayl stood to the side, his gaze purposely turned away, but she saw the bloodink on his arms swell as he clenched his muscles.

"What?"

"You're finished here."

"But what do I do now?" Her words were quiet. Desperate.

"You keep smiling, Sylah."

CHAPTER SIX

The battle we wage is not merely for the Sandstorm, but for every citizen in this land. It is a war of ideals, of integrity, in the face of discrimination. Some of you will die in this fight. But it will be a death gained in emancipation, and Anyme will welcome you to the sky, freely. It is our right to claim for ourselves the same freedom given to every Ember in this empire. It is our time to reclaim the power they have stolen from us. Now is the time to lift our nation from the quicksand of injustice.

We will not descend into indifference like our ancestors. We will soar.

And we will harvest their red blood in retribution.

—Azim Ikila, leader of the Sandstorm

Hassa watched Sylah leave Turin's from her bedroom window on the first floor of the maiden house. Though Hassa didn't work for Turin, she rented a bed in the dormitory to stay close to Marigold. From her vantage point she had watched Sylah pay off her debt and buy another stash with the money she had won from the Ring.

Sylah put another joba seed in her mouth before her weaving gait disappeared off into the distance. Hassa rubbed her eyes and sighed.

Someone touched Hassa's shoulder, and she jumped.

Are you ready? It was Marigold.

Marigold wasn't her parent, though they came close to it. They'd been the one to cut Hassa out of her mother's cooling body. They'd tried to hide Hassa's mother's pregnancy from Turin, tried to get her out of the city through the tunnels only Ghostings knew about and used, but the Ember who had impregnated her mother had been the son of an imir. An imir's power, though diluted compared to the wardens', was far reaching as they governed the twelve districts outside of Nar-Ruta at the wardens' behest. Hassa's father's money got him the information he needed.

When money is everything, everything is for sale.

There was half a chance Hassa's blood would have run red. And if that were the case, Marigold would have slaughtered her and left her body for the tidewind. Better to be dead than hunted by Embers who wouldn't tolerate an unlawful babe. Coupling of different blood colors was illegal. If caught, that is. And no sensible officer would raid a maiden house. Half of the court would end up sentenced.

If she'd been born a red-blooded Ember, Marigold wouldn't have been able to hide it. She might have been able to pretend Hassa was a Duster, but a Ghosting looking after a Duster child? It was unheard of. Dusters shunned Ghostings almost as much as Embers did.

Hassa gave Sylah one more glance as she walked away.

You should take your coat, it might take all night, Marigold signed as they pulled on their own jacket. It was black, just in case anyone caught them in the dark tunnels.

Hassa nodded. Marigold took care of her, even if it wasn't for reasons as pure as a parent's love. Ghosting children were rare and sacred. But in Marigold's case protection had quickly turned to affection, though they rarely showed it. There was a detachment to Marigold's emotions that Hassa recognized as a product of being a nightworker at Turin's. It meant Marigold's features were often schooled into a smile. But never when they were alone. When they were alone, Marigold threw away the grin from their features like soiled underwear.

Their face was blank now, their wrist idly stroking the growth of beard across their chin.

Hassa went to the box under her bed and withdrew her coat between her limbs. The room was tiled with beds, close as they were. The dormitory housed all the Ghostings who worked for

Turin—and Hassa, for a fee—though the beds were empty now. Despite the wardens claiming the Day of Descent a national holiday, Turin still made money. Hassa was glad Marigold hadn't been requested that night.

The coat was too large for Hassa, but the billowing fabric covered her brown servant attire, and for that she was glad. Hassa was small, and skinny, with a shaved head, another requirement of her servant uniform. She was beautiful too, she knew that from what she saw in the mirror, though she recognized that she had too many sharp edges and not enough filling.

She slipped a limb into the pockets of her coat and felt the packet of the hormone herbs there. Hassa had been taking them for years, transitioning into the body that felt right for her. Reaffirming surgery was also readily available throughout the empire, but it was certainly not a requirement. Anyone could identify as a woman, man, or musawa without exception. And Hassa had always been a woman.

Marigold sighed softly, and Hassa looked up at them. They were smiling, not the fraudulent type reserved for the Embers, but a genuine, open smile that Hassa rarely saw. Their eyes were filled with love. Ghostings believed that musawa were born with two spirits, both man and woman, and Hassa felt the weight of two sets of eyes looking back at her now.

Anyme bless you, my child, how seventeen years have gone faster than I could have imagined.

Anyme was a musawa deity the empire prayed to, though the Ghostings worshipped them differently. Anyme wasn't the all-seeing God the Embers preached and the Dusters repeated, but an energy fueled by their ancestors' spirits. It was a guiding force of the path unseen.

Hassa touched her limb against Marigold's forearm, before signing, *Time may move quickly, but every second of it I remain grateful to you for giving me life.*

The emotion ebbed from Marigold's face, causing their soft features to droop. The memory of Hassa's birth was a bloody one, and it reminded them of the horrors of the empire.

We should go. The elders won't wait for us, Marigold signed.

No, they won't, Hassa agreed. Tardiness was a sin not tolerated among the four Ghosting elders.

Let's go.

SYLAH HAD BEEN wandering the streets in a daze for some time. She didn't realize how late into the night it was until sand whipped around her face, threatening to draw blood. Once Sylah had paid off her debt to Turin, she'd bought the last of Turin's hoard of seeds. The price was higher than a Ghosting would trade for, but Sylah didn't have the patience to shop elsewhere. It had been too long since her last taste.

Fifty slabs. Gone. Their weight replaced by red beads of ecstasy.

Just one more. She slipped the seed into her mouth, nearly biting down on her own fingers in haste. As the juice burst against her gums, she felt the little sparks of pleasure that seemed to last less and less each time.

She'd just have to take more.

The moon was a bright beacon in the sky, but even its light grew hazy as the tidewind began to pick up. Sylah sat slumped against the ruins of a Ghosting home, the limestone wall shifting in the wind. Across the way was an abattoir. Unlike the other villas around it, this building was in constant use. It was cleaned of blue sand but covered in blood no one could see.

It wasn't the kind of abattoir used for slaughtering animals, although some people thought of its victims as less than meat. It was the Ghosting abattoir where babies were brought to be mutilated, their tongues and hands dried on sticks and then sent to the Embers to tally with the number of babies born. Embers kept a close eye on the population of Ghostings and made sure none were born without their knowledge. An auditor would make the trip across the river to inspect all newborns and book them for their mutilation within a few mooncycles of their birth. The horrors of the Embers knew no limits. Sometimes she hated the color of her own blood so much, she wanted to bleed it all out.

She forced herself to turn her head, away from the screams of the babies she could hear in her mind.

Sylah knew that she needed to find proper shelter soon, but her limbs were moving sluggishly through her drug-induced state.

"Don't want to be like ol' Mugs . . ." Sylah had once found the remains of the joba dealer who hadn't found shelter in the night. A vision of their chewed-up remains, torn apart by the tidewind, kept flashing beneath her eyelids. Death by tidewind, yet another cruel way for Dusters to die. It had never been this bad before.

Her hands moved first, splayed wide in front of her eyes as if they alone had the urge to survive. It seemed an age before her feet followed suit.

The street she was on was deserted. Only a few of the houses were occupied, and those that were had their wooden shutters down.

"Hello, will you let me in?" Her banging on the wood was drowned out by the gusts of the tidewind.

Hassa knew Sylah was about to die. The tidewind had been claiming more victims recently, and Sylah was next.

It was luck that Hassa had seen her at all. The tunnels under the Dredge opened out in countless places, so when Hassa emerged and saw Sylah slumped against a crumbling wall she knew she had to get help before the tidewind killed her.

Will you help? Sylah's out there, I need to drag her to safety, Hassa signed to Marigold.

You know it is forbidden. We cannot let them know that we use the tunnels. It's bad enough that the Warden of Crime uses his minions to crawl around the few routes he knows about. We cannot risk it. She's a liability anyway, let the tidewind take her.

Hassa wanted to argue, but she had no time. Marigold had never approved of her relationship with Sylah; they thought she distracted Hassa from the true cause. No matter their differences, Sylah was a friend, but she couldn't drag her alone. Hassa signed at Marigold to let them know where she was going and disappeared into the darkness.

By the time Hassa appeared at Lio's villa, it was nearly half past eleven, but the tidewind had already picked up. Lio's tidewind shutters were down, but still Hassa pounded on the door until someone answered.

Sylah's mother was a fierce woman, she had little time for anyone and even less time for Ghostings. Lio opened the door, just a crack. She didn't want the sand blowing in to soil her living room. Sylah's mother looked like she'd been crying. Better than the scorn of disgust Hassa was expecting.

"Hassa?"

You need to help me get Sylah now, she's in the Dredge, Hassa signed firmly, mouthing her words alongside.

"I don't understand you." Lio shook her head, her usual frown growing between her brows.

"Who is it?" Another voice called out from the living quarters of the villa. They appeared in the crack of runelight behind Lio.

"This Ghosting girl that hangs out with Sylah a lot. I don't know what she's saying, though, she looks agitated."

Hassa waved at the man behind Lio. Maybe he'd be more help. He pulled open the door marginally.

"Hello, is something wrong with Sylah?" The man wasn't tall, but he was built dangerously. Cords of muscle rippled around his bare arms, and his darks eyes glinted, not unattractively. Hassa wondered who he was as she nodded.

"Is Sylah outside? Out there?"

Again, she nodded.

"Oh, Anyme help us," Lio muttered. "One child back and another child trying to pass into the sky."

Can you shut up and come and help me? Hassa was pissed.

"I'll get the metal protector. Where was she? The Duster Quarter?" the man said.

Hassa shook her head.

"The Dredge? Okay, I have to be quick," he said. "North, south, east—east? Thank you for letting me know. I'll need the space in the metal protector to bring her back, so I'll take it from here."

Hassa watched him don the metal tube and dash out into the night. She didn't trust him, so she followed him under the tunnels as he made his way toward Sylah.

SYLAH HEARD THE faint call of the clockmaster. It was half a strike past eleven. The tidewind wasn't meant to have started yet, but it already tugged at her clothing. The wind would eventually build to a crescendo that ripped skin right from the bone. She smiled wryly, imagining the scandal, an Ember body found on the wrong side of the Ruta River. Her smile dropped as she thought about the aftermath of policing that would disrupt the whole of the Dredge. Embers would always protect one of their own, even if she hadn't been raised by them.

She opened her mouth to spit, but sand flew into her lungs, making her cough.

"Sylah!"

It took her some time to make out the noise.

"Sylah!"

The voice was faint, but she could sense the direction it came from. The wind was too strong for her to walk into the midst of the tornado, so she called out, "I'm here!"

"Sylah?" Their voice was being eaten by the gales. She saw a figure ahead of her. They wore a primitive metal body protector, a metal tube with slits for eyes. Body protectors were a common addition to every household, just in case an emergency required you to go outside in the tidewind.

Her savior had spotted her. When the wind paused for an inhale, she dashed out into the road and under the body protector.

It was not made for two.

"Hello, Jond." They were cheek to cheek. In every sense.

"Hello, Sylah. Nice night to be out." She couldn't help but grin until the wind began battering the sides of the metal and she was reminded of the danger an inch away.

They didn't speak again as they shuffled toward the Duster Quarter. Sand flew through the eye slits, blinding them more than once. Sylah didn't ask how he knew where she lived. She'd recognized the runebullet dents in the body protector and realized it was her mother's.

The shutters were down as they approached her mother's house, and Sylah could almost feel Lio's disapproval through the wood.

Once the shutter to the door was open, Sylah and Jond shuffled in and freed themselves from the body protector. Jond slipped out of their cocoon first, letting go of Sylah's hand. She hadn't even realized he was holding it. Sand had swirled in with the open door, a gust of wind wreaking havoc in the moments before the shutters and doors were closed.

The three of them looked at one another. Sylah was pleased to see Jond was tired from the worry, the skin beneath his eyes sagging with concern. Lio on the other hand looked unimpressed. Thin eyebrows bordered her small eyes, set deep into her skull. Her narrow lips, pulled thinner from disregard, were chapped and chewed, seeping a small amount of blue blood. She kept her hair shaved to the skull, a remnant of her time working as a servant in the Wardens' Keep.

"You'll be cleaning that up later," was all Lio said.

"I know," Sylah drawled, a yawn catching her mid-speech. The day's events hit her like a weight. She still heard Loot's words in her mind, his lips parting in a smile as he spoke. *Don't come back.* How would she make money now?

Lio smiled lightly at Jond. It was the most joy Sylah had ever seen on her mother's face. The two of them had already been reacquainted. The red rims around Lio's eyes told Sylah as much.

"I'll heat up the groundnut stew," Lio said.

Sylah's stomach lurched at the thought of food, and bile began to rise up her throat. As much as the joba seed gave, it took far more. Food rarely stayed inside her long, particularly during the moments of respite between each seed, when every part of her, including her bowels, seemed to quiver.

Once Lio left the hallway, Jond rounded on Sylah. "Were you trying to get yourself killed?"

"I don't think so. I got lost."

"You got lost? In a city you've lived in for six years?" He was incredulous.

"It's possible."

"It was the drugs, wasn't it? Those seeds you take?"

Sylah waved him away. He had no right to ask after her welfare. He hadn't cared enough to come find her two years ago, so why start now? Maybe it would have been better if he'd left her to the tidewind's wrath. If she'd taken a handful more seeds she wouldn't even know death when it came. The thought didn't shock her like it should have.

"What are you doing here anyway?" She turned the questioning on him.

Jond exhaled, letting go of his irritation and concern. "You could thank me for saving you, you know." He gave her a lopsided grin, and it made her stomach squirm in an entirely different way from the joba seed urges—though both were needs.

"Who said I wanted to be saved? How did you even find me?" she said, ignoring the feeling.

"Everyone wants to be saved, Sylah, you more than anyone."

Sylah snorted out a laugh, then sobered. "Are you staying here from now on?" She thought of her single bed and wasn't entirely opposed to it.

He chuckled darkly like he read her mind. "No, I'm set up in the Ember Quarter, it's closer to the Keep for the trials . . . plus I've got to act the part, be the Ember they see on the outside, even if I'm a Duster in my heart, you know?"

Sylah did know, though the part she had acted was very different from his, the part of a downtrodden Duster.

"How did Mama react when she saw you after thinking you dead for so long?"

Lio had always loved Jond the most. His eyes crinkled in the corners, and he dropped his voice. "Anger and love often get confused."

Each Stolen had been assigned one dedicated guardian. Sylah's was Lio, Jond's was a woman called Vona.

Blue blood burst through Vona's mouth as the runebullet entered her skull.

Sylah squeezed her eyes shut from the memory, and she started to reach for her satchel, where her joba seeds lay. Jond touched her on the wrist, and she jumped.

"Lio was happy, and a little sad, I think. Sometimes hope does that to you, makes you a little sad, right?"

Sylah watched him in silence, torn between suspicion and genuine happiness that their earlier meeting had not been a drug-induced dream. She settled on a growl and stormed away into the living room of the house. It was a little larger than the Ghosting villas still in use in the Dredge; those used as homes were often just the one room. Lio's home had four: two rooms upstairs, two rooms downstairs. A stove out back and a small joba tree out front. Just ordinary.

Sylah sank into a wicker chair and put her dirty feet up onto the table. Jond followed her in.

"What do you want, Jond?"

"I told you, Sylah, we have until tomorrow night to sign up to the Aktibar—"

Lio entered the room carrying a tray. Sylah took her feet off the table.

"Eat your food."

Lio's stare settled on Sylah until her hand reached for the kissrah. The bread was the texture of gauze but thinner. Sylah tore away a few layers and used her fingers and thumb to soak up the groundnut stew with the bread. It was both utensil and sustenance. The food was lukewarm; Lio hadn't checked the temperature.

"You should enter the Aktibar." Lio spoke once Sylah had finished half of the stew. Though her stomach churned, Sylah's mind was a little clearer after having eaten.

"You told her?" Sylah was annoyed.

"Well, when someone comes back from the dead, they owe you some answers," Lio said dryly as she spooned three sugars into her coffee. "I talked it through with Jond earlier; I think you should do it. You were the only child out of the Stolen that I truly believed could have gone all the way."

"What?" Sylah couldn't believe her ears, mouth, eyes, or nose. Jond bristled.

"But there's nothing left of the Sandstorm."

"Jond has been telling me to the contrary." Lio sipped her coffee. She didn't wince at the scalding liquid.

"How can you just replace them?" The words spat out her mouth toward Jond.

The silence was too loud. Sylah needed to get out. She ran up the stairs in a few bounds.

The only barrier between her and her mother's sleeping quarters was a flimsy curtain, and she shoved it to the side in frustration. Their rooms were separated by more than just the cloth. Sylah's side was messy, her bed rarely slept in, with the faint mildew smell of clothes put away before they had dried.

Lio's was bare and regimentally tidy. A small oil painting of the Sanctuary hung from a rusty frame by her bed. The picture of the white farmhouse was the only thing that suggested the room was occupied.

Sylah clutched her satchel as she fell onto her bed. Thoughts of the Sandstorm swirled like a hurricane through her mind. Guilt and shame seeped into tears down her cheek.

How could her mother so willingly forget Papa? She had always been one of the fiercest supporters of the cause, had forever seen Sylah as the asset she was.

Sylah's bed crackled beneath her as she shifted heavily on the straw. The stuffing needed changing, but she hadn't gotten around to it for . . . mooncycles? It might have been a year, she wasn't sure. Her fingers slipped under the eru leather cover of her satchel to the seed packet within. She instantly felt safer.

Something in the bag scratched her hand. She pulled it out, and she cursed as a thin red line of blood blossomed on the edge of her finger. Three fights in the Ring and not a drop spilled, but a paper cut brings down the almighty Sylah.

She stuck the finger in her mouth and rummaged in her bag for bandages. She always carried them. The wound didn't warrant it, but society did.

Once her finger was tightly bound, she pulled out the offensive culprit.

"I should have traded you for more seeds," she hissed at the map. At that present moment, she couldn't recollect why she hadn't. She unrolled it and looked at it one more time, the tear along the edge more intriguing than ever. Did she now collect broken things?

"Sylah?"

Sylah rolled up the map and tucked it in her bag.

"What?"

"Don't 'what' me." The reply was out of Lio's mouth before she could stop it. She entered Sylah's room and exhaled. Started again. "I know we don't share blood,"—her mouth twisted in distaste—"but you are my daughter, and I think . . . I think I have wronged you."

Sylah had no words.

"Close your mouth before you catch a fly." Lio moved onto the bed next to Sylah. "After everyone died, I thought it was over. I didn't push you like I should have." Lio laughed a sharp and painful sound. "We hadn't even completed your training, we still didn't know how to teach you to bloodwerk. We needed an Ember to teach you, but Azim couldn't bear the thought of asking one."

"And the Sandstorm does now?" Sylah leaned forward. If they knew how to bloodwerk, maybe they could teach her?

Lio shook her head once. "No, but Jond says they have a plan. They'll figure it out."

Sylah snorted. "Sure, because it's that easy."

Sylah thought of the paper she had traded one dull afternoon in the Maroon followed by an evening spent with a piece of charcoal and a runelamp. She had then pierced her skin with a stick and tried to replicate the bloodwerk language, to no avail.

A frown rippled across Lio's face. "Anyway, as I was saying." Another exhale. "It was wrong to turn our backs on everything we stood for. I think you should enter the Aktibar. It is time we had someone with a Duster's heart ruling this empire, even if it can't be one of us."

"It could be Jond."

A quirk of the eyebrow, no response.

"He's been training for the last two years." Sylah played with a loose piece of straw in her mattress.

"So have you."

"I—" Sylah swallowed the lie. "You know about the Ring."

Lio snorted. "Of course, I'm not a fool. You get fired from every apprenticeship you get, but still come home with enough slabs to buy the food."

The piece of straw pulled apart in Sylah's hand. She noticed her fingers were quivering; it was time for another joba seed.

"No one can replace Papa Azim."

"No." Lio patted Sylah's lap with a stiff hand. "No, they can't. But that doesn't mean this new revolution can't pick up where he left off."

"Do you really think that?"

Lio rubbed her razor-thin brows. "Papa Azim had a way of bringing people together through their oppression. He identified it, harnessed it, and used it to fuel us to develop a better tomorrow. But the collective pain wasn't anything new. Dusters have wanted to reclaim the power of our community for a long time." When Papa preached, you could hear the capital letters. Reclaim. Power. It gave the words purpose. Sylah heard them now in her mother's speech.

Lio continued, "Though the conditions in which we live are worse than ever, the community is tired. They have no one to fight for them. Not since the revolt of the hundred, ten years ago in the coal mines of Jin-Hidal, have the Dusters come together in defiance of their masters. But the wardens slaughtered them like they did our family, like they do with *every* uprising. Until all we can do is obey. Obedience is killing us, Sylah."

Sylah thought of Loot and how his criminal operation lived symbiotically with the wardens. His reign was a type of rebellion, and he drew the unsatisfied to him like Papa had. But unlike Papa, his ideals benefited no one but himself.

"There's still the problem that there's just Jond and me. Even if one of us did win, we'd only control the guild of strength. What about duty, truth, knowledge? How will we make any change without the rest of the guilds on our side?"

Lio shrugged, an unusual movement for her tense shoulders. They moved up and down mechanically.

"Papa was cautious by picking twelve of you, three chances for the win. But there wasn't ever a guarantee that would happen. Remember Fatyma's arithmetic? Couldn't add numbers. There was no chance she was ever going to win the Aktibar for knowledge."

Sylah laughed as she remembered Fatyma throwing the abacus

across the room more than once. Her twin, Hussain, had tried to teach her, but she never listened. Sylah pulled on the glass beads in her bangs, one from each of them.

Lio huffed through her nose and smiled. "Change can start off small."

When Sylah's own grin had grown stale, she looked around the room and took in the life she was leading. She was satisfied, wasn't she? Lio watched her with narrowed eyes. Neither of them liked each other all that much, but that wasn't for want of trying. A year ago Sylah had bought Lio a vase for her nameday. Her mother scolded her over wasting money and sent her to trade it. That was the last time Sylah tried to make her adoptive mother love her.

"Mama, why don't you love me?" Once she spoke the words, she realized the question had been her companion for some years.

Lio frowned.

"Love? Oh, what a silly child you can be. I love you more than the child I gave up, and do you know why? We chose you, all twelve of you. We plucked you out from your Ember homes and bonded you to us with something stronger than blood. Purpose."

The words didn't make Sylah feel any better.

"Did you not see purpose for the child you gave up?"

The slap took Sylah unawares, pushed her backward on the bed. She accepted the pain. *Bruises fade, but resilience doesn't,* as Papa used to say.

Then Lio said something unexpected.

"I . . . I'm sorry."

Sylah held a hand to her stinging cheek. She wondered if Lio would have slapped her blood daughter this way. Sylah reached into her satchel pocket. Just to count them. It was a reminder that they were all she needed.

Lio stood up and lifted the curtain that led to her room and the stairs beyond.

"I try not to think of the child I left behind." Her face was cast in shadow, but when she turned to Sylah her eyes were haunted. "We vowed never to tell the Stolen whose crib we had taken you from and whose child we left behind." She was pulling on a frayed piece of the curtain, worrying a hole into the fabric. "The Duster decoys gave us time to run, time to hide. Most of the babies were killed once they were discovered to have blue blood. We only knew one who was still alive. She was my real daughter, the girl I left behind when we stole you."

Sylah had never heard this before. Nor had she ever heard her mother speak so softly.

"Where is she?" Jealousy thrummed through her as quickly as joba seed juice.

"Here in the city . . . in the Keep."

"In the Keep? You mean . . ."

"Yes."

"The girl is now Uka Elsari's daughter."

"Uka Elsari?" Sylah had seen the woman run up the five hundred steps to claim her title of warden from her mother, Yona Elsari, mere strikes before.

"You see why you must do this, Sylah? Your grandmother and mother have set up your dynasty and you will follow in their footsteps. You *will* win the Aktibar. It is in your blood."

But that meant . . .

"You are the true daughter of the Warden of Strength."

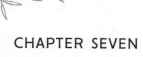

CHAPTER SEVEN

Today I woke to find the world has changed. My daughter gone. In her place they've left a maggot. She masquerades as my own, but I see her for who she is. A blue-blooded brood with no place in my family. I would have killed her, but I cannot let them know that I have been compromised.

My own home invaded, penetrated by the stink of their misplaced justice. Others have been taken, we don't know how many. They call themselves the Sandstorm. I know this from the note they left on my desk. Blue ink, the insolence. Another ripping offense, I'll have to stitch them together in order to tear them apart again.

—Uka Elsari's journal, year 403

Anoor's fingers drummed on her chin in time with the band. The guitar was soft and melodious, the singer wailing in a minor key. Anoor added the percussion.

She ached for something she could dance to. Not that her mother would let her. She was to sit and smile and sip her wine under the watchful eyes of the court as they chatted and drank and smoked.

A haze of radish-leaf smog shrouded them in opulence, the smoke more expensive than the finest of silks. The redder the smoke, the more expensive the leaf, and Anoor could barely see them swaying on the dance floor through the red fog. The dancers' chins were erect, arms adrift in the current of their self-importance. Every one of the Embers.

Despite the Keep opening its doors to all citizens of the empire earlier that day, the invitation was short-lived and confined to the few strikes of the wardens' descent. It didn't take long for the fortress to be cleared of all rabble and the blood scours put back into place. Now anyone who entered was subjected to a finger prick, their blood documented. If it was red they were let through. Order had been righted, quickly and efficiently. Now the Keep was occupied by Embers and their Ghosting servants. And Anoor, of course.

A sigh trumpeted from her.

The great veranda had been decked out for the night's festivities. Woven banners of kente cloth in yellows, reds, and greens hung above the wardens' table. Bright stars of gold and iron hung in clusters below the runelamps and chandeliers. As the tidewind shook the world, the stars gently tinkled.

The roof on the veranda protected the revelry from the raging storm beyond. It was operated by gears covered in bloodwerk; no one had looked up as the metal sheeting slid into place and locked out the night sky. To Anoor, it felt like a cold metal collar sliding around her neck.

"Miss Elsari, you are looking . . . well."

"Anoor, you must let me know the name of your tailor . . ."

"What is that? Looks delicious . . ."

"How are your studies going? Have you settled on a guild?"

No one stopped for long. Not a second longer than courtesy required. As if her mother's displeasure with her was contagious.

Uka Elsari, Warden of Strength, sat on the dais with the other three wardens who had ascended that day. She was dressed in gray from head to toe, and her cropped afro had been pulled away from her head with a single silver band. Anoor could see *the vein* throbbing on her forehead as her mother talked to the other wardens. It appeared every time Uka spoke to someone she deemed less intelligent than she was. It was always there when she spoke to Anoor.

Anoor wondered what had galled her mother that evening. Pura Dumo, the newly appointed Warden of Truth, was talking earnestly to Uka as she sat stoically beside him.

As Warden of Truth, he was believed to be the divine force of justice in the land. He was the head of the Abosom, a devout sect of Anyme's followers. He also governed the legal system and the religious rites of the empire, as they were one and the same. Pura wore the white cowl that signified the Abosom, except his hem was sprayed gold. Anoor noted the detail to raise it with her tailor another time. The embellishment would look perfect on her purple dress.

Pura picked a piece of spinach out of his white beard. You could always tell what his last meal had been.

Anoor grimaced. Pura's long face, elongated by the trail of his beard, and his greedy eyes that peppered it, had always sent shivers down her spine.

To the right of Uka was Wern Aldina, of undefinable age; Anoor was convinced she was at least two hundred years old. This was her third term as Warden of Knowledge, meaning she'd been in the court for at least fifty years, swapping between the role of disciple and warden. Anoor always wondered how she had won the Aktibar with such cloudy eyes—three times, no less. As Warden of Knowledge she managed the education structure within the empire. Her work usually kept her on the south side of the river, as there was only one school on the other. Dusters went to school until they were ten, before being assigned their guilds. Ghostings weren't educated at all.

The final warden was probably the most powerful of all. Aveed Elreeno, Warden of Duty, sat on Uka's left, the youngest of the wardens at thirty-seven years old. They had long, wavy hair that fell down their broad shoulders. Every now and then they would flick it backward with an annoyed expression. Aveed had the largest fleet of underlings. The plantations, the trade routes, the sewers. All down to the Warden of Duty.

One day soon Anoor would have to specialize: duty, strength, truth, or knowledge. She wasn't good at any of them.

The tables surrounding the wardens were filled with sycophants and imirs, though they were one and the same to Anoor. The imirs' roles were hereditary, passed on from parent to child, with one true purpose—to be the wardens' eyes and ears in every corner of the land. The twelve of them made up the Noble Court.

The imirs and their families wore their distinctive kente flags proudly as sashes, wraps, and headscarves. Anoor noted which flag was closest to the wardens, and who had been shunned to the back.

Oh dear, looks like Jin-Kutan didn't make their tax quota, they are practically seated in the privy.

Anoor was seated in the center of the great veranda. Not too close to assume favoritism, and not too far to raise questions. She was quite pleased with her position, really. It gave her full view of the entrance where servants were bringing out the food, their day's holiday having come to an end.

Right on cue large trays carried by Ghosting servants on their residual limbs appeared through the bloodwerk-activated doors. Anoor could see the rise and fall of their chests caused by running back and forth from the kitchens on the other side of the Keep, an architectural flaw in the Keep's design that the wardens would never admit.

There were a few Ember servants too, but no Dusters. The Keep had banned them from being servants eighteen years ago. So some low-ranked Embers, those not related to imirs or without a self-made fortune, ended up working there.

Maybe she'd go and check on the time. After one more kofta. Just the one.

SYLAH HAD DRUNK a bottle of firerum. Maybe two. She wasn't sure, but somehow she had another bottle in her hand. It sloshed as she weaved through the streets. The tidewind had done its work, casting the world in blue dust.

"Dusters! Time to clean!" Her bellows bounced around the empty quarter. "Get up!" She choked on her joba seed and swallowed it. Her coughing woke the resident of a nearby villa. Their tidewind shutter opened.

"Aho, get your ass out of the Duster Quarter. Go, go, you, get down to the Dredge."

"I don't belong here nor there, you won't believe where I do belong. But that's my secret." She choked on another joba seed. How many did she have in her mouth? She stuck her finger in just to check. By the time she had counted them—four—the angry Duster had gone.

The Dredge seemed as good a destination as any; the Maroon would have the shutters down on the outside, but the firerum flowing on the inside, which was exactly what Sylah needed, as she had somehow managed to pick up an empty bottle of firerum. It *may* have been full when she picked it up, she wasn't sure.

The Maroon was still busy from the day's revelry, with more patrons than usual sipping firerum in the runelight. A group of Ghostings peddled their goods in the corner.

"Does no one sleep in this city?" she mumbled as she took a seat at the bar. The revelations of the day weighed on her shoulders, and she slumped down with a sigh.

The Sandstorm, Jond, the Ring, and to top it all off I'm the fucking daughter of the Warden of Strength.

"I need to forget the day, someone get me a bottle of firerum," she shouted at the bar staff, slamming down money she had stolen from Lio's purse. The slabs were scooped up and replaced with a bottle of amber firerum.

Sylah sipped from a dirty shot glass and wondered if they drank from golden goblets in the Keep. They wouldn't drink firerum there. Firerum was a drink for Dusters and Ghostings. Brewed from the sugarcane in Jin-Sukar and smuggled in by the Warden of Crime, it was a plantation drink that had become popular among the lower classes.

If she squinted hard enough, the finger smudge on the lip of the glass looked embossed. If she closed her eyes completely, it turned into an emblem of the guild of strength. She was born for a life dipped in gold, not drenched in blood. She knew where she needed to go.

Sylah stood up, and the floor came up to meet her.

When she blinked again, Hassa was above her.

How many joba seeds have you had?

Sylah let three seeds dribble out of her mouth onto the floor. "Two?"

Get up, I'll help you home.

"Okay, my home is across the river, in a big bed with Ghosting servants and my own cook."

Hassa raised an eyebrow. *Fine, let's go there then.*

HASSA WAS TIRED. She hadn't slept for over a day. The elders would expect her to be back at work at dawn. She needed the last few strikes of the night for sleep, not dragging Sylah through the streets. She thought it was over once the man in the villa had found Sylah. But while Hassa was completing her final task of the night, there Sylah was, drinking in the Maroon.

Hassa had been trying to lead Sylah toward the Duster Quarter for some time. She had been quizzing Hassa incessantly about her job in the Keep. Like many Ghostings, Hassa had Ember masters. The kente sash around her waist was patterned in the wardens' colors identifying her as a servant of the wardens.

What type of wine did they drink? How many Ghostings served the wardens? What did they eat for breakfast? The questions slurred together, and half the time Hassa hadn't finished signing before Sylah went on to the next one.

Sylah, stop. Hassa came to a halt and pulled on Sylah's arm to swing her around. She stumbled and would have fallen if Hassa hadn't caught her.

"What did you do that for?"

Be quiet. There's a patrol up ahead. I need you to act sober for five minutes while they pass us.

Sylah followed Hassa's gaze. The purple blazers moved as one, their distinctive *thud, thud, thud* on the tarmac of the Duster Quarter. Hassa felt the air shift as they drew closer.

Sylah was swinging her head between the platoon and the oppressive black structure of the Tongue.

"Doesn't matter, I'm not going that way."

It is late, you need to go to sleep, Sylah. Hassa pushed her in the small of her back, but Sylah balked and strode toward the bridge.

Hassa had to run up to Sylah and stop in front of her before she would look at her signing. *Where are you going, Sylah?*

"I told you, I'm going home."

That's the wrong way.

Sylah didn't respond, and Hassa found herself running to keep up with her again.

Okay, so where is that exactly?

"Over there."

Hassa thought Sylah pointed at the Keep, but her hand wasn't very steady. When they got to the track of the trotro, Hassa reached for Sylah's hand between her wrists. *Please just come back with me, Sylah. You're going to get yourself arrested if the officers catch you wandering around the Ember Quarter like you are.*

"Hassa, I'm fine." Sylah began to walk across the Tongue, the metal bridge a menacing sight in the dark.

Sylah, please. Hassa moved to grab her satchel, where she knew Sylah still had a stash of joba seeds. The eru leather flap opened, and the remnant of the tidewind did the rest. Her few items rolled around the trotro track.

"See, you've caused a mess now."

Hassa bent down to help Sylah collect her few possessions and saw a roll of parchment. It looked old. Sylah stuffed it in her bag before Hassa could read it. Her ability to read was slow at the best of times. Like all Ghostings, she wasn't given any schooling, but the Ghosting elders took over the matter themselves, teaching every Ghosting child when they could.

Hassa looked away. The joba seeds sat in a clear latex packet between them. There were enough there to kill her. Easily. All Hassa had to do was kick them off the bridge. But Sylah was fast, very fast.

Hassa swung her foot too late. Sylah clutched the red beads like a child's toy against her breast.

"I'm fine, Hassa. Just leave me be."

Hassa reached for her one more time. She didn't want to give up on her friend.

"Get off me." Sylah flung Hassa's limb away like a child. "It must be past your bedtime."

Sylah, stop.

But she wouldn't. She crossed the Tongue murmuring to herself until she disappeared into the distance.

Oh, Sylah, I hope no one finds out you're one of the Stolen.

THREE KOFTAS LINED Anoor's pocket as she walked. The grease made stains on the inside of her ruffled dress. She didn't mind, she'd just buy another.

She made her way down the cloisters away from the great veranda, her green dress swirling around her like limp seaweed. The seamstress had only wanted to add one row of ruffles around the waist, but Anoor had asked for five. The final design created layers of bunched-up material from her waist to where the dress pooled around her silver-tipped sandals.

Hexagonal windows lined the corridor, giving her glimpses of the city of Nar-Ruta beyond the Keep. The tidewind had just abated, leaving the full expanse of the empire clear under the moonlit sky. Whitestone villas spread out below her like rows of teeth. The teeth got smaller, squatter, the farther she looked. Her eyes lingered on the molars at the back, decayed, forgotten, left to rot. Was that where her family had once lived? She pulled her woven shawl over her shoulders, though she wasn't cold.

The clock was situated in the middle of the entrance hall. It was a grotesque thing, all wire cogs and bloodwerk runes so old they were black. Anoor had often pondered how the runes in the clock worked. Many studied them, but none succeeded in replicating the workings and mechanisms. The inventor had died some four hundred years ago.

"Ah, Miss Elsari."

"First clockmaster." Anoor nodded. There were only a handful of people who had the ability to read the time from the three spinning arrows. The first clockmaster had studied over a decade for the role and had been an immovable presence next to the clock for as long as Anoor could remember.

"It is three quarters past fourth strike." His milky eyes blinking up at her from his podium beside the clock. He'd bellow the time across the courtyard at every half strike, the chant would then be carried by the other clockmasters toward the edge of the city.

Anoor felt the weight of the time settle on her shoulders and grew weary. That was odd, the tidewind had only just begun to quieten down for the night. The wind had been getting stronger recently, lasting longer than it ought to. Anoor loved to wake up early and watch the servants dust the Keep, but with the dust growing thicker, now it took them over a strike to clear it.

"Anoor! You cannot just leave without telling me." Gorn's face appeared from behind the clock like a geometry book. Square neck, boxy shoulders, and a small triangle mouth. Gorn's servant attire always managed to look pristine, as if she had pressed it just that moment. It might have been that time had blurred Anoor's memories of Gorn, but she had always seemed ageless, despite being older than Anoor's grandmother. She was taller than Anoor by at least three handspans, but she had the ability to make Anoor feel half that again.

"Gorn, I just went to find out the time. Kofta?"

"No, thank you. You've stained your dress."

"Yes, I suppose I have." She hoped the tailor could find the exact fabric again; it had taken her two mooncycles to ship it in from Jin-Noon. "I'm going to turn in for the night."

"Anoor, you know your mother wanted you to stay all night."

"Well." Anoor exhaled slowly. "I simply cannot shame her by wearing a stained dress."

"Anoor . . ."

"Gorn, I'm tired. I smiled, I clapped, I bowed, I did all the warden asked of me."

The clockmaster cleared his throat beside Anoor, and Gorn saw him as if for the first time. She grabbed Anoor with sharpened nails and dragged her into an alcove.

"Ouch, you're going to draw blood."

Gorn dropped her hand. "Anoor, I'm just trying to protect you, you know when she gets mad—"

"Shh." Anoor's eyes widened. "Do you hear that?" She held up a finger to Gorn's lips. She had to reach quite high.

They both leaned forward, and Gorn heard the soft groaning Anoor was referring to.

"Someone's having sex," Anoor mouthed and pointed to the alcove over. "Just there, can you believe the audacity of it?" She clapped her hand over her mouth. "Maybe they're long-lost lovers? Or maybe they fell in love on the dance floor and now they're to be wed!"

"Or maybe they are intoxicated with firerum and are as primitive as Dusters."

Anoor prickled at that. "I'm going to bed." She had a zine she wanted to finish before daybreak. The stories were included weekly in *The People's Gazette*, a newspaper run by the guild of duty. The main character, Inquisitor Abena, was a fierce Ember woman whose investigative skills were unmatched across the empire. The series documented her solving high-profile crimes. The most recent edition, "Sweet Red Wine," followed her to the vineyards of Jin-Eynab. Someone had hidden the body in a vat of grapes and then served the bloody red wine to their guests. Anoor thought she knew who the murderer was, but she needed to finish the story to prove herself right.

Gorn rolled her eyes and crossed her arms. Anoor knew she had won. She always won. Gorn was her servant, after all.

ANOOR HATED THE tunnels that led to her chambers. She only used them during the night, when the tidewind raged or in its aftermath, when the debris blocked the path to her rooms.

Every day the servants placed waxy red flowers in tall vases that lined the damp walls. Instead of masking the smell of mold, the cloying perfume mixed with the stench, sticking to the back of her throat.

They had reached the end of the tunnel where a narrow set of stairs led to the back of the kitchens on the eastern side of the Keep. Anoor's chambers were one more flight up.

She hadn't resided in the Elsari household, hadn't for some years.

"I'm just going to stop in the kitchen and see who's working."

"Anoor,"—Gorn dug her fingertips into the bags beneath her eyes—"you know your mother doesn't want you to make friends with the servants."

"Well, this one time, maybe you don't inform her." Anoor's voice was light, if a little brittle.

Gorn didn't respond.

The kitchens fed all the citizens who resided in the Keep: members of the court, servants, and the wardens themselves. There were sometimes more than two hundred servants working in the kitchens at once. But today it had dwindled as the last of the food had circulated at the party.

Anoor walked into the kitchen and felt a rare pang of belonging. She had spent many strikes down here as a child.

"Anoor!" A young man with a pockmarked face and bright, intelligent eyes waved at her from across the hearth.

"How are you, Kwame?" Anoor said as she walked over to him. Kwame was one of the few friends she had, though her mother's influence had drawn them apart.

He was covered in flour, but he hugged her anyway. His guild token, which he wore around his neck, pressed against Anoor's cheek. "Haven't seen you for a few mooncycles."

"School has been busy with Choice Day coming up after the Aktibar."

"Going with knowledge, truth, or duty?"

Anoor smarted that he had left out strength. "Not sure yet."

"You'll figure it out." He went back to kneading.

"Just started your shift?"

"Yes, bread doesn't bake itself. Well, it does, I suppose, but you have to put it in, and I guess add wood to the fire . . . Oh, hello, Gorn." Kwame straightened up slightly and brushed some flour off his servant attire.

"Your father keeping well, Kwame? His hip better?" Gorn asked, not unkindly.

Anoor started. She never thought of Gorn knowing other servants. She never saw her talking to anyone else, and she never seemed to go anywhere unless by Anoor's side. It felt odd that she would have her own life away from Anoor. But it made sense: both Gorn and Kwame were Ember servants.

"Yes, much better. Thank you for the salve," Kwame said with a bow of his head.

"Not a problem." Gorn gave him a curt nod. "We must excuse ourselves. Miss Elsari is feeling a little tired this evening."

Kwame turned back to Anoor and winked. "The party still going on?"

"Oh, I think it will be for a few more strikes yet."

"All right, well, good night. I'll send up some fresh milk bread for when you wake."

Anoor squealed, her cheeks dimpling. "Thank you, Kwame."

THEY CONTINUED UP the stairs to her chambers. The walk always made her knees ache. She never missed her mother's home, but tonight she was longing for the bloodwerk elevator that had once terrified her as a child. One day she scratched off one of the bloodwerk runes and the whole cage dropped. They were lucky they were only a few handspans off the ground. Her mother and grandmother were with them. If they had been at the top, she would have wiped out the entire Elsari family.

Gorn unlocked the doors to her chambers. The air was cool, the smell familiar. She shrugged off her dress as she walked toward her bedroom.

"Anoor, are you going to leave that there?"

"Well, it's sheep fodder now, would you mind throwing it out tomorrow? And have Hiba stop by. I'll need her to measure me for a new dress."

Anoor didn't hear Gorn respond. She closed her bedroom door and leaned on it and exhaled. It had been a long day. She began to remove her jewelry, piece by piece. The rings clanked on the floor as she dropped them. She should really put them away in her dressing room, but Gorn could do that tomorrow. The inkwell came off last. Her mother had presented it to her on her twelfth nameday. Pure platinum, the manacle wrapped around her wrist in an intricate woven pattern, like the finest wicker. The top of the inkwell fanned out like a metal cuff, just below her elbow. It was an unusual style, but it had to be to hide the catchment on the inside. The matching stylus hung on a golden chain between her breasts.

Anoor looked down at the jewelry, and her shoulders slumped. Choice Day, but what was she going to pick? She thought of the zine by her bed and wondered if she could train to be an inquisitor. She loved solving crimes in fiction, and it couldn't be that difficult in real life. But to do so she'd have to choose the guild of strength and train under her mother's lackeys.

Her thoughts clouded with the memory of pain, but she pushed it away and cradled her arms around herself. Her undergarments shimmered in the breeze. She looked up, and the brightness of the moon caught her attention. The window was open. *The window was open?*

Her heart lurched inside her chest, the koftas threatening a second appearance.

Someone was in her room.

"Are you Uka Elsari's daughter?"

The woman jumped down from the window with the stealth of a desert fox.

"Answer me."

Anoor opened her mouth to reply.

"Are you the Warden of Strength's daughter? Tell me." Her hair kept her face in shadow. It cascaded down her back in plaits filled with beads and dirty fabrics.

"Are you here to kill me?" Anoor was surprised she wasn't scared. Someone must have figured out who she was. Maybe she could ask the girl before she killed Anoor.

"No, I . . . I just wanted to meet you." Her voice was rough, uncomfortable to listen to.

"That's what all the assassins say."

"You've met more than one?"

"No, I've read about them, though." Anoor jutted her chin to the stack of zines by her bed. Their brightly colored pages and scandalous covers promised drama and discourse as the stories unfurled.

The woman took another step forward.

"I wouldn't if I were you," Anoor warned her.

"Don't tell me what to do."

"I mean it, I wouldn't take another step forward."

The assassin wasn't listening.

So when she triggered the bloodwerk trap, the paperweight hit the assassin square in the middle of her forehead.

The assassin crumpled to the ground.

CHAPTER EIGHT

Inquisitor Abena didn't have a weapon, but she had a plan. That was all Abena ever needed.

"Give me the key," she said as she cornered the stable hand.

"I can't, my master, he'll kill me." The boy cowered under Abena's shadow.

She cocked her head to the side, her curls bouncing on her shoulder. "Are you not afraid I might kill you, Duster?"

The boy's eyes fluttered. That was fear all right. He took another step backward, right where Abena needed him.

Thunk!

The stone swung out from the rafters in the ceiling, activated by the boy's weight. It knocked him unconscious. Blue blood blossomed where the stone had hit him.

Abena bent down to retrieve her trap. She'd used the bloodwerk runes Gi and Ba to drive the stone and supplementary runes to pressure-trigger it.

"They don't call me the best Inquisitor in the empire for nothing." She smiled and pulled the key out of the boy's pocket.

—"The Kori Bird and the Key" from the tales of Inquisitor Abena, featured in *The People's Gazette*

Anoor had never tested that rune trap before. She read about the concept from the tales of Inquisitor Abena. The woman was a genius.

The girl lay sprawled on the floor, red blood dotting her long black braids. The glass paperweight her father had gotten her for her fourth nameday had worked perfectly to knock her out.

She dressed like the Dusters Anoor saw from a distance, in a dirty gray tunic and blue woven pantaloons, tied at the waist with string—practical, unkempt clothing made from cheap material with faded patterns. The outfit must have been part of her undercover mission, as the small wound on her skull confirmed her Ember blood. And she would have had to be an Ember to get through the blood scour at the entrance to the Keep. Despite the baggy and unflattering clothing, Anoor could still detect the muscle beneath.

"Now where have you come from?" Anoor circled the body. "If you're not an assassin sent to kill me, then maybe . . ." She clapped, her hazel eyes shining. "You're a thief trying to steal my jewels."

"Anoor? What's going on? Did you fall out of bed again?" Gorn knocked on her bedroom door with even, persistent taps.

"I'm fine, go back to bed." The knocks didn't stop, so Anoor shuffled to the door and opened it a crack.

"What is going on?"

"Nothing, I tripped over my undergarments."

"Did you hurt yourself? I can get the bandages."

"No, I'm fine, just a heavy fall."

"Okay, I'll wake you at tenth strike for classes tomorrow." Gorn turned away.

"Oh, one thing." Anoor held her elbow in her other hand. "Please, could I get some more blood?"

"I drew some earlier for you. Why do you need more now?"

Anoor waited with her hand held out.

Gorn's disapproval was palpable, but she eventually withdrew her stylus. Her inkwell was plain copper, green and rusted in areas that made Anoor wince. The stylus inserted into the gap above her vein. The blood ran through the groove in the center and pooled in the tip where Anoor held a small vial.

"Thank you, Gorn, good night."

Anoor closed the door in Gorn's face and turned to face the intruder, the warm vial of blood clutched between her hands.

There was just a smear of red blood where the assassin had once been. Anoor rushed to the window to look for the body. She must have fallen out.

"Hello, there." The girl snuck up behind Anoor and held her neck in an elbow vise. "Don't scream." Her breath reeked.

Anoor tried to gurgle at her.

"Don't try to speak yet. I'm going to step backward, and you're going to tell me the safest way out."

Anoor tried to warn her.

The trap was triggered again. This time, it was the paperweight from her fifth nameday that knocked the girl on the forehead. She fell like a sack of apples.

"Curse the blood! I hope I haven't killed you." Anoor knelt down and checked her pulse. It was there, constant and strong. She'd have a terrible headache when she woke. Another lump, the size of an egg, grew by her right temple.

Her mind was brimming with all the possibilities for the girl's backstory. Villain, victim, vandal? Anoor thought about the vineyard murders in the zine she was reading. The assassin from that story was an undercover Ember working the field; maybe the girl was like her. It would explain her threadbare clothing.

A snore escaped the girl, making Anoor jump. Her eyes crinkled at the corners in delight at her own fear.

"What do I do with you?" She pushed a braid away from the sleeping girl's face. The braids were filthy, some woven with even filthier trinkets and beads. "I should probably get an officer."

But if she called an officer, they would summon her mother, and she would invade the chambers she had so carefully made Uka-free.

All officers of the army reported to Uka. As the Warden of Strength she was to maintain the peace, enact the law, and prevent criminal activity. Each officer was like a claw on her many talons.

But Anoor had to do something with the assassin. She looked at the vial of blood she had taken from Gorn for this purpose. "I better tie you up."

Anoor dragged her by her feet to her dressing room. Despite the girl's height, it was as if the intruder had hollow bones. She was so light Anoor could imagine her flying away, her long limbs and fingers lifting her in the breeze like a kori. Anoor often watched the small blue birds circling above the Keep.

The girl's feet thudded on the floor as Anoor dropped them.

"Sorry!" She winced and braced herself for Gorn's wrath. Nothing. Thank the blood. "I'll be right back," she whispered.

Anoor gathered the hem of her undergarments in one hand and hopped toward her dressing table across the room. She pulled out a hairpin from her curls and pricked the underside of her arm, making a minuscule wound she could hide under her sleeve. She added the small dot of her own blue blood into the vial of Gorn's red blood and shook it.

The blue drop disappeared in moments, the color diluted by the swirling crimson. By putting in her own blood she added a unique genetic signature to the bloodwerk. This allowed her to control the blood as if it were her own. So if the assassin was a master at bloodwerk, which Anoor assumed she probably was, then she would have to be very careful when drawing the runes. Any flaw and the criminal would take advantage of it. By adding her genetic signature it also ensured that Anoor was the only person who would be able to release the bloodwerk runes. Well, her and Gorn. And she had to take special care Gorn didn't find out about the intruder.

Anoor slotted Gorn's red blood into the catchment within her inkwell and slid it over her wrist. The stylus around her neck came off and fit into the slot which, for all Embers, inserted straight into the vein. And for Anoor, did not.

She grimaced as she stuffed a stocking into the girl's mouth and wrapped the gag with a scarf. She quickly drew bloodwerk runes keeping the gag in place. The wardrobe was well insulated with copious amounts of clothes and shoes, but she didn't want to take any chances. She tied her hands and legs, finishing the knots with a series of runes to keep them secure.

When that was done, Anoor looked down at the girl, mentally checking off all the things that Inquisitor Abena did in her zines.

"Ah, your pockets," Anoor chastised herself. She hastily patted the girl down for weapons, finding nothing. The assassin had a satchel hanging across one shoulder that Anoor untangled and emptied onto the floor. She discovered a packet of joba seeds, and she disposed of them outside the window in distaste.

There was an old map, not very up to date, but to be expected with an assassin; they always had maps in the zines. They needed to know where their mark was. And what was that, a knife? Anoor reached for it, and her heart sank in disappointment. It was just a rusty old spoon. What kind of assassin didn't have a weapon?

She placed the spoon on the torn edge of the map, holding the curled edge down. Her fingers trailed along the parchment of her prison: the Wardens' Keep. The southernmost point of the whole of the empire. Her gaze ran along the shore through the inky blue waves of the Marion Sea. She laughed in delight when she saw the gray sketch of the Tannin in the waves. Gorn had told her stories of the sea monster since she'd been a babe.

She began to roll up the map, but as she moved the spoon from the top right corner, she saw something unexpected. The smudge of another land shorn away.

Her finger traced the jagged edge.

"No," she whispered her disbelief. There was nothing beyond the empire. Was there?

SYLAH OPENED HER eyes to darkness. Her hands were bound in front of her with strips of cloth and bloodwerk runes. Her feet were similarly restricted, and her mouth was gagged.

The sound of gentle breathing drew her eyes to the dressing-room door. The usurper slept, slumped against the exit, her head lolling backward. Her breathing was gentle, her lips slightly parted in a smile. It enraged Sylah all the more.

She bucked against the restraints as quietly as she could, but they held fast. She could feel the quivering brought on by her joba seed withdrawal jerking her limbs long after she had stopped struggling. Her satchel was by the girl's feet. Sylah shuffled forward on her butt.

The girl started and looked around, her eyes wide and full of dreams Sylah couldn't see. She settled back down in the next breath.

Sylah ground her teeth, pushing tight the strip of cloth around her mouth. She needed to sign up for the Aktibar. Seeing how this girl lived set Sylah's decision in stone. It was time for Sylah to re-join the fight.

She let the decision settle deep into her bones. Already she felt the familiar warmth of belonging to something greater. She had yearned for that feeling of belonging more than anything else.

For now, all Sylah could do was wait for the girl to release the restraints; then she'd be out of there.

"Anoor, are you ready for breakfast?" The words were muffled, and it took Anoor quite some time to understand what Gorn was saying.

She opened her eyes to darkness.

Where was she?

"Oh, Ending Fire!" She wiped the drool from her face and sat up rod-straight. "Coming, Gorn!" Anoor pushed open the ward-robe door and tripped over her feet, landing on the bedroom carpet. "I'm okay, I'm okay."

"Anoor, are you coming?" Gorn sounded annoyed.

"Yes, yes." Anoor turned to shut the wardrobe door, until she noticed black eyes glittering at her in the shadows. "Oh, hello." Anoor waved.

The girl growled, a primitive sound in the back of her throat.

"I'm just going to go get us some breakfast. I'm sure you're very hungry."

Another growl. Her father had always taught her if she ever met a rabid dog to match aggression with aggression. Anoor inhaled and bared her teeth with a growl of her own.

"Then we'll get down to the real task at hand. Why you're here." Anoor hoped her stare was menacing. She closed the wardrobe door slowly.

Gorn didn't have to say anything about Anoor's appearance. A lift of the eyebrow was enough.

"I fell asleep."

"You should let me comb out your curls after your bath."

"I'm not twelve anymore, Gorn."

Gorn snorted. She handed Anoor her breakfast. Eggs, with chopped-up goat cheese and fried beans in butter.

"Where's the milk bread?"

"They didn't send it up."

"Kwame promised. I want toast."

Gorn's face was blank as she stared at Anoor. Like a piece of brown parchment, crinkled lines pushed smooth.

"I will go and get you some toast."

"Oh, Gorn, thank you."

"Get dressed!" Gorn shouted back as she left the chambers.

Anoor hurried back into her bedroom. She had about three minutes before Gorn returned from the kitchens below.

"Okay, so I've got you some food . . ." Anoor announced as she walked into the dressing room. "No cutlery, though . . . and I have to take the plate back, so . . ." Anoor pushed her eggs onto the floor by the captive's face. "Sorry."

Anoor went back into the bedroom and brought back a jug of water and her waste bin.

"This is for drinking." Anoor held up the jug. "This is for . . . you know." She set the waste bin by the assassin's feet.

Black diamonds tracked her movements. Sharp and shining.

"I have to go to class now. If I don't, they report it to my mother . . . and well . . . that doesn't go well."

Nothing.

"Okay, I'm going to release the gag now." She tiptoed toward the girl's face. The intruder's plaits pooled around her neck and down her back. Anoor repressed the urge to ask her about the beads and trinkets that hid in them like jewels. They were nothing like the jewelry Anoor wore, which was heavy with opulence. She couldn't fathom why anyone would choose to wear such filthy junk in their hair. "There's no point screaming, though, because no one will be able to hear you. No one's allowed in my chambers, and Gorn will be with me. When I get back we can talk about why you are here."

Anoor reached over and released the gag. Only the person whose blood had drawn the runes would be able to release them.

The assassin lunged for her seconds after being freed, with

gnashing teeth. Anoor ran to the back of the closet, her shoulders pressed against her hanging frocks.

"Did you just try and bite me?" Anoor held a hand to her mouth, but really she should have covered her ears. A scream erupted from the girl, and it rattled Anoor's brain.

Anoor jumped on the tied-up assassin and pushed the gag back in her mouth.

"Stop it, stop it."

"Anoor?" Gorn was at her door. "I've got your toast."

"Gughn fughin ghil oo." Now that the gag was back in place, the assassin's shouts were muffled.

Anoor added an extra rune to the front of the gag as the woman squirmed beneath her. Once it was done, she slammed the dressing room door.

"Anoor? I'm coming in." Gorn appeared in the doorway just as the wardrobe clicked in place. "Anoor! You're not ready at all. You're going to be late."

"I only need five minutes."

Gorn inhaled, surely praying to Anyme for strength.

"Five minutes. Promise!"

"Here, take your toast. Eat and dress."

"Yes, Gorn."

The toast could have really done with some eggs.

ANOOR COULDN'T STOP thinking about her intruder. Her speed, her grace. The way her body moved through the air like the water in the garden fountains. Between that and the unexplained bit of land on the map, her mind was teeming with possibilities.

"Anoor, please recite the four principal runes." Nuhan was a surly teacher, even though as a guild member of knowledge he was a dedicated master of bloodwerk. His features were scythe-like, straight and narrow with a sharp nose that he peered down at her over.

"*Gi, Ba, Ru, Kha*," she replied curtly. He thought she was stupid, he always had. Her bloodwerk had always been weak, the power in the runes fading quicker than most. He didn't realize it was because she was using secondhand blood. She had stopped being ashamed of her Duster blood a long time ago. It was easy to when no one knew except her mother and Gorn. However, her inadequate skill in bloodwerk was still a source of embarrassment.

"And their purpose?" Some of the Embers in the room snickered.

"Pull negative, pull positive, push negative, push positive."

"Explain the positive and negative predisposition." He was talking to her as if she hadn't taken this class for three years. Longer than anyone else present, though her Choice Day was soon. She had turned twenty last mooncycle.

"Positive reacts outward, negative inward. So a negative pull drags an object toward the rune, a positive pull drags the rune toward objects it's directed at. Similarly, a negative push presses objects away from the rune, a positive push presses the rune away from the object." She recited his own words back to him word for word.

"Come to the front of the class and demonstrate." Master Nuhan loved picking on her when Gorn fell asleep. Right on cue her bodyguard, servant, and protector began snoring.

She wasn't the only Ember in the class with a chaperone, but she was the oldest. Most Embers, even the ones as high up the social order as she, had been given protection their whole lives. Ever since the Night of the Stolen. No one talked about it, but everyone knew the story despite the wardens trying to hide it. Little did they know they had a Duster right in the heart of the Keep.

Her hips got stuck in her foldaway desk as she stood, earning a few more smirks from her classmates. Despite being the warden's daughter, they had still found cause to tease her for her appearance and lack of bloodwerk skills. When she eventually shuffled her way to the front of the class, she was sweaty and distraught.

Master Nuhan handed her four colored bricks.

"Which one should I bloodwerk on?"

"Whichever one you want, that shouldn't be the hard bit really." She tried to laugh with the class. When they stopped, she picked up the blue block and slotted in her stylus. With shaking hands, she drew the rune *Gi* in Gorn's blood.

"*Gi*, pull negative." The blue block was directly pointing at the red one. It took a couple of trembling steps toward the blue block then slammed against it with a click.

She looked at Master Nuhan, and he raised a gray eyebrow indicating she should go on.

Pulling apart the blocks was easy as the rune she had drawn contained her blood. She wiped away the rune with the rag on the side and began again.

"*Ba*, pull positive."

She positioned the rune to point at a red block. The block bucked in her hand instantly, and as she let go the blue block skated backward on the table, attracted to the red block by the rune.

"Now, *Ru*." Master Nuhan looked bored like the rest of the class. Some were experimenting with their blood on their desks. They too had hoped she'd fail the basics.

She performed *Ru* with no trouble, pushing the red block away. *Kha* should have been just as easy, but when the blue block she had drawn on didn't move backward, her heart sank. Master Nuhan instantly perked up.

"Ah, a fault." His voice was as sharp as an eru's tooth. "In the foundational basics."

He peered at the rune, his nose crinkling in distaste as he looked at her blood. Gorn's blood.

She knew it was technically perfect, it always was, but using secondhand blood meant her bloodwerk was temperamental. The blood's power always deteriorated as time passed, something about being away from the host's body. It was all speculation, really. Anoor had never found any research on the process, and there was no way the wardens wanted anyone knowing using someone else's blood was possible.

When she'd first discovered this conundrum in her bloodwerk, she'd tried to track down the man who'd made her inkwell to see if he had a solution. It was then that she'd discovered he'd died suddenly the day after making her present. Heart failure, they'd said.

Her mother was careful.

"Ah I see it, you missed a line on the top of the rune." He wiped the evidence away with the rag. "Using charcoal only, I want you to draw out the foundational runes five hundred times for three days' time."

It was a ridiculous task, it would take her strikes, days even. She opened her mouth to protest.

"Class dismissed. I'm letting you go early, as I know some of you are wanting to enter yourself into the Aktibar. They're taking last names now in the courtyard."

At least five of the older kids leaped from their seats. Anoor was the last to leave. Gorn was awake and waiting for her by the door.

"Anoor?" Master Nuhan called her over.

"Yes, Master?"

"I just wanted to check, well, you know." He coughed. "About the Aktibar, I assume you are not entering yourself." Anoor flushed with shame, then anger. White coal anger.

"Why do you ask that, Master?" Her voice was contained, tight.

"Well, I'd advise against it, that's all. You're not terribly strong." He coughed. "In bloodwerk or I assume in fitness." He widened his eyes as if his stare wasn't big enough to take her in. "Don't want you to bring shame on your family with some foolish notion of following your heritage."

It was her mother. Without a doubt she had put the master up to this. Anoor had no intention of entering the trials.

She had enough going on with the stranger she'd hidden in her wardrobe.

"Master, I have no intention of entering."

Relief washed over him, and Anoor recognized the smell of it.

"Send my regards to my mother," Anoor said to the master. She missed his affronted expression, but she knew she'd pay for it tomorrow.

By the blood she hated him. Maybe hate was too strong a word. She hated her mother. No, hate wasn't strong enough.

Tears dashed down her cheeks as she strode away from the classroom. Gorn gave her the space to grieve her pride.

If only she had the strength to stand up to him, to *her*. Be as confident and as frightening as the stranger in her room. She was tired of being the victim in the story.

The seeds of a plan began to germinate in her mind. The roots twisted over themselves, creating an impossible pattern that she could barely follow, let alone pull off.

Or could she?

CHAPTER NINE

Consumption of joba seeds and the color of blood directly correlate, my research concludes. The infirmary in the Duster Quarter has documented a substantial number of Duster deaths due to the drug. Though there is no infirmary in the Dredge, my interviews with healers who have made the journey suggest the drug use is an epidemic that is prevalent among Dusters there. Fewer Ghostings seem to rely on the vice, and it is my belief that their time spent with their masters enforces a stronger sense of morality.

—Anoor Elsari, extract from her essay
"The Drug Blossoming Among Dusters"

Shards of glass were being hammered into the base of Sylah's skull. At least that's what it felt like. She'd tried screaming through the gag, but her throat grew hoarse and her voice wispy. The wardrobe was a mess, although Sylah couldn't comprehend that it was a wardrobe. It was the size of her mother's entire villa.

Shoes, suits, scarves, pantaloons had all been knocked off their shelves from her thrashing. Egg was smeared across the walls in clumps. She'd aimed for the most opulent dresses. Dresses that should be hers. Dresses that *were* hers by right.

She'd learned a lot about her keeper while time had stopped. Once the runelamp in the corner had flickered on two strikes ago—five, six, ten; who knew what time the clockmaster called— she'd surveyed her clothing with interest. The girl liked things that sparkled. Pearlescent glitter, made from the scales of lava fish, clung to flowing gowns and suits. Sylah wondered how many Dusters had lost their lives to the brutal waves of the Marion Sea just to scour the depths for the glittering fish. At least they could rest easy knowing their hard work adorned the dresses of the nobility. Sylah didn't belong there, among the ghosts of the Dusters.

She was not born to sparkle. She was born to burn.

"Argh." Sylah threw another clump of eggs with her tied-up hands. The action bruised her shoulder, but it was worth it for the Dusters who were no longer here to fight.

Her anger turned her thoughts to Jond. He'd be worried about her. She needed to get out and sign up for the Aktibar before it was too late. Her stomach suddenly lurched.

Skies above, she needed a joba seed. The little brat had stolen them from her bag. Sylah only realized they were missing after she'd spent a good amount of time rolling on the satchel to coax them out. Now she had a bruised tit, a throbbing head, and a fractured ego. How had that girl bested her? Bloodwerk, of course. How did the girl do it? She was a Duster, wasn't she?

Sylah didn't remember deciding to infiltrate the Keep. After Lio had told her the truth, Sylah topped off her intoxication with a bottle of firerum or three. The thought bubbled up out of the depths of her inebriation. She had to see her. The girl who stole her life.

Sylah followed a group of partygoers through the blood scour at the Keep's gate.

"Next." The officer was a brute. A brute of the brutish kind.

"Hello."

"Name?"

"Lylah of Ood-Raynib." The firerum told her the disguise was brilliant, the joba seeds cackled at her trickery.

"Something funny?"

"Ah, no." She covered her mouth with her hand to suppress her smile.

Master Brute called behind him, "Rija, you have a Lylah of Ood-Raynib?" There was a pause as Rija rummaged in the back office logs.

"No."

"First time?" The officer looked at her, but it took Sylah a while to realize he was talking to her.

"Oh. Yes."

"Okay. Sign your name here."

A pen. She was holding a pen. She'd only ever signed a cross before.

"That's . . . an interesting shape." The brute of all brutes frowned.

"Thanks." Maybe the officer wasn't so bad. Sylah was quite impressed with her squiggle herself. It kind of looked like a flower.

The officer grabbed her wrist, and she was thankful for the long sleeves that hid her guild mark. She lifted her thumb for him.

Master Brute frowned. "We don't take it from the thumb. It's too important a finger, especially if you're in and out of here every day." Was he suspicious? Probably. "We take it from the third finger."

Sylah nodded like they were discussing the weather. He had to forcibly pry her finger from her fist. A sharp pinprick followed. She blinked. Red blood blossomed. He waited for it to form a bead and then smeared it next to her signature.

"You can go now." He waved her away with a shake of his hand. "Next."

She was in. She expected to feel some sort of relief, redemption, remembrance. But it was just the hum of the joba seed soaring through her veins.

Now she was trapped in a wardrobe among an offensive amount of glitter. She needed a seed more than she'd ever needed anything in her life. Corners were sharper, colors clearer; they hurt her eyes.

Why had she come here? The question bounced around the cavernous space in her mind.

Up and down.

Up and down.

Up

and

down.

The door opened and Sylah hissed at the bright light.

Like the moon, the girl's face peered down at her, beaming from ear to ear. Her hair was a cloud of short brown curls around her face. There were smaller moons within the first—large round eyes, button nose, the perfect pout.

"Hello." She waved, as if they were out for tea, not capturer and captive. Sylah hoped her eyes conveyed "fuck you."

"You've made quite a mess in here. I'll certainly have to clean that up before Gorn comes." She picked up a pair of gaudy heels. "Oh, my favorite shoes!" She cradled them like a babe before placing each heel back on the shelf.

"Are you thirsty? Hungry?"

Fuck you. Fuck you. Fuck you.

"Well, I can't take your gag off until you promise not to scream. In turn, you have my word, as a citizen of the Wardens' Empire, to not hurt you."

It was like she was reciting the words from a book. She turned around and dragged in a tray of drinks and food. Sylah's stomach churned and growled at the same time. If she was being really honest, she'd trade that tray and both her hands for a joba seed.

"Do you promise?" The girl held up a glass of water. Sylah's throat was drier than the blue sand dunes of the Farsai Desert.

Sylah nodded once.

The girl sucked on her plump bottom lip and surveyed her. Then, with swift hands she reached forward and pulled off the gag. The runes released at her touch. The girl held up the water to her mouth and Sylah downed it in one gulp.

"Fuck you," Sylah said, slamming her head against the girl's forehead. Then she began to scream. "Help me, she's kidnapped me!"

The girl, albeit a little dazed, threw herself at Sylah, her weight winding her.

"Get off." Sylah was trying to breathe, but the girl was so damn heavy and Sylah was so weak from joba seed cravings.

"Stop it. Stop it!" She was trying to put her hands on Sylah's mouth.

"Let me go, you lump." Sylah bit on her hand as the girl tried to clamp it shut. Part of Sylah's mind noticed that she hadn't broken the skin. Damn it, she was hoping to prove the girl was a Duster.

"Please stop biting me. No, stop it. That hurts!"

"Just let me go, I'll sign up for the Aktibar, and then, if you want, I'll come back." Of course she wouldn't.

"You can't. No, stop squirming, listen. You can't because it's over. The sign-up finished up half a strike ago."

Sylah deflated. It's strange how hope can fill you up. She had once thought joba seeds were enough. Enough to feel, enough to hide, enough to disregard the guilt that smoldered in her heart. But it wasn't enough. Disappointment doused the fire that had sparked within her.

"A dancer's grace, a killer's instinct, an Ember's blood, a Duster's heart." The words seeped out of her into the empty space where hope had bloomed. Eighteen years being a part of the Sandstorm, twelve years being trained and harnessed for their purpose. Gone, in one moment. The decision to sign up for the Aktibar had been robbed from her. All because of this bloodforsaken usurper in front of her.

"Anoor?" *Knock. Knock. Knock.* "Everything okay?"

The girl, who Sylah now realized was called Anoor, hissed at Sylah to shut up before going to answer the door. Sylah wasn't screaming anymore. She was empty.

The girl returned to the wardrobe a few seconds later.

"I had to pretend that I was rehearsing for the summertime opera." She looked shaken. "Curse the blood, I'll have to audition now."

She looked at Sylah as if remembering she was there. "Please don't scream again, they'll kill you, you know."

"Is it true?"

"What?"

"That the Aktibar sign-up is over?"

"Yes, well, no, it'll be open again in ten years." She said the words as if they were some comfort to Sylah. There was another sharp rap at the door. It filled the room with an echo of authority. The girl, Anoor, gulped.

"Please be very, very quiet, she will kill you, there'd be no mercy for either of us."

Sylah was curled up on the floor, and although Anoor no longer lay on her, she felt the weight of failure even more keenly. Her body trembled with the distinctive need for a joba seed, but for once her mind didn't notice.

Shapes and shadows moved in the gap between the wardrobe doors. The murmurs between Anoor and her guest were just out of reach. Sylah didn't mind.

It was not until the gray suit caught her eye that she realized who the woman was. She wore the same color clothing from the Day of Descent. Sylah sat up and pressed her cheek against the wood of the door.

"Do you realize what you have done?"

"No, mother." Anoor was sprawled on the floor.

"Do not call me that when we're alone. It's bad enough I have had to continue this charade for so long in public." The slap slammed against Anoor's cheek.

"Yes, Warden." There were no tears in her voice.

"You know you won't even get through the first round?" When Anoor didn't reply, Uka spun on her heel. As soon as the door shut, Sylah pushed open the wardrobe with her shoulder and fell onto the plush bedroom carpet. She attempted to squirm toward the door in the wake of Uka's scent—lilies and radish leaf smoke. Her mother, her *real* mother, just a few handspans away.

Would she recognize me?

Anoor started to laugh, big belly laughs that jiggled through her in happy ripples and quivered the curls around her face.

"What's going on?" Sylah rolled over to face Anoor.

"She . . . she . . . was so angry!" Tears squeezed out of her eyes in mirth.

"And that is funny because?"

Anoor didn't reply; she couldn't get the words out. Sylah waited for the laughing to stop.

"You signed up for the Aktibar?" Sylah asked, bitterness twisting her mouth.

"Yes," she answered, wiping her eyes with a lace handkerchief, but the corners of her lips quivered, threatening to lift again.

"To become the Disciple of Strength?"

"Yes, it's quite funny, really." Anoor sat up and leaned on the bed. "It was you, actually."

"What was me?" Sylah tried to sound threatening, but pieces of the plush carpet kept wafting into her mouth. She tried to push herself up.

"You made me realize I could do it." Anoor squared her shoulders. "So I've decided to keep you."

"Keep me? You realize I am not a pet."

"Well, it's that or I turn you in." Anoor wet her lips with her tongue. All humor was gone from her face.

Sylah wished her hands were free so she could push the heel of her palm into her eyes. The girl was crazy.

"Where are all my joba seeds?"

"Oh, I threw them out the window."

Sylah's mouth clamped shut.

"What were you doing here?" Anoor continued.

"You threw my joba seeds out of the window?"

"Yes, I said that already." She cocked her head at Sylah.

The growl started deep in Sylah's throat and worked its way into her limbs. She buckled and thrashed her way toward Anoor, who suddenly scuttled away, faster than anyone would have thought she could.

"Stop it, stop it, stop it." Her screech was wild, but not as wild as Sylah. "They will kill you, don't you understand?"

Slowly Sylah began to quieten. Her knees turned to jelly, and her muscles wouldn't move when she commanded them. The water, the fucking water. The girl had put something in it.

"Whachyagivmeh?" Her spittle showered the carpet, followed by her head, then darkness.

WHERE WAS SHE? She felt dark and small. She reached for Papa. No, he was dead. Dead and gone.

HE WAS COMING for her. Loot. He was chasing her down with his bare hands. She didn't mean to win. Yes, she did. She needed to win, to save them. His yellow suit morphed into manicured nails, filed to a point. No, not nails. Spider legs with razor-blade feet. He scuttled up her skin, slashing her down to the bone. Blood poured out of her into wine goblets that the wardens drank. She tried to scream but instead vomit bubbled out of her mouth into the bucket beside her. The bucket was already half full. Her whole body convulsed with each retch, as if her organs were trying to claw their way out.

SHE WAS A baby. She recognized the shapes around her, but she knew it couldn't be a memory.

Mama and Papa stood in the shadow of the Keep, but she wasn't in Lio's arms. Instead they held an empty bundle of cloth. The hole where the baby's face should have been leaked blue blood. It oozed and trickled onto the ground, the ground where Sylah lay. She felt the absence from the cloth so keenly, she wailed and cried and flung her fatty limbs. But they couldn't hear her.

Azim and Lio's gaze never moved from the building above.

SHE WAS SCATTERED across the land, little bits of her. She hurt and ached and waited. Then as the moon rose, she rose. Ferocious and beautiful, she pirouetted through the city of Nar-Ruta. Devouring and cleansing all she touched. Because she was the tidewind, and she was here to destroy.

A GIRL STOOD above her. She remembered her name. Anoor. She held a wet cloth to Sylah's face, concern dampening her pretty eyes. Sylah tried to be scared. Tried to be angry. But instead, she let her poisoner tend to her and went back to sleep.

THERE WAS SOMETHING different, something missing. Sylah felt it in the way the air moved around her.

"You're awake." Anoor sat on a stool next to the bucket, which had been thankfully empty for some time.

"What did you poison me with?" Sylah asked.

Anoor looked hurt.

"Poison you? I gave you a drug to aid your withdrawal. With the amount of joba seeds you had in your pocket, I knew it'd be bad." She dragged her perch closer. "Kwame, he's a friend of mine from the kitchens, he had a cousin who went through the same thing, so he helped me make the draft. Two parts milk honey, one part verd leaf, a dash of vinegar, and a lot of water to flush it through."

Sylah lost interest halfway through the story. Thankfully, she was no longer bound, so she was able to throw in a yawn.

"I feel like eru dung." Her stomach ached from the retching, and her body was still sticky with sweat.

"Yes." Anoor nodded. "It will continue for some time. Kwame says one joba seed can take up to a week to leave your system but depending on how much you took your body will try and right the balance of the drug's absence for some time. It's a dangerous drug, didn't your parents teach you that?"

Sylah laughed, and it hurt her throat.

"No, I had no idea actually."

Anoor missed the sarcasm in Sylah's tone and continued with a quick lecture. "Joba seeds affect the receptors in your brain; once the body becomes used to the drug, it requires more and more to get a sufficient high. But the more you have, the more your body starts to expel the foreign drug through your system. Normally heart failure, but sometimes it's the seizures that'll do it. You know, swallowing your tongue." Anoor grimaced.

"Lucky Ghostings," Sylah interjected.

Anoor recoiled at the crude joke.

"It's not funny. It's a serious addiction, I did an essay on the effect joba seeds have on Dusters and Ghostings. The withdrawal is going to be hard to get through as your brain receptors take a while to recover. You've affected the nerve center, quite fundamentally. They've become reliant on a drug you're no longer taking. So you may lose motor skills, suffer from seizures, feel nauseous. The list goes on."

"Maiden's tits, better get a joba seed in me quick then." Sylah ran her hand through her hair. And stopped.

"Where the fuck has my hair gone?" The short stubble, so like her mother's, spiked her with tiny daggers.

"Well, I suppose it's fair to say, that it's somewhere in the rubbish fill a few leagues outside of Nar-Ruta by now." Anoor was busying herself with folding and refolding a pair of red pantaloons. Sylah turned her dark eyes to her.

"You cut off my hair?"

"Yes, well, you started tearing it out in your sleep, it was all matted with blood and gore. Oh, and the smell . . . it got me thinking, an Ember servant would be as good a disguise as any. And you'd need a shaven head for that . . ."

"You cut off my hair?"

"Are you listening?" The lump sighed, actually sighed. "I had to make you a good disguise in order to—"

"You cut off my hair?"

Irritation wrinkled between Anoor's brows. The utter gall of it.

"Yes. I had to." She was speaking slowly, drawing out the truth like a blood scour. "You can help me compete in the Aktibar, be my trainer. You can use your assassin skills to train me to fight . . ."

Sylah reached for her hair. She tried to pull on it, but there was nothing there. She pushed her scalp backward, drawing her eyes out, her forehead taut.

"You want me to teach you?" A whisper.

"I can give you things, anything. Money? Jewelry? Gemstones? Clothes?"

"Monkey's balls, do you think I want any of this hideous shit? You took away everything from me. Everything I had." Sylah tried to claw at Anoor's face, but her hands had begun to quiver. She looked at them in horror as they eventually went slack.

"It's the joba seeds. Your muscles won't always obey you until your receptors heal." Anoor was quiet.

"Aghh," Sylah screamed. Fat tears fell down her face, pooling across her ears into the bare landscape of her memories.

"I'll leave you." Anoor scurried off.

Sylah cried for some time. The sobs were like waves of the Marion Sea crashing against rocks on the shore. Breaking her into rubble. Into sand. Into dust.

CHAPTER TEN

Anyme, who resides in the sky,
Ruler of all, fealty to none,
Absolve us of our sins,
So we can join you forth,
In your nation above,
Forever remembering the wrath,
The Ending Fire wrought,
On those sinners, whose transgressions,
You traded, for their souls,
In your name we pray:
The blood, the power, the life.

—Prayer recited by the Abosom

"Gorn, I'm going to the library." Anoor locked the assassin in and left. The sound of the girl keening through the dressing room door had made her wince. She needed to go out.

Gorn appeared in the hallway. "Are you feeling better?"

"Yes, thank you." The assassin had been suffering for two days, and Anoor feigned illness to take care of her. Anoor had noticed the red staining on her teeth from the moment they'd first met, but she hadn't anticipated withdrawal like this. The symptoms roiled in on a sea of vomit, sweat, and tears. The draft Anoor was giving her was meant to lessen the effects of the cravings, but the vomiting and shaking still seemed horrific to Anoor.

The first night the girl fought phantoms in her mind, thrashing against her restraints until her wrists bled. Anoor removed them then, but when Anoor returned a strike later the girl started pulling her hair out at the root. Clumps of matted braids fell around the dressing room like dead leaves shedding in autumn.

Anoor winced at the memory. She'd *had* to shave the girl's hair just to protect her.

"I'm going to the library," Anoor repeated.

Gorn reached for her shawl hanging on a peg. "I'll come with you."

"No, I'll be fine, I've got my papers in here, I'm just going to settle in for some studying." Anoor patted her bag, feeling the bulge of the rolled-up map beneath her books. "Choice Day will come around quickly once the Aktibar's over." The lie was a simple one, but Anoor didn't look Gorn in the eye.

Gorn opened her mouth to speak. Closed it. Tried again. "So it isn't true then. That you signed up for the Aktibar?"

"Well . . ."

Gorn hissed, "That's what you were doing? When you went for a walk around the courtyard? I thought you wanted some time alone, not to sneak your way to the sign-up sheet."

Anoor lifted her chin. "I did not *sneak*. I walked in very calmly."

Gorn exhaled and rubbed the back of her neck. "Oh, Anoor . . ."

"I'm going to the library." Anoor stomped to the door.

"What for? You've chosen your guild, it seems," Gorn said but Anoor didn't respond. Gorn sighed in defeat, and when she spoke again she sounded weary and sad. "Do you need anything from the market today?"

"Yes, would you mind picking up more verd leaf and milk honey?"

"Still not sleeping?"

"And, Gorn,"—a thought came to mind—"would you stop by the cocoa stall and buy some chocolate?"

"I can do that."

"A big box please."

"Always."

"Make it two."

"If it pleases you."

"Thank you, I'll be back soon."

THE LIBRARY WAS on the western side of the Keep, past the great veranda and the clock, in the business district. It housed the courthouse, the warden offices, and the schoolrooms.

The courthouse was at the forefront of the building, with whitestone statues of the founding four wardens standing watch beside the large oak doors. The wardens had led the first group of citizens to the shores of the empire, while the world beyond was claimed by fire from the sky: the Ending Fire. All that survived was in the hull of their ships. The faces of the statues had been rubbed smooth by those who passed them by, and now they were white shadows of the people they once were.

Anoor continued up the stairs, where she was greeted by the familiar smells of books and ink.

"Ah, Miss Elsari, I was going to send this to your chambers— the latest zine's just landed. And oh, it's a real good one. I won't give it away but Souz ends up married to both men, one of them finds out when she's in bed with the other. She then gets pregnant but it's neither of their children. Can you believe it? I won't ruin the ending but it doesn't end happy with the baby dead and all and Abena back on the case . . ."

"Hello, Bisma, how are you?"

When the librarian grinned, his eyebrows did the smiling for him: they lifted his features up toward his afro hair. His hair was still dark despite his age, but his face was as weather-worn as a sun-dried tomato. "Oh, doing well, doing well."

"Thank you for the zine, how much do I owe you?" Anoor didn't often handle money, but she could send Gorn up later.

"Don't worry, this one was worth it, especially that scene in the cemetery, the way Abena ends up fighting both of them and stealing their wallets. Anyway, I'll let you read it before I spill the whole plot."

Anoor laughed, "Thank you, Bisma."

"Choice Day coming up, eh?" He nodded toward her bag full of books.

"Yes, I was actually hoping to brush up on my history before making my decision."

"Aho, leaning toward knowledge then?"

She gave him a nonchalant shrug.

"What are you looking for, particularly?"

"I'm interested in any of the earliest recordings about the continent, maps, details on the people who once lived here, maybe even about the Ending Fire?"

He frowned. "I see." He scratched his wispy beard, "I'll be as honest as the tidewind's wrath, there isn't much in the way of history here. We have a few early texts but nothing that'll tell you much beyond what you've already been taught in school. You'd be better off trying the warden library. Why don't you ask your mother to get you in?" The warden library was off limits to everyone except the wardens themselves and maybe the odd trusted adviser. It wasn't Bisma's fault he didn't know Anoor didn't fall into that category.

"Ah, thank you, Bisma. I might just do that . . . another time."

His eyes crinkled with the wisdom of other people's stories. "Anything we do have will be on the third stack, second row."

"Thank you, Bisma."

Anoor took the zine from his outstretched hand and made her way through the library. The public library was rarely used anymore; the wardens had no interest in its upkeep and so the quality of the books within had never been all that great. Embers were given the texts they needed to learn from in their classes, and anything beyond that was deemed unnecessary. Anoor was one of the few people who frequented the library, and even then, that was mostly to collect her zines from Bisma.

It was a claustrophobic room, a forgotten corner of the Keep, with too many books and too little space. The bookshelves were made from an assortment of materials, some rubber wood, others oak; a few of the shelves were even made from crumbling limestone. All had to be greased every mooncycle with peppermint oil to ward off the cockroaches who loved to scuttle between the tomes. Anoor avoided the library on that day; besides the smell that burned her nostrils, the fleeing cockroaches were enough to give her nightmares.

She found the history section and selected three of the oldest volumes there: *Masters at Work, The Soil We Toil,* and *A Geography of the Empire.* They weren't very thick books, and inspecting the spines, she thought they looked like they'd never been opened. She took a seat in the reading station around the corner, which was wholly unoccupied. A plume of dust wafted from the books as she dropped them onto the table. And then she withdrew from her bag the main reason she was in the library in the first place: the assassin's map and the small flourish in the corner that looked like land.

STRIKES LATER AND she'd found nothing. Not a trace of the land across the sea. The closest she had gotten to understanding the fragment on the assassin's map was an extract from a diary belonging to a master of knowledge from three hundred years ago. The entries had been copied and added to a collection of stories in *Masters at Work.*

The Ending Fire engulfed the world. It rained from the sky and devoured the land. The last surviving people carried all they could to the deck of their boat. Animals, plants, food, clothes. It is estimated that 2,000 people left the mainland, but only half of them survived. Those who did survive claimed that the sea monster, the Tannin, devoured the others, though it is likely a fallacy caused by the trauma they experienced. Others believed that Anyme called them to the sky as a sacrifice—a more probable account.

The only remainder of civilization after the fire destroyed the world was what they carried in the hull of their boats. The Marion Sea churned and fire hailed, but the founding wardens prevailed. Bringing the Wardens' Empire to the coast of their new land.

It was the story that was told to every citizen from the day they were born. But if the land had been destroyed, how did the assassin have a map indicating otherwise? It didn't make sense. Could it be from *before* the Ending Fire? But how did it survive, if everything else, every person, animal, and plant, died? Plus, the map was made with papyrus paper, a plant that grew in abundance in the empire.

Anoor rubbed the back of her neck. Maybe the flourish in the corner wasn't land, it was something else, a mistake maybe.

She went back to the row of books and tried some others. Again, nothing. More than forty volumes she scoured through, and not a word on the land beyond the sea. The absence was telling.

How can there be nothing, not an ink dot, on the world before the Ending Fire? Those who founded the empire survived, so why didn't they document the world that once was?

Anoor was stricken that she had never had these thoughts before. She prided herself on her curious nature, something she'd learned from her years reading Inquisitor Abena's tales. But this ignorance was gargantuan, a gaping hole of nothingness in her knowledge.

Anoor pushed the books away; she was getting a headache. She'd found no answers, only questions.

But the trip hadn't been a complete waste of time. She'd also used the time to put together a robust backstory for her new trainer. She had forged three letters from a lesser Ember house in the made-up village of Ood-Adab. One of the letters was a request for a place in the household for a young woman whose uncle simply did not have the time or means to support her. Anoor could picture him, twisted and gnarled, with lingering hands and persistent bad breath, as she wrote about his niece with no parents to speak for her, both having died in a tragic eru accident when she was fourteen. The poor girl had to turn to the joba seeds just to make it through the day.

She yawned, her jaw creaking. It was time to head back. Maybe the assassin had stopped crying and she could get some answers from her. Anoor started to leave and then turned back. She picked up *Masters at Work* along with one or two other volumes and placed them in her bag. She wasn't going to give up the search just yet.

HASSA WATCHED THE warden's daughter leave the library before slipping out of the shadows herself. The library wasn't on her remit to clean that day, but when she saw where Anoor Elsari was headed, she'd offered to take over from the Ghosting who was there. They'd obliged, as Ghostings got few breaks.

Anoor had left a pile of books on the side. Hassa looked at them before putting them back on the shelf. Foolish. Anyone would be able to see that she was searching.

Searching for the truth.

Sylah had been missing for two days. Hassa had checked her mother's house twice, and each time Lio was increasingly agitated by Hassa's presence.

"I told you I haven't seen her," Lio had repeated just that morning. Though her words were nonchalant, her features were haggard from lack of sleep and worry.

The man Hassa had seen before lingered behind Lio, shifting from foot to foot; he too looked haggard.

It was Hassa's fault that Sylah was probably dead, her corpse so battered by the tidewind that Hassa hadn't been able to find any sign of her when she had searched the Ember Quarter the next night. Guilt had burrowed its way into her chest, like a desert fox hiding from the tidewind. And just when she thought she was burrowed hollow, an Ember servant approached her.

"Can you mix up a draft? Two parts milk honey, one part verd leaf, a dash of vinegar, with half a cup of water?" The servant was Gorn Rieya, Anoor Elsari's chief of chambers.

Hassa nodded, her mind reeling as she mixed up the drink with a practiced hand. The withdrawal remedy was often needed at Maiden Turin's when overexcited clients ate too many joba seeds.

But that was in the Dredge, away from prying eyes. It was unlikely an Ember would brazenly suffer from joba seed withdrawal, especially the warden's daughter. That's when Hassa started following her. She lingered outside her chambers all day until, finally, Anoor Elsari emerged.

Everyone thought the library was always empty; even the librarian had stopped seeing Ghostings anymore. Not from his lack of eyesight, though he often forgot to wear his spectacles, but because *no one* saw them. But they were there, in every room in the Keep. Listening, but not speaking. Hearing, but not telling.

Sylah, where is she keeping you? Hassa thought, but the next words sent a searing blade of panic through her. *And why?*

CHAPTER ELEVEN

Joba trees are deciduous plants that thrive in the sand of the Wardens' Empire. They range in size from small shrubs to large trees with canopies that stretch up to 250 handspans, as can be seen in the courtyard. Their flowering season is during the sixth mooncycle when large red flowers bloom, followed by the joba fruit three weeks later. The fruit is as red and glossy as the flower before it, and hardy in order to withstand the tidewind. The thick skin can only be breached by burning the fruit in a furnace. It has been found that the seeds inside are an effective painkiller and natural high, requiring strong policing of the drug. The difficulty in obtaining and harvesting the seeds makes the drug all the more profitable for crime lords.

—*The Soil We Toil* by Warden Iko

The room was spinning. Sylah's tears had dried, but the incessant swirling of the room made her want to shed more. She bit her cheek until it bled. The taste of salty iron was a poor replacement for the joba seed she craved. Sylah hugged her knees to her chest and rocked slowly back and forward, against the movement of the room.

"Fuck. Fuck. Fuck," she chanted.

Whether it was the swearing or the rhythm of the movement, she began to feel better. She unraveled her long limbs from her cocoon and stretched her aching muscles.

Her stomach roiled.

"No, no, no, no, no." Sylah could feel the bile rise up. "No!" She swallowed it and waited.

After ten minutes her stomach settled and Sylah began to think through her options. Despite the aching muscles, the headache, shaking limbs, churning stomach, her mind was clear. And with it, her memories. She pushed them away with enough mental force to rattle her brain.

So I'm stuck in a dressing room of a deranged brat who thinks I can train her to win the Aktibar. The Aktibar I missed signing up for because of her.

Anger eclipsed her mind, and suddenly Sylah's hands went slack. Sylah looked at her useless fingers, willing them to move, but instead spasms prickled up and down her forearms.

It was the joba seeds, or the lack of them. Her body couldn't function without the drug anymore. It didn't know how to. Sylah breathed in and out slowly until her hands gained mobility.

Okay, let's try this again. Aktibar, no longer an option. But she said she could give me anything. What do I want?

Red beads flashed behind her eyelids. A field of joba seeds, all hers. Sylah reveled in the daydream. When she opened her eyes, she considered what the girl had said. Jewelry? Gemstones? Clothes?

Sylah's laugh was harsh as she imagined what it would be like to care about such frivolous things. Her eyes scanned the racks of clothes in front of her.

Sylah stood, her legs like a newborn goat's, and took shaking steps toward the rack of clothes. She'd never seen such luxurious materials up close before. They were extravagant and repugnant in equal measure.

Sylah donned the most expensive dress in the closet, two of them, in fact. This first dress was made exclusively of bows. Big sweeping green bows. There must have been a hundred of them, all stitched together to make a landscaped mess of material. The other dress was a frothy chaos of lace in purple and green. It reminded Sylah of a weeping bruise.

The dresses were so baggy on her she could have probably slipped into a third. Her straight body was so different from Anoor's curves. The hems ended three handspans off the ground, and with the heels she had strapped herself into, she couldn't have looked more ridiculous.

The mirror at the end of the room agreed. She didn't recognize herself. Skeletal and bald. Eyes rimmed red from crying. Limbs quivering from withdrawal. She tried to squint and see herself as she would have been if she'd been brought up within the walls of the Keep. Was that sick in the corner of her mouth? Probably. She ran her hand over her scalp, down to the scar at the base of her neck.

THEY HAD BEEN *scoring the rubber trees for strikes. The Stolen and their foster parents worked as a unit, each with a scythe scraping the bark diagonally until a white substance hemorrhaged into the buckets below. The Stolen's chant hummed through the leaves.*

"Stolen, sharpened, the hidden key,
We'll destroy the empire and set you free,
Churned up from the shadows to tear it apart,
A dancer's grace, a killer's instinct, an Ember's blood, a Duster's heart."

It was hard and dusty work, but the sun had set long ago. Papa whistled through his teeth, and the Stolen changed routine. They retraced their steps, collecting the buckets that had overflowed with latex. Thirty buckets in total, a good haul.

"We reaped a lot this day." Papa Azim was pleased, his lips almost lifted at the corners. He was tall, impossibly tall, tall-as-two-buildings tall. Not in physical height, in presence, even though he was a quiet man—silent in his fierceness, a sandstorm in the night. His cheeks were slightly dimpled, skin dark from working the fields. And he had the softest eyes, brown like two coffee beans, toasted and warm.

He made them call him Papa Azim, though none of his blood ran through their bodies. But he loved them, and it was a love born from purpose and struggle.

Sylah grinned with the rest of the Stolen and basked in his happiness.

Then he lifted his hand high and brought his scythe to meet it. He slashed the sharpened end through his palm. It required a lot of effort to break the skin. Sylah knew because it was her turn next.

All of them cut their hands, one by one. They circled the buckets, shaking droplets of their blood into the curdling latex. Red and blue congealing.

"The handles of the overseers' whips, the tires of the trolleys that carry food away from our starving, the shoes that trample over our dead. It is our blood that carries these deeds forward."

Guilt ran down Sylah's cheeks and dripped onto the floor. She closed her eyes and listened as Papa Azim preached, the lilt of his voice like a lullaby, mesmerizing her young mind.

"It is our responsibility now. And our blood that will stop it. For we must fight for our lives and our liberties. In a battle, the last battle, the only battle. And we name it now, so it sears into our flesh, the moment to come, the rebellion that will destroy the Embers and the empire they stand upon. The Duster's last stand. And it starts with you, my Stolen children, you are our last hope, you are the Final Strife."

"The Final Strife," the Stolen chanted. "The Final Strife. The Final Strife."

Sylah chewed the corner of her lip until it bled. She watched the blood ooze and trickle down her lip. Then with a shaking finger she dipped her finger into the small wound. The smallest of wounds.

"The Final Strife."

She was taller, her eyes sharper, the colors clearer. This time they didn't hurt so much, her symptoms forgotten in the light of her memory.

She was to be the scythe against the neck of the empire. She was Papa Azim's last hope.

I will be again.

Sylah knew what she wanted from Anoor. Pride eclipsed her need for joba seeds for the first time in six years. After all, she was the Final Strife, and she would take up the title once more.

There was a knock on the wardrobe door. Sylah wiped the blood from her mouth and smeared it on the dress.

"Oh, that looks nice."

The girl meant it, she really did.

Sylah snorted. "You have interesting taste in clothes."

"Thank you, I design a lot of them myself."

"You like green."

"I do." She held out a steaming cup of tea.

"Are you going to drug me again?"

Anoor winced. "No, I think I may have added a bit too much verd leaf last time. It aids the withdrawal."

"Sip from it first." She'd played enough poison games with Loot to know the basics.

Her eyes lit up in delight. "Of course."

It was the daintiest of sips, and it made Sylah hate her all the more. "Give it to me." Sylah took the tea and drank it down. It was hot, but it soothed her glowing rage. "I have a price."

"Okay, name it."

"I'll teach you to fight, but you have to teach me to bloodwerk."

Anoor was shocked. "You don't know how to bloodwerk?"

"No, you could say I lived a sheltered life. You can bloodwerk, though?"

"Of course I can bloodwerk," Anoor answered quickly. "All Embers have the power in their blood, so it'll be simple enough to teach you." Her curls bobbed around her as she nodded. "So I teach you how to bloodwerk. Is that all?"

"You will do and listen to everything I say."

"Okay . . ."

"You must follow my training regime."

"Up to a point."

"What point is that?"

She pulled out some letters from her bejeweled bag. "I've created a backstory for you. You will be my chambermaid. It's the only way you will be able to get access to teach me. My mother is quite strict about my acquaintances; she's never let me have a chambermaid before." Anoor swallowed. "But I am of age to run my own household now. This way she can't disagree with me without taking it up with the Warden of Duty. Though she won't like it . . . the Warden of Strength isn't used to not getting her way."

Sylah felt her eyebrow twitch. "What is she like? Warden Uka?" she asked lightly.

"I think she's a good warden, maybe, I guess . . . everyone's afraid of her. She's quite mean, and she doesn't like me all that much." From what she'd seen, Sylah agreed with her.

"Fine, I'll do the chambermaid farce, but I won't be cleaning a thing."

"But it'll be expected that you contribute to the running of my household."

Sylah huffed through her nose.

"And what do my duties entail?"

"A chambermaid is required to clean the chamber. Gorn has been doing these tasks so far, but it's more proper to have a chambermaid. You'll support the chief of chambers. That's Gorn. You'll bring up my food, prepare my clothes, brush my hair—"

"Nope."

"Do the laundry."

"Nuh-uh."

"Clean the privy—"

"Okay, let's stop right there. Here's how it will go. I understand the need to keep up this facade. But—" Sylah slammed her hand on the floor. "Anything behind closed doors like the bed-making and clothes-selecting nonsense is all you. Including the privy. To everyone else, I'll happily play the chambermaid."

"Fine." Anoor pouted. "But you need to learn to be subservient in public."

"Fine." Sylah's mouth twisted in a bitter scowl. "I get freedom to leave at any time."

"After the working day and during your lunch break."

"All right."

"All right, then."

Anoor beamed. "Here's the backstory. I made up this character, Uncle Gallo, he's been—"

"Is it in that letter?"

"Yes."

"Then you don't need to repeat it. I can read." Sylah snatched the letter from Anoor's hand, reveling in the look of hurt on her face.

"I didn't know your name, so I left it blank," Anoor said in a small voice.

"Lylah of Ood-Raynib."

"Is that a lie?"

"Yes."

"What's your real name?"

Sylah thought about it. Papa Azim had named her; he named all the Stolen with names of power, names that would one day be paired with the title of warden. It might not be her that would own that title, but if she learned to bloodwerk, maybe it would be Jond. Sylah pushed her shoulders back and lifted her chin. "Sylah Alyana of Ood-Zaynib."

Anoor laughed, revealing dimples and an infectious smile. "Is that a lie too?"

"No."

"Oh, okay."

"I will teach you to fight and you will teach me to bloodwerk."

"You have to promise not to kill me."

"Why would I try and kill you?"

"Because you're an assassin."

Sylah laughed. It was a great honking sound that pushed its way through her nose. "You think I'm an assassin?"

"Why else would you be here? You asked who I was, I assumed to confirm your target," she said as if discussing the tidewind. "Who hired you? Can you tell me? Was it to hurt my mother? Or for another reason . . . ?"

Sylah's mind jumped through the possibilities of truths and lies. Why was she here? Honesty wasn't going to protect her.

"Yes, I was sent here to kill you, to hurt your mother, but I cannot tell you who sent me."

Anoor clapped, her eyes widening. "I knew it! Will your client send more after me?"

"No, it was a one-time thing; if I failed, I was to disappear. No contact, no payment."

"Why don't you know how to bloodwerk if you're some great assassin?"

Sylah's patience was finer than a river reed.

"I was taught to master the physical arts in a Sanc—farm in the north."

"An assassin school?"

Was she delighted? She sounded delighted.

"Skies above, enough about me. That isn't what I agreed to. In fact, no more questions, I'm adding that to the deal." Sylah's hand twitched to pull her plaits and the trinkets she had woven there. Her eyes smarted at the loss.

"Oh. Okay." Anoor's head bobbed.

The silence pulled tighter than a cornrow.

"Okay, so it's a deal. When I get to the final trial, I will teach you to bloodwerk."

"*Before.*"

"But—"

"No compromise. Every night I will teach you to fight. And every night you will teach me to bloodwerk until the end of the Aktibar."

"No joba seeds."

"What?"

"Your brain needs to stabilize, it needs to get used to surviving without the drug before you cause irreparable damage."

"I can't agree to that." Sylah's hands shook, and she clasped them together in a silent prayer.

"It's part of the deal." Anoor lifted her nose, and Sylah imagined it was a technique she used on a lot of servants.

Could she do it? For Jond maybe.

"You'll need to get me a lot of this tea."

Anoor nodded. "I can get you some, but you'll have to be careful with the amount you take. Verd leaf is a drug in itself; it mimics the effects of the joba seed to a much lesser extent. It'll help control the spasms and nausea, until you can cope without it." Anoor met her stare.

For the Sandstorm, and all the Dusters in oppression.

"Fine."

"Fine."

"What's that?" Sylah pointed to the box under Anoor's letters.

"Oh, of course, this is for you." Anoor handed her the box as if it were the most precious thing in the world. There was a green bow on the top, hastily stuck on with tree gum.

Sylah tore the box open and threw the lid to the side.

"The first row are coffee, the second whiskey, and the final row, they're stuffed with plantain. Those ones are my favorites."

"You got me chocolates?"

Anoor took her confusion for gratitude. "To thank you, for becoming my teacher. My grandmother had a teacher too, you know, she managed to convince the general of the army to train—"

"You capture me, lock me in your wardrobe, shave my head, then buy me chocolates? And you want me to do what with them?"

"Eat them, silly."

"But they're mine, so I can do whatever I would like?"

"Sure."

Sylah put her fist into the box and crushed the chocolates in her hand, their fillings seeping between her fingers. With deliberate slowness she smeared the chocolate down the dresses she was wearing.

Anoor looked on in horror, and tears filled her eyes. She didn't deserve the self-pity; if anyone in that room did, it was Sylah.

Sylah repeated this until there was only one chocolate left. A plantain one. She licked her lips and put it in her mouth. She'd never had chocolate before. Dusters couldn't afford it. There wasn't even a shop that sold chocolate across the river, much less a box this big. Sylah couldn't fathom how many times she'd have to fight in the Ring to get enough slabs to buy one. Here Anoor was buying it like it was nothing, gifting it to Sylah like it would right all the wrongs.

It coated her tongue with a velvety sweetness that was all at once sickly and instantly addictive. Part of her wished she hadn't wasted the rest, but the hurt in Anoor's eyes was worth it.

Like chocolate could ever make up for the life Anoor had stolen from her.

"You're right, these are delicious." Sylah smiled for the first time in days. The cut in the corner of her mouth split open. But she no longer needed to hide her blood. She was in a nest of Embers, and for once she wasn't the one out of place. "Where's your privy? I'd like to freshen up."

PART TWO

INVADE

The land we stand on was once barren—stripped bare by the Ending Fire. Until the founding wardens arrived and blessed the soil, birthing the home we call the Wardens' Empire. As you eat your meals, give thanks to the founding wardens who have taken their place next to Anyme in the sky.

Appreciate the home you have in life. And the home you will earn in death.

—Abosom blessing the guests on the great veranda
on the Day of Descent

THE STORY OF THE ORIGINS OF THE AKTIBAR AS SPOKEN BY GRIOT SHETH

The spoken word has been transcribed onto the page;
the ◊ symbol represents the beating of the griot's drum.

To mark the trials that are to come, let me tell its tale. Back to the start. Back to the beginning, when the founding wardens set sail.

◊ ◊ ◊

Before they were wardens, they were leaders, and before they were leaders, they were captains of ships.

◊

As captains, they led the survivors of the Ending Fire to the land that we call home.

Eight ships left the mainland, as down, down, down rained the Ending Fire.

Down, down, down, down.

Drowned!

Less than a thousand survived the journey to the ground beneath our feet.

◊

As leaders they built an empire on the backs of Ghostings and Dusters, using their whips and runeguns to keep them working.

Crack, crack, crack, crack.

Cowed!

Though you can't see the blood, it's there, blue and clear, in every whitestone brick. In every building near.

◊

As wardens they claimed their power and assembled the guilds to maintain order, prosperity, and peace.

Truth, duty, strength, knowledge.

Empire!

The only land left in the world, not destroyed by the Ending Fire.

◊

But power among Embers is a volatile thing, blessed as they are with bloodwerk. So one day other Embers rose up from their villas and asked, "Who are you to hold dominion over me?"

The four wardens emerged from their Keep.

"Because I am the strongest," one said.

"Because I am the most honorable," said another.

"Because I am the most trustworthy," the third acclaimed.

"Because I am the cleverest," added the fourth.

They lay claim to the four attributes most revered by the God Anyme.

The Embers heard their holy words and were subdued, until the youngest of them spoke out: "We must prove it."

◊

So six trials were decided for each guild. Six for strength, six for duty, six for knowledge, six for truth. All across six mooncycles.

◊

They like the number six, no?

◊

The competition commenced. Embers over the age of fifteen entering from all over the land. Still the founding wardens won their place, retaining their titles. But to those who came in second, they offered up a role. An apprenticeship like no other—the title of disciple was bestowed.

"For ten years you will learn all there is in the guild you now belong to. When we step down, you will rise up. The trials will then commence again to discover the next disciple, and so the cycle will continue."

Those hungry for power were sated, knowing that their opportunity would come again.

◊

This is the story of the first Aktibar, and why, every ten years, the Embers compete to find the best among the red.

CHAPTER TWELVE

TWENTY-FOUR DAYS
UNTIL THE TRIAL OF AEROFIELD

This report seeks permission to develop a further three (3) duty chutes connecting the cities of Jin-Wonta, Jin-Sukar, and Jin-Laham. The tubes will be manufactured in Jin-Hidal under the existing duty service contract and installed by Duster laborers five (5) handspans below ground.

A master of bloodwerk has been procured from the guild of knowledge to assist the operation, and mark the tubes with the necessary runes to transport messages along the tunnels. The chutes will increase communication between the three provinces on the east coast of the empire, that currently have only eru-messenger services.

—Bill 237, proposal to develop additional duty chutes

The dress pinched Sylah's armpits, making her sweat despite the chill in the air. The brown wool hung a handspan off the ground, and the waist sagged somewhere below her flat chest, but it was the simplest garment Anoor had. Anoor's gowns and suits were far too extravagant for a lesser Ember household servant like the identity she had concocted for Sylah.

Anoor would have to send off for Sylah's uniform. The obnoxious scarlet pinafores worn by the Ember servants were enough to make Sylah gag. The overlarge collars patterned with the wardens' kente colors were like a choker of iron—reminding them who their masters were. As if she could ever forget.

The duty office was a dire thing. It sat on the outskirts of the courtyard like a forgotten runt. The building was squat and tidewind worn, so unlike the well-kept whitestone of the main building.

Thwum. Thwum.

The duty chutes made Sylah jump, the canisters filled with letters that traveled back and forth toward the other cities of the empire, pushed by bloodwerk.

Thwum. Thwum.

Sylah flinched again. Her hearing, like her other senses, had been cleared of the fog of her joba-fueled days. She didn't like it.

As well as managing the postal service, the duty office was also in charge of receiving the new servants for the Keep. So Sylah was told.

The traveling basket under her arms was filled with trinkets she'd found lying around Anoor's room. A book, a paperweight, some leftovers from lunch. Things her "character" might have needed en route to Nar-Ruta. Of course, the falsified letters of recommendation sat atop it all.

Anoor had pointed her in the right direction and then hung back under the cloisters—just in case her presence roused "suspicions." The girl was living a griot tale.

She was just about to join the queue when there was a tap on her shoulder. Sylah slipped into a Nuba defensive stance automatically.

"Hassa?" Sylah's eyes bulged in their puffy sockets.

Sylah, are you okay? What's going on? Why are you dressed like that?

The questions were signed so quickly it took Sylah a minute for her mind to catch up.

"I'm fine," Sylah said and pulled Hassa away from the interested stares of those ahead of her in the queue.

An Ember, talking to a Ghosting? Impossible, they all thought. But Hassa had taught Sylah that anyone could learn the language; it's just that no one tried.

She dragged Hassa to the edge of the branches of the joba tree in the courtyard.

Sylah, I've been so worried.

And it was true, she did look worried. Her little mouth was

pulled into a taut line, the bags under her eyes as wrinkled as her beige servant dress that only Ghostings wore.

"I'm sorry, it's a long story, and I'm in the middle of unraveling it. I'm going to be a servant."

A servant? Hassa shook her head in disbelief.

How was Sylah going to explain that she was going to be a servant when Hassa thought she was a Duster, and Dusters were no longer allowed in the Keep, ever since the Night of the Stolen. Ever since *she* was stolen.

Sylah opened her mouth to garble out a lie.

Don't.

"What?"

Don't lie. I know you're an Ember. I know who you are.

"What?" Sylah's stomach dropped through her quivering intestines to her feet.

Sylah, do you know how many times I've had to help you home?

Sylah shrugged, refusing to feel shame.

No, you wouldn't remember, and if you don't remember that, do you think it's possible that at some point during the hundreds of journeys, you might have let something slip?

Shit.

"Who knows?"

You have few friends. I'm not sure whether that makes you lucky or not.

Sylah's face puckered with the stress of the last few strikes, and she used her fingers to push the frown lines away.

Now will you tell me what you're doing here?

"Not right now, it's a long story." Sylah's eyes flickered to the cloisters.

Your mother, and that friend of yours. You need to tell them you're alive.

Sylah winced. "I will, but first I need to make sure that's still the case." An officer came in from the main gate and sent a look their way. Sylah's muscles trembled, and it wasn't just from withdrawal.

"Can you tell them? Tell them I'm alive?"

Hassa rolled her eyes. *Your mother is just the worst, though. She doesn't understand me and doesn't even try to. She tried to sweep me away with a broom this morning.*

"I know, I'm sorry." It was the type of apology that one person does for a collective. A pathetic assurance that everyone was sorry for the bigotry committed, even if they didn't show it. It was the apology of the bystander, and Sylah regretted it as soon as it came out of her mouth.

Hassa frowned. *Go. Tell me more later.*

Sylah nodded and ran back into the duty office line.

"NAME?" THE MASTER of duty peered down at her. She was spiky and twiglike, a joba tree in winter.

"Sylah of Ood-Adab." The taste of her verd leaf tea still filled her mouth and she resisted spitting on the floor.

The master of duty's gaze dribbled down the list in front of her. Sylah practiced her pout like Anoor taught her.

"No, I'm afraid you're not in the servant's registry."

"Master, please can you check again, I have this letter and I've traveled so far." Sylah stuffed the letter through the bars of the counter with shaking hands. Damn those joba seeds.

The master snatched the letter away from her with a hiss.

"Elsari residence?" Her branches quivered.

"Yes, Master."

"Kika, you heard anything from above about a new servant joining the Elsari residence?" She looked at the paper in front of her. "Anoor. Yes, that one. No?"

Sylah couldn't hear Kika's response.

"Says here she was instructed to come. No, not the warden, the daughter . . . Anoor. Yes, her . . . No I haven't heard either." A sly smile crept onto the bark of her face. "Sorry, miss, no job for you here."

Sylah was stumped. It was meant to go easier than this. She felt herself get hot with anger as the master of duty waved a hand at her to move out of the queue. This was her opportunity to leave, ditch Anoor and go back to her old life.

"Oh, Sylah, there you are!" Anoor appeared behind her in the queue. She gave Sylah a hug, which she half returned. "Is there some trouble here, Master?"

"Ergh, well. I had no orders to let in a new servant."

Unlike Sylah, Anoor was a natural actor.

"Yes, yes, I sent the notice to you mooncycles ago."

"Does your mother know? We've always had strict instructions never to hire more staff into your chambers."

"Master, do you know what age I turned on my last nameday?"

"Ergh."

"Twenty. So, under the household rules set out by your patron, the Warden of Duty, I am of age to run my own home."

Anoor rounded on her, and despite her small stature, the master snapped like a twig.

"Ah, yes, Miss Elsari."

"Now give her a token."

"Yes, miss." She pushed forward a golden coin hammered with the guild of duty. It made Sylah want to scratch the same sign burned onto her wrist.

Sylah picked it up and slipped it into her pocket. The token would get her into Ember taverns, Ember shops, Ember schools. It was heavy next to her thigh, but she felt lighter.

Anoor tugged on her arm, pulling her away from the front of the queue.

"Oh, dearest Sylah, I hope you haven't been put off from your first foray into the city." Anoor linked arms with Sylah, and she tried not to shrug her off. Sylah knew it was all part of the act, but she hated being so close to the imposter. "It honestly is the most beautiful time of year for you to visit. The tidewind has been a touch on the strong side, but I'm sure it'll calm down soon."

Anoor leaned in to Sylah's ear. Sylah tried not to recoil. The girl smelled like sandalwood.

"Smile."

Sylah jolted at the change of tone. She didn't realize she'd been frowning. Each step she'd been taking was a conscious effort to prevent her from going back to punch the master's teeth through her skull.

"Smile less, smile less!" Anoor suddenly cried.

"What do you mean?"

"You look deranged when you smile like that. By the blood, that was terrifying." She held a hand on her heart then shot a sheepish grin Sylah's way.

"You realize we're not actual friends, right?" Anoor faltered in her walk but didn't respond. There were no smiles, fake or real, after that.

They had to go through the whole facade one more time for Gorn. Gorn was not happy with the new arrangement, but there was little she could do. In the end, Anoor sent Gorn to request more bedding just to end the conversation.

And then they were finally alone in Anoor's chambers.

Sylah bounced onto the four-poster bed. There were more cushions on the bed than in the entire Duster Quarter.

"I want a bed like this," Sylah declared.

"Well, you can't, this was specially shipped from Jin-Noon. It'll take seven mooncycles for them to make it and ship it out."

Sylah fell backward onto the velvet covers. They were the softest thing she'd ever touched. "I'll be long gone by then." And she would be. In six mooncycles the Aktibar would be over, and the winner would be crowned.

Sylah looked around, still marveling at how crisp everything was. She missed the blurred edges she'd grown accustomed to. But now the haze from her usual joba seed high had lifted, she could finally *see* the chambers for the first time.

The room was even more opulent than Loot's lair. Gold dripped from every surface, and if it wasn't gold it was ruby, or emerald, or the glittering scales of the lava fish. Sylah was both disgusted and enthralled by it.

Could this have been my life?

A ceiling lamp created in the shape of an upside-down joba tree hung above the gold-gilded four-poster bed. The carpet was a plush amber with thick coils of cotton begging to be walked on.

She got up and sank her toes into it. Then she walked into the dressing room that had been her prison. Her fingers grazed the bloodwerk runes on the door that had kept her trapped. Anoor must have figured out how to use someone else's blood. If that was the case, then the knowledge of how to bloodwerk was more important than ever. Sylah needed to get hold of Anoor's inkwell. And if she was using an Ember's blood, then *anyone* could bloodwerk with the right tools and education. Sylah's mind reeled with the implications.

The dressing room had been cleaned.

Sylah began tearing clothing down from the racks.

"What are you doing?" Anoor screamed. Actually screamed.

"Well, we'll need an area to train in, and this seems as good a space as any."

Her lip quivered, but she eventually nodded. "But be careful! That is an expensive scarf." She clutched the silk that Sylah had thrown to her ample chest. "Can you be a bit more delicate?"

"No." Sylah threw a glittering ruby boot at her. "This is actually very therapeutic for me." Down came a rack of dresses. "Some might say it's a bit of an invasion of privacy. Not us, though? Right?" A chandelier of emerald necklaces was kicked to the wayside. "We're best buds, pen pals." She was smiling maniacally. "So close, you even did my hair. How kind!" She ran a hand over her shaven head. "Ah!" The muscle in Sylah's arm went slack, her hand hanging limply from her body. "Argh." Sylah dropped to the ground, her muscles in her legs going weak too. Anoor ran to her and helped to prop her up against a shoe rack.

"I'll make the tea."

Sylah sat there looking at her limbs all piled on top of one another, like kindling waiting to be lit, prickling in anticipation of the fire. By the time Anoor returned with the glass of verd leaf tea, Sylah had already gained mobility in her arms.

"How long is this going to last?" Sylah asked, sipping the drink. Anoor had cooled it with cold water.

"How many joba seeds did you chew in a week?"

Sylah snorted. "About four or five a day." More. Much more.

"A day?" Anoor gasped with extravagant hysteria.

Sylah tried to shrug. "I like the feel of it."

"Well, Kwame's cousin had been chewing three a week, and her muscle spasms were really bad for a mooncycle, but they plagued her for five more after that. She'd been caught having an illicit"—Anoor tried to wink but both her eyes closed—"affair with a Duster and they sentenced her to five lashes and sent the Duster to the rack. So she turned to joba seeds, sourced from across the river, of course—"

"What worsens the symptoms?"

"Pardon?"

"Why did my muscles suddenly stop working?"

It was Anoor's turn to shrug. "Not really sure." Anoor looked down. "When I wrote that paper there was a bit of research that said stress and anger could bring on spasms. They make the blood pump faster, and so the nerve transmitters go into overdrive. And if they're still trying to stabilize without the drug, then the body shuts down. It protects itself by rerouting all the efforts to the brain. The limbs are the first to be affected." She smiled. "But at least you'll still be able to think clearly."

"Fucking maiden's tits," Sylah growled.

Anoor bristled.

"What? Don't like my language?"

Anoor's shoulders limped upward. It was a noncommittal "no."

"Well, fuck you and your fucking maiden's tits."

Knock. Knock. Knock.

Gorn arrived as if she were a bad-language detector. Anoor cast a furtive glance at Sylah.

"I'll go see what she wants." Anoor opened the door to Gorn's sour face.

"Hello, Gorn."

"Hello, Anoor. Dinner is ready in the dining room. I took the liberty to set another place setting. The bedding I have left in the foyer for now, until we can make suitable living arrangements for your . . . chambermaid."

"She will sleep in here with me."

"Indeed?"

"Yes, if you could set up a pallet while we dine, I'd be grateful, Gorn."

Gorn looked at her coolly.

"Yes, Miss Elsari." She spun on her heel and left.

Anoor shut the door.

"Well, she hates you," Anoor said as Sylah came up behind her.

"It's a very natural reaction to me." Sylah pushed past Anoor and made her own way to the dining room. With the joba seeds no longer stealing her appetite, Sylah was *hungry.*

The dining room had the empty feeling of belonging to someone who normally dines alone. An oak table sat in the center of the room, cast in the spotlight of a runelamp above. There were six chairs, but only one with a worn cushion. A tall gold vase sat in the corner of the room filled with dried wheat and lavender. A taxidermy kori bird hung from a wall, its blue feathers spread wide as if in flight. Sylah felt the kori's azure glass eyes follow her as she entered.

Sylah could not believe the array of food in front of her. Stuffed yams, dates drizzled in honey, roast lamb, quail eggs covered in goat's curds, deep-fried plantain. There was enough to feed the entire Duster Quarter.

"Well, aren't you going to dig in?" Anoor had moved past Sylah and was stacking her plate high. A scoop from here, a scoop from there, an extra scoop to top it all off.

"No." Sylah pointed to the deep-fried plantain. "Nope." Another dish was refused. "Definitely not." The sugared plums stuffed with cheese were also condemned.

"Oh, you don't like this food? I'm sure the cook can fry up something else." Anoor, eager to please, opened her mouth to call back Gorn.

Sylah held out a hand to stop her. "You promised you'd do anything I said to get you through to the final of the Aktibar, right?"

Anoor didn't hesitate. Her round head bobbed up and down like a joba fruit in a tidewind. "Call back Gorn, ask her to remove everything from this table other than the roast meat and vegetables. The ones that haven't been fried."

Anoor looked crestfallen. "But—"

"Fresh food will help you develop stronger muscles. It will give you the energy and nutrition to build a foundation of strength. You don't see an eru eating fried plantain, and they're all muscle."

"But . . . but they're lizards." Anoor looked like she was going to cry.

Sylah nodded. "Well done, yes, they are. But think of them as your end goal. They are large, lithe creatures, built of muscle and power."

Anoor said nothing for a second, then with sudden determination she called out.

"Gorn!"

The woman turned up a moment later.

"Please can you inform the cook of my change in diet. I will only require fresh vegetables and meat, simply cooked. Please remove these from the table."

"Anoor? Are you quite sure?"

"Yes. Get rid of it." Anoor looked away.

Gorn looked at Sylah, the plates, and back to Sylah.

"May I ask what Sylah's duties will be?"

"She's had a long trip, she will report to you tomorrow," Anoor said, still steadfastly avoiding anyone's eye.

Once Gorn had cleared the plates, Sylah rounded on her.

"Report to that sour plum? You didn't tell me she'd be the one assigning my jobs."

Anoor smiled at the sour plum reference.

"It was implied, she's the chief of chambers, after all."

Sylah opened her mouth to snap back, but it was then that Gorn returned.

It wasn't until the sun dipped beyond the horizon and Gorn had excused herself for bed that the real work began. Sylah had spent much of the evening rearranging the wardrobe to suit Anoor's training needs.

"You can't run, fight, box, or fence. What can you do?" Sylah held her head in her hands.

"I can swim. But I suppose I haven't done that in a while. Mother told me I embarrass her when I wear a bathing suit, so she banned me from lessons." She spoke the anecdote quickly, as if she were simply commenting on the weather.

"Why would that embarrass her?" Sylah said, confused at why anyone would be embarrassed by Anoor's curves.

"You know . . . I'm . . ." Anoor ran her hands down the waves of her body. "And she's . . ."

Anoor flicked a wrist toward Sylah's willow frame.

Sylah cocked her head but didn't say anything.

"Oh!" Anoor brightened. "I'm pretty good at archery."

"Archery?" Sylah thought of her sister Fareen and her bow and arrows. She reached for the plait that contained one of Fareen's old bow strings, but her fingers met air. Her fingers trembled with the loss.

"Well, when my mother realized I hadn't . . . inherited the fortitude to exceed in every sport imaginable, she found me something I could do that was . . . stationary." Anoor fiddled with the hem of her silk blouse. "I think it was meant to be an insult, but in the end I was very good. I can bring up my bow set and show you."

"That's something, at least, but let's maybe keep the bow and arrows out of the bedchamber for now."

Sylah ran her hand over her shaved skull.

"Right, we have six rounds to get you through in six mooncycles. Aerofield, tactics, stealth, mind, bloodwerk, and combat, in that order. The first round commences at the end of the mooncycle. That's just under four weeks away . . ." Sylah rocked back on her heels. Four weeks. They had four weeks to prepare for the first task.

"Yes." Anoor simply smiled.

Brat.

Sylah stood up with a rush of blood to her head.

"Time to get to work. Tonight, we're going to learn some basic stretches and how to focus the mind. But starting tomorrow we need to increase your fitness. Before the Keep wakes, we will run around the courtyard once and up the five hundred steps, the next day twice, then thrice, and so on."

Anoor's smile had fallen.

"If you're as good at archery as you think you are, the first trial should at least be easier than the others."

"I suppose." Her voice was quite small. "It does sound like a lot of work."

"Yes, Anoor, it is." She threw her name at her like an insult. "It's going to be a fucking great deal of work, but you know what? You chose this." Sylah's arm began to shake, and she recognized the prickling of the early stages of a seizure. The oncoming weakness in her muscles. The nausea that lurched up from her toes to the tip of her tongue. "You chose this. You chose to do this to me."

Anoor's eyes flashed.

"Yes, I trapped you. Yes, I shaved your hair. But no, I did not do this to you." She pushed her curling bangs out of her eyes. "*You* did this to you. Even if you had made it to the sign-up, you weren't going to get very far in the state you were in. Red stains on your teeth are one of the last stages of addiction. You were a few seeds away from death. So don't hold that over my head." It was one of the longest speeches Anoor had made to anyone ever. Her breath came out in short, quivering puffs and her eyes threatened to leak. Suddenly she peeled away from Sylah.

"Where are you going?" Sylah's voice was stony.

"Bed."

"No, you're not, we have a deal. That means you need to start training *tonight*. Then you need to start teaching me how to bloodwerk."

"But I need nine strikes' sleep."

"Nine?" Sylah was incredulous. Papa had trained them to survive on fewer than three strikes of sleep, and since his passing she'd rarely got through five strikes of the clock.

Anoor hung her head. "I read for two strikes, sleep for nine, then go to school. Every day the same thing. Sometimes the library and at the end of the week I ride Boey, my eru, around the gardens for two strikes . . ." There was horror in her words. Sylah was about to disrupt everything in her life.

She'd asked for it.

"Now we have a new routine. We'll be cutting out the reading and shortening the sleeping. You don't need more than six strikes to sleep."

Anoor opened her mouth to argue, but Sylah cut her off.

"If you want to get to the final trial, you have to fight for it. Simple as that." The girl was a fool if she thought it was going to be easy.

Anoor paused, then a small smile crept up her face with a flicker of confidence.

"All right. Let's start then."

Sylah stretched out her aching muscles. It would be the first time in six years that she would fight without a joba seed. She had begun to rely on the drug to dull the pain of a fight and block out the chaos of her mind. Now she'd have to confront both.

SYLAH NEED NOT have worried, they never got to any fighting. After two strikes she could see that Anoor was at her limit. They hadn't even got around to warming up; all Sylah had done was try to focus Anoor into battle wrath, the meditative state that would aid her Nuba formations. Anoor was drenched in sweat, despite not moving.

"Am I doing it?"

"Can you lift your arm with just anger?"

"No."

"Then try again."

Anoor tried one more time, her muscles tensing, her shoulders nearly reaching her ears. Sylah could hear her using the breathing exercises she had instructed. Then she collapsed, the breath going out of her.

"Time to stop. Now, bloodwerk." Sylah sat down and crossed her legs in front of Anoor.

"Give me a moment."

"Well, if you want to get some sleep before the dawn run, we had better start now." Anoor groaned.

"Where's your inkwell then? Get it out and we'll begin with the basics."

Sylah narrowed her eyes.

"I haven't got one, can't I just use yours?" The question was loaded. Sylah would have loved to take a look at Anoor's inkwell, just to prove her theory she was using someone else's blood.

"You haven't got one?" Anoor gasped. "No, you can't use mine. Besides being . . . unhygienic,"—her heart-shaped mouth twisted— "it all depends on the distance of your vein so the stylus can slot directly into it. How do you not have an inkwell?" Sylah looked away.

"I had a sheltered upbringing, I told you."

"Okay, well you'll need to get one tomorrow."

"Where?"

"You'll have to buy one at an armorsmith. Show them your birth certificate and token; they have to track inkwells and register them against the Ember's name."

"Oh. I lost my birth certificate."

"Well, you'll have to find it or apply for a new one. It takes two mooncycles," Anoor said flatly.

"I think I know someone who might know someone." Sylah's mind was whirling. This was going to be tricky.

"Oh, really? Are they a smuggler? Do they know the Warden of Crime?" She was practically bouncing up and down, her eyes gleaming. "I read a story about him once and asked my mother why the wardens didn't arrest him. She told me he was more valuable alive." She frowned, a memory rippling through her until a greedy smile pushed it away. "Is it true he unified all the crime lords in the empire? I heard that he killed those that opposed him by poisoning their coffee."

"Tea." The correction came out of her mouth before she could stop it.

"Oh, Ending Fire. You *do* know the Warden of Crime? Was he the one to train all the assassins at the assassin school you went to?"

Sylah ground her teeth together. Anoor had the ability to turn every lesson into a farce. "No. No questions, remember. Can we get back to it?"

Anoor pouted.

"I suppose today we can practice with paper and charcoal. Oh!" She held a hand to her mouth. "I forgot I need to write out the basic runes five hundred times by tomorrow for Master Nuhan. You must help me." Anoor handed some paper and charcoal to Sylah, thinking nothing of it. The paper was thick, soft, creamy, weighty. Not traded in dark corners of the Dredge. The charcoal was shaved to a point, not something found on the floor between some rubble.

"What are you looking at?" Anoor asked. Sylah didn't realize she had been staring at the paper and smiling.

"We'll start with the basics, the four foundational runes—"

"How did you remove my gag without another bloodwerk rune?"

"Ah, good question," Anoor said, smiling despite the interruption. "Blood recognizes blood."

"Huh?" Now that threw a desert fox into the chicken's den.

"Because I was using my blood, which allowed me to release the binds."

But it wasn't her blood. How could it be? She was a Duster, wasn't she?

"Do you want a notebook so you can write this down?" Anoor asked, pulling Sylah from her musings.

"I just prefer to, you know, *listen*. Take it in." It was illegal for a Duster to write, so none of the Stolen had ever learned the basics. Reading was taught in Duster schools, through Ember-prescribed texts, but not writing. Writing was an offense punishable by ripping.

Reading wasn't an easy hobby either. Books were rare, unless you were Loot, who had the means to scour the empire through his network of Gummers and spies. His library was the only one on the other side of the river. You could buy zines for a slab a page at the market, but Sylah couldn't stand the hyperbolic nature of the storytelling. She found the optimistic narrative and obvious plotlines mundane. Anoor clearly did not.

"Okay." Anoor frowned, then launched back into her lecture.

By the end of the two strikes Sylah could draw out the wobbly outlines of *Gi, Ba, Ru,* and *Kha*. She found the charcoal uncomfortable to hold, but once she approached it logically, like she would a weapon, she grew accustomed to the shape.

The runes would be used as a weapon one day, used by Jond to break down the empire. Sylah hid her cruel smile. Jond would be disappointed that Sylah hadn't signed up for the Aktibar, but he'd forgive her when she brought him the missing link in his success. Bloodwerk.

This was what Papa meant by purpose. It filled her in a different way than joba seeds, more tangible, fiercer.

"Well, that's a hundred repetitions, that will just have to do for Master Nuhan for now." Anoor cracked a yawn and stumbled to bed. Sylah's pallet was next to Anoor's ostentatious four-poster. The pallet was smaller, cobbled together with what Gorn could procure under duress, but it was the plushest bed she'd ever seen. She desperately wanted to slip under the covers, but it had been nearly four days since Jond or her mother had heard from her. She needed to get to them.

Sylah waited until Anoor was whimpering softly in her sleep. The runelamp she insisted on leaving on all night cast her in a warm glow. Sylah slipped out the bedroom door and tiptoed across the hallway.

She made it past Gorn's door before she heard the door squeak behind her.

"Sylah?" Gorn appeared. It occurred to Sylah she must sleep fully clothed, her dark red pinafore still unwrinkled.

"I was just, erm, looking for the kitchen, felt a little hungry."

"The fresh meat and vegetables didn't fill you up?" The question was dripping with sarcasm. "I'll show you the way tomorrow. It's late now. Return to the bedchamber." Sylah clenched her fists and smiled lightly.

"Of course." She retraced her steps. Tomorrow was another day.

CHAPTER THIRTEEN

TWENTY-THREE DAYS
UNTIL THE TRIAL OF AEROFIELD

I have followed the life of the man who calls himself the Warden of Crime. I watched him navigate the crime lords across the empire to become their leader. Yesterday, I held an audience with him. My officers will not arrest those that wear his symbol. In turn we take a share of his profits from his smuggling ventures, including the distribution of joba seeds and firerum.

It is important that the Nowerks believe that there is a resistance to our rule. The belief that someone else is opposing our law has lessened uprisings within the plantations. Hope is an important driver in productivity.

—Yona Elsari, Warden of Strength, year 403

Anoor had made it a third of the distance Sylah wanted her to run.

"I can't do it." The words burst out with the last of her breath. She collapsed onto the ground. Sylah stood over her, looking down at Anoor's heaving body in distaste.

"Get up."

"I can't," she whined.

"*Now*," Sylah barked. Anoor simply flinched and curled up in a ball. Sylah growled and rolled her eyes to the sky. The clockmaster called sixth bell, the sun having risen over a strike ago. The Keep was already waking from its slumber.

Sylah tried a different tack. She crouched down and laid a hand stiffly on Anoor's shoulder.

"It will get easier, but you can't give up. Each step you take today is one you'll be thankful of tomorrow."

Anoor uncurled slightly.

"Does it really get easier?"

Sylah had to stop herself from spitting on her. As if everything in her life hadn't been easy already. "Yes, it does." Sylah held out a hand for her. After some hesitation Anoor grasped it and pulled herself up.

When they got back to her chambers, Anoor had to get ready for class, leaving Sylah in the hands of Gorn.

"I'll be with Anoor all day, but I've taken the liberty of putting together a shopping list of items you need to buy from the Ember Market." Gorn handed her a scroll. It was so long it unraveled to halfway down Sylah's shin.

"Oh." Sylah wanted to claw the smug look off Gorn's face. "I had some errands to run in the city myself today."

"How fortunate. Now you can do both."

"Yes, how fortunate." Sylah's smile was as sickly as honey. Her eyes scanned the list. It varied from the practical to the outright ridiculous. There was no way Anoor needed three different types of salt.

"Where can I find these things?"

"I'm sure you can figure it out." Gorn's grin was toothy. "Ah, Anoor, there you are. Don't want to be late for class." Anoor's eyes flickered to the scroll and then to the floor.

"See you later, Sylah."

As soon as the door shut, Sylah screamed curses.

"Stupid rich girl with her stupid face, and her stupid servant. Argh!" She tore the scroll in two. Then into three. It would have been into four if her hands hadn't begun to weaken.

She then spent the next half a strike putting the scroll back together again with tree gum, the curses now directed at herself.

SOMEONE WAS FOLLOWING her. They were doing a good job of it too, but Sylah could see their shadow hop along the rooftops alongside her. She rearranged her headscarf, feigning vanity in a window, while scanning the surrounding buildings in the reflection. The Tongue wasn't far; she'd feel much safer on the Duster side of town. She pulled the shawl she had borrowed from Anoor tighter around her shoulders. It draped over her crimson pinafore, hiding more of her servants' garb.

The uniform allowed her to blend in throughout the Keep but would be a target on the other side of the river. She'd like to avoid being spat on before she reached her mama's.

Sylah's skin prickled as she heard the telltale sound of officers' boots. A platoon was walking toward her. She pressed her back against the glass in the hope of making herself invisible. Their voices reached her first.

"My shift ends in two strikes, do you fancy heading for a drink later? The Sphinx Tavern has just had a cask of red wine in from Jin-Eynab."

"Yeah? That sounds good. Got to get home before the children finish school, though."

"I always forget you have critters. Hard to believe anyone had the God-given guts to sleep with you."

"Hey!"

There were twelve of them, walking casually out of formation, their hands loosely by their sides and not on their runeguns like Sylah was used to seeing.

One of them waved at Sylah as she cowered against the glass.

"You all right there, miss?" A skinny officer tipped his soft cap in Sylah's direction.

Were they talking to her?

"Y . . . yes, thank you, officer," Sylah managed to spit out.

One of his colleagues elbowed him in the ribs, a young woman with cornrows ending in long plaits to her waist. Sylah's fingers twitched for hers.

"Stop flirting," the woman officer said as they passed Sylah.

"I wasn't flirting! Besides, she's a servant, I'm not about to go *that* low. An Ember servant is so . . ."

"So?"

"Weird?"

"My mum's a servant in the Keep."

"Oh, well, I mean, I just mean that Embers are made to be better, right? And Ghostings are meant to serve . . . So it just seems odd them taking up a Ghosting's job."

"There aren't enough Ghostings to fill the jobs."

"Ah, yes, that cursed sleeping sickness . . ."

Their words grew more muffled the farther they walked. It took several breaths for Sylah to push away from the window and stand on her feet. A wave of dizziness ran through her, and she craved a joba seed.

"Fuck." She exhaled the word with a sigh.

That's when she heard it. The loaded silence. Whoever had been following her was still there. She leaned down toward the straps of her sandals where her skirt hid the paperknife she had tied against her ankle. It was the sharpest weapon she could find in Anoor's chambers.

"Eeyah!" She pulled out the knife, timed perfectly to imbed in the side of her attacker as he landed beside her. It was a Nuba attack move, but instead of her fist, it was a paperknife. At the last second she veered to the left.

"Jond. I nearly killed you."

He launched himself at her in a hug. He smelled of basil and jasmine and home.

"The Ghosting, she tried to tell us, she kept pointing across the river, but I wasn't sure, so I thought I'd come and see, I've been wandering the Ember Quarter since the tidewind ended." He was rambling, his hands gesticulating along with his words. For a brief moment he paused. "I thought you were dead." He raised his eyes to catch her gaze.

"So you know how it feels," she said, her chin tilted to the right as she surveyed him.

He stopped, his mouth dropping open as he held her at arm's length. "Sylah . . ." His hand reached out to her head. It was the sudden breeze across her scalp that told her the scarf had fallen down. She quickly wrapped it back up.

"No, let me see." He pulled down the headscarf with gentle hands. Sylah wouldn't meet his eye. Suddenly his warm hands were running through what remained of her hair.

"Sylah, you're beautiful."

She snorted, pushing his hands away.

"You and I both know I am not."

"Sylah, your hair was not your identity. If anything, it was hiding you away, holding you back." He trailed her jaw with his finger, and she shuddered, her knees knocking together. She would need more verd leaf tea soon. Or a joba seed. But as she looked at the softened features of Jond's face as he looked at her, she knew she couldn't break the promise to Anoor.

He needed to be warden.

"Tell me everything," he asked. So she did.

THE REST OF the morning was spent collecting all of the items on Gorn's list. Together they managed the majority of what she had asked for. Unfortunately, only one type of salt could be found, sourced from the salt flats of Ood-Lopah. Poor Anoor.

"And we'll finally be able to bloodwerk." Jond had repeated that three times already.

"Yes, I know."

"I wonder how she does it."

"Because she's a Duster?"

He nodded, adding another item to Sylah's basket and crossing it off the list.

"I've been thinking about that myself. Sometimes I wonder if Mama got it wrong, but then I see how she acts. Oh, she's annoying, I'll give you that, but she seems different than the other Embers. More . . . thoughtful, I guess."

"Really?"

Sylah nodded.

"Her inkwell, it's quite big, so I have a theory she's using someone else's blood."

"You think that's possible?" Jond's eyes widened, and he faltered in his step. "If that's true . . . we could . . . the Dusters . . . the Sandstorm."

"What? Harvest an army?" Sylah laughed and patted Jond on the shoulder. "First let's figure out how to actually do it."

He nodded, but his mind was far away.

"You should have seen the way her mother treated her. I know Papa used violence to train us, but this, it was vicious."

Jond frowned, as if trying to recollect that memory. "I wonder why Uka kept her alive."

"I'm not sure. Papa told us all the Duster decoys had been killed . . . Anyway, I'll find out."

They were left to their own thoughts while Sylah collected a pot of sandalwood oil from a merchant.

"I'm sorry, Sylah," Jond said once Sylah had paid. His hand reached out and clung to her wrist. His fingers slipped under her sleeve and brushed the silvered scar of her brand.

"For what?" His fingers tingled.

He looked so sad.

"I'm sorry that you're not going to be joining the Aktibar like we dreamed."

She thought about his words for some time, the flow of the market moving around them.

"I hadn't dreamed that dream for six years. Once Papa . . . once everyone died, I knew it was over. Besides, you got the training from the new Sandstorm; if I became warden, I'd have no idea what to do."

"I'd have helped," he interjected.

"I know, but this way, I can help. I can teach you to bloodwerk, and you can win."

"But we won't be doing it together."

"We will, in our own way." Sylah gently pried Jond's hand away from her wrist and set off walking again. "I need to check in with the haberdashery to see if any of the fabric she ordered has come in."

The fabric stall was a sprawling menagerie of material. It was on the edge of the market, closest to the Tongue. The rows of clothing were empty of shoppers.

"Anoor would love this." Sylah held up a gold and green jacket in distaste. "Honestly, you should see the stuff she wears."

"May I help you?" The shop owner appeared out of nowhere. Jond sniggered behind her.

"I'm to check with the owner, a Miss . . ." Sylah looked at her list, "Kopa about an order for Miss Anoor Elsari?"

"That's me." Miss Kopa took the gold jacket out of Sylah's hand and returned it to the rack. Sylah was surprised to see a brand on her wrist. The tailor was a Duster.

Although a lot of Dusters worked in the market, they rarely owned their own stalls, particularly one as big as this one. Embers wouldn't buy from a Duster, so instead the Warden of Duty assigned Ember figureheads to own all the shops, and reap the profits. Because obviously it was okay if the person packing your groceries had blue blood if the shop was owned by an Ember, so it was still *pure*. Sylah wondered if the tailor got much business.

The seller nodded curtly and said she'd check in the back.

"No, it hasn't arrived yet, you should try again tomorrow." She turned away.

"Wait." Sylah stopped her. "Do you have any cheap pantaloons and a tunic? Something less . . . obvious?" Sylah's hand ran up and down her crimson pinafore.

The woman gave her a curt nod and then returned. "Will these do?"

One week ago, Sylah would have balked at the luxury of the material, but now she'd met Anoor and understood what the word really meant: the patterned clothes were . . . plain.

"Do you have somewhere to change?"

The woman jutted her head to the corner of the shop.

Sylah felt lighter once she'd removed the servant uniform.

"Thank you, can you put it on Anoor Elsari's tab?" Sylah said to the tailor, who simply gave a tired nod. Sylah turned to Jond.

"Okay, that's everything, let's go."

As Sylah and Jond walked toward the Duster Quarter, they saw a familiar face at the far end of the Tongue.

Hello, Sylah.

"Hassa!" Sylah grasped her shoulders.

You going to tell me what's going on yet? Hassa jutted her chin at Jond, who stood there openmouthed. *Who is this guy, anyway?*

"Jond, meet Hassa. She's a friend."

Hassa quirked an eyebrow. *And your drug dealer.*

"She says pleasure to meet you."

"We've met . . ." Jond said. "You can actually understand Ghostings?"

"Yes, it's not hard."

Especially when there's something you have to trade.

"Since when?"

"I've been learning for a few years."

Six years you've followed me around.

"What's she saying?"

Hassa rolled her eyes.

"Jond, she can't speak, but she's not deaf. She can hear you."

Jond was perturbed. "Oh, of course, I'm sorry. Thank you for all your help finding Sylah. I'm Jond." He held out his hand to shake.

Sylah slapped her palm on her forehead. "You are the worst."

He really is. Is he your boyfriend?

"Oh, no."

"What did she ask? What did you ask?"

Tell him I think he's very pretty.

"She thinks you're very pretty."

Jond's smile was jaunty, a little vain. "Thanks."

"You working?"

Yes, I should really get back to the Keep, where you now also work, for some strange reason.

"Are you still talking about me?"

Tell him yes, we're discussing how much I would buy him for.

Sylah snorted and ignored him.

"I made a deal with the daughter of Uka Elsari," Sylah said softly by way of explanation. "She's asked me to help her train for the Aktibar."

I heard she'd signed up. Why did she pick you?

The lie came to Sylah quickly, and she wondered if Anoor was already rubbing off on her. "Anoor heard about me at the Ring."

Hassa looked at her coolly. *That's it?*

Sylah's gaze bounced between Hassa's dark eyes.

"I'm acting as her servant as I train her. Apparently, trainers are common, but her mother wouldn't like it, so we needed a cover."

I'm sure she wouldn't. The warden doesn't like people around her daughter.

Hassa's eyes flickered to Jond's bored expression. Sylah didn't want Jond to figure out that Hassa knew she was one of the Stolen; that Sylah had let it slip was too much shame for her to bear.

"So I'll be seeing you around the Keep? Maybe we could meet up?"

Maybe. Hassa's smile was sly. *I've got to go. See you soon, my friend. And be careful, the Keep is full of spiders.*

"See you soon, Hassa."

The girl waved her limb and gave Jond a wink.

The Keep is full of spiders. The thought tugged on Sylah's mind, and she thought of Uka, and how she'd hurt Anoor.

The trotro rattled past, the sound drowning out any more questions Jond might have had. As they neared the end of the Tongue, Sylah's eyes were drawn to the swirling mass of blue quicksand in the Ruta River below.

"Does that look like it's moving faster than usual?"

"Not sure, don't really know the city well enough, I guess," Jond replied.

"Hmmm." She shelved that worry for another day. She looked at Jond from the corner of her eye. "So when do I meet the new Sandstorm leader? I can chew into them about why you didn't come for me sooner."

"Sylah, it wasn't my choice, at first I didn't know you were alive, and then when I found out, they wouldn't let me see you."

"There is nothing and no one that would have stopped me finding you, Jond." It was the simple truth.

"The new leader, he's forceful, he has a plan."

"Papa's plan."

"Similar."

"What aren't you telling me, Jond? Just spit it out."

"I can't, they won't let me."

She stopped, causing the flow of traffic behind her to curse and push past. "Jond Alnua, are you flaming joking right now?"

He rolled his eyes and dragged her forward. "Sorry," he apologized to a particularly angry person who was pulling a cart of vegetables behind them. "Honestly, Sylah."

"Well?" She scuffed her feet through the dust.

"It's confidential, the new leader is very . . . covert."

"Covert? How many people are there now?" She would have stopped again if Jond weren't still holding her hand.

"A few."

"A few?" She scowled at him.

He shrugged.

"I can't know?" Anger flashed behind her eyes. She needed a joba se—verd tea. She needed verd tea.

"No. Not until you've proved your worth. If you want to join again, I mean."

"Skies above, I assumed being one of the Stolen, I would have had membership for life . . ."

"It doesn't work that way." They'd come to the edge of the Duster Quarter. Sylah cast one last look at the Ruta River. The bubbling, whirling blue sand was a reflection of her thoughts.

"Move out!" The shout was harsh and loud, followed by the drumbeat of boots pounding the earth roads.

"Sylah, move!" Jond hissed, pulling her out of the way of a patrol on pursuit.

They held their runeguns out, leveled at a young Duster who was weaving through the crowd. Something glittered against his chest. A gold cuff of some kind.

"An inkwell . . ."

Sylah whistled through her teeth. The boy had guts to steal an inkwell from an Ember in broad daylight. Guts or an addled mind. Melted down, the gold from the inkwell would be worth enough to feed a Duster for a year. Perhaps it was desperation that fueled his madness.

The crowd held their breath as the captain of the platoon paused and held up his fist to signal gunfire. The officers drew the runes on their guns that activated the force of the bullet. Fourteen bullets flew through the air in quick succession.

One of them found its mark.

Blue blood sprayed across the joba tree in the courtyard of a Duster's home. The blood marked the bark like ink, dripping down to the patch of carefully tended sand below.

"Fucking Embers." Jond spat.

"Fucking Embers," Sylah agreed. Her hand squeezed the basket of Anoor's wares so tightly her knuckles tried to burst through the flesh.

The officers didn't even claim the body. They just retrieved the inkwell and left him there.

"Let's go." Sylah tugged on Jond's sleeve.

They pulled away from the crowds and down the first street that led to her home. The joba plants out front were well tended if not entirely tree sized.

"Hello, Sylah!" Her neighbor Rata waved from her courtyard. Her joba plant was the largest on the street.

"Hello, Rata."

"Not seen you around for a while, heard about the glasskeep, didn't like you working in the Dredge anyway. Nasty place. You know they found two bodies yesterday morning? Stripped to the bone from the tidewind. To the bone! Can you imagine?" She gesticulated with her dusting brush. The angry bristles shivered in agreement.

Jond looked at Sylah sidelong.

"No, I can't imagine." Sylah rubbed her eyes.

"I've been out every morning between fifth strike and eighth strike, cleaning the house and the courtyard. Can you believe it?"

"No, I can't believe it."

"The tidewind is worse than I've ever seen it. And you know I'm advancing in years, so I've seen a fair few more than you." She laughed in hiccups, the brush quivering away in mirth. At fifty, Rata wasn't much older than Lio.

"Look, Rata, I better get going." Sylah couldn't even summon a smile for the musawa.

"Oh, yes, send my love to Lio. Let me know if she needs help dusting. I haven't seen her out for a while." She hiccupped, her brush waving them away.

"Why didn't you introduce me to that delightful lady?" Jond said as Sylah pulled him along.

"Don't start. You're lucky we got away so quick; once I was caught there for a full strike. She ended up teaching me the best techniques to clean each leaf of the joba tree."

Sylah demonstrated a few moves, and they were still laughing when Lio opened the door.

"I heard you weren't dead." Lio sucked the joy out of them both in seconds. Her mouth was split into a sharp line. Sharper than a scythe.

"Hi, Mama." Sylah stood awkwardly in the doorway.

"Hello." Jond waved sheepishly. "I found her."

"I see that." Lio crossed her arms. The silence stretched, until Lio eventually deflated. The anger whooshed out of her in a sigh of relief. "I suspect there's a story to tell. I'll heat up the stew."

SYLAH STAYED WITH Lio for another two strikes. Her mother hadn't shown a twitch of surprise as Sylah recollected her story. Lio had questions but was most curious about Anoor. "What does she look like? Is she clever? Funny? What's she *like*?" Sylah felt uncomfortable answering that. *Sniveling, spoiled, annoying, whiny mess* didn't really roll off the tongue.

Before she left, she went to her room to collect a few possessions. It wasn't until she stood beside her bed that she realized she had nothing to collect. Her room was sparse, devoid of sentimental things; she had held all her treasured items in her hair. Now they were gone too.

She lifted up her straw mattress, the only space in the room she had to store things, and riffled through her clothing. Most of it was dirty, covered in sweat and sometimes blue blood from the Ring. Her fingers brushed up on a crunchy item in a pocket. At first she recoiled, expecting it to be a cockroach, then she recollected what it was and reached in.

She pulled out the parchment and blanched. It was covered in charcoal smears that were meant to be runes. Sylah had tried in secret for years to figure out the technique to bloodwerk. Turns out it was precision, something she wasn't great at, unless it related to fighting.

If the officers found this in a raid, her mother would be dead just for having the written word so obviously inscribed under her roof. Sylah would be fine, despite doing the deed; her red blood granted her freedom in the eyes of the law—though her Duster acquaintances might cut her down for the deception. Loot certainly would. Sylah stuffed the paper in her basket to burn later. There was still a small bulge in the pocket of her old pantaloons. Two small somethings.

The little balls rolled into the middle of her palm. Encrusted with cotton fluff and the unidentifiable bits that collect in pockets, Sylah could see that the seeds were stale, their red skin slightly dimmed. She put one between a forefinger and thumb. Without thinking it went into her mouth.

"Sylah, are you ready?" Jond's voice called out.

Jond. The Sandstorm. Anoor.

The seed flew out the window with a trail of spit. Sylah clawed at her tongue to remove any residue. Thankfully, the skin hadn't cracked. Only one seed left. She pocketed it.

"Yes, coming." She bounded down the stairs and out to the street beyond.

"EXPLAIN THIS AGAIN," Jond asked for the hundredth time.

"Inkwells are unique to the wearer. The slot for the stylus needs to be over a vein. We can't just go buy one, they have to be made specifically for each person," Sylah said. They were both on their way to Loot's lair, deep in the Dredge.

"And you think this Loot guy will know someone?"

"He's the only person I can think of who would."

"But he calls himself the Warden of Crime, as if it's a real title—he realizes it isn't, right?"

"I'd lower your voice if I were you. We're in his quarter now. His guild members, we call them Gummers, are everywhere. Plus he's the only warden who Dredge-dwellers truly listen to."

Jond looked over his shoulder as if a Gummer was about to jump him.

"Right . . . I like this guy less and less."

"Good, he's not to be liked. Too dangerous for that," Sylah said.

Jond sniffed, and probably regretted it.

"And this Warden of Crime . . . he lives around here?" Jond gestured to the decrepit remains of the limestone villas.

"No, he lives in the Intestines."

Jond's step faltered. "Wait, what?"

Sylah chuckled. "It's the tunnels under the city. He calls them the Intestines."

"Oh."

"We're here." Sylah waved to the watcher at the door. "Hi, Fayl. How's it hurting?"

"Good, Sylah, you? Who's this you got with you? Got yourself a bit of hustle?"

Sylah snorted and Jond blushed.

"Jond, this is Fayl; Fayl, this is Jond. Jond is my . . . step-brother."

Jond frowned.

"Didn't know you had a brother!" Fayl clapped Jond on the back.

"More like a childhood friend," Jond replied, casting a look Sylah's way.

"What mood is he in?" Sylah said.

"Well, Sylah, I'll be as true as the blood with you, he's said not to let you in." The watcher rubbed his hand over his chin.

"Maiden's tits. I'm not here to sign up for the Ring!" Sylah's arm twitched. "Look, if you could ask one of the Gummers to just check with him? Explain it's not about the Ring? Tell him I'd owe him a favor."

"A favor?" Fayl's eyes widened.

"I have to, Fayl. If he can get me what I need."

He dropped his voice. "Sylah, don't do this." Fayl's concern was strong enough for him to warn Sylah against his husband.

"No other choice."

"None?"

"No."

The big man looked unhappy, but he eventually went down the stairs.

Jond watched Fayl's retreating back. "What's so scary about a favor, Sylah?"

She shrugged, and he narrowed his eyes at her.

"Loot's favors tend to be a bit . . ." She was at a loss for words. "Creative."

"Creative?"

"Yes, often pointless, always dangerous, sometimes deadly. He can call in his debt at any time, and it lasts until he says it does."

"Essentially you become his slave for an immeasurable amount of time."

Sylah's mouth twisted, her hand slipping toward the top of her neck where her braids used to be. "What's new?"

Fayl reappeared, and from his resigned look Sylah knew the barter had been successful.

Jond was silent as Sylah turned them left, left, right, middle, through the Intestines. It wasn't until the amber glow from the runelamps began to brighten that he spoke.

"We don't need to do this, Sylah. *You* don't need to do this." He reached out and grasped her shoulder.

"Oh, stop your whining, we both know I'm going to do it." Sylah continued a touch softer. "Don't make my sacrifice worthless."

They entered the Belly, flanked by Gummers on either side. Sylah gave them a wide smile, denting their menacing facade.

"Ah, Sylah." Loot stepped into the runelight. "Nice to see you, and you've brought company." Loot smiled at them both. Not one speck of blue dust marred his yellow suit. It was so bright it was hard to look at.

Jond's eyes widened, whether from Loot's opulent attire or the vast array of books, Sylah wasn't sure.

"Hi, Loot." Sylah's heart was beating a little faster than usual. She felt the prickling of a spasm and tried to slow her breathing.

"Come, have some tea."

Jond walked stiffly beside Sylah as they took a seat. The poisoned tea was poured by a silent Ghosting servant, their shaved head a replica of Sylah's. The handle of the teapot was large enough for their limb as they carefully poured the hot liquid into flowery teacups.

"Nice headscarf." Loot tipped his head in her direction.

"Thanks, trying a new look."

Loot's eyes sparkled like the spider pin he wore on his breast. He knew, somehow, he knew.

"So, Sylah, I've heard you're interested in entering a contract with me?" He crossed his legs, keeping perfectly balanced on his stool.

"Yes, well, if you can get me what I want." Sylah sipped her tea again, keeping her eyes level with Loot.

"Does this have something to do with your tight-lipped step-brother here?"

"No, well, yes, a bit."

"Oh, do tell." Loot leaned forward, his long nails clicking against his teacup.

"We can't." Jond woke from his brief slumber, throwing the words across the table like a dagger. Loot studied him.

"How am I going to get you what you need?"

"You don't." Jond turned to Sylah. "Sylah, let's leave now."

"No, Jond," Sylah shot back. "Loot, we need someone who can make us inkwells."

"What would two Dusters like you need inkwells for?" A sly grin crept up toward his ears.

"We don't." Jond tugged on Sylah's sleeve. "Please, let's go." She shrugged him off.

"We can't tell you."

"Well, there's no fun in that." Loot's white teeth gleamed in the light. He spun the spider brooch on his lapel.

"Can you do it? Can you find someone who can make us ink-wells?"

"Of course I can do it. Come back in a strike. Dina, bring through the contract." Sylah didn't see who had written it up, but she was still shocked to see Loot so brazenly commit a crime.

"A Duster wrote that?" she breathed.

"You want an inkwell, one of the hardest things to acquire and without a doubt a ripping offense for everyone involved in this room, and you're worried who wrote the contract?"

"Writing's a ripping offense too."

"And that's my specialty." He put the paper in front of Sylah. She glanced it over. *In exchange for one favor to be redeemed at a later date, Sylah Alyana will receive two inkwells—*

"And stylus, he's missed the stylus," Jond interrupted her thoughts.

"Surely they come as a package?" Sylah asked Loot, and his only response was a wink.

"Dina, would you add in stylus?" The contract was whipped away and returned a moment later. *A favor is defined as a debt of equal or greater worth than the request. The Warden of Crime may call on you at any time in the next three years to fulfill this debt and you will have 24 strikes to complete it. Forfeit of this debt is death—*

"Death? Sylah, really? Death?" Jond's whisper cut through her thoughts.

"Fancy breaking the law together?" Loot handed Sylah a pen.

A pen! She didn't even know there were any on this side of the river. She put it between finger and thumb and signed at the bottom of the page. The second signature she'd ever written, it still looked pretty good to her. Loot followed hers with a dignified flourish.

"See you in a strike." He placed two clear vials of liquid on the table. Sylah downed one. Jond looked at her questioningly.

"Drink it, it's the antidote to the poison in the tea," Sylah hissed.

Jond's eyes widened into two fufu bowls. He reached shaking fingers to the vial before drinking it.

A strike later they returned. Fayl led them down to a darkened side room Sylah had never been in before. A cloaked man, with skin like coal and eyes just as brittle, stood behind a makeshift workbench. The crackling fire was bordered by an assortment of tools burning red with heat. Sylah wondered if it was hot enough to crack the skin of a joba fruit.

The man refused to look either of them in the eye, as if seeing them, truly seeing them, would make the crime a reality. He grunted at them to hold out their wrists.

Both inkwells would cover their brands.

A strike later the smith dunked two inkwells into a bucket, the hissing water cooling the molten metal. He pulled them out with tongs.

"Money?" He barked at Fayl, who had watched the whole process.

"I'll take you to Loot," Fayl said to the smith, his hands on his dagger by his side. "Sylah, you can make your own way out?"

She nodded, still mesmerized by the intricate piece of metal on the table.

The metal was still warm to the touch, but she couldn't help her fingers running over it. She'd never dreamed that she would one day bloodwerk. One day be one of them. An Ember, like she was meant to be.

An Ember with a Duster's heart. Papa's voice whispered in her mind, full of pride.

She picked up the inkwell. Decorative vines wrapped around the wrist, embossed with beautiful precision. Without a doubt a request from Loot. Poison ivy. Sylah didn't mind; it made the inkwell a unique piece of jewelry. Even the stylus was in the style of an ivy leaf pulled to a point. The final key to being a true Ember.

Jond was trying his on, flexing his hand in its grasp. His was simpler, plain but sturdy. One clean sheet of metal that molded around the base of his hand like a fabric cuff with a slot for the stylus to insert into his vein underneath.

They looked at each other and grinned like two desert foxes that had just caught their prey.

Papa, we did it. We're going to take them all down. Every Ember who thought Dusters were lesser.

The sun had begun to dip in the sky, but it wasn't until Sylah heard the clockmaster screech "sixth strike" that she realized how late she was.

"Maiden's tits, I've got to run. She'll be wondering where I've gone." Sylah started to speed up, but the onslaught of Dredge-dwellers heading home for dinner stalled her.

"Shit, I'll have to hop the rooftops."

"I'll see you tomorrow?"

"Yes, twelfth strike, during my lunch break. We should meet in the Ember Quarter so we can practice." She pointed at her empty wrist, the inkwell safely hidden in her basket. "The water tower?"

Jond nodded. "Anyme go with you."

"And you." She ran up the nearest ladder and skipped across the roofs, her curses echoing behind her.

CHAPTER FOURTEEN

TWENTY-THREE DAYS
UNTIL THE TRIAL OF AEROFIELD

Bloodwerk is a skill mastered only by Embers. The power bestowed by the God Anyme is what makes Ember blood superior. This book documents the four foundational runes of Ba, Ru, Kha, and Gi, as well as the hundred and fifteen supplementary runes that can alter the purpose, direction, and nature of the bloodwerk.

—Introduction to the *Book of Blood*

Sylah ran up the stairs, the basket bashing against her hip with each step. She was almost breathless by the time she reached Anoor's chambers.

Dinner had already been served. A cold plate of greens and chicken sat on the corner of the counter in the hall. She felt queasy just looking at it. The nausea brought on by her body's detoxification from the joba seeds still came in waves. She fingered the seed in her pocket.

Anoor's bedroom door opened a crack. Her red-rimmed eyes widened at Sylah's presence.

"You came back!" She ran at Sylah and wrapped her in a hug.

"Get off! You're crushing all the wares I spent the day collecting."

"But the market closed strikes ago, I thought you weren't coming back."

"I had some personal things to attend to," Sylah said.

"Personal things?" Of course Gorn just had to appear right then and there. Her shaved gray hair was so fine it made the veins at her temple seem even more pronounced.

"Yes, I had to send a letter to my uncle—"

"Uncle Gallo." Anoor nodded deeply.

"We have a duty office here; they would have sent your letter via the duty chutes," said Gorn.

"Well, I had to write it first, and I suppose I thought I should get to know the city." Sylah sighed dramatically. "But I'm afraid I got a little lost."

Gorn opened her mouth to question her poor show further, but Anoor cut her off.

"Gorn, would you mind putting away Sylah's purchases? I need her help with my homework."

Sylah held out the basket and smiled lightly.

Gorn took it and turned away, her shoulders rigid.

"I really thought you weren't coming back." Anoor shut the door behind them. She was in her loose training clothes: black cotton pantaloons, flexible leather shoes, and fingerless gloves to protect her knuckles. Sweat glazed her brow.

"You were training?"

"Yes." Her smile was infectious, like a virus Sylah didn't want to catch, though she felt the corners of her lips lift.

"Show me."

Two strikes later Sylah was still refining Anoor's basic Dambe arm stances.

"Okay, okay, enough. Time to bloodwerk." Anoor waved Sylah's hands away from her waist where they had been desperately trying to get her muscles to suck in, suck in.

"Guess what?" Sylah walked over to her disregarded coat.

"What?" Sylah pulled out her inkwell and stylus.

"You got one!" Anoor clapped her hands and reached for it.

"It's very pretty, where did you get it?"

"A friend helped me."

"A friend? Are they an assassin too?"

"Absolutely."

Anoor's eyes gleamed with the hunger for adventure.

Sylah laughed. "You read too many zines."

Anoor flashed her teeth at her.

They sat down and recapped yesterday's teachings. This time Anoor demonstrated with her own bloodwerk on a pair of shoes. The blood that came out of her stylus was definitely red.

She drew the rune for *Ru*, and it pushed away from the opposite shoe. Sylah couldn't help but gasp. The other foundational runes followed.

"So as I just demonstrated, those are the four basic runes in practice. Every other type of bloodwerk, such as runelamps, just manipulates these. The basic principle is *Gi* and *Ba* coupled with the supplementary rune repeating until the friction between them creates a glow."

"Everything that can bloodwerk is based on those four runes?"

"Exactly."

"How did the booby trap work? The one that knocked me out?"

"Well, that was based on those zines that you so casually dismissed." She smiled smugly, and Sylah scowled remembering the pain at the base of her skull.

And the side of her temple.

"I used a supplementary rune based on weight and manipulated *Ba* to create a pressure sensor."

"Why didn't it trigger every time you went to the window? Or Gorn when she cleaned?"

"Because blood recognizes blood."

But that didn't make sense; if it wasn't her blood, then how . . . Sylah's head started to pound. Was she using *Gorn's* blood?

"Right." Sylah rubbed her brow. "What in the name of the warden are you talking about?"

Anoor's smile dropped.

"Look, let's just practice the basics first, we can come back to the other runes later."

Sylah's palms started to sweat. "Can you show me how to use it?" Sylah held out the inkwell to Anoor.

Her hazel eyes twinkled as she strapped the inkwell to Sylah's wrist with soft, nimble fingers.

"Brace yourself, they say it hurts the first time. After a while the vein will swell, and the nerves will deaden." The stylus threaded between her finger and thumb through the carefully positioned hole in the inkwell. The needle at the top of the stylus was so fine Sylah barely felt it when it pierced her skin.

Then the blood began to flow, slowly, sluggishly finding its way down the stylus to the tip where it pooled into a tiny bead of blood. Like a ruby on a ring.

"Try it! Draw on the shoe." Anoor passed her the shoe. "Try *Ru*." It took Sylah three tries to get the rune right. Okay, twenty tries. But when she did, the other shoe pushed away with much more force than Anoor's demonstration.

"By Anyme, you have a lot of power in your veins! Look how far it went." Anoor was beaming, her eyes crinkling as she praised Sylah over and over again.

"I can't believe I just did that." Sylah laughed, a soft, happy sort of laugh that made her feel lighter than she had in mooncycles.

Papa would be so proud of me. Doing what none of the others could. She imagined his smile as she showed him her bloodwerk. His eyes would have gleamed with glory as the path to the five hundred steps grew ever clearer. Finally, one of the Stolen would become a warden.

Jond would reach the top, Sylah would make sure of it.

"Let's try it again." And so they did, over and over again. It took Sylah a long time to master *Ru*, and she still had to refer to her paper copy in order to replicate the shape.

"No, no. You're not elongating the top left flick enough. Here, let me show you." Anoor drew out *Ru* for her once again, but this time the shoes trembled but didn't budge.

"Oh." Anoor didn't look surprised. "I think we should stop for tonight."

"Why? What's happened? Why won't it move?" Sylah picked up the shoe; the rune looked faultless. Anoor evaded her stare and started packing up her notes. "It happens sometimes."

"Will it happen to me? Can my bloodwerk just stop working?"

"You can exert your body, cause yourself to pass out from loss of blood. Or the runes can dry out over time, the blood crusting and fading. But if you put a supplementary protection, it shouldn't fade for a mooncycle or longer."

"But will it stop, like yours did?"

"No, I've not heard it happen to anyone else." She disappeared into the privy, abruptly ending the conversation.

SYLAH GOT READY for bed. For the last six years she had slept in whichever clothes she'd fallen asleep in. Now she had fine cotton to wear at night. Cotton, the currency of Jin-Noon. She and Lio had passed the fields when they traveled from Ood-Zaynib to Nar-Ruta. Like a fleece on the landscape, the cotton crocheted up sand dunes for leagues around, protected by the tidewind from sheer glass greenhouses so the cotton bolls weren't swept away. It unnerved her, how soft and warm it was. She looked for blue blood in the tendrils of the hem. The blood of the plantation workers who had harvested the crop. Sylah couldn't wait to see the fields burn when Jond became warden.

She was bursting for the privy, but Anoor had occupied the bathroom for a century, maybe more. Hopping from foot to foot, she walked over to the desk in the corner and began to open the drawers, partly to distract herself, partly to cause a mess. She dipped a pen in ink and practiced her signature on a scrap of paper. She'd never get over the freedom of writing. Tilting her head to the left, she surveyed her handiwork. It was getting better, she decided.

A familiar paper slipped under her fingers as she moved around the papers on the desk. The map. She'd almost forgotten it.

Anoor must have taken it when she had drugged her that first night. She came out of the privy and noticed where Sylah was sitting, all the drawers of her desk spilling open with its contents.

"What are you doing?"

"Just reclaiming what was stolen." Sylah tapped the map on the desk.

Anoor looked sheepish. "I didn't steal it. It's right there, isn't it?"

"So you *borrowed* my map then?"

"Exactly."

"You can't just steal things from people. It's not your place to just come in and take anything you want from people's lives."

"What do you mean people's lives? I took it out of your bag, after you tried to kill me, if I might remind you." She had her teacher voice on.

"Whatever, just don't take my stuff." Sylah began to roll it up. "What's this?" Notes slipped out from underneath it.

"Nothing." Anoor came over and started to clear up the paper.

Sylah ripped it from her grasp.

"The Ending Fire . . . no known life . . . the founding wardens . . . what is this?"

"I did a bit of research." Anoor looked down at her hands as she took the notes from Sylah for a second time.

"Why?"

"Where did you get this?" Anoor countered, pointing to the map.

"I found it. Doesn't matter, though, it's just some old junk."

"Is it?"

Sylah's gaze slipped to the top right corner.

"Where did you find it?"

Sylah didn't answer for some time. "In the Dredge."

"The Dredge?" Soapy suds twinkled in the fine hair framing her face. "Oh, you mean the old Ghosting Quarter."

"If you like." Sylah started to roll up the map.

"What are you going to do with it?"

Sylah shrugged. "Trade it, probably."

Anoor crossed her arms over her bosom. Without her undergarments lifting them up, the swell of her chest swayed. "You can't trade it, it's important."

Sylah lifted her eyes to Anoor's. "Why? What do you know?"

Anoor opened her mouth to speak. Closed it. Opened it again. Closed it.

"Are you going to speak or should I start the applause for this highly entertaining mime show? You should be a griot."

Anoor's eyelashes fluttered, her eyes creased at the corners. "The thing is, I don't know anything."

"Well, that settles that. I need to go to the privy." Sylah stood.

"But that's the important bit." Anoor's hand gesticulated before her, as if somehow, by moving the air in earnest, she could convey what she meant.

"What do you mean?"

"I went to the library and there was nothing there about it."

A pause. Anoor's hands splayed wide, her feet arched forward, so close to the cliff of understanding.

"Did you go to the right place?"

Anoor's hands dropped to her side in frustration. "Yes, Sylah, I went to the right place—"

"And there were no books?"

"There were books, of course," She explained as if talking to a child. "But nothing *in* them. Nothing but a few sentences on the Ending Fire, and a bit about the founding wardens. No other details, nothing at all."

That *was* interesting . . .

"Maybe they didn't write books back then."

"But the story is taught in every school. How do the masters of knowledge know the facts? It must have been recorded somewhere."

Sylah dismissed Anoor's conjecture with a wave of the hand. "You're getting carried away. Besides, I've got to use the privy."

Sylah shut the bathroom door and leaned against it. Her fingers worried the grooves in the wood, the cool marble chilling her feet. Her full bladder was a thing of the past as her mind whirled through the implications of what Anoor had told her.

"Keep focused," she whispered to herself. "All you need to do is learn to bloodwerk and get out, leave the girl to her tales."

But the truth had a way of shifting the sand dunes of her life, and Sylah wasn't ready for a new landscape.

THE MORROW BROUGHT a bitter wind and a fresh film of thick blue dust. The tidewind must have lasted longer than its usual two strikes as the sand had piled up into miniature dunes in the courtyard and the servants had yet to clear it away. The Ghostings began to stir after Anoor's second lap of the courtyard.

"You're already improving," Sylah noted, the compliment quirking Anoor's lips.

"I still think I'm going to throw up." She did promptly after.

Despite brushing her teeth, Anoor could still taste the acrid remains of her breakfast at the back of her throat as she sat in the schoolroom. The run hadn't felt any better than the day before, but Sylah insisted she'd improved. Anoor was pretty sure she was lying.

"AND THAT WAS how the plants evolved over time to withstand the tidewind. Any questions?" Master Fadel had drawn the transformation of a type of tree on the board. It might have been a rubber tree, or an oak, but Anoor hadn't been paying attention. Suddenly, a question struck her. Her arm shot to the sky.

"Yes, Miss Elsari?"

"Did the founding wardens bring the plants with them? When they sailed across the seas?" Anoor asked.

Someone in the back row groaned. They all wanted the lesson to be over.

"Yes, they propagated the plants when they arrived, and over time, they grew hardy. That was one of the many things they brought with them in their ships."

Anoor sat up straighter in her seat. Again, her hand shot through the air with the speed of one of her arrows.

"Yes?"

Master Fadel cleared her throat, waiting. She was used to Anoor's capricious questions.

"Where did the founding wardens sail from?"

There was laughter to her left.

"Here she goes again." Someone behind her murmured, "Off in dreamland asking things no one cares about . . ."

Master Fadel looked bewildered. "Why, from the mainland, of course."

"Where exactly is the mainland?" Anoor pressed.

"It's gone now, the Ending Fire destroyed it." Chatter had sprung up from the corners of the room. Master Fadel was losing their attention, and she knew it. "Anoor, if you have questions about history, may I suggest you approach Master Guna, who specializes in that *subject*?" She drew out the word "subject" like a curse. "We're here to learn biology."

"But Master—"

"No." The word was a whip to the rampant eru of their attention.

Anoor couldn't help the sigh that seeped out of her like the stale air escaping a jar. The master didn't seem all that concerned about Anoor's prying. She settled back in her chair and let the matter lie. Maybe Sylah was right, and there was nothing to the nothingness.

Master Fadel continued her lesson, and Anoor's mind drifted away, out of the Keep and up to the sky where she settled among her thoughts.

If I can win the Aktibar maybe I can ask the wardens. They must know about the mainland.

She imagined her classmates, those who had laughed at her for years, cheering from the bottom of the five hundred steps as she ascended after winning the Aktibar. She smiled. She would show them. She was going to be the next Warden of Strength, and their teasing and mocking would cease as she reigned with the tenacity of Inquisitor Abena, like in her zines. She would bring justice to the people, *all* people.

"Anoor?"

How much time had passed?

"Yes, Master?" She pushed herself up in her seat.

"Did you hear what I said?"

"No, Master."

Laughter. Laughs that would one day turn to cheers.

"Quieten down, class," Master Fadel said without authority. "I was asking the class who intended to select the guild of knowledge on Choice Day. As you know the guild is the most esteemed and, in my opinion, the supreme attribute among the four. Given your . . . lack of interest, Anoor, I assume you won't be selecting knowledge. Is there anyone else who I will be welcoming to the fold?"

Anoor let the insult settle on her shoulders until the master's stare moved on.

"I will be joining the guild of knowledge," someone spoke up.

Anoor turned to look at the speaker. It was Tanu. She had once been a close companion to Anoor, her only Ember friend growing up. But as Tanu's interests led her to textbooks, Anoor's led her to zines, and eventually their lack of commonality pulled them apart.

Tanu ran her hand through the black curls at the top of her head. She had shaved the sides, which accentuated her high cheekbones and hawklike features. She tilted back in her chair and surveyed the room.

Tanu continued, now she had everyone's attention. "I expect I'll be the next Disciple of Knowledge."

No one was surprised.

"Oh ho! A competitor, how exciting. Any others in the class?" The master's eyes gleamed with the fever of an experienced gambler. There was no doubt that she was taking stock; it was said that the Aktibar was the busiest time for the betting houses.

Anoor raised her hand. They'd find out soon enough once the first day of the trials was upon them.

"I signed up for the Aktibar for strength."

The silence was heavy with disbelief.

"You signed up for the Aktibar for . . . strength?" Master Fadel repeated.

Some students looked at her as if for the first time. A few shot her a shred of respect, the rest had brows creased in concern. She realized they thought she'd gone mad.

Maybe she had.

CHAPTER FIFTEEN

TWENTY-TWO DAYS
UNTIL THE TRIAL OF AEROFIELD

It is estimated that fifty percent of Ghostings have died in the last five years from the sleeping sickness. The disease appears to strike suddenly in the night, killing Ghostings in their slumber. Given its nature, I will not allow any of the healers or masters of knowledge to study the illness, lest it mutate and become a threat to Embers. Ghostings will continue to dispose of the dead immediately and mark sites that are infected with a black cross.

—Memo from the Warden of Knowledge, Ollia, year 256

"It was so strange, like a strike or so after we started, her blood-werk failed— No, you're missing the flick on the left." Jond was even worse at this than her.

"Maybe you're right, she's using someone else's blood, and that's just what happens."

"Yeah, maybe. Or I'm wrong and she's not a Duster at all, just an Ember with weird blood—no, do that again." They'd been practicing for a strike, and Sylah was a little lightheaded. It was quite pleasant as it distracted her from her persistent nausea.

"Okay, I better go back, my lunch break's over. She was practically crying yesterday when I turned up late for dinner." Sylah sighed, rubbing her brows.

"She seems like a lot of hard work."

"I guess she is," Sylah agreed. "But half the time I think she's just role playing a character she's read about. Like she thinks that's what the world expects of her."

Jond started to laugh, but Sylah's frown cut him off. He cleared his throat.

"Well, you better head back then . . . I'll see you tomorrow?"

"Yes, first strike, same place every day. I'll teach you what she's taught me." Sylah stood, brushing the sand from her uniform. She hadn't bothered changing from her servant garb. The clothes arrived clean and pressed every morning. Besides, she was getting quite used to the swishy skirts and the way Jond's eyes lingered on her legs.

The view from the water tower was more breathtaking while sober. Shame clouded her mind when she thought of their first reconciliation at the top of the steps. This had been their childhood hideout, and now it was fulfilling that purpose once more. Sylah looked back at Jond crouching on the ground, his brows furrowed in concentration.

And there next to him she saw Fareen, another one of the Stolen, in her mind's eye.

Her heart burst like a ripe tomato, her chest shredded by bullet wounds leaking red blood onto the blue sand.

Sylah squeezed her eyes tight and felt the prickling of an oncoming spasm spread across her shoulder blades. Her mouth flooded with saliva as her cravings kicked in. Her fingers slipped into the pocket where she kept the joba seed she'd found in her room.

She kept it with her at all times. Just in case.

She began to withdraw it between her finger and thumb.

"Sylah?"

Jond. Warden Jond. Aktibar. Bloodwerk. Deal with Anoor. The thoughts rattled through her, and she released the seed, pulling out her hand from her pocket.

"I'm f . . . fine." Spasms rippled across her torso. Jond was next to her in a breath, guiding her to the floor.

"Sylah, breathe, slowly, there you go." He rubbed her back tenderly, leaving an altogether different type of prickling sensation.

She looked into his eyes.

He really was attractive.

"Thanks," he said, throwing in a crooked smile.

"Did I say that out loud?"

Jond laughed. "Yes, you did. Are you okay now?"

"Yes, I'm okay, I'm okay."

Sylah pushed herself to her feet and stumbled. "I'm okay," she repeated when Jond reached out to steady her.

"Is it the joba seeds?" Jond asked softly.

Sylah didn't want to admit it, not to him. Without the drug eclipsing her guilt it was hard to confront the addiction she had. Has.

"Yes, but I'm all right. They shouldn't last much longer. The drug's out of my system now, it's just that my brain needs to stabilize."

"Stabilize?"

"It's the word Anoor used. Apparently, it needs to adapt to cope without the drug . . ." Sylah trailed off. "I'm going to go."

"Are you sure you're all right, though?" His voice was tender, and for some reason it made Sylah crave a joba seed more.

"Yes. Bye, Jond."

Sylah jumped down from the water tower to the barn roof, and onto the cobbled street of the Ember Quarter.

It didn't take Sylah long to realize she was being watched.

She felt it from the way the wind blew. Chilly and suspicious.

"Jond?" She asked the shadows caused by the midday sun. But she knew it wasn't him.

Nothing. Even the kori birds kept their beaks shut as they watched from the branches of the joba trees above.

For a second she thought she saw a smudge in the treetops. Too big to be a bird. Too small to be a person. There were desert lions in the Farsai, but few ever ventured into the city. Either way she broke into a run.

Whoever it was didn't follow her into the Keep. The morning runs had helped Sylah's stamina.

After her blood scour at the gate, Sylah walked through the courtyard, circling the gigantic joba tree that webbed out in the middle. Today a young girl sat bowed in front of it, her white robes indicating she was an Abosom, a priest who followed and preached the teachings of Anyme.

Sylah drifted toward her melodic prayers.

"We thank thee for what you give us, Anyme, we praise thee for where you lead us. Anyme, we serve thee for how you punish us. The blood, the power, the life—"

The Abosom stopped, startled by Sylah's presence. "Sorry, didn't mean to disturb you." Sylah remembered where she was and added, "I'm new here, I've never met an Abosom before." She painted a grin on her face and tried to make her eyes rounder like Anoor's.

"Do not worry, child." The woman, because she was much older than Sylah originally thought, stood. A deep cut on her hand dripped crimson onto the cobblestones, her sacrifice to Anyme, the God of the Sky. Silvered scars lined her arm and hand. The Abosom dedicated their life to pursuing Anyme's attention in the hope of protecting the empire from their wrath. Those who believed in Anyme thought that sacrifice would signal Anyme's blessed attention to manifest their prayers. That was the currency of the God of the empire, blood, and sacrifice.

Sylah preferred to put her faith into the Sandstorm. Into Jond.

The Abosom continued, "The tidewind claimed another last night. I do not know why Anyme is punishing us so." She wrapped herself in her white cowl, not noticing or caring that her hand streaked it red. Her feet were bare and made very little sound as she slipped away.

Sylah lingered, watching the stain of blood drip down the bone-white bark.

HASSA WATCHED SYLAH jump down from the water tower from her perch in the tree. The Ghosting elders had instructed her to source more charcoal to make black paint, but she'd been waylaid when she'd spotted Sylah in a side street. The market could wait.

A few minutes later the boy, Jond, appeared. He wore a loose-fitting black tunic and tight pantaloons that carved out his calves.

Hassa appreciated them from her viewpoint above. Her gaze followed him across the street toward the Tongue.

He must be one of the Stolen. He knew Sylah before her time in Nar-Ruta. And if he was, then that meant the Sandstorm were back. But what was he doing with Sylah? And what was Sylah *really* doing at the Keep?

Hassa had the separate threads of their story but couldn't see the tapestry whole.

She didn't believe the elders when they told her Sylah had traded a favor with the Warden of Crime. She even sought out the Ghosting who served the tea to Sylah in the Belly. Hassa waited in the Intestines until she saw the Ghosting she was looking for, who confirmed what the elders said.

Hassa couldn't believe Sylah would be so reckless—so utterly stupid. A contract with Loot would get her killed.

She checked the street before making her way, lithely and quickly, down the joba tree. Hassa set aside her concern for Sylah for a later time. She had things to do.

BEFORE DINNER, SYLAH arranged to meet Anoor in the training grounds, which had a familiar smell. Sweat, iron, and egos. It was like being back at the Sanctuary.

The area backed onto the army barracks, giving them easy access for the officers to train at all strikes. Weights and weapons lined the walls with multiple training rings stacked side by side in the middle. It was no surprise that a lot of the aerofield weapons were being put to good use, considering the first trial of the Aktibar was only three weeks away. Sylah watched a group of young Embers take turns practicing throwing daggers. They were laughing, and it struck her as odd. When the Stolen trained, they trained in silence; they focused their minds with total dedication.

"Want a go?" A cocky competitor interrupted her thoughts. The boy was a few years younger than Sylah, and his body still a way off its full size. He'd be tall, she realized—tall but stupid. He waved a dagger in his hand, and it gleamed.

Everything gleamed in the Keep. It dripped with luxury and opulence.

It made her rage.

All she wanted to do was take the dagger and fling it into his treacherous Ember heart. She wouldn't miss; she was one of the Sandstorm. The blood would soil his silks, but who trained in silks anyway?

"Sylah!" Anoor rounded the corner waving frantically. Slung through one shoulder she held a bow the size of her whole body. Sylah walked toward her briskly; the farther she was from the boy, the safer he would be.

"Could we maybe go somewhere else to train? It's a little busy here," Sylah said.

Anoor looked past Sylah at the group of Embers who were exchanging glances their way. "Well, we could go into the gardens, I guess."

"Yes, yes, let's go." Sylah swept her arm out for Anoor to lead the way.

Sylah hadn't been in the gardens yet. They were located at the back of the Keep and not visible to outsiders.

Gardens was a misnomer, suggestive of a well-maintained and structured space, perhaps big enough to do a lap or two around, like the Ember Parkside Gardens or even the Duster Quarter Green that had a few potted plants here and there. But the Keep's gardens weren't what Sylah understood the word "garden" to mean; they spanned for leagues toward the horizon where a wild and rich forest grew out of the blue sand of the Farsai Desert. Preceding the forest were orchards full of gleaming red fruit and fountains teeming with fish. Landscaped hills were being pruned, their spring flowers sprinkled like powder on the landscape. The gardener's tools were like weapons themselves; they had to be to be able to cut through the tough skin of the empire's fauna, evolved to withstand the winds. The tidewind takes and takes.

"Are those apples?" Sylah asked, her pace increasing as she walked toward the fruit.

"Yes, but they're not ripe yet."

Sylah had never seen one up close before.

"This place is beautiful." The word sounded too dull to describe such organic artistry.

"Yeah, I guess." Anoor shrugged. "I used to swim in the lake during summer . . ."

Sylah wanted to scream. The girl didn't know how good she had it. Sylah clenched her fists beside her and breathed through her nose. She didn't want to have another spasm today. The last one had left her muscles weak and aching.

When Jond is warden, we'll balance the scales. We'll make sure Dusters rise to the top.

"That was before Mother asked me to stop wearing a bathing suit," Anoor continued.

Sylah remembered Anoor mentioning her mother's cruelty before. Especially cruelty based on something that should be celebrated. Anoor's curves were beautiful. She looked away before she spotted Sylah surveying her.

"What's that?" Sylah noticed gray concrete towers looming beyond the forest on the left. They marred the landscape with their foreboding presence blocking out the view of the sea beyond.

"That's the new arena to house the trials. Mother had it built over the last ten years . . ."

"The Aktibar?"

"Do you know any other trials?" Anoor laughed prettily. Sylah thought of the trials Dusters were more likely to face, the ones that ended in the rack. She shook the thought away.

"Well, I can tell you it's a trial being around you." Although Sylah sounded serious, her eyes shone with a mischievous glint. "I want to see it," she added. "Come on, extra practice." And with that Sylah launched into a swift jog toward the arena.

THE GRAY MONSTROSITY got bigger and bigger the closer she got. A set of stairs lit by runelamps led the way to rows and rows of seats, held in place by eight pillars, each the width of a villa. The competitors would fight on the rough terrain down below. Like flies in a spider's web. She wondered if Jond and the Sandstorm knew about it.

"Do we get to skip running tomorrow?" Anoor appeared moments later, sweat dripping from her brow, her bow still hanging limply over one arm.

"This thing is huge." Sylah raised her voice as if to fill the cavernous space. "Bugs, they're just going to look like bugs from here." She couldn't believe she hadn't seen it before; the gray towers seemed impossible to hide, but the Keep was set on top of a hill, masking the arena beyond.

"Mother said there are a hundred thousand seats. And then enough standing room at the back for half that again."

"Standing room?" Sylah asked but answered her own question. "Ah, of course, for Dusters and Ghostings." Sylah's mouth twisted with scorn.

Anoor didn't reply, but Sylah felt her eyes assessing her. Measuring her.

"Let's go down there," Sylah said.

Sylah flew down the steps two at a time, the runelamps activating with each lunge.

When she finally landed in the basin of the arena, the lights had been activated throughout, filling the space with a rich red glow.

"Skies above. This place is ridiculous." Her voice echoed outward into the hungry corners of the arena. Aerofield targets littered the space. All the competitors had to do was chose their weapon and hit the targets. It was ready. Waiting for bloodshed.

"Hey, you can't be here. Hello! Please leave." An officer was barreling toward her, his half-eaten flatbread in one hand. He waved it at her as if the toasty smell would somehow ward her away.

"Is that for me?" She fluttered her eyelashes and reached out and grabbed the bread, stuffing the remains in her mouth before he could blink.

"What . . . did you just eat my bread?"

Sylah grinned and winked. It would have been cute if she didn't still have a mouthful of food.

"Sorry, sir, I thought you were offering it to me." She shot him her "Anoor eyes" and pushed out her flat chest.

"You ate my bread?"

Sylah turned her expression to mortified and wobbled her lip at the horror, the sheer horror, of eating his bread. She was getting good at this.

"I'm so sorry, sir—"

"Hello, Officer Min!" Anoor entered like a steaming kettle, each puff taking her closer to the boiling point.

"Ah, Miss Elsari, your mother didn't mention you were coming down. I saw the lights come on and rushed over." His hand still held the ghost of his dinner. "I was just conversing with your servant."

"Sylah." She winked at him. Anoor grabbed her by the arm.

"Min, we'll be going now." She started marching away with Sylah, who was waving madly at Min.

"What was that? I was having fun, practicing my character and all that," Sylah said, blowing Min a final kiss.

"You looked like you were having another seizure."

"I was flirting!"

THE EDGE OF the forest was the perfect spot to practice archery. The light from the gardens bled in from the east, while the protection of the tall trees hid them from prying eyes.

Sylah noticed another building growing out of the landscape. "What's that?"

"It's one of the southern watch towers facing the Marion Sea, but it's been abandoned for some time."

"Yeah, bit pointless watching the sea."

"Unless there's something beyond it."

They looked at each other, their suspicions lingering between them. Sylah broke eye contact and looked away.

"Show me what you can do then." Sylah crossed her arms and leaned back on the trunk of a tree. "Get an arrow into that sapling on the left . . . no, the one farther away . . . yes . . . and I'll be ecstatic."

"Ecstatic? That would be something to see." Something seemed to come over Anoor, something Sylah hadn't seen before. Her shoulders pulled back and her chin lifted half a handspan. Was it confidence?

She pulled the bow string and shut her eyes, her breathing steady.

"Have you fallen asleep?" Sylah called out from her slumped position.

Anoor didn't respond.

Sylah yawned.

The bow twanged, hitting the sapling in the center. Sylah couldn't hide her shock.

Then another. And another. And one more, because why not?

Three of the four met their mark.

"That is something we can work with at least." Sylah's relief was immense.

Anoor couldn't help the squeal that escaped her. Sylah pushed herself away from the tree.

"Try the tree back there . . . the one to the left." Anoor hit it squarely in its bark chest. "The one farther back . . ."

And on it went, Sylah adjusting her position and advising her with her aim. By the end Anoor was hitting every target with ease.

"Well done," Sylah said somewhat begrudgingly. "At the trial you have ten chances to hit five targets. If you repeat what you did just now, you'll be fine."

"That's it?" Anoor's feet pitter-pattered on the ground in excitement.

"Do you know *anything* about the Aktibar?"

Anoor shrugged. "I know that I'll be tested on my aerofield skills . . . ?"

Sylah ground her teeth then continued. "The arena will be set up with five targets. Each competitor will get the choice of one weapon from those provided." Sylah held up a hand to Anoor's open mouth. "Don't worry there will be lots of different bows, but we'll practice with a few just in case. When your name is called you will stand on the podium and take your shots. You'll have five minutes."

"Five minutes?"

Sylah winced at her shriek. "That's plenty of time, you'll speed up with more practice. But only the top hundred contestants will make it through to the next round."

"You mean if everyone uses five shots to hit the five targets and I use six then I'm . . . out?"

"Yes, but you don't have to worry, that won't happen. So many people sign up to the first trial for the glory. Half won't even be able to hit one target. And the other half will choose the wrong weapon. You'll do fine, but we'll aim for a hundred percent anyway? Right?"

Anoor's lip wobbled.

"Right?" Sylah barked. Anoor had to win; if she didn't Sylah would be out on her ass, and no closer to learning enough bloodwerk for Jond to pass that trial.

Anoor inclined her head. When she next looked up at Sylah, her eyes sparkled with determination.

"Let's go again. We've only got three weeks—" Sylah felt a shiver spread across the back of her neck and spun around.

"What is it?" Anoor asked.

"Nothing," Sylah said, searching through the trees. It wasn't until she smelled the salt air that she remembered how close they were to the cliffs on the edge of the Marion Sea.

Was there a world out there watching her?

SYLAH KNOCKED ON her mother's door. It felt strange just walking in, even though she'd only lived away for one week. The time had passed in a routine of working, training, and sleeping. She was surprised at how little she missed the villa that had been her home for six years. It alarmed her to realize how quickly the Keep had come to feel like home. It was meant to be, after all.

"Hi, Mama."

"You staying for dinner?" Lio asked.

"I thought I might. I told Anoor I'd be late."

"Okay, come in, I'm making fufu."

Sylah could see the yams ready to be mashed in the corner, the pestle and mortar ready to go.

Jond sat at the table.

"Jond, what are you doing here?"

"Missed home cooking." His grin was wolfish.

It should have disturbed her, him sitting there like it was his own home. But it didn't.

They had been a family once, all twelve of the Stolen and their dedicated foster parents. Jond's parent was Vona, though really they all took care of one another. Weapons needed to be cared for, the hilts kept clean, the blades protected. Sylah had let herself get a little rusty over the years, but she remembered the drumbeat of their song: *a dancer's grace, a killer's instinct, an Ember's blood, a Duster's heart.*

At least Jond would now take up the fight, and level the Keep to dust.

Sylah sank into the wicker chair.

Lio began to pound the fufu behind her.

"How's training going?"

Sylah shrugged and pulled her tunic around her. She missed the warmth of the long sleeves of her uniform.

"She's still too slow and unfit, and I'm not sure I will get her past the next trial, but we'll see. Her aerofield skills are good."

"Good, good, we need to make sure she gets better. There is so much about bloodwerk we just don't know."

Sylah agreed. Every lesson with Anoor seemed to breed more questions.

"How is practice going?" Sylah asked Jond.

"Not bad, I still can't work the *Ba* rune very well. It's the left—"

"—Flick right? Yeah, that's really hard to get right with a stylus."

"Yesterday I passed out from trying."

"Jond, you need to be careful, she warned me about this. Some people have bled out completely in the past."

He waved her away and reached for his firerum.

"Can I get one of those?" Sylah called to her mother behind her.

"Help yourself."

She tried to, but Jond had gotten there before her. He pulled out the glass from the cupboard by the stove and poured her a healthy shot.

"May Anyme absolve me of my sins." Jond's voice was rough, but his smile warm.

"May Anyme absolve me of my *many* sins." Sylah matched his grin.

They clinked glasses.

The firerum burned her throat, she'd never realized how much.

Lio served the fufu in a steaming bowl of soup. The three of them sat around the table and used their fingers to separate pieces of the gelatinous fufu into clumps that would carry the soup to their mouths.

"It's good, Mama."

"Reminds me of home." Jond smiled.

Sylah wasn't sure which home he was referring to.

"Have you ever thought about the world beyond the Marion Sea?"

The question opened a gulf between them.

Lio put her hand down. "The Marion Sea? There's nothing there. The Ending Fire destroyed it all."

Jond frowned. "Yeah. Nothing. Just water and more water. And apparently some monsters." He laughed, and Lio joined in.

"Maybe."

Lio snorted. "Maybe? Don't you think we'd know by now if there was more land out there?"

It was a good point.

"And what of the tidewind?" Jond added. "If there was more land, no one would be able to get to it without dying during the winds."

Again, another good point.

"And"—another addition from Lio—"if the Ending Fire was a pile of dung—because who can trust the word of an Ember—why does it matter? There's no one out there. If there was, they would have found us."

"We're on our own," Jond said through a mouthful of fufu.

Sylah looked around the table at the last survivors of the Sandstorm she had known.

We're on our own.

CHAPTER SIXTEEN

THE TRIAL OF AEROFIELD

Nowerks, do not attempt to pass this barrier. Seats are for Embers only. If a Nowerk is found beyond this line, they will be subjected to twenty lashes and expelled from the arena for all future trials.

—Sign posted on the back row of the arena

The first day of the Aktibar was upon them; the last three weeks had flown by like the arrows from Anoor's bow.

Nar-Ruta bubbled and fizzed like its namesake river. Servants had been up before dawn sweeping away the copious remains of the dust from the tidewind the night before. It had come in thick and fast, as fevered as the nerves of the competitors.

There were two hundred competitors, all told. Most were Anoor's age, but there were some who were nearing middling years. All looked fierce as they stood proud in the arena. The experienced competitors wore goat's leather, clearly worn out from field practice. Others wore stiff suits with no give in the elbows, and one even wore a crushed velvet dress. But there was one thing that tied all the competitors together—their red blood.

It should have been me.

The thought struck Sylah between her eyes, and she shook it away.

No, this was Jond's time now. She would help him achieve his goal.

Sylah spotted him in the crowd of competitors and smiled. The contours of his muscles rippled beneath his black fighting leathers.

Sylah dragged her eyes away. The arena was full, the nobility concentrated toward the front. Every important Ember throughout the empire had gotten a seat. Even the imirs from the farthest cities came for the competition. Most would stay for the whole six mooncycles, leaving their subordinates to govern their districts. Every inn on this side of the river was fully booked. Sylah even heard that some Embers were forced to rent spaces in the Duster Quarter. The horror.

The standing section was bursting with Dusters and the occasional Ghosting. Officers waved runeguns like flags, penning them in behind the iron railing. Even though they were threatened with violence, they cheered for the trial to come.

Sylah was seated a few rows in front of the standing section. As an Ember she'd been given a seat. But as a servant she'd been limited to a section at the back among a sea of shaven heads.

Anoor clung to the edge of the arena in the distance.

She had cried that morning and tried to muffle the sound in the privy lest Sylah hear her. Sylah could sense her fear from afar. It made Sylah jittery and impatient for the trial to be over. Anoor *needed* to get through.

Over the weeks Sylah had developed a grudging respect for the girl. She was a hard worker, and sometimes Sylah caught the spark of unwavering determination flickering like fire in her eyes. It prompted Sylah to ask why she decided to compete in the first place.

"Because no one thought I could. Because I want to prove them wrong. I want to prove *her* wrong."

Her—Uka Elsari. The mother who hated her.

She looked toward the stage at the far right of the arena, where the newly appointed wardens sat.

Pura, the Warden of Truth, was talking to an Abosom priest. All of the Abosom answered to him as the holy conduit to Anyme. His white beard fell to his waist and blended in with his white robes. Anoor said his breath always smelled of whiskey.

The Warden of Knowledge, Wern, watched the proceedings with a faintly disapproving expression on her wrinkly face. Her cornrows were braided into swirls and stars on her scalp. Sylah rubbed her own hand through the prickles of her hair. It had grown slightly, Gorn made a point of telling her. She'd need to shave it again soon, but she couldn't bear to.

Aveed, the Warden of Duty, had just taken their seat next to Uka. Their robe of rich reds and purples stood out starkly against Uka's gray suit. Their long hair had been groomed into two plaits that hung on either side of their painted brow, the makeup fresh and precise. Anoor claimed Aveed once called Uka "a viper in the sand" during an argument that was overhead by one of her servant friends. Aveed was Uka's biggest rival and always opposed her views. Sylah liked them marginally more than the others because of that, but her feelings were still set firmly within the realm of hatred.

The wardens' metal thrones were so polished they gleamed in the sunlight like glass. And they seemed just as fragile.

I wonder if they'd shatter, Sylah thought. She rubbed her arms as her muscles twinged. The seizures had been lessening, but cramps and muscle tremors plagued her daily. She still craved joba seeds— the lightness, the euphoria, the blessed freedom of the drug.

She bit the side of her cheek, but the rusty burst of blood didn't stop the need.

The light wind was flavored with salt from the Marion Sea and Sylah wondered, once again, if there was more out there. More land. More people.

She dragged her thoughts away from her useless pondering and back to the podium where the wardens were. A hush rippled through the crowd as the Warden of Strength stood. The soft gray suit she wore blurred the edges of her sharp lines, like early morning fog. The sleeves dipped below her inkwell and trailed on the ground.

"Welcome one and all to the first day of the Aktibar. We begin today with the first guild of the empire: strength," Uka spoke into a bloodwerk sound projector, the rune *Ru* pushing out the sound vibrations. The Embers around her erupted in bloodthirsty cheers.

Sylah wanted to burn the arena to ashes, using the Embers' bones as kindling.

THE CHEERS RATTLED her bones. Anoor wanted to cry. In fact, she'd cried earlier but had managed to hide it from Sylah, who already thought of her as a sniveling mess. She looked up to the back rows and scanned them for her. Anoor knew Sylah was up there, but she couldn't see her. The master in charge had banned anyone who wasn't a contestant from the floor of the arena.

"Please can she stay?" she had begged the master. Anoor clutched onto Sylah so tightly and she didn't care who saw. Sylah shrugged her off with a look of disgust.

"Stop being a baby. You can do this." Such words of wisdom from her trainer.

The last three weeks had been grueling. Anoor couldn't remember the last time her muscles didn't hurt. If they weren't running, they were stretching; if they weren't stretching, they were aerofield training.

Anoor smiled. Though she was sore, she'd had fun. The walls around Sylah were slowly coming down, especially when Anoor was teaching her to bloodwerk. It was in those moments that Anoor saw Sylah's raw inquisitive nature so clearly.

Now Anoor missed her presence as she stood alone and apart from the other contestants. They didn't so much avoid her as pretend she wasn't there at all. They all seemed bigger than her, stronger than her. Even the ancient ones who had signed up on a whim looked like they could outrun her. They were built like her grandmother.

Anoor glanced at her grandmother in the stand, sitting behind the newly appointed wardens. The wig she wore—the preferred fashion from a few decades ago—curled around sharp features as she surveyed Anoor below. At sixty-eight, Yona's muscles corded around her limbs like the branches of a joba tree. Uka had kept

Anoor as far away from her grandmother as possible, but when Anoor did get to see her during special occasions, Anoor found herself liking her, vying for her approval.

After all, how could *she* win *this*? She wasn't born to compete, she didn't even have red blood. What if the Embers were right, and Dusters weren't meant to rule?

"No," she said softly to herself. "I can do this. I can prove them all wrong."

A tall woman moved to stand in front of her and blocked Anoor's view of her grandmother. Anoor looked at the skin of her hair parting, the scalp stretched taut into two plaits, dyed red with henna.

"Hello, excuse me, do you mind moving to the left?"

The woman turned around and looked down—it was a fair distance to Anoor—and grinned. Anoor found herself smiling back, until the woman spoke, and her grin soured.

"Oh, hello there, little mango. Am I in your way?" The woman was fierce, a silver scar puckered by the side of her eyes.

Anoor choked on the automatic greeting that nearly bubbled up.

"Yes, and I'm trying to hear my mother speak." She dropped her voice in an attempt to sound like Sylah.

"You're the daughter?"

"Yes, now can you please move to the left?"

The woman scoffed, but she moved. Anoor still felt her gaze on her, but she'd turned her attention to her mother.

"Each contestant has a choice of aerofield weapon. They have ten chances to hit five targets. The top hundred contestants will make it through to the next round. The rest will be eliminated." They cheered again. "The trial of tactics will commence next mooncycle followed by the trial of stealth, mind, bloodwerk, and ending with combat." They were almost frothing, they were so hungry for the violence. Anoor rolled her eyes, a gesture she'd picked up from Sylah. Her mother was suddenly staring at her, but there was no way she could have seen that small act of rebellion.

"I will only accept the best. I will only train with the best. So, to the best, if you're down there, I look forward to you becoming the next Disciple of Strength." Anoor shivered. Her mother was definitely looking at her. "And should you not be the best, because after all, there can only be one, hold your head high as an Ember of the Nar-Ruta empire and tell your children and your children's children that you were a competitor in the greatest trials the world has ever seen. The Aktibar." The threat was clear.

"Curse the blood, I wish she would hurry up," Anoor murmured to herself, but she heard the woman beside her scoff again. Anoor glanced at her, and the woman winked. It was more unsettling than her scorn from earlier.

Anoor turned away; she needed to clear her head in order to reach the state of battle wrath that Sylah preached about. She was ready, ready to win this. Or at least come in the top fifty. She just needed to stop being a "spoiled brat" and hit the bull's-eye. As simple as that, really. The words in her mind were spoken in Sylah's voice, but they gave her a twisted sense of hope.

THE CROWD FINALLY quietened, and the first contestants were called forward. Jond was itching to begin. This was the culmination of his life; every second spent training with every weapon imaginable was worth it, just to stand there knowing this was it. This was his time.

He felt the weight of an empire on his back: of the hopes of a community oppressed. He would change things when he was warden. He would change them for the better, just like he was taught. The Sandstorm had grown despite the massacre of six years ago.

"Anoor Elsari." A young woman was called forward, and Jond perked up. A murmur swept through the crowd as they watched her pick up the bow and quiver. Her garish clothes drowned her, making her seem larger than she was and hiding all sense of the curves underneath, but Jond could still see how sure her footing was. She was sucking on her bottom lip, glossing it with saliva, but it was her eyes that intrigued Jond the most. They were a warm hazel, like her flawless skin, and behind them was a fierceness that contradicted her skittish demeanor, a fierceness so bright it hurt to stare at her too long.

Sylah clearly had her hands full with that one.

Anoor walked up to the target podium and raised her bow. The wooden targets were easy for Jond. He could have done them with his eyes closed when he was ten years old. The circular targets varied in height and position ranging fifty to a hundred handspans in distance. There were five targets in total, and after every competitor, they swapped them out with new ones and the spacing altered slightly.

Jond watched Anoor as she drew back the bow. Sylah had convinced Jond that Anoor was ready for it, but he still sent her luck.

For a few brief seconds all was quiet. Uka Elsari leaned forward in her throne.

The arrows flew, one after another. Each hit its target, or close enough that she certainly wasn't going to be eliminated.

"Nice," Jond said, causing a few competitors to look at him sidelong. He ignored them and let out a slow breath. Jond needed Anoor to continue competing because he needed Sylah to keep learning about bloodwerk. Without that knowledge he wouldn't make it through the bloodwerk trial.

Anoor didn't know it, but her success had gotten the Sandstorm one step closer to the Keep.

A polite patter of applause followed. Those who knew her were shocked; those who didn't assumed the skills ran in her blood. Twenty more competitors took to the podium, one failing so badly he left the arena in tears.

"Jond Alnua, you're up." There were no nerves unsteadying his hands as he walked toward his weapon of choice. A few competitors gave him dubious looks as he selected the throwing axes. It was difficult to get the range required to hit the targets with such weighty weapons, but Jond preferred the solid metal in his hands over a bow. He twirled the axes in his hand. They were well balanced, if a little worse for wear. He was cold steel as he walked up to the podium.

Jond threw the axes without ceremony, all flying true in quick succession. He knew without looking that he'd be top of the leader board.

The words that slipped out were said to himself: "A dancer's grace, a killer's instinct, an Ember's blood, a Duster's heart."

CHAPTER SEVENTEEN

TWENTY-EIGHT DAYS
UNTIL THE TRIAL OF TACTICS

Take me to the fields of Jin-Gernomi,
In the green grass you'll build a home for me.
And when the night falls and the tidewind feeds,
We'll hold each other close, love the only armor we need.

—Lyrics from *The Fields of Jin-Gernomi*

Sylah shifted in her skirt. It wasn't exactly a skirt, but trousers slit so many times they showed a scandalous amount of flesh. Her suit jacket was corseted at the bottom, cinched so tightly she could barely breathe.

When Anoor had first presented her with the outfit, she cringed, but she had to admit the effect was . . . alluring.

"Please, just wear it, it's a present. You can't not accept it."

"I can accept it, then use it as tinder."

Anoor sucked on her bottom lip and tilted her face up to Sylah.

"Just try it on, I promise you'll love it. You can't wear your servant uniform if you're coming as my guest."

"Well, that sorts that then. I won't come at all." Sylah crossed her arms and collapsed onto Anoor's bed. Despite not being the one who had competed earlier, she was surprisingly exhausted.

"You have to come. The banquet celebrates all the winners, and it's our victory."

"I'm a chambermaid, Anoor, I can't just dress up and go."

"Actually, you can; servants are allowed to be competitors."

"Anoor, I'm not a competitor," Sylah said, her head sinking lower into Anoor's pillows.

Anoor waved her hand in dismissal. "Semantics. Every competitor gets a plus-one, and you'll be mine. Besides I'm not going without you."

She laid the outfit down next to Sylah on the bed. Sylah turned her head to survey it. At least it wasn't as glittery as some of Anoor's clothes. Anoor had had it tailored in a burnt orange, a color Anoor had said she "was positive would complement your dark complexion." There was even a custom headdress that would wrap around her head and knot in a large bow at the front.

"I also got you these." Anoor was cradling something in her palm. Sylah could see the sparkle of jewelry between her fingers.

"No."

"Just look at it first," Anoor protested.

"Fine." Sylah looked at Anoor's outstretched hand. There in the center lay a cuff of silver, the two edges molded into gold leaves.

"No."

"It's not even that fancy! It's just a simple armlet. I had it made just for you; it's in the shape of a poison ivy leaf like your inkwell."

It *did* match. Maybe Jond would like it?

She sighed, and Anoor took that as conceding defeat. Which it was, eventually.

Now she found herself standing in an alcove of the great veranda watching as the competitors danced and drank and ate. Her eyelids were heavy with the white makeup used by Embers on special occasions. Anoor had applied the dashes and flicks to her face with the same determination as her fighting. It had made Sylah laugh, smudging the process more than once.

The atmosphere at the winners' banquet was almost sterile compared to the Maroon. There was no pounding from the scythes or the shrill cries from the plantation workers.

Here Anoor's glitter sparkled, her bright blue, yes blue, dress still marked her in the crowd as she twirled and spun. Embers never wore blue; it was the color of dirt and Dusters. The dress was a small rebellion, and it made Sylah smile. She knew Anoor was pretty, but there was now a lightness in her eyes that hadn't been there before. The training had lifted her out of the monotony of her life. The victory had further proved she was a serious competitor now. She had to be if Sylah was to fulfill her purpose of learning to bloodwerk for the Sandstorm. Anoor caught Sylah watching and danced toward her.

Anoor was not a good dancer. Her arms flailed around her like a baby kori bird trying to leave its nest. Her neck bobbed forward, out of rhythm with her arms, attempting to propel her toward Sylah as Embers parted away from her.

"Dance with me," Anoor asked.

"I said no the first, second, and third times, why would this be any different?"

"Because you've had more to drink."

"No, *you've* had more to drink." Sylah narrowed her eyes. "Who were you dancing with before?"

"Oh, I don't know, some distant cousin of the imir of Jin-Noon—they all want to court me, you see." Anoor leaned in as she shimmied by Sylah's side. Sylah could smell the sandalwood oil she used. "They like to get closer to my mother, it's all very fickle. Certainly not romantic." Anoor flicked an errant curl away from her eye and surveyed Sylah, though her expression was unreadable.

"Must be a hard life," Sylah drawled.

"Oh, it is." Her smile dropped.

Her self-pity was like a slap in Sylah's face. "Maiden's tits, would you just leave me alone? I came to the party like you wished. I'm doing everything we agreed on and more. Can you just leave me to drink my wine in peace?" Sylah didn't feel bad for the hurt that showed on Anoor's face. She was Anoor's captive, after all. Once Anoor had shuffled away, her scent lingered. Sylah downed the last of her drink.

The edges of her vision had pleasantly blurred, but she craved the ecstasy of a joba seed. She fingered the seed in her pocket, which she now carried with her everywhere. It was a source of both comfort and pain. Comfort because she could hold it at any moment. Pain because she knew she could *take* it at any moment.

"Sylah." Jond's voice made her jump. Beads of sweat peppered his brow. She had spotted him on the dance floor a few times. He leaned in for a hug, and Sylah hugged him back with the ferocity of someone hanging onto a float. He smelled of basil and jasmine.

"Well done today." Sylah murmured into his ear.

"Thanks." He held her at arm's length. "You look incredible."

"Three meals a day does that to a person." Sylah had gained a marginal amount of weight since being Anoor's trainer. The joba seeds had been her breakfast, lunch, and dinner, the drug stealing her appetite. Now the nausea was gone, she enjoyed food like she hadn't before.

"No, I mean"—his eyes traveled up and down her body, scoring her with his gaze—"you look *amazing*."

Sylah grimaced but bowed her head in thanks. Her hand went to the cuff on her arm, warm from her skin.

Jond looked good too, *really* good. His slim-fitting suit hinted at the muscle underneath, and his strong jawline and dark eyes only added to his allure. Jond had always had the softest hair, each curl so perfectly formed she almost reached out to twirl one. He noticed her look and quirked an eyebrow.

"Is there something on my face?"

"A faint picture of smugness, but that's all."

He grinned and pulled out a flask from his pocket.

"I figured out Papa's recipe."

"What? For the firerum he used to make?"

"Yes, so drink it slow, it's stronger than the shit they import in from Jin-Sukar." Anoor twirled out of the corner of Sylah's eye, and she downed the entire flask in three gulps. "Or don't." He shrugged and waved at a Ghosting servant to top up her wineglass.

Sylah had looked for Hassa already: they had only seen each other a few times throughout the last few weeks. Anoor's training and her chambermaid duties took up much of Sylah's time. The spare strike she did get she spent with Jond teaching him bloodwerk. Besides, Hassa always seemed to be rushing from one place to another.

"Thank you," Sylah said, looking into the Ghosting's eyes as she filled Sylah's glass to the brim. The Ghosting smiled faintly as she drifted back into the recess of the veranda, waiting to be summoned again.

When Sylah didn't speak again, Jond followed her line of sight to the dance floor.

"She did well today," Jond said.

"Yes. The other trials won't come so easily." Sylah rubbed her brow. The dance floor was getting very hazy.

"You'll do it, you'll get her through."

"I hope so." Sylah wasn't so sure; they had started training for the tactics trial, but military strategy wasn't coming easy to Anoor.

"Thank you for doing this for us—"

"Let's dance," she cut in.

"Really? I haven't danced in years."

"Come on, we know this one," Sylah said, tilting her ear to the band.

Jond listened, his grin growing with each beat of the drum. The flute player dipped into a minor melody then trilled upward in a major scale. The drums made her shoulders want to dance. The singer was melismatic, avoiding the harmony of the flute, making the song almost jaunty. Sylah and Jond mouthed the lyrics to each other. "Take me to the fields of Jin-Gernomi, in the green grass you'll build a home for me."

They both scoffed at the lyrics, just like they had done when they were children. It was an Ember song, but so many of the Sandstorm foster parents were servants in the Keep, they had the song memorized. The Sandstorm teachers used it to train them to dance, over and over again.

Jond bowed and held out his hand, and for a moment Sylah felt the itch of her mama's stare between her shoulder blades, like she was there instructing her to pinch back her shoulder blades, lift her chin high. But she was no longer ten years old.

"A dancer's grace, a killer's instinct, an Ember's blood, a Duster's heart," Sylah whispered, reaching for his hand. His palms were calloused but warm. They fit together like they had always done.

ANOOR HAD BEEN dancing with a very tall gentleman when she spotted them. A circle had grown around them as if the crowd were standing on the edge of a precipice, afraid to be dragged into the sandstorm within.

Sylah danced with the same grace she fought with, but with less anger marring her brow. They spun and pranced as if made from wisps of radish leaf smoke. Sylah's legs bent and flicked outward with precision while the man twirled around her. Her hips dipped and moved back and forth in time with the music. Sylah looked happy as she grinned at the young man who led her around the dance floor. He looked dangerous to Anoor; something about him unsettled her down to her marrow. But he was enthralled by Sylah, so he couldn't be all bad.

Sylah laughed, and Anoor was struck dumb by the sound. There was no echo of bitterness or spite in it. Anoor turned to leave; she couldn't watch the trust in Sylah's eyes as she let him catch her. There was a shout, a soft screech from a spectator, a thud. Sylah had fallen, her knee giving way beneath her. The crowd had already started moving away, the spell broken.

The man was helping her up, concern etched into his brow. He probably assumed it was the drink, not the tremors caused by the lack of joba seeds in her body. Her brain had not yet adapted to the stimulant deficiency in her nerve center, and seizures and tremors had become a regular ailment Sylah still dealt with. Though they had lessened, her muscles still shook every time they practiced, even though she tried to hide it from Anoor. It was battle wrath, the meditative state that required Sylah to be angry, but being angry agitated her nerves and brought on the tingling and lack of mobility.

Anoor thought about going to help the man, but as Sylah leaned into his embrace, Anoor realized she'd just be in the way. It was time to go to bed anyway.

SYLAH WAS DRUNK. Jond was holding her up, but she couldn't stop laughing.

"Sylah, you're taller than me, please can you at least try and walk?"

"Why?"

"Because I'm trying to get you to bed."

"Bed? With you?" The thought fizzed out of her mind and into the empty hallway between them.

"Sir, you can't just wander the Keep." An officer blocked their path. "Exit is that way."

"She lives here." Jond was surprised Sylah wasn't fearful of the officer. It unsettled him to see how a mooncycle at the Keep had already changed her. She was turning into one of them.

"Yeah?" the officer asked doubtfully.

"I live in Ood-Zaynib—"

"No Sylah, you live with Anoor Elsari." Air hissed through Jond's teeth.

"I know, I'm not stupid." Her eyebrows knitted together.

"Look, unless you can prove that she lives here—"

"She's a servant. Anoor Elsari's chambermaid."

"Where's her uniform?" The officer stifled a yawn.

"She's been at the winners' banquet." Jond was getting impatient.

"Sure, working in that outfit?" He scoffed.

In a bout of anger Jond pulled the headscarf off Sylah's head. "Look at her hair, it's shaved." Sylah's head lolled this way and that.

The officer inspected it. "Hardly. I'm going to have to ask you to leave." He idly stroked the runegun by his side with a long finger.

"Let's go back to yours, Jond," Sylah murmured in his ear. Her hot breath sent shivers down his spine.

Sylah hadn't been to his little piece of home yet, hadn't asked about it either. He found himself wondering when he'd last tidied up. Not that she was in a state to know what was two handspans in front of her anyway. She'd have to sleep it off for some time yet.

Sylah was furiously sticking her tongue out at the officer, so Jond quickened their pace and led her into the cool air. The tidewind was still a few strikes away, but the breeze seemed frantic with anticipation.

A competitor, a son of an imir for sure, thundered past them on an eru. The carriage on the eru's back was bursting with young women. Jond swallowed his disgust as they walked in the dust of their wake.

"Where are we going?" Her steps were getting surer the farther they got from the Keep; the cool air seemed to be clearing her head.

"My place isn't far, it's south of the Ember Quarter."

"How long have you lived there?"

"Not long."

THE JOBA TREES on his street were lovingly cared for. One of his neighbors had begun to decorate their tree with trinkets and jewelry. The trend had gotten out of hand, each Ember trying to prove their worth with the quality of the jewelry. Jond could barely sleep with the racket they all made in the tidewind.

"This is me." He led her up a set of stairs to his flat on the third floor of a tall villa. At one stage she had begun to shiver, so he'd put his arm around her. As he let her go and reached for the keys, she felt that loss of warmth piercingly. "Are you okay? Do you want me to walk you back to the Keep? You seem a little more aware of your surroundings now." He gave her a lopsided grin.

"Yes, I'm sure. I will stay here tonight," she said. He unlocked the door.

"I'll sleep on the floor, you take the bed."

Once they entered the hallway, he pulled the metal tidewind shutters down, the clang making her jump. She gave him a tentative smile.

She looked lost standing in the middle of his home, her orange suit so bright against his humble belongings.

"It's just the one room, there's a privy out back and stove in the corner." For some reason he felt shy and embarrassed by his homestead. "The Sandstorm had to pay out a lot for this place, but it made sense being close to the Keep. Plus, the views are great."

A wicked gleam ignited in her eyes.

"Show me."

He pulled down the hatch above him, revealing a ladder.

"After you, my *Akoma*." She snorted as she grasped his outstretched hand. Whatever tension had been between them dissipated in that moment.

Akoma. Jond hadn't called her that in six years.

She still remembered when they'd learned it. Jond's foster mother, Vona, was teaching them the basics of the human heart out of a Duster school book.

"And this is the Akoma, the largest artery in the whole body." Vona pointed to the page of a stick figure in the battered book. "It carries fresh blood away from the heart."

"The best one to slice," Sylah whispered to Jond.

He smirked beside her.

Later that day they had lain side by side watching the stars before the tidewind came. It became their nightly ritual since they learned that the twinkling lights were little sparks of fire leagues away, left over from the Ending Fire.

Jond's hand rested comfortably in hers. They lay shoulder to shoulder in the sand, their heads looking upward.

"Sylah?"

"Yes, Jond."

He shifted in the sand, moving on his side. His face was a hairsbreadth from hers. "You're my Akoma." She felt his breath on her cheek and she shivered.

"You're mine." Sylah squeezed his hand but didn't look at him. She wondered if the sparks above would ever ignite.

The view was as beautiful as he'd said. To the left was the Ruta River, the churning blue sand almost pretty in the moonlight. To the right was the Keep, the lights still burning bright. Sylah looked ahead, and her smile slipped.

"The water tower," Jond answered her unspoken question. "I may have been a bit insistent with the Sandstorm when I chose this flat."

"That's how you found me?"

"I had sat watch for two weeks."

She turned to him sharply.

"Did they order you to?"

"No, Sylah, I wanted to find you." He reached for her hand, and she let him. The alcohol still raged in her blood, but she felt more in control.

"You're lucky. I hadn't been there in a long time."

She looked at him then, truly saw him for who he was. A scar ran down the side of his face, and she reached for it with her other hand. It was darker than his skin, yet silvery and smooth like the underbelly of a fish. Her finger ran the length of it, reading the story it told. The story of a boy who was no longer a boy but a man.

Her Akoma.

PART THREE

PILLAGE

A person is guilty of theft if she/he/they deceitfully appropriates property—material or immaterial—that belongs to another with the intention of divesting the owner of said property. The penalty of those charged with theft can lead to a maximum sentence of seven years in prison.*

*Ghostings and Dusters are subjected to an immediate trial per the Starting Drum Act of 275.

—Extract from the Theft Act, reviewed year 305

THE STORY OF THE SIEGE OF THE SILENT AS SPOKEN BY GRIOT ZIBENWE

The spoken word has been transcribed onto the page;
the ◊ symbol represents the beating of the griot's drum.

Four hundred years ago, more or less, less or more. It may feel a long time to you; it may even feel small. But ask a Ghosting and they will know. They will know exactly how far this tale must go. A time when Ghostings weren't as you see them now. They had fingers to clap and tongues to row.

Today, I speak of the Siege of the Silent.

◊

Sir, I see you get up to leave. Is this story not to your liking?

Aho, my dear audience, he says he cares not for our fellow clear-blooded. Servants they are to you and to many. He wants a story of battles and blood and villains.

This story has all three, I assure you, just listen.

◊

In the Before time, blue and clear stood side by side, sowing into the blackened earth the Ending Fire left behind. Their song rang out across the land:

"Scorched by the fire of God
Burned by the skies
We are the ones that live
We will survive."

And if a child fell out of line, or a field worker fainted from the heat . . .

◊

Bang! The runeguns went . . .

◊

Crack! The whips would snap.
The Embers were as forgiving then as they are now.

◊

One day a grandfather laid down his tools. Though we know not his name, the grandfather was a Ghosting—a wise one, known among his community as an elder.
"I cannot sow another seed."

◊

Bang!

◊

Crack!
The elder was struck dead.
And though he no longer sowed seeds, his death sowed dissent instead.
That evening the Ghostings gathered; men and women and musawa. Their anger brewed and bubbled and popped. They took their scythes and knives and fists to the walls of the Wardens' Keep.
Another elder came forward and spoke through the gates.
"We lay down our anger at your feet. We ask for dignity. We ask for equality of opportunity. We ask for our freedom."
And so the Ghostings dropped the weapons they had brought to reap, forging a barricade of metal no Ember could leave.
The wardens laughed from their towers and called down below.
"You ask for dignity, yet you drop your arms. You ask for equality of opportunity, yet your blood has no power. You ask for freedom, but you are our captors."
And so the Siege of the Silent began.

◊

Two mooncycles they protested. Two mooncycles they tried, peacefully, to influence change.

Now you wanted a villain? I'll give you a thousand.

Though the wardens were locked away, they had their guilds do their bidding. Over days and weeks they recruited foot soldiers and trained them.

◊

A thousand soldiers marched on the Ghostings and cut them down.

◊

Carved the rebels out of existence.

◊

And so the first warden army was made, quelling any dissent in the empire forever more.

What of the Ghostings? You know how it ends. With scars and servitude.

◊

And silence.

CHAPTER EIGHTEEN

TWENTY-SEVEN DAYS
UNTIL THE TRIAL OF TACTICS

1 chicken
4 onions
3 cloves of garlic
1 peppashito
8 large tomatoes

2 tablespoons groundnut oil
2 pints of chicken stock
2 handfuls of peanuts,
    ground to a paste
Salt and pepper to season

~ Fry off the chicken with the onions and garlic until golden
   brown.
~ Remove from heat.
~ Fry the peppashito and tomatoes in the groundnut oil.
~ Combine both pans and add the stock and peanut paste.
~ Simmer for one strike.

—Groundnut stew recipe from
Common Food for the Uncommon Chef

Sylah hadn't come home that night. Anoor sat awake listening to the sky howl into the early morning. The tidewind was fiercer than Anoor had ever heard. At one point a piece of debris dented the metal shutters, and she let out a high-pitched scream.

To distract herself, Anoor unrolled Sylah's map once more. She didn't need to look at it, not really. Every flourish of land, every swirl of a letter was burned into her mind with the force of her memory. She had spent countless nights thinking about the torn edges along the seams.

"Why would someone draw a map with more land on?" she

murmured to herself. She'd voiced the question to Sylah many times.

"How should I know? I've told you before, it's just a scrap of shit. Throw it away," she'd say. But Anoor saw how her eyes lingered on the edge. She was just as curious as Anoor, just as hopeful maybe?

With a sigh Anoor rolled the map away, admitting defeat for the night. The tidewind had calmed, and she lifted her shutters and looked out at the morning light. A blue dust covered the horizon, but the city of Nar-Ruta still looked beautiful. Dew on her windows made the white villas sparkle, and the sky was filled with iridescent blue koris. It was dreamlike.

The Duster Quarter was already frothing with energy, an ant's nest in the distance. Sometimes she pretended that her family was still alive and lived in a villa down below. Her mother would make her fufu and groundnut stew with too much peppashito. Anoor had once asked Uka if she could try some fufu. Her mother said, "It is cheap plantation food and you eat enough food already."

Anoor began to cry, but for a moment she pretended it was from the food made by a mother she would never know. The spice made her eyes run because "mama *always* put in too much peppashito."

Anoor reached for a handkerchief from her bedside table. As she went to pull out the white cotton square, her fingers caught on the grooved edge of the false bottom of the drawer. She tugged on it, releasing the slip of wood that hid the object inside.

It had been a while since Anoor had read the journal, and her fingers shook as she ran her fingers over the blood-red leather.

The spine creaked as it opened to the page she read over and over.

I looked at the bodies of the Sandstorm for any likeness of my true daughter, but their bodies were mere shreds of meat by the time I investigated the site.

Now the hunt is over I can turn my attention to the maggot they left behind. The girl grows wider instead of higher, and despite my punishments, she refuses to excel in any of her studies. I follow the same regime that was placed on me and while I grew stronger, she grows weaker. Like the Duster she is.

I wake every morn and wonder if today is the day the maggot should die. But the predicament stands, if a warden cannot protect her own, how can she protect the empire? No one must know that my house was violated by the Sandstorm, my true daughter taken. I am an emblem of strength and, though I regret to acknowledge it, the maggot is an extension of all that I stand for. Her disappearance or death would put my influence at risk. I can hear Aveed, the incessant Disciple of Duty, questioning me now. So instead I will harden my punishment toward the girl and try to shape her into someone worthy of my approval.

Do maggots see in the dark?

Fat plops of tears landed on the page, smearing the black ink. Anoor would never see her family again.

"Mere shreds of meat . . ." It churned her stomach with grief and horror.

One of the laws the Warden of Truth had instigated many centuries ago was the requirement for all wardens and disciples to document their daily lives. The journals were then preserved in the warden library for future generations to learn from. But the library was kept locked, only accessed by bloodwerk attuned to the wardens themselves.

She hadn't accessed the library by choice when she had stolen the journal. Blood recognizes blood, but it would never recognize hers. Because she had the blue blood of the Sandstorm. She was a child of the greatest revolution the empire had ever seen. They thought it quelled, but how could it be with Anoor living and breathing in the center of the Keep.

"I'm not a maggot," Anoor growled out and snapped the book closed. Her mother hadn't looked closely enough. She was a caterpillar, and at some point, she would fly.

I can do this. Not just for me, but for the family I never knew. Maybe I can make them proud somehow.

She hid the journal away; it was stolen property and no matter who her mother was, she'd be punished. And she dreaded to think what her mother would do if she found out she had taken it.

Anoor returned her gaze to the window, her face dry of tears, her back straight. She looked beyond the Duster Quarter and beyond to the plantation fields. The map tugged at the corner of her vision on the desk by her side, but she'd exhausted herself from staring at *that* corner.

An old song called to her from the edge of her memories. She'd once heard the launderers sing it while they worked, though the echo of it was familiar to her as if she wasn't learning the words, merely unveiling them from her mind. She thought it was from before, but she couldn't be sure. She'd only been two years old.

She let it out. Softly. Slowly.

O-o the tidewind came from sky afar
The penance for the blood power.
Anyme sings, Anyme brings

The winds wept for the sky they knew
The Farsai Desert mourned anew
Churning rivers, swirling seas,
No mercy from the bruising breeze.

O-o the tidewind came from sky afar
The penance for the blood power.
Anyme sings, Anyme brings

Smoke and fire, they do bow
For the tidewind is here and now
Here and now 'til atonement's paid
The debt for power is the trade.

O-o the tidewind came from sky afar
The penance for the blood power.
Anyme sings, Anyme brings

Its cleansing wind that leaves us bare.
Succumb to nightfall and be judged fair.
The tidewind takes, the tidewind gives
Here and now, and so we live.

Anoor shivered, though the morning was warm, her own singing haunting her. She thought again of the warden library. What if there was something in there that could tell her more about the Ending Fire?

ANOOR WASN'T SURE how much time had passed as she looked out of the window, but she saw a murky orange smudge in the distance. It was Sylah, walking with sure and confident steps up through the courtyard below. Anoor let out a sigh of relief, followed by a hum of jealousy and tightening in her chest. *Where had Sylah been?*

Anoor wrapped her arms around herself and clung onto her elbows. It was time for a bath. It solved everything. Plus, she didn't want Sylah to think she'd been waiting for her to come home.

She poured a generous amount of scented oil into the marble tub. The pipes were adorned with various runes, and the plumbing was connected to a vat in the kitchens that pushed water straight into the bath.

As it filled up, Anoor collected her ointments and sponges. She chimed out a laugh when she realized half of them had been emptied by Sylah. She ought to have been more annoyed, but the memory of Sylah using shampoo as body lotion put a smile on her face.

Anoor was beneath the suds when Sylah finally made her way up to her chambers. From her light footsteps she clearly thought Anoor would still be asleep.

Anoor had left the privy door open and called through it.

"Good night?" Anoor tried to sound light in an attempt to hide the tension that had kept her up all evening. Sylah hated when Anoor showed emotion.

Sylah's tired face appeared through the doorway. She scowled when she saw where Anoor was.

"Get out, we're going for a run."

"No, we're not, I'm taking a day off today. And by the looks of it, you should too."

Sylah's scowl deepened, though Anoor noted how beautiful she looked, even with her smudged makeup and still fully clothed in the now crumpled orange suit she had given her. "My body isn't functioning entirely like it used to. I may have tried someone's home brew . . ."

"I told you that your withdrawal is going to last a while."

"I wouldn't have to if it wasn't for you."

Anoor didn't have the mental stamina to engage in the same fight again and again. The silence was filled with the sound of Anoor topping up the tub with hot water.

Sylah watched the water swirl with gleaming, tired eyes. Anoor couldn't help but wonder what exactly the cause of her exhaustion was. The tightness in her chest returned.

"There's room enough for two, you know. You look like you need it," Anoor suggested, her eyes downcast.

"I'll wait until you've finished if that's okay with you." There was a fleeting look of what Anoor thought was disgust on Sylah's face. It made her dip deeper in the water. Every day Anoor got more and more curious about Sylah. Where had she grown up? Who was this man to her?

"Who was he?" she blurted out without thinking.

Sylah didn't answer for a while. "An old family friend."

"Where do you know him—"

Sylah shut the bathroom door with a bang, leaving Anoor with the silence of her thoughts.

WHEN SYLAH WOKE, Anoor had gone, but her maddening scent had remained. Sandalwood, it was everywhere.

A fresh jug of water was on the nightstand next to the bed. Sylah ignored the glass and downed the jug in a few gulps. Her head was pounding behind her eyes, and she was sorely tempted to go back to sleep. It wasn't until she heard the clockmaster cry second strike that she realized that she'd missed her daily meeting with Jond.

"Oh, shit, I hope he doesn't read into that." First, she'd snuck out at first light without telling him, then she'd missed their daily lesson on bloodwerk. She let her head fall back onto the pillow, and her brain rattled in her skull.

The door opened without a knock.

"I'm not an idiot, I know you went to the banquet last night," Gorn trumpeted into the room, and Sylah groaned.

"I certainly did, if this headache is anything to go by."

"That is not proper for a servant."

"Why? I saw at least a dozen servants had entered the Aktibar, any Ember can enter . . ."

"You are not a competitor, you are Miss Elsari's personal servant."

"Exactly, her *personal* servant. She wanted me there, so if you have a problem with it, take it up with her."

"Oh, I assure you, I will. And if you continue to be a nuisance, I will raise the issue with the warden. I'm sure she'll be extremely interested in how you are bringing down the Elsaris' reputation."

Sylah sat up so suddenly, her brain took a while to catch up. Uka was not good news. If she believed Sylah posed a threat to her reputation, Sylah would be out. That meant Jond would be out.

Sylah couldn't let down the Sandstorm again.

"Every day at ninth strike you will report to me. Now that Anoor's classes have been paused for the Aktibar, I will be here to monitor you. You will work for me until first strike, then for the rest of the day Anoor can use you as she wishes. This is the deal we must agree upon."

Sylah nodded, there was nothing else she could do.

"First you need to cut your hair; it has grown too long for a servant."

Sylah's hand reached for her phantom plaits but caught on the uneven tufts of curls that had grown over the last four weeks. It wasn't much, but it was enough to make her status ambiguous.

"Shave and then meet me in my room. I have a list of errands for you."

Sylah scrubbed her face with cold water. Her eyes were red-rimmed but clear, her cheeks still a little too hollow but getting there. The food in the Keep was certainly helping.

She rummaged in Anoor's cabinet for a razor and lathered her head with soap. Then she carefully began to run the blade against the direction of the hair.

"Need some help?" Anoor appeared in the corner of the mirror, making Sylah jump and nick herself.

"Maiden's tits, you've only gone and stopped my bloody heart."

"Sorry."

"Where've you been?"

Anoor waved a stack of zines at her in response.

"How's your head?"

"Bleeding," Sylah answered, knowing that wasn't what she meant.

"Here, let me." Anoor took the blade from Sylah's hand and guided her to the edge of the marble bathtub.

With soft, delicate fingers Anoor's hands worked the lather into Sylah's scalp. Sylah felt her back arching into her touch. With sure, even strokes Anoor ran the blade through her short curls. A soft hum slipped out of Sylah, and she covered it with a cough.

When she was done, Anoor circled Sylah, her eyes assessing her handiwork.

"There, all done."

Her breath smelled of sandalwood too.

"Thank you," Sylah said. She regretted it as Anoor beamed at her. Over the last few weeks Sylah had found herself warming to Anoor no matter how hard she tried to resist it.

Sylah pushed past her and went to get changed into her uniform.

Gorn was true to her word and kept Sylah scrubbing, mopping, scraping for four strikes of the clock. When dinnertime tolled, Sylah went down to the kitchens to sup with the other servants for the first time.

The kitchen was made up of four brick archways, each filled with a roaring hearth where food bubbled and sizzled for the court above. Three long tables that seated at least two hundred ran across the back walls, where soup was being ladled out to the servants in waiting. The Ghostings who were serving the meal had their elbows hooked under the curved handles of the ladles, their forearm muscles straining.

It didn't look as good as the groundnut stew Lio made, but it had chicken pieces, and meat was hard to come by in the Duster Quarter.

The atmosphere was relaxed and jovial, Embers laughing and Ghostings signing to one another. An unknown muscle relaxed in her back, and Sylah felt herself at ease for the first time in a long while. Her time as a servant weighed on her shoulders, subjugation cowering her more and more each day. Though she was treated better than the Ghosting servants she had seen around the Keep, she was still bound by obedience to the Ember upper class. In the kitchens no one cared. She was invisible, just one of them.

Just one of them.

The thought struck her like one of her seizures, and she faltered. She wasn't one of them, though, not really. She had a Duster's heart. She needed to remember that. Her fingers gripped her bowl of soup—white ceramic. If traded it would have fed a Duster family for a week.

She looked around the kitchens one more time with a brittle stare: the fires, the sizzling meats, the freshly roasted coffee.

This is luxury.

Anoor's extravagant lifestyle had skewed her judgment for a time, but she wasn't going to forget the poverty she came from.

Sylah walked to the far end of the tables away from the others. For the last six years, she'd gotten used to being avoided, her red-stained teeth a sure sign of trouble. Even in the Dredge people crossed the street to avoid her. Now that the stains had faded, she no longer had that deterrent. So when a group of young servants came to sit near her, Sylah was unsettled.

"My money's on Efie for Disciple of Strength."

Sylah bowed over her soup and began to slurp noisily. The food was so bland she nearly spat it out, even the chicken didn't improve it. Had she gotten used to Anoor's fare so quickly?

"Efie, the imir of Jin-Gernomi's granddaughter? Are you joking? She might be all muscle, but she's had no formal training in the warden army, she'll fail tactics for sure."

"I bet you six slabs Efie wins."

"I'll take that bet."

"Aho, and me."

"Yeah, me too."

"I'm not betting against all of you."

"Well, you shouldn't have made a stupid bet then."

On and on they bickered, and Sylah hunkered deeper and deeper into her soup.

"Would you all shut up." She said it softly at first, trying not to rattle the pain between her eyes. Then they continued, louder than before.

So she bellowed, "Skies above! You're like a group of launderers. Will you take your chatter elsewhere and leave me to eat my meal in peace?"

After throwing looks of disdain her way, they didn't take long to leave. There was silence after that. Sylah smiled.

"Nice work." One boy hadn't left. He seemed older than Sylah by a year or two. His dark skin was pockmarked, his shaven head a little knobbly, but he had kind eyes. Sylah wasn't interested in kindness today.

Sylah mustered as much venom as she could and turned her gaze to him. "Yes?"

"Hello, I'm Kwame. Not seen you here before."

"No, you won't have."

"I think I recognize you. Are you Anoor's—I mean, Miss Elsari's—new chambermaid?"

Sylah went back to eating her soup. Salt, it needed salt.

"Will you tell her I asked after her? I hope she's doing well. I can't believe she signed up for the Aktibar. Her aerofield skills were really quite impressive."

At least the bread wasn't stale.

"She won't mind me asking after her, you see we're friends, she and I."

"Friends?"

He jumped as if spooked. "Oh, well, yes."

"She doesn't have any friends." Anoor being friends with a servant was ludicrous. "What do you do around here?"

"I'm the baker."

"Great. Can you get me some more bread?"

He nearly rose from his seat. "I'm not your servant." He laughed.

He should have been. Sylah put down her spoon.

"Kwame, can I ask, how does an Ember like yourself end up a servant in the Keep?"

He frowned, making his wide brow look even wider. "I chose duty and got assigned here."

"What are you, twenty-two, twenty-three? Why haven't you risen through the ranks?"

"Ah . . ." His eyes flickered left and right, looking for an exit.

"Oh, I see, you're incompetent."

That rattled him; he pushed his chest higher, his chin tilted back. "No, I just wasn't born into an imir family."

The answer confused Sylah. She'd never really considered wealth to be a decisive factor in an Ember's life. They had all seemed so powerful to her; certainly they were all wealthier than Dusters. Papa ingrained in them that every single Ember was part of an infection that riddled the body of the empire. And when a limb grows rotten and gangrenous, what must you do? Amputate.

They might have luxury, but did they truly have freedom? she thought as she chewed the last piece of bread with her mouth open.

"Besides, I like being a baker. But it does make me wonder why you're a chambermaid, though." He looked her up and down as he stood. "Perhaps you're incompetent?" He stepped over the bench and was gone.

Sylah snorted at his retreating back. She liked him after all.

CHAPTER NINETEEN

TWENTY-SIX DAYS
UNTIL THE TRIAL OF TACTICS

General Ahmed has died fighting a treasonous uprising that occurred in the cotton plantations of Jin-Noon. Born in Nar-Ruta in the year 377, Ahmed Alyar was second cousin to the imir of Jin-Crolah. He joined the warden army at the age of twenty and rose through the ranks to the most revered position of general, below that of his leader of the guild—the most revered Warden of Strength. He is survived by a daughter, Anoor, age seven, and his spouse, Disciple Uka Elsari.

Bless his journey to the sky as he takes up his place next to our God, Anyme.

—Obituary of General Ahmed, *The People's Gazette*, year 407

"Why weren't you at dinner?" Anoor was waiting straight-backed on her bed.

"I had it in the kitchens, like a proper servant." Sylah was tired. The day had been a long one.

"Why?"

"Gorn and I had a chat." Sylah sank onto the bed next to Anoor. She didn't need to look to feel Anoor's soft eyes gazing at her.

"Oh, she curdles my insides sometimes, I'll talk to her."

"Don't." Sylah laid a hand on Anoor's thigh. "It's fine, it's the way it's supposed to be."

Anoor was looking at Sylah's hand on her thigh and smiled. Sylah pulled away, aware of the warmth of Anoor's skin on her palm.

"We have less than four weeks until the tactics trial," Sylah said.

"Can't we have another night off?" Anoor whined.

"No, we don't know what terrain the trial will be held on, so we need to study them all. You've struggled to pick up the basic principles so far, and we need to get this right." Sylah made her way into their little training room, Anoor followed halfheartedly.

"What does tactics even mean?"

"Tactics is the strategy that achieves a goal. And your goal is to win."

Anoor sat cross-legged, and Sylah paced back and forth in front of her.

"Every tactics trial has been a team task, pitting one side against the other in unexpected terrain, and the losing team is removed from the competition."

"How will I know what to practice, if I don't know what the terrain will look like?"

"That's why we've got to practice it all. You won't find out until the day of the trial."

"Hmm." Anoor sucked on her bottom lip. "I think for the last Aktibar my mother's tactics trial was based out in the desert and her team had to steal an eru from the other team and lead it back to their base."

"Exactly, it could be anywhere, at any time. In buildings, in a lake . . . and the treasure could be an eru, crown, shoe . . . they've used all sorts of things over the last few decades, but that's not the important bit. The main thing is to understand the maneuvers and approaches that will guarantee your win. You will need to work as a team while also ensuring you don't get injured. On average only thirty make it through to the next round, despite there being fifty spaces. We will review all the previous tactics trials as well as the warden army approach to skirmishes up and down the empire, to truly understand the technique to success. Tactics is very simple really, it's all about understanding the enemy and figuring out the best strategy to attack."

"How do you know so much about the Aktibar?" Anoor's eyes were wide. Wider than usual, that is.

Sylah looked deep into them.

"My . . . father was interested in it. He told me the stories before he died."

"Tell me about him."

PAPA WAS ANGRY today. They all knew to avoid him when he was angry. When he was angry, he broke things, broke bones. "All so the spirit can mend stronger," he would say in his apology later. Sylah had loved him more in those moments.

The Stolen got good at hiding.—

"No."

Anoor recoiled as if struck. It was a look Sylah was sick of seeing, like *she* was the victim.

"He died . . . I don't like to talk about it."

An almost imperceptible nod of understanding. "That's okay."

Sylah had never asked about Anoor's own father, but she'd learned from Hassa that he died when she was just seven.

"Anyway, like I said, I think we should study the previous Aktibar. I'll draw out the formations and we can study each one." Sylah had memorized them all by the age of eight.

A strike later, Sylah was still trying to convey the simplest of approaches.

"No, believe it or not 'more people' isn't the reason Harriat's team won. Look at the way they moved. What is it called?"

Anoor screwed her face up. A dumpling puckered for steaming.

"I just told you, it's called the center peel."

"It's confusing, you've drawn five blobs on the page. Can you not write the names beneath them until I understand them?"

"Just remember them." Sylah started drawing out another strategy.

"Can you just put the names at the top of the paper? What's wrong with that?"

Sylah exhaled through her nose. She closed her eyes and visualized the letters in her mind. Writing couldn't be that hard, after all. She knew how to read, so it was just copying that exact pattern—

Anoor laughed, and it was like a shard of glass in her heart.

"What is that supposed to say?" Anoor still chuckled until she saw the look on Sylah's face. Her mirth slowly turned to horror . . . then the worst thing . . . pity.

Sylah threw the pen on the floor and stormed out of the dressing room.

"Stop it, stop that right now," Sylah hissed at Anoor, who had followed her into the bedroom.

"Stop what?" She laid her hand on Sylah's lower back.

Sylah wanted to shrug her off, but she didn't, she let her hand linger. There was something raw and vulnerable in the soft spot below one's ribs.

"The pity, I can't bear it."

"I didn't realize. I'm sorry, I didn't know you couldn't write the common tongue. You manage to write the runes so well, I just didn't think." Anoor looked shocked. She should be; Sylah and Jond were probably the only two Embers who didn't know how to write in the whole of the empire. "I don't understand, why didn't you go to school?"

Because she'd been taught by Dusters, and Dusters weren't taught how to write, they barely got an education at all. Their schooling ended at ten years old when they went for their branding.

Anoor waited for Sylah to speak, to think.

"Papa . . . he didn't know how to either, none of us did. So no one could teach us."

Anoor nodded, though she clearly wanted to ask more. "It's even more impressive that you picked up the bloodwerk runes so quickly."

"Practice." Sylah smiled.

"I wish . . . I wish you would tell me what happened to you." Anoor must have seen something in Sylah's face, as she quickly added, "Eventually, eventually." She patted Sylah's hand. "Every day we'll do a strike of training, a strike of bloodwerk and a strike of writing. You'll pick it up in no time."

Gratitude lifted the corners of Sylah's lips.

She's giving me a gift, expecting nothing in return. The thought perturbed Sylah until she realized it was because this had never happened to her before. Her eyes shone as they met Anoor's. Their eyes locked and a spark, not unlike the prickling of withdrawal, spread down her spine.

Anoor looked away first, her eyes slipping toward the paper Sylah had been drawing on.

"The shapes look a bit like a shantra board." She tilted her head to the left as she surveyed the paper.

Sylah scoffed and opened her mouth to retort. Then she paused and grabbed Anoor's wrists. "You have got a brain in there after all!"

Anoor grinned widely despite the insult.

"I do?"

"Yes. Do you have a shantra board?"

"No." Anoor's shoulders drooped. "But I know where we can get one."

"Lead the way."

ANOOR LED SYLAH to her favorite place in the Keep. They walked through the cloisters—where the clockmaster informed Anoor it was half a strike past ten at night—toward the western side of the Keep where the library was.

"Hello again, Bisma," Anoor greeted the librarian.

"Oh hello, Miss Elsari." Red sauce coated his mustache from the stuffed flatbread in his hand. His eyes slipped over Sylah as if she weren't there. Sometimes Anoor forgot she was a servant in everyone's eyes. Anoor wondered if it galled her.

"You here to enter the tournament?"

"Just to watch, actually."

"Go on through then, it's a tense one today."

Sylah snorted beside her.

Between the racks of books and forgotten words was a collection of tables. Sometimes Anoor sat there to read the latest zine when she couldn't wait to go all the way back to her chambers. Sylah pulled a face as she surveyed the library.

Every third night between the strikes of nine and ten a group of servants came down to play shantra.

There were eight of them today, two groups of four, clustered around two boards. The silence was fraught with a thoughtful tension.

"Fucking skies above, *this* is what servants spend their nights doing?"

They all looked up at Sylah's rude intervention. Eight faces split in a scowl.

"Sorry," Anoor said on Sylah's behalf as she dropped her eyes to her feet.

"Anoor!"

Anoor knew that rich, deep voice, like morning coffee. She raised her gaze to Kwame's smiling face.

"Oh, I hoped you might be here." Kwame used to be Anoor's shantra partner, as the game required four players.

"You haven't played in mooncycles. We've missed you." His competitors were glaring at him, waiting for him to make the next move, but too polite to interrupt the warden's daughter.

Sylah wasn't too polite to interrupt. "Is there a spare board we could use?"

"Of course, they're all Anoor's anyway." Kwame said. "Hi by the way." He added a greeting to Sylah, which shocked Anoor until she remembered once again—Sylah was a servant.

"What does he mean they're all yours?" Sylah asked Anoor.

"Nothing," Anoor mumbled.

"She bought them all," a young girl added; Anoor was ashamed to say she didn't remember her name. "And sorted out this space in the library for us to play. The kitchens can get a bit noisy."

Sylah was looking at Anoor, and it brought out beads of sweat on her brow.

Anoor imagined what Sylah was thinking: this sad girl had to *pay* servants to be her friends? Anoor felt her skin heat up with embarrassment as she thought of her life before Sylah. Loneliness had gnawed at her heart, and she drifted, purposeless, with a few small pleasures like shantra, clothes, and jewelry. Oh, and food. She missed fried food desperately.

Anoor hunched her shoulders and went to pull out the stack of shantra boards. One of the other servants was instructing a new player, and Anoor listened in.

"A shantra board is made up of three different colors, patterned with diamonds. Each team has thirty-one counters, ten of each color and one black piece. The black piece is known as the egg." He held out a small black counter, which glittered. "The aim of the game is to steal the egg from the opposing team, but each counter can only move onto their corresponding color. And only red counters can collect the egg."

Fundamentally it was a game of strategy, and Anoor guessed that was why Sylah had asked about it. Anoor set up the board on the table next to Kwame.

"We need more players," Sylah said to the room, whose attention had gone back to their own games. Kwame looked up.

"I'll play, if you can wait until I finish here."

"Me too," said his partner, the young girl . . . Was her name Yero? Anoor really couldn't remember.

"Fine, we'll wait," Sylah said slumping into a chair.

Sylah surveyed the stacks around her. "This library is about as useful as a Ghosting singer," she grunted. "Embers really know how to run a library . . ."

"Why do you hate Embers so much?" Anoor asked quietly, slipping into a chair beside her.

"What?" The question took Sylah unawares. "I don't hate Embers." But Anoor wasn't sure that was true. "I *am* an Ember."

"But I've seen the way your face screws up when you see the court ride in on their erus. Is it because you're a servant and not part of the court?"

Sylah laughed. "No, I would rather be a servant than one of them."

"Then why?"

"I just think there's a lot of wealth this side of the river," was the sentence Sylah finally settled on.

"Not everyone is wealthy here."

"I'm not just talking about money," Sylah countered.

"But you can't hate people because of their blood color. It doesn't make sense."

A cockroach scuttled across the floor, and Sylah's foot flattened it with a crunch.

"That was disgusting."

"What, this?" Sylah presented the insect's entrails on the bottom of her foot, lifting it toward Anoor, who recoiled.

"Get it away from me."

"You've gone green."

"Because that's really repulsive."

"Repulsive?" Sylah cocked her head to the side. "White bone bursting from the thigh leaving the rest of the flesh looking like mincemeat . . . a runebullet bursting through a chest cavity . . . the film that covers the eyes of the dead when the life leaves them . . ."

Anoor lifted her hand to her mouth.

Sylah paused, thinking. "Maybe those things are repulsive."

"Have you seen those things?" Anoor's hand still hovered by her face, as if at any second it might be needed to contain her bile.

Sylah smiled, a wide smile that showed all her teeth, free from red blemishes. "Of course not." Sylah scraped the entrails on the leg of the chair. "But it isn't a very good library, is it?" Sylah put her feet up on the table, knocking some of the books off the edge.

"WE'RE READY," KWAME said, his voice a little tentative.

They played with Kwame and Wero—not Yero—until just before the tidewind. The other servants had to make it back to their homes in the Ember Quarter before the tidewind struck.

"See the way they approached the egg in the center? What does that look like to you?" Sylah had said during the first game.

Anoor looked at the formation, the two groups of counters on either side.

"Center peel," Anoor whispered. "Oh, it's just like the trial of tactics!"

"Exactly."

As soon as Kwame realized they were learning about military strategy for the tactics trial, he threw himself enthusiastically into the game. They swapped partners to "learn about teamwork," they cleared the board halfway through "to prepare for the unexpected," and they turned the board every new game to "adapt to new terrain."

Anoor immersed herself into every new challenge, and with each movement on the board she took herself one step closer to winning the next trial. She wouldn't go back to her old life. She couldn't.

Anoor learned more about tactics in that one night than she had in the four weeks prior. They went back to the library every third day after that.

HASSA WAS TIRED. She moved around the Maroon with hunched shoulders, her satchel bursting with goods, but no one buying. She moved the bag farther up her shoulder with her limb and slid her other wrist into the gaping belly of her bag. Her arm moved around, feeling the shapes of the objects inside with the soft bit of flesh at the end of her wrist.

Hassa didn't need fingers, no Ghosting did. Their shared disability meant there were few things that Ghostings hadn't adapted to use. Except threading a needle, though Hassa had gotten close once or twice. She hated that her money was spent at haberdasheries who took advantage of Ghostings' inability to sew.

Hassa felt for the remaining objects in her bag: tree gum, milk honey leaf, some crockery, and a bag of joba seeds. The last packet in her bag wasn't for sale. The dried leaves were the hormone herbs Hassa steeped in hot water twice a day to support the growth of the body that was right for her.

Hassa withdrew her limb and accidentally withdrew the bag of joba seeds. She hastened to place it back in the bag. Though she hated selling joba seeds, she knew half the people in the Maroon would happily claim the packet as their own.

It made her think of Sylah.

She missed her company, her sardonic quips, her unique ability to stumble through life without dying, despite the close calls Hassa had saved her from. But at the same time Hassa was relieved. Sylah was finally clean. She'd been trying to sell Sylah painted watermelon seeds for over a year, but she always figured it out. And Sylah had said it herself: "If you don't take my money, someone else will," and Hassa needed the money for the elders.

Marigold arrived, their eyes wide and blinking fast. It was rare to see Marigold this agitated; the musawa was the most level-headed person Hassa knew. Something was wrong.

They found them, they signed, their arms dashing back and forth over their torso with each fervent word.

What?

Hassa's eyes burned, but she didn't cry. Her signs were firm, slicing through the air with practicality. *Are the tunnels compromised?*

No, the army found them near the Lakes of Jin-Dinil. Marigold's mouth puckered in contempt.

How?

The pregnant one, she gave birth. Her cries called the officers. It gave them away.

Hassa grimaced. She had known the Ghosting was too pregnant to travel. *Did anyone survive?*

They took all the young ones who were yet to be maimed. They were sent straight to the abattoir. The rest were slaughtered. An example for any other Ghosting trying to flee the fate of our ancestors' penance.

Hassa bowed, a small gesture acknowledging all the lives lost.

We will need to find a new route out of the tunnels, somewhere far from the Central Lakes, Marigold continued.

Yes.

We'll need to make a few trips during the night, scout out the best route.

Yes. Hassa nodded assent again.

It's getting too dangerous.

Hassa didn't sign back, because she had heard them—the cause of their danger.

Thud. Thud. Thud.

Officers were above the Maroon.

Hassa pulled her satchel off her shoulder and threw it into the chaos of bodies in the center of the dance floor. The dancers had heard the boots too; they knew what was coming.

"It's a raid!"

"A raid! Quick, hide the firerum."

"Under the hatch."

"Grab the joba seeds, swallow them!"

The Maroon door was kicked open with excessive force. There was a moment where everyone held their breath as the officers made their way down the stairs.

The purple blazers of the army rippled out across the tavern.

"Empty pockets, empty bags, I want to see everything you've got. And if you're hiding anything, we will find it. We will search you down to your marrow," the captain of the platoon shouted. His short curls were twisted into coils above a thick brow and strong jawline. He would have been attractive if he didn't hold everyone's life in his hands.

Hassa shivered, and Marigold touched her arm.

Keep your eyes lowered now, child.

Hassa knew the routine: be as invisible as you can be.

There were twelve officers working under the captain's orders, and they began to probe the quaking Dusters and Ghostings with practiced brutality. Hands grabbed and slapped and punched. Runeguns were pointed left and right—Hassa was sure that if they used bloodwerk to release the bullets, they'd hit everyone including themselves.

It had been years since the Maroon was last raided. The officers often kept their violent intrusions to single dwellings or taverns not frequented by Loot's Gummers.

Hassa saw the outline of black, shiny boots enter her vision. Her dirty toes curled over the lip of her too-small rubber sandals. She felt the officer's hot breath on her shaven scalp.

"Hello there, Ghostings. Not peddling your junk today?" His small hands slithered over Hassa's baggy uniform searching for hidden pockets.

Hassa shook her head slowly, with purpose. No sudden movements.

His hand ran along the kente waistband in the colors of the Keep.

"Servant for the wardens, are we?"

Sometimes, Hassa thought, but she didn't respond.

The officer kicked her in the shin.

"You really are the dregs of the empire. Even if you had a tongue, I bet you couldn't talk. Too stupid."

Eventually the officer moved on.

Hassa added her rage to the burning coals that were always glowing white in her mind. Ghostings were the dregs of the empire because Embers made them that way. Even Dusters thought they were lesser. They were all wrong. They didn't know the truth.

Hassa saw a glint of gold from the corner of her eye as one of the Gummers presented his crime guild token to the captain with a confident swagger. The captain reached for the coin in the Gummer's outstretched hand.

"You think this cheap bit of metal's going to save you? Don't give a shit who you are." The token was thrown to the sticky ground, not far from Hassa's satchel.

The Gummer's mouth fell open to reveal bright red teeth.

"But I'm a Gummer, I work for the Warden of Crime. You normally"—he looked around and dropped his voice—"let us go."

"Aho, do we now? Saying we're corrupt, are you?" The captain pressed the nose of his runegun into the Gummer's jugular.

"N . . . n . . . no of course not."

"Oh, I see. You're saying the Warden of Strength is corrupt?"

"No!"

"Officers, I think we have a defamation trial on our hands. Fetch the Starting Drum. This one's going on the rack."

There was an inhale of breath as the Gummer collapsed to the ground at his sentence.

"The rack? But he didn't do anything!" someone whispered, someone naive.

Someone stupid.

The captain turned to the voice, but when he couldn't identify them from the group, he turned back to the Gummer on the floor.

"Someone inform the ripper," the captain said with a wide smile. The officers' answering grins were slices of white in the darkness of the Maroon.

They dragged the Gummer out, the officers pushing and kicking anyone who got in their way.

Hassa's breathing was still shallow long after they had gone.

Hassa? Marigold had retrieved her satchel with their feet, offering Hassa the strap between their sandaled toes. Hassa reached for it and slipped the pack over her head.

At least they didn't take your wares.

Hassa nodded, her fear thawing.

I have to go back to Maiden Turin's, but I'll see you later? To scout the new route?

Hassa's eyes slipped to the pool of urine the Gummer had left.

Yes, we need to find another way out of this bloodforsaken city.

CHAPTER TWENTY

SIXTEEN DAYS
UNTIL THE TRIAL OF TACTICS

This Act makes provisions for the disclosure of information held by wardens and their disciples during their term as leaders of the Wardens' Empire. During their tenure, all wardens and disciples must document, to the fullest degree, their daily lives under the laws enacted by the guild of truth. This legislation will provide learning and insight for the future leaders of our empire and be stored exclusively for their use.

In the eyes of our God, Anyme, may this be so.

—Legacy Rights Act, year 216

The days passed by in a steady rhythm of work and training. The regime, so different from Sylah's life from six weeks ago, took a toll on her body and mind. She was deathly tired. Not the kind of tired that had her falling asleep in doorways, but the satisfying kind, like a hard day in the field.

If she wasn't thinking about bloodwerk runes, she was thinking about shantra; if she wasn't thinking about shantra, she was thinking about Anoor's combat training. And if her mind wasn't full already, Gorn would pile on yet another thing, and suddenly she was struggling to recollect which color soap was for silk and which was for cotton.

Bet Papa didn't think that laundry would be a part of my mission. The smile was still playing around her lips as she climbed the steps to the water tower.

Jond was already there, the noonday sun warming his skin to a deep bronze. The wind whipped around his face, ruffling his curly hair into a frenzy around him. Sylah found herself grateful for her shaven scalp. He gave her a lazy smile, and her stomach flipped.

"How's it hurting?"

"Not bad." Sylah settled her skirt around her on the stone ground. "I've got some new runes to teach you. I learned the one known as repetition last night, so we can now make runelamps."

"Great, maybe we can start a glasskeep together, selling globes."

They laughed, their imagination conjuring the unlikely image.

Jond sobered. "Before we begin, the Sandstorm have a message."

"Skies above, finally we can stop this secrecy nonsense. When do I get to meet the new leader?"

Jond shifted his feet.

"You don't. Not yet. They have a task for you."

"A task? I'm a bit busy fulfilling the last one." Sylah waved her hand at their inkwells.

"And they appreciate that," he conceded with a tilt of his head. "I told them that you wanted in, that you wanted to be part of the rebellion again, but they don't trust you. Not yet. I warned you this would happen."

"How can they not trust me?"

"It's not the same, Sylah. It's different from what you remember. Papa . . . Azim, he was weak."

"Weak? Papa was weak? That's not what I remember. I remember a warrior who toiled and toiled to hone us into what we are: weapons."

"He was too emotional, he loved us. You know how love makes you do . . . crazy things." He avoided her eye.

"Papa also used pain to manipulate and hurt us into submission every day."

Jond frowned, ignoring Sylah's comment. "We are harder now. We don't let emotions hold us back."

Sylah couldn't bring herself to respond. Irony held her tongue in its grasp.

"There's a library in the Keep, where the wardens stow all their secrets."

"What?"

"Journals," he explained. "It's required by the Warden of Truth. An account of their days."

"You want me to steal books that document what the wardens eat for dinner?"

Jond exhaled through his nose. "The journals document everything, every thought, feeling, belief."

Sylah thought of the library in the Keep where they played shantra. There was no way a warden had ever stepped foot in there.

"Where is it?"

"In the business district, opposite the warden's offices."

"Are you joking?" The task was ludicrous. Impossible.

"They appreciate it's a hard task. But it has to be to show your total dedication to the cause. Your last actions . . . left their mark."

"That was six years ago, Jond."

He nodded, not very deeply.

"They'd like the most recent journals from the current wardens." Jond spread his hands wide, as if to say he did everything he could.

Sylah got up and started to pace.

"I'm not sure I understand." She so desperately wanted to pull on her braids, to yank out her frustration at the root. "First, they find you, not me, and train *you* for the Aktibar. Secondly, they send you to get me to sign up for the Aktibar. Thricely—and yes, I just used the word 'thricely,' Anoor told me it's a word—they won't let me officially rejoin until I complete some sort of task?"

Jond shrugged. "We're the Final Strife, Sylah, it's not our place to question."

The Final Strife. The words tugged on the invisible leash between herself and the Sandstorm. A Sandstorm she no longer knew. It was the reason she was here, teaching Jond to bloodwerk, it was the reason she had given up her quest for oblivion—which she'd been good at too.

Red beads of ecstasy flickered beneath her eyelids when she blinked and her mouth filled with saliva. Her tongue probed the gap between her teeth. The hole ached.

But now the Sandstorm want . . . more.

Sylah cricked her neck, the muscles rippling over the scar at the bottom of her hairline. She felt the tautness of the invisible leash go slack, just a little.

"Maiden's tits, we're just pieces on a shantra board, aren't we? Is this really the Sandstorm you want to be a part of, Jond?"

He was silent for some time, watching her with unreadable eyes as she stood in front of him with her hands on her hips.

"No, the Sandstorm I wanted to be a part of is dead." He said the words softly, but Sylah recognized the undertone of accusation. "But these people, they believe too, they believe in us."

"Us? You mean you. I'm just a thief, it seems."

Jond's hand reached for her and clung on to her wrist, *hard*.

"Us," he said firmly. "You can't turn away from what you were trained for. The Stolen, you and me, we are the last hope at bringing down the Embers. Just because you won't be warden doesn't mean you don't have a part to play in the plan."

"The plan?" Sylah scoffed. "What do you know of Papa's plan?"

"There is and was only ever one plan, Sylah: an end to all Embers."

Sylah nodded, but her mind bubbled with unexpected thoughts.

She thought of what Kwame had said to her, about how he'd had no choice in his career. More choice than Dusters and Ghostings, but still, it wasn't what Sylah had expected. Did he deserve to die too? The wardens, yes, but the servants?

"And how will the Sandstorm achieve it? When you're in power?"

Jond thought for less than a blink. "There are steps we will take."

"Tell me." Maybe they would spare those like Kwame.

Jond didn't respond.

"Jond?" Oh, to have a joba seed.

Still, his lips pressed shut into an impenetrable line.

The secrecy galled her. She was one of them. She was a Stolen. She had fought and bled and burned for the Sandstorm. Maybe not in the last six years, but she was making up for it, she was trying.

Her anger dissipated, replaced by guilt. These were her people; it wasn't her place to question. They were trying to make a difference.

"Fine."

Reluctantly Jond's lips parted, and Sylah watched them. "They want the journals before your contract with Anoor ends."

Sylah nodded. Disobedience wasn't an option. Without the Sandstorm she would drift back to her old life, and though it called to her every day, fighting for the Sandstorm was more important than that. It gave her hope that there was a way out of the empire's current existence.

She looked in the direction of the plantation fields. Though she couldn't see them, she felt the pain that emanated from there like a second pulse. She'd been attuned to it from a young age.

The Sandstorm *needed* to fight the empire. If not, everything she was doing, every second she spent with Anoor, was wasted. The thought unsettled her more than anything Jond had said.

Love may give you strength, but retribution gives you purpose.

"HAVE YOU SEEN Hassa?" she asked the first Ghosting servant she saw. They shook their head in response. She asked another.

"Hassa, she's short, kind of pointy-faced, not ugly, though. Actually, yeah, I think she's pretty— No?"

And another.

"Hassa, she's small, seventeen years old?"

Nothing. No one would help her or point her in the right direction. Hassa was the one person who would know exactly how to get into the warden library—Ghostings could get anywhere.

Sylah missed her friend more than the joba seeds she'd carried. Maybe.

At the Sanctuary, Sylah had had lots of foster siblings. It wasn't the same as a normal family, though she had little to compare it to. Each faction was close due to the grueling regime the Sandstorm put them through, and there was a healthy (she did wonder if that was the right word) competition between knowledge, strength, duty, and truth. Each thought their guild the better. Just like the wardens themselves.

But there was one Stolen whom Sylah felt true sister feelings for: Fareen. She chewed her lip, bit her tongue, bared her teeth, anything to stop the memory that threatened to—

SYLAH HAD HATED Fareen. Fareen followed her around, copied what she did, tried to sneak away with Jond and Sylah all the time.

She was sweet, sickly sweet, always bringing Sylah little gifts she thought she'd like: a stick in the shape of a knife, a piece of whitestone, an extra portion of fried plantain she'd been given in the kitchens—because no one said no to Fareen.

She didn't have the face you'd imagine, she didn't have the soft eyes of Papa or the easy laugh like Jond. Her eyes were small, like two round pebbles in a face a little too long. Her cheeks were hollow, making her gangly stature seem more skeleton-like. A raised scar ran down the side of her cheek, a remnant from her before-life, where no one could attest the cause. But her smile was where her personality lived. It was kind, thoughtful, a little tentative.

It was her smile that had finally brought Sylah around. She loved Fareen fiercely.

"I brought you a kori feather." Fareen was nine when she presented Sylah with her gift. "It's a tailfeather," she rushed on. "I found it while I was tapping rubber."

Sylah was braiding her hair into little chains around her head. Lio had handed over the task to her gladly, and Sylah didn't miss the yanking of her scalp as Lio braided. Sylah's plaits weren't as neat, but at least her skull didn't feel bruised for days afterward.

"That's pretty." And it was; the blue color shone in the morning light.

"The iridescence is caused by light waves combining with one another, it's a phenomenon known as interference." Fareen's knowledge was never condescending; it was as if she was in awe herself of the things she found in her head. Sylah had often thought that she should have been training for knowledge instead of strength like she and Jond were.

"Interesting," Sylah said. "Shall we put it in your hair?"

"Oh, no, Sylah, it's a gift for you, shall we put it in your hair?"

Sylah smiled. "Okay."
That was the first piece that she braided into her hair.

Sylah now wanted a joba seed more than she wanted her friend. She gave up looking and headed back to the launderers, stopping at the kitchen for a mug of verd leaf tea.

THREE DAYS LATER and Sylah still hadn't found Hassa. Instead, she threw herself into Anoor's training. After all, if Anoor didn't continue to the final, Sylah wouldn't know enough bloodwerk to ensure Jond got there too. There'd be no "plan" without Jond as disciple.

Anoor's skills improved. She mastered most of the Dambe boxing exercises and some Laambe open-hand techniques, though they were as pretty as an eru turd. The Nuba formations were still beyond her, but she managed to master a semblance of the meditative state of battle wrath.

"When are we going to start using real weapons?" She waved the broomstick in Sylah's face.

"That doesn't seem like focus to me."

"I mean it, why can't we fight with real metal?"

"We can start training with real weapons when you can knock me off my feet." Sylah laid the challenge out while she leaned on her own weapon, a smelly mop.

"You promise? If I can lay you on the ground, you'll let us move on to real weapons?"

Sylah nodded, rubbing her face.

"I promis—"

"Quick, I can hear Gorn coming."

Sylah spun around, ready to use the mop as a prop in some exquisite acting. All of a sudden, she was on the floor, the ceiling of the dressing room the only thing in her vision. That was until the grinning face of Anoor appeared above her.

"When can we go to the training grounds?"

Sylah growled.

"That was a cheap trick."

Anoor offered her a hand to pull her up.

"You promised." Her cheeks dimpled with smugness.

"Indeed, I did," Sylah conceded, rubbing the hip she had landed on.

"Can we go now? We've got a strike until the tidewind."

"Fine. We can go collect some weapons now."

They were getting better at creeping past Gorn at night. It was a routine they had practiced during their nights at the library with the other servants.

Once they made their way out of their chambers, Sylah made them jog to the training grounds. It was still Anoor's designated training time, after all. The training grounds were lit by the red haze of runelamps in striped panels above them. The army barracks sat in shadow behind, lights out having been called two strikes ago.

A few officers were still using the odd apparatus. One captain stood legs apart, sweat dripping down his back into the folds of his pantaloons as he drew arrow after arrow.

"Sexually frustrated much?" Sylah said under her breath, and Anoor giggled into cupped hands.

Sylah moved through the room with the swagger of someone more comfortable among metal than people. She stopped in front of a display wall of practice weapons.

"They're a bit worse for wear." She inspected a sword. The blade had hundreds of tiny nicks and dents in the metal. Papa would have beaten them if they had let their equipment fall into such disrepair.

"But they're better than a broom, though." Anoor reached for a set of throwing knives.

"We won't need them. Pick only melee weapons, close proximity." Sylah picked up an axe. "You'll get a choice during the final combat, so we'll try a few things, see what you fight with best."

After taking a selection of weapons, Sylah directed them to the padded terrain used for combat.

"Okay, let's start with the sword. Dambe rotation one, but instead of your fist, lunge with the sword."

Anoor separated her legs with confidence and crouched into the attack stance. She tried to lunge, but the sword nosedived into the floor, flinging her rigid arm backward. Sylah leaped out of the way as the sword catapulted through the air toward her.

"Fucking arse hair!" Sylah screeched. "That was why we've been using a broom."

Anoor's shoulders slumped as she went to retrieve the sword.

"Let's try the spear."

Sylah nearly lost a toe during that attempt.

"Okay, okay, the spear was a bad choice." Sylah kicked the wooden handle to the side.

"Let's try with the jambiya."

"The what?"

"The curved dagger," Sylah said through gritted teeth.

Anoor managed to stay standing as she lunged with the short weapon.

"I like this one! Stab, stab, stab." She lunged across the mat toward Sylah, grinning all the while.

"You won't be doing much damage with that weak wrist." The voice made Sylah jump. The captain who had been shooting arrows earlier walked up to Anoor. He kept his hair in coils that brushed the tips of his large ears. He was nearing his middle years, and gray speckled the twists of his hair. Sylah supposed he was attractive, but she was certain he knew it. He scratched his wide nose as he observed Anoor's technique.

"Training for the Aktibar, right?"

Anoor dropped the jambiya and held her elbows close to her chest. She nodded once.

"I think I remember you, the warden's daughter? I am competing as well."

Sylah didn't recognize him, though there had been more than two hundred Embers at the first trial. Still Anoor didn't speak.

"You should try it with the curve facing inward, it'll give you more control."

"Thanks for the tip . . . Captain," Anoor said quietly.

"Yanis, call me Yanis. You better be heading in soon. The tide-wind's wrath has been fierce lately . . ." He raised a dismissive hand to the sky. "I'll see you on the arena floor." He smiled at Anoor as he walked away.

"Are you quite done?" Sylah said once Yanis had left and Anoor stood silently looking after him.

She nodded sheepishly.

"Come on, pick up the weapons, we'll have to train somewhere more private if you're going to drool over every person who shows an interest."

Anoor started to protest, but Sylah wouldn't hear it.

That night Sylah dreamed of Jond. The wardens' journals poured from his mouth like blood.

And drowned her.

"IT'S THE AKTIBAR for duty today, right?" Sylah asked Anoor, knowing the answer. Every week it rotated between the four guilds. The first week had been the aerofield trial for strength, the second had been the first trial for knowledge—on biology of all things. All the competitors had to dissect one fish and one mammal. Sylah smelled the blood in the air, and it had reminded her of the rack.

"Yes, I think it's on tax."

Sylah tried not to grimace as she picked a piece of omelet off Anoor's plate. Her own breakfast of verd leaf tea was cooling in a mug beside her. Sylah was tired; the Sandstorm's task still plagued her nightmares. It had been over a week, and she was no closer to getting into the warden's library.

"And all the wardens go, right?"

Fewer people in the business district—this could be her chance.

"Yes, why, do you want to go to the trial?"

Sylah didn't, but it would get her out of her tasks for Gorn, and maybe she could slip away to scout the library.

"Let's go."

"Really? You didn't seem bothered about the trial of knowledge."

Sylah screwed up her face. "Too fishy."

Anoor laughed her laugh of clouds and cotton.

"That's true," Anoor said. "There was this girl that I used to know, Tanu, apparently she dissected a goat and a lava fish in twenty minutes. They each had to present the anatomy to the audience, and Warden Wern looked like she had sucked on a lemon as Tanu beat her record by five whole minutes."

"Five *whole* minutes." Sylah rolled her eyes.

"Yes."

"Not half? Or quarter, but whole ones. Who would have thought?"

Anoor's smile faltered as she caught up on Sylah's teasing.

"Oh," and she laughed her laugh again. This time it was rain on glass.

"Can we go?"

"If you want, though I can't imagine it'll be interesting. We'll need to get to the arena by midday."

Sylah began clearing up Anoor's meal to take to the kitchens. She'd have to miss her lunchtime meeting with Jond, but he'd understand; it was for the cause, after all.

"I'll meet you in the gardens just before twelfth strike. Gorn's asked me to sort out laundry today. Practice the first Nuba formation, it's getting better."

Anoor nodded, her pride at Sylah's words beaming across her face.

THE AKTIBAR FOR duty was dull. The seats of the arena were half full of drowsy audience members, all watching the desks below with increasing boredom. The standing area at the back was sparse, but Sylah scanned it for any Dusters or Ghostings she knew. Still no sign of Hassa.

Even the wardens looked bored. Sylah had barely taken her eyes off them. Aveed watched the trial from the podium with sharp eyes, sometimes pacing back and forth to observe the different competitors. Wern looked asleep in her chair, her gnarled walking stick resting on her knees. Uka was so statuelike, Sylah wasn't sure she had blinked. And Pura was openly cleaning his nails.

"This is shit," Sylah grunted.

"You're the one who wanted to come," Anoor whispered. The arena was silent except for the clicking of the competitors' abacuses and the soft sound of snores. They were sitting at the back, the only seats reserved for Ember servants. Anoor had suggested it.

"What do the wardens do all day when the Aktibar is on?"

Anoor turned to Sylah, her voice still lowered. "After the Day of Descent, the disciple's prior Shadow Court take over. The handover is fairly smooth as they've had ten years to choose their senior officials. So the new skeleton court manages the empire while the Aktibar narrows down the next disciple. After the Day of Ascent, where the disciples join the court, the new Shadow Court will be chosen by the new disciple. And they'll be a full court up until the next Aktibar—unless someone dies."

Sylah nodded; she remembered that during Yona's Day of Descent, there had only been three wardens ascending. The Warden of Knowledge had died during his tenure and his disciple's Shadow Court had already taken over.

"They go to court? Every day?"

"Well, there are two courts, the Noble Court made up of the imirs or their representatives, and the Upper Court of the wardens and their disciples. Technically there's a third court, the Shadow Court run by the disciple, but that is run separately. Both are adjourned during an Aktibar day, but the rest of the time they're in session."

"And the wardens belong to both courts?"

Anoor sighed through her nose. "The wardens are the court; they technically oversee both."

Sylah's brain was frazzled.

"And I'm guessing people can't just watch?"

"The court? No." Anoor laughed. "Though I expect it's as dull as this."

Sylah wasn't so sure.

"Is there any documentation of what happens at court? Does anyone, you know, share the details?"

Someone in the row ahead hissed at them to be quiet. He had the fevered expression of a gambling man. That was one way to make the trial more interesting.

"Well?" Sylah pressed, ignoring the dirty looks from in front.

"There are documents from the Noble Court, forms and such—you can find them in the Keep's library. But the Upper Court . . . the only thing that covers that would be the journals in the warden library." Anoor shivered from an invisible breeze.

Sylah sat up straighter. "The warden library?"

Why hadn't she thought of asking Anoor before? Had she so readily forgotten that the girl had been raised as Uka's daughter?

"Yes, it's locked with bloodwerk runes, attuned to the blood of the wardens and their disciples."

Perfect. And because Uka was Sylah's *real* mother . . . blood recognizes blood.

"Why do you want to know all this?" Anoor asked, suspicion marring her brow.

"Just think it might be important to know what your future could look like." The lie came out easily, but Sylah didn't remember feeling a pang of guilt before.

Sylah stretched her arms above her head. "I've got to go. Remembered something I haven't done for Gorn."

Anoor let out a relieved sigh. "Anyme, yes, my bottom is numb."

IT TOOK SYLAH four tries to find the warden library. She wasn't as familiar with the western side of the Keep and the busybodies who rushed past her every which way. She'd had to press herself against the wall more than once as an imir escorted by an entourage of officers made their way to the Noble Court. The trial of tax had long finished by the time she found it.

Now she stood in front of the stone door, her tongue between her teeth as she tried to understand the bloodwerk runes that marked it. Anoor was only halfway through teaching her the supplementary runes that could manipulate the four foundational runes. Supplementary runes influenced the forces of bloodwerk with directions, activations, safety, and protection. They were part of the language that built the *Book of Blood*. There was so much she could do to customize the push and pull of bloodwerk.

"What are you doing?"

The voice made her jump. It was cool, light. The last time she had heard it, it had been announcing the trial of aerofield.

"Are you deaf, servant?" Uka stood in the doorway of her office across the way. Sylah hadn't realized it was her office until she noticed the family portrait hanging beyond Uka's gray afro.

"Hello?"

Here was her mother, ten handspans away, and she couldn't speak, couldn't move. Her gray outfit of the day was a patterned blouse and loose trousers. She was pretty, prettier than Sylah had realized, as her face was often puckered in a frown. Sylah looked for a resemblance.

She hadn't been sure what she was going to feel when she finally came face-to-face with her mother. Hate—for all the Dusters and Ghostings she had killed across the empire. Or love—for being the daughter she brought to term.

Sylah hadn't been prepared for indifference. For pity.

The Sandstorm are going to kill you and everyone like you.

"I got lost, I'll be on my way, Warden." The prickling of a tremor began in the center of her back and traveled down her arms. She clasped her hands in front of her to hide it.

"Be on your way then," was the only thing her mother responded with before turning on her heel and shutting her office door. Sylah set her shaking limbs moving.

Her tongue probed the empty space where a joba seed should be.

CHAPTER TWENTY-ONE

TWO DAYS
UNTIL THE TRIAL OF TACTICS

Three births in the last mooncycle. Bringing the total birth number to eight this year—down by fifty percent from last year. The Ghosting numbers dwindle further. I supervised the severing of their limbs and tongue. Enclosed as proof.

—Report by Auditor Julp

Sylah returned from a bloodwerk session with Jond to find Anoor sitting hunched over her desk. Sylah groaned when she saw what she was looking at.

"Not the map, *again*." Sylah had listened to Anoor's theories that something was amiss and believed most of them. But they'd found no proof. Nothing at all, and like Jond had said, once he was warden they'd have all the secrets at their disposal. She seated herself. "Anoor, you only have two days until the trial of tactics; please can you concentrate on that?"

"I've found something."

"Really?" Sylah exhaled through her nose and sat up. She noticed the book Anoor was holding. The book was old, the title worn and the paint flecked. *The Soil We Toil* had been hovering around Anoor's chambers for some time. Sylah had used it as a doorstop more than once.

"I picked this up that night you arrived, I was so curious about the map and—"

Sylah waved her hand to speed up the process.

"Oh . . . right . . . well." Anoor held out the book to Sylah. "I noticed this was written during Warden Iko's term as it mentioned her leading the guild of knowledge in the introduction."

"Warden Iko . . ." Sylah tugged on her earlobe. "I don't know her."

Anoor's eyes gleamed. "Me neither, so I looked her up. She was the Warden of Knowledge from nearly three hundred and fifty years ago."

"Have you trained today at all?"

"No." She held the book under Sylah's eyes once more. "I kept reading and look, I found something."

"'The rubber tree, a native species to the land, was discovered when the empire was inhabited by the founding wardens. The trees can be tapped to produce sap . . .'"

Sylah rubbed her eyes. "Anoor, can you please explain why you didn't practice today, and instead are showing me this?"

"This first bit, Sylah. Native, they're *native* to the land." Anoor's grin grew triumphant. That *was* interesting. The Ending Fire was meant to have killed all life except the boats the wardens had captained containing Embers, Dusters, and Ghostings.

"That means—"

"We have proof, we have proof that the rubber trees were here before the wardens," Anoor interrupted her.

"And that means—"

"The Ending Fire didn't wipe them out."

"Which means—"

"Other things might have survived the Ending Fire."

"Or . . ."

"The Ending Fire didn't happen at all . . ." Anoor reached for Sylah's hand, the truth a fearsome thing between them. "What do we do now?"

It was a kernel of evidence, but it wasn't enough. A thought struck Sylah, oily with an ulterior motive.

"We need to get into the warden library."

Anoor slumped. "We can't, Sylah. I was thinking about it before, and there's just no way."

Would Anoor admit her blood wouldn't get them in? Could Sylah admit hers could?

"We can, and we must." For Jond, for the Sandstorm. "Please."

Sylah never said "please" and Anoor knew it.

"We can try," Anoor conceded. "During the tidewind."

THE LETTER THAT came in the morning halted their planning to get into the warden library. Creamy paper, with a red wax seal with the guild of strength stamped on the envelope.

Sylah had gone to collect Anoor's breakfast, so she hadn't seen the messenger drop it off.

"What is it? Is it about the trial? Have they told you what the terrain is?" Sylah put Anoor's plate of eggs down on the dining table with a clang.

Anoor's fingers were shaking as she handed over the letter.

"It's at midnight."

"That's okay, we knew it was going to be tomorrow, they've just moved it to the evening to catch you off guard." Sylah scanned the letter.

"Sylah, it's at *midnight*."

"Wait . . . midnight?" Realization dawned on her.

Anoor nodded miserably and pushed away the plate of food Sylah had brought. "It isn't supposed to be until tomorrow at midday. We were going to practice with Kwame tonight . . . Sylah . . . the tidewind . . ."

"The tidewind . . ." Sylah sat down, or did her legs collapse underneath her? She began to eat Anoor's bread.

"Each competitor has been given two strikes with a master armorsmith to create bespoke tidewind protection." Anoor's eyes were wide as she spoke. "It's the kind only ever given to the night officers required to travel during the tidewind."

The armor was designed to cover every element of the officers' bodies in order to protect them from the winds. It had fewer joints for the sand to work its way in, and the helmets had glass visors to protect their eyes. Still, a lot of night officers died.

In all their planning, they hadn't planned for this.

"Will you come with me?"

"To the armor fitting? Anoor . . . I have to work." She wanted to see Jond, tell him about her plans to access the library.

Gorn appeared in the dining room doorway. "Sylah, I need you to—"

"Gorn, I need Sylah for the rest of the day." Anoor's voice had an edge to it that Sylah recognized as fear blunted into anger.

"But—"

"No, the trial of tactics is tonight."

"Tonight?"

"Yes, at midnight, and I need her to help me prepare."

Gorn stood, a statue of resolute disapproval. She nodded once. "Good luck." She left to continue whatever task she had concocted for Sylah.

THE MASTER ARMORSMITH'S workshop was to the left of the training grounds in the Keep. The shop had been cleared of all the usual work required by the army, to make way for the competitors' requirements. A large circular forge burned bright orange in the center; the heat from it was stifling, making it almost hard to breathe. The copper chimney above the forge pumped smoke up through the rafters of the villa and away to the sky. Armor stands lined the far wall with half-finished breastplates and chain mail.

It struck Sylah that the Wardens' Empire was always prepared to go to war, but she wasn't sure who with.

"Name?" the smith asked Anoor.

"Anoor Elsari."

"Stand to the left." And so they shuffled to the left, thankfully away from the forge, their backs pressing against the cool whitestone of the smithy's walls.

Sylah wasn't sure why she was here. Anoor had been miserable with the news that the trial was going to take place in the tidewind, and she was under some sort of false illusion that Sylah was her emotional support.

Sylah snorted and spat on the ground near her feet. It drew a few stares, none more so than Anoor, who was incredulous.

"I wish you wouldn't do that."

"Your wish has not been granted."

Anoor pulled a face at her, ready to launch into a debate about the issues of phlegm, when Sylah interrupted her.

"Got to go." A Ghosting she recognized moved around the forge with a dustpan and brush strapped to either limb.

"Hassa!"

The Ghosting looked up with a wry smile as if she'd been expecting Sylah to find her here. She unstrapped her equipment.

Hello, Sylah.

"I haven't seen you in weeks, how are you?"

I'm well, and you?

"I'm . . . well too." Sylah looked around them, but no one paid the Ember and Ghosting much heed. It was as if their servant attire cloaked them in invisibility.

Still teaching the warden's daughter to fight?

Sylah rubbed her neck. "Trying to."

Does she know who you are yet?

"Hassa," Sylah hissed, "can we not talk about that here?" Sylah's eyes darted up and around the room once more. No one blinked their way.

As you wish, Hassa signed, though her smile was playful.

"Quite the operation they have here." Sylah waved her hands around the forge. There were at least fifty armorsmiths working in teams with servants to fit and style all the competitors' armor. They used bloodwerk-operated presses to mold the metal around their bodies.

A young woman with red hair pulled into two plaits was instructing a disgruntled armorsmith to their left.

"I want flowers, embossed around the front and back, and I want the armor to be rose gold."

"Miss, we don't have the required chemicals to oxidize the metal rose gold." The armorsmith was pleading.

"Find it."

"We can—"

"I am Efie Montera, the granddaughter of the imir of Jin-Gernomi, do you *realize* that? And this . . . is what I want."

The armorsmith's shoulders seemed to cave inward. He slipped away to source the chemicals.

Sylah laughed. "She looks like fun."

Lots and lots of fun, Hassa added.

"What's that?" Sylah pointed to a smear of black on Hassa's arm.

Paint. We lost another to the sleeping sickness. I was there to help burn their belongings.

Sylah took an instinctive step back, then cursed herself when she saw Hassa's hurt expression.

"I'm sorry, are you all right? Did you know them?"

Yes, I knew them was all Hassa replied with. There was a glint of anger in her friend's eye. *Your master is looking for you.*

Hassa pointed an arm to Anoor, who was looking wildly around the room.

Sylah scowled.

"She's *not* my master."

They're all masters to me, Sylah. Even you. With that, she returned to her sweeping.

CHAPTER TWENTY-TWO

THE TRIAL OF TACTICS

Those Embers assigned to the guild of duty can now apply to be the wardens' griot. Have you got what it takes to make the leaders of the Empire laugh? Have you got the skills to entertain a crowd? Please sign up on the sheet below.

—Audition notice found on the playhouse floor

Midnight came around faster than Sylah expected. Anoor had been gray with nerves when Sylah had last seen her. Now she was out there, below, in the abdomen of the arena, while Sylah was so high she could barely see her. A reinforced glass screen, which must have taken mooncycles to create, separated the four sides of the seated audience from the elements below. The crowd's cheering echoed eerily in the inverted fish tank.

Two teams had been selected by the griot, who made a jest of the whole thing by picking names out of his different orifices. The wardens' griots were a parody of everything the true blue-blooded griots stood for. They mimed and jested and acted like fools, which would be all well and good if they ever actually told stories. Instead, the Ember griots were a poor replica of their Duster counterparts.

Anoor's name appeared by the griot's ear, joining the same team as Jond. Uka watched on with pained impatience, but the audience cheered along with the farce.

Kwame laughed so hard beside Sylah that she almost got up and left. The servant sought her out and plonked himself next to her as if they were friends. Every day he sat next to her at dinner with the other servants; every day she bared her teeth at him, but he wouldn't go away.

Sylah looked down at the arena floor and grimaced. Anoor's armor stood out like a tree in a barren land. Bright green—"the armorsmith had never done it before, can you believe it? I got the idea from this girl who made hers pink!"—the metal had been oxidized to assault all of Sylah's senses with its vivacity. Her helm, another design of Anoor's, was admittedly a work of art. Two gilded kori birds in flight swept across her ears.

Jond's armor was simpler, but he'd still chosen a lavish filigree of gold and silver. His helm was shaped like the open jaw of a desert fox, the canines on either side of his forehead, the ears pinned back at the top of his head. It was beautiful and deadly. It suited him.

Sylah's eyes swung between the two competitors. They had half a strike before the tidewind struck.

"What are you going to do first?" Sylah had incessantly quizzed Anoor that evening.

"Build a shelter."

"Exactly, no point having a strategy when you're all dead."

The two flags had begun to flap, welcoming the wind to come. The arena had been transformed. Mounds of sand blocked the teams' views of each other, and rubble and scraps of metal were scattered on the ground. They'd be like daggers in the tidewind.

Uka began to speak.

"Competitors and audience members. We continue with the second trial of the Aktibar: tactics."

Roar ... roar ... roar. The crowd's cheers spun round and round.

"BEING A WARDEN of Strength is not just about the might of your muscles, but the might of your intellect. So today we put your theory to the test. Two teams battle to win the flag from the other. Each member has a baton, for defense or offense. The losing team will be eliminated." Uka reveled in the cries of the crowd. Her arms spread wide as she spoke into the sound projector. Her gray ensemble was skin-tight, the suit collar coming to sharp points, like daggers resting on her breasts.

The crowd was hungry. Anoor was not. She felt very, very sick. Uka continued.

"The trial of the stealth will be announced next mooncycle for the remaining competitors. Followed by the trials of mind, bloodwerk, and combat."

Her team's armor clanked around her, each of them itching to begin. One competitor's armor was rose gold, and Anoor could see the wisps of henna-dyed hair through the helm.

"You ready?" a voice said to her right.

Anoor jumped.

"Do I know you?" she said, peering into the depths of their helmet.

The competitor took it off, revealing short twists of hair and an attractive face. It was the captain she had met in the training barracks who had given her pointers on the jambiya.

"Yanis," he reminded her.

"I remember. Nice design." She nodded toward the scorpion embellishment of his helm. The pincers curved around each ear with the poisonous tail curling around the neck guard.

"Thanks, you too." His smile was warm.

The wind had started to build; any second now they would be thrown into the beautiful chaos of the tidewind. A few short weeks ago Anoor had never been outside at night. Tonight, she was going to battle in the tidewind.

Cold sweat trickled down her back.

"Do you know him?" Yanis asked.

Anoor followed his gauntleted hand toward a competitor whose eyes burrowed into her. He looked away when he saw her looking, but she recognized him. It was Sylah's friend.

"He's a friend of a friend."

Yanis quirked an eyebrow before donning his helmet once more. It was nearly time.

There were forty-five competitors in their group. Sylah had told her to take her time and listen to the others' opinions before going in with hers.

"Sometimes other people are right; just make sure you don't listen to the people who are wrong." Anoor whispered Sylah's words into her helmet.

"Begin." Her mother screamed the word just as the wind picked up.

THE SMELL OF urine permeated the air. Someone had pissed themselves. Already. Jond sighed into his helmet. The wind hadn't even really kicked in yet.

"Right—"

"I say we try 'rabbit in the hat.'" A young woman with pink armor began scouring her plan into the dirt on the arena floor. "We keep two groups of twelve, here and here . . ." She pointed to the two makeshift sand dunes she had drawn on the ground. "Then the final group defends until the last moment, until we rush up behind the others." Most of the team were nodding.

Jond ground his teeth. "Wrong." He stepped up. "We do that, and they'll skewer us in the middle. You see that mound of terrain— that gives them the advantage." The group debated for a while, their voices getting louder and louder as the tidewind picked up.

Jond suddenly realized he couldn't see Anoor. She needed to make it through this round so Sylah could carry out her task, but in seconds he'd lost her. Then she crept into the corner of his vision dragging a large metal sheet.

He ran over to help her.

"What are you doing?" He had to shout to make himself heard.

"Making shelter."

Oh, she was clever. The rest of them had launched themselves into an argument, and she had quietly gone off and began to build the one thing that would help keep them alive. He ran over to the others, who were still arguing.

"We need to build a shelter." He had to follow the shout with hand gestures until they understood.

The group began to spring into action. Within ten minutes a ramshackle hut had been created out of the metal sheeting and other bits of rubble they could cobble together to keep the roof on. It was crowded but they'd all got in.

"Where has she gone now?" he hissed into his helmet. Anoor wasn't in the hut. He shouldered his way out.

"What are you doing?"

She was still dragging metal across the course. She'd had to go farther afield to get it.

"We need to cover up the flag," she shouted at him.

He understood. It was pointless coming up with a strategy if the flag blew away and into the hand of their enemies. It was already spinning out of control in the wind.

He ran to help her complete her task, picking up errant pieces of wood and metal that he found littered around the flag. Another competitor—a tall man with a scorpion helm—saw what they were doing and joined in. Together they created a small tentlike structure that protected the flag from blowing away. He hoped it lasted.

Once they were done, they ran back together across the area into the shelter where their team was still arguing. Anoor hung back from the group and let them shout it out. Jond watched her. He could only see her eyes, but she was assessing, listening. Eventually she spoke.

"Speed." No one heard her, so she tried again. "Speed will be the only thing that will win this."

A few of the competitors closest to her heard her but shrugged her off. Jond stepped up.

"Listen to her," he commanded the group. A few had already begun to look at him sideways as if he were the leader. "Go on."

"We need to stop arguing and start doing. There are no strategies I can think of that will give us the advantage here, except maybe war-swarm."

"That's ridiculous, war-swarm leaves no one protecting the

flag, it would be suicide." The arrogance of the woman who'd spoken first was dwindling to outright fear.

"Suicide would be continuing to debate in this ramshackle hut until the tidewind rips it up and spits us out," Jond added. "I think she's right. We need to rush them. If we're lucky, they will be doing the same thing as us right now—arguing."

"We need to make it quick. Go in as a group." Anoor's voice had gotten stronger with Jond's support. "We need to do it when the tidewind is strongest, so they're surprised."

The group began to growl and hiss, and some were shaking their heads. There was a strong smell of piss again.

"Time for talking is over, unless someone has a better idea; speak now." Jond was losing his patience. When no one spoke up again, he began to delegate. Anoor spoke up every now and again, to give her advice, but let him do most of the leading. After all, he was here to win, and he couldn't trust her to follow through.

It came time for the approach. A few of the competitors volunteered to protect the flag, and it made Jond bristle. It was clear those competitors thought they'd be able to cruise to victory in this trial just by being part of the team that stayed with the flag. He had to hope the next trials weeded them out.

Anoor was part of his unit alongside the scorpion man. It meant he could keep her alive at least.

"Ready?" He looked at her, and she nodded. The baton in her hand was steady. As one, their unit launched out into the tidewind.

SYLAH SCREAMED ALONG with the rest of the crowd. She could see Anoor rush out of their base just in time for their makeshift shelter to come crashing down in a gust of wind. The other team hadn't fared any better. They had attempted to burrow into the sand to protect themselves. Like a herd of eru bedding down for the night, the team had sunk themselves deep into the ground, with just their helmets sticking out. A good technique for surviving the night, but not for winning the trial.

"War-swarm, they're using war-swarm," Sylah whispered to herself. She and Anoor had discussed the strategy once but dismissed it as suicide. That was before they knew they were fighting during the tidewind. War-swarm might be the only thing that could win it.

"What does that mean?" Kwame said next to her. "Is it the one where you circle the enemy from the left? The strategy you used to beat me last week?"

"No, no, we didn't practice it. We talked about it briefly, but never thought it would be useful. Essentially the group splits into smaller factions and rushes the enemy in an 'S' formation," Sylah said.

"Wow," Kwame said. "Brave."

"Hmm."

"You seem to know a lot about the Aktibar, where you from again?"

"Ood-Zaynib. My father was interested in the trials."

"A gambling man then?"

"Sure." Why won't he shut up?

Kwame slurped on a flask of whiskey and offered some to Sylah. She hated herself for reaching for it.

"Thanks." She wiped the back of her hand across her mouth.

"Where's Anoor?" He paused to scream at someone who stood up to block their view.

"Short one, on the edge. Bright green armor."

"Green? Cool."

"Not really."

"Oh." He squinted. "Who's that with her?"

"Her protector."

Kwame looked at her strangely. "Her protector? As in, she hired him?" Sylah didn't respond, so he shrugged and took another shot from his flask.

The arena suddenly flooded with glittering blue particles of sand. For a second Sylah lost Anoor altogether, only to find her faction twenty paces away from the flag a moment later.

"She's actually going to do it," Sylah murmured to herself. The other team hadn't had the sense to cover their flag, so it was already leaning into Anoor's outstretched hand as she plucked it from the earth.

"Left, look left!" Sylah screamed as if she could hear her. The opposing team had seen the oncoming attack and had leaped out of their sand cocoons. They were coming in hard on the left, batons raised.

The tidewind rose again, and when it settled for a brief second, Sylah saw blood. She breathed easier when she saw the red color.

"Now that . . . is disgusting," Kwame commented, taking another swig. One of the competitors had knocked someone's helmet off, and the tidewind had come in and grated their flesh off their bones.

Sylah looked for Anoor, but she was no longer holding the flag. Another faction of her team had come in and taken it and was running the last leg back to their base.

"Ten paces, come on, you can do it . . ."

She screamed, Kwame whooped, the arena roared.

Anoor's team had won.

CHAPTER TWENTY-THREE

TWENTY-EIGHT DAYS
UNTIL THE TRIAL OF MIND

The difference between Dusters and Ghostings is that the clear-blooded failed where we will not. Four hundred years ago the clear-blooded rose up to fight the empire and they faltered in their execution. We will not falter. Our hands must remain steady as we wield the Stolen against the families that gave them life.

Red must fight red if we are to succeed in purging Embers from the world.

War will come: to bring order. To bring equality. To bring peace.

—Azim, leader of the Sandstorm, year 414

Hassa had watched the trial from the standing section at the back of the arena. She hadn't wanted to attend—she found the trials a farce—but the elders had insisted. She needed to go give them her report.

Hassa hadn't expected the satisfaction she got from seeing the Dusters' team win.

Anoor Elsari, who would have thought you had it in you? she thought.

With the trial over, the Ghostings and Dusters were being herded out through the narrow entrances at the back, away from the Embers, who milled in their plush seats. Some had even brought full picnics with Jin-Eynab wine and stuffed dates. Hassa's stomach growled as she looked at them.

Something sharp jutted her in the chin. She recognized the cold metal of a runegun and the metallic smell of old bloodwerk on the barrel.

"Stop milling around, Ghosting. Get going." The officer pushed her roughly toward the exit.

The crowd of Dusters chattered excitedly.

"And then the one with the pink armor. Did you see her knock out the guy with the broken baton?"

"I was so impressed with the strategy of the winning team . . ."

"I knew they'd win . . ."

Hassa's stomach soured. They were enjoying themselves. It was the reason Hassa hated the trials so much. In the face of entertainment Dusters forgot who the real enemy was.

Ghostings never did.

Hassa shouldered her way through a group taking bets.

"Watch out, you Ghosting runt!"

She bared her teeth at the man who spoke before she slipped away through the crowd. She'd been called worse. Despite their similarities, Ghostings were the most hated race in the empire. It was what the Embers wanted, it was why they still punished the Ghostings through mutilation. It segregated them, vilified them.

Hassa's phantom fingers twitched. She so rarely felt the nerve damage there anymore, but occasionally the ghost of her fingers would reach outward, stretching toward the horizon. As if she could touch the sun.

As if she could burn.

SYLAH WAITED FOR Anoor in her room. The Embers were keen to make acquaintance with the final forty competitors of the Aktibar. They needed to know who to bet on.

Sylah sat down at Anoor's desk and pulled out a sheet of parchment. She wet the nib of the pen and rested the flesh of her palm on the paper like Anoor had taught her. It still quivered out of her grasp, but Anoor's teachings over the last two mooncycles had already improved her ability to command the alphabet.

Warden of Strength, Jond Alnua. She drew the words out slowly, with care. Curling her words like Anoor had taught her.

What was she doing? This was dangerous. She lit a candle to burn the page.

"What are you writing?"

Sylah jumped out of her skin, one hand stilling her heart as the other turned over the paper. "Anoor! You scared the hairs off my skin. I am now bald. Everywhere."

Anoor laughed, a delighted sound. "Sorry. Did you see? We won." Anoor had taken off her armor, but she still held her helmet in her hand. She looked so different from the girl she had first met. Her eyes were lighter, still hazel, of course, but brighter, her face eager to smile. The exercise had improved her posture while keeping her envious curves, and she was sure-footed, confident.

"Of course I saw." Sylah wasn't prepared for the onslaught of the hug as it clanged into her. "Ow, get off, your helmet's getting blood on me."

Anoor's eyes suddenly filled with tears.

"We lost three teammates."

More Ember blood spilled—it wasn't enough.

"Good, less competition next round."

Anoor recoiled. "You can't mean that." Her hand hovered near her mouth.

Sylah thought for a second, and the truth was, she really did. More Embers who died now meant fewer for Jond to remove later. The Final Strife was here, Anoor's feelings be damned.

Anoor smiled, grief forgotten. "Can I see what you were writing?"

"No."

She made to grab it. "I want to see your progress."

Sylah slapped her palm on the paper before she could turn it over. "It. Is. Private."

Anoor backed away as if Sylah were rabid. She probably looked it.

"Fine, I'm going to wash up."

It took a while for Sylah's heartbeat to slow. She turned over the paper, but the ink had smudged. The word "warden" had transferred onto the wood of the desk. Sylah licked her fingers and scrubbed at it until the black ink lifted onto her skin. She kept casting a glance over her shoulder, but Anoor let her be.

She looked at the mess on the paper. The words blurred as if she were seeing them through tears. Still, she couldn't help but think that Papa would have been proud: one of the Sandstorm was going to get all the way. She blew out the candle and folded the paper, putting it in her basket.

Anoor came in from the privy. "I got you a new dress for the winners' banquet. I know it will suit you for sure."

"You were so sure you'd win, you got me a new dress?"

"I had the tailor make it." Anoor met her gaze steadily. "I told you, I'm going to win this."

Could she? Sylah hadn't truly considered it before. *A Duster at the top.*

She looked at her ink-stained fingers and pushed away the thought.

"I'm not coming to the winners' banquet."

Anoor put a gauntleted hand on her hip. "It doesn't matter that you're my servant. Do we have to go through this again?"

"No, Anoor. I just, I have some stuff I need to do. Take care of, before I report to Gorn later." Even though Sylah had been up all night, there was no doubt Gorn would expect her to be ready to work in the morning.

"Really? You can't come?"

Sylah could tell she was hurt but was trying to hide it. So Sylah reached for her face and cupped her cheek in her hand.

"I wish I could, but I can't. Enjoy your party. You deserve it." She let her hand drop to her side and slung her basket on her arm, not really knowing why she'd just done that.

She needed to tell Jond that she'd made a plan to get into the warden library.

JOND ANSWERED THE door after one knock.

"I've figured it out." Sylah pushed her way into his flat.

"Hello, Sylah, won't you come in? 'Congratulations, Jond, on making it through the trial of tactics.'"

Sylah looked at him in confusion. "I didn't doubt you for a second."

A warm smile spread across his face, crinkling the corners of his shining eyes. He was dressed in a sharp suit, ready for his winners' banquet. Sylah wondered what the clothes looked like on the floor.

"So you've figured what out . . . ?"

"The journals, how to get them. I've scouted it out, and I think I'll be able to get in using my blood, as I'm Uka's daughter. I'm going to go tomorrow, during the tidewind." Sylah omitted any mention of Anoor and the map. He didn't need to know she'd be there, or that there was another reason she wanted to get into the library.

"Took you long enough," he said and winced when he saw her withering expression, "I'm just saying, the Sandstorm ask me every day . . ."

"Why don't they ask me?"

"We've been through this, Sylah, they need to trust you, and right now . . . they don't."

"Why don't they trust me?"

Jond frowned and tilted his head as if the answer were obvious. "You gave up on the mission, Sylah."

"I did *not* give up, the Sandstorm was gone. *You* were gone."

She had given up. She hadn't just given up, she'd suppressed every memory of them with the aid of the joba seeds.

He laughed, not unkindly. "Look, if you get the journals then all will be well. Okay?" He held out a hand to her, leading her to a chair by his kitchen counter.

She remembered the paper. "I made you something."

Jond took it, his severe jawline softening in a smile. "You wrote this?"

"Yes, Anoor's teaching me how to write." Sylah wasn't sure why those words bubbled up guilt inside her gut.

"It's a bit . . . rough."

"Hey!" Sylah grabbed the paper out of his hand with so much force it ripped the corner. "I'm still learning."

"Clearly." He laughed.

"I could teach you too, you know," Sylah said, sensing that somehow Jond disapproved.

"That's okay, I know."

"Wait, what? The new Sandstorm taught you to write?"

He shrugged. This new Sandstorm were more connected than she knew.

"They've gained a lot of knowledge over the years," Jond conceded.

"Sounds like it."

Sylah wondered, not for the first time, about who and what the Sandstorm had become.

"I know you're frustrated," he said, reaching for her hand. "But it'll be worth it when all the Embers are gone, and the board is reset. Everyone equal. No more bloodwerk to segregate us."

"*All* of the Embers? What about us?"

What about Kwame? Annoying, insistent Kwame, who had thrust his friendship on her like a rash she couldn't shake.

Jond's fingers entwined in hers.

"We'll be exceptions."

"Will we?" She thought about what Hassa had said at the armorsmith's. *They're all masters to me, even you.*

Jond didn't answer, and Sylah wondered if he knew the answer. His hand slipped out of hers, and he changed the subject.

"Anoor has a good eye for strategy."

Sylah snorted. "I'm just a good teacher."

He nodded, his lips quirking. He ran a hand over the shadow of his beard.

"Have you got anything to drink?" she asked, just to break his stare.

"Last time you were drunk here, you passed out and snuck out before I woke up." He laughed.

Sylah looked at his armor now standing up in the corner of his flat. The desert fox helmet was terrifying up close. The teeth looked sharp enough to cut skin.

"Nice design by the way."

"You think?" He went over to it and detached the gauntlet. He brought it over to her.

It was even more exquisite up close, the gold detailing of a fox's claw carefully embossed onto each finger.

"Turn it over," Jond said.

Sylah frowned but did as he asked. It was like seeing the inside of a skeleton, the rough inner workings of the body of metal. She moved the fingers up and down. Then she saw it, the engraving on the inside of the wrist. She ran her fingers over it.

"For my Akoma," she whispered. It was what he had called her, all that time ago and then again here, in this house. She looked into his eyes, the usual arrogance softened to tenderness in his gaze.

He kissed her. Tentatively at first, a stumbling, wet, mashing together of lips. He drew away, looked for something in her eyes.

"Is this what you want?" His breath was hot.

"Yes." The assent from Sylah came out as a growl and he leaned in again, stealing her breath.

This time the kiss was surer. Basil and jasmine and urgency. An urgency she matched with each nip of her teeth. His mouth teased open her lips, his tongue stroking hers lazily. His hands roamed her body, over her breasts and the curves of her back.

He pulled her up onto the kitchen counter, the coldness of the stone underneath a balm on her blazing skin. He parted her legs and moved into the space between them, removing her clothes with sure, steady hands.

She ripped off his shirt with a growl, and he matched her sentiment as he grasped for her undergarments, leaving them in heaps around the room. His fingers found the apex of her thighs, circling her, making her ready. But she was ready, she'd been ready for him for a long time.

He grasped her waist and lifted her off the counter, the length of him inside her in moments. He held them together with the strength of his arms, her legs wrapped around his broad back, her nails sliding along his shoulder blades.

Then he was moving within her.

"Jond." Her voice was sandpaper rough. He leaned into her lips as she murmured his name again. Their bodies moved in rhythm, a drumbeat of lust thrumming through their muscles. Her breasts were beaded with sweat, and he licked them, teased them, with his tongue.

"I love you," he murmured into her ear. "I love you, I love you, I love you."

The words shivered down her veins toward her heart—her Akoma.

Sylah groaned at the deepness of her pleasure as he moved to a steady beat, faster than her heart but slower than her need. She wanted all of him.

And he gave it to her.

THEY LAY ENTWINED in each other, their limbs sticky with sweat. Jond's nose rested in the sensitive area below her ear, and she delighted in his warm, even breaths on her skin. She felt them lengthen into sleep.

A small smile lingered on her lips. She'd needed this. It had been two mooncycles since she'd bedded anyone, and the release had been satisfying, if brief.

Her hands slipped into the curls of his hair. She felt a pang of jealousy.

The curls were longer than hers.

DAWN SPLIT THE sky in two, cracking the dark of night with the yolk of the morning sun. Sylah woke to the smell of coffee beans roasting, but when she looked up, Jond was nowhere to be seen. There was a note on the counter next to a mug of coffee.

Gone out, stay as long as you like. Look forward to the delivery tomorrow.

"Delivery?" she asked herself. "Oh, the journals."

Tonight. They'd sneak into the library tonight.

Sylah stared at Jond's tight, neat handwriting. There was so much she wanted to know about the six years they'd been apart.

What did you *do in that time?* The voice in her mind sneered. She was making up for it. She would prove herself to the Sandstorm, to Jond. Then he could tell her everything.

A yawn cracked her jaw. From the fatigue in her bones, she knew she'd only slept a handful of strikes. She took a gulp of the coffee and winced. It was cold.

"Time to get back to it."

Sylah began to search for her clothes.

CHAPTER TWENTY-FOUR

TWENTY-SEVEN DAYS
UNTIL THE TRIAL OF MIND

There are only three things a Duster needs to be taught: basic arithmetic in order to manage the market stalls, reading in order to follow written orders, and the religious sermons in order to preserve their soul for the afterlife in the sky. This can be taught to all Duster children by the time they are ten, ahead of their branding.

Ghostings need not go to school at all. As long as they can listen, they can follow their master's orders.

—Extract from *Education: The Greatest Gift*
by Wern Aldina, Warden of Knowledge

It looked like Anoor had been back from the winners' banquet for some time. She'd even put her own clothes away instead of leaving them in a pile beside her bed until Sylah had to remind her *she* wasn't going to pick them up.

"Where've you been?" she demanded, an errant curl pulsating beside her temple.

"I had some business in the city."

"That family friend again?" She was trying to probe with the subtlety of a cantering eru. Sylah was tired.

"Remember the deal." Those three words had always stopped her questions before.

"I'm just asking. All seems a bit sneaky. I know you're a trained assassin and all that, but why are you meeting him? Is he an assassin too?"

An assassin for every Ember in the empire, Sylah thought. Instead, she stared out of the window, waiting for the questions to stop.

"Why's your uniform ripped?"

Sylah looked in the direction Anoor was pointing. The clasp on the top of the pinafore had frayed, keeping the strap on by a thread.

"Must have fallen."

Onto a very, very beautiful man.

Anoor let out an annoyed sigh. "Fine, don't tell me."

"We're going to sneak into the warden library tonight," Sylah said, breaking the silence.

"Tonight?"

"Yes."

The map lay open on Anoor's desk, and it looked like she'd been studying it for the hundredth time.

"Tonight." She nodded deeply, her eyes lighting with mischief.

"That's what I said."

At least with Anoor by her side, if Sylah was caught she'd be given a much lighter punishment. She would just be the servant doing her master's bidding.

"Sylah?" Gorn called through Anoor's bedroom door.

Sylah groaned. "Back to work. See you tonight."

ONCE THE TIDEWIND began to batter against the shuttered windows of the Keep, Anoor and Sylah left their chambers.

Sweat was still drying on Sylah's brow, cooling her fevered skin. They'd trained for three strikes, Anoor learning the second Nuba formation. She'd failed every time, but every time she got up and tried again. Sylah respected that.

They were both wearing their training clothes: head-to-toe black cotton. It reminded Sylah of one of the stories she'd read in Anoor's zines, the Inquisitor sneaking through the night in dark clothes trying to solve a murder or some such.

Gorn didn't wake as they slipped past her room. The door made a creak as it opened, and they froze for one bated breath, but she didn't emerge.

"Step one. We made it out of your chambers."

Anoor leaned on the back of the door catching her breath.

"That was the easiest bit," Anoor said.

"I guess."

"Come on, we haven't got long."

They made it down to the tunnels beneath the Keep. Sylah had rarely used them, as she was often still training with Anoor during the tidewind. The red runelamp that lit their path reminded Sylah of the Intestines in the Dredge. Her thoughts turned to Loot and soured. When was he going to cash in his favor?

Her eyes caught on a shape engraved into the stone below the lamp. "Is that a rune?"

"Yes, good spot." Anoor had her teacher's voice on. "That rune is featured in a few places around the Keep . . . in the older buildings." She stroked it with her finger. "It never fades, never crumbles . . . and yet we have no idea what it does. There's no blood in the grooves either. It's like the clock in the cloisters, written in runes we don't recognize. They're not featured in the *Book of Blood*. And no one can replicate it."

"Don't you think that's strange?"

Anoor frowned. "Yes, I suppose it is."

Sylah's fingers ran over the engraving.

"I wonder who drew them."

Someone moved in the darkness behind them. Sylah spun on her heel, searching through the shadows. The face that emerged was ethereal. A Ghosting.

"Oh, hello." Anoor's body relaxed, her shoulders drawing down and the air pushing out of her in a *whoosh*.

The Ghosting paused, their gaze shifted between the two of them, confused at being addressed. They had a basket of laundry between their arms.

"Sorry, please don't let us stop you," Sylah said with a placating hand toward the tunnel behind them.

A furtive glance, prey being freed by a predator. Sylah smiled with what she hoped was reassurance. The Ghosting moved on, faster than was really necessary.

"Phew, thought we were going to be caught then." Anoor held a hand to her chest.

"We still might be; we need a reason why we're out here in the dark."

They stood still, both thinking.

"We're going for a late-night snack."

"The kitchens are behind us," Sylah replied dryly.

"Okay, how about we are going to visit my mother?"

"Really? You want her involved?"

"I could say I had a nightmare, and I needed my mother."

They both burst out laughing, the lie so ludicrous it brought tears to Sylah's eyes.

"Let's just say we're out for a walk. You couldn't sleep, okay?" Sylah said, wiping her eyes with the heel of her hand.

Anoor nodded.

They continued on down the tunnel, Anoor leading the way as the tidewind rattled above them.

"It's three floors above, past the court and the warden offices. There might be a couple of officers patrolling."

"Do you think you can get past them by batting your eyelashes?" Sylah asked, her voice low as they climbed the stairs out of the tunnels.

"I do not bat my eyelashes."

Sylah exhaled through her nose in response.

"We could take a shortcut."

"A shortcut? What type of shortcut?"

"It means going outside."

"Oh, I see." Sylah nodded, considering. "I'll try to muster some tears for your passing over ceremony."

Anoor put her hand on her hip. "If we exit at this door here, swing round to the left and head through the cloisters, we'll only be outside for ten paces."

"Have you ever been outside in the tidewind?"

"No. Have you?"

"Yes, we were . . . camping . . ." A training exercise. "All I had with me was water, string, a blanket, some dried meat and kindling." All Papa had given her. "Home was at least twenty-four strikes away by foot."

Anoor's hand had drifted to her mouth, but Sylah didn't notice; she was caught by the memory.

"I used my sandals to make a tube, binding them with the string. Then I buried myself like an eru in the tidewind. The tube sometimes got filled with sand and I'd choke on it . . ." Anoor gasped beside her, pulling Sylah back to the present.

Sylah coughed into her hand and smiled wryly. "I was fine, I survived."

Not all of the Stolen had. Fatyma had died. Her twin, Hussain, was never the same again. Papa had called Fatyma weak. She hadn't yet reached her seventh nameday.

"That sounds awful."

Sylah could tell Anoor was holding back her questions. She bit on her lower lip.

"But you survived, and you could again."

Sylah growled in the back of her throat. "We'll have to be quick, very quick."

"I understand that."

Sylah looked at her, her face determined. Beautiful in its fierceness, so much so that the runelight seemed to shimmer about her.

"Let's go."

They crept through the hallway and took a side staircase down to ground level. Like the rest of the doors and windows in the Keep, the metal shutters were down.

"You know which way we're going, right? Turn left and run until you reach the next door." Anoor's afro was quivering with her nerves, or maybe excitement.

"Yes, yes. I'll close this shutter behind us, but you've got to open the next one as you'll be ahead. There's a pulley like this on the outside. Got it?"

Anoor nodded, not trusting herself to speak. She'd never been out in the tidewind before. She'd never even been out of the Keep at night before.

The wind hammered against the shutter, making Anoor jump. Sylah rolled her eyes at her. They waited for a lull, and when Sylah heard a brief respite from the hailing sand she pulled open the shutter with a grunt.

"Go!"

Anoor stumbled out into the cold night air and Sylah followed.

The glistening blue sand swirled around them, but Sylah knew that it was just a foreshadowing of what was to come. She ran toward the door until she realized Anoor hadn't moved. She just stood there like a lump of lard. Her mouth open, she looked up at the sky as if she hadn't been outside before.

"What are you doing? Run!" Sylah booted her in the shin. Anoor jumped, and the movement broke the spell that had come over her. In seconds the wind had whipped into such a frenzy that Sylah's cheeks felt scraped raw.

"Hurry!" Sylah got to the door first and held it open for Anoor as she ran. At the back of her mind she noted how much quicker she had gotten. With one final lunge Anoor breached the doorway. Sylah shut the door behind her.

"You are the worst fucking partner in crime I have ever worked with."

Anoor lay panting on the floor, but she couldn't help the smile that spread across her face. "So we're partners in crime now? Can I give you a nickname?"

Sylah held back the spit that worked its way around her mouth. "Come on, kori bird. Let's go raid the warden library."

"Why am I a kori?"

"Have you ever seen a kori caught in a tidewind? They pin their wings to their side and stop flying. Just let the tidewind take them."

Anoor was giggling.

"I'm not that stupid."

"Present circumstances contradict that statement . . ."

"Hey! Okay, well, if I'm a kori, then you're . . . you're"—she looked Sylah up and down, and Sylah waited patiently for the insult—"a tall joba tree!" she finished, pointing her finger with a flourish.

"Impressive wordplay there." Sylah chuckled. "Shh." She held out a hand, pausing their footsteps.

"What?"

"I said shh." Sylah could hear talking up ahead. "Let me go check," she mouthed to Anoor, who nodded, her face shrouded in fear. Sylah crept ahead, toward the light she saw leaking out of the crack in a door. She heard murmuring and instinctively leaped away in sure, easy gallops.

"Pura's in his office. He's talking to someone. We need to be really quiet as we go past," Sylah said, panting.

They crept past the Warden of Truth's door. It was slightly ajar and Sylah paused, listening in. Anoor pulled on her sleeve, but there was no budging her.

"Well, if the tidewind gets much worse, we'll have to impose a curfew. Maybe bring forward the Day of Ascent. Ten Nowerks died last night." Pura, the Warden of Truth, spoke softly, his deep voice an incessant hum.

"Let a few more of them die. It is their own fault for not finding shelter."

Sylah recognized the voice of the Warden of Duty, Aveed.

"Change is coming, Aveed. Can't you feel it? Can't you feel the tidewind's shake?"

"Yes, I feel it." Aveed exhaled.

"I think we have a year at the most," Pura said.

"Before what?"

"Before we are under siege from the sky."

"Anyme help us." Aveed's voice wobbled.

"If Anyme could help us, they would have by now. Instead, the tidewind gets worse day by day, and no amount of sacrifice to Anyme will stop it . . ."

"Maybe it is just a bad season."

"Yes, let us hope."

Sylah remembered the last "bad season" two years ago. The tidewind wasn't as strong as it was now.

"Sylah!" Anoor hissed and practically dragged Sylah away from the door just in time. Aveed swung it open, red runelight pooling out into the corridor. Anoor had pushed Sylah into the alcove of her mother's study door, hoping Aveed would turn the other way.

Their bodies were pressed tightly together as if it might make their bulk suddenly become invisible. Unfortunately, Aveed, Warden of Duty, turned precisely toward the way they had come. In seconds Aveed would see their bodies pressed against the door.

"Aveed," Pura called. "Have you filled the Keep's supply

cache?" The question paused Aveed long enough for Anoor and Sylah to untie their limbs from each other and scuttle down the corridor. They needed somewhere to hide.

"My mother's office will be open," Anoor mouthed to Sylah, and in a few footsteps they entered. They didn't hear Aveed's reply before they closed the door.

Once the door was closed, they both gasped for air as if they had been underwater. Anoor fumbled in the dark for the runelamp. She pulled on the bloodwerk lever that connected the series of runes, illuminating her foolish grin. Sylah took in their surroundings.

The office was bare, just two desks and an oppressive painting hanging above the larger desk. She read the inscription.

Yona Elsari, 1st term as Warden of Strength, 38, pictured with her daughter, Disciple of Strength Uka Elsari, 15, the youngest competitor to win the Aktibar.

Anoor was no longer smiling; her eyes were watching her mother's painted ones with an aching sadness that Sylah felt in her core. Their severe cheekbones and deep-set eyes were mirrored in Sylah's face—so different from Anoor's rounded features.

"How did you know the office would be open?" Sylah asked.

"They have an open-door rule, technically, so anyone in the empire can petition the wardens. But really only Embers can access the Keep. Ghostings can, of course, but the wardens can't understand them. Of the Embers only the nobility will ever be granted an audience. Their doors might be open, but their ears are very much closed."

"Hmm."

Anoor was still looking at the painting, her shoulders slumped from the weight of the dynasty in front of her.

"I won't be like that, you know," Anoor parted the silence.

"Oh yeah?"

"I'll listen to them all. Dusters, Ghostings too."

Sylah was looking at Anoor and believed every word. For a short while she was sad that Anoor's dream would never come to fruition.

"Let's go, I think Aveed's gone."

As they turned to leave, Sylah paused and threw a rude gesture at the oil painting. Anoor's smile overflowed with warmth. The sight filled Sylah to the brim.

ANOOR FELT THE prickle of her family's eyes on her back, despite now being in the corridor. The image of her mother and grandmother haunted her every time she saw the painting. Uka had caught her staring at it once.

"I'll have one made for you."

Anoor was shocked by her mother's generosity—until the painting arrived. She found it nailed to her bedroom wall.

It was a painting of a baby, no older than two, lying in a field of blue daisies. To everyone else it was a painting that signified youth and celebrated life. To Anoor it was a reminder that she would never be the baby in the picture—Uka's true daughter.

From afar the blue daisies looked like a field of blue blood. Intentional, Anoor was sure.

Sylah poked Anoor in the ribs.

"Are you all right? You look weird."

"Yes, I'm fine."

They reached the stone door of the warden library. Anoor hadn't been in the library since the night her mother locked her in it seven years ago, just to see how long she would last in the dark. Another game she played with her. She looked at Sylah, whose eyes were focused on the door, and pushed the memory and the fear it brought away.

Anoor knew she wasn't going to be able to get Sylah in with her blood, or Gorn's blood for that matter. But she wanted the adventure more than anything. It was nice to spend time with Sylah outside of the training room.

"The runes go there, right?" Sylah pointed to the slab of slate where a door handle should have been.

Anoor nodded, still mute.

"Are you going to try, or are we going to wait until Aveed comes back?" Sylah hissed impatiently.

Anoor withdrew her stylus and slowly drew the combination of runes. Sylah watched the bloodwerk intently. *At least she's interested in learning*, Anoor thought.

"What rune is that?"

"It's a supplementary rune we call inspect. It matches with the supplementary rune on the other side of the door, triggering *Ba*."

When Anoor finished, she looked miserably at the wall.

"Oh, I must have done something wrong," Anoor said quietly after nothing happened for a few minutes. She wiped off the blood and tried again.

"That's odd, they must have changed the rune sequence. Maybe it isn't triggered by blood," Anoor concluded for Sylah's benefit.

"Can I try?" Sylah was shifting her feet impatiently. "You know, good practice, as I haven't seen that rune before."

Anoor shrugged her shoulders. They would be missing their bloodwerk training this evening, after all. Anoor coached Sylah through the sequence. No matter how many times she tried, the door didn't budge. Wouldn't budge.

"Are you getting light-headed? We should stop, you're losing too much blood." Anoor patted her arm. "Come on, let's go before the tidewind stops."

Sylah was looking at the door, a strange expression on her face.

"That's right, isn't it?" she said to Anoor, who inspected her latest attempt.

"That looks pretty good." It was close to perfect.

"One more try." As Sylah said it, she wobbled.

"No, you've lost too much blood. Pull out your stylus and put pressure on the inkwell, we can't wait for the skin to scab." Anoor was sterner than she'd ever been with Sylah. The shock of it seemed to push her into action.

Anoor had been watching Sylah cope with the withdrawal symptoms silently over the last few weeks. She felt helpless, so she did what she could, ordering in verd leaf tea for the kitchens and stocking her bathroom with eucalyptus oils so she could soak her muscles and ease the tremors.

But now as Sylah leaned on Anoor with an ailment she knew

how to fix, she felt that she had finally earned the smallest amount of trust. Anoor led them back through the tunnels to their chambers.

SYLAH DIDN'T SLEEP that night. Anoor kept feeding her mashed-up grains and lentils "to increase your iron levels" and sugared water "to keep up your energy." The dizziness began to fade, but the frustration at her poor bloodwerk skills remained. Why couldn't she get it right? She'd have to work twice as hard to make sure Jond won the bloodwerk trial.

Her thoughts turned to the snippets of conversation she'd heard. The tidewind. It was getting worse, and the wardens were worried.

But that wasn't Sylah's problem; her problem was figuring out how to get into the warden library. Hassa was the only option, but the girl was so elusive. Sylah would try to track her down in the Dredge the next day.

At some point in the early morning Sylah's eyes drooped, only to open a moment later. Anoor must have thought she was asleep, as Sylah watched in her peripheral vision as she removed a red leather-bound book from her bedside drawer. Sylah wasn't sure what it was, but she tucked the piece of information in her mind for later.

CHAPTER TWENTY-FIVE

TWENTY-SIX DAYS
UNTIL THE TRIAL OF MIND

NOWERK JAIL COLLAPSES

The jail, set into the cliffside behind the Keep, has collapsed during the tidewind. The prisoners, some two hundred, all perished. The building, constructed of limestone, was at capacity at the time and will not be rebuilt. Instead, the Warden of Strength has promised incarceration reforms which will see fewer Dusters and Ghostings jailed and trials expedited. The change has been welcomed by Nowerks around the empire.

—Article from *The People's Gazette*, year 275

For a disorientating second Sylah woke and reached for her satchel. She thought she was back in the Duster Quarter, and her finger lurched for the pocket where she kept her joba seeds. They met air.

"Morning."

The voice was bright and chipper. Sylah groaned and rolled over, jamming her face into the soft cotton of her pillow. It smelled like sandalwood.

"I went for a run already and did three meditative sessions in battle wrath."

That had Sylah opening her eyes. "Already?"

The mind trial was the third test in the Aktibar, so Sylah had Anoor meditating more often than usual. The fact that she'd done so without Sylah's prompt was a triumph.

Anoor's proud face looked down at her, curls matted with sweat twirled around her temples.

Sylah sat up and looked outside. It was well past dawn.

"I let you sleep for longer because of last night. I'm sure you were tired."

"Thank you." A yawn carried her words away. "What time is it?"

"Eighth strike."

"Urgh." Sylah swung her legs out of the pallet bed and into the velvet slippers she had "borrowed" from Anoor. Her feet didn't quite fit, so she'd jammed the back of them down with her heel. They were *very* comfy.

"A letter came for you," Anoor said, and Sylah's head snapped to the paper in her hand.

"For me?"

"Unless you know someone else named Sylah who lives in our chambers?" Anoor's smile was crooked.

Our chambers. The thought sparked something in Sylah.

"Here you go." She handed it over reluctantly, and Sylah could tell she was waiting for her to open it. Sylah's thumb ran over the wax seal: a cross in a circle. Her heartbeat quickened. It was the emblem of the guild of crime.

"Do you mind? I'd like to read this in private."

Anoor's smile drooped.

"All right, I'll just go wash up . . ."

Sylah turned away from her and opened the letter. The wax broke with a satisfying crunch.

The instructions were simple.

Sylah,

Someone has hired my services and I require you to deliver their purchase. Pickup is at noon on the morrow from Maiden Turin. Drop-off is at the arena one strike before the Aktibar of knowledge begins on the second week of the mooncycle. The client will be wearing a black silk scarf around their neck.

Yours,
Loot, Warden of Crime

He'd known where to find her. The ink shook from the tremors in her hands. How much did Loot know? Had Sylah let something slip, just like she had with Hassa?

No, if Loot knows who I am, he'd have leveraged it sooner.

Sylah let out a breath and read the letter again.

He'd signed it, he had actually signed it. The man was fearless. Either that, or he knew he had impunity to the wardens' rule.

"It's the Aktibar of knowledge next week, right?" Sylah asked Anoor through the privy door.

"Yes, it's a theory test on elements, even more boring than watching tax calculations. With that at least you could see the abacus. This one is just people answering questions."

"Want to go?"

"Why?" Anoor appeared in the doorway of the bathroom, soap suds peppering her face. "Just thinking about it puts me to sleep."

"Let's just give it a try. If it's boring, we'll leave."

Anoor, ever ready to please, bobbed her head up and down. "Okay."

Sylah scrunched the letter into her fist and hid it in her pocket to burn later.

"I might have a way to get into the warden library."

"How?" Anoor bounced on her heels.

"I know a Ghosting servant. I'm going to try and figure out how they clean the room, then maybe we can sneak in."

"You can speak Ghosting?"

Sylah shrugged. "I can't sign it. The language is unique to their limbs, and fingers just get in the way. But I can understand it."

"I heard they had a language, but I didn't really think it was true . . . and you've managed to learn it?"

"Anoor, they're people just like me and you. Of course they have a language." Sometimes Embers were so stupid. Even Dusters pretending to be Embers.

"I have to go to the Dredge to find her." Find Hassa and pick up whatever illegal parcel Loot had Sylah smuggling.

"I want to come."

"No." Sylah shook her head.

"Why?" Anoor cocked her head to the left and said, "I'll tell Gorn."

"What?" Here was the girl who had trapped her in a cupboard. Sylah had seen her lying in wait beneath the grins and smiles. "Are you threatening me?"

She lifted her chin. "Yes."

Sylah was dumbfounded. And a little proud.

She laughed. "You know I'm going to train you twice as hard tonight because of that?"

Still Anoor stood, a pillar that would not be moved.

"Fine. You can come."

Anoor squealed, and Sylah instantly regretted the decision. "Tomorrow."

"Tomorrow." Anoor nodded with so much force, Sylah thought her head would fall off.

"ANOOR, YOU CANNOT wear that." It was the next day, and Sylah had been trying to get Anoor to change for half a strike.

She twirled, and the lime green monstrosity moved with her. "Why not, isn't it lovely? It's a new dress I ordered." If anything, it drowned her out, detracting from her curves, and adding new bumps where she didn't need them.

There were no words to describe the hideousness of the dress.

"Anoor, you have to change."

She pouted. "Why? Don't you like it?"

"No, I don't. Personally, I think you should burn it and put the tailor to death, but that's not the reason. We don't want you to stick out. The Dredge has its own ecosystem of rules."

"You mean the rules made by the Warden of Crime?"

"Yes, his Gummers rule the Dredge, with or without the *real* wardens' say."

"Gummers?"

Sylah ground her teeth. "Guild members, they call them Gummers in the Dredge."

"Oh. Gummers." The words sounded overpronounced on her lips. "Why is it called the Dredge?"

"I think once people called it the Edge, as it was the furthest quarter away from the Keep. Plus it's the part of the city where the forgotten live, the people at the bottom of the barrel."

Anoor paused, thinking. Then she reached for another dress. "What about this?" It was all froth and lace.

"Still green . . ."

"Or this?"

"Fewer bows."

"Maybe I could dress as a lesser noble."

"Too rich."

"Oh, I know, maybe I could go as a servant?" She pulled out Sylah's uniform.

"Not unless you want to shave your head."

Anoor dipped her chin and folded Sylah's dress carefully, pulling the corners taut as she tucked it away.

Sylah exhaled through her nose. "Just wear your black training gear, something plain, inconspicuous, take off all the jewelry, and tie back your hair. Most people can't afford the oils you use to keep your curls looking like that."

"Like what?"

Soft curls that perfectly framed her face. Perfectly touchable. "You know what I mean." Sylah scowled. "Stop fishing for compliments."

Anoor's smile was wicked.

"Now get changed."

Finally dressed and ready to go, they made their way to the courtyard, although they had to head back once Sylah realized Anoor had slipped on bright orange earrings that hung like two scarves from her ears.

"They were really cheap. Gorn got them for me for my nameday."

"Stop whining."

"I'm not, I'm just saying, I don't know why I couldn't wear just a little bit of color."

Sylah rounded on her. "Anoor, I told you, we don't want people noticing us, the fewer jewels you wear the better."

Anoor's foot quivered as if she were about to stamp it on the cobbled courtyard ground.

Sylah raised her eyebrow at her, daring her.

After a moment she spun on her heel.

Sylah growled, "Where are you going?"

"To the stables, of course."

"Anoor, we're not taking an eru."

"What?"

Sylah ground her teeth. "We. Are. Not. Taking. An. Eru."

"You expect me to *walk*?"

IT WAS AN agonizingly slow walk across the Tongue. Anoor stopped every five minutes to gawk at every little thing. Sylah was shocked to see how little Anoor knew of the city she'd grown up in.

"What is that *smell*?" Her nose crinkled delicately.

Her privilege made Sylah yearn for a joba seed. It had been a while since her cravings had come on so strong, and she bit the tattered side of her cheek before speaking.

"That, Anoor, is the smell of the rubber plantations."

"It smells like rotten cheese."

"Yes, it does."

"Why does it smell so bad?"

"Because the Dredge is the quarter closest to the rubber plantations."

"Oh. What do rubber plantations look like?"

That stopped Sylah, her eyes going distant. "Blood is everywhere. It pours from the trees and from the backs of the Dusters who mine them. Even the Ember overseers drip blood, but only from their whips." Sylah's voice was low and fierce, and Anoor's eyes had gone wide as she listened. "So breathe that smell in and appreciate it. Savor it and be thankful. For everything you own, everything you wear is because of those Dusters, because of the blood that runs thick and sluggish down every row of rubber trees and pools at your feet."

Anoor looked at the ground as if she could see the blood there, seeping between her toes. She stepped forward gingerly, her mouth still agape. Sylah was thankful for the silence, however brief she knew it was going to be.

"Look, I'm going in here—" Sylah was interrupted.

"Is this a maiden's house?"

"Yes. Now—"

"As in people pay for . . . ?"

"Yes. I'm—"

"They have an eru stable! Why couldn't we have ridden here?"

"Anoor!" Sylah didn't mean to shout so loud. People on the peripheral of the maiden's house turned to stare. Sylah cursed. "You need to stay out here for five minutes, okay? I'm going to go in and get something."

Anoor nodded, clearly scolded.

"Don't move from this spot. If you hear a patrol coming, keep your eyes downcast, and whatever you do, don't greet them or talk to them. Okay?"

Another head bob; it looked odd without her hair bouncing around her.

Two of the villas on either side of the maiden house had recently crumbled in the tidewind. Sylah was shocked to see the decimation the winds brought in such a short space of time. She walked over the rubble that leaked onto the street, toward the door.

She had no idea what was waiting inside. She'd brought her basket, but if it was as illegal as she imagined, the package would have to travel somewhere a bit more intimate.

The door opened before Sylah could knock.

"Hello, Sylah." Turin's radish leaf cigar was down to the tip, the red ash fluttering to the ground by her bare feet.

"Hello, Turin."

"Haven't seen you at the Ring for a while." She looked at Sylah from the corners of her amber eyes.

"No, I followed other prospects."

"I can see, you're looking well, I can no longer count your ribs through your tunic. And are those *breasts*?"

Turin surveyed her with prying eyes. Taking stock. Sylah ignored her embarrassment and pressed on.

"I'm here to collect the package for Loot."

Turin opened the door wider, and Sylah felt the temperature rise as she walked into the maiden's house.

Turin waved her onto the sofa and perched opposite on a chair. "Marigold! That wretched nightworker is always disappearing. Marigold, can you get the letter on the dresser in my room?" She stubbed her cigar butt into the side of the eru leather chair. The burned hole joined other freckles that marred the leather. She smiled slightly as it sizzled.

A letter? That was worse than anything she'd imagined. If an officer stopped her with a handwritten letter, she would be put on the rack. No. No, they couldn't because she wasn't a Duster. She was an Ember, she reminded herself.

"Want one?" Turin offered Sylah a cigar from a carved bone box.

She shook her head.

"Ah, Marigold, there you are, did you hear me? Get the letter from my dresser."

Sylah took the opportunity to address Marigold. Though they had rarely spoken to each other, Sylah knew Marigold was the one to raise Hassa since she was a babe.

"Marigold, have you seen Hassa?"

Turin sighed, and it was clear she didn't like Sylah talking to her nightworkers. Marigold's shrewd eyes flickered between her master and Sylah before answering.

Yes, they signed, their face expressionless.

"Can you tell me where she is?"

Marigold hesitated, and Sylah got the distinct sense that the musawa didn't approve of Hassa's relationship with her. It was rare, maybe unique, that a Ghosting and an Ember were friends. Marigold was within their right to be wary; Ghostings suffered at the hands of everyone, and Sylah couldn't promise that she hadn't contributed to that.

She is due to meet me here soon. Marigold signed so quickly that Sylah nearly missed their meaning.

"Okay, thank you." Sylah pushed all the gratitude she could into those three words.

"Marigold, the letter, now please." Turin was still smiling, but her words had bite. The Ghosting left the room sharply.

Sylah looked at the burn mark on the chair in silence. She

could hear the soft *thump, thump, thump* of someone taking their pleasure in the room behind her.

"It always baffled me why you decided to learn the Ghosting language," Turin asked.

Sylah shrugged. "I needed to learn how to order more joba seeds."

"Most people can do that without learning what the Ghostings have to say. Their communication was, after all, sacrificed after the Siege of the Silent."

"That was four hundred years ago."

Turin nodded politely. "Still, I petitioned to have their language taken away from them, but there's not much they can do. They are made for servitude, and I can't have the Embers taking their feet, can I?" She laughed.

Sylah's leg began to tremble, her anger given life.

Marigold returned with the letter tucked under their armpit. They handed it to Maiden Turin, who handed it to Sylah.

"Don't lose it now. I lost one of my nightworkers trying to get this information." Her voice was the forlorn sound of someone losing profits.

"I won't." Sylah tried not to grind her teeth.

It was then that Hassa appeared. Sylah had never been more glad to see her friend.

"Hassa!"

The girl's eyes flickered to Turin and back to Sylah.

Outside, she signed with the twist of her shoulder and limb.

"Thank you for your time, Turin."

The maiden stood, and a plume of her fragrance drifted toward Sylah. She smelled of clean sheets and radish leaves, a heady combination.

"Goodbye, Sylah." Turin slipped away to another room.

Sylah stood dazed.

Hassa tapped her on the shoulder. *She's gone.*

"Huh?"

Turin, she's gone. You understand now why she gets so much business.

"I don't know what you're talking about."

Then why are you standing around looking like a paying customer?

"Oh, shut up."

Hassa walked with Sylah to the door. *How are you doing?*

"I'm doing okay, I might have brought a friend along, by the way. We have some questions for you," Sylah warned Hassa as they exited the maiden house.

Hassa's smile was crooked. *You don't have friends.*

"I guess that's still true."

Where is this friend of yours?

"Oh, fuck."

Anoor was nowhere to be seen.

ANOOR HAD NEVER crossed the Tongue before. In all her twenty years she had only left the walls of the Keep twice. She'd read plenty of stories about the seashores of the northern coast and the fields in the eastern plains. Gorn hailed from one of the smaller villages in the west and used to tell Anoor bedtime stories of the desert lions that roamed her village.

But nothing prepared her for stepping into the painting she had looked upon for most of her life. Even the Ruta River captivated her. The bubbling blue sand looked warm and welcoming as it swirled into waves and eddies. She knew it was quicksand, but seeing it up close, she had to stop herself from diving in.

Now she was in the Ghosting Quarter, the Dredge as Sylah called it, and she understood why Sylah had made her change. These Dusters and Ghostings had nothing.

Anoor's hand tinkled the slabs she had in her pocket. She'd stashed them when Sylah wasn't looking in the hope that she could buy a memento of their trip. She realized now how much she'd misjudged the destination.

"Are you lost?" asked a man crouched in the crumbling remains of a Ghosting home.

"No, I'm just waiting for a friend."

"Aho, a friend."

"Yes, a friend."

He winked and smiled at her. His teeth were a deep red. He was a joba seed user. She felt a prickle of fear.

"Can I trouble you for some money?" He pushed himself away from the doorframe. Blue sand glittered around him from the crevices in the roof. He took a step toward her.

"I . . . I don't have any money."

"But you've got a debt to pay. See the ground over there? That's my land."

Anoor looked at the dusty ground where Sylah had left her. Did Sylah know it was private property?

"Eeyah, there's a trespassing fine in this quarter. We are policed by a different warden."

Anoor swallowed and stuffed her hands deeper in her pockets. "H . . . how much is the fine?"

"Three slabs."

She deflated in relief, she had ten times that in just one hand.

She counted the money in her hand and handed the slabs over to him.

"Three slabs for each foot."

Anoor frowned.

"But I'll give you a discount, all in for ten slabs."

She backed away slowly, but he moved in step with her.

"What's wrong, girlie? Ain't used to paying your way in life?"

He cackled, and it looked like his mouth was filled with blood.

Anoor looked behind her, but Sylah was nowhere to be seen. She'd disappeared into the house and hadn't returned.

Anoor ran as fast as she could, and she only stopped when she could no longer hear the calls of "girlie" on the wind.

She looked back the way she'd come. The morning sun beat down on her exposed neck, and she placed her hand on the hot skin.

"Curse the blood, now I'm lost." The streets were deserted. Suspiciously so, she thought.

She backed into an empty doorway to wait for Sylah. It was an old building, made from limestone and not reinforced by blood-werk runes, like some of the other relics in the empire. She traced her finger down the crumbling wall and wondered how long the walls had stood for.

So many of the villas in the Ghosting Quarter had been decimated by the tidewind and not rebuilt. She appreciated why it was now called the Dredge and not the Ghosting Quarter; she had seen so few Ghostings.

It was then that she heard the drum.

Bang-dera-bang-dera-bang.

It vibrated her chest and set her hair on end.

Bang-dera-bang-dera-bang.

She followed the sound of it, and it grew louder. Was it a party? A street festival?

Bang-dera-bang-dera-bang.

There was a crowd of Dusters up ahead. Anoor weaved between them, searching for the source of the beat. Her arms loosened, ready to dance.

But no one was smiling. No one was dancing.

Someone was standing on a podium up ahead. A captain of the army. At least if the man who had been chasing her turned up now, she'd have someone to protect her.

The drum stopped, and the captain spoke.

"In the name of the four wardens, blessed by Anyme, our God in the Sky, we bring forth the accused."

A young woman, no older than Anoor, was dragged through the crowd by two officers. She hung limp, like a knitted doll, her dark hair obscuring her face.

"And so we begin the trial of Gala of Nar-Ruta."

Trial? This wasn't how trials went. Normally they were held in the great veranda and overseen by the Warden of Truth's guild members. Some went on for days.

"The accused was found consorting with a citizen outside of their blood color. A crime punishable by death. May Anyme be our guide. May Anyme absolve you of your sins."

"Death?" Anoor whispered against her palm. "Death?"

The woman had made love to an Ember and she was being put to death? This was a menial crime, and warranted five lashes, maybe a week or two in jail. Not death.

That's for Embers, a voice said in her mind. The truth of it sickened her.

There was a jail near the army barracks in the Keep; it was often empty. But Dusters weren't allowed there. Anoor knew that the jail that housed Dusters and Ghostings had collapsed behind the Keep over a hundred years ago, bringing on reforms.

This didn't look like reforms.

Anoor had thought the wooden monstrosity behind the captain was part of the stage. A scenic backdrop maybe. She made a horrified cry, turning a few heads, as the prisoner was brought onto the podium and strapped into four shackles, spreading her star-shaped. Her clothing was torn, as if her arrest had been violent, and dark blue bruises blossomed on scraps of skin.

Someone coughed. Such a mundane sound in the face of such violence.

The crowd parted, and a tall woman with a blue blazer walked to the stage. Her face was solemn, verging on bored. Her hand snaked out, and she pulled on a lever next to the rack where the prisoner was strapped.

Click.

Click.

Click.

The staccato of the wheel turning struck Anoor in the heart. And with every notch the victim's body was stretched further. The jaws of the table opening wider, and wider . . . Anoor couldn't look away, didn't want to look.

The skin around her midriff grew taut, her cries turning into screams of pain. But Anoor could barely hear it over the silence of the crowd. Their silence was the most horrifying sound of all. They had seen this happen before.

Anoor vomited when her organs burst from her midriff. The Dusters around her stepped back with looks of disdain.

She had never seen so much blood. Blue, the blood of her people. In the Keep, Ember blood was manipulated to create power; here Duster blood was spilled to instill fear.

Power and fear. Red and blue.

It wasn't only the gore that raised the bile to her throat, or the cries of the dying woman. It was the realization that if she won the Aktibar, she'd be the one turning the notches on every rack in every city, even if her hands weren't moving the wheel.

CHAPTER TWENTY-SIX

TWENTY-SIX DAYS
UNTIL THE TRIAL OF MIND

We have increased patrols in the area in case other Ghostings take it upon themselves to try to avoid their penance.

—Missive from the imir of Jin-Dinil

Sylah could smell the iron in the air. There had been a ripping. Hassa was on Sylah's heels as they searched the streets for Anoor.

The square had cleared, but the stains of blue blood marred the podium. The body, what remained of it, would have been taken by the family. The night's tidewind would remove the rest.

Sylah hawked in the back of her throat and spat, the globule landing where the officer would have stood.

Hassa came up behind her, her shaved head glistening in the noonday heat. *Is that her?*

Sylah dragged her gaze to where Hassa's limb pointed. Anoor was crumpled in a heap on the ground, a mound of vomit by her feet.

Sylah ran over. "Anoor? Are you okay?"

Her eyes were puffy, and it took her a while to focus them on Sylah's face. "Sylah?"

"How's it hurting?" Sylah crossed her legs and sat down next to her.

Anoor smiled lightly and inclined her head to the vomit. "Not bad. You?" Tears still flowed freely down her face.

"So you saw a ripping."

A small caw escaped her lips as she nodded.

"Not very nice, huh."

She shook her head. A pause. "Who's that?"

"Oh, this? This is Hassa. Say hello, Hassa."

Hassa waved, a shy smile on her face.

"Is she going to help us get into the library?"

Sylah groaned. "I haven't actually managed to ask her yet."

What is she talking about?

"Oh." Anoor perked up. "Will you help us get into the warden library?"

"Stop. Talking." Sylah looked around for any listeners.

Why do you want to get into the library? Hassa's jaw was clenched.

"I thought that was the whole point, to ask her?" Anoor, so innocent, still sitting by her pool of vomit.

"Because what we're doing could be seen as treason," Sylah hissed quietly, ignoring Hassa, who was signing frantically in the corner of her vision.

"Well, it's not like she could tell anyone."

"I don't want the Gummers hearing this. Plus, there are still officers on patrol."

Anoor shuddered, clearly thinking back to the ripping.

Hassa slapped Sylah on the arm with her wrist and signed, *Stop ignoring me.*

"Okay, okay, let's go walk back to the Ember Quarter where we can talk."

A lump formed in Sylah's throat. Since when did she trust the ears in the Ember Quarter before the Dredge?

They walked silently through the streets, toward the Duster Quarter and up across the Tongue, each of them muted by their own thoughts.

The basket by Sylah's waist felt heavy on her hip, though it only contained the letter. Was it bribery, blackmail, or bounty?

Sylah felt Hassa's stare and locked eyes with her. Her expression was guarded and curious.

How was she going to explain why they needed to get into the warden library? Her mission from the Sandstorm was long overdue.

Anoor sniffed beside her.

"Are you okay?"

Anoor's mouth was parted as she looked at the Ruta River below the Tongue. The trotro rattled past, filled with vegetables for the Ember Market.

"This river separates so much more than just land." Anoor's voice was soft, thoughtful. "It's like the rack, it splits the city in two. Blood oozing out."

They walked in silence after that.

THEY WERE NEARLY at the Keep when Sylah spoke.

"We need to get into the library."

Her words gave Anoor unwarranted permission to launch into an explanation, the moroseness from the ripping momentarily forgotten.

"Sylah found this map in the Dredge in an old Ghosting dwelling with a piece of land that shouldn't be there if the Ending Fire burned everything, so we think there's something the wardens know that they're not telling the citizens and we want to read the journals in the library but we don't know how to get in."

"Breathe," Sylah demanded.

Hassa's eyes had narrowed to slits. *Sylah, can we talk over here for a second?* Hassa tilted her head toward a courtyard cast in shadow, thirty handspans away.

"Be right back," Sylah said to Anoor.

Why do you really need to get into the library? I can't imagine you give two shits about a map.

Sylah recoiled. "I do. Don't you think it's weird that there's a map with unrecognizable land on it? How would the artist know what to draw?" Sylah's voice was low; though the street was empty, they stood in front of an Ember villa.

That's the only reason you need to get into the library? Nothing to do with the Sandstorm?

"I don't know what you're talking about, the Sandstorm are dead."

Hassa just tilted her head, waiting.

Sylah opened her mouth to deny it, then her shoulders drooped in defeat.

"What do you know?"

Not much. I guessed that friend of yours, Jond, was another of the Stolen. But I'm not sure why you're training the girl, or why you need to get into the library.

Sylah looked backward, just to double-check Anoor hadn't drifted any closer. The girl was watching a kori bird in the joba tree above her.

"Bloodwerk. She's teaching me to bloodwerk in exchange for the training."

And then you teach your friend? For the trial of bloodwerk?

"Yes."

And the library?

"I need to steal journals for the Sandstorm. If I do the task, they'll induct me back into the rebellion."

And you want that?

"Yes." Sylah's response was fierce.

I don't think this is a good idea. I've heard things from the elders . . . about this Sandstorm, not good things—

"I don't care, it's where I belong." Sylah said the words to reassure herself more than anything.

Anoor, she knows nothing?

Sylah shook her head. "But the map I found, the land on it . . . that's all true. Please, Hassa, will you help me?"

Hassa's eyes seemed to burrow into Sylah's, searching, probing. Then with a sharp nod she gave her assent.

What do you need?

"How do Ghostings clean the warden library?"

HASSA SAID GOODBYE to them at the Keep's gates, agreeing to meet them later. Being the warden's daughter meant Anoor could enter through the side gate assigned to the wardens and their families—forgoing the blood scour. Hassa wasn't even allowed to use the front gate. She had to use the Ghosting entrance down a dirt track to the left.

Hassa hated the Keep. The tall walls scared her more than anything else she had seen in the empire. Their menacing presence represented everything about the wardens' rule. Segregated and oppressive.

She watched Sylah and Anoor disappear within. They were crawling closer to the truth. The map, though. Hassa wanted—needed—to see that map.

"The Ghosting entrance is that way," an officer interrupted her thoughts.

She turned to look at him, to capture his essence. When the world thinks you can't talk, people reveal things in the depths of their irises they would ordinarily keep hidden.

He met her gaze then dropped it away. Behind him someone had scrawled the words she had heard more than once.

If your blood runs red, go straight ahead.
If your blood runs blue, you're not coming through.
Translucent hue, who are you, who are you, who are you?

We'd tell you exactly who we are, if only we could, Hassa thought. The words, starting in the throats of the officers, had crawled across the river into the mouths of countless children. A nursery rhyme, they thought. Isn't that how propaganda starts?

She stepped away from the front gate with a triumphant smile. It turned a few heads.

The servants' entrance was manned by a surly chief of chambers who had missed her calling as an officer, so had taken up the next best thing.

"Eeyah, eeyah," she screeched as Hassa made her way through the gate. "What do you think you're doing? You need to sign in first."

Hassa stopped and ground her teeth. She kept her eyes down and her shoulders slumped.

"Here, you need to stamp your elbow against your name." She was chewing on a radish leaf. Hassa knew that smell: it reminded her of home.

The sign-in book was a smattering of names against blobs of ink. All names were inanimate objects, animals or plants. Nice and easy to remember for the Embers.

The chief of chambers began to read them out, assuming Hassa couldn't understand the writing. Ghostings were officially never taught how, but the elders taught those who wanted to learn.

Hassa flapped her wrist when the woman got to "Honey." Hassa stamped her elbow in the ink pad, the sound hiding the growl of disgust in her throat and pressed it to the page.

Honey had left the city two years ago; Hassa was the one to guide them out. The Embers didn't know it, though, and Hassa simply slipped into her role at the Keep when she needed to. Hassa had a dozen aliases just like it across different Ember households. Once she changed her kente sash around her stomach, the Embers never noticed the difference between one Ghosting and another.

The chief of chambers waved her through after she was satisfied with Hassa's signature.

That was the thing about being undocumented: Hassa could get anywhere, and the Embers had no idea.

THEY CLEAN THE *library every fourth day between third and second strike in the afternoon. The Warden of Duty lets them in, and an officer stands guard while the cleaning is completed.*

Anoor watched, openmouthed, a small frown between her brows while she tried with all her might to understand Hassa.

They were in the dining room of Anoor's chambers, Gorn having disappeared to the kitchens below while Sylah set the table. Hassa appeared shortly after Gorn left.

"When will they next clean it?"

Tomorrow.

"What's Hassa saying?" Anoor whined.

"But how do we get past the officer?" Sylah asked.

Hassa shrugged her small shoulders. *Why don't you kill him? Isn't that what the Sandstorm would do?* Hassa's lips quirked.

"Shut. Up."

You're the one who is so desperate to join them.

Sylah frowned at her friend's disapproval.

"Going back to the matter at hand. Will the other Ghostings let us in? And not tell anyone?"

Of course, who could we tell anyway? Her eyes glinted.

"Sylah, please fill me in." Anoor's whine had progressed to a high-pitched drone.

I want to see the map.

"Why?"

You found it in the ruins in the Dredge, in a Ghosting dwelling, yes?

"I did."

I want to see it.

"Anoor, will you get the map?"

Anoor gave Sylah an angry glance.

"I'll fill you in, I promise. It's just . . . we don't have much time until Gorn gets back."

Anoor grumbled something about being left out as she ducked out of the room.

What was in the letter that Marigold gave you? Hassa suddenly asked.

"Not sure. I just have to deliver it."

My friend died getting that information. The Ember strangled her in her bed. Turin watched through the wall and collected the information. She then let the man go.

"I'm sorry, but I'm really just the messenger here."

Messengers carry guilt too.

"What are you two talking about?" Anoor said as she returned with the map.

"Nothing."

Anoor laid the map out on the table. "Here it is." And she pointed to the top right corner.

Some of it is missing.

"Exactly."

You didn't say it wasn't whole.

"It could be that the rip is from where I pulled it from the frame I found it in, but it wouldn't explain that patch of land, right there." Sylah's hand joined Anoor's at the top of the map.

Hassa's features always moved precisely; it was important to convey her meaning and message. But now her eyes were shining, beads of sweat sprinkling her brow. She was fevered, excited.

It was then that the door unlocked. Hassa darted to the shadows and Sylah rolled up the map and tucked it between her breasts in her pinafore.

"The table's not set," Gorn grunted as she entered with the steaming food.

"Oh, sorry," Sylah mumbled, rushing to get the crockery from the drawers in the dresser in the hall.

"What are you doing here?" Gorn nearly dropped the tray of food as she spotted Hassa crouching in the corner, her eyes wide like prey caught in a net.

"I asked for a Ghosting to help arrange my clothing. I want it sorted in color order and Sylah was busy." The lie slipped smoothly out of Anoor's mouth with confidence. Sylah was envious at the ease with which she lied.

Gorn let it pass, either accepting the lie or knowing she wouldn't get the truth.

"Go to the bedchamber then, there is no clothing in here."

Hassa bowed her head, but Sylah caught the irritation pooling in her eyes. She was going to have to sort through Anoor's dresses for at least half a strike. Sylah muffled her laugh.

CHAPTER TWENTY-SEVEN

TWENTY-FIVE DAYS
UNTIL THE TRIAL OF MIND

Today, I begin my term as the Disciple of Strength. I am the youngest competitor to have won the Aktibar, the youngest disciple in the four hundred years of the Wardens' Empire. My mother has not yet congratulated me. She never will.

—Uka Elsari's journal, year 391

The next day Anoor dressed even more formally than usual. Suits were generally favored by the imirs and wardens. She needed to make sure that if they got caught, she was recognized as the warden's daughter. She wore purple wide-leg trousers that trailed slightly on the ground. The matching blazer was the same plum color, a few shades darker than the army uniform. Anoor let the silk slip through her fingers like water as she walked.

"You know what to do?" Sylah asked her as they rounded the corner to the offices.

"No."

"Anoor, we've been through this." Sylah exhaled through her nose sharply.

Anoor grinned.

"Oh, you're joking."

"Yes, Sylah. We have been through it. A hundred times."

It had been Anoor's idea, though she'd later admitted to stealing it from a zine. The guard was the problem, so all they had to do was make the guard the solution. Sylah tugged on the officer's uniform. It was slightly too short in the legs and arms, but it was the only one she could find at the launderers.

When she first put the purple uniform on, Anoor caught the horrified look in Sylah's eyes as she stood in the mirror.

"You look good," Anoor said tentatively.

The fear in Sylah's eyes disappeared and was replaced by a crooked grin.

"I don't look half bad, do I?" A purple headscarf was wrapped under the black helmet she wore, hiding her shaven status.

Anoor taught Sylah some basic military commands and formations based on what she had learned in the Keep.

"Just look important, that's the main thing."

"I don't have a baton or a whip."

Anoor frowned and then marched into the bathroom.

"Here," she said, handing over what she'd gone to collect.

"Anoor, you can't be serious."

"What? The handle is black and long, like a baton. Just tuck it in your pocket so no one can see the sponge."

"It's a backscratcher."

"No." Anoor tucked it into her trousers and winked. "It's a baton."

All Sylah had to do was relieve the guard on duty and take his place. They were nearing the library.

"Aveed is still in their office," Sylah whispered.

"Yes, well, it is the middle of the day," Anoor said back.

"But, Anoor, we didn't think about your mother. Her office is opposite the library, right?"

Anoor faltered in her step, and Sylah caught her. For a second Anoor was back there, in the dark, locked in with no food or water. No light. Her mother's favorite punishment.

"If she's there, we keep on walking. Okay?"

Anoor dragged her head up and down.

"Is there any way her office door will be closed?" Sylah asked.

Anoor shook her head left and right.

"Not unless she's in a meeting."

They neared the Warden of Strength's office. Anoor could see the door was open. Her legs felt leaden, unmoving. She wondered if this was what Sylah's withdrawals felt like. Sylah dragged her forward.

"The office is empty. We continue with the plan," she said out of the corner of her mouth.

THE GUARD STANDING in the doorway looked at Sylah as she approached.

"There's been some mix-up in the barracks. I've been sent to take up your position."

"Huh?" the guard responded. She was a little smaller than Sylah, though her eyes held the same dangerous tinge.

"Who are you?" the guard asked.

There were only three hundred officers regularly at the Keep; the rest patrolled the empire, enforcing the law in the other cities and putting down any rebellions or coups. They had known it was likely the officer would ask Sylah's name. Hassa had spent a strike listening in the barracks just for the purpose.

"I'm Ejo Donara. My regiment just came in from patrol in Jin-Dinil." Sylah's legs threatened to seize; she could feel a tingle starting at the base of her heel. The withdrawals were always exacerbated by adrenalin. All she had to do was not move a muscle.

"Jin-Dinil? Where those Ghostings were caught trying to smuggle out babies who hadn't been severed? Heard one of the babies was an Ember, a result of a maiden house coupling. Is that true?" The questions were bloodthirsty and took Sylah unaware.

She tried not to look back at where she knew Anoor was hovering. She didn't know the answer. In the end she settled on a nod.

"I'm glad they didn't leave any of them alive. Ghostings got to do their penance, the reminder stops others rebelling, you know? There'll be no Ghostings left with half of them dying from the sleeping sickness and the other half trying to leave. Where were they going to go anyway?"

Sylah was thinking precisely that. Did Hassa know anything about this? Could Hassa have *helped* them? Was that where she disappeared to all the time? Sylah tucked the questions in a corner of her mind for later.

"You're to head down to the mess hall for lunch. Fried tilapia is particularly good today."

Sylah hoped the lure of food was enough.

"Tilapia, you say? Well, if the general says you're to sub in, then I think I'll head down to the mess hall like you suggest." She smiled and moved out of the open doorway.

Sylah looked at Anoor once the officer was out of earshot.

"Just like the scene in *The Missing General*," Sylah said.

"I knew you were reading my zines. Isn't Inquisitor Abena the best?"

The Ghostings cleaning the library paused as Sylah and Anoor entered. Hassa had warned the Ghostings, but neither of the two men greeted them as they stood in the center of the room. They returned to their cleaning, the straps of their cleaning implements tight on their forearms.

Books lined the walls like wallpaper, floor to ceiling. Most of them were bound in red leather. Some were larger than was physically possible to hold in two hands. The room smelled of coffee and ink. All of it, the taste of the dust on her tongue, the walls, the feel of the books, echoed in Sylah's mind, reminding her of a place she had been before.

"All the red volumes are the diaries of wardens past." Anoor walked to the farthest bookcase. "Each warden writes about five to ten books in their time. These are my mother's." Anoor indicated the fresher-looking books nearest to the front.

There, in front of her, was the truth about Sylah's heritage. She ran a finger along the spines of the books full of her mother's words.

"We should take as many of the oldest ones as we can find," Anoor continued. "But we need to be careful, not take too many, and cover any obvious gaps."

Anoor got straight to work, mounting a nearby ladder and pulling out a journal from the back.

Sylah lingered in front of her mother's memories. The Sandstorm task that had taken over her mind for so long would finally be fulfilled. She just needed to steal one of each of the most recent journals from the current wardens. She pulled out the first and began to read.

Today, I begin my term as the Disciple of Strength. Uka's writing was contained and precise, the pen nib pressed down too forcefully, leaving scours as well as ink.

"Sylah, come on, we have to hurry up—why are you reading those?"

Sylah ignored her, flicking through the pages of her mother's memoir.

"It's missing. The most recent journal is missing," Sylah said to herself. It would have journaled the years when Sylah was stolen. She swore. She'd have to take an older one and hope the Sandstorm were happy with that. Thankfully, the most recent journals for the other three wardens were there. Sylah shoved them into the blazer she wore. She was thankful for her flat chest. She hoped Anoor wouldn't notice.

"What are you doing? Come help me."

Red covers littered the ground between them until the floor looked as though it were covered in pools of blood.

"This one looks really old," Anoor said, holding up a battered book.

"Yes, let's take that one. Maybe that one too? It looks a little yellowed."

"Okay, we should tidy up and go."

The Ghostings were already on the move, putting the volumes back as quickly as they had scattered them.

"Thank you," Anoor turned to them and said. They bowed their heads in response.

It was then that Sylah remembered what the library reminded her of. The Belly, Loot's headquarters.

"SYLAH, WAKE UP."

Sylah didn't remember falling asleep, in Anoor's bed of all places. Once they had returned to their chambers, the thrill of the day's adventure was enough to carry them through into the early strikes of the morning.

Thankfully, Anoor didn't notice the extra texts Sylah had stolen. Sylah pored over her mother's journal, reading and rereading about her first few years as a disciple. The text was formal, dry, and very disappointing. When Sylah's lids began to droop, her own bed ten handspans away seemed too far a journey.

"Sylah, wake up."

"Fugh off."

Anoor crawled over the bedcovers to Sylah. The four-poster was so big Sylah didn't feel her presence until it was too late.

The journal smacked against her head with a thump. Sylah hoped it wasn't one of the diaries she needed to take to the Sandstorm.

"I will kill you with my bare hands."

Anoor was grinning above her. Her night scarf that protected her curls was wound tightly around her head. It was a fluorescent green that hurt to look at. Unpractical, garish, and completely Anoor.

"Have you found something?" Sylah groaned as she sat up.

"No."

"Don't tell me you woke me up to tell me you didn't find anything."

"Well . . ."

"I've changed my mind, I will kill you with a dagger, and peel your skin first."

"The thing is . . . neither of the journals are that old. This one"—she waved the one she had used as a weapon against Sylah's head—"is from three hundred years ago. It's the oldest journal there. But nothing. It's so mundane." She giggled into her hand. "Except for this one sex scene."

Anoor was scandalized, and her laughter had Sylah reaching for the journal. Together they read the passage together and laughed until they cried.

"He was as well-endowed as an eru in heat . . ."

"His balls were as hairy as a desert monkey's back . . ."

But nothing helped them discern the truth of the empire. The laughter at least eased their disappointment.

IT WAS TIME for Sylah to deliver the journals to the Sandstorm. Sylah slipped out during her lunch break, the four journals hidden in her basket. With Loot's letter also taking up residence in her belongings, she was beginning to feel like a duty chute.

Jond was already awake when she arrived at his flat.

"Sylah?"

"Delivery." She waved the spine of a journal in his face.

His face went slack in shock.

"You did it? You actually did it?"

"Did you doubt me?" Sylah entered his hall.

"Not exactly."

"You did! You doubted me!"

Thwack.

Pura's journal hit him on the backside. His eyebrows shot to the sky.

"Did you just smack me on the ass with a warden's journal?"

Sylah's grin was mischievous.

"Well, you asked for this," Jond said, his voice rough.

"For what?"

His answering growl sent thrills down Sylah's spine, and when he launched himself at her, she let herself be caught in his arms. His teeth grazed her neck and she groaned, her fingers finding his hair and pulling hard.

Sylah's other hand found his chest and pushed him backward toward his bed. Their clothes were off by the time they touched the sheets.

IT WAS LUNCHTIME, and Sylah had disappeared like she always did at that time.

Spending her brief time off as far away from me as possible. The thought dampened Anoor's mood.

Anoor thought the previous day's adventure had shifted something between them. The friendship that Sylah had been resisting for so long grew raw and heady; she even slept in Anoor's bed. But in the morning, Sylah was back in her pallet, the carefree nature of the night before forgotten.

Anoor sighed and drummed her fingers on the journal in front of her. Gorn appeared in her bedroom doorway and sensed her glum mood.

"Why don't you go to the library? The latest zine will be out, and I'm sure Bisma would have picked it up for you." Anoor didn't have much time to read zines anymore, and she couldn't believe that she had forgotten to get the next installment of Inquisitor Abena's adventures.

"I think I will," Anoor said, getting up to leave.

A smile threatened to lift Gorn's rigid lips.

"Do you want me to come with you?" she asked, the question maybe a little hopeful.

"No, I'll be all right." Anoor was thinking about heading to the tower to train after picking up the zine. The mind trial was just over three weeks away, and the stealth trial could be announced at any time.

Gorn sniffed before turning on her heel and leaving.

Anoor left her chambers and walked through the Keep quickly. Every time she saw an officer, she heard the *click, click, click* of the rack. At one point she thought she recognized the captain who had given the order on that ill-fated day in the Dredge. She was forced to press herself against the cloisters until he passed.

By the time she reached the library she was sweating.

"Miss Elsari," Bisma greeted her with open arms. "You've missed two zines. I nearly sent a Ghosting to your chambers, but you know what? Couldn't find one."

"Hello, Bisma, how are you?"

"Well, you won't believe what happens in the most recent tale . . . Abena discovers a Duster sent the letter to the imir and—guess what? Though I don't want to spoil the ending . . ."

He rushed on before Anoor could respond.

"Abena had him arrested and he goes to trial."

Anoor winced. Trial. *That ridiculous farce wasn't a trial.*

Bisma reached down below his desk, his back creaking like a door, and pulled out the two zines. He pressed them into Anoor's hand with a smile.

"Don't worry about payment, a gift from me for doing so well in the Aktibar. I've been watching you."

Anoor shifted her feet. It felt like the whole world was watching her sometimes.

"Thank you, Bisma. I might go sit and read some."

He nodded deeply and waved her away. "Enjoy, enjoy, but come tell me when you get to the section when Abena's ex-husband appears from the chest. It's a shocker."

The zines distracted her for some time, pulling her from the pressures of the Aktibar and her complicated relationship with Sylah.

"SYLAH, THIS ISN'T the most recent journal. This was from Uka Elsari's first term as disciple."

Skies above, that didn't take him long. Sylah rolled over in the bed to find Jond hunched over the book in question.

"So?"

"So?" He was incredulous. "The Sandstorm gave you specific instructions, you didn't follow them."

Sylah felt her anger pound her heart like a drumbeat; it brought on the beginning of a tremor.

"It was the only one there."

"Are you sure?"

"Maiden's tits, Jond. Yes, I'm sure. This is it, this is my task fulfilled. Right?"

Jond tilted his head.

"Is that a yes or a no?"

"I don't know, okay?" he said, matching her fever. "Master Inansi is very particular about this stuff, wants things to be carried out properly. There was something they needed in the journal, in that particular one."

"Master Inansi?" Sylah repeated, and Jond jerked.

"Pretend I didn't say that."

Sylah hadn't heard the name before, but she filed it away just in case.

"This is getting ridiculous, Jond." Sylah slumped back on the bed. "I'm beginning to think you don't want me back in the Sandstorm because I was always better than you." The comment was snide, uncalled for, but it hit Jond in the stomach. She regretted it instantly.

He breathed through the gut punch of the insult before he answered. "Sylah, this isn't a club, it's a covert operation of the most serious kind. Every day we commit treason, every day we trade with life."

Sylah didn't answer. Her thoughts drifted to Anoor. Sylah had woken up next to her that morning, the soft rays of dawn burnishing her face a dark bronze. The journals were scattered around them still, and Sylah carefully and quietly hid the four she needed in her basket before creeping back into her own bed. She could barely meet Anoor's gaze that morning for the guilt that churned her stomach.

"Sylah?"

She was jolted back into the room.

"See, half the time you don't seem to care," Jond said softly.

"Of course I care," she said, but she wasn't sure whether he was referring to himself or the Sandstorm.

Sylah heard the call of second strike and jumped out of bed and began to dress.

"I have to go. My lunch break is over."

"Fine, I'll deliver the journals to the Sandstorm. I'll let you know what they say."

He looked up, but Sylah was already gone.

CHAPTER TWENTY-EIGHT

FOURTEEN DAYS
UNTIL THE TRIAL OF MIND

We have now eliminated nine of the Duster decoys the Sandstorm left behind. Some of the families offered the children up willingly. Others hid them from us until a blood scour proved their heritage. No one suspects Anoor. We must keep it that way if my reign is to be successful.

I will find the Sandstorm and destroy them.

—Uka Elsari's journal, year 405

Sylah woke to Anoor sniffing.

"What's happened?" Sylah asked, rising from her pallet.

"Someone died in the courtyard. I . . . I can see their guts."

Sylah rubbed the sleep from her eyes and joined Anoor by the window.

"Yes, those are guts, all right." It was a tidewind murder, that was clear.

"Why did they go out during the tidewind?" Anoor turned her tear-streaked face to Sylah's.

She shrugged. "No idea."

"I knew the tidewind could cause death. I've never seen it, though." Anoor hugged her elbows.

Sylah thought about what she'd overheard the wardens say

when they tried to sneak into the library for the first time. *I think we have a year at the most . . . before we are under siege from the sky.*

Sylah let her eyes linger on the red blood in the courtyard. It must have been an Ember servant—maybe she had known them. At least it was one fewer Ember for Jond to kill. For some reason, the thought soured her stomach, and she looked away to find the gates of the Keep open.

Officers were taking their positions ready for the audience members to arrive later that day for the third Aktibar of knowledge. One officer was gesticulating at a Ghosting to clean up the body and the blood.

The wardens' journals littered the floor where Anoor had flung them the night before. She was studying them as closely as she had the map, hoping to glean the truth of what lay beyond the sea. Sylah was starting to doubt their suspicions, but she let the girl waste her time searching. There were no repercussions from stealing the journals, nor were there any rewards from the Sandstorm.

Eleven days had passed since Sylah delivered Jond the volumes, and although they practiced their bloodwerk together every lunchtime, he did not mention the Sandstorm and Sylah did not ask. She had enough on her mind with Anoor's mind training and the letter from Loot.

Drop-off is at the arena a strike before the Aktibar of knowledge begins on the second week of the mooncycle. The client will be wearing a black silk scarf around their neck, the instructions had said.

Sylah guarded the letter meticulously, even taking it with her when she went about her work or visited Jond. Sylah was glad the Aktibar of knowledge was today, so she could finally deliver it and be done with Loot's favor. For now.

That morning Sylah drank two cups of verd leaf tea.

"Do you still need to drink that much?" Anoor asked her.

Sylah didn't want to admit the muscle seizures still afflicted her, especially when she was nervous or angry. She began to think the problem was permanent.

"I like the taste," Sylah replied.

THE YOUNG WOMAN was waiting for her at the side of the arena between an oak tree and a cherry shrub. She was wearing a black scarf around her neck as Loot had instructed.

"You're late," she growled. Her features were crowlike, black eyes darting left and right.

"You're welcome," Sylah said as she withdrew the letter from between her breasts. She pressed it into the stranger's hand.

The girl seemed shocked to see it there. Then she tore open the wax seal, which Sylah had somehow managed to refrain from doing, and scanned its contents.

Sylah leaned forward; she couldn't see the full details, but it looked like a list of some kind. The girl brought out a set of matches and set the letter alight. The paper burned orange, then black, until all that remained was ash. Sylah was relieved.

The crow girl didn't say goodbye as she slipped away.

"Rude," Sylah said to her retreating back.

ANOOR MANAGED TO get them second-row seats. Sylah could see her from the top of the arena steps, her hair pulled into two buns, adorned with yellow ribbons. As Sylah ran down the stairs, Anoor turned to wave at her as if she detected Sylah's gaze.

"A bit closer than the servants' row," Sylah commented as she sat down.

"One of the few perks of the name Elsari."

"I suppose." A perk *she* should have had.

The arena was a little busier than it had been at the Aktibar for duty, though there were still empty seats. The audience buzzed with anticipation as the competitors entered.

The remaining thirty contenders filed in and took their places at the desks assigned to them. There were no pencils or pens on the plain wooden desks, no exam papers or dissecting tools. Instead, each competitor had a single bell.

"What are they for?" Sylah pointed.

"The bells? They're to indicate they know the answer. Each one has a bloodwerk combination that links it to the leader board up there. You see it?" Anoor pointed to the large wooden screen a hundred handspans away. There were thirty names lit up by rune-lights. "This is the trial of elements, so it's all about what they know about . . . stuff like materials and things."

Sylah snorted.

"And the bells?"

"The thing is,"—Anoor smiled slightly—"when you get thirty of the smartest people in the empire competing, you need to make it a little bit harder. So when the competitors know the answer, they ring the bell. The corresponding rune under their name on the leader board lights up, and the first person to ring the bell gets to answer. The first fifteen to get ten answers correct go through to the next round."

Sylah understood the excitement in the arena. It was going to be a quick-fire round. She looked at the podium and saw Wern, the Warden of Knowledge, hobble toward the sound projector.

"Welcome, ladies, gentlemen, and musawa. Today we challenge our competitors on their knowledge of the earth and its materials, an important aspect of ensuring the future prosperity of the Wardens' Empire." Wern's voice croaked and crackled around the arena, amplified by the bloodwerk runes in the sound projector.

Sylah looked toward the floor of the arena. All the competitors sat patiently, waiting for the first question. It was then that she noticed the girl with the black scarf, sitting with her back straight at one of the desks. She was one of them, a competitor.

Sylah barely registered that the trial had commenced until she saw the girl reach forward and ring her bell.

"Iron," she answered.

Sylah swung her head back to Wern, who nodded and continued with the next question.

"What is the composition of the sand in the Farsai Desert?"

Again, the girl with the black scarf rang her bell first. Her name lit up on the leader board, turning her name into a beacon.

"Silica, magnetite, saphridiam, and limestone." She answered correctly again.

One question after the other, the girl answered first.

"Last one. Come on, Tanu," Anoor whispered next to Sylah.

"You know her?" Sylah asked.

"Yes, that's Tanu AlKhabbir, she . . . used to be a friend. We grew up together."

"Who is she?" Sylah asked.

"She's the daughter of Pura's tailor."

"How did she end up knowing you?"

"The schoolrooms were a little quiet in the Keep. They let some servants' children attend."

She answered one of the questions before Wern had even finished it. The audience murmured. She must have realized her mistake as she let the next question be answered by another.

"This Tanu, did she always plan on entering the Aktibar?"

"Oh, yes, it's all she ever talked about."

Tanu answered the final question correctly and became the first competitor to move on to the next trial. The crowd cheered.

Sylah thought of the letter and the Ghosting who had lost their life for the knowledge.

AFTER WATCHING THE Aktibar for knowledge, Sylah said she had some errands to run in town. Anoor watched her leave the courtyard from her bedroom window. She hadn't changed out of her servant garb.

Suspicion inched its way up her back. Was she going to see the family friend—Jond Alnua? Anoor had looked up his name in the competitors' list in the training grounds. Without realizing it, she ran out of her chambers and down the stairs to the eru stables. She stopped at the kitchens on the way. She couldn't meet Boey empty-handed.

Her mother had allowed her to buy an eru when she was twelve years old. Anoor had gone to the eru bazaar with Gorn in tow and bought the brightest, bluest one she could find.

Her mother locked her up for ten strikes for that. Blue was a dirty color, undesirable, like the color of her blood. But Anoor got to keep Boey all the same. And she loved her fiercely.

Boey huffed into Anoor's hand looking for the yam she always brought her.

"All right, all right." Anoor laughed, reaching into her pocket. The eru chomped it down in two gulps.

"Miss Elsari? Do you want us to saddle Boey?" a stable girl asked.

Anoor nodded; she preferred to use a saddle rather than drive the drawn carriage. She'd only used the carriage once, and that was to test it across the courtyard. Anoor was never allowed to go far, so it was only a weekly occurrence around the gardens, although she loved to ride. Well, this was before training took over her life. Now she was of age, there wasn't much her mother could do to stop her leaving the Keep.

It didn't take long for Anoor to be saddled and ready. It was a practiced rhythm between her and the stable girl, who she'd never caught the name of.

"What's your name?"

"Name, Miss Elsari?"

"Yes, you're always here helping me, but I don't know your name."

The girl gave a small smile. Her hair was newly shaved and her red pinafore freshly pressed, despite the conditions she worked in.

"I'm Atu."

"Thank you for helping, Atu."

She ducked her head shyly and opened the stable door to let Anoor out.

Anoor waved at the officers guarding the door, who recognized her and let her out to the Ember Quarter. Soon she was hot on Sylah's trail.

The eru shrilled a low whistle, her clawed feet carrying them forward at high speed as Anoor urged her onward. She easily overtook the slower erus ferrying Embers to and from the market in carriages.

Anoor spotted Sylah ahead, her shaved head bowed, her shoulders hunched. Sylah took a left off the main road, toward a residential street of Ember houses.

Boey followed, but Anoor slowed her, as she was now the only eru on the street. She hoped Sylah would not turn around. Why hadn't she thought of wearing a disguise? Inquisitor Abena would have worn a disguise.

Anoor hesitated at the mouth of the street. She watched from a distance as Sylah knocked on the door of a small dwelling halfway down the street. The joba tree was unkempt, its branches encroaching on the neighbors' pristine courtyard, which must have annoyed them no end. Their own joba tree was protected by a fence.

The door opened to the face of Jond Alnua.

His arms snaked around Sylah's neck and brought her into a tight embrace as he pulled her inside. His mouth found hers and lingered. Then the door shut.

Anoor recoiled from the scene, her back straightening, her mouth opening. Boey whined underneath her.

"I'm okay." Anoor patted Boey, the movement reassuring her. "I'm okay."

The eru shifted on her feet.

"Yes, let's go home."

Anoor dashed the tears off her cheeks and picked up the reins.

"She knew the answers, Jond, like she'd been given them in advance, like I had given them to her."

"So what?" Jond's fingers danced across Sylah's navel.

"So *what?*" Sylah pushed his hands away and sat up in the bed. "Loot managed to get the answers, he's managed to play the game."

"And?"

"His power is absolute."

"Then why did he need you?"

Sylah's eyes flickered left and right, her mouth parted in thought. Jond licked his own lips in remembrance of her taste.

She slumped.

"I don't know."

"Stop worrying about it."

Jond leaned into the hollow crook of her neck and began kissing the sensitive skin that used to be protected by her hair.

"I think I'll keep an eye on that girl Tanu. Find out what connection she has to Loot." She leaned into his caress.

"The Sandstorm won't like that," he murmured into her skin.

"Well, don't tell them, then." Her neck muscles tensed, and he pulled away.

Jond inhaled. The air hissed between his teeth. "Sylah . . ."

She swung her legs out of bed and rested her elbows on her knees.

"I know you have to tell them . . . about me. I know they don't trust me yet. But I've done *everything* they asked."

"I'm working on it, it's just tough."

"I know, I killed—"

"It was an accident."

She dropped her chin.

Jond reached for her hand. "I don't tell them about . . . this."

Her head snapped toward him, and for a second she saw the ghost of her braids fall over her face, reminding her of the family she no longer had. She closed her eyes to the memory, her tongue running along the gap where a joba seed should be. When she opened her eyes, Jond was watching her, assessing her.

She cleared her throat and spoke.

"I remember what it felt like . . . being part of something bigger. Something that carries you along like a grain of sand. You can't fight it—you don't want to—because alone you are just one grain. Together you are the desert."

ANOOR WAS SITTING at her desk when Sylah entered. She hadn't changed into her training gear yet, and her ridiculous outfit of the day rippled around her in bows and pleats. She still looked beautiful despite the ostentatious embellishments. The room was a mess, as if Anoor had been searching for something.

Sylah's eyebrows tangled together. "Why aren't you dressed?"

"You're late." Anoor didn't turn around.

"I'm always late." Sylah went to the pile of clothes that were her only belongings and pulled out her training clothes. She noticed that her spare servant uniform was missing.

"Where have you been?"

Was that anger in Anoor's tone?

"I had some errands to run in town, and then I went for dinner."

"What errands? Gorn said she hadn't sent you for anything today."

"They're personal. I had already done my time with Gorn."

"So what errands?"

"I told you, they were personal."

Anoor was silent. Sylah ignored her and began to get changed.

"Let's take a break from meditation and work on your balance today. We're still waiting to hear on the trial for stealth, but at least we know it'll be something . . . stealthy." Sylah strode into the training room. Sylah was already through her second set of stretches by the time Anoor followed her.

She watched Sylah move through the routine. Each movement was precise and contained, each muscle awakened one by one.

"How are you so good at this?"

"Practice."

"We've been practicing for three mooncycles, and I've not once managed to touch you with any weapon."

"I was trained from a young age."

"But why? And where?"

"Are you going to join in or are we going to have a tea party and gossip?"

Anoor met Sylah's eyes. There was something beyond the darkness of her pupils that made Sylah stop.

"You can't ignore me every time I ask a question about you."

"I can and I will. It's what we agreed."

"Where do you go every day?" She was insistent.

"Nowhere."

"How come you can fight like you do?"

"Because I can."

"How did your father die?"

"Peace, Anoor. Where has this come from?"

"These are simple questions, Sylah." Anoor's head cocked to the left.

"Well, I don't want to talk about it." Sylah moved into a low lunge, stretching her calf muscles.

"We had a deal."

"Talking about my life wasn't part of the deal, in fact, it was the opposite, Anoor." Her leg went up against her head in a high stretch.

"This was." Anoor held the joba seed between her finger and thumb.

Sylah's leg thudded to the ground.

"Where did you get that?"

"I found it in the dress pocket of your uniform."

"Why were you rummaging through my clothes?"

"I was cleaning. I was upholding my end of the bargain. Besides, the real question is why did you have it in the first place?"

Sylah growled; her leg had started to spasm from the rage roiling in her blood.

"You know the deal. No seeds. You agreed, Sylah."

Sylah leaned on the wall for support.

"I can't believe you've been doing them this whole time."

"I haven't."

"And I'm supposed to believe that?" Anoor gesticulated with the seed.

"Yes, you are."

"Okay, well, you won't mind if—"

"Don't."

Anoor crushed the joba seed between her forefinger and thumb. The juice painted her hand crimson.

Sylah was the husk left behind. Her knees almost gave way beneath her, but her anger held her up. Knowing the seed was there and not taking it was Sylah's biggest accomplishment each day. And now it was gone.

"What did you just do?"

"Joba seeds are disgusting. Only Nowerks take them."

"Don't you dare use that word." It was almost a whisper. The word tugged on something feral inside her. A wild anger that was about to burst out.

"What?" Anoor stepped back, confused by the direction of the conversation.

"What makes you any different from them? Huh?" Sylah stepped forward into the gap Anoor had made between them.

"You think Embers don't take joba seeds? You think I haven't seen them in the maiden houses and the taverns? They try and hide their status, but we all know, they don't have the brand that sets Dusters apart, they don't have the scars that Ghostings bear."

"More Nowerks die from joba seed abuse than anything else." Anoor was defensive, and it riled Sylah up more.

How could the girl be so naive?

"Stop saying that word," Sylah growled, and Anoor flinched. "Why do you think more die, Anoor?"

She didn't answer, too scared probably. Good. She should be scared, she was in the den of the predators. Sylah might have forgotten it for a time, grown comfortable almost, but now in the face of Anoor's blind ignorance Sylah felt the fear and forged it into anger. It was what the Sandstorm were trained to do, and Sylah felt Papa's presence in the room as she spoke.

"Dusters and Ghostings can't afford the teeth whitening that the Embers use. They can't afford the verd leaf tea I drink every day to aid the withdrawal. They aren't given the education to understand the dangers of the drug. No one cares to tell them, to help them. And who is it that elevates the joba tree, keeps planting them around the empire? Have you thought about that? Who benefits the most from a drug that decimates half the population and keeps them placid?"

Sylah was talking too much, letting too much truth show. But Sylah wanted Anoor to see the reality of the empire so badly, so she would understand what it was that Sylah had spent her life fighting for and running from once she thought it was lost.

"We had a deal, no joba seeds." Anoor's resolve was weakening. She turned her pity toward Sylah. "Look at what the seeds have done to you, Sylah. Your legs are shaking."

It was true, Sylah could feel a seizure coming on. She wanted to lunge for Anoor, but she instead went for something that would cut much deeper. "I will tell you once again, I will tell you these four words and I beg you to listen."

Anoor looked like she was holding her breath.

"We are not friends."

Tears pooled in Anoor's eyes. Truth is a hard thing to bear. It is raw and powerful and painful. Especially when the truth is twisted by anger into a lie.

She fled, leaving Sylah alone with her shame. Because the truth was, Anoor had come to mean more to Sylah than she'd realized. It was the first time that Sylah had come to understand how much she wanted Anoor to truly, deeply *understand* her.

So that one day, she would forgive her when the Sandstorm burned it all.

SYLAH NEEDED TO get out of the Keep. First, she raided Anoor's purse.

The tidewind was nearing, so Sylah picked up her pace as she crossed the Tongue. The argument with Anoor had left her shaken. It was frustrating how little Anoor knew of the world. How could she expect to be a good warden if she didn't see the empire for what it was?

Sylah faltered and tripped over her slipper.

She isn't going to win, Jond is. Like we planned. The Sandstorm will know how to rule, how to change things. She thrust the thought against the image of Anoor at the top of the five hundred steps.

But who are the Sandstorm? The question came unbidden from the depths of her doubt.

"The Final Strife." She murmured the words and they grounded her. "I am the Final Strife, and I will see the empire turn to ash."

Sylah entered the Dredge. To her right three villas were painted with black crosses. The occupants were dead from the sleeping sickness. The tidewind hadn't sanded the paint away, which meant the deaths were recent.

A platoon of officers turned down the street ahead, and Sylah ducked into the Maroon.

The Maroon was beginning to fill up as the plantation workers made their way back from the fields. A wizened old man hunkered in the corner like an ornament. Sylah wasn't convinced that he wasn't. His scythe stood tall beside him; it had as many notches in the wood as wrinkles in his brow. The blade, however, had been cared for and polished. It shone like an emblem of his survival. And it was. Very few plantation workers made it to retirement.

"Have there been any Ghostings around today? I need to trade."

The barmaids looked up from their game of shantra.

"No, not seen them for a while. Sleeping sickness taking a lot of them recently."

Sylah swore and left the tavern, her feet dragging all the way to Maiden Turin's.

"Sylah . . ." Turin's amber eyes penetrated Sylah's. She wore a dark red paint across her lips, a little smudged.

"Can I buy some joba seeds?"

"You know I don't do business on the doorstep, Sylah."

Sylah trailed in the maiden's radish leaf smoke.

"Forty slabs." Turin withdrew the packet from her brassiere. It was warm to the touch.

Sylah didn't dispute the increase in cost. It was a pittance compared to what she had stolen from Anoor. She handed over the slabs.

The seeds were heavy in her pocket, heavier than they had any right to be. But just having them there was a balm to her fraught nerves. No matter what happened, with the Sandstorm or Anoor, she always had oblivion to fall back on.

Sylah left the maiden house and walked into the street, just like she had done many moons ago. She withdrew a joba seed and rolled it between her finger and thumb. Her eyes focused beyond the seed at the decrepit state of the Dredge. It had been a place where she found solace for so long. Now it seemed so much dirtier. Soiled. Not like the pristine halls of the Keep, cleaned by Ember servants just like her. Servants the Sandstorm would one day destroy.

"Dredge-dwellers deserve more than the life the empire thrusts upon them." She murmured the words to herself, spitting them out in anger.

But at what cost?

The wind began to lift the debris from the ruins in the Dredge—a precursor to the tidewind. Sylah quickened her pace.

The Ruta River below the Tongue swirled and bubbled with the same feeling of angst that ran through Sylah's veins. She watched the quicksand churn, the joba seed slowly making its way to her mouth, the packet clutched in her other hand.

Alone you are a grain of sand, together you are the desert. Her own words came back to haunt her.

She couldn't go back to the person she was before Jond reappeared. Slowly, she tipped the joba seeds into the river below. She watched the river consume the seeds one by one. She balled up the packet into a fist and felt the bulge of a seed in hiding. She withdrew it and pocketed it. Just because she could.

"Get out of the way," a Duster screamed at her from behind.

The trotro was three or four handspans behind her. She hadn't heard it. Hadn't seen it.

Suddenly she was pushed to the ground out of the way of the tracks.

"Maiden's tits." She looked up into the face of a very bemused Hassa.

Death wish?

"Something like that."

Thought you'd stopped the seeds?

"What were you doing? Following me?"

Yes.

"Oh. Why?"

We need to talk.

"Hassa, the tidewind's about to break, and to be honest, I've had a really rough day."

Hassa squeezed her brows as if she had a headache. *You have to meet me here tomorrow. Seventh strike.*

"Why?"

Just promise me you'll be here. Hassa touched her limb to Sylah's arm. It was as close to pleading as she was going to get.

"Okay."

Hassa looked relieved. *You won't make it back to the Keep before the tidewind breaks. Go to Jond's.*

"How do you know where Jond lives?" Sylah rounded on her, but the Ghosting had disappeared into the darkness. Sylah didn't hear her go.

ANOOR FLED TO the library.

Bisma sensed she was in no mood to talk. He handed over the latest zines solemnly, his eyes lingering on her puffy cheeks.

Anoor's fingers trailed the stacks of books as she made her way to the sitting area. The zines felt heavy in her hands. Once she had idolized Inquisitor Abena, wanted to be her. But every day Sylah made her see more and more of the world she lived in. From the rippings to the wealth imbalance, and the system of oppression against Nowerks—no, Dusters and Ghostings. It shook Anoor to the core. It was hard to see the Inquisitor in the same light she once had.

A book's spine piqued her interest: *The Evolution of the Judiciary System*. Old Anoor would have just walked by. But now she wanted to learn, now she wanted to do better.

Strikes went by, and Anoor's pile of reading grew, as did her horror. It was like a film of ignorance had covered her view of the empire like latex, so tight that she didn't even know it was there.

She would have stayed there all night if her cramps hadn't come. She dreaded going back to face the anger in Sylah's gaze. Sylah had hated her in that moment, truly *hated* her. She had felt it like the burning of a flame. The invisible blisters it left still brought her pain.

Now that her mooncycle bleeds had come, she needed to get home. Anoor lived in fear of being caught out when they started. It was why she liked wearing blue, just in case she wasn't close enough to her chambers to stanch the flow.

She pulled together a few volumes and checked them out with Bisma, her brisk goodbye surely offending him, but she felt a moistening between her legs that needed urgent attention. Anoor part-ran, part-waddled back to her rooms. She didn't even realize she had left the zines neglected on the library desk.

SYLAH HAD TWO options. Turn left down the small lanes of the Duster Quarter or cross the river to the edge of the Ember Quarter. Jond or Lio's. In the end the wind made the decision for her, pushing her farther across the Tongue to the Ember Quarter.

Sylah knocked on the shutters and hoped Jond could hear her. "Jond? Jond? Will you let me in?"

A few seconds passed before the shutters started to judder upward.

A bleary-eyed Jond peered from behind his door. "Sylah?"

"How's it hurting?"

"What you doing here?"

"Can I stay here tonight?"

"Stay?" His mouth quirked up into a smile, pushing his ears back into his unkempt curls.

"Yes, please."

He moved out of the doorway to let her pass. Once he had locked up, he joined her by the kitchen counter. Sylah had already got out the firerum and was sipping her second shot.

"That kind of night?"

Her shoulders drooped, her teeth worrying the corner of her mouth. "Jond, do you ever think about what Papa would have thought about all this?"

Jond didn't reply straightaway; he busied himself with pouring his own drink. "All what exactly?"

"You know, me and you."

He coughed on his drink. "Well—"

"Not that kind of me and you. I mean, the Sandstorm . . . Anoor."

"What's this about, Sylah?"

"I don't know, I guess I'm just wondering if we're doing the right thing . . ."

"Huh?"

Sylah cocked her head at him. "She thinks I'm helping her to win, Jond."

"Are you forgetting that she abducted you and stopped you from fighting in the Aktibar?"

"I know, I know, but she's one of us, in a way. She's a Duster."

"No, she isn't. She's one of them. You've said it yourself, she believes what they believe, that Embers are better."

Sylah thought of their argument earlier. She'd used the word "Nowerk" like she was commenting on the weather.

"It doesn't matter anyway; we both know she's not going to win. She'll never be good enough for the final trial." Jond poured Sylah another drink.

It was true, there was no way Anoor was going to win. Not against Jond or anyone else. But for a brief moment Sylah couldn't help thinking of a world where Anoor did win—a Duster leading the empire. Anoor wouldn't have the Sandstorm to guide her, but maybe Sylah could teach her. The thought unsettled her. She downed her drink. It burned her throat more than usual.

"After all, she was bred to be a decoy. A decoy for you. She was always going to be collateral damage." Jond sipped his drink, assessing her.

Sylah's stomach churned, and it wasn't the firerum.

"And when I win, there will be more of that. We need to cleanse the empire, Sylah, rid it of the Embers that have brought so many Nowerks to their knees."

There was that word again. That insult. It didn't sound reclaimed on Jond's tongue, it sounded cruel. Bitter.

"Is more violence the answer?"

Jond looked at her, his glass frozen in front of his lips.

"The Final Strife is here," he eventually said.

Sylah nodded with less conviction than Jond's fevered expression. She had always been so sure of her place in the Final Strife—that she was the blade on the neck of the empire. But when she closed her eyes, it wasn't the wardens' blood she had on her hands, but Anoor's. Bright blue with life.

CHAPTER TWENTY-NINE

THIRTEEN DAYS
UNTIL THE TRIAL OF MIND

Take up the Embers' burden,
And reap your own rewards:
Dissent from the blue,
Malice from the clear,
The hate of those you guard,
The blame of those who fear.
It is the Embers' burden,
To guide the citizens and lead,
Until Anyme calls,
Will we be free from this deed.

—*An Ember's Burden*, lyrics by Anj Ubdul

The messenger woke her up. She didn't know it was a messenger until Jond returned with an envelope in his hand.

"What time is it?" The sheets had tangled their way around Sylah's long legs. She lay nude and spread-eagled among them.

"Not sure, looks around sixth strike, but the clockmaster hasn't called yet."

Sylah groaned. "What is it?"

"It's the instructions for the trial of stealth." Jond sounded bemused.

"What? Give it here." Sylah grabbed it out of Jond's hand and began to read.

"The trial of stealth will begin upon reading this letter."

Sylah sucked in a breath.

"You have until the beginning of the final trial to retrieve your weapon from the north watch tower. There are twenty weapons and forty competitors. The weapon will be your aid in the trial of combat. You cannot be seen by the armored guards who watch over the room where they are kept. If you are seen, you are disqualified. If you fail to retrieve your weapon you are disqualified. Choose wisely . . . Regards, Warden of Strength, Uka Elsari."

Sylah's eyes were flicking left to right, thinking through the implications.

Jond leaned on the kitchen counter, his trail of navel hair just visible behind their discarded glasses from last night. "So the trial runs up until combat, and the weapon you select is the weapon you have to fight with?"

"Sounds like it." Sylah folded the letter back into the envelope, running her thumb over the wax seal of the guild of strength.

"Want to come with me to scout the place?" He moved to turn the stove on for breakfast, his bare backside making Sylah crave coffee beans.

"I better get back to Anoor, she'll be worried about all this." Sylah dreaded facing up to the words she'd said in anger.

"Of course." He said it lightly, but he didn't kiss her goodbye.

THE CLOCKMASTER CRIED sixth strike when Sylah left Jond's apartment. The streets of the Ember Quarter were quiet except for the Ghosting cleaners dusting the joba trees that lined them.

Sylah dragged her feet through the entrance toward the courtyard into the Keep; shame made her footsteps leaden. Would Anoor forgive her?

"I looked everywhere for you," a voice said to her right.

"Anoor?"

She was in her training gear and had clearly been running around their usual circuit. "I went right up to the Tongue and couldn't find you," she said like she was commenting on the weather.

"Were you running?"

"Where have you been?"

"I . . . I stayed with a friend."

Anoor crossed her arms. "What friend?"

"Let's not do this again, Anoor." Sylah continued the walk back to their chambers, Anoor falling into step beside her. They walked in silence. The apology they both wanted to voice hung heavy in the air between them. It was stifling.

Anoor went straight into her bedroom to get changed. Sylah sighed and followed her in.

Sylah slumped on her bed, exhausted by her warring emotions. She raised a hand to her forehead to rub away the stress lines there.

"You got the letter about the trial of stealth?" Sylah asked to fill the silence.

"How did you know?" Anoor called from the dressing room.

Sylah looked around. "It's on your desk."

"Oh." Anoor reappeared in a gown of sea blue. She sat stiffly next to Sylah on the edge of her bed, and the gown threatened to devour her too. "What are we going to do?" The question was said with the blandness of plain jollof rice.

"I'm not sure yet."

"I need the jambiya, it's the only thing I can passably fight with." The words were flung like an accusation. Sylah lowered her eyes.

"I said I haven't figured it out yet."

"You're supposed to get me through the Aktibar. Come up with a plan, then."

"Anoor, the instructions have only just come in—"

"You're not trying hard enough."

Anoor was done hiding her anger at Sylah. Now it was blazing, lit by the green center of her hazel eyes. But there was hurt there too. *We are not friends.* The words popped like a bubble in Sylah's memory, and she flinched.

Anoor got up and began to pace, putting space between her and Sylah. The sea foam ruffles of her dress bounced with each footstep, and it would have been funny if Sylah wasn't so distracted by the angry pout of her lips.

"Calm down." Sylah regretted the words as soon as she said them.

When has anyone ever calmed down after being told to?

Anoor's anger was feral. Sylah cocked her head at her.

"You want to hit me, don't you?"

Anoor didn't respond, but Sylah saw the moment in her eyes when she focused and slipped into battle wrath. Sylah launched herself at her. They grappled on the floor, Anoor getting Sylah's elbow under her back, but Sylah had her neck in a deadlock in seconds.

Sylah pushed Anoor away once she'd tapped the floor in defeat. She wiped her brow in surprise. Sylah was sweating.

Anoor didn't move from her sprawled position. Sylah waited.

"I'm sorry I went through your clothes."

"I'm sorry I said we weren't . . . friends."

Anoor sat up, the tension between them going slack as she smiled.

"Friends?"

Sylah growled. "I'm going to regret admitting that, aren't I?"

Anoor's mischievous grin turned thoughtful, and she asked, "Why don't you like the word . . . you know, the word I said."

Sylah turned to look at her. "It's a very cruel word, Anoor. It's used to separate, to make Dusters and Ghostings feel other, to make them feel less than whole. You shouldn't use it. They're just like you."

Exactly like you.

Anoor blinked slowly. "I didn't know. Everyone in the Keep uses the word."

"Precisely my point."

Anoor sat up and hugged her knees. "Are you going to eat that?" Anoor inclined her head toward the seed in Sylah's fingers.

Sylah was shocked to see it there. She had been rolling it around in her fingers and thinking. "No."

"Okay." Anoor didn't say anything more, though her eyes never left Sylah's.

Sylah exhaled, giving her a small gift of truth. "The seeds made me feel alive."

"I understand."

"No, you don't, you don't really."

"No, I suppose not," Anoor conceded. "I've always felt alive."

"I believe that."

"Even when my mother beats me or when the Embers bully me. I always feel the blood running through my veins."

Sylah stiffened and looked at Anoor from the corner of her eye. She sparkled in the sunrise. "Too alive."

"Too alive."

The pause ached.

"It was my fault," Sylah said.

"What was?"

"It was my fault my family died. I was the reason all of them were slaughtered."

"You don't have to tell me any more." She shuffled over to Sylah and rested her head on her shoulder. Her hair smelled of sandalwood. Sylah reached for it then faltered.

"I know. One day I will, Anoor. One day I will tell you everything." Even if it meant losing her.

"Thank you." She smiled, and Sylah felt lighter.

She put the joba seed back in her pocket.

"I was never going to take it, you know. It was a spite seed." She smiled wryly.

"A spite seed?"

"Yeah, a seed taken purely out of spite. And if I died from taking it, then it would have been your fault."

"Sylah?"

"Yes?"

"You're a maiden's tit sometimes."

Sylah gasped.

"Did you just swear?"

SEVENTH STRIKE CAME and went, but still Hassa waited. The bag she wore dug into the welts across her back. Welts administered by the Ember chief of chambers in the Keep after they had caught her in the wrong room. She rubbed her shoulder with her limb and winced. *Made for servitude.*

She'd heard Turin say the words to Sylah. Turin, a woman who was too stupid to learn their language. A woman who was a servant to people's desires. But Hassa didn't judge Turin as harshly as she would have liked. The woman had taken Hassa in, an undocumented Ghosting, the bastard of an Ember.

Turin had protected Hassa as a babe, driven by the guilt of her mother's death. Hassa had no doubt Turin had sold her mother's whereabouts to her father, the result of which was her murder. Marigold cut Hassa from the womb, because Ghostings protected their own.

"Aho, I've got something to trade. What have you got, Ghosting?" The Duster came up behind her holding a battered book.

She nodded. Ghostings always had something to trade. She grasped the book between her limbs and turned it over.

It was old, she wasn't sure how old; she'd have to show it to the elders.

"You got any tree gum? The market was out."

She did. She gave a sharp nod of assent and opened her bag. The Duster peered in as if it were a market stall.

"Eeyah, what's that?"

She shouldered him away.

"Okay, okay." He backed away, and she continued rummaging.

She used her right limb to rummage in her bag, pushing the pot of tree gum upward for her left limb to pincer it together. She passed it to the trader.

"Thanks." He ambled off, muttering to himself about the creepiness of Ghostings. As if she had no ears. No voice.

Fucking idiot, she signed at his back.

Seventh strike had long passed. Sylah still hadn't turned up. She wasn't coming.

Hassa closed her bag, her phantom fingers resting on the other half of a rolled-up map before she turned on her heel and left.

CHAPTER THIRTY

TEN DAYS
UNTIL THE TRIAL OF MIND

The sand of the Farsai Desert is made up of four main elements: silica, magnetite, saphridiam, and limestone. Saphridiam is what gives the sand its blue hue. When melted into glass, the majority of the color burns away, leaving a sheen of its previous color. If the Glasskeeper is skilled enough, a secondary forging can leach away the color completely, though this increases the price of the products.

—Extract from *Shards and Sand* by Glasskeeper Runa

"Where are you taking me?" Sylah held Anoor's hand as she dragged her through the gardens.

"Remember when we were training for aerofield? There was that tower that faced the Marion Sea."

"Yes."

"Well, I went exploring, and I think it's a better space for us to train."

"Really?"

"I moved our stuff in yesterday."

Anoor clapped her hands together, her eyes lighting. It had been three days since their fight. Three days of Sylah patching up what she had broken but admitting their friendship had brought a lightness to their days. It eased the tension of guilt and shame that surrounded them both.

"We're going to be training in an abandoned tower. How spooky."

"Not really, I cleaned it out."

"You cleaned something? Gorn will be scandalized." Anoor's grin was wolfish.

The forest at the back of the gardens was peaceful. Even the foreboding gray legs of the arena disappeared once they walked under the canopy of leaves.

The tower was surrounded by a small moat of moss. The white-stone hadn't been washed in some time, and the blue sand dragged in from the tidewind coated the walls. One windowpane had been sanded down completely, the glass shards filed away to join their family as grains on the wind.

"It doesn't look . . . great." Anoor chewed her bottom lip.

"It's fine. The door locks, the floorboards are sound. It'll protect us from the tidewind too. I chased away a rat nest or two . . . which brings the total number down to eleven, but what can you do?"

Anoor laughed.

"Go on, after you." Sylah pushed open the door. It creaked with the sound of old knees bending.

Anoor jutted her chin and marched forward. A loose floorboard caught her unaware, but she stabilized herself and kept on going. Sylah didn't realize grace could be taught until that moment. Her movements were surer, elegant.

Stairs led them to a circular room. It had been heaped with sand when Sylah first entered it, but she had painstakingly swept it away until her hands were raw. The window and shutters on this floor were still intact but open.

Sylah drew a charcoal ring in the center of the room. It replicated the combat trial in size.

Blue sand fell on Sylah's shaved head as Anoor jumped up and down.

"Argh, stop it. I didn't get around to dusting the beams."

"But it's so great. We can properly train here. Like properly."

"I know, I know."

"Look at that jambiya, it's not blunt at all!" She swung her head to Sylah. "Thank you."

"You can thank me later." Sylah looked at the jambiya hanging on the wall. She had asked Jond to procure it for her, and though he grumbled about it, he'd come through.

"Sylah, have you thought about the trial of stealth?"

"Of course I have. Don't worry, I'm working on it."

Sylah had nothing. She'd stayed up all strikes of the night trying to figure out a way to enter the tower.

The first competitor had claimed their weapon yesterday. She'd sauntered into the great veranda with a golden dagger strapped to the waist of her rose gold armour.

"Efie of Jin-Gernomi, the granddaughter of the imir. Remember my face, remember my name," she'd boomed to the watching crowd, her henna-dyed hair streaming behind her. Sylah didn't care where she was from; she was more interested in how she'd done what none other had so far achieved.

Twelve guards, two hundred steps, one exit, and two windows. The watch tower was impenetrable. Sylah had even been surveying the shift patterns of the guards, but they were so efficient there was no advantage there.

A dozen competitors had already failed at scaling the wall. One competitor posed as one of the guards on duty and failed miserably. Another hid in the alcoves of the tower until the tidewind brought them death. Someone else tried distracting the guards by setting off a bonfire in the courtyard; that earned him a night in the Ember jail instead. But Efie of Jin-Gernomi . . . How did she do it?

"Apparently Efie landed on the roof with an aeroglider." Anoor broke through Sylah's thoughts.

"How do you know that?"

"Kwame's cousin's from Jin-Gernomi. The hills make it the perfect place for aerogliding."

"When did you see Kwame?" Sylah crossed her arms.

"I stopped by the kitchens last night."

Sylah clenched her jaw. "Stop eating candied yams, Anoor, it's not going to help you gain muscle."

"I only had one . . ."

"One, perfect. Let's assume you mean ten. So ten push-ups please."

Anoor muttered something under her breath.

"That's a mean mouth you've got there. Really dishing out the swear words now."

FIVE MORE COMPETITORS won their weapons the following week. Thankfully, none claimed a jambiya, but it didn't stop Anoor's frustration.

"You're supposed to help me win. It's like you're not even *trying*." They were in the tower. It was hot and stuffy, and they were both at the end of their tether.

"I'm sorry, but I'm not an inquisitor from one of your zines, I can't just manifest the perfect solution—"

"Don't say it like that. I know you read the latest Inquisitor Abena story too."

"I can't just turn you into an incredible climber overnight. Did you see the last guy? He literally free-climbed the whole tower with his fingertips. That's years of training. Years."

"Well, figure it out, because right now you're not keeping up your end of the bargain."

"What?" Sylah's voice was quiet. Simmering.

"You were supposed to get me through these trials, and I was supposed to teach you bloodwerk. We're nearly through the entire *Book of Blood*, so I'm certainly keeping up my side." Anoor's eyes were wild.

"Oh, poor rich girl in her tower. For once something isn't going exactly how you imagined it."

"Imagined it? Not for one second did I imagine that I'd be learning from someone as—as mean as you."

"It's not my fault that the only way you could get anyone to stomach teaching you was to trick them into it. Don't worry, I don't forget the deal we stuck for one minute."

They looked at each other, both breathing heavier than after their morning run.

"I feel sorry for you." Anoor's words were quiet, but her cheeks shook as she spoke. "I feel sorry for the hate you harbor in your chest. That hate has never had a vessel quite like you. You tell me I wallow in self-pity but can't see your own guilt that eats away at your heart. I don't know what you did or why you did it. You think that guilt transcends you, makes you better than the rest of us." Each word stung like the gust of the tidewind, grating her raw. "Sometimes I wondered whether the joba seeds were the only thing keeping you alive, because the rest of you is dead. Deader than that seed you roll in your pocket."

Sylah laughed. She laughed heavily, with spit and phlegm. It coughed out of her and into the awkward silence.

Anoor looked at her, her lips pert. "Why are you laughing?"

"Because it's so true." Sylah laughed some more. "And also, you're a total asshole."

Anoor recoiled.

"An asshole?"

"Yes, you know, that puckered bit of flesh that spouts shit? That's you." Tears of mirth leaked from Sylah's eyes.

Anoor's laughter started to bubble up too, and she was tinkling along with Sylah's snorts until their laughter rattled to a halt like the trotro.

"Sorry, I didn't mean it."

Sylah looked up sharply. "You did, and that's okay." The grin she gave her was evil. "Pick up the sword."

Anoor slumped. She hated the sword. They trained for an extra strike that night.

"You're leaning too far to the left, it's unbalancing you."

"That's because I'm used to the jambiya. Can we go back to that?" Anoor panted.

"But imagine if there aren't any in that tower and you have to use a sword?"

"Then I'll cut it down and turn it into a jambiya." Anoor stuck her tongue out at Sylah and she rolled her eyes.

"Come again." Sylah launched herself at Anoor, pressing her attack on the left side. "You see what happens when you favor your left arm, it puts you off balance."

"Urgh." Anoor pressed forward, trying hard to block Sylah's oncoming attacks. Their swords clanged against each other.

"Push harder," Sylah hissed at her. "You're using your weight and not your strength."

Anoor bared her teeth; it was adorable.

She lunged again, but Sylah blocked and pushed her back. Then Anoor returned, stronger, faster. Sylah tried to slip into battle wrath, but the meditative state was always more elusive without the stimulant of the joba seeds. She felt the telltale signs of a seizure, starting with the prickling across her back. It quickly moved into tremors, and then she lost mobility completely.

Sylah's sword fell to the ground.

"Sylah, are you all right?" Anoor rushed toward her, the flask of verd leaf tea she had made in her hand. "Here, drink this."

Sylah drank from the flask gratefully, but her mobility was already back. The episodes were getting shorter, but no less frequent.

"You nearly beat me," Sylah said.

Anoor shook her head miserably. "No, I didn't. But thanks for saying it."

Sylah laughed and sat up. She began to stretch the affected muscles, glad they were finally cooperating.

"Do you think you would have won the Aktibar?" Anoor asked.

Yes, and I was going to destroy everyone you know.

"Not like this." Not without joba seeds.

"Why did you want to enter?"

Sylah was about to dismiss the question, but then she thought about it. "I wanted a better world. I wanted this world to burn."

Anoor nodded. "Like a joba fruit." She reached a hand down to help Sylah up.

"What?"

"Sometimes fire is what's needed for new life to bloom."

And like the shell of a joba fruit, Sylah felt something inside her crack under Anoor's gaze. It unfurled with a warmth of feeling, more intoxicating than the seeds within.

PART FOUR

ASSIMILATION

Tell them they are lesser.
And they will feel lesser.
Show them they are nothing.
And they will be nothing.
Take their identity.
And they will be no one.

—Writing confiscated from the Dredge.
The writer and date of the poem are unknown.

The story of Anyme and the Spider as spoken by Griot Sheth

The spoken word has been transcribed onto the page;
the ◊ symbol represents the beating of the griot's drum.

Tomorrow we celebrate Ardae, the day Anyme climbed into the sky to watch from above and guide us through life. I tell not the story preached by the Abosom or the words chanted by the Embers, but the words carried from griot to griot. You chose which is fact, but does truth need faith and faith need truth?

◊

Anyme was a musawa. Neither man nor woman, but both and none. Anyme was clever. Anyme was smart. Anyme knew every person, plant, and animal by heart.

One day Anyme said to the sky, "Why are you up there, so high, so high?"

"Because I am wise and clever and I have earned my place above," the sky replied.

◊

Centuries passed and Anyme became full of knowledge, wise and clever. So Anyme returned to the sky.

"Why are you up there, so high, so high?"

"Because I take care of the world below, I know my duty," the sky replied.

◊

Anyme wandered the earth, caring for all beings. Anyme learned of obligation and responsibility. So Anyme returned to the sky.

"Why are you up there, so high, so high?"

"Because I am merciful and true."

◊

Anyme drew followers, named the Abosom, who preached the sky's truth.

So Anyme returned to the sky.

"Why are you up there, so high, so high?"

"Because I am strong."

◊

Anyme created the most powerful of regimes, the Nuba martial art, and trained for centuries and grew strong.

So Anyme returned to the sky.

"I have done all you have done and more. I am clever, and trustworthy, strong and dutiful. I have earned my place in the sky."

"It is true, Anyme, you have done all I have done, and more. I welcome you above."

◊

And so Anyme climbed the tallest joba tree they could find and took their place in the sky, a shining beacon to watch and guide.

Anyme's children down below watched the musawa they knew become a God and every day they bowed at the roots of the joba tree and prayed. And so, do you see, the joba tree became the gateway to the one who sees.

◊

And here is where the tale ends for some and many, but not for us. Because when Anyme climbed above, alone they were not. Inside Anyme's pocket, another did ride.

◊

A silver spider. So small was its body, but so large was its mind.

◊

"Who are you?" boomed the sky and Anyme, for they had become one.

"I have earned my place," the silver spider said. "I was with Anyme all this time. I aged and saw and fought and more."

Anyme knew the truth in the words, and so the spider joined Anyme above and wove clouds of web and silver moonlight, and fog so thick no one could see.

◊

So, every Ardae we give our offering to our God, Anyme the merciful, the just and all-seeing. Our ancient one who guides us. But don't forget the spider too. A little piece of cheese or a grape or a few.

CHAPTER THIRTY-ONE

FOUR DAYS
UNTIL THE TRIAL OF MIND

*My daughter is like me in so many ways. And yet, I do not see the
fire burning in her eyes when I look at her. Therefore, I cannot help
but look at her in disappointment.*

—The journal of Yona Elsari, year 417

Hassa moved through the Maroon with practiced silence. The
griot was coming to the end of his tale, and though Hassa didn't
want to leave, she knew she had to meet Marigold. Every time the
griot came to the Maroon, Hassa made sure she was there. Not
because the elders told her to spy or because she needed to trade,
though she did. It was because of the stories. Sometimes fantasti-
cal, occasionally humorous, always educational.

"Anyme knew the truth in the words, and so the spider joined
Anyme above."

She knew the tale of the spider God, though the Abosom would
call it blasphemy. Some Dusters, and even some Embers, still
worshipped the insect, the darkness to Anyme's light. They left
treats and offerings to both Gods during Ardae.

Ardae. A big day for the Ghostings. Made bigger by the Aktibar and the imirs who were visiting the capital city. Ghostings across the empire would wait on their Ember masters with fine wines and finer food. Then, once their bellies were bloated, their thirsts quenched, Hassa would slip out into the tunnels, and the night would really begin.

They had a hundred rescues planned. Some were pregnant, others were not, all were willing to risk death rather than stay in Nar-Ruta. A hundred Ghostings was the most they had ever tried to lead out of the city at once. There would be a surge of sleeping sickness crosses found in the morning and a lot of empty pyres to burn.

And for Hassa, a lot of people to guide through the tunnels.

She ascended the stairs to the street bathed in the full moon's light. She looked at the Keep, a beacon of runelights in the distance. The preparations had taken up much of Hassa's time. She hadn't seen or heard from Sylah in a week, not since she missed their meeting. She wondered if she and Anoor were still searching for the truth.

"YOU'RE NOT CONCENTRATING. Empty your mind. Connect to the ground," Sylah barked.

"I'm trying." Anoor puffed out as she balanced in Nuba formation three: both hands raised upward to the sky, her right leg flexed in a half twist behind her. When used in combat, the body weight from her back foot would propel her forward into a very violent kick.

They were in the tower, as was their new nightly routine. The tower protected them while the tidewind battered the world outside. Then they would slip back to their beds aching from the night's training. Often Sylah would find she was light-headed from the bloodwerk practice, though she would never admit it to Anoor. Anyway, it aided her sleep.

Sylah took off her sandal and threw it at Anoor. It slapped against her thigh.

"Curse the blood, what did you do that for?" Anoor screeched, and she toppled to the floor.

"See, you've dropped the stance. I told you, you're not concentrating. You haven't reached battle wrath. You need to be able to connect with your muscles in a way that will block out all other distraction."

"But we've done this formation three hundred times now."

"Exactly, and you still can't get it right. The mind trial is in three days, Anoor, and we have no idea what's coming."

"Last time they made the competitors swim across an eel-infested lake." She picked up Sylah's sandal and walked it back over to her.

"Do you see my point? If you can train your mind to block out distraction and isolate your muscles, you'd be able to swim that lake ten times over."

"Anyway, the trial's in four days."

"No, three."

"No, four," Anoor repeated. "It's Ardae tomorrow, we have an extra day."

"It's Ardae?"

Ardae, a day of family and celebrations. Sylah swallowed and rubbed her hand through her shaved scalp. She felt the glimmer of braids moving through her fingers and she craved to touch them again. She'd forgotten, how had she forgotten? A year had moved so quickly.

"An extra day. More time to practice. Get back to it."

Anoor sighed but moved back into formation.

SYLAH COULD SMELL blood in the air, and for once it wasn't a ripping.

Their morning run had slowed to a limping jog, then a walk as their sweat cooled their heaving chests. As they turned the corner toward the courtyard, Sylah saw the cause of the iron on her tongue.

Three Abosoms stood at the foot of the joba tree, red blood dripping from their wrists to the ground. Offerings of plantain and dried fish were cradled in the gnarled knots of the tree's roots;

even a sacrificial goat had been slaughtered and hung from one of the lower branches.

Sylah couldn't get the image of the goat out of her mind as they walked back to their chambers together.

"What are you going to do for Ardae?" Anoor asked softly as they climbed the stairs up from the kitchens. "The servants normally have quite a good party during the tidewind. Sometimes I go."

"I think I'll just enjoy the time off. Gorn said I'm excused from duty today."

"She must be starting to like you!" Anoor laughed, and Sylah tried to join in.

"I'll be going to my mother's chambers," Anoor continued. "Do you have a large family?"

She tried to slip the question in innocently, but Sylah had noticed how Anoor had begun to pry more and more.

"Some. Not many."

"You mentioned a mother." Had she? She needed to be more careful. "Does she live in Nar-Ruta?"

Sylah gave a nonchalant shrug.

"Maybe you can visit them, if they're not far."

Sylah opened the door to Anoor's chambers and stalked to their bedroom.

"I'm taking a bath. Do you want help getting dressed or are you okay?"

Anoor shook her head, smiling faintly. She was probably remembering the first and last time Sylah had tried to help dress her. She'd thought a ruffled suit jacket was a skirt and got it halfway over Anoor's legs before she realized. Anoor fell into a fit of giggles, the suit jacket still wrapped tight around her leg. In fairness, the sleeves were very long.

Sylah went to the bath and began to fill it. She was still mesmerized by the bloodwerk runes that pushed the water from the kitchens below. Now she could read them, they only fascinated her more. She went over to the shelving unit by the sink and lifted out the sandalwood oil. Pouring a healthy amount into the bath, maybe a bit too much, she slipped off her clothes.

Submerging herself into a bath was one of the most blissful feelings Sylah could think of. Well, second most—joba seeds would always come first. The hot water lapped over her shoulders and tickled the back of her neck, soothing the scar that she had gained that awful day six years ago. It still hurt, not physically, but the aching bruised her soul in an irrevocable way.

She heard Anoor moving around in the bedroom and dressing room, which had been restored to its "rightful" calling, as Anoor had put it. Sylah hadn't closed the door and could see Anoor moving frantically in the slip of light.

"What are you doing?" Sylah called out. She watched as Anoor's shadow paused, her sheepish face tilting into view.

"I have too many clothes."

"Yes, you do." Sylah nodded, slipping deeper into the bath until the tip of her chin was submerged. Anoor held her gaze and didn't stray to her body. It galled Sylah.

"And with it being Ardae . . ."

"Also stating another fact that doesn't explain your actions."

"I'm giving some away. To the Dusters, across the river. I'll have them dropped off at the Dredge."

Sylah held back her laugh, though it desperately wanted to come out. The image of Dusters in the Dredge wearing one of Anoor's combinations of ruffles and bows was enough to set her crying. They'd cut up the expensive fabric and turn them into tablecloths.

"That's a nice idea."

"What is it? You think it's silly? Oh, you think it's silly, don't you?"

"No . . . no, I didn't say that, did I? I think it's a lovely idea. But aren't you going to be late for your mother's Ardae lunch?"

Her smile was all teeth. "Oh, well, I'll get Gorn to organize taking the clothes across the river later."

"I can do it." There'd be some fancy table settings this Ardae.

"But it's your day off."

"I don't mind," Sylah said.

"Okay, well, I'll see you later for training. I better go." Fear of her mother had overtaken the rebellious streak in Anoor's eyes.

"Yes, see you later." Sylah didn't hear Anoor's reply as she sunk her whole head under the water.

ARDAE. SYLAH DIDN'T want to think about it. It seemed Embers didn't know how to celebrate like the Dusters in the north of the city. In the Duster Quarter, the day would be filled with fried yams and laughter. Offerings to Anyme would be made with firerum, and the Maroon would pull down their tidewind shutters so the party could continue until the early strikes.

At the Sanctuary, it had also been a special day. It was their only day off from training in the whole year. They'd have a feast of fufu and groundnut stew. Each Stolen would be given a small glass of firerum to toast with, and with no Abosom to bless their meals, Papa would do it himself in his booming voice.

"WE ALL SURVIVED the Ending Fire, Embers, Dusters, and Ghostings, because Anyme made us equal in the sky's eye. So, we will rise and we will fight for our place. We thank Anyme for guiding us down this path. Anyme bless." He held his shot of firerum high.

"Anyme bless," they called back and drank their shots in time with him.

The alcohol fizzed in her veins. Jond was seated next to Sylah, his teeth shining white in the moonlight. Jond had just turned sixteen. He was older by two years, but he drank the firerum without flinching. Fareen sat opposite them both.

"I've got a surprise for you," he whispered under his breath. Sylah could tell Fareen was trying to listen.

"What surprise?"

"Come with me." He held out his hand and winked.

Sylah shot Fareen an apologetic look as they slinked away.

"Jond, where are you taking me?"

"Shhh."

"Jond, why are you taking me to the barn?"

Huda, the eru, was asleep, her tail hooked under her claws.

"Just a little farther." They stopped in a pool of darkness. Sylah reached for his hand. It was sweaty like her own. "Can I?" he whispered, and she tasted the firerum in his breath.

She nodded, leaning in to him as his hands slipped around to the small of her back.

He broke away from her kiss and reached for her hand.

"Blessings this Ardae," he said, the epithet that accompanied a gift. She looked at what he had placed in her hand.

It was a small braid of red and blue thread.

"It's for your hair," he whispered. "An Ember's blood, a Duster's heart." He murmured the words against her cheek.

Sylah pushed herself up and reached for a zine. There were stacks of colorful zines around the chambers, always within reach of a cozy chair or the bath.

"Inquisitor Abena and the Hundred Paths." Sylah murmured the title and began reading. She got three pages in before giving up. If she could predict the ending that fast, it wasn't worth reading in her eyes. She reached for another.

"Oh."

Her hand touched a hardback book. She leaned out of the marble bathtub, hooking her arms over the edge. The title read *A History of the Rights of a Citizen*. Anoor had been reading more and more recently, learning about the privilege she was raised in. It made Sylah proud.

She looked at the next book in the stack. It was one of the red leather-bound journals from the library. Not the oldest one, which they pored strikes into, but a journal they pulled from the middle. Anoor must have been reading it in the bath before she got waylaid by her research. Sylah went to the folded page and picked up where Anoor had left off.

"Blah blah . . . I don't care what you had for breakfast."

"Interesting . . . This Warden of Truth, Gada, was in power a hundred and fifty years ago." Sylah skimmed through the pages, looking for something, anything.

We found a Ghosting that hadn't suffered the penance. We cut out their tongue before they could tell the truth. They were only seven years of age, but my guild's purpose is to hide the truth and not bare it.

Sylah swallowed and continued.

I have fired the auditor who missed their birth on the register and have increased a sweep of all villas in Nar-Ruta to ensure every Ghosting is found and maimed, as is the way. To protect the truth.

Sylah swallowed and thought of Hassa. She had missed her meeting with her but searched for her in the Keep every chance she got. The girl seemed to be a part-time servant, because whenever she asked another Ghosting, they weren't sure where she was.

Sylah kept reading. She read until the bath water went cold, though she didn't notice. There was nothing else of note until she got to the end. In the final pages, one sentence stood out to her. She read it over and over again, her lips moving.

One of my masters of truth attended to a report in a small fishing village in Ood-Rahabe. A boat arrived from the mainland, though decimated by the sea and the tidewind; only one messenger survived. We killed her and killed those who had seen her.

A messenger, from the mainland.

Sylah lurched forward, bath water splashing over the sides of the tub onto the tiled floor.

"Skies above, Anoor was right. Anoor was fucking right."

Sylah turned the page of the journal, but there were only two sentences left of the entry.

We left the Ghostings who saw the messenger alive. We need servants as much as silence, and they provide both.

Sylah reached for her towel.

It was time to find Hassa.

ANOOR WAS IN her mother's chambers. Like the rest of the wardens' rooms in the Keep, they overlooked the gardens.

There were few things Anoor had inherited from her adoptive mother. She didn't have her skill for physical exercise, her presence, nor her affinity for leadership, but she had gotten one thing: her taste for opulence. A fountain adorned the foyer, filled with fat carp and blooming lily pads. Each chandelier was made of intricate glass art, shining runelight across the room. Despite the lavishness, it didn't feel lived in. Maybe the oil paintings of famous battles that lined the walls sucked out all the warmth. Red and blue blood warring in rebellions of the past. Incense floated around the empty space in between the frames, like fog on a battlefield.

Anoor searched for any presence of her father in the room's design. There was none, like her adoptive father had never existed. Anoor had hazy memories of the man who raised her in her early years. A man with a beard that tickled and eyes that laughed. Fragments and feelings merged into the soft strokes of an oil painting in her mind. Love. He was the only person ever to love Anoor.

The battlefield saw an end to that. A scythe through the throat from a plantation uprising in the coastal north of the empire, one of the few that had gained real traction in recent years. It had been fourteen years since Ahmed died.

"Anoor, how lovely to see you." Rasa was one of Uka's two chiefs of chambers. She reminded Anoor of a palm frond, the leaves of her hair fanning out around her stick figure. Her mother's rooms sprawled up the expanse of the west of the Keep, and it required a small armada to navigate its smooth running.

"Hi, Rasa."

"I'm afraid your mother's been called to an urgent meeting this morning. She won't be long. Your grandmother is due presently."

"That's okay, I will wait for her in her living room."

"Please, do go right ahead. You do know the way?"

Of course she knew the way, it was her family home. "Yes, thank you, I can guide myself."

As she walked toward her mother's living room, it became apparent that Rasa had no intention of letting Anoor walk around the chambers by herself. Rasa followed ten handspans behind. They walked down the wide corridor toward the formal lounge. Anoor paused in the doorway of her old bedroom.

It was exactly the same. Untouched. Not because of sentiment, Anoor was sure, but as a threat that she could end up back there should her mother wish it. The room was bare but for the small oil painting beside the bed: the image of the babe among a field of blue daises. Anoor shuddered. It was of Uka's true child, the Ember who had been stolen.

Anoor had examined that painting her whole life, and though it hadn't aged like she had, its immortality faded. Once the babe's gray eyes haunted her nightmares; now it collected dust in the recess of her memories.

An involuntary shiver racked her body. She disguised it as a cough and carried on.

The double doors in front of her were open, the smell of lilies making her instinctively recoil. They were her mother's favorite flower, and the scent clung to the nightmares in Anoor's mind. They were everywhere, blooming from vases and potted in gold planters. White, so white they made her eyes hurt to look at them. Each flower had its pollen painstakingly removed. Of course her mother wouldn't want them to stain her white carpet.

Anoor perched herself on the edge of the brown eru leather sofa. Her muted outfit of pale yellow for once blended in with the soft colors of the room. This wasn't what she had planned to wear. She was going to wear an emerald blazer with panels of lace and green silk that fell to her waist above wide-legged pantaloons that matched. Her tailor worked on the combination for over six mooncycles. The earrings were Anoor's idea; they matched the tassels around the edge of the sleeves but dipped farther to the shoulders. They were perfect.

But as she had looked at herself in the mirror, she thought of the ripping still so fresh in her mind, the injustice of the empire laid so obviously bare like the fresh cadaver of a corpse. Her research into the empire's inner workings swirled through her thoughts constantly.

And as she looked at her reflection, the injustice of it all blurred her vision. All she wanted to do was give it all away, her clothes, her jewelry, every last thing. So she'd changed into a plain dress of yellow flowers and thrown all of her favorite clothes into a basket.

She wished Sylah had got to see her in her emerald outfit before she changed, though, but Anoor didn't want to parade into the bathroom. She found it hard enough to keep her eyes steady on Sylah's face.

"Rasa, please would you brew some coffee?"

"Coffee, Miss?" Rasa pursed her lips.

"Yes, well, you told me I have a bit of a wait, so some refreshments would be nice." Anoor's hands were shaking. She clenched them together.

"Yes, miss."

"Oh, and Rasa, please bring me anything sweet you might have. Even better if it's also fried."

She nodded curtly.

As soon as Rasa left the room, Anoor made her way to the bookcase at the back. Not for the books, though her fingers ached to touch them, but for the weapons cabinet beside it. She cast a furtive glance behind her as her fingers rummaged for the latch she had once blasted to pieces with bloodwerk. She found it and gave it a sharp pull. It relinquished a satisfying click, the door giving way to a waft of stale air. The cupboard was smaller than she remembered. She wasn't sure how she ever fitted in. The weapons that lined it were long gone. Anoor wondered what her mother had done with them. She looked for her blood in the grooves of the wood, for any remnant of the horrible incident that happened six years ago, the last time she lived in the Elsari residence. The last time she let her mother lock her up.

"I will not let her darkness overcome me," Anoor whispered to herself.

Her heart raced, and her body broke out in a cold sweat. A low moan escaped her, and tears began to seep from her eyes. She was not sure how long she rocked to and fro on her heels, but footsteps eventually brought her out of her haze. She pushed the door closed and with it blocked out the memory.

"Looking for a book, miss?" Rasa's voice sounded a little brittle. She placed the tray of coffee and biscuits on the table.

"Yes." Anoor could feel her hair shaking around her, the traitorous curls quivering with each heartbeat. She slowed her breathing, loosened her shoulders, and tried to embody the meditative state of battle wrath. She dragged her finger along the spines of the books with mild interest. Stiff with disuse, the books had been dusted—her mother would have her servants' heads if they hadn't—but Anoor could see the discoloration of the wooden shelf beneath them. They hadn't been opened in years.

A love of stories, that's what she'd gotten from her father. The bookcase had been lovingly organized with a specificity that only her father knew. He was here, in the books—a folded corner, a pencil mark, a thumbprint of ink. She ran her thumb over some of the titles. *The Embers in the Castle, A Hundred Sparks of Fire, A Letter for an Officer.* The third title made Anoor blush when she recollected the romantic encounters within.

Once her father died, Gorn had taken up the mantle of storyteller. She sat by Anoor's bed every night trying to inject her voice with adventure and intrigue. Eventually Gorn gave up, after she realized Anoor was faking sleep to speed up the routine, and brought Anoor her very first zine.

Anoor smiled, remembered the delight reflected in Gorn's eyes when she asked for the next installment in the series. Anoor had a tantrum when she realized she'd have to wait for a week for it to be published in *The People's Gazette.*

She laughed at the memory. Anoor returned to reading her zines, but she saw them for what they were: tales that glorified the army's power.

But tales all the same.

"What are you doing?" Rasa asked.

"Reminiscing." And it was true. Her father's memory lifted her out of the horrors of the past.

I will not let her darkness overcome me.

"Right. Shall I pour the coffee?"

"Yes, please. No sugar for me."

"Me neither."

Anoor turned at the sound of her grandmother's voice and grinned.

"Grandmother."

Uka had kept Anoor away from her grandmother, Yona, for most of her life, but Ardae had always been an exception. Age was an important attribute of the religion, and paying respect to elders was a requirement on days like Ardae. Uka couldn't disrespect the Abosom without snubbing Warden Pura and so was forced to keep up appearances.

Yona wore a deep mustard dress simply adorned with a small black diamond brooch of a spider on her breast. The collar was high, the sleeves long—Yona's signature style, along with a new wig for every formal occasion.

Today her hair fell in perfect curls reaching her waist. Anoor wondered for the first time how many Dusters had gone bald at her grandmother's whim.

"Anoor." Yona greeted her without ceremony. She didn't care for formalities. Throughout her tenure, she'd been openly critical about the guild of truth and the power of the Abosom within it. "Your mother is still working?"

"Yes." Anoor took a seat on the sofa next to her.

Anoor didn't think her grandmother knew the truth about her blood, but Uka had said enough to cultivate disinterest in Yona for her granddaughter, and she never strove for a relationship with her, despite Anoor's yearnings.

"I've been watching your progress," Yona said. Yona's accent was more guttural than the melodic tone of those born in Nar-Ruta. Anoor learned that she had traveled south to Nar-Ruta for the Aktibar when she was in her mid-twenties.

"Yes?" Anoor stopped her hand before she reached for a biscuit.

"You did well in aerofield."

"Thank you."

"And tactics, I heard you helped decide on the strategy."

Anoor didn't ask how she knew.

"And stealth? You have a plan to retrieve a weapon?"

"Yes." Anoor hoped Sylah did.

"Uka has asked me to dissuade you from continuing."

Anoor flinched.

"Oh, that surprises you?" Yona continued.

"I just thought—"

"Because you made it through two trials, you wouldn't sully the Elsari name?" Her laugh was stiff. She ran a hand through the borrowed hair at her waist. "I happen to think the Aktibar is good for you. Of course, you won't win. But I've seen you running in the mornings." She sipped her coffee.

"Thank you."

"Speak with purpose, girl."

"Thank you, Grandmother. I will bring respect to the Elsari ancestors."

Yona gave a mocking smile. "Of course."

Anoor wasn't sure whether it was the rush of the coffee or of the praise but the words seeped out of her and into the empty room. "Yona, why were we"—Anoor waved her hand as if to encompass the empire—"the only people to survive the Ending Fire?"

Yona sat up a little straighter. Or maybe Anoor imagined it.

"Are you not schooled in the story of the Ending Fire?"

"Yes."

"Then why don't you ask your masters? Or do I need to speak to the Warden of Knowledge about the quality of your schooling?"

"No, no." Anoor spoke quickly, trying to de-escalate the situation. "I was just wondering if you have any more information. I . . . I had an assignment on it."

"Who assigned it to you?" She leaned toward Anoor.

"No, I mean, I assigned it to myself. I was just doing some research on . . . on stealth, and the question just came up. In my mind. It came up in my mind."

Yona looked at Anoor, her wrinkles pushed smooth. "I see. I didn't realize the story of the Ending Fire was a deciding factor in how to get up a tower and retrieve a weapon."

Anoor sank deeper into the sofa, cradling her mug.

"Sacrifice," Yona said after a brief silence. "Our ancestors traded their sacrifice for prosperity."

The skin around Anoor's collarbone prickled, and she shivered.

"What do you mean, Grandmother?"

Yona's eyes flashed.

"Did you know that I was expecting two children in my womb when I was pregnant? It runs in our family. I myself was a twin once."

Anoor did not know either of those facts.

"The boy when he was born . . . he was sickly." Yona looked through Anoor to a memory. "And Uka was strong, as strong as an eru." Yona smiled then, her teeth shining.

"Did he die?"

The door opened, interrupting their conversation. Uka stood in the doorway, and Yona's gaze shifted to her daughter's and back to Anoor's.

"With sacrifice comes prosperity."

Uka frowned but didn't comment, as she swept into the room.

"Daughter." Yona stood to greet Uka with a peck on either cheek. She would never refer to her as "Warden," despite decorum dictating it.

"Warden," Anoor said quietly, though she didn't lean in for a kiss. There was no point; her mother wouldn't touch her. Not with affection anyway; a slap or a kick was perfectly fine, but not in front of others.

Uka was wearing a white robe, a more fitted version of the swathes of white fabric the Abosom wore. It was the one time of the year Uka did not wear gray. Despite the lightness of her attire, it was as if darkness swelled in Anoor's mind when she arrived.

"Shall we begin lunch? The Abosom is in the dining hall ready to bless the meal."

They all moved out of the lounge, Anoor, the forgotten puppy trailing behind, her mother and Yona in conversation.

"Anoor, why are you dragging your feet so?" Yona paused in the hallway, looking back at her.

Anoor started, then hurried along the hallway toward her mother and grandmother.

"We were just discussing the merits of the blood scour that Uka introduced during her first term as warden. It is good to keep an eye on the inhabitants of the empire, don't you think?"

Yona was inviting her into the conversation. *Her.* Anoor. She spoke before the conversation passed her by.

"I think it raises a lot of questions around freedom of movement."

Uka's eyes snapped toward Anoor with the sound of a whip, though she knew it was only in her mind.

"Freedom of movement?"

"Yes." Damn her curls quivering away. "Blood scours turn identities into permits. Closing off areas of the empire, like the Keep, exacerbates differences between the citizens. It allows for fragmentation within a unified state." The words rushed out of her.

"Interesting," Yona said before Uka could cut in. "Uka, you always told me Anoor was somewhat simple, but I'm beginning to think more and more that she is not. You might consider her viewpoint as it may help quench the dissent among the Nowerks."

Anoor winced at the word, hearing the insult within it for the first time.

"There is no dissent among the Nowerks," Uka snapped.

"Indeed? I hear that the peace I brokered with the crime lord has . . . fractured and he is taking . . . liberties."

Uka inhaled sharply.

"And didn't I hear that a group of Ghostings were caught fleeing the city? With babies they refused to give to the abattoir?" Yona spoke as if commenting on the weather.

"Mother," Uka said through clenched teeth. "Let us speak of this another day."

They reached the dining hall where the table was laid out with fried plantains and rice, stuffed tomatoes with goat's cheese, roasted sweet roots, and in the center of it all, a whole roast lamb.

The Abosom was large, swaddled in reams of white fabric, his lips glistening with the oil of the food he had clearly started eating while he waited. His prayer mat was laid out beneath him, pointing toward the joba tree, the conduit to Anyme.

Anoor chose the farthest seat from the window. Uka and Yona sat side by side opposite her.

"Please, bless this meal. I'm hungry." Yona waved her hand toward the food.

The Abosom bowed over the prayer mat. Either his knees buckled or he let his body guide him to the floor. After a deep breath he spoke.

"Anyme, we thank thee for what you give us. We praise thee for where you lead us."

Yona yawned, and Anoor's laugh caught in her throat at Uka's deadly stare.

Anoor wondered how her real family celebrated Ardae, if they celebrated at all. Would *they* have been proud of her achievements in the Aktibar? A Duster as a warden; did they even let themselves hope?

Anoor glanced at Uka and shuddered, thinking of all the rippings the woman authorized. Hope was all Anoor had. She needed to end the cycle of oppression that fueled the empire.

The Abosom droned on: "On this sacred day, we thank Anyme for their guidance in the sky. We celebrate the light you give to guide us. We petition you to watch over us in your realm of beauty and chaos, of sunlight and rain, and protect the Elsari family. Guide them in the way of wisdom and knowing. Teach them to lead and to follow. Set a seat for them in the sky, for they pray one day to be worthy. The blood, the power, the life."

"The blood, the power, the life," they all murmured as one, though Anoor thought she heard Yona say something like "the brood, the flower, the kite."

Yona's dark eyes glimmered above the roast lamb that separated them.

"Shall we eat?" Yona said.

"Mother, we need to thank the Abosom," Uka scolded her, and for a second Anoor felt the echo of a normal family.

The Abosom was sweating, and he dabbed his jowls with his robe.

"Warden, it is no worry. I thank you for the honor of blessing your table. I will take my leave."

He rolled up his prayer mat, which took longer than it should have, and left the dining hall.

"Finally. Let's eat," Yona said.

Uka rubbed her brows, and it reminded Anoor of Sylah's exasperated expression. "You know the Abosom will report how you treated him to Pura. I'm going to get it in the neck from him tomorrow."

"Pura's an idiot. Yams?"

Anoor jumped at being addressed yet again.

"Yes, thank you." She had already added them to her plate, but she piled on another spoonful. This was the most conversation she'd had with her grandmother in years.

"Tell me, Anoor, what do you think of the guild of truth?" Yona asked.

Anoor's eyes darted to her mother then away again.

"I think the Abosom have a lot of jurisdiction . . ."

"Ha. The girl speaks truth."

"Mother, I cannot start a coup against one of my own just because you don't like him," Uka hissed, though her venom appeared to be directed at Anoor.

"A coup? No one's suggesting a coup, you silly girl."

Anoor tried not to laugh as she committed the insult to memory. Her grandmother calling her mother a silly girl was the best Ardae gift anyone could ask for.

"Have him killed, that's what we used to do when I was in charge." Yona winked at Anoor.

Was she being serious? Anoor couldn't tell.

"Mother, can we please talk about *anything* else."

"Indeed, how about the sleeping sickness epidemic? Seems like we're losing more and more Ghostings each day. How are you handling that?"

Uka growled into her food.

Anoor allowed herself a small smile. This was the best Ardae she'd ever had.

CHAPTER THIRTY-TWO

FOUR DAYS
UNTIL THE TRIAL OF MIND

Erus are oviparous. They lay eggs twice a year. The humidity of Jin-Sahalia provides the ideal conditions for breeding. The city's eru market is famous for the riding breeds, developed for speed, agility, and endurance.

—Extract from *Know Your Steed* by H. Kolm

Sylah needed to find Hassa. Somehow the Ghostings were connected to the truth. She had spent another two strikes going through the journal but had reaped no more clues.

When Sylah entered the bedroom after her bath, she stopped in her tracks.

"Maiden's tits . . ."

She was desperate to find Hassa as soon as possible, but three baskets of Anoor's belongings were piled high. Jewelry, headpieces, scarfs, pantaloons, suits, dresses, all of her prized possessions. Sylah regretted agreeing to help her with this.

Walking into the nearly empty dressing room, she found three simple outfits hanging on the rack. One was a gray suit, another a pale red dress, and the third was her training gear.

"Oh, Anoor," Sylah said softly. She rifled through the clothing she was discarding and pulled out a pile of gold and green material that Sylah thought might be a dress. She tucked the dress into one of Anoor's now empty drawers. "You've got to keep something nice for the winners' banquet."

She looked at the baskets and cursed. She'd have to take an eru. Sylah hated traveling by eru.

Sylah located Anoor's eru, named Boey as the stall indicated in silver swirling letters. Anoor's carriage was by the side, and it was as ostentatious as Sylah predicted. Made of thin steel to protect from the tidewind, the edges of the carriage swirled with gilded flowers of gold and silver. The driver's seat, a lip on the front of the carriage, was cushioned with a velvet throw. If Sylah drove that into the Duster Quarter, she'd only be left with wheels.

"Fuck." Sylah dumped the first basket of Anoor's belongings by her feet. "I'm going to have to ride you across the Tongue." The eru huffed as if she knew this journey was going to be uncomfortable for both of them. Driving a carriage was hard enough, but riding on top of the eru—that was near impossible. It was for Sylah, at least. She was never destined to be a part of the wardens' cavalry, and growing up, she'd always been glad that erus never factored into the Aktibar. Not that it mattered now.

"Need some help?" A small girl dressed in the red pinafore Sylah had come to detest slipped under the stall.

"Would you be able to saddle this eru for me?"

"You have permission to ride Miss Elsari's eru?"

Oh shit, Sylah had thought the girl's tone was helpful, but it turned out she was just plain old annoying.

"Yes, yes. This is her stuff. You can check with Gorn, her chief of chambers, if you want."

"I will."

Sylah ground her teeth.

"Okay, go check with her. I need to bring down another two baskets anyway."

"You'll need the carriage?"

"No, I can't drive that." Sylah waved at the big piece of jewelry on wheels. "Can you just add a couple of packs to the saddle?"

The girl nodded.

After checking with Gorn and another two trips to Anoor's chambers, Sylah was finally packed and ready to go. She jumped onto the eru—after her third try using the stirrups, mind you—and picked up the reins.

The blue eru snorted at Sylah and scuffed the floor with a clawed foot. It had been a long time since Sylah had ridden. Not since their escape from the Sanctuary. Even then, they'd had a carriage, and driving from the seat was much easier than getting used to the twisted motion of the lizard while on its back.

The Sandstorm's eru was called Huda, and she was a sweet and gentle creature. Something about Boey made Sylah think that wasn't the case with her. Boey was strong and lithe, like all the large lizards, but her snort seemed pulled back in a sneer, her blue eyes a little too intelligent.

Sylah wondered if Huda was still alive. They'd had to abandon the old lizard at the nearest town, just in case the army followed their trail all those years ago. Sylah didn't want to think of that memory. Not today, not ever.

"Have you seen Hassa recently?" she asked a Ghosting who had appeared near the stable door.

No, I'm not sure who you mean, the boy signed, moving toward the back of the barn.

It was the same answer she got from many Ghostings. They either refused to answer her or pleaded ignorance. Distrust always shifted in their eyes.

"All right, Boey, we're on an adventure. Let's go." She kicked and flicked the reins with her wrist, but the eru didn't move a handspan.

"Oh, come on, you can do it." Again, Sylah flicked her wrists.

This time the eru lurched forward, propelling them out of the stables and into the courtyard. A few Abosoms still doted around the joba tree, and she had to steer Boey away from them sharply before an offering of a life was given unintentionally.

They loped toward the gates of the Keep that were opening ahead of them. The officer waved, presumably assuming it was Anoor at the reins. There weren't any other blue erus in the stable.

Sylah waved back and galloped toward the Tongue.

HASSA WAS SCOUTING the tunnels in preparation for the night's escape. As usual, they'd go during a tidewind, though it had gotten increasingly risky with the Warden of Crime's Gummers inching ever closer to Ghosting territory. But the tunnels were theirs, they always had been.

A light flickered up ahead, and Hassa paused. The red glow got brighter, and she slipped into a sewage pipe that, thankfully, hadn't been used in some time. Ghostings didn't use runelights in the passages; it was too dangerous, and they knew their way by touch alone.

Hassa knew they were below the northernmost point of the city, where the ruins of Ghosting homes deteriorated more and more the farther you got toward the Farsai Desert, until there was no differentiation between the crumbled remains and the sand. It was all dust.

She couldn't imagine a time when the Dredge was the Ghosting Quarter, an area where they all lived, handing out wares in the market and talking with tongues. Four hundred years ago never seemed so far away.

The runelight got closer, words along with it.

"But if the Sandstorm can't get him in, what will they do then?"

"I'm sure they'll figure out a way of bribing the winner."

"Yes, I'm sure."

Two faces passed by Hassa. It was Loot's husband, Fayl. She recognized him by the size of his shadow. The other Gummer was just out of sight.

"And the Zalaam? They'll have control of the court. What then?"

"What then indeed," Fayl said with a sigh.

They disappeared into the darkness of the tunnels, their words obscuring, then the light faded out.

Hassa slipped her shoulders out of the sewage pipe first, her feet following. She'd never heard the word "Zalaam" spoken, though they had a sign for it in the Ghosting language.

Zalaam. Her lips moved, fumbling over the shapes of the letters. She should report the conversation to the elders.

Hassa made her way quickly through the passages toward the Nest, where the Ghostings met and the elders lived. Deep beneath the city, where the world was theirs.

THE HAVEN WAS somewhere under the Ruta River. Every now and then wet sand oozed through the walls, plopping to the ground in clumps. The Ruta River, like the tidewind, had been churning more ferociously of late. The elders were concerned.

The tunnel toward the Nest was lit with torches, the orange glow warmer and cheaper than runelights. Hassa could smell the flatbread cooking on the stove at the back, which was always manned and ready to provide sustenance.

The Nest twinkled and shone with trinkets and treasures piled high. Old books, mugs, toys, plates, pots, anything the Ghostings had found from *before*. Before the empire became what it now was. The relics were the real reason Ghostings traded. Too many of their ancestors' belongings had been pillaged, so over the centuries Ghostings began to trade goods recovered from the ruins.

Hassa hummed a happy sound as she moved in and out of the musty artifacts of a world long gone. The Nest itself was carved out of the same whitestone the tunnels had been built into. It was a large space, large enough for the four elders and their families to live comfortably, while also holding meetings. It was part home, part war chamber.

Hassa glanced at the carvings on the floor as she made her way through the piles of relics. After the spoken and written word were stolen from the Ghostings, they turned to a new form of history. The Nest now housed their secrets in swirls on the floor and walls, carved into the surface of the rocks. Their story, told in knife strokes.

At the moment there was only one Ghosting in the back corner near the stove. Many of the others had been sent on errands like Hassa. Tonight was a big night, after all.

Elder Dew. Hassa greeted the baker who was flipping flatbread on a hot stone. The spatula was hooked under their elbow with a horizontal handle. They set it down before signing.

Hassa, how went the scout? Elder Dew's eyes were a light brown, so light they were almost gray. Dew still wore a Ghosting servant uniform, even though they hadn't worked above ground for over two decades.

I heard Fayl and another Gummer talking in the tunnel. They spoke of the Zalaam.

War is coming, Dew signed.

War is coming, Hassa agreed. She moved up to the stove and picked up a warm flatbread between her limbs. She chewed on it slowly.

You are ready for tonight?

Hassa nodded.

Elder Dew flipped the last flatbread and turned to her.

I was searching through the belongings of our ancestors yesterday, observing and preserving as is my wont. And I noticed one item I had been working on has disappeared. Now, Hassa, do you know what it might be?

Elder Dew's tone was mild; their facial expression hadn't changed from their normal countenance of content. But Hassa knew better. Dew was mad, very mad. The Ghosting language was very subtle, and a few extra pauses between the words told Hassa all she needed to know.

I was going to bring it back.

Why did you take it?

I was just going to read it, Elder Dew.

Read it?

Yes, I wanted to study the world beyond.

Please do not insult me with your lies.

Oh, so mad. Dew had never spoken to Hassa this way before. Her chest caved, and she let the truth out.

I'm taking the map to Sylah.

The Stolen girl who's been helping the Duster in the Aktibar?

Yes, they have been looking for answers, searching for them.

I read a report somewhere. They were looking in the library in the Keep.

They're so close to the truth.

And yet you've chosen to guide them and to reveal our secrets?

They're not ours to keep, Hassa signed frantically, the hot stove making her sweat.

They'll kill us all. The wardens, they meant the wardens.

I trust Sylah. I trust her to keep the truth safe.

Why, Hassa? Our people must come first. Dew's wrist clipped the hot stone as they signed "first" with force. No pain registered on Dew's face.

I am thinking about our people. They will be good allies. We can use them, send them forth to the mainland.

Dew nodded.

It is true our free children are too young to speak for us; we will need an ambassador who can speak the common tongue.

Hassa didn't want Sylah to be sent away, but she also wanted her friend to know the truth.

Hassa, the other elders won't like this. They won't agree.

She knew that. It was why she hadn't told them. She should have known Dew would notice the map was missing.

We cannot reclaim what is ours without the help from those who oppress us.

Dew nodded, thinking, considering.

This could end us.

This could also restore us.

You are too young to be speaking like an elder. Finish your bread and go.

Hassa was relieved. The smile across Elder Dew's face was all the approval she needed.

SYLAH COULDN'T FIND Hassa. She had tied up the eru by her mother's villa and gone to search the Dredge. Sylah left Boey chewing the leaves of their neighbor's precious joba tree. She was only sorry she wasn't going to see Rata's crestfallen face as she caught Boey with a mouthful.

Turin had closed up shop for the day, the one day in the year she ever did, and the Maroon was empty. All the plantation workers had the day off and were likely spending it with their families.

They weren't alone. The thought rattled around and around Sylah's mind. It made her frantic in her search as she pushed through happy groups of families and tripped over carefully laid offerings. There was more out there. There was *more.*

She wanted to tell Jond, but by telling him she'd need to give up the other journals to the Sandstorm, and she hadn't showed the passage to Anoor yet.

The sun had begun to set, and still Sylah couldn't find her friend. For a horrible second she wondered if the sleeping sickness got her. The illness was plaguing the Ghostings en masse.

But there had been no black cross on Maiden Turin's door. That was something, at least.

As night fell, Sylah gave up.

She headed back toward her mother's house in the Duster Quarter.

"Sylah, is that your eru in front of my house?" Rata screeched.

Oh, goody, Sylah didn't miss the show after all.

"No," she replied.

"Then why are you emptying stuff from its packs?"

"They're gifts, would you like one?"

That shut her up.

"What's in them?" She crept forward from the stoop of her villa.

"Dresses, jewels, some scarfs, some shoes."

"Oh." Rata moved forward and began to pick at Anoor's clothes. "They're very fancy."

"Take them, give them out to your friends. Trade them, for all I care."

Rata placed a hand on her chest, torn between insult and gratitude.

"Thank you?"

Sylah was pleased she'd managed to get rid of the items before entering Lio's. She didn't want to see her mother look for the threads of her *real* daughter in the clothing.

Lio was already at the door by the time Sylah got there.

"You talking to Rata?" Lio said.

"Yeah, is that redred I smell?"

"I made enough for two, wasn't sure you'd come."

"Wasn't sure I'd be here."

Jond had said he might visit Lio on Ardae, but he didn't show. The new Sandstorm probably had their own tradition for the holiday, but she was still disappointed not to see his lopsided grin. Sylah was surprised to feel a spark of resentment toward the new Sandstorm.

They moved into the comfortable routine of setting up for dinner, Sylah getting the crockery out from under the sink, while her mother poured the firerum.

When it was time to eat, neither of them acknowledged it was Ardae. Instead, they looked into each other's eyes for a brief moment, their glasses held high.

"To those we lost," Lio whispered.

It had been six years to the day since her family died.

Sylah pushed all thoughts of another world from her mind and let herself feel the grief she had kept at bay all day.

Grief is like a scab, each day you heal a little more, the blood clotting, the skin stitching together. But once a year you peel back the protective crust, each time expecting a scar, but instead the blood still gushes forth.

Sylah welcomed the pain; she deserved it and more besides.

SYLAH WAS A little drunk by the time she returned to the Keep. She swerved more than usual as she led Boey across the Tongue but made it back to the stables safely.

She was late for their training session, so she went straight to the tower.

"You stink of alcohol," was the first thing Anoor said as Sylah entered the room.

"Sure do."

"Where've you been?"

"Dropping off your clothes."

"And trading them for . . . firerum?" Anoor had a hand on her hip.

"No." Sylah went over and tweaked her nose. Anoor recoiled but laughed. "I drank the firerum after I gave away your stuff. Did you have a good Ardae?"

"Same as usual. Though this time my grandmother spoke to me a bit. I think she's oddly proud of my progress in the Aktibar."

"She *should* be. No one can believe how well you're doing. I believe it, of course. I've seen you work hard."

"You think I work hard?" Anoor asked, her hazel eyes glittering.

"I didn't say that."

"You just said that."

"No, I didn't. Oh—" Sylah clapped her hands. "I found something. I found more evidence that there's a big secret that the wardens are hiding." Sylah withdrew the journal from her basket and filled Anoor in.

"The guild of truth is all about hiding the truth? No wonder they're all so sly." Anoor rocked back and forth on her heels.

"I tried to look for Hassa, but she's disappeared."

"Maybe she's gone to the mainland."

Sylah scoffed then paused. "What if this *is* the mainland? And the Wardens' Empire is a fictitious world someone had made up?"

"What if this is all a dream?"

"Or a zine?"

They laughed, their theories fizzing out.

"What do we do with this information?" Anoor asked what they were both thinking.

"All we know is that there is a secret, right?"

"Right."

"We've got to fill in the blanks. Maybe Hassa will turn up."

"Maybe."

"In the meantime, you better get training."

Anoor groaned.

"Formation three. Go." Sylah's buzz was turning into a throbbing headache.

She watched Anoor's form as she moved. In half a second she had broken formation and fallen to the floor.

"That was terrible," Sylah said, standing over Anoor's crumpled heap. "If possible, you've regressed a whole mooncycle. Did you clear your mind like I said?"

"I can't." Anoor had curled into a ball, and Sylah had flashbacks of their first run.

"Not this again. What is it? What has you distracted?"

Anoor didn't say anything for a while, then she spoke. Sylah had to lean in to hear.

"I'm so scared of her. She hates me so much. I'm worried if I fail and I'm worried if I don't."

"Your mother?"

"Yes. Today I saw the cupboard she used to lock me in. She locked me in many places, but that was the last. That was the last time I let her cage me in. I . . . I managed to get out, to free myself. What if I don't have the strength to free myself again?"

The firerum had dulled as her rage became fiercer.

"She locked you in a cupboard?" Sylah said through clenched teeth. She knew Uka had mistreated her, misused her, but this . . . *this was something Papa would have done.* The thought struck her dumb, seeing her childhood with a stranger's eyes for the first time.

They were the same, Anoor and her.

"Stand up," Sylah barked, and Anoor winced. "Use it." Sylah tried again, softly.

"Use what?" Anoor uncurled from her ball.

"Use the anger. The one true gift she has given you can take you all the way. Use it to reach battle wrath."

"Show me." Anoor's words were a challenge. So Sylah obliged. They had hauled a training dummy up from the barracks one sweaty afternoon, though they had rarely used it. Sylah stalked toward it and landed a Dambe punch that skidded the dummy a hundred handspans across the room.

She pounced across the room using her aerobatic agility to land a Laambe slap across its girth. And once the anger beneath her skin simmered to white coal, she slipped into a Nuba trance and moved fluidly through the ten Nuba formations, each one more deadly than the last. White cotton stuffing burst from the dummy's midriff.

"Show-off," Anoor muttered behind her, but Sylah wasn't done. She cracked her knuckles and leaped onto the dummy, her thighs crushing its neck. Suddenly her leg muscle spasmed, and she fell badly onto the floor.

"Are you okay?" Anoor was beside her trying to locate her pain.

"My leg . . . no, the left one . . . yes, there." Anoor's deft fingers always helped ease the spasms when they struck. She massaged her leg until they subsided.

"Wasn't quite the big finish I was going for." She gave Anoor a lopsided grin as she sat up.

The tidewind had begun to rage outside; it shook the foundations of the tower, rattling the sand in the rafters. It fell down around them in glitters of blue rain. An errant piece of debris hit the metal window shutters and made them jump.

"It's a bad one tonight," Sylah said.

Anoor was quiet for some time. Sylah watched her and listened to the wind howl.

"Who do you think of when you fight? Whose anger do you use?" Anoor asked.

Sylah thought about it. For years they had been trained to use the anger of a community, the anger of the Dusters. That still smoldered deep within, but it wasn't the main driver. She thought about Papa, about the reckoning he'd wrought on her childhood. She thought about Anoor, the girl who stole her life. But there was one anger that eclipsed them all, and it was driven by guilt and shame.

"Mine."

THE TIDEWIND WAS half a strike early. Marigold hadn't arrived yet; they were still above ground leading the last family to freedom.

Hassa wanted to pace, but the Ghostings around her were already nervous. Their journey was going to be a long one.

The tidewind's begun, are we leaving now? a young woman asked. She was leaning on the tunnel wall, her face cast in shadow, but her signing clear.

We're waiting for a few more. Hassa moved through the Ghostings and counted again, but she knew the number she'd come to. Sixty-seven. Nowhere near the hundred they had expected.

They were below an entry point to the tunnels, a few handspans north of the apothecary where Hassa bought her hormone herbs that aided her transition. Marigold should have been here by now.

I'm going up to check, Hassa signed to the nearest Ghosting, who nodded vaguely, tears of fear already streaking their face.

Hassa climbed the ladder lithely; her agility had made her invaluable to the elders. That and the fact that her birth wasn't documented anywhere in the empire. Hassa was invisible.

Once Marigold had cut Hassa from her mother's womb and tested her blood ran clear, they took her to the elders. It was there, in the Nest, where they severed Hassa's hands and tongue. The officers would have eventually found her and tested her blood in a blood scour. Then her birth would have been reported to the Auditors, sealing the same fate in a Ghosting abattoir. By doing the deed themselves, the elders created a child off the books. A spy who could go anywhere, be anything. But still a Ghosting.

It was ruthless but necessary, and she was glad of it. She'd spent her life learning from and listening to others. Her servant uniform was the perfect veneer despite her never having worked in any one place. Hassa made it her business to be everywhere and nowhere.

Hassa pushed open the trap door above the ladder. The tidewind sounded angrier than she'd ever heard it. It shook the ruins of the house she had emerged in and whipped around debris so violently she had to shield her face.

There was no way she was going to be able to make it outside. Not without killing herself. She tried to look around the villa, but sand kept flying into her eyes. She screamed in the back of her throat, a calling sound to anyone who was out beyond the walls of the villa. The tidewind swallowed Hassa's pathetic cry and howled back in response. Hassa tried again, moving toward the crumbling wall that was protecting her from the full force of the tidewind.

She heard a cry in response, though she couldn't sense the direction. She brought her wrists to her eyes and moved toward a gap in the wall. Blue talons made of desert sand clawed through the gap. Hassa laid her back against the wall and watched the wind swirl in like it was searching for prey to drag back out into the night.

The wind heaved and paused for a heartbeat. In that moment Hassa rushed to the crumbling hole and looked through, screaming all the while. She saw a group of people huddled together on the other side of the street. They were taking advantage of the brief respite and moving quickly through the open. Their steps were a strange, jerky march, and Hassa realized they held their clothing above their heads, an umbrella of eru leather and cotton giving them extra protection. It wouldn't be enough. Hassa knew that when she saw the look on Marigold's face as they locked eyes.

Go, run, run to that hole in the wall. Go. Marigold dropped their protection and signed frantically to the other Ghostings. They had seconds, mere breaths before the tidewind—

Suddenly the villa was filled with Ghostings, and Hassa had to move out of the way to let them through. Each one of them was running for their life. She shepherded them down the ladder and went to help Marigold, who was at the back of the pack.

A pregnant Ghosting was struggling to make it. Marigold was pushing them along. They had ten handspans or fewer to go. Then Hassa felt it and Marigold did too. The tidewind inhaled. With a final push, Marigold propelled the pregnant Ghosting forward, pushing them into the gap in the villa and Hassa's waiting arms before the tidewind flooded the night.

The tidewind slammed across the left side of Marigold's body, the grains of sand imprinted into their skin for a moment, entombing them in blue glass. Hassa looked away, refusing to see the flesh ripped from their bones, preferring the perfectly blue statue in her mind.

When she looked back, Marigold was gone.

CHAPTER THIRTY-THREE

ONE DAY
UNTIL THE TRIAL OF MIND

The trial of mind is a difficult one, arguably the hardest of all. As wardens we have the responsibility to bear the burden of an empire, therefore strength of mind is paramount. This Aktibar I have suggested a trial that challenges our basest instincts.

—The journal of Uka Elsari, year 421

Knock. Knock. Knock.

The sound woke Sylah with a start. She'd fallen asleep in Anoor's bed again, the journals scattered around them. Sylah had shown Anoor the sentence she'd found, and together they went back through all the other volumes to no avail. The tidewind was so loud and raged for much longer than they were used to, and it was difficult to fall asleep.

They both shot out of bed and began hiding the leather-bound books.

"Come in, Gorn."

Sylah muffled her laugh as she saw Gorn's suspicious face.

"Anoor, may I have a word?"

"Yes, sure, what is it?"

Gorn's eyes flickered to Sylah's and away. "I've been informed that your mother is on her way."

Anoor stepped back as if someone had punched her in the stomach. "When?"

"One of the servants in the kitchens overheard Rasa saying that she was going to drop by."

As if summoned by the horror in Anoor's face, the front door rattled with the strength of a sharp rap.

Sylah took Anoor's hand. "It's fine, don't worry. I'm sure she's just checking in on you."

Anoor nodded, but Sylah could tell she wasn't listening. Her hands were shaking.

"I'll answer it. Go into the living room, Anoor." Even Gorn looked more agitated than usual.

Anoor stood rooted to the spot.

"Anoor, you've got to go meet Uka in the living room," Sylah said.

She looked at Sylah, her eyes glassy. "My mother?"

"Yes, she's in the living room."

"Will you come with me?" She looked so small.

"Come with you? To see your mother?"

Anoor came alive and grabbed Sylah's hand. "Oh, yes please, having you there will help me stand up to her."

"If you say so. Come on, let's go."

UKA ELSARI. ANOOR'S mother. Her mother, a handspan away. While Anoor quivered on the outside, Sylah shook within.

She was talking to Gorn, coffee beans stewing on a metal tray in front of them. The gooey plate of kunafa wasn't enough to distract Anoor.

"I assume that's her." Uka's voice scraped along the wall toward them. "Unless she's gone and hired another maid without telling me."

"Yes, Warden, it's her." Gorn's breathing was shallow, as if Uka had sucked all of her breath. She must have, because Sylah couldn't breathe. Would she remember Sylah from outside the library? Would she recognize her child this time?

"Anoor." Uka was perched on the edge of the sofa, her combat boots firmly planted on the ground.

"Hello, Mother." The words were a sigh. Anoor sunk into the armchair opposite.

"This is the servant Gorn informed me you've hired?"

"Yes. Sylah, say hello." Anoor waved her hand between the two of them.

"Hello." The word got stuck in Sylah's throat, and she coughed. Uka leaned backward.

"Don't worry, poverty isn't contagious." The words were out of Sylah's mouth before she could stop them.

One, two, three horrified faces.

The silence went on. Sylah clutched the hem of her uniform like it was a raft in a sea of red blood.

"Sylah, where is that name from?" Uka scratched her eyebrow with a clawlike nail.

"The north."

"Near Ood-Zaynib," Anoor offered helpfully, and Sylah's stomach sunk.

"Ood-Zaynib?" Uka drummed her fingers on her thigh. "I went on a hunting trip there once."

"Indeed." The word spat out of Sylah's twisted lips.

"It was very fruitful." Uka watched Sylah carefully. She couldn't know. If she did, Sylah would be dead.

"We do have a lot of desert foxes in the north." Light and careful.

"Indeed." Uka threw the word back at Sylah with a cruel smirk.

Sylah realized with a start that Uka's eyes were a stormy gray, unlike the black depths of Sylah's. She pondered the father she would never get to meet.

Uka uncrossed her legs and reached for the coffee. "You are dismissed. Gorn, you can go too."

"No." Anoor sat up from the chair that had been slowly consuming her. "Sylah can stay."

Uka's severe gaze lingered on Anoor. "These may be your

chambers, *daughter*, but while I still breathe, my word is paramount to yours. In every corner of the empire."

"But not beyond it." Anoor uttered the words softly, under her breath.

Sylah had never seen the explosives they used to mine in the east of the empire, but she imagined they had a similar effect.

Uka recoiled, her shoulders stiff. Sylah's ears were ringing with the speed of her blood.

Then Uka laughed.

"Beyond it? Oh, dear daughter. You are welcome to travel beyond the empire, but make sure you pack enough food for a long trip. There's no land out there. In fact, please, raid the coffers, you might do me a favor heading out of the empire . . . indefinitely."

Anoor looked at Sylah, who gave a small shake of the head. Now was not the time.

"It was a pleasure to meet you, Warden." Sylah bowed deeply.

Back straight, hips locked. Lift your head high and bring your feet together. Again, Sylah. Watch Jond now. There, he's got it.

Anoor's pleading face was the last thing Sylah saw as the door shut.

"Well, I made a great first impression." Sylah was muttering to herself, but Gorn responded.

"Yes, congratulations. That was quite a scene in there."

Sylah ignored her and pressed her ear to the door.

Talons grabbed her around the wrist. "Stop that. Have you no respect?" Gorn's face was rounder than Sylah had ever seen it.

"Get off."

They stood there staring at each other, civility peeling back to reveal a bitter hatred beneath.

Sylah broke the silence first.

"I'm going to my room, then I'm heading out."

"*Her* room. You'd do well to remember that."

Sylah wanted to scream and shout, to tell Gorn the riotous truth that she was the one who belonged more than anyone else.

Her arms began to twitch. Her legs followed shortly after. She closed her eyes and tried to calm her beating heart.

Breathe. She needed to breathe or she'd have a fit right there in the hallway.

When she opened her eyes, Gorn was gone.

"You're early," Jond commented as he followed her into his own apartment. They had long since moved their bloodwerk lessons to his room since the water tower wasn't a great bed.

"Uka kicked me out, and I ran away from Gorn before she could give me any errands." She grunted. "Ah, I'm going to have to start again." She wiped the blood off the glass bulb she was working on.

"What are you doing?" He sat cross-legged on the bed next to her.

"Since Anoor taught me how to create runelamps, I've been wondering how they could be used in combat." She redrew the series of runes she'd been tinkering with. "And I realized, if I increase the pressure of *Ba*, and funnel the rune through a series of sequences that refine the light into a beam, I can . . ." The bulb exploded into a bright beam of light, but no glass shattered. It was gone in seconds.

"Fuck, Sylah, I can only see black spots now."

"That's the point. It's for combat. Next up I'm going to add shards of glass."

He began to grope around like a blind person, his hands brushing her breasts.

"Is that your nose, oh wait . . . I'm too high." He pulled up her skirt and slid his hand lower and lower. She laughed, her breath rumbling deep in her lungs.

Her toes curled when his fingers unfurled. She lay backward, letting him roam within.

"What's that?" The axe lay on its side in the corner of the room.

"What?" he murmured into her upper thigh. She pushed him off her and reached for the axe.

The handle was crafted out of tio root, a dark wood that was worth more than gold. Gold also laced the double blade in swirls, adorning the deadly steel with sunlight.

Of course, it was perfectly balanced.

"When?"

"Last night."

"Five weapons left, then." She couldn't tear her eyes away. "How?"

There was no arrogance as he told her how he'd tracked the food suppliers for days, eventually infiltrating the building underneath a food trolley and up the dumbwaiter.

"Was there a jambiya left?"

He frowned and then smirked.

"The curved dagger? Really?"

"It's what she's best at."

"Yes, there was a jambiya there."

"Good . . . good." She bobbed her head up and down. "I've got to get back, got to figure out how to get her into that tower."

"We haven't even had our lesson. Although there can't be much more to learn, right?"

"We're hardly halfway through the *Book of Blood*. There's still a lot that might come up in the test." Sylah rearranged her skirt. "Sorry I've got to run, but I do need to figure this out."

"Sylah, wait," Jond said as she got up to leave. She rolled her eyes and kissed him. He avoided her eyes and added, "I just want to check that you still remember the mission."

Sylah felt her lips curl. "Remember the mission?"

"There will be a reckoning for *every* Ember."

"I know, Jond, I remember Papa's words, even if the other Sandstorm leader doesn't deem me worthy."

"The Sandstorm, the leader . . . the journals, they just weren't enough . . . but I'm trying."

Enough. The word gave her pause.

"Will I ever be enough for them?"

The look Jond gave her was pained. "Sylah . . ."

Will they ever be enough for me?

"The Final Strife, Sylah."

Sylah didn't repeat the words, yet they quickened the beating of her heart, but this time she wasn't sure if it was from pride or fear.

SYLAH FOUND ANOOR crying when she got back. Not the incessant all-consuming sob Sylah had heard before, but a wordless, hollow cawing. She didn't know what to expect after Anoor's talk with her mother, but it wasn't this.

"Maiden's tits, she's only one woman, what could she have said to hurt you so?"

It was then that Sylah saw the letter in her hand. Anoor's dark skin was pulled so taut over her knuckles, you could see the white bone underneath. Sylah had to pry it from her grip. Her eyes scanned the words.

"They've brought forward all of the trials. Given the temper of the tidewind this season the imirs are concerned for the welfare of their districts . . . the trial of the mind is tomorrow . . ." Sylah sat down next to Anoor and put a hand on her leg. "It's okay. We knew this would be coming, it's only two days earlier. You can do it."

Anoor looked at Sylah's hand as if she had only just realized she was in the room.

"We don't have enough time. I can't win. The bloodwerk trial is in two weeks; we were meant to have another mooncycle." Her voice was shards of pain.

"But your bloodwerk is impeccable. The bloodwerk trial is always timed, and you're fast at drawing runes. I've never seen you get one wrong. You'll win that trial, no problem."

"You don't understand . . . that means the final combat trial is two weeks after that. So in one mooncycle I'll be fighting to first blood. How can I learn the rest of the Nuba formations in one mooncycle?"

She couldn't, but Sylah wasn't going to tell her that.

"You've trained for nearly four mooncycles now; you're better than any of those in the training barracks."

"It doesn't matter, it doesn't matter," Anoor was repeating under her breath. "I won't pass the mind trial."

"What? Why?"

A ragged breath in. "She told me she designed this challenge for me." Tears spilled out of Anoor's eyes onto her cheek.

Sylah absently wiped one away with her thumb and turned Anoor's face to hers. "Tell me."

A small mewl escaped her lips, but Anoor didn't divert her eyes. She leaned her head into Sylah's hand and spoke. "I told you about the cupboard and how she always locked me up."

"Yes, I've half a mind to slap her tits through her back for it."

"She always kept me in the dark. And didn't give me any food or water."

"What? How many times did she do this to you?"

"Whenever I displeased her, which was often."

"Fuck." Sylah's anger was roaring in her ears. She got up and clasped Anoor's shoulder. "Why did she stop?"

"Because I threatened to tell everyone."

"Tell them what?"

Anoor reached for the letter opener. Sylah flinched as the knife flashed. But it didn't go in her direction. Anoor slashed her own forearm. Blue blood swelled and dribbled onto the carpet.

ANOOR WATCHED SYLAH'S expression change from threatened to wary. Her arm stung as the blood dripped to the floor. Her blue blood.

Sylah's shoulders drooped, exhaustion sinking into every line on her face. She walked into the privy not saying a word, leaving Anoor to her thoughts.

Was this the stupidest thing I've ever done? Will she hate me now, knowing that I'm beneath her?

No. The word rung out in her mind with conviction, there was no way Sylah would leave her, not if she felt the same way as she did. They needed each other.

Sylah came back into the room with some gauze in her hand.

"So you're a Duster?" She wound the gauze around Anoor's cut. Once, twice, thrice. No evidence of the color beneath it.

"Yes, I am a Duster." She'd never said the words out loud,

never let herself. They didn't catch in her throat as she thought they would. "I was one of the children who were left behind to give the Sandstorm time to escape. You might not have heard of the Night of the Stolen where you're from. My mother tried her hardest to keep the story contained . . . but you know . . . the city whispers."

Sylah nodded, and Anoor was emboldened to go on.

"The Sandstorm swapped twelve Ember children with twelve of their own. My mother tracked them down and killed them all years ago. Can you imagine . . . killing your own child out of fear . . . of what? That one day there would be a reckoning? There will be." Anoor clenched her fists and reveled in the beating of her heart. It thrummed with the promise of violence. Sylah must have seen something in her eyes, something fierce, because she stepped back.

"What were the Sandstorm planning?" Sylah's voice sounded frail. Anoor wondered if the truth of her blue blood would tear them apart.

"Mother always said that they had tortured the children just to spite the Embers."

"What do you think?"

"I think they had a bigger plan. I think they were planning to overthrow the empire."

Sylah nodded slowly. "Why didn't your mother kill you? You after all were the biggest threat to her."

"It was her first term as warden; she couldn't, wouldn't let them know she had been compromised in her very chambers. Then after some time I think I became an emblem of her strength. Many imirs were targeted in the Keep, but the warden, she *protected* her own. Did you know the Sandstorm came during Ardae? They made sure the Keep was full of children."

"Yes, it's why she launched her assault on the Sandstorm during Ardae. I mean, that's what I heard."

Anoor nodded.

"I also think my father made her promise not to harm me."

All the breath went out of her, and she collapsed in a heap on the floor, her mother's words from earlier haunting her still.

"You're training with that girl."

It wasn't a question; her mother had clearly been spying on her. "Mother?"

Uka made a disgusted sound in the back of her throat.

"Mother, why are you here?"

"If you won't heed your grandmother, heed me. You need to exit the Aktibar."

All the muscles in Anoor's body ached with a weariness she hadn't felt since the first day of training.

"Anoor, are you listening to me?" Uka leaned forward and Anoor flinched.

"I am listening. That's one thing you did teach me. To shut up and listen."

"Where has this insolence come from?"

"I suspect I've always been harboring it."

Uka stood, her gray suit cloaking her in an extra shadow. She gripped Anoor's chin between her fingers.

"You ungrateful child, I ought to kill you for the way you're speaking to me."

"Do it." A part of Anoor was ashamed of the way she spoke to her mother, the Abosoms' teachings having been drilled into her since infancy and overruling the reality of their relationship, but another part cheered her on. It had Sylah's voice. "Then you'll have to explain to the rest of the wardens what happened to your true daughter. You'll have to explain everything."

The grip on Anoor's chin tightened, but she didn't break eye contact.

"You think I can't make you disappear?" She leaned in, her hot breath tickling Anoor's ear. "Watch your step, little *maggot* of mine."

The slap was sharp, and the kick was even sharper. Her two preferred forms of attack. No blood spilled.

Anoor dropped to the floor and curled around the pain in the pit of her stomach.

"Exit the Aktibar, Anoor." Uka dropped something onto Anoor's back. She winced despite the lightness of it.

Tears seeped from the corners of her eyes, but Uka wasn't done.

"This next challenge I designed just for you. I do remember how much you hated the dark."

Anoor had quivered from the words. They hurt more than the kick and slap combined.

"I'm beginning to realize my father wasn't a good man." Sylah interrupted her thoughts. She sounded like she was speaking from a place far, far away. "He hurt me in lots of ways, in ways I thought were helping to make me better . . . but . . . but they just made me smaller. I thought he loved me, but really . . . I think he saw me as a means to an end." She placed a hand in the small of Anoor's back. "But what I've learned, what I'm learning, is not to let those hurts define you. Use them like we use the anger, craft yourself from those little hurts, block by block. Build a fortress of pain, a castle even. And lord over it."

Sylah leaned in, her glittering eyes ignited with a passion Anoor had never seen before. No fury marred her face, no scorn, nor sarcastic quips. Instead, Anoor trailed her finger around Sylah's full lips, and Sylah's eyes went wide at Anoor's touch.

"Anoor." Sylah's voice was rough, a warning, a siren.

Anoor dropped her hand.

"Can I have fried yams?"

"Now?"

"In the fortress of pain. Can I have fried yams?"

Sylah laughed, breaking the tension that had started to build. "You can have a hundred, but make sure you make me some too."

Anoor smiled, her gaze falling from Sylah's and lingering on the wound covered in gauze.

"How do you know it was your father who made her promise?" Sylah prompted Anoor back to her story.

Anoor glanced at her bedside table, then back to Sylah. With jerky movements she reached over and pulled out the false drawer. Her hands cradled her mother's words as she handed the journal over.

"I read it in this."

"The missing journal . . ." Sylah breathed.

"What?"

"I noticed that there was one missing . . . in the library." Sylah's words were distracted.

"Oh." Anoor spread her hands along the leatherbound cover. "I stole it when she locked me in the library."

Sylah reached for the journal.

"Don't—" Anoor shrieked. "I don't want you to read the names she calls me."

"It can't be worse than what I call you, can it?" Sylah's lopsided grin made Anoor ache.

"I keep it to remind myself of who I don't want to be, what I cannot let myself become."

Sylah dragged her eyes away from the journal and met Anoor's. "You will never be Uka."

Anoor quaked under the tenderness in her words. She put the journal away and turned to Sylah.

"Do you hate me because I'm a Duster?"

Sylah recoiled. "Why would you say that?"

"Because my blood is dirty. The Dusters, we have no power."

Sylah stood.

"Come with me."

"Where are we going?"

"To meet your people."

AGAIN, THEY WALKED, up through the Ember Quarter and across the Tongue. Anoor let Sylah lead her, their hands intertwined.

The trotro rattled past, and Sylah stopped. "See that?"

"The trotro?"

"No, what's inside it."

Anoor had to hurry to keep up with it as it clattered away. She peered into one of the carriages. "Sandals?"

Sylah nodded. "That's power."

Anoor didn't understand, but she wanted to. So she didn't say anything.

Sylah didn't stop again until they crossed the Tongue and entered the Duster Quarter. She pointed to a group of Duster children walking hand in hand toward a building. They were dancing and chanting the blood scour song. Anoor had heard the officers' song for as long as she could remember.

"If your blood runs red, go straight ahead." Their hands clasped together and snaked forward. "If your blood runs blue, you're not coming through." They held up their arms in a cross. "Translucent hue, who are you, who are you, who are you?" They turned to their partners and clapped their hands.

"You see those children, do you know where they go?"

Anoor shook her head, something like dread crawling up her back. The air smelled of burning hair.

"They walk toward their branding. Each one of them is prepared to burn for the empire." Sylah watched them, a small smile toying her lips. "That is power."

Anoor wanted to cry. But there was no time; Sylah was walking again. The streets became dirtier, the villas crumbling. Beggars lingered in front of ruined villas and Ghostings became more visible. They were in the Dredge again.

Sylah led Anoor down some narrow steps below street level.

"This is the Maroon, a place where all the Dusters come to drink." Sylah pulled open the wood lice–infested door and shepherded Anoor in.

Anoor could tell they were Dusters by the blood-crusted welts on their backs. They nursed glasses of firerum and played games of shantra on small tables. A singer stood on a podium and hummed a morose tune that made Anoor's hairs stand on end. A drummer beat a metal spoon on an upturned pot next to her. Anoor could smell the body odor and the scent of congealed latex. They should really have burned some sandalwood.

A young girl stood at the bar cleaning greasy glasses.

"Why isn't she in school?" Anoor asked Sylah.

"School, Anoor? School?" Sylah rubbed her brows. "Education is a luxury, not a necessity. Do you understand that? Dusters are given ten years of schooling, to better their prospects for roles the Embers assign them. Burning flesh not quite the Choice Day ceremony you had in mind? Ghostings don't even get to go to school, they're entered into servitude as soon as they can walk."

Anoor had been going to school for most of her life, and she was twenty. It was a luxury, she knew that, but now she wondered if she'd been studying the wrong things. She was trying to make up for it now.

"How do you know all this?"

Sylah waved at the girl behind the bar. "You're paying," she said to Anoor.

"Sylah . . . you're not an assassin, are you?"

Anoor had doubted it for a long time. The only person who wanted her killed was her mother, and she wouldn't send an assassin and let someone else find her body swathed in blue blood. She'd be tidy, right up until the end.

Sylah downed her firerum in one, hissing through her teeth as it burned her throat.

"No, I'm not, Anoor."

"What are you?"

Sylah looked at Anoor's firerum. "You drinking this?"

Anoor shook her head. Waiting.

"I'm not an assassin."

"Okay."

"I'm a thief. I was stealing from you that night."

"But why didn't you just take my jewels and go?"

"I tried, but remember the . . . clonk." Sylah tipped her head back, reenacting the paperweight hitting her temple. Sylah grinned, but she didn't seem amused.

"Then why do you know so much about this world?"

"I grew up here, well, for the last six years."

"An Ember? In the Dredge? Why?"

Sylah shrugged. "I didn't have a lot of money. It was easier to work here."

Sylah pulled up the sleeve of her right arm, normally covered by her inkwell. But Sylah had made them take them off before coming to the Dredge. She bared the raised flesh of her brand.

"Once I got this, I could work anywhere in the Dredge."

Anoor flinched. "Who did that to you?"

This time Sylah's smile was amused, if a little pained. "Me."

Anoor hissed.

"I don't understand."

Sylah didn't respond.

"How do you know all those fighting moves?" Anoor pressed.

"Oh, that, well, there's this thing called the Ring, in the north of the Dredge. It's a fighting contest. I was the champion."

Anoor felt unsettled. It might have been the eerie song or the half-truths she felt Sylah was telling.

"Can we get two more firerums over here, please." Sylah bellowed the request, but her voice sounded like it was shaking.

"Do you think they were good people?" Anoor suddenly asked.

"Who?"

"The Sandstorm."

The firerum shots were served, and still Sylah didn't respond, though her eyes looked troubled.

Eventually she spoke. "Drink up. You'll need it for our final stop."

It took them a while to reach the plantation fields; the roads got rougher, the smell thicker. Anoor had to hold a handkerchief to her nose. She had seen the fields of rubber trees from her window for years. They had always looked so beautiful and perfect, each row neatly planted straight. But now she could smell them. Not just the latex but the sour odor of perspiration and the coppery smell of clotting blood.

"Why are we stopping?" Anoor asked as they stopped on the edge of the field.

"Look."

Anoor followed Sylah's gaze. An Ember, a master of duty to be exact, walked between the trees a few hundred handspans ahead of them. Dusters toiled all around, their scythe blades dripping white, the handles dripping blue. They bent and hacked at the bark with blunt blades until white latex oozed from the creases. At the end of each row there were overflowing buckets. When a Duster squatted over one, Anoor realized they were toilets.

An irrigation system pumped around the fields using bloodwerk. A water bucket strapped to the back of a sleeping eru was manned by another master of duty. He rationed out the water in dirty and broken cups, some of them leaking away to the ground, but he didn't give the workers another.

And from her tower on the hill, Anoor had seen the beauty, but now she saw the horror.

The master of duty barked an order, and Anoor could see his spittle in the sunlight.

Anoor flinched as his whip struck the back of an elderly man.

"Why are you showing me this, Sylah?"

"This morning you told me you wished you had power." Sylah's voice was rough. "But look, see that man. See the wound on his back?"

Anoor watched the blood ooze from the slash across his spine. It dribbled like the white latex they harvested, sluggish and thick. The skin across his back was no longer a deep brown, but a silvered gray. A shantra board of scars.

"Every day the Embers beat the backs of those below them. Still, he stands. Still, he works. That is power."

Anoor caught the old man's eyes, and she saw resentment there—but also a fierceness that hadn't dimmed in his old age. He stood up straighter under her stare, the blood pouring down his back into his pantaloons.

"Why doesn't he wear a shirt?" Anoor asked.

"Why, when it'll only get ripped?"

He broke Anoor's gaze and moved back to the bark he was hacking. Up and down his gnarled hands moved. Each swing of his scythe ripping the wound open just a little more.

Anoor let the tears fall.

SYLAH WAS QUIET as they made their way back to the Keep.

Anoor had the missing journal.

It had been there the whole time, a few handspans from where Sylah slept. Now that she thought about it, she'd seen Anoor remove it the one time she grew dizzy from bloodwerk, but her memory was hazy. Besides, she never considered that Anoor would ever steal something.

Sylah rubbed her arms, her muscles twinging. She hadn't had a verd leaf tea that morning, and she needed one. For the first time in a long while, she craved the ecstasy of a joba seed more than anything else.

More than rejoining the Sandstorm.

She repeated their conversation in the Maroon over and over in her mind. That was the moment to tell Anoor the truth. That had been her opening, but Sylah had let it pass by.

She rolled the joba seed in her pocket, the action helping to dampen the craving she felt.

"Are you okay?" Anoor asked as they stepped off the Tongue and into the Ember Quarter.

Sylah should be asking her that question, not the other way around.

"I'm fine, just . . . you know."

Anoor nodded. "Let's stop by at the kitchens and get you a verd leaf tea."

"Thank you. Not just for that, but for telling me the truth."

Anoor smiled, her eyes still puffy from crying. Sylah had held her for some time as they watched the plantation workers toil.

"What would you do, Sylah, if you were warden?"

Sylah faltered in her step.

"I would want to help the Dusters and the Ghostings, raise them up. Level the ranks."

"But how? How would you help them?"

By killing every single Ember. The words in her mind were said in Jond's voice, but they felt wrong to her.

"I would hold the Embers accountable."

"With violence?"

Sylah didn't respond, but the set of her jaw told Anoor all she needed to know.

"I would raise taxes," Anoor said. "I would set up a proper education system that benefited everyone, I would abolish blood scours and ensure equal opportunities across all guilds. No more brandings. I would close every Ghosting abattoir in the empire and pardon them for the crimes of their ancestors; they've suffered enough. I would stop the rippings and improve working conditions across the plantations. I would encourage bloodwerk inventions to mechanize some of the labor and melt down every weapon."

"And the courts? They'd just bend over and say 'do what you will'?"

"Well, yes, it'd take a long time and a lot of planning. I'd need allies to get the bills passed . . ."

"And those bloodwerk inventions you mention? You're forgetting only Embers can bloodwerk. What will happen is the Embers will continue to be the most educated, the most revered, and we're back to where we started."

"No, no, it'll take some time, but we could do it. We could change the empire for the better." Anoor was firm, her swollen eyes clear and determined.

Sylah didn't say anything; she was in awe of the woman in front of her. Anoor had solid plans to change things. It was more than Sylah had gotten from Jond.

They entered the Keep through the separate door reserved for the wardens and their families. The servants of the Keep kept fresh flowers hanging in vases on either side of the door, and the sickly sweet smell gave Sylah a headache.

On the way to Anoor's room they stopped at the kitchen to collect the verd leaf tea Sylah desperately needed.

Kwame was cleaning pots in one of the white ceramic sinks, and he looked up when he saw them.

"Sylah, you missed lunch. I've saved you a roll."

Sylah had given up trying to dissuade Kwame and let their friendship manifest.

"Anoor." He threw his arms around her, spraying soap suds from his hands.

"Hi, Kwame," Anoor said through squished cheeks.

"You look good," he said, holding her at length. "Did you hear? There's a sleeping sickness wave running through the Ghostings. They just tallied the deaths, and we lost over sixty on Ardae night. A lot of pyres burning."

"Oh, no, that's sad," Anoor said.

"We've missed you at the library."

"Sorry, we've been a bit busy training for the other trials." Anoor wrung her hands.

"Oh yes! The trial of mind tomorrow. You worried?"

"No."

Sylah wandered away from them and went to make her verd leaf tea. The container of herbs sat by one of the stoves that had a full bubbling kettle always on. She mixed in a large dollop of honey and stirred the ingredients together, watching the servants move around the kitchens.

There were a few Ghostings sitting on the floor of the kitchen using their feet to snap open beans, a mound of shells growing by their side. Sylah knew better than to ask them about Hassa, though she worried for her friend. An Ember chief of chambers stirred a large cauldron of what smelled like red pepper soup on the stove. An officer entered the kitchen and moved toward Sylah, an empty mug in his hand.

"Sorry, do you mind if I . . . ?" He waved at the kettle.

"No, please go right ahead."

Sylah watched him make his coffee, the grains of an idea blossoming in her mind.

She knew how Anoor was going to get into the tower and retrieve the jambiya.

Anoor laughed across the kitchen, and Sylah's own lips automatically lifted. She looked at her from afar. She had changed from the woman Sylah had first met. Though she had donated her opulent clothes, her spirit was more vibrant than ever.

Sylah's smile slipped. If she was going to pull this off, she'd need to talk to Loot.

CHAPTER THIRTY-FOUR

THE **TRIAL** OF MIND

Darkness is but a concept
Of blindness
In reverse
So close your eyes
And see.

—Poet Labul

The next morning Anoor slipped out of her bed without waking Sylah. It was the second night in a row Sylah had fallen asleep in her bed. Sylah convinced her to turn off the runelamp beside her bed and sleep through the night in the dark as preparation.

But as soon as darkness enveloped them, Anoor began to shiver uncontrollably. Her bowels loosened, and she worried she might soil herself as she had done every time her mother locked her away. Sylah slipped soundlessly into her bed and held her hand. Anoor got used to Sylah's snoring, and the gentle wheezing was now like a sleeping draft to her. Before long Sylah fell into a dreamless sleep.

Anoor smiled at her sleeping form, a strip of morning light running down her face from the tidewind shutters that rattled all night. Her thighs clutched the blankets, which she refused to share in her sleep. Her hair was longer than any servant's Anoor had seen, but she didn't have the heart to tell her to shave it. Even Gorn hadn't raised the issue of late, and Anoor wondered if she had softened on Sylah. With a final glance at her peaceful face, Anoor left her chambers for the cool morning breeze outside.

The dawn light clawed its way through clouds and the haze left over from the tidewind. The air was thick with dust and humidity, but instead of the sticky heat of summer the breeze was cool.

Servants dusted the blue sand off the joba tree in the courtyard. It rose like a white marbled statue, chiseled by nature. Standing beneath its immense boughs, Anoor could believe that Anyme had climbed a joba tree into the sky.

Anoor had never been overtly religious, and she wondered if she'd inherited that from her grandmother. Though as the warden's daughter—and warden's granddaughter when Yona was in power—she was forced to engage with the traditional rites like Ardae, and the blessings of the harvest.

As she stood beneath the joba tree she found herself wanting to pray but not knowing how to. Though she knew the words and the prayer stance, the action seemed false without the faith to guide her. She waved at one of the Ghostings who was dusting in the branches. He was lightly freckled, his hair a very light brown, shaven like all the other servants in the Keep.

As he saw her greet him, he paused as if struck by a runebullet, his cuffed wrist holding the attached feather duster very still. So still, the feathers seemed to defy the breeze.

"Sorry, I didn't mean to disturb you." Anoor turned away from his wide stare, the Ghosting's unease shifting to her.

Sylah had told Anoor that Ghostings prayed to Anyme differently. They believed that Anyme was not one being, but an existence that was layered on top of life like another world, and when you died you moved into the next realm. You became Anyme to guide your descendants on the other side.

Anoor tilted her head against the bark of the joba tree until she felt the bark making indents in her skin. She wondered who her ancestors were and if they would guide her. She knew it was unlikely she would succeed in the trial. The darkness and her mother, two things, one and the same, fed the creature of fear that lived in the recess of her mind.

"Ancestors, I don't know who you are, and I don't know how to pray to you, but bring me light. Please bring me light," she whispered the words against the joba tree.

She turned to leave and tripped over a loose cobblestone pushed from the earth by the roots of the tree. Arms held her up. It was the Ghosting man she had waved at.

"Oh, I'm so sorry," she said, stabilizing herself.

He inclined his head and handed Anoor a white handkerchief.

"Thank you." Anoor hadn't realized she'd been crying. "Your kindness is much appreciated." Anoor put as much warmth into the words as she could muster.

The man twitched his elbow and rotated his shoulder back once. Anoor wondered what he had said.

"I can have this laundered and returned to you?"

The man shook his head and smiled a little sadly, Anoor thought.

"Oh, okay. Thank you again."

Anoor turned and left the courtyard, finding solace in clutching the bright white handkerchief in her fist.

SYLAH WAS AWAKE when Anoor returned. She had made the bed and was sitting sternly on the edge of it.

"Not long," Sylah said by way of greeting.

Anoor nodded.

"Not long."

Anoor had an urge to read her mother's journal, to remind herself the demon in her mind was just a person, if a cruel one. She looked at her bedside cabinet and back to Sylah. No, the words were hers. Once words are let out of their confinement, a secret can latch onto emotions and distort the purity of the pain. Sylah would call it self-pity. Anoor called it self-preservation.

She looked at her inkwell on her desk, the stylus as always on a chain around her neck. She wouldn't need it this time. This time she wasn't trying to break out; she would be trying to stay in.

"How are you feeling?"

"Fine," Anoor said, sitting next to Sylah, their shoulders touching.

Sylah lifted her eyebrow.

"My mother gave me a gift, really. She revealed the trial to me before anyone else. At least I know what's coming."

"What's coming is your nightmare manifested."

"But think of the other competitors. They're pacing their chambers wondering what's coming up, whether they'll be swimming in eel-infested waters, or jumping from the highest platform into the Marion Sea. They have no idea how their minds will be challenged."

Sylah patted her knee.

"You have the most impressive way of finding the light in a dark situation."

Anoor covered Sylah's hand with her own.

"Let's hope that helps me through the trial."

THE OFFICER CAME for her just before noon and marched her across the courtyard to the great veranda. They wouldn't be competing in the arena today.

There were just thirty-three competitors left. Jond Alnua was standing apart, but Anoor observed him from afar. A woman moved in front of her line of sight, and Anoor recognized the henna-dyed hair of Efie, the granddaughter of the imir of Jin-Gernomi. It was braided in her customary plaits that ran down over her breasts. She was wearing the chest plate armor from the tactics trial. Rose gold, swirling with embossed flowers. Anoor had admired the armor when she first saw it.

Anoor wore her loose-fitting training clothes, knowing she'd need to be comfortable. She wished she had knotted her hair up above; it would have made a good pillow.

"What do you think it'll be?" a warm voice said from behind her.

She turned and saw it was Yanis. He was more handsome than she remembered. He moved to stand beside her. Although he was out of uniform, his movements were precise, as if he were marching to battle. His hair coils were freshly wound.

"I'm not sure," Anoor replied.

"You scared?"

Anoor looked at his profile, her eyes trailing the strong lines of his jaw.

"No."

"Me neither." Yanis smiled down at her from his great height, but somehow he didn't make Anoor feel small.

Anoor's mother was walking through the great veranda toward them.

"Good luck," he said.

"You too."

"Competitors," Uka greeted them. Her afro had been pulled into a tight bun on her head, and her resemblance to Yona struck a chord in Anoor that made her feel very alone despite Yanis's close proximity.

Uka continued, "Today we test your mind. We look for the strength within, for the body is just a puppet for what lies behind our eyes. As you will have seen in your correspondence from me, the Day of Ascent has been brought forward to one mooncycle and one day from today. That means those who complete this trial will enter the bloodwerk trial in two weeks' time as you may need some time to recover." She didn't smile, but her eyes did light up. "Then two weeks after that, a mere mooncycle from today, the trial of combat will commence. Be sure to collect your weapon before then." Uka looked Anoor in the eye, and her eyebrow twitched.

"Have you got a plan for the trial of stealth yet?" Yanis whispered. "I haven't got mine."

Anoor shook her head.

"Maybe we can help each other?" he suggested.

"Really?"

Someone shushed them and they returned their concentration to Uka.

"So follow me and I will lead you to your trial of mind."

The competitors each hurried to be closest to the front, but Yanis and Anoor stayed a step behind. Anoor knew what was coming, and Yanis seemed in no rush to prove his worth by competing to walk in the lily-perfumed trail of Uka.

"If we both make it through, maybe we can meet and consider ideas?" He touched her shoulder, the way a comrade might.

"Definitely."

"What do you fight best with?"

"The jambiya, actually." She looked up at him sheepishly, remembering that he'd watched her practice with it the first time.

"You must have improved then." He laughed, not unkindly.

Uka was leading them toward the back of the Keep, where the building faced the cliffs that preceded the Marion Sea.

"She's taking us to the Old Nowerk Jail," someone murmured ahead of them.

The old jail had collapsed over a hundred years ago due to the poor integrity of the structure. It housed Dusters and Ghostings, away from the Embers' jail near the army barracks. Hundreds of prisoners died.

Anoor thought back to the ripping she'd witnessed. The barbaric execution was brought in shortly after the prison collapsed. Those sentenced to lesser crimes were condemned to whippings. She was still shocked by the disparities between Ember trials and those afforded to Ghostings and Dusters. Though the books she read were biased, Anoor began to piece together a picture of the system that the Warden of Truth called "justice."

They went down two staircases toward the tunnels under the city. But instead of heading inward toward the Ruta River, they walked toward the Marion Sea, though they couldn't see it or hear it this deep underground.

They passed many officers on patrol, but Anoor didn't notice. She was concentrating on breathing.

Runelamps cast the small corridors in red light. Anoor spotted a slight flaw in one of the lamps. One of the runes was positioned slightly higher than the other, unbalancing the friction. If you looked closely enough the light it emitted pulsed like a heartbeat.

Finally, the echo of their footsteps changed, and the corridor opened out to an atrium in the shape of a hexagon. At each corner of the hexagon stood a cell carved into the limestone. Anoor looked up.

Row upon row of cells stood five stories high with ladders on wheels on either end. Like a library of cells. One could swing through the shelves and pluck a prisoner at random. But as her gaze curved around the hexagon, Anoor saw the destruction the tidewind had wrought on the limestone frame. More than half the cells had collapsed into rubble.

And in the middle of the atrium stood the three other wardens, Uka joining them.

"Urgh, the air smells of sour piss," Yanis said.

"Fear," Anoor said. "It smells of fear."

It was the last thing she said to him as they were separated and allocated to different cells.

"You are to stay within the darkness for as long as you can. The top fifteen will make it to the bloodwerk trial." Uka had softened her voice, recognizing the darkness carried more menace than anything she could say. "Knock three times on the door when you are ready to leave."

One by one the competitors were locked in their cells. Limestone doors, limestone walls. Not one crack of daylight. Forty doors closed, forty locks turned.

The darkness consumed her in moments. Panic rose in her throat when she heard the key turn in the lock, but she quashed it. Block by block, like Sylah said. Take each piece and build a castle, a fortress, to lord over.

The bricks fell into place, then the walls. She added furniture and filled the bathroom with scented oils. Finally, she imagined hundreds of plates of fried yams. Just for her and Sylah.

FOUR WALLS, ALL slick with grime Jond was glad he couldn't see. He couldn't lie flat even diagonally across two corners. The cell was too small to be called a cell. He wondered who the last occupant had been and if they survived the cave-in from the tidewind.

Jond didn't mind the darkness but there was still something strange that happened to a brain when it was starved of all stimulation.

He had been in confinement for eighteen strikes when he started hearing the voices.

How did he know it had been eighteen strikes? He counted the seconds.

At first, he thought he heard Fareen speak. But he knew she couldn't, because she was dead. Then he found himself listening, yearning for her words. She had such a sweet voice. He saw the image of her in his mind, the scar by her eye always crinkling with a smile when she spoke.

Tell Sylah the truth, Jond. The guilt will only consume you.

The guilt was the darkness, and it was in his mouth, starving him of breath.

"I can't," he gasped.

If he told her the truth, she would hate him. And he needed her to love him.

"I need her, she's all I have left." Jond let the tears come.

He thought of Sylah, not that he was ever not thinking of Sylah, but she came to him then, fully formed in the darkness in his mind. He saw her as she was before, the girl he had grown up with, her braids falling to her waist, her lithe body running through the desert.

"Run with me, Jond," she once said as they crested the valley beyond the Sanctuary all those years ago.

"Where?"

"Everywhere."

He wished he had gone everywhere with her. Azim saw them running across the dunes and shouted for them to get back to work. He slipped off his sandal and held the threat high.

Azim had it right. Azim knew pain was a crafting tool. And the pain of this guilt was just like any other. The Sandstorm had always shown him that. Jond held fast when Master Inansi told him their plan for Sylah. When he found out she was alive, all he wanted to do was run to her, run everywhere with her.

But the master showed him how carving a person was like carving a weapon. Sylah should be in the cell next to his. But Anoor proved her worth in the end. Jond still wore his inkwell, a gift he would never part with.

Tell her the truth. This time the voice was Anoor's, though it didn't pierce his heart like Fareen's did. Maybe because every day he knew she stepped closer to her death.

He couldn't hold his bladder anymore, so he let it out. He tried to aim for the wall, but it just pooled beside him, and when he sat, it soaked through his pantaloons, but he was grateful. The warmth was a distraction from his guilt.

As ANOOR DRIFTED up and away from the confines of her cell in her mind, she began to plan. She kept her eyes closed, her body tense, though there was not enough space above her head to hold Nuba formations, she embodied what she could of the meditative state of battle wrath.

Anoor had been horrified by the size of the cell. It was beyond cruel to confine anyone between these four walls. The prison she would build would be bigger, better equipped to survive the tide-wind.

If she won the position of disciple, she'd have ten years to prepare her strategy before her mother descended. In the moments between training, teaching, sleeping, and eating, Anoor had already started to scheme. She had roles for Kwame, Gorn, and Hassa already, though she'd have to convince the wardens to change the rules of the court. Anoor hoped her blue blood would be enough to convince them anyone could have a place in ruling the empire.

She'd need to form alliances. Maybe Yanis would be a good start; he seemed decent enough. He'd helped her to build the shelter in the tactics trial. Kind and thoughtful, those were the people she wanted to surround herself with.

She had planned out an advisory role for Sylah, which Anoor was sure she wouldn't take, but Anoor needed her to; she couldn't do it without her. Sylah was the reason she'd gotten this far—

A small scratch behind her brought her out of her trance. She leaped up and collided with the wall. Pain lanced her elbow.

Panic crawled its way up from her toes. Handspan by handspan it froze her muscles and pinned her to the ground. She felt her heartbeat in her ears and smelled lilies in the air. Her jaw locked, and a low moan escaped her.

As the seconds passed, she managed to move her fist, though the movement was erratic, and she reached out to knock on the door.

Knock.

She hit it once.

Knock.

She hit it twice.

Her knuckle withdrew to make the final contact with the door, to give her the freedom she so desperately craved.

Don't do it, you pile of eru dung. Sylah's voice was in Anoor's mind. She knew that, but she hesitated before hitting the door.

Get into Nuba formation three.

"I can't . . . the ceiling . . . it's too low."

Do it while kneeling.

It was a make-believe conversation, but make-believe was what was needed to conquer a creature born of darkness.

Now be calm, my little kori bird. Be calm.

Anoor smiled at the nickname that also sent shivers down her spine. So like a kori bird on the morning breeze, she opened her mouth and sang.

O-o the tidewind came from sky afar
The penance for the blood power.
Anyme sings, Anyme brings

The winds wept for the sky they knew
The Farsai Desert mourned anew
Churning rivers, swirling seas
No mercy from the bruising breeze.

O-o the tidewind came from sky afar
The penance for the blood power.
Anyme sings, Anyme brings

Smoke and fire, they do bow
For the tidewind is here and now
Here and now 'til atonement's paid
The debt for power is the trade.

O-o the tidewind came from sky afar
The penance for the blood power.
Anyme sings, Anyme brings

Its cleansing wind that leaves us bare
Succumb to nightfall and be judged fair
The tidewind takes, the tidewind gives
Here and now, and so we live.

IT HAD BEEN days, maybe weeks. Jond was so dehydrated he had sucked the urine out of his clothing long ago. He was done.

"I'm done." The words were just an exhale of air. "Let me out please." He knew if he had any water to spare, his eyes would have leaked. He would have drowned in the tears that poured from his empty eyes. He would have drowned and died in this blackness of guilt.

He crawled to the door. His knocking was weak, but someone or something stirred behind it.

Then there was light.

SHE HAD COLLAPSED long ago. Still, she sang on in her dreams. A lord of her castle.

O-o the tidewind came from sky afar
The penance for the blood power.
Anyme sings, Anyme brings.

CHAPTER THIRTY-FIVE

TWELVE DAYS
UNTIL THE TRIAL OF BLOODWERK

I find poisons to be a rewarding course of study. The silent nature of their effects and the subtlety of the concoctions require a keen eye and a keener mind. Generally, I prefer the term medicine to poison. Sometimes death is the only treatment that should be prescribed.

—The journal of the Warden of Crime

Anoor's absence from her chambers left a gaping wound of silence. Sylah could hardly bear it. She busied herself with plans for the stealth trial, turning her spying to the officers who rotated shifts at the tower. She watched who drank coffee and who drank tea. She'd even caught one brewing verd leaves and wondered if her affliction echoed her own.

Though the seizures in her muscles had lessened over time, Sylah was glad for the break in training. She hadn't successfully taught a lesson without experiencing pain of some sort.

Once Sylah knew the officers on sight and had recorded all of their meals and food preferences, she made ready to go to the Dredge. She knew she'd need slabs, so she searched Anoor's chambers for as many as she could scrounge together. Unfortunately, it looked like Anoor had been giving them away too, as her purse came out as dry as a Duster's.

"What are you doing?" Gorn stood immovable in the doorframe of the bedroom. Like Sylah, Gorn was gray with worry with Anoor still in the jail.

Sylah dropped the purse back onto the desk with her other hand spread wide like a shield against Gorn's prying. "Nothing."

"You're stealing from her." Gorn's voice was normally a bark, but today, it was barely a whisper.

"No, I needed some money for an errand."

"I provide you with the money, and I send you on errands. I have done neither today."

"It was a specific task from Anoor."

"Get out and never come back."

Sylah stepped back as if struck.

Gorn continued, "I will proceed to the warden and tell her of your crimes, but as a service to the friendship"—her lips twisted—"you have given Anoor, I will give you fair warning to leave before the warden's wrath strikes your back like a whip."

"No, no, wait, listen—" Everything was unraveling around her.

There was silence. Gorn was actually waiting, listening. There was only one thing for it: the truth.

Sylah told Gorn of her plan to help Anoor win the stealth trial and explained why the money was required. She showed her the sheets of research she had done while Anoor was locked away.

"You did all this? To help her?"

Sylah nodded.

"Do you understand why I need the money? If I come back empty-handed, you can go to the warden. Please, just let me do this."

Gorn looked at the sheets of notes, Sylah's scribbled writing legible, but barely. It had been good practice.

"Come with me." Gorn hooked a finger at Sylah and led her to her bedroom.

Sylah had never been in Gorn's room, though it looked how she imagined it. A bed pulled taut with white linens, a desk with papers organized into different compartments. There were at least two dozen zines on a bookshelf to the side of the desk. Above her bed was a framed painting of two stick figures running across sand dunes.

Gorn saw where Sylah was looking.

"Anoor drew it for me when she was seven."

Sylah couldn't recognize the features of the smaller stick figure, but she knew it was Anoor holding hands with Gorn. The painting was the only decoration in the room.

"Here, is this enough, do you think?" Gorn handed her a leather purse of slabs, the weight hard to hold up with one hand.

"That should do it." Sylah smiled.

"NOT DETECTABLE, EVEN to a trained person. Clear, quick-acting, lasts at least ten minutes, and causes no adverse effects." Sylah listed the specifics on her fingers.

"Anything else? Maybe it could make them fly?" Loot drawled at her. "It's not possible, Sylah."

"Make it possible." She'd poured out the purse Gorn had given her. A thousand slabs clattered across the table, the whitestone currency making a satisfying echo in the Belly. Some of Loot's Gummers shifted in the shadows.

"That's a lot of money there, Sylah. Found a new profession?"

"Can you do it?"

Loot flicked a wrist and Fayl appeared.

"Darling, would you mind collecting up the slabs Sylah brought? They're ruining our tea party," Loot said.

It was a vaguely concealed threat, as Sylah hadn't sipped her tea yet. She took a gulp from the flowery teacup, wondering, as usual, what game Loot was playing that day. Was there poison in it or not?

"Come back in three days."

"Loot, that's a long time. Can you speed it up?"

He picked up his teacup and ran his finger along the rim.

"Sylah, have you heard of yambrini?"

She shook her head.

"It's a poison extracted from shrimp. It's clear"—he flicked out a manicured nail—"fast acting, tasteless, and odorless." Four fingers hung in the space between them. Then he crushed his fist together and slammed it on the table. "But ain't nobody waking up from yambrini."

He smiled, and Sylah sunk deeper in her chair.

"How about the fruit of the water mint, heard of that? No? Well, let me tell you, it'll put someone to sleep in under ten minutes, but guess what? Tastes and smells like mint."

"Okay, I get it."

"Do you? Because if you did, former champion of mine, you would understand the insult in your words." He leaned back and surveyed her. "Three days is not a long time at all."

"Three days."

Sylah stood up and held out her hand. Loot held out the antidote for whatever poison he had put in the tea. She drank it and left.

THREE DAYS LATER Sylah rolled two clear vials around in her palm. Loot had said he had to distill both pepper flower and grass root to make the concoction, which he'd named sleepglass. All that time Anoor was still locked up in her cell. Three days in the darkness with no food or drink, no sliver of light. The thought of her discomfort, her thirst, was enough to set Sylah's heart racing.

She'd survived Uka's discipline—no, her abuse—and would survive this too.

Sylah thought of Papa Azim and wondered if that was his intention. She wondered if he relished their pain like Uka did, or if it pained him too. She wasn't sure which was worse, the delight in violence or the premeditated nature of crafting the Stolen to become survivors.

Either way, he didn't deserve to die.

There were only three competitors left. Jond had been the last to beg his way out after two and a half days. Sylah visited him in his home that morning.

"You look like shit."

He smiled weakly.

They were lying in his bed facing each other. It felt strange to be fully clothed on his sheets.

"How was it?" Sylah asked.

"Dark." He reached out to tuck a small curl behind her ear. Sylah knew her hair had gotten too long, but Gorn didn't mention it, and Sylah enjoyed the small act of rebellion.

Jond looked tired, his eyes a little more sunken, his beard longer than she had seen it for some time.

"Tell me." Sylah wanted to know what Anoor was experiencing.

"Small, so small I couldn't lie down. So dark I lost the sense of where I stopped and the limestone began. Then there was the thirst, the hunger . . . then the voices."

He rolled onto his back, breaking eye contact with Sylah.

"I don't want to talk about it, Sylah."

They lay there in silence until Jond reached out and intertwined his hands with hers.

"Thank you for coming to visit me," Jond said.

"I have to go, Jond." Sylah didn't want to miss Anoor's return. She pulled her hand away.

"Gorn has you busy?"

"Yes, very."

He nodded and leaned in for a parting kiss, his grin back.

His lips were comforting, and Sylah savored his desire for her as his teeth nipped her and the kiss deepened. The safety of his arms wrapped around her. Strong and protective like the walls of the Sanctuary, of the home she had grown up in, with him by her side. An errant thought crossed her mind: *was this what it was like to be trapped within those four walls of the cell?*

She broke off the kiss, the truth of her thoughts striking her dumb.

"What is it?" Jond asked.

"Nothing," she said, sitting up.

He smiled, his eyes taking her in.

"I wish I could read your mind."

Sylah snorted. "No you don't."

"I do, I wish I could delve into your memories and live through the last six years with you. I hate that time separated us."

Sylah looked at him, and for the first time saw that time wasn't all that separated them. After the massacre at the Sanctuary, Jond had healed his wounds and gone on to be trained by a new Sandstorm, more ruthless than the last, vowing to eliminate all Embers from the empire. Sylah had turned her anger toward herself and sought feeling through joba seeds and the violence of the Ring. Both on paths of destruction, Sylah inward, Jond outward.

But these differences *were* differences.

"Sylah?"

She thought of Uka's journal and how she still hadn't told Jond. What was stopping her? She was busy, that was all; once the stealth trial was over she'd deliver the journal to Jond.

"I . . . I have to go, Jond."

He could see it in her eyes, the resolution of their love. He dropped his hand from the side of her face and pushed himself back on the bed, his expression cloaked in exhaustion.

"I'll see you tomorrow?" he asked.

Sylah nodded but didn't speak.

SYLAH DIDN'T RETURN to the Keep straightaway. She tried once more to look for Hassa in the Dredge, though she was propelled by more than just the questions about the Ending Fire. She needed Hassa to help her lace the officers' food and drink for Anoor's stealth trial. Even Turin hadn't seen Hassa for days. When the sun set, Sylah headed back to the Keep.

The worry for Hassa merged with her concern for Anoor, and Sylah found herself rolling the joba seed in her pocket until she returned to the Keep. After checking the chambers to see if there was any word from Anoor, Sylah went to the kitchens for dinner.

"Sylah, over here!" Kwame waved from their usual table.

She collected her food of steamed yams and bean stew and joined him.

"Did you hear?" His mouth was full of white mashed-up yams. "Efie of Jin-Gernomi got out a strike ago."

"Really?"

"Yeah, they took her to the infirmary. Dehydration."

"I wish there was a way we could tell Anoor that she's made it, that she can come out now."

"That's the thing, isn't it? Clever trial, you don't know if what you've done is enough," Kwame said.

"Only she and someone else are left, right? What do we know about him?"

Kwame shrugged. "Not much. He's a captain in the warden army. Called Yanis Yahun. The betting houses have quite good odds on him. Much higher than Anoor, of course, but she might tip the balance after coming in in the top two."

Sylah tried the stew. It needed more peppashito.

"Where's the 'shito?"

"On the herbs rack at the back."

The thought hit Sylah like a lightning bolt over the Marion Sea.

"Kwame."

"Sylah."

"You know your way around the kitchen, right?"

"I'd think so, been working here nearly every day for the past three years." He gestured his hands wide as if surveying his own personal empire.

Sylah reached into her pocket and placed a vial on the table between them.

"How would you like to help Anoor win the trial of stealth?"

He grinned, the delight dimpling his pockmarked face.

"What do I need to do?"

Sylah outlined the plan, Kwame nodding deeply with each step.

WHEN SYLAH RETURNED to Anoor's chambers, Gorn was waiting.

"Did you find the Ghosting to help?"

"No, but I drafted in someone else," Sylah said.

"Good, that's good."

Sylah smiled at Gorn. This was the most pleasant exchange they'd ever had.

"I think I'll wait in Anoor's bedroom."

"Why don't you help me polish the silverware?"

Sylah knew it was a ploy to keep her distracted, and she was grateful.

"Sure, let's polish the silverware."

"SHE'S OUT." KWAME had found her while she was making a food order run for Gorn in the kitchens. "Anoor's out. They've taken her to the infirmary."

Sylah dropped her basket and ran. Her heart thumped so fast in her chest, it propelled her forward toward the infirmary.

Four days. Anoor had lasted four days with no water or food. She was the last competitor out. Sylah skidded into the infirmary.

"Anoor Elsari," Sylah panted at an Ember dressed in white clothing. It was starched so stiff it gave the impression that it would stand up on its own, if only the woman would let it. Whether she was an orderly or a healer, Sylah wasn't sure, nor did she care, as she gave Sylah all she needed with a wordless gesture down the hall. The infirmary stank of vinegar and peppermint. The floors were slick with cleaning fluid pushed along by a Ghosting with a sodden mop. The liquid helped Sylah slide along.

She peered into rooms as she passed them searching for Anoor. Then she saw Gorn standing vigil outside a closed door.

"How is she?"

"A healer is with her at the moment," Gorn said.

"I'm going in." Sylah was ready to push past Gorn with force, but the big woman stepped aside for her.

A healer with long, trailing locs was standing over Anoor, but Sylah paid him no heed. Her eyes were full of Anoor's sleeping form. She was gaunt, her beautiful curves sucked away by darkness and dehydration. Even her hair seemed to have lost most of its bounce. Sylah reached for a curl, but a polite cough stopped her.

"Are you a friend?"

It was a covert way of asking why a servant was in the warden's daughter's room.

"Her chambermaid," Sylah said automatically. "But yes, her friend too. Is she okay?"

"She will be," the healer said. "I've checked her for signs of injury, but she's just extremely dehydrated and suffering from exhaustion. Fluids and sleep are what she needs."

Sylah nodded.

"Four days." The healer chuckled and shook his head, his locs shifting behind his large ears. "My sister, she bet on the warden's daughter here. Believes it's in her blood."

Sylah prickled. Did he know she was a Duster? She hoped not; Uka would kill him just for the thought.

He continued, "Maybe it is, I must say I am impressed, she does seem to be following in her mother's footsteps."

Anoor's arm twitched in her sleep, and the sight of it chipped away at the whitestone of worry that Sylah had carried for four days.

"When will she wake up?"

"I've given her a sleeping tea. She should come around in a few strikes."

The healer shuffled some papers in his folder and made ready to leave.

"I wonder how long she would have stayed?" he said.

"What do you mean?"

"You didn't hear? Someone petitioned the wardens to let her out. Being the only one left, it seemed fair."

Oh, Anoor, you bonded too closely with the darkness.

"Who was it?" Sylah asked.

"Pardon?"

"Who petitioned the wardens?"

"I'm not sure, I heard that it was her chief of chambers, but that seems a tad presumptuous of a servant." The healer checked himself and cleared his throat. He mumbled a few words about "other patients" and shuffled out of the room in embarrassment.

The door was left open, and Sylah saw Gorn, whose eyes were automatically drawn to Anoor. Their gazes connected for a moment, and mutual understanding passed through them.

Gorn entered the room and shut the door.

"Fluids and sleep," she stated.

"Yes, that's what the healer said."

Gorn moved to the other side of the bed, Anoor asleep between them.

"Her mother didn't want me to take her to the infirmary, but I requested it in front of the other wardens, so she couldn't refuse."

Sylah nodded.

"I . . . I wanted to thank you." Gorn smiled lightly. "She has always been quick to smile, ever since she was a child . . . but recently . . . I don't think she's been faking it." She sighed, looking down at Anoor. "I had to pick up the pieces every time, hide the bruises, stitch the stitches, wipe away her tears. I'm glad she's doing this . . . fighting back against her."

Sylah didn't know what to say.

"She told you, didn't she?" Gorn said.

"Yes." Sylah let a sigh out her nostrils, "I know Anoor is a D—"

"Say the words and they'll likely be your last," Gorn whispered. "And not just yours. The warden has ears everywhere."

"Are you not one of them?" It was a presumptuous question, rude and insulting in equal measure.

Gorn bowed her head. "There is a thread I walk, its edges frayed nearly to dust. I must remain balanced to those who look carefully, even if all the while my mind takes a different path." Gorn looked at Anoor. "That is the cost of loving her."

Sylah had two thoughts in that moment.

One: that it was a cost Sylah was willing to pay.

Two: that Anoor had a mother who loved her after all.

CHAPTER THIRTY-SIX

EIGHT DAYS
UNTIL THE TRIAL OF BLOODWERK

Master Nuhan of the guild of knowledge has been reported missing. His husband claimed that he never returned home from teaching his last class in bloodwerk. An additional patrol will be sent out to scour the area.

—Missing person report filed by Officer Wahal, year 421

The sharp smell of vinegar tickled Anoor's nose. Was it real? Or was the darkness playing tricks on her again? Light moved on the other side of her eyelids, but it had done that before. She cracked open an eye. Yes, that was sunlight. She squeezed them shut against the brightness.

A shadow moved in front of her vision.

"Stop playing dead." Sylah's drawl was the sweetest sound she had ever heard. When she opened her eyes again, Sylah's face filled her vision. She was smiling but her eyes had thick bags underneath, heavy with worry.

"Did I lose?" Anoor croaked, then coughed. Sylah handed her a cup of water, monitoring her slow intake.

"No, you didn't lose. Maiden's tits, you came out last."

"I came first?" Anoor couldn't believe it.

"Yes, you monkey bullock."

"Will you stop swearing at me?"

"Absolutely fucking not."

They grinned at each other. Sylah trailed a finger down Anoor's face, her own gaze softening.

"Was it bad?"

Anoor didn't lie: she nodded.

"But I built my fortress and lorded over it." She gestured for Sylah, and she leaned on the bed to complete the embrace.

"I was so worried," Sylah said into her hair.

"I made us yams."

"What?"

"In the fortress I built. I made us plates and plates of fried yams."

Sylah laughed, and Anoor was eager for her to make the sound again. She squeezed her tightly before releasing her.

"I feel all right, my throat is a bit sore." Anoor pushed herself up and winced.

"What is it? Where hurts?" Sylah flapped around her like a mother hen.

"I'm fine . . . it's just . . ."

"What, cramp? I can help."

"No, you can't."

"Tell me what's wrong."

"I am dying for the privy," Anoor cried, springing out of bed.

She heard Sylah laughing from the other side of the privy door for quite some time.

Anoor recovered in the infirmary for three days; she insisted she felt fine after one day, but both Sylah and Gorn stood firm on following the healer's orders.

Something had shifted between Sylah and Gorn when Anoor went away. She wasn't sure what, but it accentuated the similarities in their stubborn personalities. Although neither Gorn nor Sylah ever mentioned it, they had clearly devised a rota so that Anoor was never alone. She enjoyed waking up and seeing one or the other by her side. Even in the dead of night, Sylah's snoring was a lullaby to Anoor's restless dreams of darkness.

Sylah had filled the room with zines, but Anoor had requested different books from the library about the history of the plantations, the accounts of the Jin-Hidal mining uprisings, army ledgers of Duster crimes. Sylah fetched her requests without a twitch of the eyebrow, but Anoor caught her approving glances. If Anoor was going to be warden, she was going to make a difference.

As much as Anoor wanted to prove she was ready to get back to training, she was also reluctant to leave the safety of the infirmary. When the healer eventually gave his blessing for her to leave, she dragged her feet all the way up to her chambers.

"What's wrong?" Sylah asked her. "I thought you'd be glad to leave that smelly place."

"I am, it's just that . . . I don't know, it felt for a minute like I won, you know?" Anoor pushed her hair out of her face. Its volume had grown during her time without her precious oils. "But there's still so much to do . . . bloodwerk . . . combat . . . and we still haven't got the weapon from the tower."

"Don't worry about that. Shall I run you a bath?"

"I *am* worried about that, though, Sylah." Anoor went to sit on the side of the marble bathtub as Sylah poured half a bottle of oil into the running water. No wonder Anoor had gotten through ten bottles in the last mooncycle.

"I told you I would figure it out. And I have," Sylah said.

"What?" Anoor shrieked, her bare feet slapping on the tiled floor as she stood.

"Get in and I'll tell you all about it."

Sylah sat on a stack of zines beside Anoor, their heads side by side but separated by the wall of the bathtub. She told Anoor of her plan and the sleeping draft she had procured, though she omitted where from, and Kwame's role in administering it. Sylah retrieved the research she had done and pointed out the different foods and drinks that they'd need to lace with the liquid depending on the time of day.

"During breakfast before the officers swap rotation is the ideal time. Kwame can be there to monitor their comings and goings and add the liquid to the coffee. He'll have to be careful and make sure no one else drinks from it during that time."

"I trust him," Anoor said.

"Yeah, well, being trustworthy and being capable are two different things. This isn't a game of shantra, this is real life."

"I guess."

"After he's done that, you'll have ten minutes to go up to the tower, retrieve the weapon, and leave again," Sylah said.

Anoor was silent for a moment.

"Let's do it tomorrow," she said in between the dripping of the faucet.

"That's too soon, Anoor."

"Why? I'm fully recovered, the healer said so. Plus, we don't have a lot of time. I need the jambiya. I *need* it."

"Are you sure?"

"Yes."

Anoor dipped her head under the water, cutting off Sylah's protests. She submerged her hair beneath the warm embrace of the tub and opened her eyes, though the perfume in the oil stung them. Sylah appeared above her, a blob of wavy shapes and gargled noises.

After a few breathless moments, Sylah left, and Anoor knew she had won. Tomorrow, then. Tomorrow, she would retrieve her weapon.

GORN HAD STOPPED giving Sylah any work. Even though Sylah still dressed like a chambermaid during the day, she was able to fully dedicate her time to Anoor. That morning their run took them past the northern tower where the weapons were kept. Anoor had lost some of her stamina from the week off running, but she was fitter than Sylah expected.

"Remember the plan? At the call of the eighth strike—"

"I wait until I see Officer Ado enter the tower," Anoor interrupted Sylah. "Then count to a hundred. At that point I can enter the tower, retrieve my weapon, and leave. I have ten minutes from when the officer enters."

Sylah nodded, and they slowed their run to a jog. They had one strike until eighth call. The air was humid and thick with anticipation. Or it might have just been the haze left over from the tidewind. Sylah heard in the kitchens that an Ember servant got caught in the tidewind last night. He survived, just, though they weren't sure he'd make it through the day. He lost all the skin from his arms and half his face. It had happened at four in the morning, when the tidewind should have been long gone two strikes prior.

Anoor darted to the right beside her, waving at someone in the distance.

"I'll be right back," she called to Sylah.

Sylah watched as she jogged up to a captain in uniform. His pressed jacket was so crisp she wondered if it would crunch between her teeth. His hair was pulled into tight coils, neatly done.

There was something familiar about him, but Sylah wasn't sure. He might have been one of the captains she had tracked during her research for the trial of stealth. Either way, he was familiar to Anoor. She watched him make her laugh. Sylah lingered for a few more moments, though jealousy eventually dragged her away, and she made her way back to their chambers.

"Hassa." Sylah spotted her coming out of the kitchens. "Hassa, you're alive."

Sylah wrapped her arms around Hassa, noticing there was less of her than usual. She pushed her to arm's length and looked in Hassa's sunken eyes. "Are you okay? Where've you been?"

I'm okay, Sylah. I've been working.

"Where? Because you haven't been working at the Keep."

Hassa shifted her feet and looked down.

No. Marigold died.

"What?"

Hassa's shoulders slumped.

"How?"

The tidewind.

Sylah winced.

"What can I do? Are you okay?"

Hassa tried to lift the corners of her mouth. *I'm okay.*

Sylah wasn't so sure.

Is there somewhere we can go? To talk?

"I need to talk to you too. Can we meet later? I have to do a thing . . . In fact I really should be going . . ."

I'm not sure where I'll be later. Here, take this. Hassa handed Sylah an eru leather sheath. *If I can come later, I'll find you.*

"Come to the gardens this evening. To the left of the arena a hundred handspans in from the trees is an abandoned watch tower. Anoor and I will be there tonight after tenth strike."

I'll try. Hassa hadn't taken her eyes away from the tube in Sylah's hand.

Sylah heard the call of half strike. She needed to get in position. Where was Anoor anyway?

As if the thought conjured her, Anoor appeared from the steps below.

"Hassa, hello." Anoor smiled at Hassa.

Hi, Anoor. Hassa waved, then she turned to Sylah once more. *Read it, Sylah, but don't tell anyone of what you see.*

Sylah tilted her head toward Anoor. "Even her?"

Hassa looked at Anoor.

I think she can keep a secret, don't you?

"Don't we need to be . . ." Anoor shifted from foot to foot looking at Sylah pointedly.

"Yes, sorry, Hassa, we have to run. See you later?"

Maybe.

"I'm sorry, Hassa, about Marigold."

Hassa nodded sadly but waved them away, touching her shoulder. *Go, go.*

Sylah and Anoor rushed off to take their positions ahead of eighth strike.

ANOOR COUNTED TO a hundred as she stood in the shadows of the cloisters. The tower was just beyond the courtyard, to the right of the joba tree.

"Sixty-three . . . sixty-four . . ."

She wondered if Sylah would have time to run here if anything went wrong. Anoor just had to trust them both: Kwame pouring the potion and Sylah drawing eyes away from him. Anoor suggested that Sylah should get on a table and dance, but she'd refused. She didn't want people to "drop dead from shock." Instead, she decided to go with pushing over a cauldron of spinach stew.

"Ninety-nine . . . a hundred."

Anoor ran across the courtyard toward the tower. Her muscles protested from the excess exercise, but she paid them no heed. The door was jammed by something heavy, and Anoor had to push her whole body weight until it would give.

"Oh, sorry." The weight blocking the doorway was the slumped form of an officer who had fallen forward onto the door instead of backward. Anoor inadvertently dragged him across the floor as she pushed the door open. He would have a few bruises for sure.

Anoor knew she didn't have long, so she crept up the stone steps to the room above. She paused. She could hear a faint tapping in the distance. It was getting louder with each passing moment, followed by a low hiss. Boots, there were *boots* on the steps above, accompanied by the puffing of breath. Someone was coming down toward her.

The spiral staircase didn't divulge any hiding spots, so Anoor had to think fast. She pulled her stylus from under her shirt and pierced it through her inkwell. Gorn's blood beaded at the nib, and she got to work on the step in front of her, drawing a series of runes. She quickly ripped the sleeve of her shirt and drew another string of bloodwerk runes. The officer was coming closer, their grumbling echoing down the steps.

"I knew I shouldn't have swapped shifts with Jina . . ."

Anoor swore and ducked back down the staircase. She propped the body of the other sleeping officer up against the wall and pushed herself flat into the corner, using the body of the officer to hide behind.

This had to work.

"Hello . . . ? Your attempt didn't work. I know you're in—"

The bloodwerk rune pushed against his boots, launching him down the stairs with force. He screamed as he tumbled down the stone steps, collapsing in a heap by the door. Anoor hoped that had been enough to knock him out, but he groaned into the ensuing silence.

She pulled out the blindfold she'd made from her ripped sleeve and crept out from the corner. With deft fingers she pulled it over his eyes and tied it at the back of his head.

"Argh, you rascal. You swine fodder. Get this off me." His hands scrabbled at the blindfold but the bloodwerk runes held it fast to his face.

Anoor wanted to apologize, but she couldn't let the officer know the sound of her voice. After all, she couldn't get *caught*.

Anoor left the officer crawling around the foyer and ran up the stairs. She needed to get the weapon and go. Time was running out. Two more officers were slumped on duty in the main room. But Anoor's eyes were drawn straight to the weapons rack at the back. The blood-red runelamps around it made the gold shine like copper. There was a spear, a mace, a pole axe, a sword, and a jambiya. Her jambiya. She walked toward it as if it called to her. The hilt was adorned with rubies set in gold. She reached out and held it in her hand. The cool metal fit her grip perfectly.

She slipped into Nuba formation one, testing the balance. Her grin was triumphant as it whistled through the air. The sword on the rack glinted at her. It was by far the most impressive weapon, but its weight and the technique required to wield it made it one of the last weapons to be claimed.

She lifted the sword off the rack, putting the jambiya down. It was lighter than she expected but still much too heavy for her. The hilt was a work of art: it had been fashioned into the roots of a joba tree, the branches reaching out across the blade in intricate gold embellishment.

"Thank you for this."

She almost dropped the sword in fear. She spun on her heel and came face-to-face with the jambiya pointed directly at her chest. She choked as she saw the face behind it.

"Hello, Anoor."

"Yanis, what are you doing?" Anoor's stomach turned sour.

"Taking my weapon."

"You know that's the one I wanted."

"Exactly, and now it's mine." His tone was mild, pleasant, his smile kindly.

"I don't understand."

"Thank you for letting me know about your plan. It really was easy to just follow you in."

"Yanis, give me the jambiya." She ground her teeth, anger building behind her eyes.

"I'm sorry, Anoor, but I can't."

Anoor brought up the sword and drew it across her body, moving into a defensive position, though her muscles struggled with the weight.

"Good footwork, your upper body has a strong foundation. But I'm guessing we don't have time to play-fight." He was complimenting her, a smile still playing around his lips.

Anoor inched closer, close enough to knock the jambiya from his hands. But the closer she got, the closer he had gotten to the stairs.

He cocked his head to the side.

"Your mother sends her regards."

The words pierced her sharper than the tip of a knife, and she stumbled back.

"What?" Her hesitation sent Yanis running down the stairs.

The scream started in the sour pit of her stomach and worked its way out. But when it reached her lips it wasn't a scream after all, it was a growl.

THE WAITING WAS the worst part. Kwame had gone back to work but assured her the deed was done. Sylah paced in their chambers waiting for Anoor to return. Had Sylah slipped up? Had she missed one of the officers? What if one of them had been sick and missed his shift?

No, if something was wrong, Sylah would know by now.

She looked down into the courtyard below, but the view from Anoor's room didn't show the northern tower. Only a quarter of a strike had passed, but it felt like longer. Sylah rubbed her brow. All she could do was wait.

Sylah remembered the tube Hassa had given her and went to retrieve it. Pulling open the leather strap, she tipped out the contents onto the desk.

"Shit."

Sylah rubbed her eyes, looked again.

"Fuck."

She reached out, touched it, felt the parchment as real as the skin on her arms.

"How?"

Sylah opened the drawer next to her and retrieved the map. She pushed it flat against the edge of the parchment.

"They fit. Maiden's tits, they fit."

Hassa had given Sylah the other piece of the map.

As SOON AS Sylah heard the door open, she jumped up and went to greet Anoor. Sylah was triumphant with the truth; a lightness of validation had settled on her. There was more out there. *More.*

"Anoor what's wrong? Wait, that's a sword."

"My mother, she took the jambiya."

"What?" Gorn appeared from her bedroom and joined them in the hall.

"What do you mean? Uka was there?"

"Yes; well, no. Yanis, she sent Yanis."

"Who's Yanis?"

"He's a competitor, and he took the jambiya. He knew I wanted it, needed it."

Sylah's blood rushed to her face.

"Kwame," Sylah simmered. "I'm going to kill him."

"No, Sylah, wait!"

But Sylah's rage gave her the speed to lope past Anoor in moments. Down the stairs she went, getting angrier each step of the way.

When she burst into the kitchen, a few people looked her way, some sensing the drama to come and drifting closer.

"Kwame," Sylah barked at him.

His face was covered in flour, and his smile dropped when he saw her expression.

"What happened? Oh, no, did it not work?"

"You sold the information, didn't you."

"What?"

"You sold her out, you told the warden what we were planning."

Kwame looked around him worriedly at the onlookers and held out a placating hand.

"Sylah, I don't know what you're talking about, but maybe lower your voice?"

"Was it for money?" Sylah was shaking. She felt the warning signs of the prickling in her legs. A seizure was coming, but she couldn't stop now. "I knew I was foolish to trust an Ember. You disgust me, you know. You act like wealth is something that separates you from the others. But you *are* rich, don't you get it? Your blood is the currency, but that wasn't enough, was it?"

Sylah fell to her knees, her right leg jerking beside her.

"You earthworm, eat shit, Kwame, eat shit." She tried to loosen her tongue to spit into the bread he was making as a big finisher, but the trembling was too much. Fingers dug into her shoulder.

"Sylah, oh, Sylah," Anoor said, kneeling beside her. "Gorn, will you help me get her up?"

Large hands joined Anoor's and lifted Sylah to a nearby seat.

Sylah hadn't taken her eyes off Kwame. He wasn't reacting like she expected. He looked horrified, but not ashamed. He rubbed at his eyes.

"Gorn, can you make a verd leaf tea?" The servants had dispersed at Anoor's intervention, the drama halted by the warden's daughter.

"Sylah, it wasn't Kwame, it was me," Anoor said quietly.

Sylah looked away from him, her gaze connecting with Anoor's. "What?"

"I told Yanis to come to the tower at eighth strike."

"Anoor? You told that guy?"

"He was the man in the courtyard earlier . . . I was trying to make allies."

Sylah's anger was punctured by Anoor's words. She sagged against the back of her chair. Gorn pushed a mug of verd leaf tea in her hands, but the seizures had already abated. Sylah turned to Kwame, but he had gone.

"I think I might have overreacted," Sylah said. "Can we go back to your chambers?" Though the other servants averted their eyes, Sylah still felt them tiptoeing around her.

"I'll find Kwame later and apologize." If he would listen.

The walk back to Anoor's chambers was solemn, Sylah all the while trying to put her disappointment into words.

"I don't need to tell you how stupid you were, do I?" was the question Sylah settled on.

"No," Anoor said quietly, closing the door behind them. Anoor ran a hand through her hair, and Sylah saw the weariness spread like a poison. She was giving up.

"I can't win this without the jambiya. We don't have enough time. Three weeks, Sylah, three weeks until the combat trial."

Sylah had to put her annoyance for Anoor's actions aside. She held Anoor's chin in her hand and tilted her face toward her.

"You can do this."

"Sylah . . ." she whispered.

"You must do this. And when you win, you need to tell everyone the truth." She guided Anoor's face to her desk where the two parts of the map connected as one.

PART FIVE

RULE

One, two, three, four
All the wardens in a row
Ruling us forever more
Watching over all below.

—Nursery rhyme sung in Ember schools

THE STORY OF THE TANNIN AS SPOKEN BY GRIOT SHETH

The spoken word has been transcribed onto the page;
the ◊ symbol represents the beating of the griot's drum.

Another mooncycle has passed, and with each passing day the empire swells and grows. But it was not always so, as you know, as you know. The story I will tell today takes us to a time before the empire was an empire, before the wardens were called wardens.

◊◊◊

Oh, don't groan and wail! You may know the story of the Ending Fire, but what of the Tannin?

◊◊◊

Oh, don't scoff and cry! Bedside stories and nursery rhymes the Tannin may be, but listen to me . . .
Listen to me.

◊◊◊

Oh, I made you jump! That's for the grumbles and heads that turned. Don't get tired of a story or it'll spook in return.
Eee, so listen to me. Listen to me.

◊

The sky began to crackle, the sun began to hide, the ground shook from beneath, and the rain came from the side.

"What could it be? What could it be?" the people howled.

The earth cracked open and lava flowed.

"What could it be? What could it be?" the people cried.

Three days passed, and many more had died.

And though they prayed and wailed and flailed, Anyme's wrath still hailed.

◊

No one knew what they had done to cause the world to come undone, but on the fourth day the Abosom claimed, "Anyme was cleansing the land," and they gave it a name.

The Ending Fire. The Ending Fire. THE ENDING FI—

◊◊◊

Ach! The people's words were stolen as they were struck by rain of sparks and flame. Bringing the pain, the Ending Fire came.

The Abosom said the fire that would fall would be enough to befall the greatest of musawa, women, and men.

There was one group, eight ships all told, who had prepared for the journey before it took hold. Some say Anyme spoke to them, the wardens who were to come, and warned them of the need for hoarding, boarding and . . . gone!

Gone into the sea, the captains led their ships, with plants and animals, mortar and brick. All they would need to start a new world. All they would need to be freed from the old. Dusters and Ghostings and Embers all together.

◊◊◊

Though the Ghostings were confined to the hull and the Dusters toiled the ropes, the Embers, as we have come to see, were leaders even then.

◊

Freed from what, you ask? Some say the God Anyme had believed now was the time to purge the world of their greed.

◊

Ey, you think you know the ending? I see you get up to leave, as if this is where we stop, the shores of the empire in sight?

Oh no, you forget, eight ships left the mainland before it sunk under the flames of Anyme's wrath. But only two made it here, to the ground where we now stand. So what happened? Where did they go? Let me fill the meat in this flatbread sandwich. Listen to me. Listen to me.

◊

The wayfarers remarked at the strange wind that carried them forward. Blue and sparkling with grains of sand, a good omen they thought.

The raging fire behind them, glittering blue up ahead.

Three weeks they moved across the open ocean. The wind was their only guide. Then one day it stung and bit, the wind rubbing the cheeks of the sailors raw. So raw their skin ripped.

Then the waves churned up and threatened to capsize the ships, twisting and turning in the sea's grip. Some of you think it was the tidewind that took them, those six vessels lost, tossed in the waves. But the griots know that another horror rose up, up, and up from the depths of the sea.

A being not of nightmares but of nightmare itself. The Tannin is the creature that holds your body captive when your mind wakes in bed. The shadows in the cupboard and the darkness in your head. Longer than the Tongue across the Ruta River, wider than the gates of the Keep.

With teeth of stone and scales of glass, the Tannin roams the Marion Sea. It roams and owns the waters, its nest, its home. And so when the ships invaded unbeknownst to them, the great serpent rose up from the sea, and chewed up six ships, while the others got free.

◊◊◊

I see disbelief in your eyes, you up there, but why don't you go for a swim, go into the Tannin's lair? I've heard the fishermen speak of a churn in the water, the flick of a fin, or a shadow, too big to slaughter.

◇◇◇

Now those who did survive, guided by the tidewind as they were, found a world ready to shape, a graveyard of ruins ready to rise.

That's the filling in our flatbread, though I didn't promise it wouldn't be rancid. As ever, I leave you a warning, don't board a ship in the Marion Sea, and don't ever, ever be stranded.

CHAPTER THIRTY-SEVEN

ONE DAY
UNTIL THE TRIAL OF BLOODWERK

Reporting sixty-seven Ghosting deaths from the sleeping sickness on Ardae night. The pyres were burned the following day beyond the plantation fields so as to not spread the disease. I oversaw them from afar, maintaining distance from the contagion.

—Memo to the Warden of Duty from Auditor Quol

"What are you doing?" Anoor came through the door in their training room, catching Sylah unawares. She pulled out her stylus and hid what she was working on behind her.

"Nothing."

"Doesn't look like nothing; show me." Anoor reached out for the glass orb with Sylah's bloodwerk on it. It jingled with the shards of glass she'd placed inside.

Anoor inspected the runes. Sylah was really proud of it. It was a new invention she called a runebomb. At first her experiments were light-based, but this new version was more dangerous. It pushed the shards of glass outward once activated by Sylah's blood. Shrapnel and light would stop anyone in their tracks.

Anoor dropped it on the floor and stepped on it, Sylah's hard work crunching under her foot.

"Skies above! I just spent the last three strikes on that!"

Anoor pressed her heel in harder over the glass, shattering it to dust. Anoor raised her eyes to Sylah's indignant expression.

"I didn't teach you to bloodwerk so you could make things like this."

"They're for protection!"

"Protection against who?"

The Embers, Sylah thought.

Anoor continued, "Things like this only ever get used on Dusters, Sylah. My father was the general of the warden army, and the only people he ever fought were Dusters who couldn't fight back. Uprisings at plantations are where their runebullets are spent. Those Dusters you showed me in the field, they're the ones who will suffer." Anoor's mouth twisted. "The coups that the imirs stir up are deadlier, but they are fought with words and legislation."

Sylah wanted to say that she'd never use the runebombs on a Duster. She'd spilled enough blue blood when she lost her family. But then she thought of Anoor and the side she resided on. Ember or Duster?

"How many of these have you created?"

Four.

"Just that one."

"Good. It's not up to you to choose who lives or dies, Sylah. Creating things like this"—she waved to the crushed glass like ice on the floor—"is the choice of death."

The little kori bird has grown wise. She marveled at the change in Anoor. She never thought that learning about the atrocities of the empire could lead to such empathy. Maybe education played a bigger part than Sylah had realized.

Sylah thought on her words for some time.

A little later they were sparring, the runebombs forgotten. At least by Anoor.

"Move to your right . . . no, block again. Harder. Yes." They had been practicing noon and night for the past week. Anoor was getting better, but she still couldn't beat Sylah.

"Anoor, come on, stop holding back. You're still too scared to hurt me."

"I don't want to hurt you." Anoor wiped the sweat from her brow.

"You can't think like that. The combat round is based on first blood. Your opponent will be looking to make you bleed. Do you understand that? And you cannot bleed in front of them," Sylah snarled at her.

"Watch me again." Sylah demonstrated how to duck and parry away from an oncoming attack by feinting. It was a move adapted from the defensive motions of Laambe, and it helped Sylah avoid being sliced in the Ring more than once.

Anoor watched her move with interest. "Fine. Then stop holding back for me. Give me everything you've got. If you want me to learn the hard way, then you need to show me what it's going to be like in that arena."

She had a point. "Are you sure?"

"You've just asked me to hurt you. Should it not be both ways?" She cocked her head at Sylah and her curls bounced.

Instead of replying, Sylah launched herself at her.

Their swords clattered together with the sound of battle, a metallic echo that whispered through their bones of pain and blood to come.

"Argh." Anoor broke contact first, whirling away with the move Sylah had taught her. Sylah stalked after her. Anoor was no longer Anoor, she was prey. Sylah swept her sword under her legs, but Anoor was one step ahead and jumped to the left. Of course, Sylah knew she would, and her sword was there a moment later.

"First strike would have been your heart," Sylah commented, but they fought on, Anoor getting more and more frustrated with every parry. "Release the anger, calm your nerves, and reach the meditative state of battle wrath." Anoor closed her eyes and Sylah knew she was mastering it.

Their swords flashed and clashed over and over, Anoor's arms shuddering beneath the weight of the weapon she detested. Sylah ground her to the back of the room, step by step. Anoor tried with all her might, but she would never best Sylah. Sylah was a product of the Sandstorm. She was born to fight. Born to sacrifice. The Final Strife.

Sylah felt her muscles spasm, the cursed withdrawals spreading out like a spiderweb. She cried out and dropped her sword. Anoor swung for her with a battle cry. The sword aimed for Sylah's neck and stopped just shy of severing her artery. Anoor's nostrils flared, her breathing heavy. Then realization hit her.

"Curse the blood, are you okay?" Her sword dropped to the ground with a clatter. Sylah placed her hand on her neck, double-checking it was still there. Blood swelled from a shallow cut.

"I'm okay." She ground her teeth in frustration. This would have never happened in the Ring. In all her six years of fighting there, not once had she let anyone slice her skin. But that was before she had turned away from the joba seeds. She hated to admit that the drug had aided her so.

Anoor was fussing over her, tears of guilt welling in her eyes.

"I'm fine, Anoor. Hey, I said I'm fine."

"I'm sorry."

"Why? You won." Sylah cupped her face in her hands. "That's what we want after all."

"But I wouldn't have if . . . you know."

"If I hadn't been addicted to joba seeds and damaged my body for life."

"Not for life, just a few more mooncycles . . ."

"I'm not sure, I think I'll always be broken. The tremors, they aren't improving anymore." They were silent for a moment. "I never thanked you, you know. For saving my life."

"I abducted you, as you constantly like to remind me . . ." Anoor smiled.

"Yes, I guess that's true. But seriously. You gave me my life back, and for that I will be eternally grateful."

"How grateful?" She had that glint in her eye.

Sylah shivered, then jumped as the tidewind shook the tower with the force of a hammer.

"Maiden's tits, it's getting strong."

They both looked at the map hanging on the wall. Anoor had painstakingly glued it back together with tree gum so the two parts were bound together again.

"What do you think is out there?" Anoor walked over to the map as she spoke.

"I wish I could ask Hassa."

Hassa hadn't come to the tower that night or the six nights after that. Sylah would let her friend grieve, but when she returned, she had *a lot* of questions for her.

Sylah joined Anoor beneath the map, though she didn't like looking at it. It made her feel dizzy, like she was standing on the edge of the Tongue looking down on the Ruta River, but instead of the river, it was a sea of lies.

The world was huge.

They had initially thought that the map was torn away equally, two halves separated over time. But when Sylah unrolled the piece Hassa had given her, it showed the scope of how small the empire was among the other islands and four continents.

The piece of map Anoor and Sylah had was only a quarter of the size of the full map, maybe less. It sprawled across the wall of the tower.

"The empire really is just one island." Anoor trailed her fingers southeast to the bottom of the map where an oblong land mass called the Wetlands lay; it was three times the size of the empire. Farther east, there was the Grasslands, and in the north, cresting the parchment, was the Winterlands.

But it was the center of the map that had Sylah reeling. Ten times the size of the empire, the Queendom of Tenio was carefully transcribed to the page. In the center of it was a town called the Zwina Academy. Small buildings that looked like libraries and courtyards surrounded a tall bell tower, bloated out of proportion to signify the town.

Anoor was looking at the same thing as she asked.

"I wonder if they have a tidewind there?"

"I don't know." Sylah looked away toward the window. "We need to go; you need to rest for the trial tomorrow."

"We can't, Sylah, the tidewind's still going."

They would die if they left now. The tidewind should have abated at second strike, and now they were trapped.

"Let's sleep here."

"What? On the stone floor? It'll be freezing!"

"We'll huddle to keep warm." Sylah dragged the dummy to the center of the room and tipped it over. "A pillow," she said.

Anoor's eyes lit up with excitement, and she was soon curled around the straw arm of the dummy she had pummeled to shreds more than once. Sylah joined her on the floor.

Their eyes locked.

"Are you cold?"

Anoor shrugged, but it wasn't a no. Sylah moved her body closer and wrapped her arms around her.

Anoor sighed into the crook of Sylah's arm, and her breath burned Sylah's skin.

"Comfortable?" Sylah asked into her hair.

"Mhmm." Her mumble was drowsy, and Sylah smiled.

She didn't go to sleep for a long time. Anoor's breath sent tingles down her arm with each exhale.

It was a feeling that Sylah didn't want to miss by sleeping.

"COMPETITORS AND AUDIENCE members. We continue with the fifth trial of the Aktibar: bloodwerk." The crowd roared at Anoor's mother. They were even more bloodthirsty than usual. "The competitors below have proven their stratagems and their minds, but they have not yet proven what makes Embers so mighty: our power." Uka smiled at the cheering crowd. Anoor simmered with anger beneath her nerves. Yanis was at the far end of the arena and she was glad of it.

Yona was sitting to Uka's right, her legs crossed, arms folded. She was smiling at Anoor, actually smiling; it must have been making her mother's blood boil.

Anoor looked around her. There were only twenty competitors left. Only twenty. Anoor knew her bloodwerk skills were exquisite, her ability to draw detailed runes from her mind was second to none in her class. But that wasn't what had held her back. Gorn's blood had always ended up failing. Blood away from a host's body too long rendered the runes useless, as she had discovered over time.

The extra three years she'd studied bloodwerk had prepared her for this moment more than anything else. She just wished she could use her own blood.

Sylah had come to her early in the morning, a vial in her hand.

"I want you to use my blood today."

"What?"

"You've said it yourself, there's a lot of power in my veins, and my bloodwerk always pushes further than Gorn's."

It was true, whenever Anoor had demonstrated by using *Kha* on an object, Sylah's object always went twice the distance.

"Are you sure?" Anoor said.

Sylah pushed the vial into her hands, their fingers brushing.

"Yes."

And so Anoor had placed Sylah's vial of blood into her inkwell ahead of the trial of bloodwerk. It was a private gift that no one would ever know about. A precious gift just for her. It gave her more confidence than she knew she could muster.

Two deep-set eyes were watching her. Jond, Sylah's friend, was still in the competition. For a fleeting moment Anoor wondered whether Sylah wanted Jond to win over her. Anoor dismissed it and wrapped her arms around herself remembering the feel of Sylah's embrace during the night.

Jond held her gaze with an unreadable expression. Was it hate?

Anoor broke the stare first and turned to her left. Efie was there, a mountain of muscle, her red braids pinned up for the first time. Again, she wore her rose gold armor.

Uka continued, "The trial will take place in three rooms. Each room can only be escaped with the use of bloodwerk runes. The four competitors who complete all three rooms first will go onto the final trial in two weeks' time, combat."

Speed, that was what Anoor needed. Speed and focus . . . Jond wouldn't stop looking at her. She felt his stare graze her skin.

"Armed with just their inkwells and their knowledge, each competitor will begin in a replica of the same room. Fifteen in total . . . but only four can win. I wish all the competitors luck and speed."

The competitors were herded to the starting line, a chalky strip of white in front of twenty wooden doors without handles. Anoor cast one look down the line at Jond and bared her teeth.

The horn blared.

Pushed open with bloodwerk runes, the wooden doors swung

wide. Anoor entered, shrugging off Jond's glare. The door slammed behind her, making her jump.

The crowd's screaming lessened to a hushed murmur as the trial began, though it was more unsettling than their cheers. Anoor blocked them out using the exercises she'd learned during Nuba practice and looked around.

The room was small and roofless, so the audience members could watch from above. The walls were made of sheets of wood, constructed just for the trial. She wondered how many Dusters had built it.

It was empty save for a barred door at the other end made of thick steel. She automatically tried it. Locked, of course. This was the test, get through the door and into the next room.

She rifled through the runes in her mind. She could use *Ba* to separate the bars, then a combination of *Kha* and *Ba* to create friction through a series of supplementary runes. The heat would blow up the lock in moments.

But who *was* Jond?

She shook her head, pushing him from her thoughts. She needed to get through this trial. She drew the runes and stood back as the friction caused the bars to explode. The door opened, and she stepped through into the second room.

THE ROOFLESS ROOMS were specks in the distance, but Sylah could see the shape of Anoor's curls and her eye line followed their shadow.

"She's doing well." Kwame sat next to Sylah.

She'd apologized over and over, but the lightness in their friendship wasn't the same as it had been. It made her ashamed to be around him, knowing she was the one to cause the fracture.

"You think so? That one to her right is ahead of her slightly—no, my right. Is that Efie, the granddaughter of the imir of Jin-Gernomi?"

"Looks like it; on the other side, who's that?"

"Jond Alnua," Sylah said. She could recognize the silhouette of him ten leagues back.

"Looks like he's last."

Sylah cursed—hadn't Jond been practicing? She'd missed a few lessons with him over the last week, but that was because of Anoor more than anything else.

She rubbed her brow, trying to press away the guilt that had burrowed there. She still hadn't given him Uka's journal. She wanted to read it first, that was all, then she'd give it to the Sandstorm. But with Anoor's training regime there had been no time to read it without Anoor seeing.

There was a flash of bright red light, and suddenly Jond was through his first room.

Sylah breathed a sigh of relief.

JOND COULDN'T GET Anoor's face out of his mind. So when he entered the second room, every bloodwerk rune he'd learned over the last four mooncycles went straight out of his head. The second room was paneled in wood too, but instead of steel bars the door at the end was glass and rotating at high speed. It was a test of precision: to slow the door down in order to pass through it, Jond would have to use the opposite rune of what was drawn on the glass. Too much force, and the glass doors would shatter.

He wasn't sure what had irritated him so much about seeing Anoor. Maybe it was because he hadn't seen Sylah in over two days, and he knew it was because she was with *her*. The brat in Sylah's place.

But after this trial Sylah was free, her bargain with Anoor Elsari complete. Sylah would get her to the final trial, and Anoor would have inadvertently taught Jond everything he needed to make it through. Though he never really needed it. Master Inansi had captured a master in bloodwerk at the start of the Aktibar, and they taught him all that Sylah could.

But the time with Sylah had been precious, a gift she had given him every day, and he would have never traded it for strikes in a cell with a master in bloodwerk. When the Sandstorm gave her a task, he thought he'd been giving her something back, something to believe in again. And it did. He saw the spark of dedication reflected in her eyes, he saw her say the words "The Final Strife" and believe them.

But then that spark had fizzled, dulled, replaced by a thoughtful expression, one that probed and questioned every step the Sandstorm took. The Stolen weren't there to question, they were there to execute.

And so when the Sandstorm asked him to trail her, he did. It was how he had known, how he had seen with his own eyes, Sylah and Anoor leaving the tower they used to train in, just that morning.

He looked at the door at the end and funneled the anger he had been trained to harness. In moments the runes came to him, and he blew the glass door into fragments. Who needed precision if you could use brute strength?

He grinned and climbed over the shards and through to the third and final room.

Enough pining. He was here to win.

ANOOR COULD TELL the power in the blood was weakening. Sylah's blood was definitely more powerful than Gorn's, but it wouldn't last much longer. Anoor walked through the glass door. She'd slowed its spinning to a sand snail's pace and entered the third room.

For a moment she thought she was looking into a mirror. It wasn't until she saw the glass panels that she realized what they'd done. She stood on a small platform above a tank filled with water. The water was so still she could see her reflection. The door out was more than twenty handspans below the surface through a glass tube.

She jumped in, the cold water rushing up her nose and making her splutter for the surface. She dipped beneath the water and tried again, just to see how long she could hold her breath.

Nope, not long enough to get to the door. She got out and sat on the platform. She needed to drop to the floor more quickly, then propel herself through the tube to the door on the other side.

Her mind flicked through the *Book of Blood*. Runes don't work on a living thing, so she'd need to write on her shoes. But she'd also have to protect the rune because of the water.

The combination began first in her head and then went onto her shoes. The left foot would drop her quickly, the right would push her away from the wall. She plunged into the water, dropping faster than she expected. She let go of the left shoe as soon as she reached the tube and angled the right shoe at the wall. It should have propelled her down the tube, but nothing happened.

The blood. The blood was too old to work. She kicked her legs, but she was too slow. Air escaped her mouth, and she felt her blood racing in her head. She was going to die in this tube.

She was going to die.

SOMETHING WAS WRONG. She'd been under the water too long. Sylah strained her eyes to see a flicker of movement, anything to indicate life. Suddenly Anoor broke the surface, but not at the exit, at the entrance. The arena seemed to have held its breath with her, and the exhalation of disappointment whooshed around. Anoor would have been first, but the delay gave Efie the lead.

Sylah watched the granddaughter of Jin-Gernomi exit the final room. A trail of water gushed out as the door opened. She'd used her armor to draw bloodwerk runes on, to guide her through the water.

When Sylah looked back to Anoor, she was bent over, redrawing runes on her shoe. Within moments she ducked under the water again.

"Come on, Anoor, come on . . ."

Both Kwame and Sylah were leaning forward in their seats. The crowd cheered; another competitor had made it through, but Sylah didn't turn to see who.

Then there was a splash, and the final door in Anoor's run opened. She flopped onto the ground with the rush of water that followed. Anoor was gasping and spluttering but alive. She had done it. She had gotten through to the final round.

ANOOR COULDN'T GET enough air. Her lungs gasped and strained, tears streamed down her face, but no one could see them because of the water dripping off her. Blue blood seeped out of a small cut in her forearm, and she clutched her hand over it.

She'd made it.

She looked for Sylah in the stands, directed her eyes to the top where she knew she would be cheering with the other servants.

Anoor looked at the leader board to see if she'd done enough. Efie was first, followed by Yanis, then her. A squelch of another competitor landing on the ground indicated the final winner of the bloodwerk trial. Anoor didn't need to turn around to know it was Jond; the hairs on her arms were already raised. The leader board flashed the runelamp next to his name in confirmation.

Efie, Yanis, Jond, and her: the four competitors. They were all that was between her and the title of disciple.

"DID YOU SEE? Did you see?"

Sylah smiled as she entered the bed chamber.

"Yes, I saw."

"I made it!" Anoor ran into Sylah's arms, knocking the breath out of her. Sylah leaned into her embrace, and despite the dampness of her clothing, her scent clung to her and Sylah inhaled it deeply.

"I nearly didn't make it."

Sylah pushed Anoor to arm's length.

"What happened? I saw you come back out of the water."

Anoor's gaze dropped to the floor. "The runes, I think I messed up, so I had to redo them."

"You? *You* messed up?"

Anoor batted Sylah's disbelief away with a smile.

"But I still won, didn't I?"

"Yes, you did."

"I wish we could celebrate at the winners' banquet, but with so few competitors left, they're holding it after every guild has completed the fifth trial. And that won't be until the day before the combat trial."

"Don't worry, I got you a reward."

"You have?"

Sylah slipped into attack mode. "Yes. More practice."

CHAPTER THIRTY-EIGHT

SEVEN DAYS
UNTIL THE TRIAL OF COMBAT

We call on all corners of the world. The Zalaam are rising. The damage they reap on our homes puts us all in danger. We request aid and your armies.
Come with haste.

—Messenger from the Zwina Academy

The days passed in a grueling routine of training and more training. That morning Sylah had realized it had been over a week since she'd seen Jond.

"I have to go into town now," Sylah said, wiping sweat from her brow.

"Oh? Has Gorn given you some errands to run?"

Sylah sensed the trap. Anoor knew Gorn had stopped giving her any tasks.

"No, I need to visit a friend."

"Can I come?"

"No."

Anoor busied herself with tidying away their weapons, and she didn't look at Sylah when she said, "Are you going to see Jond Alnua?"

Sylah held back her immediate retort; instead she went for honesty.

"Yes."

"Is he your lover?"

"I . . . I'm not sure that's the right word." Akoma, her Akoma.

"Well, do you love him?" Her voice had bite.

"Yes, but—"

"And you've been . . . intimate with him?"

"Yes, but—"

"He's your lover." She said it with the grave tone of someone being sentenced to a ripping. She was trying to force the sword into the scabbard, but she kept swinging wide.

"Anoor." Sylah took the hilt of the sword and helped her guide it through the opening. "What Jond and I have . . . is something unusual."

Anoor was looking down at the sheathed blade between them but didn't speak.

"He knew my family . . . the ones who died . . . who were murdered."

At that, Anoor looked up, shock in her eyes. It was the most Sylah had told her about the Sandstorm. Sylah continued, "Yes, I love him, but it's a complicated love born of grief and anger and loneliness."

"Are you still lonely?" Anoor's question was a whisper.

Sylah knew the way to Anoor's lips, had imagined it enough times, had imagined closing that gap between them. What she hadn't expected was the warmth and softness that enveloped her as their lips pressed together.

Where Jond was stone, immovable and safe, Anoor was the tidewind, spirited and dangerous. And like the tidewind, her essence had found its way into the cavities and emptiness of Sylah's life, relentlessly beautiful.

They broke apart, and Anoor spoke.

"Is this what you want?" Anoor's breath warmed Sylah's neck.

"More than anything."

Anoor's body pressed against Sylah's, her hands slipping under her shirt and up the cooling sweat of her lower back. Sylah arched against her touch, and Anoor took the opportunity to nip at her neck toward her collarbone. Her body was aflame as Anoor's fingers made their way down. She groaned as Anoor trailed the thick, curly hair at the apex of her thighs.

If Anoor was the tidewind, Sylah was fire.

THEY LAY WITH their backs against the dummy, their legs intertwined. Two colors swirling in veins through tangled limbs. Midday had come and gone, and Sylah hadn't gone to see Jond.

"This is a pretty good pillow, you know," Sylah said into the comfortable silence.

Anoor's laugh tinkled.

"I think I prefer my own bed."

"Of course you would, you were born into feathers and luxury." Sylah had only been teasing, but Anoor went silent.

Suddenly she sat up, her bare chest leaning against Sylah's.

"I'll give it away."

"Anoor, that's not what I meant."

"But it's not right, me having all of this and the Dusters, the Ghostings . . . they have nothing."

"Look, I understand you want to help, and living frugally is a start, but it doesn't really help the Ghostings and Dusters."

"What do you mean?" She settled her chin below Sylah's and looked up at her, hazel eyes gleaming.

"Well, think about what you'd do if you don't win—"

"You don't think I'm going to win?"

"That's not what I said, is it?" Sylah tweaked her nose. "I'm just saying . . . if you don't win, which you will, how can you work to influence the court?"

"Hmm, I'd start a rebellion." She sat up suddenly. "Maybe restart the Sandstorm."

Sylah didn't need a third Sandstorm to navigate. "Maybe." Sylah began to get up. "I do have to go, you know."

"To see him?" This time the jealousy was laid bare.

"Yes, but then I'll be right back for more . . ." Sylah leaned in and kissed Anoor's pouting lips then whispered, "Training."

Anoor's laugh painted Sylah with a foolish grin.

SYLAH HOVERED OUTSIDE Jond's villa. Her basket was heavy with the weight of the journal that rested there, made heavier with guilt. She had finally stolen it the day before and finished reading it that night. Uka's words were brutal; her hatred for Anoor ran deep. Deeper than she'd imagined. It brought tears to Sylah's eyes.

The journal was also filled with the military stratagem of the empire. It even outlined the spies, including some Dusters, she had hired in the revolt of the hundred, an uprising ten years ago in the coal mines of Jin-Hidal. The information would be priceless to the Sandstorm. But still Sylah's hand hesitated as she lifted her knuckles to Jond's door.

Jond. Her Akoma. And now there was Anoor. Anoor. Sylah could still smell her sandalwood oil on her skin.

There was that foolish grin again.

The door opened after one knock.

"Sylah," Jond said in shock. He was dressed simply, clothes one wore if they wanted to disappear in the Dredge.

Sylah dropped the smile.

"Sorry, are you going out?"

"Do you want to come in? I have time."

"Sorry it's been a while." Sylah entered Jond's chambers. Something was different about the space; though it all looked the same, it seemed emptier than before.

"Jond—"

"Coffee?" he interrupted her, and she nodded.

He moved around the kitchen with jerky movements. He handed her a mug.

"Thanks."

They sipped in silence. Jond seemed distracted, aloof.

"Not long now until the combat trial. You've finally fulfilled your contract with that brat. You're free to leave the Keep."

Sylah bristled. She wasn't sure what to say but she wasn't leaving Anoor.

Jond pulled out a bottle of firerum and poured a shot into their drinks. His expression noted her silence.

Sylah forced a laugh and changed the subject. "Coffee *and* firerum. Be careful, Jond, I may just swoon." He grinned at her, a charming smile that reminded her of Loot. It was disarming, perilous.

"I wanted to thank you for the sacrifice you have made. For your dedication to the cause." He clinked their mugs together, and he took a deep drink of the scalding liquid.

"Thanks, I guess, it wasn't all bad."

"Papa would be proud. And Fareen. If only they could see us now." Jond poured himself another shot and interlaced their fingers. Down the firerum went, again and again.

Sylah watched him. "Are you okay?"

"Yes." He wiped his mouth and poured another shot.

"Jond, I came to share some information with the Sandstorm."

"Oh, yes?"

"Anoor—"

"Don't say her name like that." His voice cracked.

"Like what?"

"Like you care for her." He said the words like an insult, but they hit like a compliment. Sylah *did* care for her, deeply.

"What is this about, Jond?"

"No, please continue, share the information you have. We'll do an information exchange, you and I."

Sylah watched him. His hands were shaking, and he steadied them on the firerum bottle, which was halfway gone.

"Okay . . ." Sylah pulled out the journals. "Anoor had the missing journal in her bedside table." Sylah placed it on the table between them. A river of red blood.

Jond raised an eyebrow, and she continued.

"I saw it there a little while ago, and I only just managed to steal it."

"How long ago?"

That was his first question?

Sylah took a deep breath and shared the second secret that had been simmering beneath her skin.

"It doesn't matter. Look, Jond, there's something else. We've found evidence that there's more land beyond the empire . . ."

"How long ago," he repeated through clenched teeth.

"Jond, did you just hear me? Anoor and I found evidence of land beyond the empire."

He waited.

"I learned the journal was there a few weeks ago."

Jond stood, his mug crashing down on the table.

"Do you think this is a game, Sylah? Do you understand what your task was? Have you forgotten the enemy here?"

She couldn't believe this was what he was upset about.

"Jond, this is so much bigger than anything the Sandstorm . . ."

"You're wrong, there is nothing more important than the Final Strife. The Embers must be eliminated," he growled at her.

"The Final Strife? We are not those three words, we are more than that. Jond, listen to yourself."

His eyes bulged, like he couldn't believe what she was saying.

"Do you know how much I have lied for you? Every day I report back to the master as if it's come from you, I've watched and waited and spied and followed." His voice was hoarse. "Every day I begged for the Sandstorm to welcome you back, even though you were the one who caused their deaths, even after you managed to miss the sign-up and get yourself captured. They wanted to kill you, Sylah . . ." His voice was pained. "And I couldn't let them kill you, I couldn't." His eyes filled with tears, and he reached for her, despite his next words striking her like a whip. "Everything is your fucking fault, Sylah."

She took a step back, her thoughts a jumble.

"They wanted to kill me?" she whispered.

He nodded.

They sat in silence for some time, until Sylah spoke.

"All this time I thought I needed the purpose of the Sandstorm to sustain me. And when . . . when I caused their deaths as you rightfully point out, I lost that purpose, and joba seeds found me. Then there was you." Sylah's face softened as she looked at her Akoma. "And you came back with the promise of that purpose again. But I don't think I was ever meant to be that grain of sand among the Sandstorm. I was meant to be forged through fire and flame into glass."

Sylah felt the freedom in her words. The severing of her ties to an organization she had never willingly joined. She closed her eyes for a blissful moment.

Jond spoke, his voice rough, his lopsided grin a ghost of an expression, trying to hide the pain in her words. "Sylah, will you go everywhere with me?"

She couldn't. She wouldn't. She inclined her head.

"No, Jond." Sylah smiled sadly, even though each word made an invisible wound in his side. "You are my Akoma, I grant you that, but you are not my heart."

She turned on her heel and left.

SYLAH SAT IN the courtyard beneath the sprawling joba tree and fondled the seed in her pocket. The sun had just set, and the tidewind would be here soon. There was grief in her freedom from the Sandstorm, and she didn't want Anoor to see it.

Part of her wondered if this was where it was always supposed to end, at the bottom of the joba tree, her body fertilizing the roots of the addiction that had destroyed her. At least the tidewind would be quick. It had claimed more and more lives in the last few weeks, its ferocity stronger than ever.

"We thank thee for what you give us, we praise thee for where you lead us. We serve thee for how you punish us. The blood, the power, the life." The murmuring came from her left. Sylah was surprised the Abosom was out so close to the coming of the tidewind.

Sylah circled the trunk of the tree to find a young woman bent in prayer. Her white cowl was wrapped tightly around her face, but with her head tipped back Sylah recognized her as the same woman she had seen here before.

Two smears of blood ran down either cheek. Her hands also dripped crimson, palms up toward the sky. She murmured the prayers to herself in a sing-song rhythm that sent shivers down Sylah's spine. Her eyes rolled in her sockets.

"Anyme, take me as your sacrifice, take me as the savior, place your wrath upon me, your chosen follower. For I will be yours. The blood, the power, the life."

Sylah tiptoed away. The Abosom was entranced by her prayer, and Sylah didn't want to interrupt her again.

Sylah entered the west wing of the Keep, a longer walk back to Anoor's, but one she needed. She was so immersed in her thoughts that she found herself drifting toward the warden library automatically, like she had when she was scouting the place. She was about to turn on her heel when she heard them.

"Another one made it across the Marion Sea," Uka said.

"Another one?" Wern replied. The Warden of Strength and the Warden of Knowledge were walking down the corridor toward her, their voices soft.

"Yes, thankfully one of my officers apprehended him before he made it beyond the coast. We have already burned the body."

"Good. Good," Wern said, her frail voice warbling.

"He had this with him."

Sylah heard the rustle of paper. She pushed herself into an alcove.

"From the Zwina Academy?"

"Yes, they're requesting aid from all corners of the land. The Zalaam are raising an army," Uka said.

The word was new to Sylah, ominous sounding. She committed it to memory; maybe Anoor would know it.

"Did anyone see them?"

"Just a couple of Nowerks."

"Dealt with?"

"Of course," Uka snorted. "I will burn the letter. The academy can take care of it."

Sylah realized too late that her hiding place was backlit by a runelamp. She moved out of the alcove and began to walk with purpose, keeping her head down.

"You! You're Anoor's servant, are you not?"

And your daughter.

"Yes, Warden." Shoulders slumped, head bowed, knees bent for a quick getaway.

"What are you doing on this side of the Keep? Anoor should keep a shorter leash on you."

"Sorry, Warden. I was just making my way to the tunnels, the tidewind looked like it was going to begin."

"So soon?" Wern asked the question to Uka, who gave her an irritated glance.

"Go back to your chambers now."

"Yes, Warden."

Uka and Wern marched on, and Sylah rushed away. She needed to tell Anoor what she'd heard.

THEY WERE IN the bath, the warm water lapping at the sides as Anoor scrubbed at her hair. Sylah realized she'd been dreaming of this moment since she'd first seen Anoor lying so brazenly in the tub over two mooncycles ago.

Sylah held out her hand for the bar of soap, but Anoor waved her off. Then her hands were in Sylah's short curls working the soap into a lather.

"They talked about the academy? The one in the center of the map?" Anoor said, and Sylah purred beneath her touch.

"Yes, it confirms what we thought, there are definitely still people living beyond the Marion Sea. Ah, that's good."

"And what was the other name you said?"

". . ."

"Sylah."

"Sylah's fallen into a blissful sleep." Sylah laughed.

Anoor stopped scrubbing her hair and splashed her with bath water.

"Hey! There are no water fights in my blissful sleep."

"Sylah, what was the name?"

"Zalaam?"

"The Zalaam, I wonder if Hassa knows more about them."

"Maybe." Sylah dunked her head, and when she surfaced Anoor landed a kiss on Sylah's mouth.

Sylah teased her lips open with her teeth and took her time to kiss her slowly, thoroughly.

"It's getting late, we should do some training," Anoor murmured beneath her, though her breasts emerged from the bathwater as she arched her back.

Sylah growled and dropped her kisses to her neck, submerging her hands to find the soft folds of skin between her thighs. Anoor's pants turned feral, and she gripped Sylah as she went deeper.

Sylah could never have enough. Even if she knew she would never be enough for her.

HASSA HOVERED BY the edge of the cavern and watched Elder Dew pack away the final items in the Nest. After a few moments Dew sighed and turned to her.

You have been clinging to the shadows in your mind for weeks. You know this is not what Marigold would have wanted, Dew signed.

Marigold would have prodded Hassa's cheeks until she smiled like they did when she was a child. The memory made Hassa's cheekbones ache.

Elder, I'm going to stay with the other Ghostings. Hassa pushed herself off the whitestone wall, the carvings in the stone leaving an imprint on her arm.

Child, it is your turn to guide the last group through the tunnels. You cannot stay, it is your duty as a watcher.

I will guide them, but I will return. There are still too many left in the city.

But we have given them the opportunity to leave. Some do not want to part with their masters.

Because they don't recognize they are *masters, Elder.*

Elder Dew took a breath.

This is because of your friend? The Stolen one?

No, but, Elder, I think she should go with you.

Absolutely not.

Hassa frowned. *You said it yourself, she would be useful. The Sandstorm are hunting her. The boy, Jond, no longer protects her from them. She knows too little to join the Sandstorm and too much to be kept alive. She has a good heart and can be an ally to the Ghostings.*

And what of the other? The Duster in the Keep?

I think she might surprise us all. Her place is here, to blow up the empire from the inside as the tidewind rages outside.

Elder Dew smiled, and Hassa saw the clean cut of their tongue.

I have always been envious of the Abosom and their faith in a God they cannot see. Today I am envious of you, child, of the faith you have in others. To be that open is to be free.

We will be free.

Elder Dew nodded. *And so will our land.*

CHAPTER THIRTY-NINE

ONE DAY
UNTIL THE TRIAL OF COMBAT

Warden Yona,

I have arrived at the coal mines of Jin-Hidal to find a serious insurrection has occurred. A hundred Dusters have confiscated the weapons hoard and have taken up arms against the Embers in revolt against their working conditions. I suspect they had help from one of our own. I have sent for additional troops to enforce order. Their punishments will be swift, their actions condemned. I will ensure no other uprisings of this nature occur during my tenure as disciple.

They will all die.

—Disciple Uka Elsari, year 411

It was the day of the winners' banquet, and Sylah had agreed, after copious amounts of begging from Anoor, that they could attend and forgo the night's training. Even though the combat trial was the very next day, there was nothing more Sylah could teach her that wouldn't take years. And they didn't have years.

They had mere strikes.

Sylah stood by the open window that once upon a time she had climbed through in a haze induced by drugs and alcohol. She watched crowds of Embers milling in the courtyard discussing winner prospects. She heard Anoor's name mentioned more than once, and her heart soared at the cadence of it. Sylah wanted her to win more than anything she'd ever wanted in her life.

She jammed her hands in her pockets. Her fingers found the

familiar shape of the joba seed and rolled it around in her fingers. She brought it up to the afternoon light, and it shone like a small bead of blood.

"What's that?" Anoor startled her as she came up beside her.

"Nothing," and that's truly what it was. Sylah didn't want to part with the joba seed, not because it still held that promise of possibility, but because it had somehow become an emblem of all she had overcome. She tucked it inside her undergarments, next to her chest.

Anoor's face was slathered in a gloopy white cream. Sylah took a step back, her hands held up in attack mode.

"Where is Anoor and what have you done with her?"

Anoor laughed. "It's a face mask. I want to look my best. It's the final winners' banquet before Ascent Day, and you know, I might not be invited to that . . ."

Similar to Descent Day, the appointing of the new disciples on the Day of Ascent rippled with festivities around the empire.

"Anoor, you're going to win."

"Do you really think so?"

Sylah thought by saying it she could make it true.

"Yes, but not with that on your face. Why is it so lumpy and patchy and"—Sylah sniffed—"smelly?"

"It's oats and avocado pear. I make it myself with a bit of honey and vinegar—"

"Sounds like a meal."

"A meal for my face. Want some?" Anoor peeled a globule off her cheek and stalked toward Sylah, her nose crinkling, eyes glinting.

"Get away from me . . . stop . . . Hey, I said stop. No, get off!"

Anoor launched herself at Sylah, and she let her pull her to the ground. Sylah held her wrists as they lunged for her face. The globule found the tip of Sylah's nose.

"Ha!" Anoor was triumphant, her grin wicked. Sylah sprung onto her heels and readied herself to return the gloop to Anoor's face when her leg began to cramp.

"Ach." Sylah fell back onto her butt, her right leg spasming before her. Anoor was there in a moment locating the pain and massaging with her deft fingers. The pain was almost worth her gentle touch.

"I'll get the tea."

"The kitchen's out."

"I'll go to the market."

"Looking like that? No, it's fine, I'm all right now. I'll go." The extra activity Sylah and Anoor had been partaking in had brought on additional tremors, and it galled Sylah that the symptoms were exacerbated by her happy state, and not just the anger of battle wrath. When would the withdrawal end?

"Are you sure?"

"Yes, Anoor, I think I can make it to the market and back again without you."

Anoor's smile was small. Sylah kissed it.

"That facemask tastes quite good." Sylah leaned in to lick her cheek, but Anoor pranced back.

"Go, go!" Anoor laughed as she flapped Sylah away.

Sylah left the Keep feeling content and light. It was a different type of ecstasy than the feeling of taking a joba seed: it filled more of the spaces in her mind and didn't leave her feeling hollow. In fact, it didn't leave her at all. The farther she walked from the Keep, the more confident she was that Anoor was there waiting for her. It was a wholly unique experience for Sylah, and she relished it.

The Tongue protruded in the distance, but Sylah wasn't going to cross it. Instead, she walked east across the Ember Quarter toward the Ember Market. The roads were busy with ambling erus moving Embers in drawn carriages.

Sylah coughed as a gold filigree carriage rolled past puffing out incense from the curtained windows. Spitting in the wake of its dust, Sylah decided to take the long way around through the quieter streets, where the only sounds were the trinkets in the joba trees moving in the breeze.

Sylah's eyes snagged on a ripple of shadows by an empty eru stable. Her heart began to beat, the hairs on her neck standing on end. The darkness moved, becoming a small figure.

Sylah let out a sigh as she spotted Hassa. Or rather, Hassa allowed herself to be found.

"Where have you been?"

Hi, Sylah.

"Are you okay?" Sylah held Hassa's shoulders and did a quick scan. Despite looking a little tired, there were no visible signs of hurt.

I've been really busy.

"Hassa, you handed me the bone-shattering truth and then disappeared."

She gave Sylah a half smile.

It's not my fault if you used it as a baton, though none of your bones appear to be shattered.

"Hassa."

Yes?

"What is going on? Tell me the truth."

A second ago you were telling me I gave you too much truth. Broken-bone truth.

"Stop being word-sneaky."

Hassa tried the signing combination.

Word-sneaky? I like that. She repeated it with a twist of her left arm, and a touch on her nose, feeling the word out. *Word-sneaky.*

Sylah almost stamped her foot, a sign she was spending too much time with Anoor.

"Hassa, what role do the Ghostings play in all of this?"

All mirth bled from Hassa's face.

Role? I guess it is a role to be the forgotten, to be a ghost in your own land. Haunting the stolen.

Sylah jumped at the word.

"What are you talking about?"

Hassa frowned and looked away for a moment. *What if I told you this tidewind was only going to get worse until everyone in the empire was wiped off this continent?*

"When? How do you know this?"

Hassa shrugged. *Everyone knows it, some people just aren't seeing it. "A bad season," they say. "It'll pass." But the tidewind takes and takes, and soon it will take us all.*

"When?"

Maybe six mooncycles, maybe even a year. We don't know.

"Who is 'we' in this story? Hassa, can you just tell me the truth?"

The elders don't want me to. After all, I am just a watcher. Hassa looked at the sky and squinted at the nearly full moon, which despite the time of day, sat side by side with the sun. *Another mooncycle gone, another story to be told.*

"You're a watcher?" Sylah thought of Fayl, Loot's watcher in the Dredge who guided guests down to the Belly and gathered information. "You're a watcher for the Ghostings? Is that how you found the map? Is that how you know things?"

Sylah waited as Hassa shifted her toes in the sand, wrestling with her loyalties in her mind.

Be careful, Sylah, the Sandstorm want you dead. I came to warn you. You should stay in tonight, go back to the Keep. I will come for you tomorrow.

Sylah didn't call after Hassa's retreating form, awestruck as she was.

In the end, the warning from Hassa was Sylah's downfall. She was struck dumb, not because of imminent death or the truth about the tidewind, but because of the words that had only just sunk in: *it is a role to be the forgotten, to be a ghost in your own land. Haunting the stolen.*

The Wardens' Empire was the Ghostings' land? The thought rattled her.

So when one of Loot's Gummers approached Sylah's stoic form, it was easy for him to slip the drug-soaked rag against Sylah's nose and mouth. She bucked once, twice. Then she was still.

FAYL'S SAD EYES were the first thing she saw when she came around. The bloodink tattoos on his neck seemed to swirl as his throat bobbed. He handed her a glass of water to rinse her mouth out from the bitter vapors of the sleeping drug. She took it, spitting the liquid onto the floor at his feet, her eyes not once leaving his.

"Where are we?" she croaked. The cloying humidity indicated they were below the city, but it wasn't the Belly, that was for sure.

A single runelamp flickered in Fayl's hand, but the walls were bare of books.

"I tried to warn you, Sylah, I told you not to enter a contract with him."

She considered tackling him, but she still felt woozy from the drug they'd given her. Better to bide her time, learn what Loot wanted from her first.

"I had no choice, Fayl." She sighed, crossing her legs and settling into the damp ground.

"You always have a choice." He looked so sad. Sentimental bastard. Suddenly he straightened. "He's coming."

A speck in the distance was getting brighter, confirming to Sylah they were in the tunnels below the city. Just from the sway of the light Sylah recognized the swagger.

"Hello there, Sylah." Loot's teeth shone like pieces of the moon in a night's sky.

"Loot. Was this really necessary?"

"Necessary? No. Fun? Certainly." He swung his hand lamp toward Fayl. "It was fun, wasn't it, Fayl?"

"Yes, Warden." His tone was lifeless.

Loot stuck out his bottom lip. "Oh, that wasn't quite the enthusiasm I was looking for, husband." He kneeled down by Sylah and ran a finger down her cheek. "Fayl likes you, you see. But no one will stop my fun. I like my fun. Ever since you defied me in the Ring I've waited for this moment. I knew you'd be mine in the end."

Sylah could smell the cinnamon on his breath.

"Can we quit the dramatics? Tell me what you want me to do. I have somewhere to be."

Anger blossomed in his eyes, and then he laughed. A booming, ear-cringing laugh that rang out in the hollow room.

"Of course, the winners' banquet. How could I forget?" He peered into the darkness behind him. "Maybe you could use a partner?"

Jond swaggered out of the shadows. Sylah's eyes went wide.

"What are you doing here?" she hissed at him. For a moment he looked guilty, but it was washed away with the same vacant look she'd seen on many Gummers. She laughed harshly. "Is this because I rejected you? You get mixed up with Loot? Seriously, Jond. I haven't got time for this."

Sylah began to stand, but Loot kicked her down. She lay spread-eagled from shock. How dare he? She tried again; this time Loot nodded for Fayl to restrain her. She let him. Although she could take Fayl, with Jond's allegiance thrown into question, she wasn't sure she could take them both.

"When you first came to me about your little project, I was angry. How stupid could one of the Stolen be to tell the Warden of Crime that you were an Ember? Stupider still to drag Jond into it."

Jond was indeed hanging his head in shame.

"Then I saw an opportunity. Fayl always tells me I'm an opportunist, you see, and it's true. I knew I would need you to do something for me in the future." He shone his torch into Sylah's eyes. "See, my friend over there had been filling me in on your little relationship with Anoor Elsari. Now she's in the way, and I need you to get rid of her."

Sylah couldn't take in what was happening. Jond was a spy for Loot? He had told him about the Stolen?

Wait. No.

No. No. No. No.

"You're the leader of the Sandstorm," Sylah whispered up into the gleaming whites of his teeth.

Loot bowed.

"Pleased to finally meet you, Sylah."

SYLAH WAS STILL as if each muscle were held down by the weight of the truth. Jond never saw her look so helpless. If he dug deep enough through his guilt, there was a small feeling of satisfaction. Her words still stung.

Master Inansi, or Loot, as Sylah knew him, was talking again.

"I've been watching you for a very long time. The Ring? That was my way of keeping you trained. All those apprenticeships in the Dredge? Organized by me. Do you think the Sandstorm would just let you disappear? People gave up their children for you."

Master Inansi was furious, his mouth twisted into a sinister smile that promised pain. He spat on the floor by Sylah's feet. She still hadn't moved. "Still, you disobeyed me. You drowned your self-pity in drugs and then got yourself captured."

He patted her on the cheek, and she flinched.

"But it worked out well in the end, didn't it? You managed to get a position in the Keep, close enough to steal a journal I've been wanting for a *very* long time. *And* you sidled up close to the Duster decoy, who we've been watching for a long time too, maybe a little too close, eh?" He stood up and brushed himself off. "It amused me to have a Duster living right under their noses for so long, but no more. Now little Miss Elsari is a threat and you, my dear, need to get rid of her. She is the only unfinished story and you know how I like my stories." The spider brooch on his lapel seemed to wink in the runelight.

"What about the others?" Sylah asked.

Was Sylah buying time? Jond watched her muscles begin to clench.

"Efie's grandfather owes me a favor, and Yanis, we have a plan for him, one of my favorite potions."

"Watch out—" Jond rushed in just in time for Sylah to launch at Master Inansi. Jond held her across the chest, Fayl holding back her legs. The look she gave Jond was worse than anything he could have imagined.

Master Inansi chuckled, having not moved from her attempted attack. But for dramatic effect he picked off a piece of invisible dirt on his lapels. The master loved his theatrics.

"Why?" Sylah croaked as she bucked against Jond's arms.

"Isn't it obvious? She's a Duster with an Ember's heart, and that just won't do. I like control, Sylah, and she is the tidewind. Impossible to harness."

"Why don't you bring her into the Sandstorm, teach her your ways? She wants to help." Sylah was almost pleading.

"She won't be seen as an equal among the nobility." Loot smiled. "We need a clear path to victory for Jond. At one time I thought it might have been you . . . but no matter."

Jond flinched.

"So I'm afraid she's just got to go."

"No." Sylah was defiant, her lips pulled back in a snarl.

"No?" Master Inansi laughed. "You know that 'no' isn't an option. Besides, you owe me a favor. You are the reason the Sanctuary was discovered. You were the reason my best competitors died."

Sylah choked.

"Oh, you think I didn't know that?" His voice dropped to a near whisper. "You think Papa Azim was the boss? I've heard all about how soft poor Papa was. No, Azim reported to me. He always did, until you got him killed."

Her gut caved in as if she had been hit by a runegun. Jond automatically reached for her.

"Fall back." Master Inansi smiled as he said it, and Jond froze mid-step. "Let's try this again, Sylah. You are going to kill Anoor. She's a threat to the entire organization. Then your debt will be wiped clean and I might even let you rejoin the ranks. We've got big plans. Very big plans."

Sylah's head was shaking, but no words were coming out of her mouth.

"Good, I'm glad we're agreed." Master Inansi clicked his fingers, and a servant moved out of the shadows. "You know how much I like pretty things, so I took the liberty of getting these made for you some weeks ago." The suit and dress were held out to Jond.

"Weeks ago?" The words were numb on her lips.

"Go enjoy the banquet," Loot said to Sylah's fallen form. "If you haven't killed her by the time the tidewind calms, then we'll finish the job. And you."

Sylah lay crumpled on the floor for some time after Loot had gone.

"Sylah?" Jond asked, wondering if she would ever get up again.

She whimpered, a sound Jond had never heard before. Jond fell to his knees beside her and reached out a hand.

"Sylah?"

There was that sound again. Mouselike, pained.

She turned to face him, and he pushed himself back, the heat of her stare sending him reeling.

"One day, Jond, I will pay you back in full for this betrayal. Oh, I won't kill you," she spat. "I've murdered enough of our family, but, Jond, what I will do to you will be worse. I will make you feel so alone, the very darkness will be your only friend. I will make you suffer."

He heard the promise in her words wrap around him, sucking his air. They watched each other, breathing heavily, two desert foxes ready to pounce. He broke the tension first and moved away.

"Get changed," he barked at her, hoping his anger eclipsed the sound of his heart breaking.

The very darkness will be your only friend.

He wondered if the words hadn't been true for some time.

CHAPTER FORTY

TWELVE STRIKES
UNTIL THE TRIAL OF COMBAT

First we traded stories for money to sustain us in hard times. Now we trade money for stories to sustain us in harder times.

—Words of the first griot, passed from griot to griot

Sylah had promised her they could stay at the winners' banquet until the tidewind struck. They trained every night and day with the sword, and Anoor was glad for the respite, even though the combat trial was tomorrow. Anoor hoped it was enough, though she knew deep down she would never be as good as the competitors who had been training since they were babes.

Anoor brushed the worry aside and continued to get ready. She wanted to look beautiful for Sylah, but she was aware she'd gotten rid of all her pretty garments.

"Bland, bland, and bland." She sighed as she looked around her stark dressing room. As she turned to leave, something caught her eye. A glint of green, a shimmer of turquoise. Anoor couldn't believe she hadn't noticed it before.

Sticking out of the drawer in her dressing room was an outfit Anoor didn't remember saving. It must have been left behind from the baskets of clothes she had given away. She pulled it out and gasped. It was perfect.

The bodice was a shimmering gold, overlaid with green lace. Running from the shoulder to the cinched waist was a large green bow, the tassels dripping to the floor. The full skirt created a wide circumference, made for twirling. The sleeves stopped at the elbow with smaller gold bows tying them in place.

Anoor had forgotten she'd commissioned it all those mooncycles ago. She'd been intending to wear it as a guest for one of the winners' banquets, before she knew she'd be one of the four guests of honor, before she knew where her path would lead her.

I am one of the four competitors left in the Aktibar. Tomorrow, I could be the next disciple.

The thought, which was once a whim, fused with the identity she carved for herself. She would do better than any warden before her. She would make the ghosts of her family proud and manifest the changes they wanted in a world ruled by Embers.

I will be a Duster warden. A blue above the red.

Her shoulders straightened and she felt herself grow taller, not outwardly, but her spirit within.

"Gorn, will you help me dress?" she called to her chief of chambers. It had been a long time since Gorn had helped Anoor to get ready.

The buttons of the dress ran from her shoulder blades down to the back of her knees, and Gorn's fingers closed each one, cinching in her waist. Anoor's chest crowned above the heart-shaped neckline. Once she was dressed, Gorn helped her plait her curls into an intricate bun at the top of her head. With her hair slicked back her eyes looked wider, her cheekbones sharper.

Anoor looked in the mirror. She'd kept her makeup simple, two white dashes beneath each eye and a dot on either side. Her ears and chest were bare of gems, as she had given away all of her jewelry. She'd even forgone her inkwell, leaving her wrist bare.

"You look beautiful, Anoor," Gorn said, and her mouth opened to speak again.

"Thank you . . . Was there something else?"

Gorn lurched forward and Anoor flinched, only to be clasped in Gorn's stiff embrace.

"I'm so proud of who you are. And I'll always be proud of what you do."

The words brought tears to Anoor's eyes.

"Thank you, Gorn." She leaned into her embrace before pulling away. Their reflection in the mirror startled Anoor. Standing as they were, side by side, faces forward, with Gorn's arm around her waist, they replicated the same stance between Yona and Uka in the portrait above her mother's desk.

It was a satisfying sight.

"Where's Sylah?" Gorn asked.

"She went to the market a while ago to get some verd leaf tea, but she should be back by now."

"Why don't you go down to the banquet? Meet some of the competitors from the other guilds? They could be your colleagues, you know."

"But Sylah . . ."

"I'll send her down. Besides, you'll look even better under the lighting in the great veranda." Gorn winked, actually winked.

But she was right. Anoor twirled to the left and right. The dress was really beautiful, Sylah was going to love it.

ANOOR WENT DOWN to the great veranda, officers nodding to her as she went. For the first time it wasn't because of her family name, but because of something she had done. If only they knew about the reforms she would bring to their ranks once she won.

The room was roiling with Ember nobles, dressed in their finery with their inkwells on proud display. Radish leaf smoke clung to the rafters of the great veranda, and wine was poured freely by servants around the dance floor.

Anoor saw Tanu dancing with a tall woman, their fingers intertwined as they twirled. Anoor was glad she was in the final of the knowledge Aktibar. If Anoor did win, it would be nice to have someone she knew, even if their friendship had faded.

Anoor watched them as they moved in the runelight, laughter

fizzing in the air around them. It was infectious, and she found herself being drawn into the swirl of chaos in the center of the room.

Cheers of "Anoor Elsari" carried through the crowd as her unknown fans realized she had arrived. She let herself be swept away by a tall noble whose inkwell was slate gray and covered most of his biceps. Then came an older gentleman whose words of encouragement and support didn't forgive his wandering hands. She moved to the churning crowds at the edge, trying desperately to escape into the world beyond the dance floor, when she saw them.

She was wearing a silver dress woven out of the most delicate lace Anoor had ever seen. It was like a waterfall cascading so close to her skin that Anoor strained her eyes to see the dark skin beneath. A band of silver wrapped around her short curls, with a single emerald drop in the center of her forehead. No makeup except the slight sheen of red paint swept across her lips. Anoor longed to kiss them.

"Sylah." She choked on the words as she saw the man she arrived with. Jond. Of course that was where she was. Tears threatened to blur the beautiful wraith before her.

She was wearing the most hideous dress Sylah had ever seen. Sylah recognized it as the dress she had saved from the Ardae donations, but if she'd known it was that ugly, she would have burned it on sight.

It was all tassels and gold glitter. And it was green. Not a subtle green. Oh, no. A nauseous, throbbing green that infested her eyesight even after she blinked away. But Sylah couldn't look away, because her heart was breaking. Breaking for what she had to do. The tears that welled in her eyes were reflected in Anoor's.

"Good luck. You have five strikes," Jond murmured beside her. She couldn't bear to look at him. If she did, she might have clawed his eyes out.

"Anoor, wait." Her call was meek and drowned out by the revelry. Damn the dress. It clung to her like a second skin, and with every stride Anoor got farther and farther away.

Anoor had stopped in the eye of the storm. Her shoulders tightened, ready to spring. Sylah grasped for her arm, but Anoor shrugged her off, her feet moving quicker than they could four mooncycles ago. Sylah followed her out of the great veranda and through to the gardens beyond.

"Skies above. When did you get so damn fast?" Sylah slipped off her jeweled shoes and discarded them in a bush. With little care for the craftsmanship of the dress, she ripped a slit up to her thigh and charged ahead, the cool air weaving through her legs as she ran. Anoor was already halfway up the tower. Sylah looked at the trail of tear droplets on the stairs leading up to their training room and paused.

When she reached the top of the steps, she withdrew her stylus and drew a series of runes on the other side of the door before entering and closing it.

This is where it ends.

Anoor was waiting for her in the center of the room. Sylah realized it wasn't sadness fueling her but rage. She knew what needed to happen. She moved into starting position.

"I see it in your eyes." Sylah inclined her head. Gave her permission.

Then Anoor exploded. She exploded with the brightness of the runebombs Sylah had been working on. Sylah blocked the first kick but let the rest find their mark. Sylah felt she deserved it and more.

"You don't get to have me and then push me aside. You don't get to do this to me. I refuse." She was screaming into the cadence of her punches, each word hurtling toward Sylah like shrapnel. "She didn't break me, and . . . neither will you. I love you, but I reject it. I. Will. Not. Be. Broken."

Each word was punctuated by a kick in the side.

But Sylah couldn't hear it. All she heard were those three words. She loved her. Anoor loved her. Something gnarled and ugly that had grown taut over the years snapped. And Sylah began to cry.

She'd had people who had loved her once, and their names clawed out of her memory as tremors racked her body.

"Mia, Hala, Bola, Khadid, Jond, Yota, Hussain, Ali, Isa,

Abrar . . ." the words tore from Sylah in gasps. "Otto, Fareen . . . Papa."

Warm arms enveloped her as her body stilled. Anoor was there with her.

ANOOR WAS DUMBSTRUCK. Sylah was crying the tears of a child lost, the wails of a daughter grieving, the screams of the wounded dying. She cried out names Anoor had never heard before with an anguish that pierced her heart. Anoor was the sole boat in her ocean, and when she knelt beside her, Sylah grasped onto her with all the strength left in her body. The tidewind had begun to rage outside the tower. Anoor held Sylah, the tidewind rattling both their bones as she sang the one lullaby she knew.

O-o the tidewind came from sky afar
The penance for the blood power.
Anyme sings, Anyme brings

The winds wept for the sky they knew
The Farsai Desert mourned anew
Churning rivers, swirling seas
No mercy from the bruising breeze

O-o the tidewind came from sky afar
The penance for the blood power.
Anyme sings, Anyme brings

Smoke and fire, they do bow
For the tidewind is here and now
Here and now 'til atonement's paid
The debt for power is the trade

O-o the tidewind came from sky afar
The penance for the blood power.
Anyme sings, Anyme brings

Its cleansing wind that leaves us bare
Succumb to nightfall and be judged fair
The tidewind takes, the tidewind gives
Here and now, and so we live.

Sylah knew that lullaby, knew the lilt of the words, the dip of the chorus. It brought her out of the dark gap where her heart should be.

"My mother used to sing that song to me." The words were raw in her ravaged throat. "Your mother, I should say."

Anoor frowned down at her, and Sylah knew it was time.

"When I was two years old, I was stolen from my crib." Sylah took a quivering breath and sat up. "I was taken from my home. From the Keep. They left a baby in my place. You."

Anoor crawled backward away from Sylah. Her nails scraped on the stone floor as she scuttled, her eyes going wide.

But Sylah didn't stop.

"I was trained in a place called the Sanctuary until I was fourteen. Trained for the Aktibar, for the sole purpose of competing in the trials and winning the title of disciple. There were twelve of us. They called us the Stolen. We were part of the Sandstorm." Sylah swallowed, ignored the fear in Anoor's face and continued on. She listed their names, each one of the Stolen and their surrogate parents. She spoke about Fareen, Jond, all of them. Her voice grew hoarse as she recounted the brutal beatings used by Azim to train them. The tidewind still pounded the walls of the tower as she reached the zenith of her tale.

"And then I killed them all."

Air hissed out between Anoor's teeth, and she looked at the door.

"I didn't mean to," Sylah added softly. "I slipped away . . . to the village." A tear fell to her lip, but Sylah didn't notice. "I was going to buy Fareen and Jond sweets for Ardae. I wanted to get there before the market closed, so I was running, and I fell." Sylah cradled her left knee, the echo of the pain as she fell on the dirt road thrumming through her.

"I split my knee, and an officer helped me up. He saw the red, and he knew, he knew that the only Embers in Ood-Zaynib that day were the overseer's family. Uka, she had never given up looking for the Sandstorm, and her platoon were there." Sylah swallowed, her throat dry, her gaze far, far away.

"I ran all the way back to the Sanctuary, leading them right to the Sandstorm. I didn't think, didn't consider leading them anywhere else. It was their downfall. I mean, *I* was their downfall. We tried to fight them; I killed many. But they had runeguns."

Sylah choked on a laugh.

"I remember thinking it was raining, I tilted my head to the sky, waiting for the water to touch my face . . . but it didn't." Her hand went to the scar at the base of her neck where the bullet had skimmed her skin. "I was lucky. Or unlucky. I'm never sure."

"Fareen . . ." A low moan emanated with her name, and Sylah couldn't continue for a moment.

The rain shower of bullets took her. Sylah was there, holding Fareen's hand, running with her to shelter. But then she dropped, and still Sylah dragged her along. She pulled her lifeless body all the way to the barn, refusing to see her spirit had left her. Lio tried to pry Sylah's fingers off her stiffened corpse, before she could get her onto Huda, the eru.

"Everyone died. Everyone except me and my mother. *Your* mother."

"Jond?" The question was quiet. Fierce.

"I didn't know until earlier this year that he survived, that the Sandstorm didn't truly die with my family but lived on through a different leader, the person who was the true leader all along . . . the Warden of Crime."

Anoor shifted her feet but said nothing.

"Jond found me, told me the truth. I was going to rejoin, sign up for the Aktibar and win." Sylah's smile was wry. "But no one accounted for you. Least of all me."

"The deal we struck? The bloodwerk, was that . . . to teach Jond?"

Sylah nodded. "He gave me purpose again. The Sandstorm gave me purpose."

"Purpose?" The word rolled off Anoor's mouth with malice.

"The task was simple, learn how to bloodwerk and in exchange I teach you. Then they asked me to steal the journals."

"What?"

Shame dried her mouth, and Sylah coughed. "I . . . I stole some journals and gave them to the Sandstorm . . . including the one in your bedside cabinet."

Anoor laughed, a brittle, painful sound.

Sylah sat against the wall like a broken doll. Her limbs still ached with the aftershocks of the seizure. "Then you said you love me and I—"

"Don't you dare say those words to me." Anoor's words sliced through the air with the sharpness of a whip. "I can never trust you. I don't want to see you ever again." She got up to leave, but when she reached the tower door it was locked. "What have you done?"

Sylah reached for the sword hanging on the wall and stood.

CHAPTER FORTY-ONE

EIGHT STRIKES
UNTIL THE TRIAL OF COMBAT

Under the city, under the roads
You'll find a path, where no one goes.
Most who find it don't come back.
Without a map, it's hard to track
But worth the risk if you're so bold
To find the wardens' hidden gold.

—Folk tale of the warden treasury beneath the city

"What have you done?" Anoor asked her again.

The runes Sylah drew with her blood locked them in, and only she could break them.

"I can't let you leave this tower." Sylah strapped the sword to her waist. "They asked me to kill you and I can't. I won't do it. This is the safest place for you." Sylah strapped a couple of throwing daggers to her arms as well.

"The Sandstorm? Why do they want to kill me?"

"You're unpredictable, they're worried you will win."

"I *will* win." Anoor stood, her arms folded across her chest. Despite the mass of bows, she looked fierce, and Sylah's heart soared to see it, even if her next words made it plummet.

"No, Anoor, you won't."

"Sylah, let me out of here right now."

"I can't, I don't care if you hate me, but this is the only thing I can think of to keep you safe."

"Sylah, everything we've worked for. The combat trial, I can't miss it." She was pleading, begging with her eyes.

"It's not worth your life."

"Where are you going?"

"I'm going to patrol the tower and take out anyone who gets too close."

Anoor slid down the wall. She realized Sylah wasn't budging.

"You are a terrible person." She didn't say the words maliciously, but they carved out a piece of Sylah's heart.

"I know, and I don't care if you hate me. But I'm not letting you die." It was true, Sylah would trade anything to keep Anoor alive, even if it meant losing her life.

"They lied to you, Sylah."

"What do you mean?"

"My mother gave me a gift once. An oil painting of a baby surrounded by blue daisies. It was of her child, the one the Sandstorm stole. Sylah, the baby had gray eyes and a small scar running down the side of her face."

"What?"

"You are not Uka's daughter."

Why did those words hurt so much? "What do you mean?"

"Well, unless I'm mistaken, you do not have a scar running down the side of your face. Do you remember if any of the other Stolen did?"

Fareen. Fareen. Fareen.

Fareen with her gray eyes like Uka's, Fareen with the big heart and the even bigger smile. Fareen who had taken a runebullet to the head.

Is this what it felt like?

HASSA FOUND SYLAH standing outside the tower with a sword across her knee. The tidewind had ended; the Sandstorm would be there soon. Sylah looked vacant but defiant. A pot determined to boil with no heat.

They found you? Hassa said as she sat down.

"Yes, they found me."

Sylah, you have to hide, the Sandstorm will want you dead just as much as Anoor. Lock yourself in with her.

"I can't, not when she looks at me like . . . Maiden's tits, how has it all come to this?" Sylah slumped forward and rested her head on the cool metal of the sword in front of her. Weapon against weapon.

"Hassa, how much do you know?"

More than you could ever guess. Hassa smiled.

"Today, I found out I'm no one. I have nothing, I am nothing."

Hassa searched Sylah's dark eyes.

"What?"

I'm looking for the Sylah I used to know.

"What are you talking about?"

This. Hassa waved her arm at Sylah's wilting form. *You're pathetic. Pathetic and soon to be dead. At least when you were taking the joba seeds you were in control of the slow death you were heading toward. Now you're just letting it happen to you.*

Sylah straightened at that, a spark of anger flickering across her features.

"I need to protect her, I can't leave, they'll be here any minute." A sharp laugh burst out of Sylah. "Papa always said that our mission is bigger than one person, that the final battle is where the most sacrifices will be made. He'd be ashamed to see me throwing it away for one person, one Duster. *Against* the Sandstorm."

Sylah turned to Hassa, and there were tears in her eyes. It startled Hassa to see it.

"But she's my one person. Don't you see? I can't let them kill her."

Hassa watched the tear roll out of Sylah's eyes, wetting the lashes and slipping down the side of her nose toward her mouth. The tears dripped over her large lips and over to her chin, pooling in her collarbone. One by one they fell.

Eventually Hassa said, *Azim was wrong, if we forget the individual, we forget ourselves. Come, my friends are waiting.*

Sylah frowned but let herself be led by Hassa toward the edges of the clearing. There were nearly fifty of them, all told. There weren't many Ghostings left in the city, and of those who were, few wanted to help an Ember, or even a Duster. But Hassa had brought everyone she could think of.

"Sylah!" Anoor's chief of chambers broke away from the gathering servants when she spotted Sylah.

"Gorn, what are you doing here? What's going on?" Sylah looked past the big woman and saw a group of Ghostings.

When I saw you had both left the great veranda, I was worried the worst had happened. That I had been too late in my warning. I recognized Anoor's chief of chambers and tried to convey the danger. Hassa frowned as another person who wasn't a Ghosting appeared. *But it seems she hasn't come alone.*

"Kwame?"

"Sylah, what's going on? Gorn said Anoor is in trouble?"

"What did you tell them?" Sylah asked Hassa.

As much as a Ghosting can. My people know the truth, of course. Hassa jutted her chin toward the pale eyes of a group of Ghostings who stood apart. *I conveyed danger and trouble. The rest of the story is yours to carve.*

Sylah nodded.

"Anoor is in trouble—" Sylah said to Kwame and Gorn.

"Shall we get an officer?" Kwame interrupted.

"No!" Both Gorn and Sylah shouted at once.

"She's in the tower behind us, but she needs to remain there, safe. There are people . . . people who are trying to rig the Aktibar, who are trying to wipe her out."

"We won't let them," Gorn said firmly.

"Anoor will try and get out, but you can't let her," Sylah warned.

"Of course, we'll make sure that no one goes in or out of the tower." Kwame stamped his heels together as if he were an officer. Together Kwame and Gorn approached the tower.

They will protect her. With a sign from Hassa, the Ghostings fanned out, surrounding the base of the tower. A seventeen-year-old girl with a regiment of Ghostings.

"Why?" The question croaked out of Sylah.

Because Anoor is one person and her space in the world is important, as is yours, despite you not realizing it. Hassa winked, and it was so unexpected Sylah laughed, though it was a broken sound.

No one held a weapon, no one would survive a fight with the Sandstorm, but Hassa knew it wouldn't come to that.

"I don't understand." Sylah turned to Hassa. "How will their deaths protect Anoor?"

Secrets are how the Sandstorm function. A massacre of fifty on the edge of the arena would be hard to hide, would it not?

Sylah nodded and looked around her. Hassa saw the knot between her shoulder blades loosening, just marginally.

The Sandstorm will not forgive you for this, Sylah. They will hunt you down. Loot is not going to take this transgression lightly.

"I know, imagine the theatrics he'll conjure for my death. The rack will seem like a blessing," Sylah grunted.

I might have a solution, Hassa said. *But you need to come with me.*

Hassa could see Sylah didn't want to leave Anoor; her eyes hadn't left the shadow watching in the top window above.

"I can't, Hassa."

They might not kill fifty, but they would kill one, and you're the one they want.

Sylah flinched, and Hassa wondered if she imagined Jond yielding the blade.

"Okay, I'll come with you."

EACH THUD OF Sylah's footsteps echoed in time with the dripping from the tunnel walls. They were deep beneath the churning quicksand of the Ruta River, farther than Sylah had ever been in the Intestines.

"Hassa, how much farther?"

The girl didn't turn, her silhouette burned at the edges of the torch she held in the crook of her elbow, the flame burning above her head.

"Hassa, we've been walking for leagues. Are we lost?" Sylah regretted leaving Anoor with every step she took.

Hassa snorted but still didn't stop. Her footsteps made no sound.

"Hassa?" Sylah tugged on the arm she was holding, causing the torch to clatter to the ground and go out. The darkness consumed them.

"Shit, sorry."

"Gah," Hassa said beside her as Sylah's splayed hands poked her in the face.

"Sorry."

Hassa huffed beside her in response.

Sylah grabbed Hassa's limb and let her lead her on. Her silvery scars were smooth but raised, as if the keloids were reaching for phantom fingers. Sylah's other hand trailed along the wet walls. Every now and then her finger would slip into a groove or a crack, reminding her of the Ruta River above.

Sylah wasn't sure how far dawn was from breaking, and for a moment she thought it was the sun up ahead until the orange hue flickered like flame.

"Hassa?" Sylah's blood pounded around and around with the drum of her heart.

Hassa's face was illuminated by the beckoning fire beyond. It was the face of a girl who had seen too much, felt too much, heard too much. The sorrow overflowed and etched into the lines of her face. Sylah cast her eyes away toward the fire that cackled and sucked its teeth. The darkness retreated, exposing the room as they entered.

"What is this place, Hassa?"

Smoke curled its way up toward a slash in the stone above. Larger than entire villas in the Duster Quarter, the room had been chipped and carved out of whitestone into a hexagon. The cavern spilled off at each corner into rooms and corridors. Sylah could smell flatbread cooking, and though it wasn't her home, she felt the essence of care from whoever lived there. No slime or mold marred any surface or item; it was all immaculately clean. Sylah wiped her hands on her silver dress and noticed she still wasn't wearing any shoes.

Sylah stood out starkly in this well-loved place.

A small sound made her jump, and she noticed four people standing in the back of the cavern behind a pile of goods.

Hassa, who is this? One of the Ghostings took a step toward Sylah. Her pale blue eyes were the most piercing color Sylah had ever seen. She was old, though not as old as the Ghosting who stood to her left. They walked with a cane strapped to their elbow and waved it as an indication they were ready to speak.

Is this her? The Stolen? The Ghosting limped forward.

The woman with blue eyes snarled.

Hassa signed next to Sylah. *Yes, Elder Dew, this is Sylah. She's the one the Sandstorm are hunting.*

How dare you bring her down here? Her blue eyes seemed to burn like ice.

"Hassa . . . ?"

Elder Reed, calm yourself, let Hassa speak, the elder with a limp said.

Hassa nodded.

Sylah, these four are the elders of the Ghostings. This is Elder Dew. Hassa pointed to the Ghosting with the crutch. *This is Elder Reed.* She pointed to blue eyes, who kept her eyes shrewdly trained on Sylah. *This is Elder Zero, and this is Elder Ravenwing.*

Sylah wasn't sure how to greet them. She knew that the Ghostings had elders, she had heard Hassa refer to them before, but she'd never actually met one. She settled for bowing her head.

"Hello . . . Elders."

Elders, Sylah is in danger. She needs to leave the city.

"Wait a minute, Hassa, I didn't agree to leave . . . Anoor—"

Hassa held up her arm, her eyes like flints.

She comes here unwilling? Elder Reed signed, her expression thunderous.

Elders, I believe Sylah will be a beneficial ally to the Ghosting cause. Her need to leave the city, Hassa shot her a look before Sylah opened her mouth to interrupt, *gives her the freedom to join the other Ghostings in the caves and onto the mainland.*

As a sacrifice for the Tannin? Elder Reed said.

No, Hassa signed, her small mouth tight. *But she speaks the common tongue and can be useful when negotiating with the academy.*

Sylah's head was whipping back and forth between the Ghostings. They spoke quickly, without the slow movements Sylah had gotten used to from Hassa, whom she now realized had been compensating for Sylah's lack of ability.

"Did you say the academy? The Ghostings are going to the mainland? Is that why this is all packed?"

Hassa sighed impatiently through her teeth and nodded.

"Where is all this stuff from?"

Every day we trade back the pieces of the heritage that we lost, Elder Dew signed to Sylah.

"What do you mean, 'lost'?"

Someone laughed softly, Sylah couldn't tell which elder.

Hassa touched her left wrist to her eyes.

Look.

Sylah followed the direction of Hassa's gaze.

"Oh."

The walls weren't just hammered, they were carved, etched with drawings that scoured the floor and up the walls, setting the room alight with history.

Some of the engravings were painted with the faded hue of old ink, and Sylah's eyes were drawn to a cluster of figures on the wall to her right. A group of Ghostings was sketched in gray, screaming, mouths open. Rippers, identified by their blue-flecked uniform, severed the Ghosting's tongues. The carvings were intricate, so finely detailed that Sylah could see the horror in the expressions of the Ghostings. Sylah reached out to touch them, to feel the grooves of their pain etched into the whitestone.

Hassa's arms pulled her back. *Don't touch them, these carvings are some of the oldest in the Nest.*

Nest. It was the first time the Ghostings had referred to the cavern Sylah found herself in. It suited the place.

They were drawn by our forebears over four hundred years ago, Hassa continued.

"Four hundred years ago?" Sylah's hand still hovered above the carvings, not touching, but feeling them.

This is the end. Start at the beginning, Hassa said.

No, it is not the end. The end has not come yet. Elder Reed chastised Hassa, and Elder Dew nodded in response, tapping their walking stick on the ground. It made a metallic sound and for the first time Sylah realized the end of the stick was filed to a point, flecks of whitestone marred the blade.

Start here. Hassa pointed toward the Nest's entrance, where Sylah, unbeknownst to her, had already walked past the truth she had so long been searching for.

There were more gray figures carved into the stone here. Families, friends, a town—a city. Sylah recognized the domed roofs of the Keep and the people within it. Ghostings, with their tongues wagging, hands gesticulating.

The next drawing was of a ship, manned by red and blue. Dusters and Embers coming from the mainland. Eight ships; four were circled by a great serpent: the Tannin. But Sylah didn't laugh at the children's stories made real in stone. She watched two ships sink beneath the Marion Sea and the Dusters and Embers storming the land. Blue and red specks filled the empire like Ardae confetti.

The next image saw the Ghostings asleep in their beds next to pyres burning in flames.

Hassa signed to Sylah. *They brought disease.*

"The sleeping sickness . . ." Sylah whispered. Though she wasn't sure the words came out as her throat constricted at a carving she couldn't quite comprehend.

A Ghosting held a knife against their wrist, their fingers drawing a gray smear on the ground. A bloodwerk rune. *Ba.*

"I don't understand." Sylah didn't see if anyone replied as she kept her eyes glued to the series of etchings that were leading her around the circumference of the Nest.

In one of the corners of the cavern clustered a series of images of Embers with their wrists slashed; a Ghosting taught them.

"But only Embers can bloodwerk?"

Hassa didn't reply, just looked back at her with eyes alight with mischief. Sylah turned back to the next engraving.

This cavern, drawn primitively, but clearly marked in a hexagon. A discussion in this very room, back when Ghostings could talk, four hundred years ago. The drawing followed the Ghostings as they grouped together outside the gates of the Keep that was now occupied by the Embers.

The truth weighed heavy on Sylah, and her legs faltered. She thought again about what Hassa had said the day before. *It is a role to be the forgotten, to be a ghost in your own land. Haunting the stolen.*

"You taught them to bloodwerk and in return they stole your land?"

Nods around the room.

The next etching was scoured with chaos and blue flecks of sand. The tidewind roiling across the empire. Sylah wondered of the significance, but her mind moved on, hungry to learn more, to see more.

"The Siege of the Silent." Sylah knew the next part, she'd been taught it like every citizen in the empire. The Ghostings had risen with bloodlust and anger against the wardens. And the empire had cut them down and vowed to remove the hands and tongues of every Ghosting forevermore.

But the siege here wasn't vengeful or fraught with anger. The drawn faces were peaceful, silent. The siege went on for two mooncycles. For two mooncycles they kept the Embers locked up. The peaceful protest turned bloody after an army of Dusters, drafted by Embers, attacked the Ghostings at night.

Their blood, like rain, ran through the streets of Nar-Ruta. The final image captured the hanging bodies of the four elders who had organized the siege, the tongue and hands of all the others beside them. Their penance.

This is the treasure beneath the ruins. A treasure we have collected and pieced together over the years.

Sylah looked at the trunks, packed ready for travel. Hassa opened one, the large handles made for Ghostings to loop their forearms under. Sylah couldn't help the hiss of shock that whistled out her teeth. They were bursting with items: books, pictures, lamps, letters, scraps of wood, pieces of crockery.

Sylah thought of all the items she had traded over the years. Items that Ghostings gratefully received but would be worthless to anyone else. Somewhere in this cavern were the goods she had used to barter for joba seeds.

These are the belongings of our ancestors.

Sylah nodded. She knew she understood, because all she could feel was shame.

"What of the Ending Fire?"

Their laughs shifted the smoke around the room.

They lie. Every day they breathe out the lie and everyone inhales it. The Ending Fire was them, they caused the chaos and destruction of our land, Elder Dew signed.

"They took away your words. They took away your hands. So you couldn't tell, couldn't write this story . . . couldn't bloodwerk."

A sea of nodding faces, like waves eroding rock in their assent.

"We need to tell everyone the truth." Sylah reached for Hassa's shoulder and clenched it hard. "We need to get your land back."

Elder Reed snorted, her blue eyes flashing. *See, I told you this was a bad idea. Her first instinct is to open her mouth.*

No, stolen child, now is not the time to bare the truth. Though it has taken us four hundred years, we have learned from our mistakes. We want our land but we want it whole. Elder Dew stamped their stick to punctuate the sentence.

"The tidewind?"

Dew nodded. *We have been moving as many of our people as possible out to a cave on the coastline. There is a Ghosting settlement there that has lived freely for some time, covertly, acquiring materials and goods—*

We learned to steal from our invaders too. This was the first time Elder Ravenwing spoke, and Sylah was taken aback by the malice in his eyes. His dark shaven hair, so unusual for a Ghosting, left a shadow on the top of his head. Raven wing indeed.

We're preparing for a journey.

Sylah's eyes flicked to the trunks and bags, then back to Elder Dew.

The tidewind, Dew continued, *it came with our invaders and now it rages more fiercely than it ever has before.*

"So you're just going to leave your land?"

Elder Reed's laugh was pained. *She understands after all.*

Hassa touched Sylah's arm, drawing her eyes to her. *The tidewind will eventually make this land unlivable. The elders are preparing to travel to the Ghosting settlement at midday when the city is distracted by the Aktibar finals. The Ghostings at the settlement are preparing for a scouting voyage to the mainland to ask for aid.*

"How do we know they will help us?"

No one answered her for a beat.

If aid cannot be found, we are prepared to move all our people if need be.

Not all of them will leave the home of our ancestors, Ravenwing signed. And Sylah was sure he would be one of those who would stay and fight the Embers. On his own if need be.

"What about your bloodwerk? Can't you teach me to stop the tidewind?"

Our knowledge was lost to us long ago. Our descendants burned all the Books of Blood, *thirteen volumes, all told. The Embers salvaged one; their bloodwerk is stunted, ugly,* Elder Reed signed.

"So the old relics, the old bloodwerk around the empire, like the clock, that was by the Ghostings?"

An incline of the head. *You cannot see the Ghosting markers, our blood is silent, transparent. Look as hard as you might at the Tongue our legacy built, but you will not see the clear blood that holds it up. What you see is apprentices we taught. The Embers.*

"The Embers as apprentices?" Sylah couldn't believe it.

Yes, we welcomed them to our land, and for years they have been trying to erase us. So we hoarded. We traded. We hid what we could. Our ancestors knew the power of the map you now own. Now it is yours. Elder Ravenwing's eyes flickered to Hassa, who shriveled.

Sylah swallowed.

"You think I should go with them?"

Hassa inclined her head. *You can help, you can speak the common tongue to the mainlanders, you can aid the Ghostings in the fight, if you wish to. The Sandstorm won't find you there.*

Sylah thought of Anoor, of her smile, her lips, the way her eyes splintered with anger as she heard the truth.

"What of Anoor? I won't leave her, she's in as much danger as me. More so."

The elders signed to each other quickly, so fast Sylah couldn't follow. Hassa shifted her feet next to her. Finally Elder Dew turned to her.

You may bring her. Come at midday, we will not wait.

THE LABYRINTH OF tunnels had led her to the entrance of the Keep, and Hassa and Sylah walked back through the gardens to the tower together.

"You've been watching me."

Yes.

"For mooncycles."

Yes. We all have.

Sylah didn't have the strength to be affronted. The night had been one of the longest of her life, the aftershocks of truth still thrumming through her.

"So everyone can bloodwerk? No matter their blood color?"

A sharp nod.

A young kori bird soared above them, the fluffy feathers a sign that the adolescent had only recently taken to the skies. Sylah watched it as it flew up through the pink morning light. The day of the Aktibar finals was upon them.

Each guild would test its competitors for the final time. Starting with strength. A fight was always the best way to draw the crowds in.

The music from the great veranda still floated across the courtyard, and as they passed the hall Sylah saw the stragglers from the night before still dancing. They laughed and twirled and spun on their heels. Did they know the ground they were dancing on belonged to another?

They reached the crop of trees that led to the tower and moved through the foliage carefully. Sylah held her breath until she saw Kwame, then it burst out of her in a sigh. Anoor was safe.

"Sylah, all okay?" Kwame was sitting straight-backed against the door, and she nodded to him.

Sylah took an inventory of the surrounding area. The Ghostings didn't meet Sylah's eyes, but they still stood their vigil. Sylah found Gorn scouting around the tower.

"No trouble?" Sylah asked.

"Nothing."

Sylah looked up at the window in the tower. She had locked

Anoor in the top room that they had renovated for their training, leaving the other floors in the disrepair they had found them in.

"Wait." Something was different.

Gorn looked in the direction where Sylah was pointing.

There was a crack in the wall that hadn't been there before, Sylah was sure of it. She leaned forward, squinted. Was that blue blood on the edge of it?

Sylah lurched forward, ran back the way she had come.

"No, no, no." The word blurred into a low moan.

"What's wrong?" Kwame asked, and Sylah dragged him away from the door and burst through it.

She loped up the tower steps, tripping when her muscles began to seize, but still she continued. She went to the second floor where she saw the crack in the wall, big enough for a person.

Blue blood marred the whitestone, dust from a hole in the ceiling above smudged the footsteps of those who had taken her. Sylah fell to her knees.

Anoor was gone.

Sylah couldn't cry; she had been drained dry of any feeling. All that filled her was a darkness so empty and desolate she barely felt the arms holding her, shaking her, screaming in her ear.

"Look, Sylah, look at the floor."

Sylah couldn't look, didn't want to see the remains of the woman she had loved. Hassa appeared in front of her.

Look, Sylah. Her face was earnest, pleading.

Sylah let her eyes slide to the floor. Let the blood come into focus.

The blood. It was shaped in the form of bloodwerk runes. Sylah was propelled out of her state of shock with clarity. She spun her head left and right.

Kwame and Gorn were chatting loudly at her, but she didn't want to hear them, not yet.

Sylah pushed past them and ran up to the final floor. The door opened at her touch. Blood recognizes blood.

There, in the middle of the room was a circle of runes with a blasted hole in the middle. Kwame waved as Sylah looked down through it.

The sound started in the darkness in her stomach, banishing it with hope. It gurgled its way up her throat and out into the empty room. Great big guffaws that had her eyes streaming, because she wasn't drained after all.

No one had entered. Anoor had escaped using her own blood.

"I can't fucking believe it." Sylah laughed.

CHAPTER FORTY-TWO

SIX STRIKES
UNTIL THE TRIAL OF COMBAT

Nuba is by far the most disciplined martial art in the empire. It requires intensive focused attention with a subtlety of movements only the very best fighters can master. But when used in hand-to-hand combat, Nuba skills become deadly.

—The army's master of weapons

Anoor could see Sylah in the tower below. She held a sword by her side like an extension of her limb. She was one of the Stolen. Anoor had known there was more to Sylah than she had ever shared, but this, this wasn't just a grain of truth she'd been hiding. This was a colossal sand dune of lies.

Anoor couldn't cry about it. Sylah had shed enough tears for the two of them. Right now, she just felt anger, and that was exactly what she needed to fuel her fury for the final trial. Heartbreak could come later.

Anoor brought her hand to her bare wrist and rubbed the empty space where her inkwell should be. She needed to get out of the tower. There was more at stake than she had ever known, and now it was imperative for her to win. The Sandstorm's rule would spill more blood.

She watched Hassa approach Sylah with Gorn and Kwame as well as a host of other Ghostings. Anoor softened to see the servants of the Keep coming to protect her. At the same time her mind ran through all the ways in which she could escape, counting her protectors, watching where they stood, roamed, looked.

When Sylah left with Hassa, Anoor sprang into action. She knew what she needed to do. It would be painstaking work, pain being the operative word.

She plucked a dagger from the wall of weapons. Taking in a deep breath, she sliced along a thin vein on her wrist in a quick, fluid motion. She needed blood, a lot of it and fast. This was going to be harder than the bloodwerk trial; at least then she'd had her stylus to navigate her blood. When Sylah's blood in her catchment had failed, she had no choice but to use her own, right under the eyes of everyone in the arena. She'd simply hunched over the shoe she was drawing on and slipped into the water with no one noticing.

Her blue blood was gushing now, and Anoor knew she didn't have long before she had to put pressure on the wound or she would faint. She dipped the tip of the knife into the cut and began to draw on the floor. This was going to be difficult.

But she'd done it before, she could do it again.

SHE WAS FOURTEEN. *Her mother had locked her in the weapons cupboard in the living room because Anoor failed her aerobatics test. Flexibility wasn't her strong suit, yet her mother still forced her to take the class.*

Anoor shifted her knees. They'd gone numb long ago, tucked as they were against her chest, the shelves behind her, door in front. Anoor let the tears flow, she let the fear take her. She hated the darkness more than anything in the world. It was the manifestation of her loneliness.

A long time passed. One day, maybe two. Her mother had forgotten about her. It was the longest time she had ever left her. She was covered in her own filth. She was hungry, thirsty, dying.

She wasn't wearing her inkwell; her mother was always careful to remove it before locking her away. Eventually Anoor got so weak, the hunger and thirst so debilitating, she decided to take fate into her own hands. Her final revenge on her mother, bestowing on her the title of murderer.

Anoor's fingers reached through the darkness toward the weapons above. She jumped as they collided with the cool metal of a knife.

She brought the knife to her wrist.

Would Inquisitor Abena give up this way?

The knife vibrated against her skin, channeling the beating of her heart.

No, Abena would not. But she would expose her mother, fight back. Anoor pressed the blade against her skin, slicing it cleanly. The darkness was filled with the sound of her dripping blood. Anoor stilled her breathing and began to smear her blood across the inside of the cupboard, in every crack, every knot of wood and weapon handle she could touch. It would be a beacon of blue blood for whoever saw it.

As the giddiness of the blood loss settled in, she started to use her blood to draw bloodwerk runes. She drew Gi slowly and carefully, not knowing where the knife edge was, but letting her muscle memory lead her.

There was a metallic clunk, and Anoor jumped. Her breath came out in short bursts as her fingers moved toward the sound. Pressed against the door was a sword, pulled from the shelf above her. It hovered as if pulled by a magnet. Or a rune. Her fingers brushed the door's surface, marring the rune Gi.

Thunk.

The sword dropped to the ground; although she couldn't see it, the air shifted as it fell, and she knew it had narrowly missed her toes.

She had no time to marvel, no time to question. Her mind was becoming sluggish, her thoughts becoming faint. She needed to get out.

She drew Ru around the lock. The door creaked and buckled. She repeated the sequence around the doorframe, each rune adding pressure to the door as it bowed against the metal lock. Light seeped into the cracks until . . .

The door blasted off the hinges, spraying splinters covered in Anoor's blood across the living room. A servant ran in. Anoor couldn't remember their name, but it was the last time she saw them alive.

Anoor knew they had gone to fetch her mother, because she could feel the march of Uka's footsteps on the wooden floor under her cheek.

"What did you do?" Uka hissed at her as Anoor blinked up at her.

Anoor lifted her head and looked at the weapons cupboard. She had thought that all her wishing had come true, that her blood finally ran red, and that's what had saved her. But when she saw the blue blood coating the inside of the cupboard, it was with a strange mix of disappointment and satisfaction.

"Get me a bandage and some soap and water. Speak to no one," Uka barked behind her at the servant who had found Anoor.

After the servant left, Uka leaned over Anoor again, her nose crinkling at the smell of excrement and urine. She lunged for Anoor, her hand clamping on the wound at her wrist.

"Oh no, you don't get to die."

"I . . . I . . . I can bloodwerk?"

"No, the cupboard must have given way." The lie was barely palatable on Uka's lips.

"Dusters can bloodwerk?" Anoor tried again, loosening her dry mouth with saliva.

Uka hissed, "No." But Anoor saw the fear in her eyes.

"You knew. Do all the wardens know?"

Uka looked at Anoor's wrist and lessened the pressure, the blue blood running over her knuckles. She sat there watching her adoptive daughter die.

"You speak a word of this to anyone and you will die." The pressure returned to Anoor's wrist.

"Why not kill me now?" she whispered.

Uka's eyes narrowed, the vein throbbing.

"I've thought of it many times, false daughter of mine. But how can I protect the empire if I can't protect my own daughter?" She choked on a laugh, and Anoor wondered if she knew how ironic her sentence was.

"Then you'll never kill me."

Uka squeezed her wrist painfully tight, and Anoor whimpered.

"You think you're clever? How about I kill those servants you run around with? How about I kill Gorn? She will be watching you, I should add. So use your blood at your peril. At their *peril."*

The horror of her mother's words was enough to silence her. Reluctantly Anoor spoke, her voice clear, unshaking, despite the earthquake within herself.

"I want my own chambers. This is the last time you lock me in the darkness." Anoor didn't voice the threat, she didn't want to give her mother purchase to hurt those she loved, but Uka sensed it anyway.

Her mother smiled, and it was the face of a merchant having made a very good deal. She gave a short nod.

It was a small win for Anoor, a small defeat against her mother.

ANOOR KNEW SHE couldn't blast through Sylah's runes, as blood recognizes blood. She could explore weak points in the doorframe, a separate object from what Sylah had presumably drawn on, but it could pull the tower down around her. She also assumed that Sylah had been very cautious; after all, she'd been taught by Anoor.

Instead Anoor focused on another way out. She created a circle of runes through a weak bit of floorboard and blasted a hole in the floor to the room below. Before she left the training room, she put on her armor and strapped on the sword she had won from the tactics trial. The only weapon and protection she was allowed in the combat trial. She jumped down to the room below and scanned the area through a crack in the wall. It wasn't large enough for Anoor to fit through, so she spent some time slowly chiseling at it with the bloodwerk rune *Kha*.

Eventually the gap was large enough for Anoor to escape. All she had to do was time it right. She watched Gorn circle the tower, followed by a group of Ghostings. She lifted the dagger high and threw it as hard as she could in the opposite direction.

It had the desired effect, drawing their attention away while she made her way out of the tower, scaling down the whitestone to the floor. The cracks in the neglected building sometimes gave beneath her grip, but she made it to the ground safely.

Dawn had come, and Anoor could hear the sound of the kori birds waking. Their sweet tune guided her through the forest, toward freedom.

Her own chambers were too risky. If Sylah managed to scale the wall to her window, then Jond could too. So Anoor went to the place she least wanted to go. Her mother's office.

The west wing of the Keep was quiet and still, the morning rota of servants only just rising to dust the remnants of debris the tide-wind had brought. Anoor made her way through the corridors as quietly as she could with the armor strapped to her. The clanging echoed through the empty rooms, and she hoped the Sandstorm wouldn't find her here. If they had infiltrated the Aktibar, Anoor didn't doubt that they had gained access to the Keep.

The room smelled of lilies and radish leaf smoke as she entered. She turned on the runelamp illuminating the oil painting of her mother and grandmother. Instead of feeling the mockery in their paintbrush expressions, Anoor felt something hotter than anger build up inside her.

"Today I reclaim my name. I am Anoor Elsari, not born but bred. Not wanted but kept. I am going to be the next Disciple of Strength, and I vow to do better than either of you."

"Is that so?" Her mother's voice raised the hairs on the back of her neck, and she turned, coming face-to-face with Uka in the doorway. Her armor made her feel protected from the terror her mother instilled in her.

She walked into her office and took a seat at her desk, creating a ripple effect of the painting behind her. The two sets of disapproving eyes were enough to bring Anoor to her knees. But she didn't fall, she stayed standing.

"I'm going to win today," Anoor said.

"I heard . . ." The smirk was less painful than Anoor expected.

"You can't stop me."

"I could." Uka opened her top drawer and pulled out her thin pipe, stuffing it with radish leaves. She only ever smoked when she was stressed. "I could kill you now." She lit the match and inhaled. "I face that decision every day I wake up."

Anoor had heard this threat before. She didn't blink at it.

"You were everything I didn't want you to be. Slow, short, lazy. You never took strength from my teachings, my discipline. They were my gifts. I wanted to strengthen you, but no, you refused to harden. Instead, you softened, turned to stories and make-believe. My mother thinks you might be worthy, somehow. She has seen something I haven't. But I suppose she doesn't feel the shame I see every time I look at you. The ravenous guilt that eats at me for letting them take my child."

Anoor took a step back. There were tears in her mother's eyes, screwed up as they were with pain.

"I didn't do that to you, though," Anoor said. "That was the Sandstorm."

Uka laughed. "But you, my changeling, my maggot, you are the vessel of those traitorous people. You are the blood, the dirty blood of those who stole from me."

Anoor's back bumped against the other desk in the room. The desk assigned to the Disciple of Strength. She took comfort in the cool wood. This was going to be hers.

"We will have to work together, you and me. Because I intend to change the empire," Anoor said.

"Again, I heard . . ." Uka took a drag from her pipe, the red smoke filling out the silence in the room. "Shouldn't you be getting in final practice with that servant of yours?" The question was mocking. It was time for Anoor to leave.

"I'll see you for assignments tomorrow," Anoor said, not quietly, but firmly. Her mother's laugh was silent, but Anoor saw the billowing of the radish leaf smoke.

Anoor ran down the corridor, not caring about the sound she made. When she burst out of the doors to the outside, she pulled off her helmet and let the air cool the sweat that beaded across her face.

Then she smiled. Her mother didn't once deny that she could win.

ANOOR HAD ONE place left to go where she thought she could be safe. She rushed through the cloisters passing the first clockmaster, who confirmed she had three more strikes until the trial of combat began.

The gray legs of the arena came into view as she ran through the gardens, giving the trees around their training tower a wide berth. The wardens built the arena out of concrete, as they couldn't mine enough whitestone bricks for the monstrosity. Concrete didn't weather well during a tidewind, so the exposed gray legs were carefully inscribed with bloodwerk runes creating a constant *push* around anything that touched it. It protected it from the weaponized grains in the tidewind. The bloodwerk was only visible once you got within fifty handspans of the arena. Anoor often wondered how much blood it took to protect a building made for spilling blood.

"Anoor Elsari, you're early." The officer at the door shuffled his feet with the pitter-patter of excitement. His face held the shadow of his first mustache.

"I know, I just like to get a feel for the place."

"What's your precombat routine? You see my brother, he's a captain, I'm just an officer, but he swears by twelve eggs from a brown hen every morn. He has two dozen brown hens."

"That's . . . a lot of eggs."

"My sister, who works as an eru driver, doesn't eat any meat or eggs at all, and she's the fastest rider on this side of the river. What's your secret?"

"I guess . . . I like to get a feel for the place, you know . . . get in early. Is the arena open?"

"Oh, sure, yes, go straight through."

"Can you make sure I'm not disturbed? I really need to . . . get in the zone. So if anyone comes looking for me, just tell them I'm not here, okay?"

The officer nodded enthusiastically.

"Of course, of course. I understand, and thanks for letting me in on your little secret routine. I'll be watching from the crowd to see if it pays off."

Anoor moved past him and into the arena beyond. The runelamps lit up as she entered the combat floor, triggered by her presence. The floor had already been swept of blue sand, with no remnants of the bloodwerk trials that had filled the space. Instead, cast in the red runelight and the burning morning sun, a charcoal ring was prepared for the competitors, with four benches lining the four corners.

A stand of bandages and water stood ominously to the side, and Anoor wondered if she would need them. Even if she lost and someone else managed to make her bleed first, she doubted they'd pause to patch her up before sending her to the rack.

She heard her own bones popping in her mind. The joints being pulled apart with her mother at the lever. She shook the image free.

The podium stood to her right. The sound projector was ready for Uka to start the final trial. Their metal thrones were empty. A Ghosting appeared behind one, making Anoor jump, her shriek echoing through the empty seats that rippled outward for infinity. The Ghosting was using a polishing cloth on the metal arms, making the metal gleam silver. They looked like runeguns in holsters.

Anoor exhaled, exhaustion settling into her bones. A whole night without sleep before the most important fight of her life.

Anoor placed her helmet on one of the benches and began her vigil.

She closed her eyes, kept her breathing steady. She emptied her mind of the chaos of the day and found the quiet rage within. Keeping her breathing steady, she moved through the Nuba formations.

A bird called overhead. Its caw broke through her thoughts.

One strike passed.

Sweat trickled down her neck as she moved fluidly through the slow movements. She could hear someone approaching, someone she knew. She knew the lilt of their walk, knew the breath that filled their lungs, the lips that spoke her name. She kept her eyes closed, retaining her balance in Nuba formation four. Back bent, right leg extended, hands pointing downward.

"Anoor."

Still Anoor refused to acknowledge Sylah.

"Anoor, please look at me."

"Have the Sandstorm sent you to finish me off?" Anoor's balance was waning; she readjusted.

"Anoor, I would never hurt you."

"Too late," Anoor murmured. "How did you find me?" She moved into formation five. Chest up, back arched, left leg bent over the right.

"The Ghostings."

Anoor nodded. Of course, the Ghosting cleaning had told Hassa.

"Then, I . . . I knocked out the officer . . . who I think is like your biggest fan or something. He really didn't want to let me past lest I ruin 'your routine.'" Sylah huffed out a laugh, but Anoor could tell it was forced.

Nuba formation six. Torso twisted, hands meeting behind the shoulder blades, neck rotating to the sky, right foot flexed off the ground.

"Anoor, I found out many things tonight. You can bloodwerk?"

"I could always bloodwerk." She'd just never told Sylah. She refused to feel guilty for the omission.

Sylah didn't reply for a moment, affronted by the truth as she was.

"Why didn't you tell me?"

Anoor wanted to laugh. The irony of Sylah's words must have struck her too as she rushed on. "Ghostings can bloodwerk too. In fact, Ghostings taught the Embers to bloodwerk." Sylah was babbling. "The empire, the ruins, it's all theirs. This land is the Ghostings'. The Ending Fire never happened."

Anoor fell from her pose. Sylah tried to help her up, but Anoor shrugged her off.

"What?" Anoor looked at her for the first time. She was a mess. She was still wearing the silver dress from the night before, the slit frayed from where she had ripped it. She wore no shoes and yet seemed not to notice, despite the welts and blisters that covered her feet. She was a sorry sight but one Anoor was still glad to see despite herself.

Sylah looked around her, confirming the arena was as empty as when she entered, but still she lowered her voice and told Anoor all she had learned. The explanation that followed shook Anoor to the core.

"We have to go, don't you see? This is our way out. We can help the Ghostings and save ourselves."

Anoor picked up the sword from the bench behind Sylah and examined the blade, looking at her reflection. What she saw gave her courage.

"No."

"Anoor, I know I have lost your trust, but this will save your life."

"No."

Sylah exhaled through her nose, her jaw clenching.

"Anoor we have to go, now, please. Please do this for me." Sylah was begging. Sylah was using *please*.

"No," Anoor said. "This news only proves the importance of this trial. Sylah, I have to win, because we know the wardens aren't preparing for the tidewind like they should be. We know so many truths now and I can fight for the Ghostings here better than I could by leaving."

"Anoor," Sylah's voice cracked and Anoor looked away from her dark eyes. "Anoor, they'll hunt you down. They'll hunt me down."

"Then go, save yourself. But I'm not leaving."

"Please." Again.

"No, Sylah." Anoor's shout echoed around the empty chairs. "You know why? I've realized a world run by people who think they are better will never be better for everyone." Anoor could taste the bitterness of her own smile. "I didn't want to fight this fight, but I was the only one who could. Not because I'm better but because I'm not one of them. And that's a start. But I will thank you for one thing. You've given me just about enough anger to ensure I win."

Nuba formation seven. Right hand reaching for left toe, hips turned to the right, left hand reaching to the sky.

"Anoor, I'm so afraid for you," Sylah whispered. Though Anoor closed her eyes, she imagined the tears pooling in Sylah's.

"You once told me to use my fear like building blocks. And that's precisely what I'm going to do. I'm going to rebuild this empire whether you're here to see it or not."

Sylah didn't respond, and after some time Anoor cracked open an eyelid to check whether she was still there. The intensity of Sylah's gaze nearly brought her to her knees.

"Remember to make us plates of fried yams," Sylah said softly.

And when Anoor didn't reply, Sylah added, "I love you, Anoor."

Anoor shut her eyes tight against the rush of feeling she felt at those words. Anger marred it all.

When she opened her eyes again, Sylah was gone.

SYLAH ROLLED THE joba seed between her finger and thumb. It was all she had left. That and the remains of her dress. Sylah patrolled the perimeter of the arena waiting and watching for the Sandstorm, avoiding the officers as they too searched for the crazy woman who'd knocked Gio out. Audience members had begun arriving, the chances of freedom shortening. The Ghostings would leave with or without her.

Sylah rubbed her brows. Anoor was right about all of it. Except one thing. Anoor *was* better. She was kind and honest and intelligent. She would break the world and build it back up again. Block by block.

Sylah's tongue probed the gap in her teeth where the joba seed belonged.

"Sylah."

She turned at the sound of his voice. Kwame had found her.

"Sylah, did you find Anoor? Did you convince her not to fight?"

Sylah shook her head, not trusting herself to speak.

"She's stubborn, that one. But maybe she'll be okay, maybe the people trying to rig the fight won't hurt her . . ." Kwame's hand reached for Sylah's shoulder and squeezed. "Is that a joba seed?"

"Yes."

"Sylah, you can't take that . . . I helped Anoor with the verd leaf remedy all those mooncycles ago. I know it was for you. Don't turn back now. You've been doing so well."

She laughed. "Have I? I still get seizures or prickling in my limbs every day. Every *single* day."

Kwame's expression clouded over. "How much did you used to take?"

Sylah shrugged. "Honestly, I'm not really sure. Sometimes I'd buy a bag of twenty and finish them in a day."

Air hissed between his teeth.

"Sylah, you probably can't cope without joba seeds. Your body has adapted to the stimulant . . . possibly forever."

It was what she thought.

"I'm damaged."

Kwame grasped her wrists, and Sylah lurched to secure the seed between her finger and thumb.

"No," he said firmly.

"I have to take it, Kwame. It's the only way I can fight them if they come for her. I need to be able to trust my body." Sylah's voice shook.

"Your tolerance will be lower, you could have a heart attack, you could die. There are so many risks."

"She's worth it."

Sylah led the joba seed to her mouth.

"Halve it!" Kwame shouted. "Don't take it all."

Sylah nodded then added, "Will you stay with me?"

Kwame smiled. "Of course."

All this time Sylah had imagined what it would be like to take a joba seed again; never had she imagined her reluctance.

Sylah put the joba seed in her mouth and bit down.

CHAPTER FORTY-THREE

THE TRIAL OF COMBAT

Odds on Disciple of Strength:

Yanis Yahun 7/5
Efie Montera 9/2
Jond Alnua 11/1
Anoor Elsari 11/1

—Master Fula's gambling house

The arena was full. It always was for the strength trials, but this time it was bloated with energy. The audience members knew the names and were chanting them in waves. Jond had heard his more than once, and it put him on edge. Healers began to enter the arena; they were always on call for any of the worst injuries. The fight was the first to blood, after all.

Anoor was seated in the corner of his vision, her bright green armor giving him a throbbing headache. She was still alive. Jond had searched for her and had found the tower Sylah had locked her in, surrounded by Ghostings. Jond could have cut them down, would have, if Fayl hadn't held him back.

"A massacre of this size could halt the Aktibar," the big man said, and he was right. Jond had come to like the master's watcher.

Jond wasn't worried about fighting Anoor; there was no way she could best him. In fact, he preferred to duel her fairly. Her death was inevitable either way; Master Inansi wouldn't let her live.

He turned his stare to Efie on the bench opposite, who was chewing the edge of her red braid, her ankles crossed in front of her. She held her helm under her arm. Its rose gold filigree looked like lace, but it was a mistake to think the warrior at all delicate. The kente flag of Jin-Gernomi was tied around her waist. She saw Jond looking and winked.

Jond's mouth twisted in response. He hated that Master Inansi had blackmailed Efie's grandfather. He wanted an honest path to victory, but Master Inansi never left anything to chance.

Yanis walked into his vision, pacing up and down. The silver helm hooked under his arm was shaped like a scorpion, the poisonous tail curving around the back, the pincers on either side of the ears. He held a flask in his hand. Jond wondered if that was the water Master Inansi had laced with valerian root. Again, nothing left to chance. Yanis gave him a cheery thumbs-up and Jond grimaced. *What an idiot.*

The griot had come out onto the stage, and Jond groaned. He hated the pageantry of the whole thing, the showmanship. He wanted to get to the fight.

The griot was introducing the competitors and doing an impression of each one. He paced along the podium like Yanis, dropping his jaw in a slack-mouthed grin. It was quite good, actually. Jond allowed himself a small smile. Yanis bobbed his head in an endearing shrug, as if to say "I can't help my charm," and Jond was sure half the people in the audience swooned.

Jond hawked in the back of his throat.

Anoor was up next, and the griot puffed out his cheeks and shrunk his stature, quivering around the stage like a scared rabbit. But looking at Anoor, there was no shyness in her demeanor, no tremble in her posture. She didn't wave, didn't smile. It was as if she were in a trance, so complete was her focus. She just stared calmly at the cheering crowd.

And cheer for her they did. Over and over. "Anoor Elsari, Anoor Elsari!"

The griot grew taller somehow and dropped his left knee as he walked, the swagger taking on the same arrogance Efie projected. She stood up and waved at the crowd, flapping her arms up so they'd increase their volume. Some of the audience members waved the kente flag of Jin-Gernomi, and she waved at them the most.

"Get on with it," Jond muttered.

Jond was up next. The griot walked as if a rod pierced his butt cheeks; he clenched his biceps and lunged across the stage. Clearly the griot had run out of material by the time he got to Jond.

The cheers for Jond were more subdued. He was an unknown Ember, not tied to the army, not a member of a warden's family, and not the grandchild of an imir. He didn't mind. They'd be cheering for him in the end. Uka stood, and Jond wasn't sure whether the griot's fear was rehearsed. He scuttled off the stage.

Uka walked toward the sound projector. She wore a sheer gunmetal dress that shimmered in the morning light. When she shifted you could see through it; a black body suit covered the areas she wanted. As she moved to speak into the projector, the throne behind her seemed to merge with her dress, creating an elaborate illusion that the gown splintered into shards of metal.

"Welcome to the final trial in the Aktibar for strength. Today we will start a new chapter. Today we will discover our next disciple to carry on my legacy, to protect and to nurture the empire and to maintain the law and order of its citizens." Uka paused, let the cheers build in crescendo, then ripple down to silence again. "The rules of the final trial are simple. A coin toss determines the fighting pairs. Each fight ends when blood is drawn. If a competitor mars the charcoal ring, or goes beyond it, they are also disqualified. Competitors must use the weapons they have chosen in the trial of stealth."

Jond saw Anoor's eyes shift to Yanis and the jambiya he held in his hand. The anger in that glance was the first time Anoor scared him.

"The winners of the first two rounds will go on to face each other. The resulting champion will be named Disciple of Strength on the Day of Ascent on the morrow."

Uka shifted to the side, pulling a coin out of her glittering silks. She called out the pairs: "Jond and Efie. Yanis and Anoor."

The chanting rattled Jond's bones as he entered the ring of combat. Efie followed, her gold dagger twirling in her hand. She took off her kente flag and waved it to the crowd. Her supporters waved their flags back, their cheers deepening when Efie wrapped it around her forehead before placing on her helm. The yellow and green colors of Jin-Gernomi were just visible above her eye line.

"Let's give them a show." Efie's words were drowned out by the sound of the crowd, but Jond read her lips.

When the horn sounded, she lunged.

JOND'S FIGHT WAS over quickly. Efie had gone in strong, her blows forcing Jond to go on the defensive as she inched him closer to the edge of the ring. He glanced behind him and saw his predicament. He needed to reclaim ground, so he pulled a move Anoor had seen Sylah do more than once. He feinted to the right, distracting his attacker, then dived into a roll, sweeping Efie's legs out from under her. The move was executed in a blink of an eye.

Efie jumped up from her sprawl quickly. Her dagger lashed out toward Jond's helm, trying to knock it from his face so she could get to the skin underneath.

She didn't get a chance as Jond's axe clattered against her armor, again and again, the force of its blows leaving dents across her beautiful breastplate. Shards of rose gold glittered on the ground, and Anoor mourned the exquisite armor.

The crowd screamed as Efie fell to her knees. Anoor wasn't sure if they were crying out of anger or out of joy. Either way it sounded bloodthirsty.

It seemed to Anoor that Efie was giving up too easily, because a moment later Jond had nicked the soft bit of skin between her helm and her chest plate. Her red blood swelled from between the crack, dribbling over the rose gold armor. His name lit up on the leader board, the runelamps so bright you could barely read his name. It didn't matter because the crowd was shouting it.

"Jond Alnua, Jond Alnua, Jond Alnua."

Jond helped Efie up, and she removed her helm for the healers who had rushed forward. Once they patched her up, Efie took a bow with a flourish, her red braids surfing the ground as she dipped low. It reminded Anoor of a griot coming to the end of a story.

Jond had already moved back to his bench, his axe balanced across his knees. He was smiling, his grin crooked and alluring.

Anoor looked up to the podium and saw Uka was leaning forward watching Jond. She clapped politely.

The charcoal ring was checked, Efie's specks of blood and armor cleaned away. Now it was Anoor's time to take her stand.

Yanis wasn't wearing his helm. Stupid and vain.

"Good luck, Anoor," he said, and Anoor hated herself for smiling back. She was just glad he couldn't see it beneath the helm.

He held the jambiya across his body in the position he'd taught her, curved inward. All of a sudden, he stumbled as if the tidewind had knocked him sideways. He stood up, planted his feet again, still smiling, but a small frown crinkled his perfect brow.

Anoor focused, pushing thoughts of him from her mind. Instead, she pulled on the anger like strings in her bow, pulling them taut, ready to release in contained movements. Just like Sylah had taught her.

The horn sounded, and Anoor lunged with the sword.

The sound of her blade crashing on his chest plate reverberated throughout the arena. He jumped back, but not fast enough to miss her side thrust. It pushed him to the ground, but he kicked dust up into her eyes as he fell. The sand glanced off the glass visor, but the moment's hesitation was enough for him to jump up.

He swayed as he tried to regain his footing. Was he drunk? On drugs?

"What did you do, Anoor? What did you do to me?" He shouted the words across the ring. He was no longer smiling. But still attractive. Asshole.

Anoor took advantage of his mania and pushed forward. He parried her blows as she swooped in low, left and right. He made an unstable stab toward the small bit of exposed skin where the gauntlet met the elbow joint, but the jambiya glanced off the metal.

Anoor blocked his next attempt and pivoted on her heel to slam the sword across his side. It was the second time she'd landed a crushing blow on that area of his armor and she could see the joints weakening at the breast plate, just like Sylah had said they would.

She just needed to hit him there a few more times to expose the skin. Then she could pierce him like she so desperately wanted. Sweat stung her eyes, blurring together with tears of anger.

She screamed, throwing her weight into another swing, but he preempted her move and slipped his feet under hers, sending her sprawling on her back.

With a growl, he launched himself toward her. Anoor's sword arm was trapped under the weight of his body as he used the jambiya to lift her helm. His smile was back, but his gaze was glassy, like the pupils were cast in ice.

She could not let him cut her.

His blade pushed the helm all the way off. The rush of air on Anoor's face was a welcome respite in the chaos of the moment. Anoor slackened her muscles, letting him savor his winning moment as the blade came down on the side of her cheek.

While he had been putting on the theatrics, Anoor had slipped her hand from her gauntlet and away from the weight of his body. The slackening of her muscles had given her the space to wriggle the hand out and around to the front of her face where she now held the hilt of the jambiya.

Whether it was the surprise or his affliction, he wasn't prepared for Anoor's counter-thrust.

"Always point the curve away from the body," Anoor said. The curved tip of the blade had pressed into Yanis's forehead, yielding the smallest drop of blood.

But it was enough.

The runelight around her name on the leader board shimmered around Yanis's dark hair.

"You cheated," he said as he rolled off her. He screamed up at Anoor's mother, "She cheated."

Uka dismissed him with a turn of her head.

Anoor whistled through her teeth.

"That must hurt."

The cheers of "Anoor Elsari" drowned out his complaints as he left the combat ground.

Anoor picked up her helm and looked around her. She was standing in the center of the ring, all four wardens clapping to her left, and a sea of people chanting her name. She let the smile spread across her face.

She had won.

She had *won*.

IT HAD BEEN a close call, even with the valerian root Master Inansi had given Yanis. But despite letting him overcome her with his weight, he had made a foolish mistake that proved he was not worthy. First blood was first blood.

The man was crying as he exited the arena, certain he'd been drugged. But there was no way he could prove it. The drug would be out of his system by the time he next pissed.

The warden had given them a short break to rehydrate and use the privy, and Jond watched as Anoor re-entered the arena from the left, her helm back on, the armor cleaned of dust. The sword rested in her hand comfortably.

Now it just came down to the two of them. Anoor and Jond. Her composure was absolute. Jond knew Sylah had been teaching her the art of Nuba, but Jond could slip into battle wrath within a breath. He had been practicing morning, noon, and night since he was four years old.

Anoor was good, but she couldn't compete with one of the Stolen.

"And now we begin the final trial. The final test to discover our Disciple of Strength," Uka spoke into the sound projector again. The audience started to stamp their feet, the sound vibrating the ground. The crowd was in a frenzy, the odds having been swayed to Efie and Yanis. No one expected the underdogs to be the final two. The Embers' front row writhed in their seats, drinking and smoking radish leaf cigars.

Jond pulled focus, found the rage he needed to harness and waited. He waited like he had done for the last twenty-two years.

It was time for it to end.

Anoor entered the ring, her stance wider than before, the sword ready in a lunge position. Jond took a breath and entered the ring.

The horn sounded, and neither of them moved.

"Come on, I'll give you the first hit," he called out to her, smiling. "We can make it look like a close call if you want."

She didn't respond, but her shoulders shook as if she were . . . laughing.

It raised the hairs on his arms as she stalked toward him.

The wind picked up around them, and in that moment she struck.

He didn't expect the strength that met him, and after deflecting the sword with a thrust of his axe, he retreated backward. He was breathing heavily already.

Anoor didn't press the attack; she just stood there, waiting, her head cocked to the left. It reminded him of Sylah so much that he almost missed the attack when it came. They parried left and right. Anoor jabbing with the sword with all her weight. She evaded every move Jond threw at her, the axe never getting close enough to skim her armor. Anoor was toying with him.

How did she get this good?

Her footwork was light, like a dancer's.

Dread curled in the pit of his stomach.

Every time he swung his axe, she blocked his blows.

It couldn't be.

"Sylah?"

"How's it hurting?" Sylah drawled back.

SYLAH HAD ALWAYS been able to best Jond, even when she was smaller than him.

The joba seed high had mellowed to a warming hum, settling her into battle wrath like slipping into a bath. Mooncycles of fighting the withdrawal seizures, and it had come down to this moment. She'd needed to win without her body giving out on her, she needed the lightness to fight Jond's dark. It was the only way.

Anoor had barely made it through the first round, and that was only because Yanis was drugged. There was no way Anoor could fight Jond and win. The Stolen were sharpened against a whetstone for years. Only a Stolen can beat a Stolen.

Jond thrust his axe in her direction, but she knew the move. If she deflected it, he'd pull her toward him with his other arm and strike her side. Instead, she sprung to the right and swiped her blade between his shoulder blades. The sword clanged against his armor.

He flipped backward and was back up again in moments, but not before she pounced on his back.

"Sylah, you won't get away with this." Their helms knocked together.

"I already have," she whispered.

He snarled and, with an impressive feat of strength, threw her over his shoulder.

She spun in the air and landed on her feet, but the sword skidded out of her grip across the ground. Sylah fed off the turmoil of the crowd; it reminded her of the Ring. At least she had Loot to thank for that.

He lunged toward her, the axe held high.

Sylah wondered if Anoor had yet woken from her slumber. If she would be watching Sylah lose for her.

No. No. No. No.

As the axe came down toward her, Sylah dove for the sword and wrapped her fingers around the hilt. In one clean motion she rolled onto her back and struck upward. Straight through the gap between his armpit and his chest plate.

It was a shallow cut, but she wanted to go deeper.

As she withdrew the blade, she held it up to the crowd. The blood ran down the tip toward the pommel, coating Sylah's hands in Jond's blood.

ANOOR HAD COME to the realization she wasn't going to win against Jond. That meant he was about to make her bleed. Everyone was about to see her Duster blood. These were her last few moments alive.

Anoor stood up; she needed the privy. Servants had begun to make ready for the final combat, ensuring the arena was clear of any blood. It gave the competitors a much-needed break. Anoor ignored the chants of her name as she walked toward the privy next to the arena entrance.

"Anoor."

A voice she recognized caught her attention. She turned to see Kwame leaning over the railing at the front. The Embers around him were unamused that he was blocking their prime position.

An officer had already been called to drag him away.

"Stop." Anoor waved away the brute who had Kwame by the arm. "It's okay, I know him."

The officer raised an eyebrow but let go of Kwame, who gave Anoor a rueful smile.

"Thanks." He rubbed his shoulder. "Can we talk? It's really *really* important. Like the most important thing you'll hear all day."

Anoor doubted that. She jerked her head toward the entrance. "Meet me by the competitors' entrance, I don't have long."

Anoor relieved herself, which took longer than she would have liked with all her armor, then went to meet Kwame.

The officer at the front entrance had changed; instead a petite young woman guarded the door to the arena floor.

"Careful." The officer stopped Anoor as she walked past. The officer's voice was deeper than she expected. "There's a woman attacking people. She apprehended one of my platoon."

"I won't go far," Anoor said. She hoped the other officer wasn't hurt.

"Hi, Anoor," Kwame said sheepishly. He was standing in the shadows of the forest, and Anoor was glad for the breather from prying eyes. "Here." He handed her a flask of water, but she shook her head; she didn't want to need the privy halfway through the fight.

"Take it, you need to stay hydrated."

She relented, taking off her helm and taking a big swig. The water was cool and refreshing.

"Thanks, I actually needed that."

Kwame took back the empty flask and shifted his feet.

"What's so important, Kwame? I'm a little bit busy."

"Anoor, what if you lose and they see your blue blood?"

"You saw the tower, then." Anoor's shoulders drooped.

He reached out and touched her gauntleted hand. "You have the coolest secret in the world." Anoor lifted her eyes to his. He wasn't turning away from her, wasn't discarding her like she feared. He was *concerned* for her.

"Is that all you came to say?"

"No." Kwame looked around. "Will you come over here? There's someone who wants to talk to you."

It was then that Anoor felt the first wave of fatigue. She leaned on Kwame for support.

"What?"

Kwame was leading her into the trees, but her feet were beginning to blur together.

She saw Sylah emerge from behind some leaves, but Sylah was gone. Gone with the Ghostings. Anoor must be dreaming.

"A little help?" Kwame said. Anoor thought he was talking to her, but she couldn't help, she couldn't lift her head. Sylah filled her whole vision, the sun leaking through the gaps in the canopy setting her short curls aflame. She was easing Anoor softly to the ground.

"Just close your eyes, Anoor, close your eyes and dream of your win."

It was an order, an order from a teacher to a student.

Sleep. And so she did.

Anoor woke with her face pressed against something moist. It smelled of earth and green. She groaned and rolled over, bringing her hand to her forehead. A clump of leaves resided there, and she pulled them off.

"What in the name of the Ending Fire happened?" Her head pounded like a stampede of erus, and her mind was as foggy as the dust they kicked up.

"Here, drink this." Kwame appeared above her, another flask in his hand.

"Aho, no, I don't think so."

"No, there isn't any poison in there, I promise."

"Why did you drug me, Kwame? Did I see Sylah? Curse the blood, the fight, I've got to get back out there." Anoor scrambled to her knees and noticed for the first time the clothes she wore.

"Where is my armor?" She picked at the front of her training clothes as if they offended her.

"Anoor, the fight already started." Kwame had the audacity to look contrite.

"What do you mean?" Anoor wasn't sure what hurt more, the anger or her head.

Kwame reached for Anoor's hand. "Sylah's gone to fight in your place."

"What in Anyme's name are you talking about?" Anoor started to get up, but Kwame held her shoulders, guiding her back to the ground.

"If Sylah isn't back in five more minutes, you're to find Hassa and leave the city."

"What has she done . . ." Anoor wanted to scream. This was her fight to lose.

"She couldn't let you risk everything, Anoor."

"So what? The two of you concocted this plan together? What, to save me?"

Kwame flinched.

"I don't know how long Sylah's planned it. She always had the second vial of sleepglass from the stealth trial. I thought it was in case I messed up on the officers' doses, but . . ." He lifted his shoulders weakly. "She couldn't let you die today, and neither could I."

Kwame scuffed the dirt with his shoe. "I didn't just do it for you, though, Anoor. You never saw me as just a servant. I know I'm not a Duster, and I can't imagine what it must be like to be on the other side of the river, but the world should be more equal than this. Now with this knowledge, the truth that everyone can bloodwerk, you can reset the scales, you know? And that's why I think you should be the next disciple."

They both heard the clanking of someone running in armor at the same time. Sylah entered the forest. The sword by her side dripped red blood.

"What happened?" Anoor demanded.

"No time. Talk later. Quick, put on the armor."

Sylah was quivering and stumbling as she flung the pieces of green armor to Anoor. Her withdrawals were worse than Anoor had ever seen them. A part of her wanted to fetch her some verd leaf tea.

"You won?" Anoor couldn't believe it.

"Put on the armor," Sylah shouted. "Help her, Kwame."

"No, I don't want this victory, it isn't mine." Anoor frowned.

"Don't be a monkey bullock, this isn't a time for pride," Sylah hissed. She had stripped to her training clothes, the warm armor a line on the ground between them.

"She's right. This isn't just about you," Kwame said.

Anoor knew it to be the truth. She was the disciple the empire needed. Anoor reached for the armor. The three of them pieced her back together into the warrior she had become.

Sylah was shivering uncontrollably now. Anoor could see her muscles were cramping, though Sylah smiled through it.

"May I be the first to congratulate you, Anoor Elsari, Disciple of Strength?" And as she grinned, Anoor saw the red seed jammed between her front teeth. The gravity of Sylah's sacrifice hit Anoor in the chest harder than Jond's axe could have done.

"Go, go." Sylah pushed her lower back through the trees.

"Take her to the infirmary," Anoor shouted to Kwame. She didn't wait for his nod before she was running, launching herself through the arena entrance and into the screams of the crowd beyond. She let herself hear them. They chanted her name and waved and cried. She could have drowned in their approval.

She looked up at the podium. Her mother wasn't clapping along with the other guild leaders; instead she stood poised at the edge of the stage, as if at any moment she was going to launch herself into the core of the arena. Her mouth was parted ever so slightly, her eyes a blank stare.

Anoor met her gaze. With a cry she thrust the sword into the air. Her mother flinched. Uka saw the move for what it was, a plunge into the beating heart of the empire as it was.

Things were about to change.

Block by block.

CHAPTER FORTY-FOUR

THE DAY OF ASCENT

Today I start my first journal as a disciple of the empire. Mother has stressed the importance of the truth. I find it ironic. I wonder how much they know. Now I have access to the warden library, I will search for the truth.

—The journal of Anoor Elsari, year 421

Sylah felt ten times heavier with the weight of exhaustion. It took her a few tries to get her eyes fully open. When she did, the sight couldn't have been sweeter.

Anoor was reading a book next to Sylah's infirmary bed. Her shoulders hunched as she leaned forward into her research. So different and yet still the same.

"How's it hurting?" Sylah croaked at Anoor. The infirmary was as sour smelling as Sylah remembered. She could hear the din of other patients and healers in the rooms beyond hers, their talking an incessant hum.

"I should be asking you that." Tears filled Anoor's eyes.

"Why are you crying?"

"Because you're alive," she murmured. She closed the book and added it to a stack beside Sylah's bed.

"Are you sure? Doesn't feel like it." Sylah tried to sit up and winced. Her muscles felt like they'd been pounded like fufu flour.

"You've been unconscious, Sylah; your heart rate dropped too low, Kwame had to carry you here. The healers weren't sure you'd wake up." Anoor stood, dashing away the tears on her cheek. "You shouldn't have taken that joba seed."

"I had to, Anoor." Sylah reached for Anoor's hand, but she was too far away.

"No, you didn't." Anoor looked at the window, the afternoon light softening her frown. "I was so angry that you took away my fight." She turned to Sylah, a small smile on her heart-shaped lips. "But I understand now. Things are already shifting."

"Are you still angry at me?" Sylah said quietly.

Anoor looked away again.

"I am angry at you for so many things. But not for that sacrifice, not for the risk you took for me."

Sylah nodded, though Anoor wasn't looking.

"The Sandstorm made a mistake leaving you."

Anoor's shoulders tensed, pulling taut the red suit she wore.

There was a knock at the door.

"Come in," Anoor said with authority.

Gorn appeared, a rare smile breaking up the straight lines of her face as she saw Sylah.

"You're awake."

"Hi, Gorn. Yes, wholly alive, though wholly in pain."

"Anoor, it's nearly time."

"Time for what?" Sylah interrupted.

"She didn't tell you? It's the Day of Ascent."

Sylah flung herself forward in the bed. "Wait, I've been out a *whole* day?"

Gorn looked bemused.

"I have to go, I have to hide. The Sandstorm . . ." Sylah swung her legs out of the bed.

"Sit down, it's fine, no one's tried to kill you yet," Anoor said, waving her back under the covers. "One of the perks of being a Disciple of Strength is that I've got my own personal guards. Where I go, they go."

Sylah sank back down, but the uneasiness didn't abate. The

hum she'd thought was the murmur of other patients must be the crowd in the courtyard below.

"We need to get you out of the city, though. Jond has disappeared. And despite the resources I now have, I don't trust anyone," Anoor said, and Sylah flinched. "The Ghosting elders have left. Hassa has marked the settlement on the map, it's a three-week journey, but they've had a head start through the tunnels. You'll need to leave by eru if you hope to catch up with them before they leave for the mainland. Boey is ready and prepared in the stable."

With each word Sylah sunk deeper and deeper into the straw mattress.

"I can't leave you."

Gorn quietly excused herself at Sylah's words.

"You must, and when you get to the settlement, you must join them on their journey to the mainland." Anoor pulled out a round medallion from her pocket. It was similar to the gold guild tokens given to Embers but larger and silver. "This is an ambassador emblem. Not only will it get you supplies on your journey with no questions asked, it will protect you if you are stopped by officers."

"An ambassador emblem?"

"Ambassadors are used by the wardens as mediators between the twelve cities and Nar-Ruta. I am allowed to name one within my Shadow Court."

Sylah reached for it. The metal was warm from being pressed against Anoor's body.

"Thank you."

"If what the Ghosting elders said to you is true, we need to figure out a way to rid the land of the tidewind."

"What about you, Anoor? The tidewind is getting worse. You could die."

"It's a risk we have to take, Sylah."

"Come with me." Sylah knew her plea was futile.

Anoor didn't reply, though she locked eyes with Sylah, her decision clear for her to see.

"What about the Sandstorm? They won't stop, Anoor."

Anoor smiled sadly and reached for Sylah's hand, intertwining it with hers. "I'll just have to set more paperweight traps."

Sylah choked on her tears, their woven hands blurring.

"Can I . . . can I come to the Ascent first?"

"I think it would be best if you didn't. Everyone will be at the Ascent. That gives you good cover to get out of the city. The streets will be clear."

Anoor reached for one of Sylah's tears and let it run over her knuckle.

"I don't want to leave you, Anoor. I love you."

"I know," she said, but didn't return the sentiment. "Come back to me, Sylah."

Sylah cupped Anoor's face in her hands.

"I will," Sylah said. She trailed her fingers over Anoor's lips, committing the shape of them to memory. Then she kissed her.

"I have to go," Anoor whispered. "And so do you. When I leave, the guards do too." She pulled away from Sylah.

Anoor didn't look back as she left the room.

SYLAH HAD A couple of things to do before she left the Keep. Her aching body protested as she made her way toward Anoor's chambers. The sack of joba seed powder in her pocket pressed against her leg.

"You should not have stopped taking the seeds without weaning yourself off them *properly*," the healer had chastised her. Then he said the words that she knew in her heart all along. "Your body is damaged; you'll continue to have ailments as your mind tries to cope with the lack of stimulant. You may have regained some sort of normalcy in the mooncycles to come, if you hadn't succumbed to the drug once more. But now your brain has reverted to adapting to the drug. In one moment, you undid moons of hard work." The healer *tsk*ed and pulled out a small bag. "I recommend you take a small dose of joba seed powder every day, a few grains added to a sweetened tea. That is all. If you don't, the seizures and tremors will return, worse than before. You could even suffer from a heart attack."

"Can I not just take verd leaf tea?"

The healer laughed harshly. "That old weed? It does nothing.

Less than nothing. It is high in caffeine, that's all. It's been a remedy among the lower classes for some time because it grows cheaply on the riverbank. Clever, eh? Who came up with that one?"

"Oh."

Sylah winced as she grabbed the bag, her muscles aching.

"Will I ever not be dependent on it? Will I ever heal?"

"It is unlikely."

Unlikely. The thought still echoed in her mind. Now the bag of powder bulged in the pocket of her pantaloons. The drug was her salvation once again. But it was different this time. This time it was survival, not oblivion, she strived for.

She walked up the stairs toward the kitchens and paused. What if, as Disciple of Strength, Anoor's chambers had moved? *No, Anoor wouldn't move, Anoor would want to stay close to the servants.*

Sylah was right, and their chambers were just as she'd left them three days before. A lifetime ago. She went through to the bedroom and pulled out the few possessions she had left. Her inkwell was there, and she strapped it to her arm. The prototypes of the runebombs she had been working on, which she stuffed in her pockets, and a journal where she'd been practicing her writing.

Sylah flicked through the innumerable babblings of "the desert fox lunged through the trees" and "the Abosom prayed in extreme weather." She ripped out a blank page and wrote Anoor a short note: the last secret she had to tell Anoor, the address to Lio's villa in the Duster Quarter. Sylah marveled at her handwriting, a gift from the woman she loved. She folded the note and left it on Anoor's pillow.

Sylah left Anoor's chambers and walked to the west side of the Keep toward the business district. With everyone out in the courtyard celebrating the Day of Ascent, the corridors were near silent. Every sound she heard reminded her of a knife unsheathing, every shadow looked like Jond.

Sylah walked down the corridor to the library, her boots echoing through the empty rooms of the offices, and stopped in front of the stone door.

Sylah withdrew her stylus and wrote the rune combination that should have given her access to the library, if Uka had been her mother. The stone remained steadfast. Sylah tried again, the runes perfectly drawn, as flawless as they had been the very first time she had drawn them. The stone door did not swing open.

Sylah rested her forehead on the uneven whitestone. The grooves dented her forehead painfully. Anoor had not lied.

Uka was not her mother.

Sylah lost the last facet of the identity she had been given.

"Blood means nothing after all," Sylah whispered against the stone.

Sylah made her way to the stables feeling lighter, different. She was rid of the weight of expectation for the first time in her life.

She could hear the rumble of the crowd as she entered the stables. The stalls were full of erus as all of the court and their families were in attendance to watch the disciples ascend.

Hassa was standing next to Boey. Sylah hugged her.

"Hi," Sylah said, squeezing her tight.

Hassa pushed her to arm's length and signed, *How are you feeling?*

"I'm okay." It was partially true. She already missed Anoor.

Anoor packed you a lot of stuff. Hassa waved at the carriage that was ready and waiting to be strapped to Boey.

Sylah peered in. The carriage was brimming with supplies, food, drink, blankets, clothes. Even a bottle of firerum.

The firerum's from me. Hassa gave Sylah a knowing glance.

"Thank you, Hassa." Sylah's heart warmed at the gesture.

Hassa pulled the map out from within the metal carriage and unrolled it on its side.

I've marked on the map where you need to go. Northeast. Follow the brightest star in the sky if you get lost.

The Wardens' Empire was such a small section of the map it was hard to see the small mark where the Ghosting settlement was.

The elders are going by foot, but they will be using the tunnels until they surface in Jin-Dinil. They will have to go the long way round, as one of our routes there has been compromised.

"How long have I got?"

The elders will be there in three weeks, give or take. They will not wait for you before leaving for the mainland.

Sylah would have to ride hard. She took the map from Hassa and rolled it up.

"Will you look after her for me? There are few people she can trust."

I will, Sylah.

Sylah hugged Hassa one more time, her small frame softening a bit more at the close contact.

"I'll see you soon," Sylah said, getting into the driving seat.

I hope so, Sylah. For all our sakes.

ANOOR COULDN'T QUITE believe she was walking the five hundred steps toward her mother. She looked down to the courtyard below at the sea of Ember faces. Her grandmother was there, in the front row, a sardonic smile on her face that Anoor took for pride. Anoor had planned a meeting with Yona tomorrow. Now that her mother could no longer keep them apart, Anoor was keen to find out what she could learn from her grandmother. If Yona didn't prove worthy of being an ally, at least she'd really annoy her mother with the meeting.

Anoor looked beyond the Embers in the courtyard and for the first time truly saw the onlooking Dusters and Ghostings pressed into pens at the back. They weren't given seats. They were given railings manned by officers. Anoor promised she would free them from their bars before long.

She hoped Sylah got away safely. Anoor had asked Boey to ride swiftly, though she knew the eru couldn't understand her. The nudge Boey gave Anoor had been full of affection, and Anoor had kissed her on the snout. She hoped they would both come back safely.

Anoor's legs started to ache. Five hundred steps were a lot of steps, no matter how hard you trained. Her knees creaked and sweat dripped down her neck into the wide collar of her red suit. One of the first things she'd done was order a new wardrobe. She made sure Gorn went to the Duster Quarter to buy her the clothes. Though the material wasn't as soft as the cotton from Jin-Noon, it was hardy and the stitching precise.

The Disciple of Truth puffed beside her. He was a large man with a circular bald patch on his head so defined that Anoor wondered if he'd shaved it in on purpose. He smiled at her, and she smiled back.

Tanu had won the title of Disciple of Knowledge. Anoor was glad of it; at least there was someone she knew. Tanu ran ahead of Anoor, the white sleeves of her suit billowing out behind her like milk froth.

The final disciple was a scrawny musawa called Faro. Their gangly legs seemed out of proportion for their body, but their mind must have been sharp if they won the Aktibar of duty. They were yet to introduce themselves to Anoor, but Tanu had said that Faro was Aveed's favorite from the very beginning of the Aktibar, nearly five mooncycles ago.

Five mooncycles. Was that all? Anoor was sure she'd been climbing the steps for half that time.

The four of them reached the pinnacle of the five hundred steps, their wardens there to greet them. Uka, in her signature gray, looked at her coolly.

"Anoor." She tilted her head in greeting.

"Warden," Anoor replied. It was the first time they had spoken since the final trial, and Anoor realized the fear she felt toward her had abated somewhat.

Oh, Anoor's knees still knocked together, but the power in her mother's threats was gone. Uka's disapproval dimmed in the light of Anoor's success. But she no longer needed her love. Not that Uka wouldn't assassinate Anoor if it came down to it. There were just bigger threats now. Her mother simply wasn't the only person who wanted to kill her anymore.

Anoor turned and took her place beside Uka.

Her breath left her in an appreciative sigh as she looked out across the city. The sky was the faded purple of a healing bruise, and she understood in that moment why Anyme had wanted to climb into the world above.

Anoor could see all the quarters of Nar-Ruta, from the plantations in the distance to the churning Ruta River that separated the wealthy from the poor. She could see the joba trees speckling courtyards in the Ember Quarter and the empty streets that wound around the Dredge. But what stole the air from her lungs wasn't just the villas in the distance, the shifting sand dunes on the horizon. No, it was the sea of brown faces, a sea of Embers and Ghostings and Dusters looking up to her with reverence.

This was power.

SYLAH COULD STILL taste Anoor on her lips.

The eru grumbled beneath her, and Sylah flicked the reins.

"Ayaah, stop it."

Boey shifted her shoulders, which altered the breeching rope connected to the carriage, sending it off balance.

"Go left, you hairy bullock, go left!"

Sylah was trying to lead Boey toward the Duster Quarter, but Sylah's driving skills were always challenged. Swearing at the beast seemed to make Boey even more incompetent. It took some time, but Sylah managed to steer the eru down the street toward her mother's home.

As Sylah hitched Boey to the small joba tree in the front of the villa, Lio opened the door. Sylah knew she wouldn't have gone to the Ascent.

"Hello, Sylah," she called out.

"Hello, Lio."

Lio flinched. "I'm just making fufu. Come in."

Sylah hesitated on the street. She looked back at Boey, who had already settled into the dusty road and gone to sleep.

"I can't be long."

Lio had already made her way inside. Sylah could hear the sound of her pestle as she pounded and pulverized the yams.

Sylah entered the house she once called home and made her way to the hearth at the back. She watched her mother for a few moments. Lio's left hand pounded the yam with a pestle while the right hand folded the sticky mess.

Thump. Fold. Thump. Fold. Thump. Fold.

Lio jutted her chin at the stove. "Don't just stand there, stir the soup."

Sylah found her feet moving before she could stop them. She stirred the bubbling soup next to her mother.

"Why did you lie to me?"

Thump. Fold. Thump. Fold. Thump. Fold.

"Sylah, we all had to make sacrifices."

"Don't give me that shit."

Thump.

"Do you remember what happened to you after we left the Sanctuary, Sylah?"

She put down the pestle, but Sylah couldn't meet her eyes.

"You stopped eating, stopped sleeping, but worst of all you stopped speaking."

Sylah stepped back from the stove as if struck, the memories bobbing to the surface in the murky swamp of her grief.

"It took you a whole year before you spoke again, and I thank Anyme every day for that Ghosting friend of yours. She taught you how to find your voice, teaching you their silent language out in the Dredge every day. Stir the soup, it's going to burn on the bottom."

Sylah nodded. "You are still not answering my question."

"When Jond returned with the news of the Sandstorm, run by Master Inansi—"

"Loot."

"Yes, Loot." She elongated the "L" with distaste. "He came to see me. He explained that Master Inansi, Loot, had plans for you. You see, we thought Papa Azim was the leader. The Sandstorm was the family we had around us. Turns out he was but a shantra piece in Master Inansi's scheme.

"He saw Azim's reports on you and didn't want to lose your talent. Jond told me it was Loot's idea to develop the Ring. To provide you with tests, keep you fit, but keep you away from the others."

It inflamed Sylah's anger. "Why did you lie to me?"

"Because he knew it would fuel you, the pride of a mother's blood, of the Warden of Strength's blood. It would make you sign up for the Aktibar by yourself and come back to the cause. Not that it went according to plan, mind you."

Lio went back to pounding the fufu.

Thump. Fold. Thump. Fold. Thump. Fold.

"Who is my family?" If the question hurt Lio, she didn't show it.

"Your family is all but wiped out. They were lower-ranking Embers who lived the last decade in disgrace. Your father died in a cell ten years ago for the murder and rape of your mother. Seems like losing their daughter caused them a few problems." The words were cruel, but not spoken cruelly.

"Anoor?"

"Yes, she's my daughter. That much is true. But Fareen, she was the child we swapped her with."

"Why?"

"He—"

"Why?"

Sylah stopped stirring the soup and turned to face her mother. She saw something she understood staring back at her. Addiction, not to the euphoric thrill of a joba seed, but to the three words that had crafted her life. Three words that had given her meaning and the blissful belief of being important.

Sylah was glad when Lio didn't respond. She didn't want to hear those words again. She turned back to the soup, and with each stir her anger faded to a simmering acceptance. She took a sip.

"It's good. A bit more peppashito and it would be perfect."

Lio nodded, the motion dropping tears into the mortar below.

That was the last thing Sylah ever said to the mother who raised her.

CHAPTER FORTY-FIVE

Patient suffered from chronic joba seed use >20 seeds a day. Clear evidence of neurotransmitter dysregulation and altered function resulting in ongoing seizures and desensitization in limbs. I recommend microdoses of joba seed powder in order to stabilize her brain's core function. This may be the only long-term solution for the patient's ailments. Overdosing is her biggest threat to survival now.

—Healer Kior's patient report on Sylah Alyana

Sylah looked up at the Keep. It was a speck in the distance, but she could see the crowds, small as ants, crawling at the bottom of the five hundred steps. Anoor was there, at the top. Could Sylah see a red smudge? Maybe. Sylah turned Boey away and didn't look back as she directed the eru through the city of Nar-Ruta.

About halfway through the Dredge, she noticed them. Hassa had told her there weren't many left. She told her their sleeping sickness ploy, borne from truth, was their means of escape. The ones left behind were those who chose to stay. Some, like Hassa, stayed to protect what was theirs. The guardians of the land, the Ghostings.

They escorted her out of the gates of the city. Past the planta-tion fields, which were empty of Dusters, who were all at the Ascent. They started to break away as she got to the open desert. Some waved their limbs, others simply left. But she felt their well wishes guiding her forward.

When they had all gone, she pushed Boey into a gallop, and they rode fast for two strikes. The farther she went, the harder it was to hold back the tears she had held tightly in her fist since leaving Lio. Everyone she had ever known was behind her.

Night fell, and Sylah knew she'd have a better night's sleep in a valley. She looked for the telltale sign of the shifting sand and navigated Boey down it.

"Aho, stop now." She slowed her down, and Boey screamed shrilly.

Boey shook her reins, and because Sylah was gripping them so tightly, she fell from the driver's seat onto the sand below.

"I really need to get better at driving."

Boey huffed in her direction.

Suddenly the eru squatted and urinated. Sylah jumped back just in time.

Sylah laughed, and it felt good. "We're going to get along fine, you and I."

When Boey was done, Sylah unhitched the carriage from the lizard's hindquarters, letting the eru find a comfortable nesting spot. After a few circles of the valley, Boey returned and settled next to the carriage. Once the tidewind started, Boey would burrow down into the sand with just her snout protruding.

Sylah looked at the sky; the sun had set long ago, the full moon a beacon in the sky. The brightest star beamed northwest just like Hassa said it would, but they had a long way to go.

It was time for Sylah to settle in for the night. The metal carriage was so full of supplies that Sylah needed to rearrange everything in order to find enough space to lie down. Anoor had provided more than fifty waterskins, enough bandages to mummify an army, and so much salt beef that Sylah wondered how many cows were contained within these four walls.

Something clattered to the floor, and Sylah jumped up with a start, banging her head on the metal roof. She cursed loudly and heard Boey bleat out a shrill in the distance.

Sylah poked her head out the door. "I'm okay."

She bent to look at the item that had caused such a ruckus.

"That crafty little kori."

Anoor had given Sylah her sword, the sword that was Anoor's by right from the tactics trial. The one Sylah used to cut down Jond. Sylah gazed at the golden blade, the hilt the bark of the joba tree with embossed branches winding down the shaft. She caught shards of her reflection in the moonlight. She looked miserable, blotchy, sad.

"No more tears," she whispered.

Boey whistled in assent.

Sylah shoved a piece of meat in her mouth and drew out the map. She estimated they were a few leagues south of Jin-Dinil, though she was going to avoid all cities until she needed supplies.

Boey pushed her snout into the carriage door and huffed.

"All right, all right. Dinner's on the way."

Once Sylah had fed the lizard, she climbed aboard the carriage and locked the doors. It was as safe as she could be in a tidewind.

SYLAH WOKE TO the sound of movement outside. The tidewind had fallen still some strikes before, and she had just managed to fall asleep. She was curled up among her supplies, a runelamp lighting the map beside her. Boey's snoring on the other side of the carriage wall indicated she was still asleep. Sylah reached for the sword, but it was wedged beneath the open container of dried meat.

Tap. Tap. Tap.

The knocks made a tinny sound against the metal side.

"Hello, can we come in?"

Sylah knew that voice. She reached for the sword, not caring about the sound it made. She opened the latch with the blade and leveled it at her guest.

"Hello, there." Loot's smiling face entered the carriage.

Boey's snout emerged from the sand, followed by her body. Her three eyelids opened in succession, and she cast a disinterested glance at the intruders who had woken her.

"You couldn't have woken up sooner?" Sylah said to Boey, and she was sure the lizard rolled her eyes.

"Pardon?" Loot was still smiling.

"Not you. This lump." Sylah jutted her chin toward Boey, who looked like she had already gone back to sleep. Sylah sighed.

"Why don't you come out of there and we'll have a nice chat?" Loot held open the door.

"Leave that behind, please." He flicked his dagger in the sword's direction. It was fine, because she needed her hands free anyway. She jumped out of the carriage, her feet shifting in the sand, but she kept her balance. Her hands hovered above her pockets. She was ready.

Jond and Fayl moved out of the shadows of their eru steeds.

"Oh, hello friends," Sylah greeted them both.

Fayl looked sad, forlorn almost.

"Sylah . . ." Fayl shook his head, his words failing him. She too was sad he was there.

Jond didn't say a word. It was as if the air around him blurred with the anger.

"What do you want, Loot?" Sylah asked, though she knew full well he wanted her life.

"First I'm going to kill you." Loot adjusted his yellow collar. "Then, naturally, Anoor . . . and once that mess is cleaned up, I think I'm going to have a big cup of tea."

"Loot, none of this matters, there's more to this world than just this empire."

"Oh, you mean the mainland Tenio?"

Both Jond and Fayl looked at Loot. *Looks like their master has been keeping secrets from them too.*

"You can kill me, Loot, but eventually you'll be dead as well. The tidewind is going to destroy this land."

"An interesting theory, but the tidewind is just another thing that ebbs and flows with the passing of time."

"Jond, didn't you tell him what the wardens were saying? It's not normal."

Loot snorted and flicked his wrist at Jond. "End her."

It was a test for Jond. Of course, it was a test. Kill the girl you love. But still Jond stepped forward, holding his axe high.

"Jond, don't do this," Sylah said.

Fayl hovered behind him, his own knife held out in case Jond didn't come through on his order. Loot watched the exchange like an audience member during a griot's story.

"Jond, stop, don't come any closer. I mean it."

Sylah backed away as he advanced, until her back was against Boey's cool blue scales.

Jond raised his axe, and Loot clapped in glee.

"Jond, I'm your Akoma."

He hesitated at the word, his jaw unclenching.

"I grow bored. Get to the main event," Loot said behind them, throwing in a yawn.

She saw Jond's eyes go flat as he swung the axe toward her neck. Sylah grabbed the pommel and threw her weight against it to counterbalance the axe's swing.

The blade glanced her cheek, but she needed the blood to activate the runebombs. She dropped to the ground as Jond stumbled back, preparing to swing again. Sylah wiped her cheek and reached into her pocket. She withdrew the three prototypes she'd been working on and threw them. Triggered by Sylah's blood, the runebombs burst into blinding light. It was the first time she'd tested them. She'd incorporated the rune *Ru* to push any nearby objects away from the bomb. But as bloodwerk doesn't work on living things, Sylah had inserted shrapnel into the glass orb. When it burst, it burst with the destruction of a hundred runebullets.

In addition to pushing the shrapnel through the glass, the rune *Ru* also pushed inanimate objects away. That meant the sand around them burst up around the bomb, and the force pushed and picked at their clothing. Before the dust could settle, Sylah reached into the carriage to retrieve her sword.

Sylah ran into the crater that the runebomb had created and looked around. The knife Fayl was holding fell victim to the bomb's force and embedded itself in the center of his body. Blue blood seeped into the sand around him. If he wasn't dead yet, he would be in moments.

Sylah didn't have time to mourn him, but she would. Fayl had always been kind to her. Except for the hunting-down-and-murdering thing. But that was only recently.

Sylah turned her attention to Jond. With his back to the blast he'd fallen forward, toward the carriage, as the axe was ripped out of his hand. He groaned and rolled onto his side. It looked like his shoulder had come out of its socket. She went to retrieve his axe, leaving nothing to chance as she stalked toward Loot.

"Oh, monkey's bullocks, did you have to survive?" Loot had been the closest to the runebombs, yet here he was crawling through the sand toward her. His suit was in tatters, the shrapnel piercing the delicate fabric and embedding in his skin.

"Ach . . . huch," he gurgled up at her. He collapsed on the ground by her feet, his back to the ground, his eyes looking upward toward the sky.

Sylah leaned down and unpinned the black diamond spider brooch on his pocket.

"Thank you for this. I've always admired it."

His watery eyes slipped to hers, and she thought she saw a ghost of a smile on his face.

"See you around, Loot." Sylah held the sword aloft, poised to make the killing blow. Anoor's voice chanted in her mind, and she tried to block it out, *had* to block it out in order to save her.

"It's not up to you to choose who lives or dies," Anoor whispered.

No, Anoor, today I do decide. I decide that you will live, and he will die.

Sylah brought the sword down on Loot's neck. The blade crunched bone and cartilage, but it went clean through.

She looked at Loot's body one last time, blinked once, twice.

If your blood runs red, go straight ahead.

If your blood runs blue, you're not coming through.

Translucent hue, who are you, who are you, who are you?

"Who are you?" The words of the chant echoed in her mind. "Who are you?"

Because Loot was bleeding. And it wasn't red or blue. It wasn't translucent.

It was yellow.

"Curse the fucking blood."

EPILOGUE

Sand. It was everywhere, in her clothes, her sandals, even in the crack of her ass.

Sylah shook her pantaloons loose, attempting to dislodge the particles wedged between her cheeks. Boey shrilled and shook her head.

"I know, I know, you're hungry."

Boey huffed in response.

"Let's stop here."

Sylah jumped down from the driver's seat, letting the reins go slack. Sylah's riding skills hadn't improved, not that it mattered much. Boey went where she wanted; most of the time it was in the direction Sylah intended. They'd come to an easy understanding.

Boey's amber eyes tracked Sylah as she got down from the carriage, her diamond-shaped head tilting. Sylah knew what the lizard wanted because Boey had gone as far as opening her third eyelid to do it. More effort.

"Fine, but you'll have to explain to Anoor why we maxed out the ambassador's credit on yams."

Sylah fished in the carriage, careful not to disturb the load. She withdrew a purple yam the size of her thigh and threw it toward Boey, who elongated her neck to catch it. She snapped it between her jaws and swallowed it in one bite. Sylah patted Boey's mottled blue scales and sat on the ground.

She was careful as she unraveled the map, the glue holding the two pieces together already cracking. She sipped the sweetened tea and grimaced, but she was glad for the joba seed powder. It had allowed her to reclaim her body for the first time in mooncycles. She looked at the map.

Her journey had taken her to the northern tip of the empire over the course of three weeks. Ood-Zaynib hadn't exactly been on route, but they had called to her: the dead. The ones she killed.

The sand was warm underfoot as she walked down the dune to the valley of her childhood home.

The Sanctuary was much the same. Built of sturdy whitestone, it hadn't yet succumbed to tidewind damage. The fields of rubber trees grew wild and tall. Much like her. Their bark had healed in the six years since she had last been there. The sour smell of latex was a wisp of a memory among the trees.

Sylah walked slowly, searching the blue ground for any hint of them. Then she saw it, a skull in the distance. She placed a hand on the bark of a tree to steady herself.

"Fuck." She jumped back, holding her hand to her chest. One, two, three tentative steps forward. There it was. A hole in the wood from the runebullet meant for her. Once she would have wished it made its mark. Not today. Not again.

She walked toward the skull, away from the hole made for her heart. The Farsai Desert made sand dunes in its eye sockets, and a sand snail now occupied the nasal cavity. She couldn't guess whose smile once opened up to the gleaming white teeth beneath.

On she walked, through her family's phantoms, the echoes of

their battle cries and final goodbyes. Six different bones she found, all too large to be the Stolen. The Embers must have taken the Stolen's bodies away and scrubbed the Sanctuary clean. They only left the remains of the blue-blooded Dusters to seep into the sand like the dirt they were.

Her heart began to pound as she neared the area where the rain of bullets had struck Fareen down. Sylah's hand went to the scar at the base of her neck. Her curls had just started to hide the keloid skin there.

"Hmmgargh gargh."

Sylah spun just in time to see Jond crest the sand dune at the top of the valley and fall over. His hands and feet were bound, his mouth gagged with silk. He rolled toward the rubber trees, coming to a rest at the base of them ten handspans away.

"Nice trip?"

His eyes shrunk into slits as he blinked the sand out of them.

"Are you flirting with me, Jond?"

"Fugh hu."

"Is it time for your pee pee?"

"Gughn fughin ghil oo."

"Oh, you sweet talker."

Sylah went over to him and dragged him up by his hair. She rolled him over to reveal the knot of bloodwerk runes holding his gag in place and released it. After all, the Sanctuary was in the middle of nowhere. It had to be.

"Are there any bodies left?" His contempt seeped out of all the cracks in his unused voice.

"I found some bones. They look like adult bones. I think they took the Stolen's away."

He cursed.

"A few more fucks and you'll be close to capturing how I'm feeling."

"What are we doing here?"

"I want to burn them. Properly."

He nodded, his eyes downcast.

"Release me and I will help."

Sylah snorted. "No chance. I'll release your feet so you can wander, but let's not have a repeat of yesterday. Boey's starting to think of you as prey, and you can't blame me if you become her next snack."

"Erus are herbivores."

"You haven't seen her when she's *really* hungry."

"Fine, Sylah, just release the bonds on my feet."

"Civility at last. I was beginning to think you'd forgotten my name. Because it's certainly not 'Fuck You.'"

It had been a rough journey. Sylah couldn't keep track of the number of times she regretted letting Jond live. But she couldn't let him go back to Nar-Ruta and threaten Anoor's reign, and she couldn't kill him. Not until she got more answers from him about Loot, about the Sandstorm, about all of it.

Yellow blood.

Sylah shuddered. So far Jond's life had reaped no rewards. He claimed he didn't know anything about the Sandstorm's plan and knew even less about Loot's origins. Sylah didn't believe him. She fingered the spider brooch in her pocket, her fingers running over the engraving on the back. "Inansi" had been carved into the center of the spider's underbelly.

"I'll gather the bones," Sylah said.

"I will attempt to collect firewood. Are you sure you can't release my hands?"

"I could." Sylah smiled. "But I won't."

Together they toiled in the afternoon sun like they were children again. There was no laughter, no grumblings about the extra duty they were forced to do for pulling a prank on Fareen. Though guilt was an invisible line that now tethered them together.

They built a fire in the Sanctuary's courtyard. The ten bodies were the foster parents, the teachers, the leaders of the Sandstorm. The original Dusters who had given up their children for a cause they believed in so wholly. Sylah wondered which bones were Papa Azim's as they placed them on the fire.

Sylah and Jond stood on opposite sides of the fire, their families' remains burning between them. The smell of rubber had returned to the Sanctuary, and it burned Sylah's nostrils. She breathed deep and embraced the pain.

The heat waves from the fire rose tall, casting a haze over the whitestone building, blurring her home like the faded edges of a dream. A nightmare.

"We should say some words," Sylah said.

"We should."

"I—" Sylah exhaled in a rush. She had no more air, no more words. "Sorry" would never be enough, "thank you" would never be true.

Jond looked at her through the smoke. The smoke that the Abosom believed carried souls to the sky. Sylah wasn't sure. Jond cleared his throat and spoke into the silence.

"Some knew you as the Sandstorm. We knew you as family." Jond's voice boomed across the valley. "A dancer's grace." He thumped his bound hands to his chest, adding percussion to his tribute. "A killer's instinct, an Ember's blood, a Duster's heart." He looked at Sylah, and she knew what he wanted her to say. He wanted her to repeat the mantra that had sustained them, more than food, more than air.

She inclined her head, let him ring out the words that churned her stomach so.

"The Final Strife."

It meant something else to her now. It meant survival, it meant freedom, it meant Anoor.

They stood by the fire until it flickered out.

"We need to bury the bones." Jond touched her arm.

The sun had begun to set. They'd spent strikes longer than she'd intended at the Sanctuary. She still needed to get to the Ghosting settlement in time for their scouting mission to the mainland. They'd need to ride up until the tidewind struck.

"Hurry."

The bones were coated with rubber wood ash from the fire, and Sylah laid them on the cooling sand while Jond scrabbled to make a hole. Embers who could afford an Abosom would have had one to perform the ceremony, to light the pyre and bless the earth with their sacred blood. But they made do with what they had. Sylah knew it was what Papa would have wanted for them: choosing their path right up to the end.

Sylah fingered a small bone between her forefinger and thumb. She wiped the ash from the chalky bone and wondered whose remains she was holding. Whose body had this bone held up and connected tissue with tissue?

Sylah went to the carriage and pulled out the sword from behind a stack of dried meat. She'd had to keep all weapons hidden from Jond. Using the tip of the blade, she pierced the bone in the center.

Sylah walked back down the valley toward Jond.

"Would you?" Sylah held out the small piece of bone.

Jond understood and knelt in the ground beside her. She released his hands then, giving him the smallest bit of trust for the task.

Slowly, carefully, he began to braid the bone into the short tufts of her curls, connecting hair with hair, rebuilding the Sylah she now was.

The bone hung just below her ear. White against black.

THE STORY WILL CONTINUE IN BOOK 2 OF

THE ENDING FIRE TRILOGY

*A piece of moonlight stretched thin, stretched taut. It spins and spins
over our memories and thoughts.
A web of lies, a net of deceit.
Now the Griot speaks. The Griot speaks.*

◊◊◊

Let us cast our eyes to the horizon beyond.

◊

Go forth, break free from those silvered bonds.

◊

Break free, I say, but always remember, what hides in a web?

◊◊◊

A spider in the center.

—Griot Sheth

DEL REY BOOKS

TURN THE PAGE FOR
A BONUS SHORT STORY,
SET BEFORE THE EVENTS OF
THE FINAL STRIFE!

ONE POISON, TWO SUGARS

ONE POISON, TWO SUGARS
LOOT YEAR 403

The Starting Drum permeated Loot's mind with its incessant beat and shook the rafters of the villa he was living in.

Bang-dera-bang-dera-bang.

He rolled over on his makeshift bed and felt the uneven floorboard probe the flesh between his ribs. He sat up, but it took a while for his brain to rejoin his skull.

"Argh." He rubbed at his temples where the Starting Drum still pounded. "Another trial. Another day."

He leaned his elbows on his knees before surveying the room around him with blurry eyes. Vials cluttered every surface of the room. Those closest to him were upended, their liquids gone, consumed the night before. He reached for the open notebook, discarded among the chaos of glass and potions.

He wrote with shaking hands.

Antidote worked, though I cannot remember falling asleep. Side effects: headache, possible unconsciousness, fatigued muscles. Recommendation for final dose: increase in valerian, caffa root, and extract of water mint.

It is ready.

Loot looked at the notebook. His penmanship was remarkable; he had Crime lord Anhid to thank for that. Anhid had taught Loot everything he knew, especially his illegal skills like writing.

Shame he has to die today, Loot thought. He liked Anhid, he really did. But the crime lord was lazy, he was losing his grip on the Dredge, and two rival crews were encroaching on Anhid's territory. And while Anhid's dominion was diminishing, Loot's ambition was growing like poison ivy, wild and all consuming.

Loot stood and made his way to the window at the front of the villa. He pulled away the metal sheeting from the glass, flooding the room with light. He held up his forearm to the sunshine and watched as his dark skin turned a slight ochre. If he squinted he could see the fine yellow veins on his dark skin throbbing with blood.

He sighed and moved away from the window, back into the embrace of the shadows of his laboratory. Shadows held secrets. It was why he had chosen the location of his future throne room. He went to it now.

The hatch at the back of the villa was open, but still Loot could smell the stale air of the tunnels seeping up. He reminded himself to buy incense. Cinnamon maybe.

With a grunt Loot lowered himself down the ladder. His foot slipped on a damp rung, and he nearly tumbled to the ground.

"Shit." The word echoed out toward the speck of rune light in the distance. "Imagine breaking my neck today. It would all be for nothing." His voice was light, full of dry humor.

"Loot, are you okay?"

Fayl moved out of the darkness below, his muscular arms enveloping Loot in a hug before his feet touched the tunnel floor.

"I'm fine, my love. I'm fine." But Loot leaned into his husband's tight embrace. Fayl's beard tousled Loot's curls as he rested his head on the intricate bloodink tattoos that wrapped up Fayl's arms and shoulder. Loot trailed a finger over the swirling blue pattern.

"You're shaking," Fayl scolded.

"It was just the antidote. I needed to make some final tweaks."

"Tweaks? Let's delay, do this another day."

"No, Fayl. We've planned for too long." Loot looked into Fayl's concerned eyes. The bags beneath were laden with worry. "Today, they die."

Fayl flinched. The big man hated violence, and Loot could only love him more for that weakness.

"Today, they die," Fayl repeated with a slow nod of the head.

Loot smiled, revealing all his teeth.

THEY HAD BEEN cleaning out the tunnels under the city for three mooncycles. It had been Loot's idea to locate his headquarters beneath the Dredge. Though the underground had been barred from citizens as unsafe, he'd found a set of rooms and tunnels that would suffice quite well.

Few people ventured in the tunnels anymore; crumbling foundations and a mazelike structure had killed off the few who had tried to find the fabled treasure beneath the city. Some areas were rumored to have pockets of exploding gas, but Loot suspected it was a lie circulated by the wardens to dissuade explorers. Still, he shared the story with anyone who would listen, kept them away from his lair.

"Loot, where do you want these?" Iko, another young member of Loot's cohort, waved a flowery teacup in his hand. Next to him was the rest of the tea set.

"Careful," Loot shouted, lurching his way toward the crockery. "That is *infinitely* precious, and it's what I'll be serving tea in later."

Iko shrugged his shoulders, his long braids swaying. "Do you want me to put it in the Belly?"

Loot scowled. He wasn't sure who first nicknamed the library the "Belly," or the tunnels that led to it the "Intestines," but either way the names had stuck. Much to Loot's chagrin.

"Yes, set it up in the *Belly*."

Loot sucked his teeth as Iko stacked the crockery carelessly atop one another.

Iko must have seen the murderous look in Loot's eyes, as he practically tiptoed out of the room to the library beyond, whispering, "Sorry, sorry."

"Don't kill Iko, we need all the people we can get." Fayl's voice held a laugh as it tickled Loot's ear.

"I know, but did you see him with the crockery? It took me three trips to steal the full set from the imir of Jin-Sukar. *Three* trips."

Fayl's eyes softened. He knew Loot lied about the tea set's origin, that the china had actually been Mama Bengo's. But Fayl didn't contradict him; instead Fayl's expression held the grief Loot refused to feel when he thought of the adoptive mother he had come to love.

But she was gone. Dead by Anhid's hand. It didn't matter that it had been Anhid who killed her, all the crime lords would pay the price. Though revenge wasn't Loot's main driver—that was power—revenge would be the syrup on the top of an already delicious cake.

"Have the invitations gone out?"

Fayl nodded. "Most, just one left, to Anhid. I thought you might want to write that personally."

"Yes, you're right."

Loot walked toward the library, and Fayl fell into step beside him.

"Do you really need to go to the Keep?" Fayl said softly.

Loot clenched his jaw and didn't respond.

"I know you want to prove your skills and reach but it seems a bit like suicide, if you're caught, or you're cut and they see your bl—"

"It's everything or nothing. I must not only appear to be powerful, I must *be* powerful." Loot's voice was clipped by the wideness of his smile. "And to be powerful, I must show them that I can get anywhere and be everywhere. Fear is what will subdue them. If not, death will."

Fayl laughed nervously. It made Loot sad to hear it, but it was necessary. Fayl was the only person alive who knew everything about him. Even the color of his blood.

They arrived at the library, and Loot walked over to his desk. The room was set alight by the glow of runelamps, all the finest quality glass, of course, their light pure and unblemished. Books lined the walls of the room, more books than most Dusters would see in a lifetime; most Embers too. Loot loved books. He didn't have any growing up. But over the last few years he had been building his collection and quietly stashing them down here.

He leafed through the notes on his desk, pages that would result in everyone in the room being treated to a ripping. But the truth was, their lives were a risk Loot was willing to take. He'd sacrifice everyone in the room if it meant he could reign.

Loot plucked out a piece of paper from the pages of his desk.

Dearest Anhid,

Loot could see the scandal in Anhid's face at not being referred to as "crime lord."

You are invited to tea at noon to hear the most wonderful news. A proposition, if you will. One that will benefit every crime lord in the empire. All of whom are required to attend. You may bring your crew.

Yours,
Loot, Warden of Crime

Aho, how Anhid's eyes would bulge to see the words "Warden of Crime" written so brazenly as if Loot was better than him.

I am, I'm better than all of them.

The invitation had already gone out to the other three crime lords of Nar-Ruta. They would bring weapons and anger. Loot would bring tea.

Loot handed the letter to Fayl.

"Make sure everyone is ready. I'll be back by noon."

LOOT WALKED LEISURELY across the Tongue with his hands in his jacket pockets. It was corduroy, richly woven with large pockets both filled and empty. The Dusters who recognized him kept their heads lowered in respect, while those who didn't still gave him a wide berth because Loot exhumed self-importance. And that was very dangerous for a Dredge-dweller. It made him a target. But today, Loot wanted to be noticed.

As he entered the Ember Quarter he felt the eyes of a platoon of soldiers narrow on him.

"Who are you?" They leered at him, approaching out of formation like a group of thugs. Their runeguns glinted in the sunlight.

"Me?" Loot acted surprised.

"You see anyone else?" The captain was a fierce woman with a cropped wig that curled behind her ears.

"Why, I do, there's you, and him, and them." Loot picked off the crowd on the Tongue behind him.

The captain scowled.

"I'm talking about you."

"Oh." Loot smiled and spread his bejeweled hands wide. "I'm the son of the imir of Jin-Gernomi."

The members of the platoon shifted their feet, slowly moving into formation, but the captain wasn't convinced.

"The son of Imir Jenda is ten years old."

Aho, a clever one here.

Loot shrugged. "I'm the *bastard* son of the imir of Jin-Gernomi. I don't often have to specify my family tree when I walk around the capital."

The captain looked unconvinced.

"Show me your arm."

Loot rolled up his sleeves with exaggerated slowness. He brandished the smooth skin of his forearms with a twirl of his wrist.

"See, no brand."

Loot had never been branded like a Duster. His birth had never been recorded.

"And if you want even more proof, look at my ring." Loot pressed the gold circle into the captain's hand. It was flesh warm, and heavy. Very heavy. "It is engraved with the imir kente pattern. You can keep it if you want."

There was a beat of silence. The captain's eyes locked with Loot's. There were flecks of ice in her gaze. The ring wasn't engraved with the imir's kente pattern and she knew it. But so goes the game of bribery.

"What were you doing on the other side of the city?" Her voice had softened, from ice to rain. She still held the ring clenched in her fist.

"Walking."

"Captain," another officer murmured beside her, "I think he's telling the truth, I heard about the imir's bastard son being in the city." The officer dropped his voice further. "And his tastes in the maiden houses across the river."

Loot battled back the smugness of his smile. He'd been building the persona for weeks, dropping into every tavern in the Ember Quarter with a story or two. Sometimes he was the bastard son, other times he was a disgruntled friend, or even a nightworker who had been paid by the fictional man.

The captain slipped the ring into her pocket, the bribe accepted. She gave him a short nod, and the platoon moved away. Loot continued walking.

Anhid had trained Loot for years, and for years Loot had learned it all: from smuggling to tax evasion, from fraud to fighting. At twenty-eight years old he was one of the most well-known deputies of any crew, tipped to take over Anhid's reign when the old man was eventually killed.

But being a crime lord wasn't enough. It never would be.

Mama Bengo had taught him that.

"You're not a follower, boy."

She called him "boy" well into his twenties.

"You are a leader. Remember that." She had rapped her cane against his fingers, and a stack of coins fell over.

"Did you hear me?"

"Yes, Mama Bengo."

"Now recount that money."

He had done so with a smile on his face, knowing that no matter his status she would always reign above.

Until she didn't. Mama Bengo had been the greatest slab counterfeiter in the empire. And when Anhid's stash had been flagged by an officer, that was it. She'd paid with her life.

"I'll do you proud, Mama," Loot said to the breeze.

He was deep in the Ember Quarter now, the villas drawing out like oil paintings across the cobbled lane. There on the horizon was the Wardens' Keep, its domed roofs thrusting up to the bright morning sky.

He walked up to the gate and gave his fake name. It wasn't

technically fake: the imir did have a bastard son, he just didn't know it.

The officers at the Keep's gates weren't too concerned; they just jotted down his name, noting who Loot was there to visit.

Security wasn't lax, precisely; it's just that the wardens' reign was so omnipotent that few had the courage to attack them in their own home. Loot would see an end to that.

"Kiha, escort this man to Imir Jenda's residential chamber."

Kiha was an officer of medium build. Their long hair was braided in two thick plaits that ran down their back.

"This way." Kiha's voice was gruff, unwelcoming. Loot grinned up at them willing Kiha's features to crack into a smile. Some people wielded their anger like weapons; Loot wielded smiles.

Kiha looked perturbed.

"What do you want? You creeping on me? I'm married."

Loot sighed out his nose but didn't drop his grin. "Me too."

Kiha walked a few steps ahead of Loot, their steps quickening. Loot didn't bother muffling his laugh, and it was carried on the wind around the joba tree in the center of the courtyard.

The five hundred steps were ahead of him, and he let himself dream of what the world looked like from that height. To have the power of the wardens at his back, and the strength of the citizens ahead of him. It was a future that wasn't too far from his grasp.

One step at a time, he reminded himself. *One step at a time.*

The cloisters that surrounded the Keep were full of bustling people. There was a group of children being heralded toward the Keep's nursery. A servant was holding a screaming child whose cries echoed around the corridors.

The babe appeared to have a recently healed wound under her gray eyes. Eyes that were filled with tears.

"Aho, little one, don't cry. Everything will be all right in the end," Loot cooed at her. The Duster maid holding the child scowled at Loot and hustled away.

"Stop dawdling," Kiha barked, and Loot skipped lightly to catch up.

Kiha led Loot through to the business district of the Keep. They passed the courtroom and the wardens' offices on their way to the residential area. Loot whistled as he walked, his hand stroking the spider brooch on his lapel. Absently he slipped his finger behind the cool metal and felt the engraving carved above the pin. The words were branded in his mind like any scar.

Inansi.

It was his true name. The name he'd been given, the brooch a family heirloom. It was the name the whole world would know someday. The name he saved for when it truly mattered.

Loot was the name of a criminal. Inansi was the name of a leader.

"We're here," Kiha said, knocking once on the wooden door. By the time it opened Kiha had already turned on their heel and disappeared down the corridor from which they had come.

"Yes?" The chief of chambers who answered the door looked bewildered to see Loot.

"I'm to meet the imir. Tell him I have news of Hila's son."

"Who?" The servant frowned, a small N appearing between his brow.

"He'll know," Loot said with an air of importance, reveling in the expression it caused on the servant's face.

Loot didn't need to talk to the imir. He'd already got into the Keep, but Loot reveled in the drama his news brought. Besides, he might one day need the imir's help.

"Wait here." The servant disappeared, returning a short while later, the N on their brow now a worried W.

"He will see you in his office."

Imir Jenda's chambers were sparsely decorated, like the room of an inn, clean but unloved. The residence was secondary to the imir's home in Jin-Gernomi.

The office was a little more lived in. Books lined the walls, and Loot found himself scanning the spines, wondering if he had any of them in his collection. He'd try to pinch a few on the way out.

"Who are you?"

The imir was beefy looking. Cow eyes, with wide shoulders and short hands like hoofs.

"Hello, imir."

"Who are you?"

Loot took a seat on the eru-leather chair opposite the desk. He stroked the armrest.

"Very high quality, *very* high quality," Loot mused.

"What do you know of Hila?" The imir's jowl wobbled ever so slightly. Beef medium-rare.

"What don't I know?"

The imir's eyes were watery and bloodshot, and Loot wondered if women were the man's only vice. He screwed up his features and spat, "You know nothing."

Loot was still stroking the eru leather. It was softer than any leather he owned, the scales carefully tanned and stretched. It must have come from Jin-Sahlia. He'd inquire about getting one for himself. He'd always fancied a throne.

The imir stood, his twisted mouth parted to call for assistance. "Get—"

"I know she's beautiful. Very beautiful indeed. Much more beautiful than your wife."

The imir sat down—or did he fall down? Loot wasn't sure. Either way the air was knocked from his lungs and he spoke breathlessly.

"You spoke of a son. A child."

"I did. I did."

The word quivered on the imir's lips, but no sound came out as he questioned, "Mine?"

"Oh, yes, no amount of henna hides the light brown hair of your family."

"Where?"

Loot winked. "Now that would be telling . . ."

If he gave the man his child's address, he'd have no leverage. Loot spotted a decanter on the side.

"It doesn't make sense, we were careful. This will ruin me. My wife. My daughter . . . my granddaughter. She's only young. So young. This will jeopardize her succession . . ."

Loot waved a hand in the imir's direction.

"Don't worry. I can keep a secret." Loot split his mouth into his widest smile. The imir stopped talking, thankfully. But his eyes narrowed.

"Here, let me pour you a drink. Settle your nerves a little," Loot said.

Loot didn't wait for the imir to respond; instead he poured himself and the imir a healthy glass of the amber whiskey and sniffed it.

"Aho, this is fine."

Loot savored the amber liquid: apples and citrus peel with a slight note of bitterness. When he looked back at the imir, the man's glass was empty. Loot wondered how many bottles Imir Jenda got through in a week.

The drink had given the imir courage, though, foolish, foolish courage.

"There is nothing stopping me from killing you right now." The foolish, foolish man withdrew a knife from his drawer and held it up with quivering hands.

"Oh, I do disagree, my good friend."

The imir stood, his chair squealing backward on the polished floor. He stabbed forward with the knife, but Loot didn't move. He was at least ten handspans short from bodily harm.

Instead, Loot poured himself another drink and smiled before saying, "I poisoned that drink that you so quickly downed."

The knife dropped to the floor.

"What?" Imir Jenda was rigid now, the fear solidifying into paralysis.

"Don't worry, though. I have the antidote." Loot slipped his hands into his pocket and brandished one of the many glass vials that lay there.

"What do you want?"

"Paper."

When the imir didn't move, Loot rolled his eyes and grabbed a page from his desk.

"Pen?"

Again, no movement. Loot grumbled and reached for a pen.

He wrote a few short sentences on the page and offered it to the imir. The imir's lips moved as he read.

"In exchange for keeping the secret of the imir of Jin-Gernomi's bastard child, the secret bearer may request a favor. A favor is defined as a debt of equal or greater worth than the request. The Warden of Crime may call on you at any time in the next thirty years to fulfill this debt, and you will have twenty-four strikes to complete it. Forfeit of this debt is the circulation of the bastard's whereabouts to the court and the death of the child's mother." Dread had seeped into the imir's voice like tea leaves, bitter and dark.

Loot reached for the paper, his lips curling, "Let me just add one more thing. You said you had a young granddaughter? Hmm, let's put her life on the line too. What is your granddaughter's name?"

"Efie Montera." The imir looked shocked he had spoken.

Loot added Efie Montera to the death threat at the end. Just in case Imir Jenda harbored no attachment to the bastard's mother anymore.

The imir took back the page.

"Who is the Warden of Crime?" he asked.

Loot bowed low, flourishing his hands like a griot.

"Why, me. Sign at the bottom please."

The imir hesitated. But only for a second. Loot knew how damaging the truth would be. Not a rumor whispered in taverns, but the flesh-and-blood truth of a child at your door. Half the imirs had bastard children, but you'd be hard pressed to find them. Most assassinated them young, as the title of imir was hereditary and having children spring up was never helpful.

The imir's signature was pretty, almost dainty. Loot admired it before rolling the contract and slipping it into his pocket.

"Thank you for that. Now if you don't mind, I'll be leaving from your balcony."

"What?"

Loot spoke slower. "There's something I need to do next door, so I'll be leaving from your balcony. Please do oblige me by moving out of the way."

The imir had regained his paralysis.

Loot sighed and pushed his chair out of the way. The man was heavy, but again Loot found himself appreciating the detailing on the furniture.

He swung open the balcony doors and stepped out.

"The antidote!" the imir cried out.

Loot smiled, "Oh, silly me, nearly forgot." Loot threw the vial to the imir, and the man drank it with slurping sounds.

The liquid was a simple sleeping draft and it would knock him cold for three strikes. Loot hadn't poisoned the whiskey, but the threat was too good an opportunity to miss. Now at least Loot was sure the imir wouldn't go to the authorities while he still had business in the Keep.

He waved back at the imir before shutting the balcony doors again. Loot looked to his right. The balcony was wide and sprawling with gold pots of trailing jasmine and roses. Loot whistled low through his teeth and rubbed his hands together.

It was a fine day for a climb.

THERE WAS A reason Loot singled out the imir of Jin-Gernomi for this particular ploy. The imir's chambers were next to Yona Elsari's, and there was no way he could talk his way into her chambers. The Warden of Strength was terrifying, her reign brutal and efficient. Crime was down, but so was morality.

Loot jumped lithely over the railing of Yona's balcony, his hands sticky with tree gum. It had helped him keep a grip on the whitestone walls between the imir's chambers and Yona's.

He withdrew a mustard handkerchief from his suit pocket and rubbed the handkerchief roughly against his palms. Then he picked the substance from out of his nails, wiping every bit of residue away. He worked methodically, the slip of silk turning black as the gum transferred from his hands to the material. *Don't want to leave a trace.*

It was said that some inquisitors had learned to discover fingerprints, and they were building a list of criminal impressions. Loot couldn't imagine the process would catch on. Not because it was labor intensive, but because inquisitors weren't so fussed about proving guilt, especially if you were born on the wrong side of the river.

The door to the balcony was open. He knew it would be, as every morning Yona Elsari took her morning coffee on the terrace before going to court, leaving it unlocked. And he knew this because he had an informant on the inside.

"Why don't you get Dilla to take something from Yona's chambers? She's a servant and your informant," Fayl had complained.

"Because Dilla is not me. And I need to prove that I have the reach to get anywhere." Loot had reached for Fayl's hand, his manicured nails squeezing a little too tight. "If I have one of my own in the Keep, will not the other crime lords? And if they ask them of my feat, will they not tell the truth and say I never went? No, Fayl, this must be me."

Loot stepped carefully into the living chambers of Yona Elsari, Warden of Strength. Her bedroom smelled strongly of copper, and Loot found himself recoiling. It reminded him of the smell in Dredge Square after a ripping.

Yona's rooms were quietly decorated. A drawing of an island hung above her bed, the soil black, the sea blue. The runelamps hung low, merging with the summer sun to create light the color of fire that warmed the shadows of the room.

Loot thought about taking the painting, but its bulk put him off. Instead, he opened one of her bedside drawers.

Now here was a treasure worth stealing. A dagger with a hilt glittering with yellow diamonds. Loot picked it up. Perfectly balanced; he expected no less. He was about to pocket it when a sound came from outside the door.

". . . I won't be long, wait for me outside."

The voice was muffled but recognizable. Though Loot had only heard her speak once—wardens rarely made it across the river—he remembered the rasping quality of her voice and the strange lilt to her words.

"Fuck," Loot sang the word like the start of a song.

He wouldn't make it out the balcony in time. The next best option was her bathroom. Loot scampered across the room. He still held the dagger in his hand as he slipped into the empty marble tub and willed himself into nonexistence.

There was a moment of silence, the padding of footsteps, then a disappointed sigh.

"That's a very terrible hiding place, thief," Yona said, devoid of emotion.

Loot winced. The game was lost.

"Come out," she commanded.

There was nothing more to it. He'd have to charm his way out. He tugged on the corners of his mouth as he stood with as much grace as he could.

"Warden Yona, the pleasure is mine." Loot bowed low while saluting. A double-charm attack.

Yona Elsari filled the doorway of her bathroom, the edge of her afro wig touching the doorframe. She wore a thick red suit that covered every inch of skin. A sword hung by her waist, unsheathed, a stroke away from drawing blood. Her eyes were hard slices of flint, ready to ignite.

"Who are you?" Yona's gaze flickered to the spider brooch on his lapel and then back to his eyes.

She hadn't called for any officers . . . maybe the game was not lost after all.

"Why, I . . . am the Warden of Crime."

Yona's eyes didn't soften, but Loot wondered if he detected a slight humor there.

"Warden of Crime?"

"Yes . . . well soon to be appointed anyway. I'm uniting the crime lords of the empire under my rule."

A small twitch of the eyebrow. Sometimes there wasn't a weapon better than the weapon of honesty.

"And what are you doing in my chambers?"

"Stealing." Loot twirled the dagger in his hand. A risky move, and he saw Yona's muscles harden to pounce. He held out a placating hand before lowering the dagger to the floor slowly. "I wanted to prove that I could steal from the Warden of Strength. A show of power."

"Theatrical," she snorted, and Loot bobbed his head with a sheepish grin.

Still, she didn't call for guards.

There was a moment of silence as they surveyed each other until Loot broke it with a polite cough.

". . . Well, I think I'll be on my way . . ."

Yona let out a laugh as if she couldn't believe his gall. Loot could hardly believe it himself.

"No, I don't think so. I think we will talk a little longer, you and I. Grab that stool and come and sit." Yona tipped her head to the three-legged stool in the corner of the privy and disappeared into her bedroom.

Loot frowned and did as she bade.

A STRIKE LATER Loot was making his way back out of the Keep, the stool tucked under his arm. His heart hammered in his chest, perplexed and terrified as he was in equal measure.

His time with Yona had been unexpected. The warden had offered a partnership. She would support his reign with a yearly donation and immunity from the law—"only my officers, mind you; if you get tied up with the Abosom, they'll be no protection"—and in return she would get a cut of his smuggling venture and he would meet with her once a mooncycle to trade information.

Loot couldn't believe his luck. The partnership was exactly what he needed to secure his reign. When he'd inquired about the dagger, she had laughed.

"No, if you must take a token, take the stool." Yona's eyes had glittered with the challenge.

How can I make a stool used to prop someone's feet up while they shit look impressive?

"Engrave your initials," he requested. She'd acquiesced with a tilt of the head, using the dagger deftly to draw Y.E. on the bottom.

By the time he made it back to the Belly it was nearly noon. Fayl was frantic.

"Where have you been?" His voice lifted in a whine. "I was so worried, I thought you'd been caught. Wait, is that a stool?"

Loot smiled and gave him a quick peck on his rough cheek. "Yes, it is. Is the tea ready?"

Fayl softened at Loot's touch.

"Yes, yes. I haven't added the . . . poison." Fayl did a comical look around, his eyes wide.

Loot laughed and walked up to the teapot.

"Don't worry, I'll handle that."

The powder was sitting heavy in his pocket, a pleasing weight. He emptied the entire contents into the tea. He stirred the hot liquid with his finger then licked it clean.

"Delicious."

Fayl's gave him a tentative grin, but Loot could see the worry underneath.

"It'll be okay, Fayl. We have a warden on our side."

"What?"

Loot swept past him, for he could see the shadow of guests arriving.

Anhid was the first to arrive, his face sour, like a babe who had sucked lemon for the first time. As suspected, he had brought with him three guards and his new deputy.

"What? You expected me to keep your role open?" Anhid barked out a laugh as he noticed Loot appraising his new heir. The man had warm brown eyes, but he didn't smile at Loot as he took his seat next to Anhid.

"Yes, sit, please do. Help yourself to tea."

"Loot we're not here for fucking tea, we're here to kill you," Anhid growled.

Loot gave him an appeasing smile. "Well, if that could wait, we have more guests."

The second crime lord of the Nar-Ruta operated out of the south of the city, in the taverns of the Ember Quarter. A risky business, the danger had seemingly sapped away at their weight, leaving the musawa a small sack of bones and wrinkles. The muscled crew they had brought made up for that. They piled into the room, standing like statues behind their crime lord.

Loot welcomed them with open arms and cups of tea. Muscle doesn't stop poison.

The final two crime lords were along not long after. A young maiden with amber eyes called Turin and an older woman with henna-dyed gray hair who controlled the majority of the empire's joba seed distribution.

"Crime lords, welcome, welcome."

The tension was palpable; thick like honey, it made the tea ever sweeter. Never before had all four crime lords and their minions come together before.

"Imagine if the pockets of exploding gas they say is down here killed us all." Loot's laughter was a little manic—probably the poison. It brought silence to the room.

"Why are we here?" the maiden asked.

"To kill him," Anhid said bluntly. "You all got the message, he fancies himself Warden of Crime."

"Yes, I do fancy myself Warden of Crime actually," Loot agreed. "But no, today isn't about killing me. No, no, no. Not me at all."

Only two of the cohort had drank from the tea.

"Would you like some sugar?" Loot prompted, adding two spoons to his. He circulated the porcelain bowl to his right. "Please relax, appreciate my hospitality. I have a proposition that will benefit you all."

"I'll say it again, we're not here for fucking tea." Anhid made to stand.

"Did I not just tell you that it is in your best interest to listen?" Loot's voice was a little sharp. Then he smiled. "It is rude to enter someone's home and not share in their hospitality. How about whiskey instead? I recently pilfered this from the imir of Jin-Gernomi. Top quality."

Anhid liked his alcohol, and whiskey was his favorite. He gave a short nod.

"Gummers, would you get Anhid a glass?"

"Gummers?" Anhid asked.

"Guild members," Loot explained with a shrug. "They shortened it to Gummers. I quite like it."

Anhid opened his mouth to protest, but Loot held up a hand.

"Partake in my hospitality, then I will tell you all." Anhid's teacup was swapped with a glass, and Loot poured him a healthy shot.

Once Anhid drank, Loot noticed that everyone else in the room did the same. Except one.

"Is it poisoned?" the maiden spoke. Though she was young, she was clever, it turned out.

"Of course not." Loot took a drink from his mug.

The maiden's eyes glittered as she followed suit.

"We have accepted your hospitality, now tell us what this is about," Anhid demanded.

"Life," Loot said honestly.

"What?" the skin-and-bones musawa said.

"I am the Warden of Crime, and you will either submit yourself to me. Or . . ." Loot held a feeble hand to his forehead, ". . . die."

The room broke into laughter and guffaws, Anhid laughing the loudest. Like Loot expected. It made it all the more dramatic. He even joined in with them.

"You see, I have the approval of the Warden of Strength to operate. This stool was stolen from her privy this very day."

Some of the smiles dropped, but some grew bigger, indulging Loot in what they thought was make-believe. Loot brandished the initials.

"Carved by the Warden herself. Who also gave me her blessing. Everyone under my rule will be immune to the laws of the empire."

The laughter stopped.

"You can't expect anyone to believe you, Loot." The henna-haired crime lord spoke for the first time. Her voice was thin and warbling.

"Oh, no, but I know for a fact that each of you has reports that placed me in the Keep this afternoon. Some of you may even have details of the very chambers I was in. I saw at least three of the maiden's spies on my way back here. Was I not carrying a stool?"

The maiden looked to Anhid before nodding.

"He was. I also had it confirmed that he came out of Warden Yona's chambers."

Anhid laughed.

"And what does that prove?"

Loot ignored him and turned to the others.

"So, do you want to join me, or not?"

The crime lords looked between them. The maiden's eyes skittered to her bodyguard, and Loot wondered if she would be the first to attack after all. Then she nodded once.

"I will join you. If my maiden house will be able to operate without threat from the warden's officers, then that benefit is worth relinquishing my power for." Though the maiden tried to hide it, Loot saw the hint of ambition in her eyes and he wondered how loyal she would be until the end. But submitting to his rule was the first step.

The other three shook their heads, Anhid adding, "Over my tidewind-scoured body will I submit to your rule, boy."

Loot's smile dropped at the name Mama Bengo had used for him.

"Do not call me boy."

Anhid's grin was oily.

Loot threw the maiden a small vial of clear liquid. He winked at her.

"Drink that."

She frowned, clearly wondering if it was a test, but she did as he asked. He withdrew a vial for himself and did the same.

"What is that?" Anhid's voice held the waver of doubt.

"An antidote."

"You poisoned us. You lied," the musawa said.

"Yes. I did."

"I submit, I submit, give me the antidote," they pleaded.

"No."

Their face went slack. Loot knew their stomach was slowly dissolving and that the pain would come soon.

Anhid had the decency not to plead, though it was a little unsatisfying. Instead he turned to his subordinates and made a sign that Loot knew meant violence. But Loot was prepared, and now he had the maiden's fighters too.

But his minions didn't move. They were held back by the new deputy, his meaty fist held high, his warm eyes glowing.

"What next? You become Warden of Crime, but what will you do with that power?" he asked.

Loot liked this man. He had vision. So Loot let his raw ambition show on his face. "One day, I'll rule it all."

The man nodded once, hearing what he wanted. He signaled for his team to relax.

Anhid spluttered, "What are you doing? Attack him."

The musawa had started to scream, screams that quickly turned to gurgles. The gray-haired joba seed dealer began to die next. Anhid clutched his stomach, waiting for the pain to come.

"The tea, it was in the tea, wasn't it? I wasn't poisoned after all." Anhid was triumphant.

Loot looked to his new recruit, the man who had, just a moment ago, been Anhid's heir.

"Kill him."

Anhid's throat was slit. A messy kill; it would take ages to clean the carpets. Well, he had a lot more subordinates now. They could do it.

Loot's smile dipped slightly as he spoke to Anhid's dying form. "Say hi to Mama Bengo, she's waiting with a knife on the other side."

Loot looked around the room. The maiden had watched the proceedings with barely a flicker of concern. The other minions and deputies who hadn't drank the tea stood slack-jawed and outnumbered.

"Welcome to the guild of crime, everyone. This is going to be fun."

Loot pushed his hands in his pockets and picked his way across the room.

"You." Loot pointed at Anhid's last heir. "What's your name?"

"Azim, Warden."

"Azim, I think we'll get along quite nicely, you and I. Quite nicely. Yes, yes I think so."

Azim nodded, a ghost of a smile on his lips.

GLOSSARY

TERMS

Abosom — The devout followers of Anyme who serve under the Warden of Truth.

aerobatics — A type of gymnastics that incorporates aerial movements.

aerofield — Ranged combat, first trial of the Aktibar for strength.

aeroglider — Wind gliding sport, commonly practiced on the hills of Jin-Gernomi.

Akoma — The largest valve in the heart.

Aktibar, the — A set of trials held every ten years to determine the next disciples.

Anyme — The genderless deity worshiped in the empire. God of the Sky.

Ardae — A religious festival celebrating the anniversary of when Anyme first climbed into the sky. It involves a blessed meal, gifts, and offerings to the God.

battle wrath — A state of focus used in the martial art of Nuba.

blood scour — Finger pinprick check points to test the color of your blood.

bloodink — Tattoos, most commonly seen on Dusters.

bloodwerk The ability to use your blood to manipulate objects by drawing runes. There are four foundational runes. The rest are supplementary runes that guide in direction, activation, safety, and protection.

bloodwerk rune—

Ba Foundational rune: A positive pull drags the rune toward an object.

Gi Foundational rune: A negative pull drags an object toward the rune.

Kha Foundational rune: A positive push presses the rune away from an object.

Ru Foundational rune: A negative push presses an object away from the rune.

Book of Blood The sacred book of bloodwerk runes.

Choice Day The day when twenty-year-old Embers are required to choose their guild.

clockmaster The role of timekeeping in the empire. The clockmaster projects the time every quarter strike through a chain of calls, starting with the First Clockmaster, based in the Keep where the only clock resides.

crime lord The leader of a criminal organization. Before Loot's reign there were four ruling in Nar-Ruta. Now they all report to Loot.

Dambe A form of boxing in which the opponents use their strong arm as if it were a spear.

Day of Ascent The day that the winners of the Aktibar ascend the five hundred steps to join their warden as the new disciple of their guild.

Day of Descent The day, once a decade, that the wardens of Nar-Ruta abdicate their places to their disciples by descending the five hundred steps.

disciples Seconds-in-command to the wardens. Leaders of the Shadow Court. They train under their specific warden for ten years before ascending to the title of warden themselves.

Dusters Citizens of the empire identified by their blue blood. The working-class tier of the caste system.

duty chute The postal tubes that run under main roads. The chutes carry messages through the twelve cities of the empire.

Embers The noble and ruling class of the empire. Only Embers are allowed to rule, receive a full education, or live in the Ember Quarter. Only Embers are taught to bloodwerk.

Ending Fire, the A phenomenon believed to have struck the world four hundred years ago, wiping out everything with lava, flame, and flooding. Nothing survived except what was on the wardens' ships.

eru Large lizard-like creatures that are trained as steeds. They can be ridden with saddles by the most experienced or driven with cart-drawn carriages.

Ghostings Citizens of the empire identified by their transparent blood, their hands and tongues are severed at birth. They are the lowest class of the empire.

griot Storyteller and truth-seeker.

guild of crime A counterfeit guild, led by Loot, that has no true jurisdiction in the empire. It is run in opposition to the true wardens. Vow: to resist and sow chaos.

guild of duty Manages the smooth running of the empire and domestic services. Vow: to nourish and maintain the land.

guild of knowledge Manages the educational system within the empire. Vow: to teach and discover all.

guild of strength Responsible for protecting and maintaining the peace. This includes the warden army. Vow: to protect and enforce the law.

guild of truth Rules the courthouse and upholds the law and religious rites. The Warden of Truth leads the Abosom. Vow: to preach and incite justice.

Gummers Members of the guild of crime, shortened from "guild members."

handspan A unit of measurement using the tip of your thumb to the tip of your little finger.

imir The twelve leaders of the cities of the Wardens' Empire. In inherited positions, the twelve imirs make up the Noble Court.

inkwell A device worn by Embers that allows them to bloodwerk. The metal cuff wraps around the wrist with a slot above a vein where a stylus is inserted. The blood then runs down a channel in the stylus to the tip of the stylus, allowing them to write with their blood.

jambiya Curved dagger.

joba fruit A red berry the size of a small plum with an extremely hard outer shell that requires a forge to crack. The flesh is often used to create dyes. The joba tree bears fruit only every sixth mooncycle.

joba seed The joba seed can be chewed, releasing a bitter juice that is a narcotic stimulant. Users of the joba seed often feel an initial rush of euphoria, followed by a dreamlike state. It is often coupled with a depressive comedown and is highly addictive. Withdrawals include seizures, sickness, and muscle cramps.

joba tree Joba trees are planted in the front garden of most Ember houses. The height of the tree indicates the status and generational wealth of the occupier. The trees are white with green leaves. They are believed to be a conduit to Anyme, as the God climbed a joba tree into the sky.

kori Small blue birds with iridescent wings.

Laambe A defensive martial art known for its open-palmed technique.

lava fish A deep-sea fish harvested for its pearlescent scales, which are used to adorn garments in glitter.

maiden The head of a brothel.

milk honey A white-leafed herb used in medicine to lessen nausea.

mooncycle A full rotation of the moon; a way to measure months.

Moonday The first day of the full moon.

musawa A third gender.

nameday The anniversary of the day you are born.

Night of the Stolen The night the Sandstorm stole twelve children from Ember houses.

nightworker Someone who works in a maiden house.

Noble Court Made up of the twelve imirs, they debate and propose changes to laws and legislation, then present them to the Upper Court.

Nowerks A slur used to refer to Ghostings and Dusters who can't bloodwerk.

Nuba A regimented code of physical formations that are implemented through strict mental codes, Nuba practice is difficult to master. The user has to reach a state of complete control and focus, known as battle wrath, in which anger fuels the Nuba artist to create precise movements that become deadly when paired with a weapon.

peppashito A red, spicy pepper sauce.

rack, the A wooden contraption that slowly tears the condemned into two. It is operated by a ripper.

radish leaf Red leaves cultivated in the desert sand that give a rush of endorphins to those who smoke them. Expensive to procure. Slightly addictive. Smoked mostly by Embers.

Ring, the An illegal wrestling competition run by the guild of crime.

rippers Executioners who operate the rack—always Dusters. The uniform is a blue jacket.

runegun Bloodwerk-operated firearm.

runelamp Bloodwerk-generated light.

sandsnail Small, white-shelled snails that live in the Farsai Desert.

saphridiam A blue mineral found in the sand of the Farsai Desert, derived from volcanic matter.

Shadow Court The court-in-waiting assigned and led by the disciple of each guild.

shantra A game of strategy. A shantra board is made up of three different colors, patterned with diamonds. Each team has thirty-one counters, ten of each color and one black piece. The black piece is known as the egg. The aim of the game is to steal the egg from the opposing team, but each counter can only move onto its corresponding color. Only red counters can collect the egg.

Siege of the Silent The rebellion is taught in schools as the reason why the Ghostings are subjected to their penance. Four hundred years ago they rebelled against the wardens by laying siege to the Wardens' Keep for two months.

slab The currency of the Wardens' Empire, made out of carved whitestone with former wardens printed on the underside.

sleepglass Poison made with pepper flower and grass roots. Undetectable, it puts the victim to sleep for a short time.

Starting Drum The drum that indicates the start of a ripping.

Stolen, the The twelve children stolen from their cribs as babes and raised by the Sandstorm.

strike A unit of time measurement; one strike is one hour.

Tannin A fabled sea monster that lives in the depths of the Marion Sea.

tidewind A nightly phenomenon that blows and whips the sand of the Farsai Desert into a deadly frenzy.

tio root A dark wood that is worth more than gold. Short, stubby plant grown by the coast, hard to cultivate.

Trolley, the The bloodwerk-operated train that carts across the Tongue, also known as the trotro.

Upper Court Made up of wardens, disciples, and their key advisers, the Upper Court is where legislation is proposed.

verd leaf A leaf harvested for its painkiller attributes. High in caffeine.

wardens The four leaders of the Empire of Nar-Ruta, each charged with representing one of the four guilds: duty, truth, knowledge, and strength.

whitestone A hard-wearing substance that can withstand the tidewind, often used to build houses.

yambrini Poison extracted from shrimp.

Zalaam, the An unknown group.

zine Short stories featured in *The People's Gazette*.

PLACES

Arena, the Newly built amphitheater that houses the trials for the Aktibar.

Belly, the The headquarters of the Warden of Crime.

Dredge, the Previously called the Ghostings Quarter, but after the Siege of the Silent, their numbers dwindled and it was taken over by businesses of ill repute.

Duster Quarter A district in the northwest side of Nar-Ruta, occupied by Dusters.

Ember Quarter A district in the south side of Nar-Ruta, between the Ruta River and the Warden's Keep, occupied by Embers.

Farsai Desert Blue sand dunes that sprawl across the center of the empire.

Great Veranda The open-air center of the Wardens' Keep where functions are held. A roof automated by bloodwerk covers it during the tidewind.

Intestines, the The tunnels that run below the city of Nar-Ruta. There is a myth that one of the tunnels leads to treasure.

Jin-Crolah A city in the north, its main export is coffee beans.

Jin-Dinil A city that surrounds the central lakes of the empire.

Jin-Eynab A city in the west, known for its wine producing.

Jin-Gernomi A city in the center-east with lots of cultivated grass hills.

Jin-Hidal A city in the center of the island that produces the empire's coal supply.

Jin-Hubab A city in the northwest of the empire where grain and flour is milled.

Jin-Kutan A city in the southeast of the empire, one day's ride from Nar-Ruta.

Jin-Laham A city in the east that mainly exports cattle.

Jin-Noon A city in the west where the majority of cotton is grown on plantations.

Jin-Sahalia A city in the north known for the best eru breeding, and eru races that the imir hosts once a year.

Jin-Sukar A city in the northeast where sugar cane is farmed.

Jin-Wonta A city in the east that exports metal and mineral deposits.

Maroon Tavern in the Dredge where plantation workers drink.

Marion Sea The volatile and highly dangerous sea surrounding the Wardens' Empire. Superstitiously believed to be haunted by a sea monster called the Tannin.

Nar-Ruta The capital city of the Wardens' Empire, in the southeast of the island.

Ood-Lopah A village where salt flats are harvested.

Ood-Rahabe A fishing village in the north of the empire.

Ood-Zaynib A village in the north of the empire, close to the Sanctuary.

Ring, the A fighting ring operated by the guild of crime situated in the north of the Dredge.

Ruta River A quicksand river that separates the Duster Quarter from the Ember Quarter.

Sanctuary, the The farmstead where the Stolen were raised, situated outside of Ood-Zaynib.

Tongue, the The black iron bridge that stands five hundred handspans above the Ruta River.

Wardens' Keep The governing center of Nar-Ruta and home to the wardens. The cobbled courtyard is adorned with the largest joba tree in the empire. Beyond that, the five hundred steps lead to a marble platform where the wardens ascend and descend. The western side of the keep houses the courtrooms, wardens' offices, wardens' chambers, library, and the schoolrooms. The eastern side houses the servant quarters, kitchens, and Anoor's chambers.

PEOPLE

Anoor Elsari Daughter of the Uka Elsari. Competitor in the Aktibar for the guild of strength. (She/Her)

Aveed Elreeno Warden of Duty. (They/Them)

Azim Ikila Former leader of the Sandstorm, deceased. (He/Him)

Bisma Oharam Librarian in the Wardens' Keep. (He/Him)

Boey Elsari Blue-scaled eru owned by Anoor. (She/Her)

Efie Montera Granddaughter of the imir of Jin-Gernomi. Competitor in the Aktibar for the guild of strength. (She/Her)

Elder Dew Ghosting elder. (They/Them)

Elder Ravenwing Ghosting elder. (He/Him)

Elder Reed Ghosting elder. (She/Her)

Elder Zero Ghosting elder. (He/Him)

Fareen Ola One of the Stolen, deceased. Has a scar running down her cheek. (She/Her)

Fayl Hisbar Watcher for the guild of crime and Loot's husband. (He/Him)

General Ahmed Uka's deceased partner, father of Anoor. (He/Him)

Gorn Rieya Anoor's chief of chambers. (She/Her)

Griot Sheth Storyteller who frequents the Maroon. (He/Him)

Griot Zibenwe Storyteller, killed on the rack for writing. (He/Him)

Hassa Ghosting servant and watcher for the elders. Friends with Sylah. (She/Her)

Inquisitor Abena Fictional main character of the zine "Tales of Inquisitor Abena." (She/Her)

Jond Alnua One of the Stolen who survived the massacre. Competitor in the Aktibar for the guild of strength. Member of the Sandstorm. (He/Him)

Kwame Muklis Ember servant who works in the kitchens of the Keep. (He/Him)

Lio Alyana Sylah's adoptive mother. Member of the Sandstorm. (She/Her)

Loot Hisbar Warden of Crime, married to Fayl. (He/Him)

Maiden Turin Owner of a maiden house in the Dredge. (She/Her)

Marigold Hassa's adoptive parent, Ghosting. (They/Them)

Master Inansi Leader of the Sandstorm. (He/Him)

Master Nuhan Teacher of bloodwerk. (He/Him)

One-ear Lazo Competitor in the wrestling contest known as the Ring. (He/Him)

Pura Dumo Warden of Truth. (He/Him)

Sylah Alyana One of the Stolen who survived the massacre. Chambermaid to Anoor Elsari. (She/Her)

Tanu AlKhabbir Competitor in the Aktibar for the guild of knowledge. (She/Her)

Uka Elsari Warden of Strength, Anoor's mother. (She/Her)

Vona Esar Jond's guardian, deceased. Member of the Sandstorm. (She/Her)

Wern Aldina Warden of Knowledge. (She/Her)

Yanis Yahun Competitor in the Aktibar for the guild of strength. Captain in the warden army. (He/Him)

Yona Elsari Former Warden of Strength; Anoor's grandmother. (She/Her)

ACKNOWLEDGMENTS

If there is one thing a griot would tell you, it is that telling the tale is only a small part of what makes a story.

Before the telling there are the wordsmiths, who define the ebb and flow of words:

Juliet Mushens, you are my superwoman, collaborator, and agent. You saw me so others could too. I cannot wait to continue growing my career with you by my side. Thank you also to the incredible team you have around you at Mushens Entertainment and for leading me to Ginger Clark, my guiding light on the other side of the pond. This book is for you all.

Tricia Narwani, I will never forget our first phone call, it was pure magic. I knew there was no one better to help me tell Sylah's story. Your faultless editing has left me in awe of your genius. My gratitude is endless. This book is for you.

Natasha Bardon, you let me slide into your DMs, offering up your time for Black aspiring writers. Little did I know you'd be my editor in the end. Fairy tales are real after all. This book is for you.

Next there are those who facilitate the telling, who beat the drum and set the stage:

Thank you to Scott Shannon and Keith Clayton and their outstanding team at Del Rey: Bree Gary, Alex Larned, Julie Leung, Ashleigh Heaton, Sabrina Shen, David Moench, Jordan Pace, Adaobi Maduka, Megan Tripp, Matt Schwartz, Catherine Bucaria,

Rob Guzman, Ellen Folan, Brittanie Black, Elizabeth Fabian, David Stevenson, Ella Laytham to name a few! It truly has been the greatest privilege to work with such an incredible team.

And to the exceptional HarperVoyager UK team: Jack Renninson, Vicky Leech, Fleur Clarke, Terence Caven, Robyn Watts, Holly MacDonald, Jaime Witcomb, Susanna Peden, Alice Hill, Mayada Ibrahim, Linda Joyce, and everyone else who's been involved. What an absolute honor it is to work alongside you.

Adekunle Adeleke, thank you for your art; you have captured the essence of Sylah like no one else could. And to Kingsley Nebechi, whose cartography graces the endpapers of this book.

A special thank-you to those from the trans community who welcomed me with open arms, in particular EM Williams and Adam Sharah. Thank you also to my sensitivity readers, Dae and Al.

This book is for all of you.

Long before the telling of the story are the ancestors who pave the way. So, to the family whose roots I have climbed:

Muma and Baba El-Arifi, you taught me everything. How to laugh until I cry and how to care deeply and loyally. Baba, you didn't get the chance to see my dreams come true, but I feel your pride every day. Not only would you be proud of me, but you'd be proud of Muma too. This book is for both of you.

To the El-Arifis and Dinsdales, and all the extended family, thank you for allowing my dreams to blossom. This book is for you.

Then there are the advocates, whose support gives the story its foundation:

Jim, phew, words won't do you justice. Thank you for pushing me to discover the parts of myself I didn't know existed. You are the reason I know who I am when I look in the mirror. It is the greatest gift anyone has ever given me. This book is for you.

Sally El-Arifi, you who listened to me tell stories since you were small. Without you there would have been blank pages. Rachel Bell, how could I have done it without you? My first reader and my forever cheerleader. With you by my side, I can do anything. Ali Rodney and Giulia Sciota, you are my energy and light. How lucky

I am to be on this journey with you. David Lowe, thank you for your endless support, and I can't wait until it's your turn. Thank you to the writing group I met at Faber Academy and the countless friends, Laura Foster, Richard Bell, Joanna Briscoe, Sarah Taylor, and many more who have picked me up and fueled my motivation. This book is for all of you.

Finally, the most important part of telling a tale is the listeners who give the story life:

Thank you for choosing to read this novel. Thank you for helping to create Hassa, Anoor, and Sylah in your mind. You don't know how much each one of you matters to me. Each of you are a part of making this Black-awkward-too-tall-for-her-own-good woman's dream come true.

This book is for you most of all.

ABOUT THE AUTHOR

SAARA EL-ARIFI's heritage is intrinsically linked to the themes she explores in her writing. She was raised in the Middle East until her formative years, when her family swapped the Abu Dhabi desert for the English Peak District hills. This change of climate taught her what it means to be Black in a white world. *The Final Strife* is Saara El-Arifi's debut novel, the first part of a trilogy inspired by Ghanaian folklore and Arabian myths.

saaraelarifi.com
Twitter: @saaraelarifi
Instagram: @saaraelarifi

ABOUT THE TYPE

This book was set in Plantin, a classic roman typeface named after the famous sixteenth-century printer Christophe Plantin (c. 1520–89). Plantin was designed in 1913 by the Monotype Corporation, based on some sixteenth-century type designs of Robert Granjon (1513–89). Plantin's even strokes and lack of contrast make it a highly legible face. It was, later, the typeface on which Times New Roman was modeled.

21982320383189

JIN-EYNAB Farsai

Duster Quarter

The Ring

The Belly

The Maroon

NAR-RUTA

The Wardens' Keep

Ember Quarter

The Arena

THE WARDE

SOUTHERN